Kitty Cooper
Harvard - 1934

LAURENCE STERNE

A SENTIMENTAL JOURNEY
THROUGH FRANCE AND ITALY

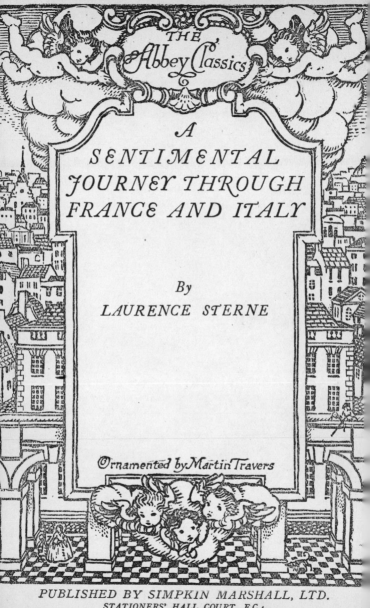

THE Abbey Classics

A
SENTIMENTAL
JOURNEY THROUGH
FRANCE AND ITALY

By
LAURENCE STERNE

Ornamented by Martin Travers

PUBLISHED BY SIMPKIN MARSHALL, LTD.
STATIONERS' HALL COURT, E.C.4

*Printed in Great Britain by*
*Hazell, Watson & Viney, Ltd., London and Aylesbury.*

# BIOGRAPHICAL NOTE

LAURENCE STERNE, the eldest son of Roger Sterne, an officer of Chudleigh's (now 34th) Foot (Border Regiment) was born in 1713. His earliest years were spent in vagabonding in the track of his father's regiment, but on the death of his father he was sent to Cambridge, where he matriculated in 1735, and graduated M.A., 1740. In 1738 he had taken orders and became vicar of Sutton-in-the-Forest in Yorkshire. In 1741 he married Elizabeth Lumley, through whose influence he became Prebendary of York. His life thereafter was a round of petty incident : " Books, painting, fiddling and shooting were my amusement," he says. In 1760 the first volume of *TRISTRAM SHANDY* appeared, and its author at once stepped into popularity : he came up to London and became a social favourite. Thereafter he spent his life in writing, flirting in London, or in travelling on the Continent. His health finally gave way, and he died in 1768 in London.

# BIBLIOGRAPHY

1. *The Case of Elijah*, a charity sermon, 1747.
2. *The Abuses of Conscience*, 1750.
3. *The Political Romance*, 1759.
4. *The Life and Opinions of Tristram Shandy*, Vols. I and II, 1759 ; Vols. III and IV, 1761 ; Vols. V and VI, 1762 ; Vols. VII and VIII, 1765 ; Vol. IX, 1767.
5. *Sermons of Mr. Yorick*, Vols. I and II, 1760 ; Vols. III and IV, 1766 ; Vols. V, VI and VII, 1769.
6. *A Sentimental Journey through France and Italy*, 1768.
7. *Letters of the late Rev. Laurence Sterne*, 1775.
8. *Letters from Yorick to Eliza*, 1775.
9. *Twelve Letters to his Friends on Various Occasions*, 1775.
10. *Seven Letters written by Sterne and his Friends* (privately printed), 1884.

First collected edition, Dublin, 7 vols., 1779.

# INTRODUCTION

THE *Sentimental Journey* was to have filled four small volumes. Only two of them were written, and within a month of their publication and enthusiastic reception their author had done for ever with sentiment and travelling. Yet, in spite of the discrepancy between the title-page, which promises that we shall be taken through Italy as well as France, and the actual contents, which leave us abruptly at a wayside inn on the Lyons road, one does not readily think of the book as among the unfinished masterpieces of literature. A masterpiece it certainly is ; but a book which is a succession of beginnings and endings, or rather of leavings-off, can hardly be called unfinished—a chain is a complete chain whatever the number of its links—and it is probable that had the fourth volume been achieved it would have closed on just such an effective aposiopesis as does the second. There is no reason, indeed, inherent in their conception why either *Tristram Shandy* or the *Sentimental Journey*, both of which open in a manner so matchless, should have been brought to a final conclusion, even had Sterne's length of days surpassed by as much as it fell short of the psalmist's arbitrarily estimated span. It was Sterne's original intention—though he may not have been altogether serious when he expressed it—to write two volumes of *Tristram* every year of his life. He did not, perhaps fortunately, fulfil that intention, publishing a mere nine volumes in about eight years ; but although there are indications that both writer and readers were growing weary of what had once so charmed them, it is likely that, had he lived, he would sooner or later have resumed the tale. Such, at any rate, was his declared purpose. "At present I am in my peaceful retreat," he wrote from Coxwold in June, 1766, "writing the ninth volume of *Tristram*. I shall publish but one this year, and the next I shall begin a new work of four volumes "—the *Journey* of course —"which when finished I shall continue

*Tristram* with fresh spirit." As for the *Sentimental Journey*, it might well have developed, without change of scale or plan, into a full and overflowing autobiography; and also without change of title, for none apter could have been found to describe the mortal career of the vagabond of feeling who was its author.

The book might be called, with equal accuracy, a fragment of autobiography with fictitious embellishments or a work of fiction with an autobiographical basis. Either description would of course be inadequate, accounting for the accidents and not the essence of the book, the soul of which is expressed in the adjective of its title and only the body in the noun ; but either would serve for a librarian's classification. For like *Tristram Shandy*, though the proportions are different, the *Sentimental Journey* is a farrago of experience (more or less transfused with fancy), pure invention, reflection, and borrowings from the books or the lips of others. The core and occasion of it were the foreign holiday on which Sterne set out in the autumn of 1765—the second of such holidays ; the first having provided material for the seventh and subsequent volumes of *Tristram*, though a residue probably found its way into the later book. In the classification of travellers which he drew up in the belated preface penned in the unsteady *desobligeant* at Calais, he assigned himself a special class of which he obviously took pride in being the only member. But like Fielding before him, and for the same reason as Fielding, he was also a " traveller of necessity." For on both occasions it was a vain quest after health which drove him abroad.

The route pursued by the physical Sterne was roughly that of his literary projection, Yorick. At Calais he, too, stayed at Dessein's hostelry, which he made fashionable for a season and famous for all time ; the authenticity of the begging Franciscan is at any rate probable, and the lady of the *remise* door was the Marquise de Lamberti, though whether those eloquent hand-pressures and speaking silences had any existance but in the willing imagination of him who described them with such exquisite art is matter for conjecture. The drummer-valet, La Fleur, whom any writer of fiction would rejoice to have created,

was actually hired at Montreuil, and it is on
his authority that we know that those incidents which read most like a sentimentalist's
inventions—that of the dead ass and that of
the unhappy Maria—were not inventions but
facts, however much of sentimental significance
they may have gained in their transmuta-
tion into literature. That in the episode of
Maria, at any rate, Sterne stuck fairly close
to fact is shown by La Fleur's account ; though
maybe the valet's memory of the event was
modified by a subsequent perusal of his master's
book. " When we came up to her, she was
grovelling in the road like an infant, and
throwing the dust upon her head—and yet few
were more lovely! Upon Sterne's accosting her
with tenderness, and raising her in his arms,
she collected herself and resumed some composure—told him her tale of misery and wept
upon his breast—my master sobbed aloud.
I saw her gently disengage herself from his
arms, and she sung him the service to the
Virgin, my poor master covered his face
with his hands, and walked by her side to the
cottage where she lived,—there he talked
earnestly to the old woman." The charming

trio, Janatone of the Montreuil inn (who also, like Maria, appears in *Tristram Shandy*), the *grisette* of the Paris glove-shop, and the *fille de chambre* of the little green purse and *Les Egarements du Cœur*, all graced the actual earth ; while that last adventure, the " case of delicacy," in which another *fille de chambre* figured, happened not to Sterne himself but to his friend, " Fish " Craufurd—at least, so Craufurd said.

The plaintive starling rose from a heraldic nest, and it can hardly be believed that Sterne obtained his passport quite in the delightful manner described by Yorick. Speaking generally, it may be conjectured that while the majority of the episodes in the *Sentimental Journey* have some foundation of historical truth, the structural arrangement and decoration in every case owe a good deal to the architect's fancy. In real life things do not happen, even to one so alert as was Sterne to the dramatic value of the least event, so patly as they happen in this book.

One scene, certainly, was a purely literary borrowing. The dwarf at the Opéra Comique had already suffered the inconveniences of his stature in the pages of Scarron. Sterne's reading was wide, and often, in the bookseller's special use of the word, curious. He acknowledged great masters, the Bible and Montaigne, Rabelais and Cervantes—though for all his protestations of devotion to these last two, to be a true Rabelaisian was as far beyond his strength as true quixotry was out of his visionary reach—but he was learned also in the bypaths, especially of French literature from the sixteenth century to his own. A good deal of the extraordinary lore which arrests while it illustrates the development of the unlucky Tristram comes from the pages of minor Renaissance writers. He leaned much on Burton, himself the prince of borrowers ; but whereas Burton acknowledged his obligations, Sterne, of easy morals, took and did not tell.

But what does it matter ? Only a heart encrusted in pedantry would seriously lay a charge of theft against light-fingered genius. If Sterne stole, what he stole became his own by a higher law than that of property. He took base metal and made it precious. It might even be urged that he was the benefactor of his prey. Who now, among "general readers," knows Béroalde de Verville or Bouchet? Who does not know, even though unknowingly, their ghosts as they walk in the pages of Sterne?

Whencesoever he took his material, the author of *Tristram Shandy* and the *Sentimental Journey* is as original a writer as any in the history of literature. He had no spiritual forbears, though a dim and occasional presage of him may be discovered in the amorous whimsicalities of Prior. Nor of the successors who have felt his influence has any been very closely of his kin : Heine, perhaps, was the nearest. So original was he that he had to invent his own epithet. He was the first sentimentalist, and very much aware of the fact. That his invention was not superfluous is proven by its ready acceptance : even his French translators had to admit that their language owned no equivalent for the new English word, though *sensible* comes very near it. In the course of time the word has become degraded : we use it now as a term of reproach, implying an emotional dishonesty which the sentimentalist himself, just because of his dishonesty, cannot perceive. It connotes the lie in the soul. But in its authentic sense—Sterne's sense—it represents something perfectly sincere which calls for no reprehension, unless we take the Erewhonian view that ill-health is a misdemeanour : for Sterne's temperament was undoubtedly bound up with his physical weakness. In that respect he has a numerous and notable kindred, the great family of consumptive artists. The difference between him and his cousins, which accounts for his isolation, lies in the candour with which he accepted his condition. The rest of them, from Prior and Watteau to Laforgue and Beardsley, were all fundamentally sentimental, but hid their misfortune from the world and themselves beneath the mask and motley of cynicism or sought to forget it in the pursuit of the ideal. Sterne, though he often wore motley, was neither a cynic nor an idealist. He was a sentimentalist, deliberately and for the most part contentedly.

Sentimentality, as Sterne understood, felt, and practised it, is an abnormal sensitiveness and reaction to emotional stimuli. The other consumptives, aware of their sensitiveness and frightened of it, have resisted their reactions, or at any rate denied them in their art. Sterne, on the other hand, not only accepted them but cultivated them and turned them into literary capital. He went out of his way to encounter stimuli against which to react. He could not live without frequent recourse to the drug of feeling. In the *Sentimental Journey*, during the intervals, which were short enough, between his immediate emotional adventures, he must needs dope his imagination with thoughts of the absent Eliza. The wonder is that, with such a temperament and such an attitude towards it, he ever produced a book ; for to let oneself be blown about by every wind of feeling is not conducive to sustained effort. He was incapable of recollecting emotion in tranquillity, for he was never tranquil. The tears must often have fallen on his page as he wrote it. " I have torn my whole frame into pieces by my feelings," he told Lord Shelborne, referring to the composition of the *Sentimental Journey* ; and less than a week later, while the book was still on the stocks, he exclaimed to Sir George Macartney: " The deuce take all sentiments !

I wish there was not one in the world ! "
Even the sentimentalist by profession was at
last driven to revolt against the effects of the
gift which he had so carefully cherished.

It may be urged that Sterne's books do not
represent sustained efforts, but are accumula-
tions of short spurts, such as are not beyond
the compass of the most volatile of tempera-
ments. It has been said, both here and
elsewhere, that they are series of episodes
rather than consistent wholes. But their
episodic character should not be over-
emphasised. The simile of beads on a string,
which has been applied to them, is not really
accurate ; or if it be allowed it must be with
the qualification that though the beads may
be separated from one another they cannot
be taken off the string, for in both books
there is a real and infrangible continuity,
besides that which is inevitably given by the
constant obtrusion of the personality of the
most personal of authors—the continuity
given by consistent characterisation. Walter
and Toby Shandy, Corporal Trim and La
Fleur could only have got their intense and
individual life from one whose imagination

B                           xvii

was strong and steady, whatever his senses may have been.

The truth is that Sterne was saved, from the literary point of view, by an intellect which was stronger than his body or his nerves. He lost his heart a hundred times, but he never lost his head. Even while he suffered from his hyperæsthesia, he could watch its processes, detached and smiling. Though it is very possible that he would have sympathised with it, he could never have become a true member of that humourless modern school of writers which has declared war on the mind and its conceptions. They are among the most remarkable phenomena, those writers, of our present intellectual anarchy. Art, they say, should be " un jaillissement spontané du réel et de l'ame " ; and the only reality is sensation. Ideas are lies, and to present life through an intellectual medium is to misrepresent it. They aim, therefore, at a direct expression of reality, as they understand it, unwarped by ideas. But of course they cannot accomplish that aim, for words themselves are ideas, unless they push it to its logical conclusion, which is dadaism or non-

sense. Few of them being prepared to do
this, their achievement is in the main a
compromise which does not banish the intellectual function but stultifies it—a hectic
incoherence of sense and style, disintegration
instead of analysis, meaningless accumulation
in place of synthesis. M. Julien Benda, who
has exposed their futility with merciless logic,
has mocked them with a question of Bossuet's :
" Le charme de sentir est-il donc si fort ? "

The charm of feeling was very strong for
Sterne, but not so strong as to conquer his
reason or his humour. He was not sufficiently sophisticated to despise the intellect,
which, if it is not the artist's most important
source, is certainly his most precious tool. He
was not even ashamed to confess to an ethical
purpose. The *Sentimental Journey*, he says,
was designed " to teach us to love the world
and our fellow-creatures better than we do—
so it runs most upon those gentler passions
and affections, which aid so much to it."
This was perhaps an afterthought, and at
any rate we do not read the book for its
message, but for its delicate silver-point
delineations and its exquisite (and purely

intellectual) registration of emotional contacts.
Sterne's fingers were ever on his own pulse,
and he counted its wayward beats for our
pleasure. Too self-conscious to be a great
lover, he was the very type of the intellectual
amorist. He was the prince of philanderers,
and the *Sentimental Journey* is the classic, the
gospel, of philandering. The scenes with
Madame de L\*\*\* at the *remise* door and with
the *grisette* in the glove-shop are perfect
exemplifications of that art, which is an
intellectual exploitation of sensibility.

Sterne's hiatuses and abruptions have
nothing to do with the gasps and spasms of
the "expressionists." They are but tricks
of a whimsical fancy, or at most the evidence
of his volatility. Many of his dashes could
be changed into commas without alteration
of sense or even of *nuance*. These things are
too characteristic of the man to be dismissed
as merely mechanical and external, but the
essence of his style is its lucid limpidity.
In that quality he has no peer but Lamb and
one other, who has something in common
and has often been compared with him, but
is in no way his debtor—Mr. George Moore.

His prose is like a leisurely ſtream of infinite meanderings. Sometimes it babbles sunlit over shallows, and sometimes its pools are deep and dark and inhabited by ſtrange life. Here the bottom is of mud, which ever and again is ſtirred to cloud and discolour the waters; and here it is a garden of bright water-flowers. There are reaches which are dull and to be hurried over. But nearly always the ſtream is intereſting, nearly always delightful, to follow.

*Francis Bickley.*

# A SENTIMENTAL
# JOURNEY

——THEY order, said I, this matter
better in France.

—You have been in France? said my
gentleman, turning quick upon me, with the
most civil triumph in the world.——Strange!
quoth I, debating the matter with myself,
that one-and-twenty miles sailing, for 'tis
absolutely no further from Dover to Calais,
should give a man these rights :——I'll look
into them : so giving up the argument,——
I went straight to my lodgings, put up half a
dozen shirts and a black pair of silk breeches ;

—"the coat I have on," said I, looking at the sleeve, " will do,"—took a place in the Dover stage ; and, the packet sailing at nine the next morning,—by three I had got sat down to my dinner upon a fricasseed chicken, so incontestibly in France, that, had I died that night of an indigestion, the whole world could not have suspended the effects of the *droits d'aubaine* ; \*—my shirts, and black pair of silk breeches,—portmanteau and all, must have gone to the King of France ;—even the little picture which I have so long worn, and so often told thee, Eliza, I would carry with me into my grave, would have been torn from my neck !—Ungenerous ! to seize upon the wreck of an unwary passenger, whom your subjects had beckoned to their coast !—by Heaven ! Sire, it is not well done ; and much does it grieve me 'tis the monarch of a people so civilized and courteous, and so renowned for sentiment and fine feelings, that I have to reason with !——

But I have scarce set a foot in your dominions—

\*All the effects of strangers (Swiss and Scots excepted) dying in France are seized by virtue of this law, though the heir be upon the spot ;—the profit of these contingencies being farmed, there is no redress.

CALAIS

WHEN I had finished my dinner, and drank the King of France's health, to satisfy my mind that I bore him no spleen, but, on the contrary, high honor for the humanity of his temper,— I rose up an inch taller for the accommodation.

—No, said I, the Bourbon is by no means a cruel race : they may be misled, like other people ; but there is a mildness in their blood. As I acknowledged this, I felt a suffusion of a finer kind upon my cheek, more warm and friendly to man than what Burgundy (at least of two livres a bottle which was such as I had been drinking) could have produced.

——Just God ! said I, kicking my portmanteau aside, what is there in this world's goods which should sharpen our spirits, and make so many kind-hearted brethren of us fall out so cruelly as we do by the way ?

When man is at peace with man, how much lighter than a feather is the heaviest of metals in his hand ! he pulls out his purse, and holding it airily and uncompress'd, looks round him, as if he sought for an object to share it with.— In doing this I felt every vessel in my frame dilate,—the arteries beat all cheerly together, and every power which sustained life performed it with so little friction, that 'twould have confounded the most *physical precieuse* in France : with all her materialism, she could scarce have called me a machine.

I'm confident, said I to myself, I should have overset her creed.

The accession of that idea carried Nature, at that time, as high as she could go ;—I was at peace with the world before, and this finish'd the treaty with myself.

—Now, was I a King of France, cried I, what a moment for an orphan to have begg'd his father's portmanteau of me !

# THE MONK

### CALAIS

I HAD scarce uttered the words, when a poor Monk, of the order of St. Francis, came into the room, to beg something for his convent. No man cares to have his virtues the sport of contingencies,—or one man may be generous, as another man is puissant ;—*sed non quoad hanc,*—or be it as it may,—for there is no regular reasoning upon the ebbs and flows of our humours, they may depend upon the same causes, for aught I know, which influence the tides themselves ;—'twould oft be no discredit to us to suppose it was so : I'm sure, at least for myself, that in many a case I should be more highly satisfied to have it said by the world—" I had had an affair with the moon, in which there was neither sin nor shame," than have it pass altogether as my own act and deed, wherein there was so much of both.

5

—But be this as it may,—the moment I caſt my eyes upon him, I was predetermined not to give him a single sous ; and, accordingly, I put my purse into my pocket, button'd it up, set myself a little more upon my centre and advanced up gravely to him. There was something, I fear, forbidding in my look : I have his figure this moment before my eyes and think there was that in it which deserved better.

The monk, as I judged from the break in his tonsure, a few scatter'd white hairs upon his temples being all that remained of it, might be about seventy ; but from his eyes, and that sort of fire which was in them, which seemed more tempered by courtesy than years, could be no more than sixty :—truth might lie between,—he was certainly sixty-five ; and the general air of his countenance, notwith-ſtanding something seem'd to have been planting wrinkles in it before their time, agreed to the account.

It was one of those heads which Guido has often painted,—mild, pale, penetrating, free from all common-place ideas of fat contented ignorance looking downwards upon the earth ;—

it look'd forwards, but look'd as if it look'd
at something beyond this world. How one
of his order came by it, Heaven above, who
let it fall upon a monk's shoulders, best
knows ; but it would have suited a Brahmin
and, had I met it upon the plains of Indostan,
I had reverenced it.

The rest of his outline may be given in a few
strokes ; one might put it into the hands of
any one to design, for 'twas neither elegant
nor otherwise, but as character and expression
made it so : it was a thin, spare form, something above the common size, if it lost not the
distinction by a bend forward in the figure,—
but it was the attitude of Intreaty ; and, as it
now stands presented to my imagination, it
gained more than it lost by it.

When he had entered the room three paces,
he stood still ; and laying his left hand upon
his breast (a slender white staff with which
he journeyed being in his right)—when I
had got close up to him, he introduced himself
with the little story of the wants of his convent,
and the poverty of his order ;—and did it
with so simple a grace,—and such an air of
deprecation was there in the whole cast of

7

his look and figure,—I was bewitch'd not to have been struck with it.—

—A better reason was, I had predetermined not to give him a single sous.

# THE MONK

## CALAIS

——'Tis very true, said I, replying to a cast upwards with his eyes, with which he had concluded his address ;—'tis very true,— and Heaven be their resource who have no other but the charity of the world ! the stock of which, I fear, is no way sufficient for the many *great claims* which are hourly made upon it.

As I pronounced the words *great claims*, he gave a slight glance with his eye downwards upon the sleeve of his tunic :—I felt the full force of the appeal ;—I acknowledge it, said I :—a coarse habit, and that but once in three years, with meagre diet,—are no great matters ; and the true point of pity is, as they can be earn'd in the world with so little industry, that your order should wish to procure them by pressing upon a fund which is the property of the lame, the blind, the aged, and the infirm !—the captive, who lies down counting over and over again the days of his afflictions, languishes also for his share of it ; and had you been of the *order of Mercy*, instead of the order of St. Francis, poor as I am, continued I, pointing at my portmanteau, full cheerfully should it have been opened to you, for the ransom of the unfortunate.——The monk made me a bow.——But of all others, resum'd I, the unfortunate of our own country, surely, have the first rights ; and I have left thousands in distress upon our own shore.——The monk gave a cordial wave with his head,—as much as to say, No doubt, there is misery enough in every corner of the world, as well as within our convent.——But we distinguish, said I, laying my hand upon the sleeve of his tunic, in return for his appeal,—we diſtinguish, my good father, betwixt those who wish only to eat the bread of their own labour—and those who eat the bread of other people's, and have no other plan in life but to get through it in sloth and ignorance, *for the love of God*.

The poor Franciscan made no reply : a hectic of a moment pass'd across his cheek, but could not tarry :—Nature seemed to have had done with her resentments in him ; he shewed none :—but letting his ſtaff fall within his arm, he press'd both his hands with resignation upon his breaſt, and retired.

## THE MONK

### CALAIS

My heart smote me the moment he shut the door.—Psha ! said I, with an air of carelessness, three several times,—but it would not do ; every ungracious syllable I had uttered crowded back into my imagination: I reflected I had no right over the poor Franciscan but to deny him ; and that the punishment of that was enough to the disappointed, without the addition of unkind language.—I considered his grey hairs :— his courteous figure seem'd to re-enter, and gently ask me what injury he had done me ? —and why I could use him thus ?—I would have given twenty livres for an advocate.— I have behaved very ill, said I, within myself ; but I have only just set out upon my travels, and shall learn better manners as I get along.

# THE DESOBLIGEANT

## CALAIS

WHEN a man is discontented with himself, it has one advantage, however, that it puts him

C                    11

into an excellent frame of mind for making a bargain. Now, there being no travelling through France and Italy without a chaise, —and Nature generally prompting us to the thing we are fittest for, I walked out into the coach-yard to buy or hire something of that kind to my purpose : an old *desobligeant*,* in the furthest corner of the court, hit my fancy at first sight ; so I instantly got into it, and finding it in tolerable harmony with my feelings, I ordered the waiter to call Monsieur Dessein, the master of the hotel ; —but Monsieur Dessein being gone to vespers, and not caring to face the Franciscan, whom I saw on the opposite side of the court, in conference with a lady just arrived at the inn, —I drew the taffeta-curtain betwixt us, and, being determined to write my journey, I took out my pen and ink, and wrote the preface to it in the *desobligeant*.

* A chaise, so called in France from its holding but one person.

# PREFACE

## IN THE DESOBLIGEANT

It must have been observed, by many a peripatetic philosopher, That Nature has set up, by her own unquestionable authority, certain boundaries and fences to circumscribe the discontent of man ; she has effected her purpose in the quietest and easiest manner, by laying him under almost insuperable obligations to work out his ease, and to sustain his sufferings at home. It is there only that she has provided him with the most suitable objects to partake of his happiness, and bear a part of that burden which, in all countries and ages, has ever been too heavy for one pair of shoulders. 'Tis true, we are endued with an imperfect power of spreading our happiness sometimes beyond *her* limits ; but 'tis so ordered, that, from the want of languages, connections, and dependencies, and, from the

13

difference in educations, customs, and habits, we lie under so many impediments in communicating our sensations out of our own sphere, as often amount to a total impossibility.

It will always follow from hence, that the balance of sentimental commerce is always against the expatriated adventurer : he must buy, what he has little occasion for, at their own price ;—his conversation will seldom be taken in exchange for theirs without a large discount,—and this, by the bye, eternally driving him into the hands of more equitable brokers, for such conversation as he can find, it requires no great spirit of divination to guess at his party.

This brings me to my point, and naturally leads me (if the see-saw of this *desobligeant* will but let me get on) into the efficient as well as final causes of travelling.

Your idle people that leave their native country, and go abroad for some reason or reasons; which may be derived from one of these general causes :—

> Infirmity of body,
> Imbecility of mind, or
> Inevitable necessity.

The two first include all those who travel by land or by water, labouring with pride, curiosity, vanity, or spleen, subdivided and combined *in infinitum*.

The third class includes the whole army of peregrine martyrs ; more especially those travellers who set out upon their travels with the benefit of the clergy, either as delinquents, travelling under the direction of governors recommended by the magistrate ;—or young gentlemen, transported by the cruelty of parents and guardians, and travelling under the direction of governors recommended by Oxford, Aberdeen, and Glasgow.

There is a fourth class, but their number is so small, that they would not deserve a distinction, were it not necessary, in a work of this nature, to observe the greatest precision and nicety, to avoid a confusion of character : and these men I speak of are such as cross the seas, and sojourn in a land of strangers, with a view of saving money for various reasons, and upon various pretences ; but, as they might also save themselves and others a great deal of unnecessary trouble by saving their money at home,—and, as their reasons for travelling are the least complex of any other species of emigrants, I shall distinguish these gentlemen by the name of

Simple Travellers.

Thus the whole circle of travellers may be reduced to the following heads :—

Idle Travellers,
Inquisitive Travellers,
Lying Travellers,
Proud Travellers,
Vain Travellers,
Splenetic Travellers ;

then follow

The Travellers of Necessity,
The Delinquent and Felonious Traveller,
The Unfortunate and Innocent Traveller,
The simple Traveller,

And last of all (if you please) The Sentimental Traveller (meaning thereby myself) who have travell'd, and of which I am now sitting down to give an account,—as much out of *Necessity*, and the *besoin de Voyager* as any one in the class.

I am well aware, at the same time, as both my travels and observations will be altogether

of a different cast from any of my forerunners,
that I might have insisted upon a whole niche
entirely to myself ;—but I should break in
upon the confines of the *Vain* Traveller, in
wishing to draw attention towards me, till
I have some better grounds for it than the
mere *Novelty of my Vehicle*. It is sufficient
for my reader, if he has been a Traveller
himself, that with study and reflection here-
upon, he may be able to determine his own
place and rank in the catalogue ;—it will be
one step towards knowing himself, as it is
great odds but he retains some tincture and
resemblance of what he imbibed or carried
out, to the present hour.

The man who first transplanted the grape of
Burgundy to the Cape of Good Hope (observe
he was a Dutchman) never dreamt of drinking
the same wine at the Cape that the same grape
produced upon the French mountains,—he
was too phlegmatic for that ;—but, undoubtedly he expected to drink some sort of
vinous liquor ; but whether good, bad, or
indifferent,—he knew enough of this world
to know that it did not depend upon his
choice, but that what is generally called

17

*chance* was to decide his success : however, he hoped for the best ; and in these hopes, by an intemperate confidence in the fortitude of his head, and the depth of his discretion, *Mynheer* might possibly overset both in his new vine-yard ; and, by discovering his nakedness, become a laughing-stock to his people.

Even so it fares with the poor Traveller sailing and posting through the politer king-doms of the globe, in pursuit of knowledge and improvements.

Knowledge and improvements are to be got by sailing and posting for that purpose ; but whether useful knowledge and real improvements are all a lottery ;—and, even where the adventurer is successful, the acquired stock must be used with caution and sobriety, to turn to any profit :—but, as the chances run prodigiously the other way, both as to the acquisition and application, I am of opinion, That a man would act as wisely, if he could prevail upon himself to live con-tented without foreign knowledge or foreign improvements, especially if he lives in a country that has no absolute want of either ;—and, indeed, much grief of heart has it oft

and many a time cost me, when I have observed
how many a foul step the Inquisitive Traveller
has measured, to see sights and look into
discoveries, all which, as Sancho Pança said
to Don Quixote, they might have seen dry-
shod at home. It is an age so full of light,
that there is scarce a country or corner of
Europe, whose beams are not crossed and
interchanged with others.—Knowledge, in
most of its branches, and in most affairs, is
like music in an Italian street, whereof those
may partake who pay nothing.—But there is
no nation under Heaven,—and God is my
record (before whose tribunal I must one
day come and give an account of this work)—
that I do not speak it vauntingly,—But there
is no nation under Heaven abounding with
more variety of learning,—where the sciences
may be more fitly woo'd, or more surely won,
than here—where Art is encouraged, and will
soon rise high,—where Nature (take her
altogether) has so little to answer for,—and,
to close all, where there is more wit and variety
of character to feed the mind with :—Where,
then, my dear countrymen, are you going ?—

————We are only looking at this chaise,

said they.——Your most obedient servant, said I, skipping out of it, and pulling off my hat.——We were wondering, said one of them, who, I found, was an *Inquisitive Traveller*,—what could occasion its motion.—'Twas the agitation, said I, coolly, of writing a preface.——I never heard, said the other, who was a *Simple Traveller*, of a preface wrote in a *desobligeant*.——It would have been better, said I, in a *vis-a-vis*.

*As an Englishman does not travel to see Englishmen*, I retired to my room.

## CALAIS

I PERCEIVED that something darken'd the passage more than myself, as I stepp'd along it to my room ; it was effectually Mons. Dessein, the master of the hotel, who had just returned from vespers, and, with his hat under his arm, was most complaisantly following me, to put me in mind of my wants. I had wrote myself pretty well out of conceit with the *desobligeant* ; and Mons. Dessein

speaking of it with a shrug, as if it would
no way suit me, it immediately ſtruck my
fancy that it belonged to some *Innocent
Traveller*, who, on his return home, had left
it to Mons. Dessein's honor to make the
moſt of. Four months had elapsed since it
had finished its career of Europe in the corner
of Mons. Dessein's coach-yard : and having
sallied out from thence but a vampt-up
business at the firſt, though it had been twice
taken to pieces on Mount Sennis, it had not
profited much by its adventures,—but by
none so little as the ſtanding so many months
unpitied in the corner of Mons. Desscin's
coach-yard. Much, indeed, was not to be
said for it,—but something might,—and, when
a few words will rescue Misery out of her
diſtress, I hate the man who can be a churl
of them.

—Now, was I the maſter of this hotel, said
I, laying the point of my fore-finger on Mons.
Dessein's breaſt, I would inevitably make a
point of getting rid of this unfortunate *desobligeant* ; it ſtands swinging reproaches at
you every time you pass by it.

*Mon Dieu !* said Mons. Dessein,—I have

no interest.——Except the interest, said I, which men of a certain turn of mind take, Mons. Dessein, in their own sensations,— I'm persuaded, to a man who feels for others as well as for himself, every rainy night, disguise it as you will, must cast a damp upon your spirits. You suffer, Mons. Dessein, as much as the machine.

I have always observed, when there is as much *sour* as *sweet* in a compliment, that an Englishman is eternally at a loss within himself whether to take it or let it alone ; a Frenchman never is ; Mons. Dessein made me a bow.

*C'est bien vrai*, said he.—But, in this case, I should only exchange one disquietude for another, and with loss. Figure to yourself, my dear Sir, that in giving you a chaise which would fall to pieces before you had got half way to Paris,—figure to yourself how much I should suffer, in giving an ill impression of myself to a man of honor, and lying at the mercy, as I must do, *d'un homme d'esprit.*

The dose was made up exactly after my own prescription ; so I could not help taking it,— and returning Mons. Dessein his bow, without more casuistry we walk'd together towards his *remise*, to take a view of his magazine of chaises.

## IN THE STREET

### CALAIS

It must needs be a hostile kind of a world, when the buyer (if it be but of a sorry post-chaise) cannot go forth with the seller thereof into the street, to terminate the difference betwixt them, but he instantly falls into the same frame of mind, and views his conventionist with the same sort of eye, as if he was going along with him to Hyde Park Corner to fight a duel. For my own part, being but a poor swordsman, and no way a match for Mons. Dessein, I felt the rotation of all the movements within me, to which the situation is incident ;—I looked at Monsieur Dessein through and through,—eyed him as he walked along in profile,—then *en face ;*—thought he looked like a Jew,—then a Turk,—disliked his wig,—cursed him by my gods,—wished him at the Devil !

—And is all this to be lighted up in the heart for a beggarly account of three or four Louis d'ors, which is the most I can be overreached in ?—Base passion ! said I, turning myself about, as a man naturally does upon a sudden reverse of sentiment,—base, ungentle passion ! thy hand is against every man, and every man's hand against thee.——Heaven forbid ! said she, raising her hand up to her forehead for I had turned full in front upon the lady whom I had seen in conference with the monk :—she had followed us unperceived. ——Heaven forbid, indeed ! said I, offering her my own ;—she had a black pair of silk gloves, open only at the thumb and two forefingers, so accepted it without reserve,—and I led her up to the door of the *remise*.

Monsieur Dessein had *diabled* the key above fifty times before he found out he had come with a wrong one in his hand : we were as impatient as himself to have it open'd ; and so attentive to the obstacle, that I continued holding her hand almost without knowing it : so that Mons. Dessein left us together, with her hand in mine, and with our faces turned towards the door of the *remise*, and said he would be back in five minutes.

Now, a colloquy of five minutes, in such a situation, is worth one of as many ages, with your faces turned towards the street. In the latter case, 'tis drawn from the objects and occurrences without ;—when your eyes are fixed upon a dead blank,—you draw purely from yourselves. A silence of a single moment, upon Mons. Dessein's leaving us, had been fatal to the situation,—she had infallibly turned about ;—so I began the conversation instantly.

—But what were the temptations (as I write not to apologize for the weaknesses of my heart in this tour,—but to give an account of them)—shall be described with the same simplicity with which I felt them.

# THE REMISE DOOR

## CALAIS

WHEN I told the reader that I did not care to get out of the *desobligeant*, because I saw the monk in close conference with the lady just arrived at the inn, I told him the truth ; but I did not tell him the whole truth ; for I was full as much restrained by the appearance and figure of the lady he was talking to. Suspicion crossed my brain, and said, he was telling her what had passed ; something jarred upon it within me,—I wished him at his convent.

When the heart flies out before the understanding, it saves the judgment a world of pains.—I was certain she was of a better order of beings :—however, I thought no more of her, but went on and wrote my preface.

The impression returned upon my encounter with her in the street, a guarded frankness with which she gave me her hand, shewed, I thought, her good education and her good sense ; and, as I led her on, I felt a pleasurable ductility about her, which spread a calmness over all my spirits.

——Good God ! how a man might lead such a creature as this round the world with him !

I had not yet seen her face,—'twas not material ; for the drawing was instantly set about, and, long before we had got to the door of the *remise*, *Fancy* had finish'd the whole head, and pleased herself as much with its fitting her goddess, as if she had dived into the Tiber for it ;—but thou art seduced, and a seducing slut ; and albeit thou cheatest us seven times a day with thy pictures and images, yet with so many charms dost thou do it, and thou deckest out thy pictures in the shapes of so many angels of light, 'tis a shame to break with thee.

When we had got to the door of the *remise*, she withdrew her hand from across her forehead, and let me see the original :—it was a face of about six-and-twenty,—of a clear transparent brown, simply set off without

D      

rouge or powder ;—it was not critically handsome, but there was that in it which, in the frame of mind I was in, attached me much more to it,—it was interesting ; I fancied it wore the characters of a widow'd look, and in that state of its declension which had passed the two first paroxysms of sorrow, and was quietly beginning to reconcile itself to its loss ;—but a thousand other distresses might have traced the same lines : I wish'd to know what they had been,—and was ready to inquire (had the same *bon ton* of conversation permitted as in the days of Esdras)— " *What aileth thee ? and why art thou disquieted ? and why is thy understanding troubled ?* "— In a word, I felt benevolence for her, and resolv'd, some way or other, to throw in my mite of courtesy,—if not of service.

Such were my temptations ;—and in this disposition to give way to them, was I left alone with the lady, with her hand in mine, and with our faces both turned closer to the door of the *remise* than what was absolutely necessary.

## THE REMISE DOOR

### CALAIS

THIS certainly, fair lady, said I, raising her hand up a little lightly as I began, must be one of Fortune's whimsical doings ; to take two utter strangers by their hands,—of different sexes, and perhaps, from different corners of the globe, and in one moment place them together in such a cordial situation as Friendship herself could scarce have achieved for them, had she projected it for a month.——

——And your reflection upon it shews how much, Monsieur, she has embarrassed you by the adventure.

When the situation is what we would wish, nothing is so ill-timed as to hint at the circumstances which make it so.——You thank Fortune, continued she,—you had reason,— the heart knew it, and was satisfied ; and who but an English philosopher would have sent notice of it to the brain to reverse the judgment?

In saying this, she disengaged her hand, with a look which I thought a sufficient commentary upon the text.

It is a miserable picture which I am going to give of the weakness of my heart, by owning that it suffered a pain, which worthier occasions could not have inflicted.—I was mortified with the loss of her hand ; and the manner in which I had lost it, carried neither oil nor wine to the wound : I never felt the pain of a peevish inferiority so miserably in my life.

The triumphs of a true feminine heart are short upon these discomfitures. In a very few seconds she laid her hand upon the cuff of my coat in order to finish her reply ; so, some way or other, God knows how, I regained my situation.

——She had nothing to add.

I forthwith began to model a different conversation for the lady, thinking, from the spirit as well as moral of this, that I had been mistaken in her character ; but, upon turning her face towards me, the spirit which had animated the reply was fled,—the muscles relaxed, and I saw the same unprotected look of distress which first won me to her interest :—melancholy ! to see such sprightliness the prey of sorrow,—I pitied her from my soul ; and, though it may seem ridiculous enough to a torpid heart,—I could have taken her into my arms, and cherished her, though it was in the open street, without blushing.

The pulsations of the arteries along my fingers pressing across hers, told her what was passing within me. She looked down:— a silence of some moments followed.

I fear, in this interval, I must have made some slight efforts towards a closer compression of her hand, from a subtle sensation I felt in the palm of my own,—not as if she was going to withdraw hers,—but as if she thought about it ;—and I had infallibly lost it a second time, had not instinct, more than reason, directed me to the last resource in these dangers,—to hold it loosely, and in a manner as if I was every moment going to release it of myself : so she let it continue till Mons. Dessein returned with the key ; and, in the meantime, I set myself to consider how I should undo the ill impressions which the poor monk's

31

story, in case he had told it her, must have planted in her breast against me.

## THE SNUFF-BOX

### CALAIS

THE good old monk was within six paces of us as the idea of him cross'd my mind ; and was advancing towards us a little out of the line, as if uncertain whether he should break in upon us or no.——He stopp'd, however, as soon as he came up to us, with a world of frankness, and, having a horn snuff-box in his hand, he presented it open to me.—— You shall taste mine, said I, pulling out my box (which was a small tortoise one), and putting it into his hand.——'Tis most excellent, said the monk.—Then do me the favour, I replied, to accept of the box and all ; and when you take a pinch out of it, sometimes recollect it was the peace-offering of a man who once used you unkindly, but not from his heart.

The poor monk blush'd as red as scarlet. *Mon Dieu !* said he, pressing his hands together —you never used me unkindly.——I should think, said the lady, he is not likely.——I blush'd in my turn ; but from what movements, I leave to the few who feel, to analyse. —Excuse me, Madam, replied I,—I treated him most unkindly ; and from no provocations.——'Tis impossible, said the lady.—— My God ! cried the monk, with a warmth of asseveration which seemed not to belong to him,—the fault was in me, and in the indiscretion of my zeal.——The lady opposed it ; and I joined with her,—in maintaining it was impossible that a spirit so regulated as his could give offence to any.

I knew not that contention could be rendered so sweet and pleasurable a thing to the nerves as I then felt it. We remained silent, without any sensation of that foolish pain which takes place, when, in such a circle, you look for ten minutes in one another's faces without saying a word. Whilst this lasted the monk rubb'd his horn-box upon the sleeve of his tunic ; and as soon as it had acquired a little air of brightness by the friction, he made a low bow, and said, 'Twas too late to say whether it was the weakness or goodness of our tempers which had involved us in this contest ;—but, be it as it would,— he begged we might exchange boxes.—In saying this, he presented his to me with one hand, as he took mine from me in the other ; and having kissed it,—with a stream of good-nature in his eyes, he put it into his bosom,— and took his leave.

I guard this box as I would the instrumental parts of my religion, to help my mind on to something better. In truth, I seldom go abroad without it ; and oft and many a time have I called up by it the courteous spirit of its owner to regulate my own, in the justlings of the world : they had found full employment for his, as I learnt from his story, till about the forty-fifth year of his age, when, upon some military services ill requited, and meeting at the same time with a disappointment in the tenderest of passions, he abandoned the sword and the sex together, and took sanctuary, not so much in his convent as in himself.

I feel a damp upon my spirits as I am going to add, that in my last return through Calais, upon inquiring after Father Lorenzo, I heard he had been dead near three months ; and was buried, not in his convent, but according to his desire, in a little cemetery belonging to it, about two leagues off. I had a strong desire to see where they had laid him,—when, upon pulling out his little horn-box, as I sat by his grave, and plucking up a nettle or two at the head of it, which had no business to grow there, they all struck together so forcibly upon my affections, that I burst into a flood of tears ;—but I am as weak as a woman ; and I beg the world not to smile, but pity me.

## THE REMISE DOOR

### CALAIS

I HAD never quitted the lady's hand all this
time ; and had held it so long, that it would
have been indecent to have let it go, without
first pressing it to my lips : the blood and
spirits, which had suffered a revulsion from
her, crowded back to her as I did it.

Now the two travellers, who had spoke to
me in the coach-yard, happened at that crisis
to be passing by, and observing our com-
munications naturally took it into their heads
that we must be *man and wife* at least ; so
stopping as soon as they came up to the door
of the *remise*, the one of them, who was the
Inquisitive Traveller, ask'd us, if we set out
for Paris the next morning ?——I could only
answer for myself, I said ;—and the lady
added, she was for Amiens.——We dined
there yesterday, said the Simple Traveller.

——You go directly through the town, added the other, in your road to Paris.——I was going to return a thousand thanks for the intelligence *that Amiens was on the road to Paris ;* but, upon pulling out my poor monk's little horn-box to take a pinch of snuff, I made them a quiet bow, and wished them a good passage to Dover.——They left us alone.

——Now where would be the harm, said I to myself, if I was to beg of this distressed lady to accept of half my chaise ?——and what mighty mischief could ensue ?

Every dirty passion and bad propensity in my nature took the alarm as I stated the proposition ;——It will oblige you to have a third horse, said *Avarice*, which will put twenty livres out of your pocket.——You know not what she is, said *Caution ;* or what scrapes the affair may draw you into, whisper'd *Cowardice.*

——Depend upon it, Yorick, said *Discretion*, 'twill be said you went off with a mistress ; and came, by assignation, to Calais for that purpose.

——You can never after, cried *Hypocrisy*, aloud, shew your face in the world ;——nor rise, quoth *Meanness*, in the church ;—nor be any thing in it, said *Pride*, but a lousy prebendary.

But 'tis a civil thing, said I ;—and as I generally act from the first impulse, and therefore seldom listen to these cabals, which serve no purpose that I know of, but to encompass the heart with adamant,—I turn'd instantly about to the lady,——

But she had glided off unperceived, as the cause was pleading, and had made ten or a dozen paces down the street by the time I had made the determination ; so I set off after her with a long stride, to make her the proposal with the best address I was master of ; but observing she walk'd with her cheek half resting upon the palm of her hand,—with the slow, short-measur'd step of thoughtfulness, and with her eyes, as she went step by step, fixed upon the ground, it struck me she was trying the same cause herself.—God help her ! said I, she has some mother-in-law, or tartufish aunt, or nonsensical old woman, to consult upon the occasion, as well as myself : so not caring to interrupt the process, and deeming it more gallant to take her at discretion than surprise, I faced about, and took a short turn or two before the door of the *remise*, whilſt she walk'd musing on one side.

## IN THE STREET

### CALAIS

HAVING, on firſt sight of the lady, settled the affair in my fancy, "that she was of the bettcr order of beings";—and then laid it down as a second axiom, as indisputable as the firſt, That she was a widow, and wore a chara&ter of diſtress,—I went no further; I got ground enough for the situation which pleased me;—and had she remained close beside my elbow till midnight, I should have held true to my syſtem, and considered her only under that general idea.

She had scarce got twenty paces distant from me, ere something within me called out for a more particular inquiry ;—it brought on the idea of a further separation :—I might possibly never see her more :—the heart is for saving what it can ; and I wanted the traces through which my wishes might find their way to her, in case I should never rejoin her myself. In a word, I wish'd to know her name,—her family,—her condition ;—and as I knew the place to which she was going, I wanted to know from whence she came : but there was no coming at all this intelligence : a hundred little delicacies stood in the way. I form'd a score different plans.—There was no such thing as a man's asking her directly ; —the thing was impossible.

A little French *debonaire* captain, who came dancing down the street, shewed me it was the easiest thing in the world ;—for, popping in betwixt us, just as the lady was returning back to the door of the *remise*, he introduced himself to my acquaintance, and before he had well got announced, begg'd I would do him the honor to present him to the lady.—I had not been presented myself ;

—so turning about to her, he did it just as well, by asking her if she had come from Paris?——No ; she was going that route, she said.——*Vous n'etez pas de Londre?*—— She was not, she replied.——Then Madame must have come through Flanders.—*Apparamment vous etez Flammande?* said the French captain,—The lady answered, she was.—— *Peut etre de Lisle?* added he.——She answered, she was not of Lisle,——Nor Arras? —nor Cambray?—nor Ghent?—nor Brussels? ——She answered, she was of Brussels.

——He had had the honor, he said, to be at the bombardment of it last war ;—that it was finely situated, *pour cela*,—and full of noblesse when the Imperialists were driven out by the French (the lady made a slight curtsey) ;— so giving her an account of the affair, and of the share he had had in it,—he begg'd the honor to know her name,—so made his bow.

——*Et Madame a son Mari?* said he, looking back when he had made two steps,—and without staying for an answer,—danced down the street.

Had I served seven years' apprenticeship to good-breeding, I could not have done as much.

## THE REMISE

### CALAIS

As the little French captain left us, Mons. Dessein came up with the key of the *remise* in his hand, and forthwith let us into his magazine of chaises.

The first object which caught my eye, as Mons. Dessein open'd the door of the *remise*, was another old tatter'd *desobligeant*; and notwithstanding it was the exact picture of that which had hit my fancy so much in the coach-yard but an hour before,—the very sight of it stirr'd up a disagreeable sensation within me now ; and I thought 'twas a churlish beast into whose heart the idea could first enter to construct such a machine ; nor had I much more charity for the man who could think of using it.

I observed the lady was as little taken with it as myself : so Mons. Dessein led us on to a couple of chaises which stood abreast, telling us, as he recommended them, that they had been purchased by my Lord A. and B. to go the *grand tour*, but had gone no further than Paris ; so were, in all respects, as good as new.—They were too good ;—so I pass'd on to a third, which stood behind, and forth-with began to chaffer for the price.——But 'twill scarce hold two, said I, opening the door and getting in.——Have the goodness, Madam, said Mons. Dessein, offering his arm, to step in.—The lady hesitated half a second, and stepp'd in ; and the waiter that moment beckoning to speak to Mons. Dessein he shut the door of the chaise upon us, and left us.

## THE REMISE DOOR

### CALAIS

*C'est bien comique*, 'tis very droll, said the lady smiling, from the reflection that this

E

was the second time we had been left together
by a parcel of nonsensical contingencies,—
*c'est bien comique*, said she.

——There wants nothing, said I, to make
it so, but the comic use which the gallantry of
a Frenchman would put it to,—to make love
the first moment,—and an offer of his person
the second.

——'Tis their *fort*, replied the lady.

——It is supposed so at least ;—and how
it has come to pass, continued I, I know not ;
but they have certainly got the credit of
understanding more of love, and making it
better than any other nation upon earth ;
but for my own part, I think them arrant
bunglers ; and, in truth, the worst set of
marksmen that ever tried Cupid's patience.

—To think of making love by *sentiments* !

I should as soon think of making a genteel
suit of clothes out of remnants ;—and to do
it,—pop,—at first sight by declaration,—is
submitting the offer and themselves with it,
to be sifted with all their *pours* and *contres*
by an unheated mind.

The lady attended as if she expected I
should go on.

——Consider then, Madam, continued I, laying my hand upon hers,——

That grave people hate Love for the name's sake,——

That selfish people hate it for their own,——

Hypocrites for Heaven's,——

And that all of us, both old and young, being ten times worse frightened than hurt by the very *report*,——

What a want of knowledge in this branch of commerce a man betrays, who ever lets the word come out of his lips till an hour or two at least after the time that his silence upon it becomes tormenting ! A course of small, quiet attentions, not so pointed as to alarm, —nor so vague as to be misunderstood,— with now and then a look of kindness, and little or nothing said upon it,—leaves Nature for your mistress, and she fashions it to her mind.

——Then I solemnly declare, said the lady, blushing,—you have been making love to me all this while.

## THE REMISE

### CALAIS

MONSIEUR DESSEIN came back to let us out of the chaise, and acquaint the lady that Count de L ***, her brother, was just arrived at the hotel. Though I had infinite good-will for the lady, I cannot say that I rejoiced in my heart at the event,—and could not help telling her so ;—for it is fatal to a proposal, Madam, said I, that I was going to make you.

——You need not tell me what the proposal was, said she, laying her hand upon both mine, as she interrupted me.—A man, my good Sir, has seldom an offer of Kindness to make to a woman, but she has a presentiment of it some moments before.

——Nature arms her with it, said I, for immediate preservation.——But I think, said she, looking in my face, I had no evil to apprehend ;—and, to deal frankly with you, had determined to accept it.—If I had—(she stopped a moment)—I believe your good-will would have drawn a story from me, which would have made pity the only dangerous thing in the journey.

In saying this, she suffered me to kiss her hand twice ; and, with a look of sensibility mixed with concern, she got out of the chaise, —and bid adieu.

## IN THE STREET

### CALAIS

I never finished a twelve-guinea bargain so expeditiously in my life. My time seemed heavy upon the loss of the lady ; and knowing every moment of it would be as two, till I put myself into motion,—I ordered post-horses directly, and walked towards the hotel.

Lord! said I, hearing the town-clock strike four, and recollecting that I had been little more than a single hour in Calais,—

What a large volume of adventures may be grasped within this little span of life by him who interests his heart in every thing, and who, having eyes to see what time and chance are perpetually holding out to him as he journeyeth on his way, misses nothing he can *fairly* lay his hands on!

—If this won't turn out something,—another will;—no matter,—'tis an assay upon human nature;—I get my labour for my pains,—'tis enough;—the pleasure of the experiment has kept my senses and the best part of my blood awake, and laid the gross to sleep.

I pity the man who can travel from *Dan* to *Beersheba*, and cry, 'Tis all barren;—and so it is: and so is all the world to him who will not cultivate the fruits it offers. I declare, said I, clapping my hands cheerily together, that was I in a desert, I would find

48

out wherewith in it to call forth my affections :
—if I could not do better, I would fasten
them upon some sweet myrtle, or seek some
melancholy cypress to connect myself to ;—
I would court their shade, and greet them
kindly for their protection ;—I would cut
my name upon them, and swear they were
the loveliest trees throughout the desert ;
if their leaves withered, I would teach myself
to mourn :—and when they rejoiced, I would
rejoice along with them.

The learned Smelfungus travelled from
Boulogne to Paris,—from Paris to Rome,—
and so on ;—but he set out with the spleen
and jaundice ; and every object he pass'd
by was discoloured or distorted.—He wrote
an account of them ; but 'twas nothing but the
account of his miserable feelings.

I met Smelfungus in the grand portico of
the Pantheon :—he was just coming out of
it.—*'Tis nothing but a huge cock-pit,** said he
——I wish you had said nothing worse of
the Venus of Medicis, replied I ;—for in
passing through Florence, I had heard he
had fallen foul upon the goddess, and used

* Vide S——'s Travels.

her worse than a common strumpet, without the least provocation in nature.

I popp'd upon Smelfungus again at Turin, in his return home ; and a sad tale of sorrowful adventures he had to tell, " wherein he spoke of moving accidents by flood and field, and of the cannibals who each other eat : the Anthropophagi."—He had been flay'd alive, and bedevil'd, and used worse than St. Bartholomew at every stage he had come at.——

I'll tell it, cried Smelfungus, to the world. ——You had better tell it, said I, to your physician.

Mundungus, with an immense fortune, made the whole tour ; going on from Rome to Naples,—from Naples to Venice,—from Venice to Vienna,—to Dresden, to Berlin, without one generous connection or pleasurable anecdote to tell of ; but he had travell'd straight on, looking neither to his right hand nor his left, lest Love or Pity should seduce him out of his road.

Peace be to them, if it is to be found ; but Heaven itself, was it possible to get there with such tempers, would want objects to give it ;—every gentle spirit would come flying upon the wings of Love to hail their arrival.—Nothing would the souls of Smelfungus and Mundungus hear of, but fresh anthems of joy, fresh raptures of love, and fresh congratulations of their common felicity. —I heartily pity them : they have brought up no faculties for this work : and was the happiest mansion in Heaven to be allotted to Smelfungus and Mundungus, they would be so far from being happy, that the souls of Smelfungus and Mundungus would do penance there to all eternity !

## MONTRIUL

I HAD once loſt my portmanteau from behind my chaise, and twice got out in the rain, and one of the times up to the knees in dirt, to help the poſtillion to tie it on, without being able to find out what was wanting.—Nor was it till I got to Montriul, upon the landlord's asking me if I wanted not a servant, that it occurred to me that *that* was the very thing.

A servant! that I do, most sadly, quoth I. ——Because Monsieur, said the landlord, there is a clever young fellow, who would be very proud of the honor to serve an Englishman.——But why an English one more than any other?——They are so generous, said the landlord.——I'll be shot if this is not a livre out of my pocket, quoth I to myself, this very night.——But they have wherewithal to be so, Monsieur, added he.——Set down one livre more for that, quoth I.—— It was but laſt night, said the landlord, *qu'un my Lord Anglois presentoit un ecu a la fille de chambre.*——*Tant pis, pour Madamoiselle Janatone,* said I.

Now Janatone being the landlord's daughter, and the landlord supposing I was young in French, took the liberty to inform me, I should not have said *tant pis;*—but *tant mieux.*—*Tant mieux, toujours, Monsieur,* said he, when there is anything to be got, *tant pis,* when there is nothing.——It comes to the same thing, said I.—*Pardonnez moi,* said the landlord.

I cannot take a fitter opportunity to observe once for all, that *tant pis* and *tant mieux* being two of the great hinges in French conversation, a stranger would do well to set himself right in the use of them, before he gets to Paris.

A prompt French Marquis at our Ambassador's table, demanded of Mr. H——, if he was H—— the poet?——No, said Mr. H——, mildly.——*Tant pis*, replied the Marquis.

——It is H—— the historian, said another. ——*Tant mieux*, said the Marquis.——And Mr. H——, who is a man of an excellent heart, return'd thanks for both.

When the landlord had set me right in this matter, he called in La Fleur, which was the name of the young man he had spoke of,— saying only first, That as for his talents, he would presume to say nothing—Monsieur was the best judge what would suit him ; but for the fidelity of La Fleur, he would stand responsible in all he was worth.

The landlord delivered this in a manner which instantly set my mind to the business I was upon ;—and La Fleur, who stood waiting without, in that breathless expectation which every son of Nature of us have felt in our turns, came in.

MONTRIUL

I AM apt to be taken with all kinds of people at first sight ; but never more so than when a poor Devil comes to offer his service to so poor a Devil as myself ; and as I know this weakness, I always suffer my judgment to draw back something on that very account,— and this more or less, according to the mood I am in, and the case ;—and I may add, the gender too of the person I am to govern.

When La Fleur entered the room, after every discount I could make for my soul, the genuine look and air of the fellow determined the matter at once in his favor ; so I hired him first,—and then began to enquire what he could do.—But I shall find out his talents, quoth I, as I want them ;—besides, a Frenchman can do every thing.

Now poor La Fleur could do nothing in the world but beat a drum, and play a march or two upon the fife. I was determined to make his talents do : and can't say my weakness was ever so insulted by my wisdom as in the attempt.

La Fleur had set out early in life, as gallantly as moſt Frenchmen do, with *serving* for a few years : at the end of which, having satisfied the sentiment, and found, moreover, that the honor of beating a drum was likely to be its own reward, as it open'd no further track of glory to him,—he retired *a ses terres,* and lived *comme il plaisoit a Dieu ;*—that is to say, upon nothing.

———And so, quoth Wisdom, you have hired a drummer to attend you in this tour of yours through France and Italy !———Pshaw ! said I, and do not one half of our gentry go with a humdrum *compagnon du voiage* the same round, and have the piper and the Devil and all ιο pay besides ? When man can extricate himself with an *equivoque* in such an unequal match,—he is not ill off.———But you can do something else, La Fleur ? said I. ———*O qu'oui !* he could make spatterdashes, and play a little upon the fiddle.———Bravo ! said Wisdom———Why I play a bass myself, said I ;—we shall do very well. You can shave and dress a wig a little, La Fleur ?—

He had all the dispositions in the world.——
It is enough for Heaven, said I, interrupting
him,—and ought to be enough for me.——
So supper coming in, and having a frisky
English spaniel, on one side of my chair, and
a French valet, with as much hilarity in his
countenance as ever Nature painted in one,
on the other,—I was satisfied to my heart's
content with my empire ; and if monarchs
knew what they would be at, they might be as
satisfied as I was.

### MONTRIUL

As La Fleur went the whole tour of France
and Italy with me, and will be often upon the
stage, I must interest the reader a little further
in his behalf, by saying, that I had never less
reason to repent of the impulses which generally
do determine me, than in regard to this fellow ;
—he was a faithful, affectionate, simple soul as
ever trudged after the heels of a philosopher ;
and notwithstanding his talents of drum-
beating and spatterdash-making, which, though

very good in themselves, happened to be of no great service to me, yet was I hourly recompensed by the festivity of his temper ; —it supplied all defects :—I had a constant resource in his looks in all difficulties and distresses of my own—(I was going to have added, of his too) ; but La Fleur was out of the reach of every thing ; for whether it was hunger or thirst, or cold or nakedness, or watchings, or whatever stripes of ill luck La Fleur met with in our journeyings, there was no index in his physiognomy to point them out by,—he was eternally the same ; so that if I am a piece of a philosopher, which Satan now and then puts into my head I am,—it always mortifies the pride of the conceit, by reflecting how much I owe to the complexional philosophy of this poor fellow, for shaming me into one of a better kind. With all this, La Fleur had a small cast of the coxcomb ;—but he seemed, at first sight, to be more a coxcomb of nature than of art ; and before I had been three days in Paris with him,—he seemed to be no coxcomb at all.

### MONTRIUL

THE next morning, La Fleur entering upon his employment, I delivered to him the key of my portmanteau, with an inventory of my half a dozen shirts and a silk pair of breeches : and bid him fasten all upon the chaise,——get the horses put to,——and desire the landlord to come in with his bill.

——*C'est un garcon de bonne fortune*, said the landlord, pointing thro' the window, to half a dozen wenches who had got round about La Fleur, and were most kindly taking their leave of him as the postillion was leading out the horses. La Fleur kissed all their hands round and round again, and thrice he wiped his eyes, and thrice he promised he would bring them all pardons from Rome.

—The young fellow, said the landlord, is beloved by all the town ; and there is scarce a corner in Montriul where the want of him will not be felt. He has but one misfortune in the world, continued he, " He is always in love."——I am heartily glad of it, said I ;

58

'twill save me the trouble every night of putting my breeches under my head. In saying this, I was making not so much La Fleur's eloge as my own, having been in love with one Princess or other almost all my life, and I hope I shall go on so till I die, being firmly persuaded, that if ever I do a mean action, it must be in some interval betwixt one passion and another : whilst this inter-regnum lasts, I always perceive my heart locked up,—I can scarce find in it to give misery a sixpence : and therefore I always get out of it as fast as I can ; and the moment I am rekindled, I am all generosity and good-will again ; and would do any thing in the world, either for or with any one, if they will but satisfy me there is no sin in it.

—But in saying this,—sure I am commend-ing the passion,—not myself.

## A FRAGMENT

———The town of Abdera, notwithstanding Democritus lived there, trying all the powers of irony and laughter to reclaim it, was the vilest and most profligate town in all Thrace. What for poisons, conspiracies, and assassinations,—libels, pasquinades, and tumults, there was no going there by day ;—'twas worse by night.

Now, when things were at the worst, it came to pass, that the Andromeda of Euripides being represented at Abdera, the whole orchestra was delighted with it ; but of all the passages which delighted them, nothing operated more upon their imaginations than the tender strokes of nature which the poet had wrought up in that pathetic speech of Perseus, *O Cupid, prince of Gods and men*, &c. Every man almost spoke pure iambics the next day, and talk'd of nothing but Perseus his pathetic address,—" O Cupid, prince of

Gods and men ! " in every street of Abdera,
in every house,—" O Cupid ! Cupid ! "—
in every mouth, like the natural notes of some
sweet melody which drop from it, whether it
will or no,—nothing but " Cupid ! Cupid !
prince of Gods and men ! "—The fire
caught,—and the whole city, like the heart of
one man, open'd itself to Love.

No pharmacopolist could sell one grain of
helebore,—not a single armourer had a heart
to forge one instrument of death ;—Friendship and Virtue met together, and kiss'd each
other in the street ;—the golden age returned,
and hung over the town of Abdera ;—every
Abderite took his oaten pipe ; and every
Abderitish woman left her purple web, and
chastely sat her down, and listened to the song.

—'Twas only in the power, says the Fragment, of the God whose empire extendeth
from heaven to earth, and even to the depths
of the sea, to have done this.

### MONTRIUL

WHEN all is ready, and every article is
disputed and paid for at the inn, unless you

are a little soured by the adventure, there is always a matter to compound at the door, before you can get into your chaise, and that is, with the sons and daughters of poverty who surround you. Let no man say, " Let them go to the Devil ! "—'tis a cruel journey to send a few miserables ; and they have had sufferings enow without it. I always think it better to take a few sous out in my hand ; and I would counsel every gentle traveller to do so likewise ; he need not be so exact in setting down his motives for giving them :—they will be register'd elsewhere.

For my own part, there is no man gives so little as I do ; for few, that I know, have so little to give : but as this was the first public act of my charity in France, I took the more notice of it.

——A well-a-way ! said I,—I have but eight sous in the world, shewing them in my hand, and there are eight poor men and eight poor women for 'em.

A poor tatter'd soul, without a shirt on, instantly withdrew his claim, by retiring two steps out of the circle, and making a disqualifying bow on his part. Had the whole parterre cried out, *Place aux dames*, with one voice, it would not have conveyed the sentiment of a deference for the sex with half the effect.

Just Heaven ! for what wise reasons hast thou ordered it, that beggary and urbanity, which are at such variance in other countries, should find a way to be at unity in this ?

I insisted upon presenting him with a single sous, merely for his *politesse*.

A poor little dwarfish, brisk fellow, who stood over against me in the circle, putting something first under his arm, which had once been a hat, took his snuff-box out of his pocket, and generously offer'd a pinch on both sides of him : it was a gift of consequence, and modestly declined.—The poor little fellow press'd it upon them with a nod of welcomeness.——*Prenez-en*,——*prenez*, said he, looking another way ; so they each took a pinch. ——Pity thy box should ever want one, said I to myself ; so I put a couple of sous into it, —taking a small pinch out of his box to enhance their value, as I did it.——He felt the weight of the second obligation more than of the first, —'twas doing him an honor,—the other was only doing him a charity ;—and he made me a bow to the ground for it.

——Here ! said I to an old soldier with one hand, who had been campaign'd and worn out to death in the service,—here's a couple of sous for thee.——*Vive le Roi !* said the old soldier.

I had then but three sous left : so I gave one, simply *pour l'amour de Dieu*, which was the footing on which it was begg'd.——The poor woman had a dislocated hip ; so it could not be well upon any other motive.

*Mon cher en tres-charitable, Monsieur.*—— There's no opposing this, said I.

*My Lord Anglois ;*—the very sound was worth the money ;—so I gave *my last sous for it*. But, in the eagerness of giving, I had overlooked a *pauvre honteux*, who had no one to ask a sous for him, and who, I believe, would have perish'd ere he could have ask'd one for himself ; he stood by the chaise, a little without the circle, and wiped a tear from a face which I thought had seen better days. ——Good God ! said I, and I have not one single sous left to give him.——But you have a thousand ! cried all the powers of Nature, ſtirring within me ;—so I gave him——no matter what,—I am ashamed to say *how much* now,—and was ashamed to think how little then ; so if the reader can form any conjecture of my disposition, as these two fixed points are given him, he may judge within a livre or two what was the precise sum.

I could afford nothing for the rest, but *Dieu vous benisse.——Et le bon Dieu vous benisse encore*, said the old soldier, the dwarf, etc. The *pauvre honteux* could say nothing,—he pull'd out a little handkerchief, and wiped his face as he turned away ;—and I thought he thanked me more than them all.

## THE BIDET

Having settled all these little matters, I got into my poſt-chaise with more ease than ever

I got into a post-chaise in my life ; and La
Fleur having got one large jack-boot on the
far side of a little *bidet*,* and another on this
(for I count nothing of his legs) he canter'd
away before me as happy and as perpendicular
as a prince.

—But what is happiness ! what is grandeur
in this painted scene of life !—A dead ass,
before we had got a league, put a sudden stop
to La Fleur's career ;—his bidet would not
pass by it,—a contention arose betwixt them,
and the poor fellow was kick'd out of his
jack-boots the very first kick.

La Fleur bore his fall like a French
Christian, saying neither more nor less upon
it than *Diable !* so presently got up, and came
to the charge again astride his bidet, beating
him up to it as he would have beat his drum.

The bidet flew from one side of the road to
the other, then back again, then this way,—
then that way, and, in short, every way but
by the dead ass :—La Fleur insisted upon the
thing,—and the bidet threw him.

——What's the matter, La Fleur, said I,
with this bidet of thine ?——*Monsieur*, said

* Post-horse.

66

he, *c'est un cheval le plus opiniatre du monde.*
——Nay, if he is a conceited beast, he must
go his own way, replied I.——So La Fleur
got off him, and giving him a good sound
lash, the bidet took me at my word, and away
he scampered back to Montriul.——*Peste!*
said La Fleur.

It is not *mal-a-propos* to take notice here,
that though La Fleur availed himself but of two
different terms of exclamation in this encounter,
—namely, *Diable!* and *Peste!* that there are,
nevertheless, three in the French language,
like the positive, comparative, and superlative,
one or the other of which serve for every
unexpected throw of the dice in life.

*Le Diable!* which is the first and positive
degree, is generally used in ordinary emotions
of the mind, where small things only fall out
contrary to your expectations,—such as—
the throwing one's doublets,—La Fleur's
being kick'd off his horse, and so forth.—
Cuckoldom, for the same reason, is always—
*Le Diable!*

But, in cases where the cast has something
provoking in it, as in that of the Bidet's
running away after, and leaving La Fleur

aground in jack-boots,—'tis the second degree :

'Tis then *Peste* !

And for the third—

——But here my heart is wrung with pity and fellow-feeling, when I reflect what miseries must have been their lot, and how bitterly so refined a people must have smarted to have forced them upon the use of it.

—Grant me, O ye powers which touch the tongue with eloquence in distress !—whatever is my *cast*, grant me but decent words to exclaim in, and I will give my nature way.

—But as these were not to be had in France, I resolved to take every evil just as it befel me, without any exclamation at all.

La Fleur, who had made no such covenant with himself, followed the Bidet with his eyes till it was got out of sight,—and then, you may imagine, if you please, with what word he closed the whole affair.

As there was no hunting down a frighten'd horse in jack-boots, there remained no alternative but taking La Fleur either behind the chaise, or into it.—

I preferred the latter, and, in half an hour, we got to the post-house at Nampont.

NAMPONT

## THE DEAD ASS

——And this, said he, putting the remains of a crust into his wallet,—and this should have been thy portion, said he, hadst thou been alive to have shared it with me.——I thought, by the accent, it had been an apostrophe to his child ; but 'twas to his ass, and to the very ass we had seen dead in the road, which had occasioned La Fleur's misadventure. The man seemed to lament it much ; and it instantly brought into my mind Sancho's lamentation for his ; but he did it with more true touches of nature.

The mourner was sitting upon a stone bench

at the door, with the ass's panel and its bridle on one side, which he took up from time to time,—then laid them down,—look'd at them, and shook his head. He then took his crust of bread out of his wallet again, as if to eat it, held it some time in his hand,—then laid it upon the bit of his ass's bridle,—look'd wistfully at the little arrangement he had made,—and then gave a sigh.

The simplicity of his grief drew numbers about him, and La Fleur among the rest, whilst the horses were getting ready : as I continued sitting in the post-chaise, I could see and hear over their heads.

——He said he had come last from Spain, where he had been from the furthest borders of Franconia ; and had got so far on his return home when his ass died. Every one seemed desirous to know what business could have taken so old and poor a man so far a journey from his own home.

——It had pleased Heaven, he said, to bless him with three sons, the finest lads in all Germany ; but having, in one week, lost two of the eldest of them by the small-pox, and the youngest falling ill of the same distemper, he was afraid of being bereft of them all ; and made a vow, if Heaven would not take him from him also, he would go, in gratitude, to St. Iago in Spain.

When the mourner got thus far on his story, he stopp'd to pay Nature his tribute,—and wept bitterly.

He said, Heaven had accepted the conditions, and that he had set out from his cottage with this poor creature, who had been a patient partner of his journey ;—that it had eat the same bread with him all the way, and was unto him as a friend.

Every body who stood about, heard the poor fellow with concern.—La Fleur offered him money.——The mourner said he did not want it ;—it was not the value of the ass, but the loss of him. The ass, he said, he was assured, loved him ;—and, upon this, told them a long story of a mischance upon their passage over the Pyrenean Mountains, which had separated them from each other three days ; during which time the ass had sought him as much as he had sought the ass ; and that they had scarce either eat or drank till they met.

——Thou haſt one comfort, friend, said I, at leaſt, in the loss of thy poor beaſt,—I'm sure thou haſt been a merciful maſter to him. ——Alas! said the mourner, I thought so when he was alive ;—but now that he is dead, I think otherwise.—I fear the weight of myself and my afflictions together, have been too much for him,—they have shortened the poor creature's days, and I fear I have them to answer for.——Shame on the world! said I to myself.——Did we but love each other as this poor soul loved his ass,—'twould be something.——

## THE POSTILLION

THE concern which the poor fellow's ſtory threw me into, required some attention ;

the postillion paid not the least to it, but set off upon the *pavé* in a full gallop.

The thirstiest soul in the most sandy desert of Arabia could not have wished more for a cup of cold water than mine did for grave and quiet movements ; and I should have had an high opinion of the postillion, had he but stolen off with me in something like a pensive pace.——On the contrary, as the mourner finished his lamentation, the fellow gave an unfeeling lash to each of his beasts, and set off clattering like a thousand Devils.

I called to him as loud as I could, for Heaven's sake to go slower :——and the louder I called, the more unmercifully he gallopped. ——The deuce take him and his gallopping tóo, said I, he'll go on tearing my nerves to pieces till he has worked me into a foolish passion, and then he'll go slow, that I may enjoy the sweets of it.

The postillion managed the point to a miracle : by the time he had got to the foot of a steep hill, about half a league from Nampont,——he had put me out of temper with him,——and then with myself for being so.

My case then required a different treatment ; and a good rattling gallop would have been of real service to me.

——Then, prithee, get on,—get on, my good lad, said I.

——The postillion pointed to the hill,—— I then tried to return back to the story of the poor German and his ass ;—but I had broke the clue,—and could no more get into it again than the postillion could into a trot.

——The deuce go, said I, with it all ! Here am I, sitting as candidly disposed to make the best of the worst as ever wight was, and all runs counter.

There is one sweet lenitive at least for evils, which Nature holds out to us : so I took it kindly at her hands, and fell asleep ; and the first word which roused me was Amiens.

——Bless me ! said I, rubbing my eyes,— this is the very town where my poor lady is to come.

### AMIENS

THE words were scarce out of my mouth, when the Count de L***'s post-chaise, with his sister in it, drove hastily by ; she had just time to make me a bow of recognition,—and of that particular kind of it which told me she had not yet done with me. She was as good as her look ; for, before I quite finished my supper, her brother's servant came into the room with a billet, in which she said she had taken the liberty to charge me with a letter, which I was to present myself to Madame R*** the first morning I had nothing to do at Paris. There was only added, she was sorry, but from what *penchant* she had not considered, that she had been prevented telling me her story,—that she still owed it me ; and if my route should ever lay through Brussels, and I had not by then forgot the name of Madame de L***,—that Madame de L*** would be glad to discharge her obligation.

G

———Then I will meet thee, said I, fair
spirit ! at Brussels ;—'tis only returning from
Italy, through Germany to Holland, by the
route of Flanders, home ;—'twill scarce be
ten posts out of my way ; but were it ten
thousand ! with what a moral delight will it
crown my journey, in sharing in the sickening
incidents of a tale of misery told to me by such
a sufferer ! To see her weep, and, though
I cannot dry up the fountain of her tears, what
an exquisite sensation is there still left, in
wiping them away from off the cheeks of the
first and fairest of women, as I'm sitting with
my handkerchief in my hand in silence the
whole night beside her !

There was nothing wrong in the sentiment ;
and yet I instantly reproached my heart with
it in the bitterest and most reprobate of
expressions.

It had ever, as I told the reader, been one of
the singular blessings of my life, to be almost
every hour of it miserably in love with some
one : and my last flame happening to be
blown out by a whiff of jealousy on the sudden
turn of a corner, I had lighted it up afresh
at the pure taper of Eliza but about three

months before,—swearing, as I did it, that it should laſt me through the whole journey. —Why should I dissemble the matter? I had sworn to her eternal fidelity ;—she had a right to my whole heart :—to divide my affections was to lessen them ;—to expose them, was to risk them ; where there is risk, there may be loss :—and what wilt thou have, Yorick, to answer to a heart so full of truſt and confidence,—so good, so gentle, and un-reproaching !

———I will not go to Brussels, replied I, interrupting myself ;—but my imagination went on,—I recalled her looks at that crisis of our separation, when neither of us had power to say adieu ! I look'd at the picture she had tied in a black ribband about my neck,—and blush'd as I look'd at it.—I would have given the world to have kiss'd it,—but was ashamed ; and shall this tender flower, said I, pressing it between my hands,—shall it be smitten to its very root,—and smitten, Yorick ! by thee, who haſt promised to shelter it in thy breaſt ?

Eternal Fountain of Happiness ! said I, kneeling down upon the ground,—be thou my witness,—and every pure spirit which taſtes it, be my witness also, that I would not travel to Brussels, unless Eliza went along with me, did the road lead me towards Heaven !

In transports of this kind, the heart, in spite of the understanding, will always say too much.

## THE LETTER

### AMIENS

FORTUNE had not smiled upon La Fleur ; for he had been unsuccessful in his feats of chivalry,—and not one thing had offered to signalize his zeal for my service from the time he had entered into it, which was almost four-and-twenty hours. The poor soul burn'd with impatience ; and the Count de L***'s servant coming with the letter, being the first practicable occasion which offered, La Fleur had laid hold of it, and, in order to do honor to his master, had taken him into a back-parlour in the *auberge*, and treated him with a cup or two of the best wine in Picardy ; and the Count de L***'s servant, in return, and not to be behind-hand in politeness with La Fleur, had taken him back with him to the Count's hotel. La Fleur's *prevenancy* (for there was a passport in his very looks) soon set every servant in the kitchen at ease with him ; and as a Frenchman, whatever be his talents, has no sort of prudery in shewing them, La Fleur, in less than five minutes, had pulled out his fife, and, leading off the dance himself with the first note, set the *fille de chambre*, the *maitre de hotel*, the cook, the scullion, and all the household, dogs and cats, besides an old monkey, a dancing ! I suppose there never was a merrier kitchen since the flood.

Madame de L***, in passing from her brother's apartments to her own, hearing so much jollity below stairs, rung up her *fille de chambre* to ask about it ; and hearing it was the English gentleman's servant who had set the whole house merry with his pipe, she ordered him up.

As the poor fellow could not present himself empty, he had loaden'd himself in going up stairs with a thousand compliments to Madame de L\*\*\*, on the part of his master, —added a long apocrypha of inquiries after Madame de L\*\*\*'s health, told her that Monsieur his master was *au desespoire* for her re-establishment from the fatigues of her journey,—and, to close all, that Monsieur had received the letter which Madame had done him the honour.——And he has done me the honour, said Madame de L\*\*\*, interrupting La Fleur, to send a billet in return.

Madame de L\*\*\* had said this with such a tone of reliance upon the fact, that La Fleur had not power to disappoint her expectations ; —he trembled for my honour,—and, possibly might not altogether be unconcerned for his own, as a man capable of being attached to a master who could be wanting *en egards vis a vis d'une femme !* so that, when Madame de L\*\*\* asked La Fleur if he had brought a letter,——*O qu'oui*, said La Fleur ; so laying down his hat upon the ground, and taking hold of the flap of his right side-pocket with his left hand, he began to search for the letter

with his right ;—then contrarywise.—*Diable !*
—then sought every pocket, pocket by pocket,
round, not forgetting his fob ;—*Peste !*—
then La Fleur emptied them upon the floor,—
pulled out a dirty cravat,—a handkerchief,—
a comb,—a whip-lash,—a night-cap,—then
gave a peep into his hat,—*Quelle etourderie !*
He had left the letter upon the table in the
*auberge ;*—he would run for it, and be back
with it in three minutes.

I had just finished my supper when La
Fleur came in to give me an account of his
adventure : he told the whole story simply as
it was ; and only added, that if Monsieur had
forgot (*par hazard*) to answer Madame's
letter, the arrangement gave him an opportunity to recover the *pas faux ;*—and if not
that things were only as they were.

Now, I was not altogether sure of my
*etiquette*, whether I ought to have wrote or
no ; but if I had,—a Devil himself could
not have been angry : 'twas but the officious
zeal of a well-meaning creature for my honour ;
and however he might have mistook the road
or embarrassed me in so doing,—his heart
was in no fault,—I was under no necessity to

write—and what weighed more than all,—
he did not look as if he had done amiss.

——'Tis all very well, La Fleur, said I.
—'Twas sufficient. La Fleur flew out of
the room like lightning, and return'd with
pen, ink, and paper, in his hand ; and coming
up to the table, laid them close before me, with
such a delight in his countenance, that I
could not help taking up the pen.

I began, and began again ; and though I
had nothing to say, and that nothing might
have been expressed in half a dozen lines, I
made half a dozen different beginnings, and
could no way please myself.

In short, I was in no mood to write.

La Fleur stepped out and brought a little
water in a glass to dilute my ink,—then fetched
sand and seal-wax.—It was all one ; I wrote,
and blotted, and tore off, and burnt, and wrote
again.—*Le Diable l'emporte!* said I half to
myself,—I cannot write this self-same letter,
throwing the pen down despairingly as I
said it.

As soon as I had cast down my pen, La
Fleur advanced with the most respectful
carriage up to the table, and making a thousand

apologies for the liberty he was going to take, told me he had a letter in his pocket, wrote by a drummer in his regiment to a corporal's wife, which, he durst say, would suit the occasion.

I had a mind to let the poor fellow have his humour,——Then prithee, said I, let me see it.

La Fleur instantly pulled out a little dirty pocket-book, cramm'd full of small letters and billet-doux in a sad condition, and laying it upon the table, and then untying the string which held them all together, run them over, one by one, till he came to the letter in question, —*La voila*, said he, clapping his hands ; so unfolding it first, he laid it before me, and retired three steps from the table whilst I read it.

### THE LETTER

Madame,

JE suis penetré de la douleur la plus vive, et reduit en meme temps au desespoir par ce retour imprevu du Corporal, qui rend notre entrevue de ce soir la chose du monde la plus impossible.

Mais vive la joie ! et toute la mienne sera de penser a vous.

L'amour n'est *rien* sans sentiment.

Et le sentiment est encore *moins* sans amour.

On dit qu'on ne doit jamais se desesperer. On dit aussi que Monsieur le Corporal monte le garde Mercredi : alors ce sera mon tour.

*Chacun a son tour.*

En attendant—Vive l'amour ! et vive la bagatelle !

Je suis, Madame,
Avec toutes les sentiments les
plus respectueux et les plus
tendres, tout a vous,
JAQUES ROQUE.

It was but changing the Corporal into the Count—and saying nothing about mounting guard on Wednesday,—and the letter was neither right nor wrong ;—so to gratify the poor fellow, who stood trembling for my honor, his own, and the honor of his letter,—

I took the cream gently off it,—and, whipping it up in my own way,—seal'd it up, and sent it to Madame de L*** ; and the next morning we pursued our journey to Paris.

## PARIS

WHEN a man can contest the point by dint of equipage, and carry on all floundering before him with half a dozen lackies and a couple of cooks,—'tis very well in such a place as Paris,—he may drive in at which end of the street he will.

A poor prince, who is weak in cavalry, and whose whole infantry does not exceed a single man, had best quit the field, and signalize himself in the cabinet, if he can get up into it, —I say *up into it*,—for there is no descending perpendicularly amongst 'em with a " *Me voici, mes enfans,*"—here I am,--whatever many may think.

I own, my first sensations, as soon as I was left solitary and alone in my own chamber in the hotel, were far from being so flattering as I had prefigured them.   I walked up gravely

to the window in my dusty black coat, and
looking through the glass, saw all the world
in yellow, blue, and green, running at the ring
of pleasure.——The old with broken lances
and in helmets which had lost their vizards ;——
the young in armour bright, which shone like
gold, beplumed with each gay feather of the
east,——all,——all,——tilting at it like fascinated
knights in tournaments of yore for fame and
love.

——Alas, poor Yorick ! cried I, what art
thou doing here ? On the very first onset of
all this glittering clatter, thou art reduced to
an atom ;——seek,——seek some winding alley,
with a tourniquet at the end of it, where chariot
never rolled, nor flambeaux shot its rays ;——
there thou mayest solace thy soul in converse
sweet with some kind grisset of a barber's
wife, and get into such coteries !——

——May I perish ! if I do, said I, pulling
out a letter which I had to present to Madame
de R***.——I'll wait upon this lady the very
first thing I do. So I called La Fleur to go
seek me a barber directly,——and come back
and brush my coat.

## THE WIG

### PARIS

WHEN the barber came, he absolutely refused to have any thing to do with my wig: 'twas either above or below his art : I had nothing to do but to take one ready made of his own recommendation.

——But I fear, friend, said I, this buckle won't stand.——You may immerge it, replied he, into the ocean, and it will stand.

What a great scale is every thing upon in this city ! thought I.—The utmost stretch of an English periwig-maker's ideas could have gone no further than to have " dipped it into a pail of water."—What difference ! 'tis like time to eternity !

I confess I do hate all cold conceptions as I do the puny ideas which engender them; and am generally so struck with the great works of Nature, that, for my own part, if I could help it, I never would make a comparison less

87

than a mountain at least. All that can be said against the French sublime in this instance of it, is this :—That the grandeur is *more* in the *word*, and *less* in the *thing*. No doubt the ocean fills the mind with vast ideas ; but Paris being so far inland, it was not likely I should run post a hundred miles out of it to try the experiment :—the Parisian barber meant nothing.

The pail of water standing beside the great deep, makes certainly but a sorry figure in speech ;—but 'twill be said,—it has one advantage—'tis in the next room, and the truth of the buckle may be tried in it, without more ado, in a single moment.

In honest truth, and upon a more candid revision of the matter, *The French expression professes more than it performs*.

I think I can see the precise and distinguishing marks of national characters more in these nonsensical *minutiæ*, than in the most important matters of state ; where great men of all nations talk and talk so much alike, that I would not give nine-pence to chuse among them.

I was so long in getting from under my

barber's hands, that it was too late to think of going with my letter to Madame R*** that night : but, when a man is once dressed at all points for going out, his reflections turn to little account ; so taking down the name of the Hotel de Modene, where I lodged, I walked forth, without any determination where to go ;—I shall consider of that, said I, as I walk along.

## THE PULSE

### PARIS

HAIL, ye small sweet courtesies of life, for smooth do ye make the road of it ! like grace and beauty, which beget inclinatons to love at first sight : 'tis ye who open this door, and let the stranger in.

———Pray, Madame, said I, have the goodness to tell me which way I must turn to go to the opera comique.———Most willingly, Monsieur, said she, laying aside her work.

I had given a cast with my eye into half a dozen shops as I came along, in search of a face not likely to be disordered by such an interruption ; till, at last, this hitting my fancy, I had walked in.

She was working a pair of ruffles as she sat in a low chair on the far side of the shop facing the door.

———*Tres volontieres ;* most willingly, said she, laying her work down upon a chair next her, and rising up from the low chair she was sitting in, with so cheerful a movement and so cheerful a look, that, had I been laying out fifty Louis d'ors with her, I should have said—— " This woman is grateful."

You must turn, Monsieur, said she, going with me to the door of the shop, and pointing the way down the street I was to take,—you must turn first to your left hand,—*mais prenez guarde,*—there are two turns ; and be so good as to take the second,—then go down a little way, and you'll see a church, and when you are past it, give yourself the trouble to turn directly to the right, and that will lead you to the foot of the *pont neuf*, which you must cross, and there any one will do himself the pleasure to shew you.

She repeated her instructions three times over to me, with the same good-natur'd patience the third time as the first ;—and if *tones and manners* have a meaning, which certainly they have, unless to hearts which shut them out,—she seemed really interested that I should not lose myself.

I will not suppose it was the woman's beauty, nowithstanding she was the handsomest grisset, I think, I ever saw, which had much to do with the sense I had of her courtesy ; only I remember, when I told her how much I was obliged to her, that I looked very full in her eyes,—and that I repeated my thanks as often as she had done her instructions.

I had not got ten paces from the door, before I found I had forgot every tittle of what she had said :—so looking back, and seeing her still standing in the door of the shop, as if to look whether I went right or

not,—I returned back, to ask her whether the
firſt turn was to my right or left, for that I
had absolutely forgot.——Is it possible ! said
she, half laughing.—'Tis very possible, replied
I, when a man is thinking more of a woman
than of her good advice.

As this was the real truth, she took it, as
every woman takes a matter of right, with a
slight curtsey.

——*Attendez,* said she, laying her hand
upon my arm to detain me, whilſt she called
a lad out of the back shop to get ready a parcel
of gloves.  I am juſt going to send him, said
she, with a packet into that quarter ; and if
you will have the complaisance to ſtep in, it
will be ready in a moment, and he shall attend
you to the place.  So I walked in with her to
the far side of the shop ;  and taking up the
ruffle in my hands which she laid upon the
chair, as if I had a mind to sit, she sat down
herself in her low chair, and I inſtantly sat
myself down beside her.

He will be ready, Monsieur, said she, in a
moment.——And in that moment, replied I,
moſt willingly would I say something very
civil to you for all these courtesies.  Any

one may do a casual act of good-nature, but a continuation of them shews it is a part of the temperature ; and, certainly, added I, if it is the same blood which comes from the heart, which descends to the extremes (touching her wrist) I am sure you must have one of the best pulses of any woman in the world. Feel it, said she, holding out her arm. So laying down my hat, I took hold of her fingers in one hand, and applied the two fore-fingers of my other to the artery.——

Would to Heaven ! my dear Eugenius, thou hadst passed by, and beheld me sitting in my black coat, and in my lack-a-day-sical manner, counting the throbs of it, one by one, with as much true devotion as if I had been watching the critical ebb or flow of her fever ! How wouldst thou have laughed and moralized upon my new profession !—and thou shouldst have laughed and moralized on—Trust me, my dear Eugenius, I should have said " there are worse occupations in this world *than feeling a woman's pulse.*"—But a grisset's ! thou wouldst have said,—and in an open shop, Yorick !—

—So much the better : for when my views

are direct, Eugenius, I care not if all the world saw me feel it.

## THE HUSBAND

### PARIS

I HAD counted twenty pulsations, and was going on fast towards the fortieth, when her husband coming unexpected from a back-parlour into the shop, put me a little out in my reckoning.———'Twas nobody but her husband, she said—so I began a fresh score— Monsieur is so good, quoth she, as he passed by us, as to give himself the trouble of feeling my pulse.———The husband took off his hat, and making me a bow, said, I did him too much honor ; and having said that, he put on his hat and walked out.

94

Good God ! said I to myself, as he went out,
—and can this man be the husband of this
woman !

Let it not torment the few who know what
muſt have been the grounds of this exclamation, if I explain it to those who do not.

In London, a shopkeeper and a shopkeeper's wife seem to be one bone and one
flesh.  In the several endowments of mind
and body, sometimes the one, sometimes the
other has it, so as in general to be upon a par,
and to tally with each other as nearly as a man
and wife need to do.

In Paris, there are scarce two orders of
beings more different, for the legislative and
executive powers of the shop not reſting in
the husband, he seldom comes there :—in
some dark and dismal room behind, he sits
commerceless in his thrum night-cap, the
same rough son of Nature that Nature left
him.

The genius of a people where nothing but
the monarchy is *salique*, having ceded this
department, with sundry others, totally to the
women—by a continual higgling with customers of all ranks and sizes from morning to

night, like so many rough pebbles shook long together in a bag, by amicable collisions, they have worn down their asperities and sharp angles, and not only become round and smooth, but will receive, some of them, a polish like a brilliant—Monsieur *le Marli* is little better than the stone under your foot.

—Surely,—surely, man! it is not good for thee to sit alone ; thou wast for social intercourse and gentle greetings ; and this improvement of our natures from it, I appeal to, as my evidence.

—And how does it beat, Monsieur? said she.——With all the benignity, said I, looking quietly in her eyes, that I expected.——She was going to say something civil in return, but the lad came into the shop with the gloves.—*A propos*, said I, I want a couple of pair myself.

## THE GLOVES

### PARIS

THE beautiful grisset rose up when I said this, and, going behind the counter, reached down a parcel, and untied it : I advanced to the side over-against her : they were all too large. The beautiful grisset measured them one by one across my hand.—It would not alter the dimensions.—She begged I would try a single pair, which seemed to be the least.—She held it open ;—my hand slipped into it at once.—It will not do, said I, shaking my head a little.—No, said she, doing the same thing.

There are certain combined looks of simple subtlety,—where whim, and sense, and seriousness, and nonsense, are so blended, that all the languages of Babel set loose together, could not express them :—they are communicated and caught so instantaneously, that

97

you can scarce say which party is the infector.
I leave it to your men of words to swell pages
about it,—it is enough in the present to say
again, the gloves would not do ; so folding
our hands within our arms, we both loll'd
upon the counter ;—it was narrow, and there
was just room for the parcel to lay between us.

The beautiful grisset looked sometimes at
the gloves, then sideways to the window, then
at the gloves,—and then at me. I was not
disposed to break silence ;—I followed her
example : so I looked at the gloves, then to
the window, then at the gloves, and then at
her—and so on alternately.

I found I lost considerably in every attack :
—she had a quick black eye, and shot through
two such long and silken eye-lashes with such
penetration, that she looked into my very
heart and veins.—It may seem strange ; but
I could actually feel she did.

It is no matter, said I, taking up a couple of
the pairs next me, and putting them into my
pocket.

I was sensible the beautiful grisset had not
asked a single livre above the price. I wished
she had asked a livre more ; and was puzzling

my brains how to bring the matter about.—
Do you think, my dear Sir, said she, mistaking
my embarrassment, that I could ask a *sous*
too much of a stranger—and of a stranger
whose politeness, more than his want of
gloves, has done me the honor to lay himself
at my mercy?—*M'en croyez capable?*—Faith!
not I, said I; and if you were, you are welcome.
So counting the money into her hand, and
with a lower bow than one generally makes to
a shopkeeper's wife, I went out; and her lad
with his parcel followed me.

## THE TRANSLATION

### PARIS

THERE was nobody in the box I was let into,
but a kindly old French officer. I love the

character, not only because I honor the man whose manners are softened by a profession which makes bad men worse, but that I once knew one,—for he is no more,—and why should I not rescue one page from violation by writing his name in it, and telling the world it was Captain Tobias Shandy, the dearest of my flock and friends, whose philanthropy I never think of at this long distance from his death, but my eyes gush out tears. For his sake, I have a predilection for the whole corps of veterans ; and so I strode over the two back rows of benches, and placed myself beside him.

The old officer was reading attentively a small pamphlet (it might be the book of the opera) with a large pair of spectacles. As soon as I sat down, he took his spectacles off, and putting them into a shagreen case, returned them and the book into his pocket together. I half rose up, and made him a bow.

Translate this into any civilized language in the world, the sense is this :—

" Here's a poor stranger come into the box ; he seems as if he knew nobody ; and is never likely, was he to be seven years in Paris, if every man he comes near keeps his spectacles upon his nose :—'tis shutting the door of conversation absolutely in his face, and using him worse than a German."

The French officer might as well have said it all aloud : and if he had, I should in course have put the bow I made him into French too, and told him, " I was sensible of his attention and returned him a thousand thanks for it."

There is not a secret so aiding to the progress of sociality, as to get master of this *short hand*, and to be quick in rendering the several turns of looks and limbs, with all their inflections and delineations, into plain words. For my own part, by long habitude, I do it so mechanically, that when I walk the streets of London, I go translating all the way ; and have more than once stood behind the circle, where not three words have been said, and have brought off twenty different dialogues with me, which I could have fairly wrote down and sworn to.

I was going one evening to Martini's concert at Milan, and was just entering the door of the hall, when the Marquisina de F*** was coming out, in a sort of a hurry :—she was

almost upon me before I saw her : so I gave a
spring to one side, to let her pass.  She had
done the same, and on the same side too : so
we ran our heads together : she instantly got
to the other side to get out : I was just as
unfortunate as she had been ;  for I had
sprung to that side, and opposed her passage
again.  We both flew together to the other
side, and then back,—and so on :—it was
ridiculous ;  we both blushed intolerably ;
so I did at last the thing I should have done at
first ;—I stood stock still, and the Marquisina
had no more difficulty.  I had no power to go
into the room till I had made her so much
reparation as wait and to follow her with my
eye to the end of the passage.  She looked
back twice, and walked along it rather sideways, as if she would make room for any one
coming up stairs to pass her.—No, said I,
that's a vile translation : the Marquisina has
a right to the best apology I can make her ;
and that opening is left for me to do it in :—
so I ran and begged pardon for the embarrassment I had given her, saying it was my intention to have made her way.  She answered she
was guided by the same intention towards

me ;—so we reciprocally thanked each other. She was at the top of the stairs ; and seeing no *chichesbee* near her, I begged to hand her to her coach ; so we went down the stairs, stopping at every third step to talk of the concert and the adventure.—Upon my word, Madam, said I, when I handed her in, I made six different efforts to let you go out.—And I made six efforts, replied she, to let you enter.—I wish to Heaven you would make a seventh, said I.—With all my heart, said she, making room.—Life is too short to be long about the forms of it ;—so I instantly stepped in, and she carried me home with her.—— And what became of the concert ? St. Cecilia, who, I suppose, was at it, knows more than I.

I will only add, that the connection which arose out of the translation, gave me more pleasure than any one I had the honour to make in Italy.

# THE DWARF

### PARIS

I HAD never heard the remark made by any one in my life, except by one ; and who that was, will probably come out in this chapter; so that being pretty much unprepossessed, there muſt have been grounds for what ſtruck me the moment I caſt my eyes over the *parterre*,— and that was, the unaccountable sport of Nature in forming such numbers of dwarfs.— No doubt, she sports at certain times in almoſt every corner of the world ; but in Paris, there is no end to her amusements.—The goddess seems almoſt as merry as she is wise.

As I carried my idea out of the opera comique with me, I measured every body I saw walking in the ſtreets by it.—Melancholy application ! especially where the size was extremely little,—the face extremely dark,— the eyes quick,—the nose long,—the teeth white,—the jaw prominent,—to see so many miserables, by force of accidents, driven out of their own proper class into the very verge of another, which it gives me pain to write down : —every third man a pigmy ?—some by ricketty heads and hump backs ;—others by bandy-legs ;—a third set arrested by the hand of Nature in the sixth and seventh years of their growth ;—a fourth, in their perfect and natural state, like dwarf apple-trees ; from the first rudiments and stamina of their existence, never meant to grow higher.

A Medical Traveller might say, 'tis owing to undue bandages ;—a Splenetic one, to want of air ;—and an Inquisitive Traveller, to fortify the system, may measure the height of their houses, the narrowness of their streets, and in how few feet square in the sixth and seventh stories such numbers of the *Bourgoisie* eat and sleep together. But I remember, Mr. Shandy the Elder, who accounted for nothing like any body else, in speaking one evening of these matters, averred, That children, like other animals, might be increased almost to any size, provided they came right into the world ; but the misery was, the citizens of Paris were so coop'd up, that they had not actually room enough to get them.——I do not call it getting any thing, said he ;——'tis getting nothing.——Nay, continued he, rising in his argument, 'tis getting worse than nothing, when all you have got, after twenty or five-and-twenty years of the tenderest care and most nutritious aliment bestowed upon it, shall not at last be as high as my leg. Now, Mr. Shandy being very short, there could be nothing more said of it.

As this is not a work of reasoning, I leave the solution as I found it, and content myself with the truth only of the remark, which is verified in every lane and bye-lane of Paris. I was walking down that which leads from the Carousal to the Palais Royal, and observing a little boy in some distress at the side of the gutter which ran down the middle of it, I took hold of his hand, and help'd him over. Upon turning up his face to look at him after, I perceived he was about forty.——Never mind, said I, some good body will do as much for me when I am ninety.

I feel some little principles within me, which incline me to be merciful towards this poor blighted part of my species, who have neither size nor strength to get on in the world. —I cannot bear to see one of them trod upon ; and had scarce got seated beside my old French officer ere the disgust was exercised, by seeing the very thing happen under the box we sat in.

At the end of the orchestra, and betwixt that and the first side-box, there is a small esplanade left, where, when the house is full, numbers of all ranks take sanctuary. Though you stand, as in the *parterre*, you pay the same price as in the orchestra. A poor defenceless being of this order, had got thrust, some how or other, into this luckless place ;—the night was hot, and he was surrounded by beings two feet and a half higher than himself. The dwarf suffered inexpressibly on all sides ; but the thing which incommoded him most, was a tall, corpulent German, near seven feet high, who stood directly betwixt him and all possibility of his seeing either the stage or the actors. The poor dwarf did all he could to get a peep at what was going forwards, by seeking for some little opening betwixt the German's arm and his body, trying first on

I

one side, then on the other ; but the German
stood square in the most unaccommodating
posture that can be imagined :—the dwarf
might as well have been placed at the bottom
of the deepest draw-well in Paris ; so he
civilly reach'd up his hand to the German's
sleeve, and told him his distress.—The
German turn'd his head back, look'd down
upon him as Goliah did upon David,—and
unfeelingly resumed his posture.

I was just then taking a pinch of snuff out of
my monk's little horn box.—And how would
thy meek and courteous spirit, my dear monk !
so temper'd to *bear and forbear !*—how sweetly
would it have leant an ear to this poor soul's
complaint.

The old French officer seeing me lift up
my eyes with an emotion, as I made the
apostrophe, took the liberty to ask me what
was the matter ?——I told him the story in
three words, and added, how inhuman it was.

By this time the dwarf was driven to
extremes, and in his first transports, which are
generally unreasonable, had told the German
he would cut off his long queue with his
knife.——The German look'd back coolly,

and told him he was welcome, if he could reach it.

An injury sharpened by an insult, be it to whom it will, makes every man of sentiment a party : I could have leap'd out of the box to have redressed it.—The old French officer did it with much less confusion ; for leaning a little over, and nodding to a sentinel, and pointing at the same time with his finger at the diſtress,—the sentinel made his way to it. —There was no occasion to tell the grievance —the thing told itself ; so thruſting back the German inſtantly with his musket,—he took the poor dwarf by the hand, and placed him before him.——This is noble ! said I, clapping my hands together.——And yet you would not permit this, said the old officer, in England.

——In England, dear Sir, said I, *we sit all at our ease.*

The old French officer would have set me at unity with myself, in case I had been at variance,—by saying it was a *bon mot ;*—and as a *bon mot* is always worth something in Paris, he offered me a pinch of snuff.

# THE ROSE

### PARIS

IT was now my turn to ask the old French officer, " What was the matter ? " for a cry of " *Haussez les mains, Monsieur l'Abbé*," re-echoed from a dozen different parts of the *parterre*, was as unintelligible to me as my apostrophe to the monk had been to him.

He told me it was some poor Abbé in one of the upper *loges*, who he supposed had got planted *perdu* behind a couple of grissets, in order to see the opera, and that the *parterre* espying him, were insisting upon his holding up both his hands during the representation. ——And can it be supposed, said I, that an ecclesiastick would pick the grisset's pockets ? ——The old French officer smiled, and whispering in my ear, opened a door of knowledge which I had no idea of——

——Good God ! said I, turning pale with astonishment,—is it possible, that a people so smit with sentiment should at the same time be so unclean, and so unlike themselves.— *Quelle grossierté!* added I.

———The French officer told me it was an illiberal sarcasm at the church, which had begun in the theatre about the time the Tartuffe was given in it, by Moliere :—but, like other remains of Gothic manners, was declining. —Every nation, continued he, have their refinements and *grossiertés*, in which they take the lead, and lose it of one another by turns ;—that he had been in most countries, but never in one where he found not some delicacies, which others seemed to want. *Le pour et le contre se trouvent en chaque nation;* there is a balance, said he, of good and bad everywhere ; and nothing but the knowing it is so, can emancipate one half of the world from the prepossession which it holds against the other :—that the advantage of travel, as it regarded the *sçavoir vivre*, was by seeing a great deal both of men and manners : it taught us mutual toleration ; and mutual toleration, concluded he, making me a bow, taught us mutual love.

The old French officer delivered this with an

air of such candour and good sense, as coincided with my first favorable impressions of his character :—I thought I loved the man ; but I fear I mistook the object :—'twas my own way of thinking,—the difference was, I could not have expressed it half so well.

It is alike troublesome to both the rider and his beast,—if the latter goes pricking up his ears, and starting all the way at every object which he never saw before.—I have as little torment of this kind as any creature alive ; and yet I honestly confess, that many a thing gave me pain, and that I blush'd at many a word the first month,—which I found inconsequent and perfectly innocent the second.

Madame de Rambouliet, after an acquaintance of about six weeks with her, had done me the honor to take me in her coach about two leagues out of town.—Of all women, Madame de Rambouliet is the most correct ;—and I never wish to see one of more virtues and purity of heart.—In our return back, Madame de Rambouliet desired me to pull the cord.—— I asked her if she wanted any thing ?—— *Rein que pour pisser*, said Madame de Rambouliet.

Grieve not, gentle traveller, to let Madame de Rambouliet p—ss on.—And ye fair mystic nymphs, go each one *pluck your rose*, and scatter them in your path,—for Madame de Rambouliet did no more.—I handed Madame de Rambouliet out of the coach ; and had I been the priest of the chaste *Castalia*, I could not have served at her fountain with a more respectful decorum.

## THE FILLE DE CHAMBRE

### PARIS

WHAT the old French officer had delivered upon travelling, bringing Polonius's advice to his son, upon the same subject, into my head—and that bringing in Hamlet,—and Hamlet the rest of Shakespeare's Works, I stopt at the Quai de Conti, in my return home, to purchase the whole set.

The bookseller said he had not a set in the world.——*Comment !* said I, taking one up out

of a set which lay upon the counter betwixt us.
——He said, they were sent him only to be
got bound ; and were to be sent back to
Versailles in the morning to the Count de
B***.

——And does the Count de B***, said I,
read Shakespeare ?—*C'est un* Esprit *fort*, replied
the bookseller.—He loves English books ;
and what is more to his honor, Monsieur, he
loves the English too.——You speak this so
civilly, said I, that it is enough to oblige an
Englishman to lay out a Louis d'or or two at
your shop.——The bookseller made a bow,
and was going to say something, when a
young decent girl, about twenty, who by her
air and dress seemed to be *fille de chambre*
to some devout woman of fashion, came
into the shop and asked for *Les Egarements du
Cœur & de l'Esprit*. The bookseller gave her
the book directly ; she pulled out a little
green satin purse, run round with a ribband of
the same colour, and putting her finger and
thumb into it, she took out the money and
paid for it. As I had nothing more to stay
me in the shop, we both walk'd out of the door
together.

———And what have you to do, my dear, said I, with *The Wanderings of the Heart*, who scarce know yet you have one ? nor, 'till Love has first told you it, or some faithless shepherd has made it ache, canst thou ever be sure it is so.———*La Dieu m'en guarde!* said the girl.———With reason, said I ; for if it is a good one, 'tis a pity it should be stolen ; 'tis a little treasure to thee, and gives a better air to your face, than if it was dress'd out with pearls.

The young girl listened with a submissive attention, holding her satin purse by its ribband in her hand all the time.———'Tis a very small one, said I, taking hold of the bottom of it—(she held it towards me)—and there is very little in it, my dear, said I ; but be but as good as thou art handsome, and Heaven will fill it. I had a parcel of crowns in my hand to pay for Shakespeare ; and as she had let go the purse entirely, I put a single one in ; and tying up the ribband in a bow-knot, returned it to her.

The young girl made me more a humble curtsey than a low one :—'twas one of those quiet, thankful sinkings, where the spirit bows itself down,—the body does no more than tell it. I never gave a girl a crown in my life which gave me half the pleasure.

My advice, my dear, would not have been worth a pin to you, said I, if I had not given this along with it : but now, when you see the crown, you'll remember it ;—so don't, my dear, lay it out in ribbands.

——Upon my word, Sir, said the girl, earnestly, I am incapable ;—in saying which as is usual in little bargains of honor, she gave me her hand :—*En verité, Monsieur, je mettrai cet argent apart*, said she.

When a virtuous convention is made betwixt man and woman, it sanctified their most private walks ; so notwithstanding it was dusky, yet as both our roads lay the same way, we made no scruple of walking along the Quai de Conti together.

She made me a second curtsey in setting off ; and before we got twenty yards from the door, as if she had not done enough before, she made a sort of a little stop, to tell me again —she thank'd me.

—It was a small tribute, I told her, which I could not avoid paying to virtue, and would

not be mistaken in the person I had been
rendering it to for the world ; but I see
innocence, my dear, in your face,—and foul
befal the man who ever lays a snare in its
way !

The girl seem'd affeéted, some way or other,
with what I said ;—she gave a low sigh :—
I found I was not empowered to enquire at all
after it,—so said nothing more till I got to
the corner of the Rue de Nevers, where we
were to part.

——But, is this the way, my dear, said I, to
the Hotel de Modene ?——She told me it was ;
—or that I may go by the Rue de Gueneguault,
which was the next turn.——Then I'll go, my
dear, by the Rue de Gueneguault, said I, for
two reasons : first, I shall please myself ;
and next, I shall give you the proteétion of my
company as far on your way as I can.——The
girl was sensible I was civil,—and said, She
wish'd the Hotel de Modene was in the
Rue de St. Pierre.——You live there ? said
I.——She told me she was *fille de chambre*
to Madame R***.——Good God ! said I, 'tis
the very lady for whom I have brought a letter
from Amiens.——The girl told me that

Madame R***, she believed, expected a stranger with a letter, and was impatient to see him.——So I desired the girl to present my compliments to Madame R***, and say I would certainly wait upon her in the morning.

We stood still at the corner of the Rue de Nevers whilst this pass'd.——We then stopped a moment whilst she disposed of her *Egarements du Cœur*, &c., more commodiously than carrying them in her hand :——they were two volumes ; so I held the second for her whilst she put the first into her pocket ; and then she held her pocket, and I put in the other after it.

'Tis sweet to feel by what fine-spun threads our affections are drawn together !

We set off afresh ; and as she took her third step, the girl put her hand within my arm.——I was just bidding her,——but she did it of herself, with that undeliberating simplicity, which shew'd it was out of her head that she had never seen me before. For my own part, I felt the conviction of consanguinity so strongly, that I could not help turning half round to look in her face, and see if I could trace out any thing in it of a family likeness.—Tut, said I, are we not all relations ?

When we arrived at the turning up of the Rue de Gueneguault, I stopp'd to bid her adieu for good and all : the girl would thank me again for my company and kindness.— She bid me adieu twice ;—I repeated it as often ; and so cordial was the parting between us, that had it happened any where else, I'm not sure but I should have signed it with a kiss of charity, as warm and holy as an apostle.

But in Paris, as none kiss each other but the men,—I did what amounted to the same thing,—

I bid God bless her !

## THE PASSPORT

### PARIS

When I got home to my hotel, La Fleur told me I had been inquired after by the

Lieutenant de Police.——The deuce take it, said I,—I know the reason. It is time the reader should know it ; for in the order of things in which it happened, it was omitted ; not that it was out of my head ; but, that had I told it then, it might have been forgot now ; —and now is the time I want it.

I had left London with so much precipitation, that it never entered my mind that we were at war with France ; and had reached Dover, and looked through my glass at the hills beyond Boulogne, before the idea presented itself ; and with this in its train, that there was no getting there without a passport. Go but to the end of a street, I have a mortal aversion for returning back no wiser than I set out ; and as this was one of the greatest efforts I had ever made for knowledge, I could less bear the thoughts of it ; so hearing the Count de *** had hired the packet, I begg'd he would take me in his *suite*. The Count had some little knowledge of me, so made little or no difficulty,—only said, his inclination to serve me could reach no farther than Calais, as he was to return by way of Brussels to Paris ; however, when I had once pass'd there, I might get to Paris without interruption ; but that in Paris I must make friends and shift for myself.——Let me get to Paris, Monsieur le Count, said I,—and I shall do very well. So I embark'd, and never thought more of the matter.

When La Fleur told me the Lieutenant de Police had been enquiring after me,—the thing instantly recurred ;—and by the time La Fleur had well told me, the master of the hotel came into my room to tell me the same thing, with this addition to it, that my passport had been particularly asked after : the master of the hotel concluded with saying he hoped I had one.——Not I, faith ! said I.

The master of the hotel retired three steps from me, as from an infected person, as I declared this ;—and poor La Fleur advanced three steps towards me, and with that sort of movement which a good soul makes to succour a distress'd one : the fellow won my heart by it ; and from that single *trait*, I knew his character as perfectly, and could rely upon it as firmly, as if he had served me with fidelity for seven years.

*Mon Seigneur !* cried the master of the

hotel ;—but recollecting himself as he made the exclamation, he instantly changed the tone of it—If Monsieur, said he, has not a passport (*apparemment*) in all likelihood he has friends in Paris who can procure him one. —Not that I know of, quoth I, with an air of indifference.——Then, *certes*, replied he, you'll be sent to the Bastile, or the Chatelet, *au moins*.——Poo ! said I, the King of France is a good-natured soul,—he'll hurt nobody.—— *Cela n'empeche pas*, said he,—you will certainly be sent to the Bastile to-morrow morning.—— But I've taken your lodgings for a month, answer'd I ; and I'll not quit them a day before the time for all the Kings of France in the world.——La Fleur whispered in my ear, —That nobody could oppose the King of France.

*Pardi*, said my host, *ces Messieurs Anglois sont des gens tres extraordinaires ;*—and having both said and sworn it,—he went out.

## THE PASSPORT

### THE HOTEL AT PARIS

I COULD not find in my heart to torture La
Fleur's with a serious look upon the subject of
my embarrassment, which was the reason I
had treated it so cavalierly ; and to shew him
how light it lay upon my mind, I dropped the
subject entirely ; and whilst he waited upon
me at supper, talk'd to him with more than
usual gaiety about Paris, and of the *opera
comique*.—La Fleur had been there himself,
and had followed me through the streets as
far as the bookseller's shop ; but seeing me
come out with the young *fille de chambre*, and
that we walk'd down the Quai de Conti
together, La Fleur deem'd it unnecessary to
follow me a step further,—so making his own
reflections upon it, he took a shorter cut,—
and got to the hotel in time to be inform'd
of the affair of the police against my arrival.

As soon as the honest creature had taken

K       123

away, and gone down to sup himself, I then began to think a little seriously about my situation.

——And here, I know, Eugenius, thou wilt smile at the remembrance of a short dialogue which pass'd betwixt us the moment I was going to set out :——I muſt tell it here.

Eugenius, knowing that I was as little ſubjeƈt to be overburthen'd with money as thought, had drawn me aside to interrogate me how much I had taken care for. Upon telling him the exaƈt sum, Eugenius shook his head, and said, it would not do ; so pull'd out his purse, in order to empty it into mine. ——I've enough, in conscience, Eugenius, said I.——Indeed, Yorick you have not, replied Eugenius ;——I know France and Italy better than you.——But you don't consider, Eugenius, said I, refusing his offer, that before I have been three days in Paris, I shall take care to say or do something or other for which I shall get clapp'd up into the Baſtile, and that I shall live there a couple of months entirely at the King of France's expence.——I beg pardon, said Eugenius, dryly : really, I had forgot that resource.

Now the event I treated gaily, came seriously to my door.

Is it folly, or *nonchalance*, or philosophy, or pertinacity ;—or what is it in me, that, after all, when La Fleur had gone down stairs, and I was quite alone, I could not bring down my mind to think of it otherwise than I had then spoken of it to Eugenius ?

—And as for the Baſtile,—the terror is in the word.—Make the moſt of it you can, said I to myself, the Baſtile is but another word for a tower ;—and a tower is but another word for a house you can't get out of.—Mercy on the gouty ! for they are in it twice a year.—But with nine livres a day, and pen and ink and paper and patience, albeit a man can't get out, he may do very well within,—at leaſt for a month or six weeks ; at the end of which, if he is a harmless fellow, his innocence appears, and he comes out a better and wiser man than he went in.

I had some occasion (I forgot what) to ſtep into the court-yard, as I settled this account ; and remember I walk'd down ſtairs in no small triumph with the conceit of my reasoning.——Beshrew the *sombre* pencil ! said I, vauntingly,—for I envy not its power, which paints the evils of life with so hard and deadly a colouring. The mind sits terrified at the objects she has magnified herself, and blackened : reduce them to their proper size and hue, she overlooks them.———'Tis true said I, correcting the proposition,—the Bastile is not an evil to be despised.—But strip it of its towers,—fill up the fosse,—unbarricade the doors,—call it simply a confinement, and suppose 'tis some tyrant of a distemper,— and not of a man, which holds you in it,—the evil vanishes, and you bear the other half without complaint.

I was interrupted in the hey-day of this soliloquy, with a voice which I took to be of a child, which complained " it could not get out."—I look'd up and down the passage, and seeing neither man, woman, nor child, I went out without further attention.

In my return back through the passage, I heard the same words repeated twice over ; and looking up, I saw it was a starling hung in a little cage.—" I can't get out,—I can't get out," said the starling.

I stood looking at the bird : and to every

person who came through the passage, it ran
fluttering to the side towards which they
approach'd it, with the same lamentation of its
captivity,—" I can't get out," said the ſtarling.
——God help thee ! said I,—but I'll let thee
out, coſt what it will ; so I turned about the
cage to get the door: it was twiſted and
double twiſted so faſt with wire, there was no
getting it open without pulling the cage to
pieces.—I took both hands to it.

The bird flew to the place where I was
attempting his deliverance, and thruſting his
head through the trellis, pressed his breaſt
against it, as if impatient.—I fear, poor
creature, said I, I cannot set thee at liberty.
——" No," said the ſtarling ; " I can't get
" out,—I can't get out," said the ſtarling.

I vow I never had my affections more
tenderly awakened ; nor do I remember an
incident in my life where the dissipated
spirits to which my reason had been a bubble,
were so suddenly call'd home. Mechanical
as the notes were, yet so true in tune to nature
were they chanted, that in one moment they
overthrew all my syſtematic reasonings upon
the Baſtile ; and I heavily walk'd up stairs,

unsaying every word I had said in going down them.

Disguise thyself as thou wilt, still, Slavery said I,—still thou art a bitter draught! and though thousands in all ages have been made to drink of thee, thou art no less bitter on that account.—'Tis thou, thrice sweet and gracious goddess, addressing myself to *Liberty*, whom all in public or in private worship, whose taste is grateful, and ever will be so, till *Nature* herself shall change. No *tint* of words can spot thy snowy mantle, or chymic power turn thy sceptre into iron ;—with thee to smile upon him as he eats his crust, the swain is happier than his monarch, from whose court thou art exiled.—Gracious Heaven! cried I, kneeling down upon the last step but one in my ascent, grant me but health, thou great Bestower of it, and give me but this fair goddess as my companion,—and shower down thy mitres, if it seems good unto thy Divine Providence, upon those heads which are aching for them!

## THE CAPTIVE

### PARIS

THE bird in his cage pursued me into my room. I sat down close by my table, and, leaning my head upon my hand, I began to figure to myself the miseries of confinement. I was in a right frame for it, and so I gave full scope to my imagination.

I was going to begin with the millions of my fellow-creatures born to no inheritance but slavery ; but finding, however affecting the picture was, that I could not bring it near me, and that the multitude of sad groups in it did but distract me.

—I took a single captive ; and having first shut him up in his dungeon, I then look'd through the twilight of his grated door to take his picture.

I beheld his body half wasted away with long expectation and confinement, and felt what kind of sickness of the heart it was which arises from hope deferred. Upon looking nearer, I saw him pale and feverish ; in thirty years the western breeze had not once fanned his blood ;—he had seen no sun, no moon, in all that time ;—nor had the voice of friend or kinsman breathed through his lattice !—His children !——

But here my heart began to bleed ; and I was forced to go on with another part of the portrait.

He was sitting upon the ground upon a little straw, in the furthest corner of his dungeon, which was alternately his chair and bed : a little calendar of small sticks were laid at the head, notched all over with the dismal days and nights he had passed there :—he had one of these little sticks in his hand, and, with a rusty nail, he was etching another day of misery to add to the heap.   As I darkened the little light he had, he lifted up a hopeless eye towards the door, then cast it down,—shook his head, and went on with his work of affliction. I heard his chains upon his legs, as he turned his body to lay his little stick upon the bundle. —He gave a deep sigh.—I saw the Iron enter into his soul !—I burst into tears.——I could not sustain the picture of confinement which my fancy had drawn.—I started up from my chair, and, calling La Fleur,—I bid him bespeak me a remise, and have it ready at the door of the hotel by nine in the morning.

—I'll go directly, said I, myself to Monsieur le Duc de Choiseul.

La Fleur would have put me to bed ; but not willing he should see any thing upon my cheek which would cost the honest fellow a heart-ache,—I told him I would go to bed by myself,—and bid him go do the same.

## THE STARLING

### ROAD TO VERSAILLES

I got into my remise the hour I proposed. La Fleur got up behind, and I bid the coachman make the best of his way to Versailles.

As there was nothing in this road, or rather

nothing which I look for in travelling, I cannot fill up the blank better than with a short history of this self-same bird, which became the subject of the last chapter.

Whilst the Honourable Mr. *** was waiting for a wind at Dover, it had been caught upon the cliffs before it could well fly, by an English lad who was his groom ; who, not caring to destroy it, had taken it in his breast into the packet ;—and, by course of feeding it, and taking it once under his protection, in a day or two grew fond of it, and got it safe along with him to Paris.

At Paris, the lad had laid out a livre in a little cage for the starling ; and as he had little to do better the five months his master staid there, he taught it in his mother's tongue, the four simple words—(and no more)—to which I owned myself so much its debtor.

Upon his master's going on for Italy, the lad had given it to the master of the hotel. But his little song for liberty being in an *unknown* language at Paris, the bird had little or no store set by him :—so La Fleur bought both him and his cage for me for a bottle of Burgundy.

In my return from Italy, I brought him with me to the country in whose language he had learned his notes ; and telling the story of him to Lord A—, Lord A. begged the bird of me ; in a week Lord A. gave him to Lord B— ; Lord B. made a present of him to Lord C— ; and Lord C.'s gentleman sold him to Lord D.'s for a shilling :—Lord D. gave him to Lord E. and so on, half round the alphabet. From that rank he passed into the lower house, and passed the hands of as many commoners.—But as all these wanted to get in, and my bird wanted to get out, he had almost as little store set by him in London as in Paris.

It is impossible but many of my readers must have heard of him ; and if any by mere chance have ever seen him,—I beg leave to inform them that the bird was my bird,—or some vile copy set up to represent him.

I have nothing farther to add upon him, but that from that time to this, I have borne this poor starling as the crest to my arms.—— And let the herald's officers twist his neck about if they dare.

133

## THE ADDRESS

VERSAILLES

I SHOULD not like to have my enemy take a view of my mind when I am going to ask protection of any man ; for which reason I generally endeavour to protect myself : but this going to Monsieur le Duc de C***, was an act of compulsion ;—had it been an act of choice, I should have done it, I suppose, like other people.

How many mean plans of dirty address, as I went along, did my servile heart form ! I deserved the Baſtile for every one of them.

Then nothing would serve me, when I got within sight of Versailles, but putting words and sentences together, and conceiving attitudes and tones to writhe myself into Monsieur le Duc de C***'s good grace.—This will do, said I.—Just as well, retorted I again, as a coat carried up to him by an adventurous tailor without taking his measure.—Fool ! con-

tinued I,—see Monsieur le Duc's face first ;
—observe what character is written in it ;—
take notice in what posture he stands to hear
you ;—mark the turns and expressions of
his body and limbs ;—and for the tone,—
the first sound which comes from his lips will
give it to you ; and from all these together
you'll compound an address at once upon the
spot, which cannot disgust the Duke ;—the
ingredients are his own, and most likely to go
down.

Well ! said I, I wish it well over.—Coward
again ! as if man to man was not equal throughout the whole surface of the globe ; and if in
the field, why not face to face in the cabinet
too ? and trust me, Yorick, whenever it is not
so, man is false to himself, and betrays his own
succours ten times where nature does it once.
Go to the Duc de C*** with the Bastile in
thy looks ;—my life for it, thou wilt be sent
back to Paris in half-an-hour with an escort.

I believe so, said I.—Then I'll go to the
Duke, by Heaven ! with all the gaiety and
debonairness in the world.

—And there you are wrong again, replied I.
——A heart at ease Yorick, flies into no

extremes,—'tis ever on its centre.—Well !
well ! cried I, as the coachman turned in at
the gates, I find I shall do very well : and by
the time he had wheeled round the court, and
brought me up to the door, I found myself
so much the better for my own lecture, that
I neither ascended the steps like a victim to
justice, who was to part with life upon the top-
most,—nor did I mount them with a skip
and a couple of strides, as I do when I fly up,
Eliza ! to thee, to meet it.

As I entered the door of the saloon, I was
met by a person who possibly might be the
*maitre d'hotel*, but had more the air of one of
the under-secretaries, who told me the Duc de
C*** was busy.—I am utterly ignorant, said
I, of the forms of obtaining an audience, being
an absolute stranger, and, what is worse in the
present conjuncture of affairs, being an Englishman too.——He replied, that did not increase
the difficulty.—I made him a slight bow, and
told him I had something of importance to
say to Monsieur le Duc.   The secretary looked
towards the stairs, as if he was about to leave
me to carry up this account to some one.—
But I must not mislead you, said I,—for what

I have to say is of no manner of importance to Monsieur le Duc de C\*\*\*, but of great importance to myself.——*C'est une autre affaire*, replied he.——Not at all, said I, to a man of gallantry. But pray, good Sir, continued I, when can a stranger hope to have *accesse* ?——In not less than two hours, said he, looking at his watch.——The number of equipages in the court-yard seemed to justify the calculation, that I could have no nearer a prospect ;—and as walking backwards and forwards in the saloon, without a soul to commune with, was for the time as bad as being in the Bastile itself, I instantly went back to my remise, and bid the coachman drive me to the *Cordon Bleu*, which was the nearest hotel.

I think there is a fatality in it ;—I seldom go to the place I set out for.

## LE PATISSER

### VERSAILLES

Before I had got half way down the street, I changed my mind : as I am at Versailles, thought I, I might as well take a view of the town ; so I pulled the cord, and ordered the coachman to drive round some of the principal streets.—I suppose the town is not very large said I.—The coachman begged pardon for setting me right, and told me it was very superb ; and that numbers of the first dukes and marquisses and counts had hotels.—The Count de B\*\*\*, of whom the bookseller at the Quai de Conti had spoke so handsomely the night before, came instantly into my mind. —And why should I not go, thought I, to the Count de B\*\*\*, who has so high an idea of English books and English men,—and tell him my story ? So I changed my mind a second time. In truth, it was the third ; for I had intended that day for Madame de

138

R\*\*\*, in the Rue St. Pierre, and had devoutly sent her word by her *fille de chambre* that I would assuredly wait upon her ;—but I am governed by circumstances ;—I cannot govern them : so seeing a man standing with a basket on the other side of the street, as if he had something to sell, I bid La Fleur go up to him, and inquire for the Count's hotel.

La Fleur returned a little pale ; and told me it was a Chevalier de St. Louis selling *patés*. —It is impossible, La Fleur, said I.—La Fleur could no more account for the phænomenon than myself ; but persisted in his story : he had seen the croix set in gold, with its red ribband, he said, tied to his button-hole ; and had looked into the basket, and seen the *patés* which the Chevalier was selling ; so could not be mistaken in that.

Such a reverse in a man's life awakens a better principle than curiosity : I could not help looking for some time at him as I sat in his *remise*. The more I looked at him, his croix, and his basket, the stronger they wove themselves into my brain.—I got out of the *remise*, and went towards him.

L     

He was begirt with a clean linen apron which fell below his knees, and with a sort of a bib that went half way up his breaſt. Upon the top of this, but a little below the hem, hung his croix. His basket of little *patés* was covered over with a white damask napkin : another of the same kind was spread at the bottom ; and there was such a look of *propreté* and neatness throughout, that one might have bought his *patés* of him as much from appetite as sentiment.

He made an offer of them to neither ; but ſtood ſtill with them at the corner of a hotel, for those to buy who chose it, without solicitation.

He was about forty-eight ;—of a sedate look, something approaching to gravity. I did not wonder.——I went up rather to the basket than him, and having lifted up the napkin, and taken one of his *patés* into my hand,—I begged he would explain the appearance which affeᶜted me.

He told me in a few words, that the beſt part of his life had passed in the service ; in which, after spending a small patrimony, he had obtained a company and the croix with it ; but that, at the conclusion of the laſt peace,

his regiment being reformed, and the whole
corps, with those of some other regiments,
left without any provision, he found himself
in a wide world without friends, without a
livre ;—and indeed, said he, without any
thing but this :—(pointing, as he said it, to
his croix).——The poor Chevalier won my
pity ; and he finished the scene by winning
my esteem too.

The King, he said, was the most generous of
princes ; but his generosity could neither
relieve nor reward every one ; and it was only
his misfortune to be amongst the number.
He had a little wife, he said, whom he loved,
who did the *patisserie ;* and added, he felt no
dishonor in defending her and himself from
want in this way,—unless Providence had
offered him a better.

It would be wicked to withhold a pleasure
from the good, in passing over what happened
to this poor Chevalier of St. Louis about nine
months after.

It seems he usually took his stand near the
iron gates which lead up to the palace ; and
as his croix had caught the eye of numbers,
numbers had made the same inquiry which

I had done.—He had told the same story and always with so much modesty and good sense, that it had reached at last the king's ears ;—who hearing the Chevalier had been a gallant officer, and respected by the whole regiment as a man of honour and integrity,— he broke up his little trade by a pension of fifteen hundred livres a-year.

As I have told this to please the reader, I beg he will allow me to relate another, out of its order, to please myself ;—the two stories reflect light upon each other,—and 'tis a pity they should be parted.

## THE SWORD

### RENNES

WHEN states and empires have their periods of declension, and feel in their turns what distress and poverty is,—I stop not to tell the causes which gradually brought the house d'E*** in Britanny into decay. The Marquis d'E*** had fought up against his condition with great firmness ; wishing to preserve, and still shew to the world some little fragments of what his ancestors had been ; their indiscretions had put it out of his power. There was enough left for the little exigencies of obscurity.—But he had two boys who looked up to him for light ;—he thought they deserved it. He had tried his sword,—it could not open the way,—the mounting was too expensive,—and simple economy was not a match for it :—there was no resource but commerce.

In any other province in France save Britanny, this was smiting the root for ever on the little tree his pride and affection wished to see re-blossom.—But in Britanny, there being a provision for this, he availed himself of it ; and taking an occasion when the states were assembled at Rennes, the Marquis, attended with his two boys, entered the court ; and having pleaded the right of an ancient law of the duchy, which, though seldom claimed, he said, was no less in force, he took his sword from his side :—Here, said he, take it ; and be trusty guardians of it till better times put me in condition to reclaim it.

The president accepted the Marquis's sword ;—he staid a few minutes to see it deposited in the archives of his house, and departed.

The Marquis and his whole family embarked the next day for Martinico, and in about nineteen or twenty years of successful application to business, with some unlooked-for bequests from distant branches of his house, returned home to reclaim his nobility, and to support it.

It was an incident of good fortune which will never happen to any traveller but a sentimental one, that I should be at Rennes at the very time of this solemn requisition. I call it solemn ;—it was so to me.

The Marquis entered the court with his whole family : he supported his lady ;—his eldest son supported his sister, and his youngest was at the other extreme of the line next his mother ;—he put his handkerchief to his face twice.—

—There was a dead silence. When the Marquis had approached within six paces of the tribunal, he gave the Marchioness to his youngest son, and advancing three steps before his family,—he reclaimed his sword. His sword was given him : and the moment he got it into his hand, he drew it almost out of the scabbard :—'twas the shining face of a friend he had once given up :—he looked attentively along it, beginning at the hilt, as if to see whether it was the same,—when observing a little rust which it had contracted near the point, he brought it near his eye, and bending his head down over it,—I think I saw a tear fall upon the place, I could not be deceived by what followed.

" I shall find," said he, " some other way to get it off."

When the Marquis had said this, he returned his sword into his scabbard, made a bow to the guardians of it,—and, with his wife and daughter, and his two sons following him, walked out.

O how I envied his feelings

## THE PASSPORT

### VERSAILLES

I FOUND no difficulty in getting admittance to Monsieur le Count de B***. The set of Shakespeares was laid upon the table, and he was tumbling them over. I walked up close to the table, and giving firſt such a look at the books as to make him conceive I knew what they were,—I told him I had come without any one to present me, knowing I should meet with a friend in his apartment, who, I truſted, would do it for me ;—It is my countryman the great Shakespeare, said I, pointing to his works, *et ayez la bonté, mon cher ami,* apoſtrophizing his spirit, added I, *de me faire cet honneur-là.*—

The Count smiled at the singularity of the introduction ; and seeing I looked a little pale and sickly, insiſted upon my taking an armchair ; so I sat down ; and to save him conjeƈtures upon a visit so out of all rule, I

146

told him simply of the incident in the bookseller's shop, and how that had impelled me
rather to go to him with the story of a little
embarrassment I was under, than to any other
man in France.——And what is your embarrassment ? let me hear it, said the Count.——
So I told him the story just as I have told it
the reader.

——And the master of my hotel, said I, as I
concluded it, will needs have it, Monsieur le
Count, that I should be sent to the Bastile ;——
but I have no apprehensions, continued I,——
for in falling into the hands of the most
polished people in the world. and being
conscious I was a true man, and not come to
spy the nakedness of the land, I scarce thought
I lay at their mercy.——It does not suit the
gallantry of the French, Monsieur le Count,
said I, to shew it against invalids.

An animated blush came into the Count de
B***'s cheeks as I spoke this—*Ne craignez
rien*—Don't fear, said he.—Indeed I don't,
replied I again.—Besides, continued I a little
sportingly, I have come laughing all the way
from London to Paris ; and I do not think
Monsieur le Duc de Choiseul is such an

enemy to mirth, as to send me back crying for my pains.

—My application to you, Monsieur le Count de B*** (making him a low bow) is to desire he will not.

The Count heard me with great good-nature, or I had not said half as much,—and once or twice said,—*C'est bien dit.* So I rested my cause there,—and determined to say no more about it.

The Count led the discourse : we talked of indifferent things,—of books, and politics, and men ; and then of women.——God bless them all ! said I, after much discourse about them,—there is not a man upon earth who loves them so much as I do. After all the foibles I have seen, and all the satires I have read against them, still I love them ; being firmly persuaded that a man who has not a sort of an affection for the whole sex, is incapable of ever loving a single one as he ought.

*Heh bien ! Monsieur l'Anglois,* said the Count, gaily ;—you are not come to spy the nakedness of the land ;—I believe you ;— *ni encore,* I dare say, *that* of our women : but

148

permit me to conjecture,—if, *par hazard*, they fell into your way, that the prospect would not affect you.

I have something within me which cannot bear the shock of the least indecent insinuation : in the sportability of chit-chat I have often endeavoured to conquer it, and with infinite pain have hazarded a thousand things to a dozen of the sex together,—the least of which I could not venture to a single one to gain Heaven.

Excuse me, Monsieur le Count, said I :— as for the nakedness of your land, if I saw it, I should cast my eyes over it with tears in them ;—and for that of your women (blushing at the idea he had excited in me) I am so evangelical in this, and have such a fellow-feeling for whatever is *weak* about them, that I would cover it with a garment, if I knew how to throw it on ;—but I could wish, continued I, to spy the *nakedness* of their hearts, and, through the different disguises of customs, climates, and religion, find out what is good in them to fashion my own by ;—and, therefore, am I come.

It is for this reason, Monsieur le Count,

continued I, that I have not seen the Palais
Royal, nor the Luxembourg,—nor the Façade
of the Louvre,—nor have attempted to swell
the catalogues we have of pictures, statues, and
churches.—I conceive every fair being as a
temple, and would rather enter in, and see the
original drawings, and loose sketches hung up
in it, than the Transfiguration of Raphæl
itself.

The thirst of this, continued I, as impatient
as that which inflames the breast of the con-
noisseur, has led me from my own home into
France,—and from France will lead me through
Italy ;—'tis a quiet journey of the heart in
pursuit of *Nature*, and those affections which
arise out of her, which make us love each
other,—and the world, better than we do.

The Count said a great many civil things
to me upon the occasion ; and added, very
politely, how much he stood obliged to
Shakespeare for making me known to him.——
But, *à-propos*, said he ;—Shakespeare is full
of great things ;—he forgot the small punctilio
of announcing your name :—it puts you under
a necessity of doing it yourself.

## THE PASSPORT

### VERSAILLES

THERE is not a more perplexing affair in life to me, than to set about telling any one who I am,—for there is scarce any body I cannot give a better account of than myself ; and I have often wish'd I could do it in a single word,—and have an end of it. It was the only time and occasion in my life I could accomplish this to any purpose ;—for Shakespeare lying upon the table, and recollecting I was in his books, I took up Hamlet, and turning immediately to the grave-digger's scene in the fifth act, I laid my finger upon *Yorick* ; and advancing the book to the Count, with my finger all the way over the name,—*Me voici !* said I.

Now, whether the idea of poor Yorick's skull was put out of the Count's mind by the reality of my own, or by what magic he could drop a period of seven or eight hundred years, makes nothing in this account ; 'tis certain, the French conceive better than they combine ;— I wonder at nothing in this world, and the less at this ; inasmuch as one of the firſt of our own church, for whose candour and paternal sentiments I have the higheſt veneration, fell into the same mistake in the very same case :— " He could not bear," he said, " to look into sermons wrote by the King of Denmark's jeſter."—Good, my Lord ! said I ; but there are two Yoricks. The Yorick your Lordship thinks of, has been dead and buried eight hundred years ago : he flourish'd in Horwendillus's court ;—the other Yorick is myself, who have flourish'd, my Lord, in no court.——He shook his head.——Good God ! said I, you might as well confound Alexander the Great with Alexander the Coppersmith, my Lord !——'Twas all one, he replied.

——If Alexander, King of Macedon, could have translated your Lordship, said I, I'm sure your Lordship would not have said so.

The poor Count de B*** fell but into the same *error*.

——*Et, Monsieur, eſt il Yorick ?* cried the Count.——*Je le suis*, said I.——*Vous ?*———

*Moi——moi qui ai l'honneur de vous parler,
Monsieur le Comte.——Mon Dieu !* said he,
embracing me,—*Vous etes Yorick ?*

The Count inftantly put the Shakespeare
into his pocket, and left me alone in his room.

## THE PASSPORT

### VERSAILLES

I COULD not conceive why the Count de
B\*\*\* had gone so abruptly out of the room,
any more than I could conceive why he had
put the Shakespeare into his pocket.—*Mysteries
which muft explain themselves, are not worth
the loss of time which a conjecture about them
takes up :* 'twas better to read Shakespeare ;
so taking up " *Much Ado about Nothing,*" I
transported myself inftantly from the chair

I sat in to Messina in Sicily, and got so busy with Don Pedro, and Benedict, and Beatrice, that I thought not of Versailles, the Count, or the passport.

Sweet pliability of man's spirit, that can at once surrender itself to illusions which cheat expectation and sorrow of their weary moments! —Long,—long since had ye number'd out my days, had I not trod so great a part of them upon this enchanted ground. When my way is too rough for my feet, or too steep for my strength, I get off it, to some smooth velvet path which fancy has scatter'd over with rose-buds of delights ; and, having taken a few turns in it, come back strengthen'd and refresh'd.—When evils press sore upon me, and there is no retreat from them in this world, then I take a new course ;—I leave it,— and, as I have a clearer idea of the Elysian Fields than I have of Heaven, I force myself, like Æneas, into them ;—I see him meet the pensive shade of his forsaken Dido, and wish to recognize it ;—I see the injured spirit wave her head, and turn off silent from the author of her miseries and dishonors ;—I loose the feelings for myself in hers, and in those affections which were wont to make me mourn for her when I was at school.

*Surely, this is not walking in a vain shadow,—nor does man disquiet himself* in vain *by it :*—he oftener does so in trusting the issue of his commotions to reason only.—I can safely say for myself, I was never able to conquer any one single bad sensation in my heart so decisively, as by beating up as fast as I could for some kindly and gentle sensation to fight it upon its own ground.

When I had got to the end of the third act, the Count de B*** entered with my passport in his hand. Mons. le Duc de C***, said the Count, is as good a prophet, I dare say, as he is a statesman.——*Un homme qui rit,* said the Duke, *ne sera jamais dangereux.*——Had it been for any one but the King's jester, added the Count, I could not have got it these two hours.——*Pardonnez moi,* Mons. le Count, said I, I am not the King's jester.——But you are Yorick ?——Yes.——*Et vous plaisantez ?*——I answered, Indeed I did jest,—but was not paid for it ;—'twas entirely at my own expence.

We have no jester at court, Mons. le Count,

M 155

said I ; the laſt we had was in the licentious reign of Charles II. ;—since which time, our manners have been so gradually refining, that our court at present is so full of patriots, who wish for *nothing* but the honors and wealth of our country ;—and our ladies are all so chaſte, so spotless, so good, so devout,—there is nothing for a jeſter to make a jeſt of.

*Voila un persiflage !* cried the Count.

# THE PASSPORT

## VERSAILLES

As the passport was directed to all lieutenant-governors, governors, and commandants of cities, generals of armies, juſticiaries, and all officers of juſtice, to let Mr. Yorick the

King's jester, and his baggage, travel quietly along,—I own the triumph of obtaining the passport was not a little tarnish'd by the figure I cut in it.—But there is nothing unmix'd in this world ; and some of the gravest of our divines have carried it so far as to affirm, that enjoyment itself was attended even with a sigh,—and that the greatest *they knew of*, terminated, *in a general way*, in little better than a convulsion.

I remember the grave and learned Bevoriskius, in his Commentary upon the Generations from Adam, very naturally breaks off in the middle of a note, to give an account to the world of a couple of sparrows upon the outedge of his window, which had incommoded him all the time he wrote ; and, at last, had entirely taken him off from his genealogy.

——'Tis strange ! writes Bevoriskius, but the facts are certain ; for I have had the curiosity to mark them down, one by one, with my pen ;—but the cock-sparrow, during the little time that I could have finished the other half of this note, has actually interrupted me with the reiteration of his caresses three-and-twenty times and a half.

How merciful, adds Bevoriskius, is Heaven to his creatures !

Ill-fated Yorick ! that the gravest of thy brethren should be able to write that to the world, which stains thy face with crimson to copy, even in thy study.

But this is nothing to my travels ;—so I twice,—twice beg pardon for it.

## CHARACTER

### VERSAILLES

AND how do you find the French ? said the Count de B***, after he had given me the passport.

The reader may suppose, that, after so

obliging a proof of courtesy, I could not be at a loss to say something handsome to the inquiry.

——*Mais passe, pour cela.*——Speak frankly, said he : do you find all the urbanity in the French which the world give us the honor of ? ——I had found every thing, I said, which confirmed it.——*Vraiment,* said the Count, *les François sont polis.*——To an excess, replied I.

The Count took notice of the word *excesse ;* and would have it I meant more than I said. I defended myself a long time, as well as I could, against it ;—he insisted I had a reserve, and that I would speak my opinion frankly.

I believe, Mons. le Count, said I, that man has a certain compass, as well as an instrument ; and that the social and other calls have occasion, by turns, for every key in him ; so that, if you begin a note too high or too low, there must be want either in the upper or under part, to fill up the system of harmony.——The Count de B*** did not understand music ; so desired me to explain it some other way. ——A polish'd nation, my dear Count, said I, makes everyone its debtor ; and besides,

Urbanity itself, like the fair sex, has so
many charms, it goes against the heart
to say it can do ill ; and yet, I believe,
there is but a certain line of perfection
that man, take him altogether, is em-
power'd to arrive at ;—if he gets beyond,
he rather exchanges qualities than gets them.
I must not presume to say how far this has
affected the French in the subject we are
speaking of ;—but should it ever be the case
of the English, in the progress of their refinements, to arrive at the same polish which
distinguishes the French, if we did not lose
the *politesse du cœur*, which inclines men more
to humane actions than courteous ones,—we
should at least lose that distinct variety and
originality of character, which distinguishes
them not only from each other, but from all
the world besides.

I had a few of King William's shillings, as
smooth as glass, in my pocket, and foreseeing
they would be of use in the illustration of my
hypothesis, I had got them into my hand, when
I had proceeded so far :—

See, Mons. le Count, said I, rising up, and
laying them before him upon the table,—by

jingling and rubbing one against another for seventy years together in one body's pocket or another's, they are become so much alike you can scarce distinguish one shilling from another.

The English, like ancient medals, kept more apart, and passing but few people's hands, preserve the first sharpness which the fine hand of Nature has given them ;—they are not so pleasant to feel,—but, in return, the legend is so visible, that, at the first look, you see whose image and superscription they bear. But the French, Mons. le Count, added I, (wishing to soften what I had said) have so many excellencies, they can the better spare this ;—they are a loyal, a gallant, a generous, an ingenious, and a good-temper'd people as is under Heaven ;—if they have a fault, they are too *serious*.

*Mon Dieu !* cried the Count, rising out of his chair.

*Mais vous plaisantez*, said he, correcting his exclamation.——I laid my hand upon my breast, and, with earnest gravity, assured him it was my most settled opinion.

——The Count said he was mortified, he

could not stay to hear my reasons, being engaged to go that moment to dine with the Duc de C***.

But, if it is not too far to come to Versailles, to eat your soup with me, I beg, before you leave France, I may have the pleasure of knowing you retract your opinion,—or in what manner you support it.—But if you do support it, *Mons. Anglois*, said he, you must do it with all your powers, because you have the whole world against you.——I promised the Count I would do myself the honor of dining with him before I set out for Italy;—so took my leave.

## THE TEMPTATION

### PARIS

WHEN I alighted at the hotel, the porter told me a young woman with a band-box had been that moment inquiring for me.——I do not know, said the porter, whether she is gone away or not.——I took the key of my chamber of him, and went upstairs ; and, when I had got within ten steps of the top of the landing before my door, I met her coming easily down.

It was the fair *fille de chambre* I had walked along the Quai de Conti with : Madame de R\*\*\* had sent her upon some commission to a *marchante des modes* within a step or two of the hotel de Modene ; and, as I had fail'd in waiting upon her, had bid her inquire if I had left Paris ; and, if so, whether I had not left a letter addressed to her.

As the fair *fille de chambre* was so near my door, she returned back, and went into the room with me for a moment or two whilst I wrote a card.

It was a fine still evening in the latter end of the month of May,—the crimson window-curtains (which were of the same colour as those of the bed) were drawn close,—the sun was setting, and reflected through them so warm a tint into the fair *fille de chambre's* face,—I thought she blush'd ;—the idea of it made me blush myself ;—we were quite alone, and that superinduced a second blush before the first could get off.

There is a sort of a pleasing half-guilty blush, where the blood is more in fault than the man ;—'tis sent impetuous from the heart, and virtue flies after it,—not to call it back, but to make the sensation of it more delicious to the nerves ;—'tis associated.

But I'll not describe it ;—I felt something at first within me which was not in strict unison with the lesson of virtue I had given her the night before ;—I sought five minutes for a card ; I knew I had not one. I took up a pen,—I laid it down again,—my hand trembled :—the Devil was in me.

I know as well as any one he is an adversary ; whom, if we resist, he will fly from us ; but I seldom resist him at all, from a terror that, though I may conquer, I may still get a hurt in the combat ;—so I give up the triumph for security ; and, instead of thinking to make him fly, I generally fly myself.

The fair *fille de chambre* came close up to the bureau, where I was looking for a card,— took up first the pen I cast down, then offer'd to hold me the ink ; she offer'd it so sweetly, I was going to accept it, but I durst not ;——— I have nothing, my dear, said I, to write upon. ———Write it, said she, simply, upon any thing.

———I was just going to cry out, Then I will write it, fair girl, upon thy lips !

———If I do, said I, I shall perish ; so I took her by the hand, and led her to the door, and begg'd she would not forget the lesson I had given her.———She said, indeed she would not, and as she uttered it with some earnestness, she turn'd about, and gave me both her hands, closed together, into mine ;—it was impossible not to compress them in that situation ;—I wish'd to let them go ; and, all the time I held them, I kept arguing within myself against it,—and still I held them on.—In two minutes I found I had all the battle to fight over again ;—and I felt my legs and every limb about me tremble at the idea.

The foot of the bed was within a yard and a half of the place where we were standing.— I had still hold of her hands—(and how it happened, I can give no account) ; but I neither asked her, nor drew her, nor did I think of the bed ;—but so it did happen, we both sat down.

I'll juft shew you, said the fair *fille de chambre*, the little purse I have been making to-day to hold your crown. So she put her hand into her right pocket, which was next me, and felt for it some time ;—then into the left. ——" She had loft it."——I never bore expeftation more quietly ;—it was in her right pocket at laft ; she pull'd it out ; it was of green taffeta, lined with a little bit of white quilted satin, and juft big enough to hold the crown :—she put it into my hand ; it was pretty ; and I held it ten minutes, with the back of my hand refting upon her lap, looking sometimes at the purse, sometimes on one side of it.

A ftitch or two had broke out in the gathers of my ftock ; the fair *fille de chambre*, without saying a word, took out her little housewife, threaded a small needle, and sewed it up. I foresaw it would hazard the glory of the day, and, as she passed her hand in silence across and across my neck in the manœuvre, I felt the laurels shake which fancy had wreathed about my head.

A ftrap had given way in her walk, and the

buckle of her shoe was just falling off.——
See, said the *fille de chambre*, holding up her
foot,——I could not from my soul but fasten
the buckle in return ; and, putting in the
strap,—and lifting up the other foot with it,
when I had done, to see both were right, in
doing it so suddenly, it unavoidably threw the
fair *fille de chambre* off her centre,—and then—

## THE CONQUEST

Yes,—and then——Ye, whose clay-cold
heads and lukewarm hearts can argue down
or mask your passions, tell me, what trespass,
is it that man should have them ? or how his
spirit stands answerable to the Father of
spirits but for his conduct under them ?

If nature has so wove her web of kindness

that some threads of love and desire are entangled with the piece,—must the whole web be rent in drawing them out ?—Whip me such stoics, great Governor of Nature ! said I to myself :—wherever thy Providence shall place me for the trials of my virtue ; whatever is my danger,—whatever is my situation, —let me feel the movements which rise out of it, and which belong to me as a man,—and if I govern them as a good one, I will trust the issues to thy justice ; for thou hast made us, and not we ourselves.

As I finished my address, I raised the fair *fille de chambre* up by the hand, and led her out of the room :—she stood by me till I locked the door and put the key in my pocket, —*and then*,—the victory being quite decisive —and not till then, I pressed my lips to her cheek, and, taking her by the hand again, led her safe to the gate of the hotel.

## THE MYSTERY

### PARIS

IF a man knows the heart, he will know it was impossible to go back instantly to my chamber ;—it was touching a cold key with a flat third to it, upon the close of a piece of music, which had called forth my affections ; therefore, when I let go the hand of the *fille de chambre*, I remain'd at the gate of the hotel for some time, looking at every one who pass'd by, and forming conjectures upon them, till my attention got fix'd upon a single object which confounded all kind of reasoning upon him.

It was a tall figure, of a philosophic, serious, adust look, which pass'd and repass'd sedately along the street, making a turn of about sixty paces on each side of the gate of the hotel.— The man was about fifty-two, had a small cane under his arm, was dress'd in a dark drab-

169

coloured coat, waistcoat, and breeches, which
seem'd to have seen some years' service ;—
they were still clean, and there was a little air
of frugal *propreté* throughout him. By his
pulling off his hat, and his attitude of accosting
a good many in his way, I saw he was asking
charity ; so I got a sous or two out of my
pocket ready to give him, as he took me in
his turn. He pass'd by me without asking
any thing,—and yet did not go five steps
farther before he ask'd charity of a little
woman.—I was much more likely to have
given of the two. He had scarce done with
the woman, when he pull'd his hat off to
another who was coming the same way. An
ancient gentleman came slowly, and, after
him, a young smart one. He let them both
pass, and ask'd nothing : I stood observing
him half-an-hour ; in which time he had made
a dozen turns backwards and forwards, and
found that he invariably pursued the same
plan.

There were two things very singular in
this, which set my brain to work, and to no
purpose ;—the first was, Why the man should
*only* tell his story to the sex ;—and secondly,

What kind of story it was, and what species of eloquence it could be, which soften'd the hearts of the women, which he knew 'twas to no purpose to practise upon the men.

There were two other circumstances which entangled this mystery :—the one was, He told every woman what he had to say, in her ear, and in a way which had much more the air of a secret than a petition :—the other was, It was always successful ;—he never stopp'd a woman but she pull'd out her purse, and immediately gave him something.

I could form no system to explain the phænomenon.

I had got a riddle to amuse me for the rest of the evening ; so I walk'd up stairs to my chamber.

## THE CASE OF CONSCIENCE

PARIS

I was immediately followed up by the master of the hotel, who came into my room to tell me I must provide lodgings elsewhere.—— How so, friend ? said I.——He answer'd, I had a young woman lock'd up with me two hours that evening in my bedchamber, and 'twas against the rules of his house.——Very well, said I, we'll all part friends then,—for the girl is no worse,—and I am no worse,— and you will be just as I found you.—It was enough, he said, to overthrow the credit of his hotel.—*Voyez vous, Monsieur*, said he, pointing to the foot of the bed we had been sitting upon. ——I own it had something of the appearance of an evidence ; but my pride not suffering me to enter into any detail of the case, I exhorted him to let his soul sleep in peace, as I resolved to let mine do that night, and that I would discharge what I owed him at breakfast.

———I should not have minded, Monsieur, said he, if you had had twenty girls,———'Tis a score more, replied I, interrupting him, than I ever reckon'd upon.———Provided, added he, it had been but in a morning.———And does the difference of the time of the day at Paris, make a difference in the sin ?———It made a difference, he said, in the scandal.———I like a good distinction in my heart ; and cannot say I was intolerably out of temper with the man.———I own it necessary, resumed the master of the hotel, that a stranger at Paris should have the opportunities presented to him of buying lace and silk stockings, and ruffles, *et tout cela ;*—and 'tis nothing if a woman comes with a band-box.———O' my conscience, said I, she had one ; but I never look'd into it.———Then, Monsieur, said he, has bought nothing.———Not one earthly thing, replied I.———Because, said he, I could recommend you to one who would use you *en conscience.*———But I must see her this night, said I.——— He made me a low bow, and walk'd down.

Now shall I triumph over this *maitre d'hotel,* cried I ;—and what then ?   Then I shall let him see I know he is a dirty fellow.—And what then ?—What then !—I was too near myself to say it was for the sake of others.—I had no good answer left ;—there was more of spleen than of principle in my project, and I was sick of it before the execution.

In a few minutes the grisset came in with her box of lace.——I'll buy nothing, however, said I, within myself.

The grisset would shew me every thing.—I was hard to please : she would not seem to see it. She open'd her little magazine, and laid all her laces, one after another, before me ; —unfolded and folded them up again, one by one, with the most patient sweetness.—I might buy,—or not ;—she would let me have every thing at my own price :—the poor creature seem'd anxious to get a penny ; and laid herself out to win me, and not so much in a manner which seem'd artful, as in one I felt simple and caressing.

If there is not a fund of honest cullibility in man, so much the worse ;—my heart relented, and I gave up my second resolution as quietly as the first.—Why should I chastise one for the trespass of another ?   If thou art tributary to this tyrant of an hoſt, thought I, looking up in her face, so much harder is thy bread.

If I had not had more than four Louis d'ors in my purse, there was no such thing as rising up and shewing her the door till I had first laid three of them out in a pair of ruffles.

—The maſter of the hotel will share the profit with her ;—no matter,—then I have only paid, as many a poor soul has *paid* before me, for an aćt he *could* not do, or think of.

## THE RIDDLE

### PARIS

WHEN La Fleur came up to wait upon me at supper, he told me how sorry the maſter of the hotel was, for his affront to me in bidding me change my lodgings.

A man who values a good night's rest will not lie down with enmity in his heart, if he can help it.—So I bid La Fleur tell the master of the hotel, that I was sorry, on my side, for the occasion I had given him ;—and you may tell him, if you will, La Fleur, added I, that if the young woman should call again, I shall not see her.

This was a sacrifice not to him, but myself, having resolv'd, after so narrow an escape, to run no more risks, but to leave Paris, if it was possible, with all the virtue I entered it.

*C'est deroger à noblesse, Monsieur*, said La Fleur, making me a bow down to the ground as he said it.—*Et encore, Monsieur*, said he, may change his sentiments ;—and if (*par hazard*) he should like to amuse himself,——I find no amusement in it, said I, interrupting him.

——*Mon Dieu !* said La Fleur,—and took away.

In an hour's time he came to put me to bed, and was more than commonly officious : —something hung upon his lips to say to me, or ask me, which he could not get off : I could not conceive what it was ; and indeed gave myself little trouble to find it out, as I

176

had another riddle so much more interesting upon my mind, which was that of the man's asking charity before the door of the hotel. —I would have given any thing to have got to the bottom of it ; and that not out of curiosity,—'tis so low a principle of enquiry, in general, I would not purchase the gratification of it with a two-sous piece ;—but a secret, I thought, which so soon and so certainly soften'd the heart of every woman you came near, was a secret at least equal to the philosopher's stone : had I had both the Indies, I would have given up one to have been master of it.

I toss'd and turn'd it almost all night long in my brains, to no manner of purpose ; and when I awoke in the morning, I found my spirits as much troubled with my *dreams*, as ever the King of Babylon had been with his ; and I will not hesitate to affirm, it would have puzzled all the wise men of Paris as much as those of Chaldea, to have given its interpretation.

## LE DIMANCHE

### PARIS

It was Sunday ; and when La Fleur came in, in the morning, with my coffee and roll and butter, he had got himself so gallantly array'd, I scarce knew him.

I had covenanted at Montriul to give him a new hat with a silver button and loop, and four Louis d'ors *pour s'adoniser*, when we got to Paris ; and the poor fellow, to do him justice, had done wonders with it.

He had bought a bright, clean, good scarlet coat, and a pair of breeches of the same.—— They were not a crown worse, he said, for the wearing.—I wish'd him hang'd for telling me.——They look'd so fresh, that though I knew the thing could not be done, yet I would rather have imposed upon my fancy with thinking I had bought them new for the fellow, than that they had come out of the Rue de Friperie.

178

This is a nicety which makes not the heart sore at Paris.

He had purchased, moreover, a handsome blue satin waistcoat, fancifully enough embroidered ;—This was indeed something the worse for the service it had done, but 'twas clean scour'd,—the gold had been touch'd up, and, upon the whole, was rather showy than otherwise ;—and as the blue was not violent, it suited with the coat and breeches very well : he had squeez'd out of the money moreover, a new bag and a *solitaire ;* and had insisted with the *fripier* upon a gold pair of garters to his breeches knees.—He had purchased muslin ruffles *bien brodées,* with four livres of his own money ;—and a pair of white silk stockings for five more ;— and, to top all, Nature had given him a handsome figure, without costing him a sous.

He entered the room thus set off, with his hair drest in the first style, and with a handsome *bouquet* in his breast.—In a word, there was that look of festivity in everything about him, which at once put me in mind it was Sunday— and by combining both together, it instantly struck me, that the favor he wish'd to ask

179

of me the night before, was to spend the day as every body in Paris spent it besides. I had scarce made the conjecture, when La Fleur, with infinite humility, but with a look of trust, as if I should not refuse him, begg'd I would grant him the day, *pour faire le gallant vis-à-vis de sa maitresse.*

Now it was the very thing I intended to do myself *vis-à-vis* Madame de R***.—I had retained the *remise* on purpose for it, and it would not have mortified my vanity to have had a servant so well dress'd as La Fleur was, to have got up behind it : I never could have worse spared him.

But we must *feel*, not argue, in these embarrassments ;—the sons and daughters of Service part with liberty, but not with nature, in their contracts; they are flesh and blood, and have their little vanities and wishes in the midst of the house of bondage, as well as their taskmasters ;—no doubt, they have set their self-denials at a price,—and their expectations are so unreasonable, that I would often disappoint them, but that their condition puts it so much in my power to do it.

*Behold,—Behold, I am the servant,*—disarms me at once of the powers of a Master.

——Thou shalt go, La Fleur, said I.

—And what Mistress, La Fleur, said I, canst thou have pick'd up in so little a time at Paris ?——La Fleur laid his hand upon his breast, and said, 'Twas a *petite demoiselle*, at Monsieur le Count de B\*\*\*'s.—La Fleur had a heart made for society ; and to speak the truth of him, let as few occasions slip him as his master,—so that, somehow or other,— but how,—Heaven knows,—he had connected himself with the *demoiselle* upon the landing of the staircase, during the time I was taken up with my passport ; and as there was time enough for me to win the Count to my interest, La Fleur had contrived to make it do to win the maid to his. The family, it seems, was to be at Paris that day, and he had made a party with her, and two or three more of the Count's household, upon the *boulevards*.

Happy people ! that once a week at least are sure to lay down all your cares together, and dance and sing, and sport away the weights of grievance, which bow down the spirit of other nations to the earth.

## THE FRAGMENT

### PARIS

La Fleur had left me something to amuse myself with for the day more than I had bargained for, or could have entered either into his head or mine.

He had brought the little print of butter upon a currant-leaf ; and, as the morning was warm, and he had a good step to bring it, he had begged a sheet of waste paper to put betwixt the currant-leaf and his hand.—As that was plate sufficient, I bade him lay it upon the table as it was ; and as I resolved to stay within all day, I ordered him to call upon the *traiteur*, to bespeak my dinner, and leave me to breakfast by myself.

When I had finished the butter, I threw the currant-leaf out of the window, and was going to do the same by the waste paper ;—but, stopping to read a line first, and that drawing me on to a second and third,—I thought it better worth ; so I shut the window, and drawing a chair up to it, I sat down to read it.

It was in the old French of Rabelais's time ; and, for aught I know, might have been wrote by him : it was, moreover, in a Gothic letter, and that so faded and gone off by damps and length of time, it cost me infinite trouble to make any thing of it.—I threw it down ; and then wrote a letter to Eugenius, —then I took it up again, and embroiled my patience with it afresh ;—and then, to cure that, I wrote a letter to Eliza.—Still it kept hold of me ; and the difficulty of understanding it, increased but the desire.

I got my dinner ; and after I had enlightened my mind with a bottle of Burgundy, I at it again ;—and after two or three hours' poring over it, with almost as deep attention as ever Gruter or Jacob Spon did upon a nonsensical inscription, I thought I made sense of it ; but to make sure of it, the best way, I imagined, was to turn it into English, and see how it would look then ;—so I went on leisurely as a trifling man does, sometimes writing a sentence,—then taking a turn or two,—and then looking how the world went, out of the window ; so that it was nine o'clock at night before I had done it.—I then began, and read it as follows :—

## THE FRAGMENT

### PARIS

——Now as the Notary's wife disputed the point with the Notary with too much heat,—— I wish, said the Notary (throwing down the parchment), that there was another Notary here, only to set down and attest all´this.

——And what would you do then, Monsieur ? said she, rising haſtily up.—The Notary's wife was a little fume of a woman, and the Notary thought it well to avoid a hurricane by a mild reply.——I would go, answered he, to bed.———You may go to the Devil, answered the Notary's wife.

Now there happening to be but one bed in the house, the other two rooms being unfurnished, as is the custom at Paris, and the Notary not caring to lie in the same bed with a woman who had but that moment sent him pell-mell to the Devil, went forth with his hat, and cane, and short cloak, the night being very windy, and walk'd out ill at ease towards the Pont Neuf.

Of all the bridges which were ever built, the whole world who have pass'd over the Pont Neuf must own, that it is the noblest,—the finest,—the grandest,—the lightest,—the longest,—the broadest, that ever conjoin'd land and land together upon the face of the terraqueous globe.—

> *By this it seems as if the author of the Fragment had not been a Frenchman.*

The worst fault which Divines and the Doctors of the Sorbonne can allege against it, is, that if there is but a cap-full of wind in or about Paris, 'tis more blasphemously *sacre Dieu*'d there than in any other aperture of the whole city,—and with reason, good and cogent,

Messieurs ; for it comes against you without crying *garde d'eau*, and with such unpremeditable puffs, that of the few who cross it with their hats on, not one in fifty but hazards two livres and a half, which is its full worth.

The poor Notary, just as he was passing by the sentry, instinctively clapp'd his cane to the side of it ; but in raising it up, the point of his cane catching hold of the loop of the sentinel's hat, hoisted it over the spikes of the ballustrade clear into the Seine.

——*'Tis an ill wind*, said a boatman, who catch'd it, *which blows nobody any good*.

The sentry, being a Gascon, incontinently twirl'd up his whiskers, and levell'd his arquebuse.

Arquebuses in those days went off with matches ; and an old woman's paper lantern at the end of the bridge happening to be blown out, she had borrowed the sentry's match to light it ;—it gave a moment's time for the Gascon's blood to run cool, and turn the accident better to his advantage.—*'Tis an ill wind*, said he, catching off the Notary's castor, and legitimating the capture with the boatman's adage.

The poor Notary cross'd the bridge, and passing along the Rue de Dauphine into the Fauxbourgh of St. Germain, lamented himself as he walked along in this manner :—

Luckless man that I am ! said the Notary, to be the sport of hurricanes all my days !—to be born to have the storm of ill language levell'd against me and my profession wherever I go !—to be forced into marriage by the thunder of the church to a tempest of a woman !—to be driven forth out of my house by domestic winds, and despoil'd of my castor by pontific ones !—to be here, bare-headed, in a windy-night, at the mercy of the ebbs and flows of accidents !—Where am I to lay my head ?—Miserable man ! what wind in the two-and-thirty points in the whole compass can blow unto thee, as it does to the rest of thy fellow-creatures, good !

As the Notary was passing on by a dark passage, complaining in this sort, a voice called out to a girl, to bid her run for the next Notary.—Now the Notary being the next, and availing himself of his situation, walk'd up the passage to the door, and passing through an old sort of a saloon, was ushered

O  187

into a large chamber, dismantled of every thing but a long military pike,—a breast-plate,—a rusty old sword, and bandoleer, hung up equidistant in four different places against the wall.

An old personage, who had heretofore been a gentleman, and unless decay of fortune taints the blood along with it, was a gentleman at that time, lay supporting his head upon his hand, in his bed ; a little table with a taper burning was set close beside it, and close by the table was placed a chair :—the Notary sat him down in it ; and pulling out his ink-horn and a sheet or two of paper which he had in his pocket, he placed them before him, and dipping his pen in his ink, and leaning his breast over the table, he disposed every thing to make the gentleman's last will and testament. ——Alas ! Monsieur le Notaire, said the gentleman, raising himself up a little, I have nothing to bequeath, which will pay the expence of bequeathing, except the history of myself, which I could not die in peace unless I left it as a legacy to the world ; the profits arising out of it I bequeath to you for the pains of taking it from me.—It is a story so uncommon, it must be read by all mankind ;—it will make the fortunes of your house.——The Notary dipp'd his pen into his inkhorn.—— Almighty Director of every event in my life ! said the old gentleman, looking up earnestly and raising his hands towards Heaven,— Thou, whose hand has led me on through such a labyrinth of strange passages down into this scene of desolation, assist the decaying memory of an old, infirm, and broken-hearted man !—Direct my tongue by the spirit of thy eternal truth, that this stranger may set down nought but what is written in that *Book*, from whose records, said he, clasping his hands together, I am to be condemn'd or acquitted !——The Notary held up the point of his pen betwixt the taper and his eye.

——It is a story, Monsieur le Notaire, said the gentleman, which will arouse up every affection in nature ;—it will kill the humane, and touch the heart of cruelty herself with pity.——

The Notary was inflamed with a desire to begin, and put his pen a third time into his inkhorn !—and the old gentleman, turning a little more towards the Notary, began to dictate his story in these words :——

——And where is the rest of it, La Fleur? said I,—as he just then entered the room.

## THE FRAGMENT, AND THE BOUQUET *

### PARIS

WHEN La Fleur came close up to the table, and was made to comprehend what I wanted, he told me there were only two other sheets of it, which he had wrapped round the stalks of a *bouquet* to keep it together, which he had presented to the *demoiselle* upon the *boulevards*.

——Then prithee, La Fleur, said I, step back to her, to the Count de B***'s hotel, and *see*

* Nosegay.

*if thou canst get it.*——There is no doubt of it, said La Fleur ;—and away he flew.

In a very little time the poor fellow came back, quite out of breath, with deeper marks of disappointment in his looks, than could arise from the simple irreparability of the fragment. *Juste ciel !* in less than two minutes that the poor fellow had taken his last tender farewell of her—his faithless mistress had given his *gage d'amour* to one of the Count's footmen,—the footman to a young sempstress,—and the sempstress to a fiddler, with my fragment at the end of it.—Our misfortunes were involved together ;—I gave a sigh,—and La Fleur echo'd it back again to my ear.

——How perfidious ! cried La Fleur.—— How unlucky ! said I.

——I should not have been mortified, Monsieur, quoth La Fleur, if she had lost it. ——Nor I, La Fleur, said I, had I found it.

Whether I did or no, will be seen hereafter.

## THE ACT OF CHARITY

PARIS

THE man who either disdains or fears to walk up a dark entry, may be an excellent good man, and fit for a hundred things ; but he will not do to make a good Sentimental Traveller. I count little of the many things I see pass at broad noon-day, in large and open streets.—Nature is shy, and hates to act before spectators ; but in such an unobserved corner you sometimes see a single short scene of hers, worth all the sentiments of a dozen French plays compounded together, —and yet they are *absolutely* fine ;—and whenever I have a more brilliant affair upon my hands than common, as they suit a preacher just as well as a hero, I generally make my sermon out of 'em ;—and for the text,— " Cappadocia, Pontus and Asia, Phrygia and Pamphylia,"—is as good as any one in the Bible.

There is a long dark passage issuing out
from the *Opera Comique* into a narrow street ;
'tis trod by a few who humbly wait for a
*fiacre*,\* or wish to get off quietly o'foot when
the opera is done.  At the end of it, towards
the theatre, 'tis lighted by a small candle, the
light of which is almost lost before you get
half way down, but near the door ;—'tis
more for ornament than use : you see it as a
fix'd star of the least magnitude ; it burns,—
but does little good to the world, that we know
of.

In returning along this passage, I discern'd,
as I approach'd within five or six paces of the
door, two ladies standing arm in arm, with
their backs against the wall, waiting, as I
imagined, for a *fiacre* :—as they were next the
door, I thought they had a prior right ; so
edged myself up within a yard or little more
of them, and quietly took my stand.—I was in
black, and scarce seen.

The lady next me was a tall lean figure of a
woman, of about thirty-six ; the other, of the
same size and make, of about forty : there was
no mark of wife or widow in any one part of

\* Hackney-coach.

either of them ;—they seem'd to be two upright vestal sisters, unsapp'd by caresses, unbroke in upon by tender salutations. I could have wish'd to have made them happy ; —their happiness was destin'd, that night, to come from another quarter.

A low voice, with a good turn of expression, and sweet cadence at the end of it, begg'd for a twelve-sous piece betwixt them, for the love of Heaven. I thought it singular that a beggar should fix the quota of an alms,—and that the sum should be twelve times as much as what is usually given in the dark. They both seem'd astonish'd at it as much as myself. ——Twelve sous ! said one.——A twelve-sous piece ! said the other,—and made no reply.

——The poor man said, he knew not how to ask less of ladies of their rank ; and bow'd down his head to the ground.

——Poo ! said they,—we have no money. The beggar remained silent for a moment or two, and renew'd his supplication.

——Do not, my fair young ladies, said he, stop your good ears against me.——Upon my word, honest man ! said the younger, we

have no change.——Then God bless you !
said the poor man, and multiply those joys
which you can give to others, without change !
——I observed the eldest sister put her hand
into her pocket.——I'll see, said she, if I
have a sous !——A sous ! give twelve, said
the supplicant ; Nature has been bountiful
to you ; be bountiful to a poor man.

——I would friend, with all my heart, said
the younger, if I had it.

——My fair charitable ! said he, addressing
himself to the elder,——What is it but your
goodness and humanity which makes your
bright eyes so sweet, that they outshine the
morning, even in this dark passage ! and what
was it which made the Marquis de Santerre
and his brother say so much of you both as
they just pass'd by ?

The two ladies seemed much affected ; and
impulsively at the same time they both put
their hands into their pocket, and each took
out a twelve-sous piece.

The contest betwixt them and the poor
supplicant was no more,——it was continued
betwixt themselves, which of the two should
give the twelve-sous piece in charity ;——and,

to end the dispute, they both gave it together, and the man went away.

## THE RIDDLE EXPLAINED

### PARIS

I STEPPED hastily after him : it was the very man whose success in asking charity of the women before the door of the hotel had so puzzled me ;—and I found at once his secret, or at least the basis of it :—'twas flattery.

Delicious essence ! how refreshing art thou to Nature ! how strongly are all its powers and all its weaknesses on thy side ! how sweetly dost thou mix with the blood, and help it thro' the most difficult and tortuous passages to the heart !

The poor man, as he was not straiten'd for

196

time, had given it here in a larger dose : 'tis certain he had a way of bringing it into less form, for the many sudden cases he had to do with in the ſtreets ; but how he contrived to correct, sweeten, concentre, and qualify it,—I vex not my spirit with the inquiry ;— it is enough, the beggar gained two twelve-sous pieces,—and they can beſt tell the reſt who have gained much greater matters by it.

### PARIS

We get forwards in the world, not so much by doing services as receiving them : you take a withering twig, and put it in the ground ; and then you water it, because you have planted it.

Mons. le Count de B***, merely because he had done me one kindness in the affair of my passport, would go on and do me another, the few days he was at Paris, in making me known to a few people of rank ; and they were to present me to you others, and so on.

I had got the maſter of my *secret* juſt in time to turn these honors to some little account;

otherwise, as is commonly the case, I should have din'd or supp'd a single time or two round ; and then, by *translating* French looks and attitudes into plain English, I should presently have seen that I had gold out of the *couvert* * of some more entertaining guest ; and, in course, should have resigned all my places, one after another, merely upon the principle that I could not keep them.——As it was, things did not go much amiss.

I had the honour of being introduced to the old Marquis de B***. In days of yore he had signaliz'd himself by some small feats of chivalry in the *Cour d'Amour*, and had dress'd himself out to the idea of tilts and tournaments ever since.——The Marquis de B*** wish'd to have it thought the affair was somewhere else than in his brain. "He could like to take a trip to England ; " and ask'd much of the English ladies.——Stay where you are, I beseech you, Mons. le Marquis, said I.——*Les Messieurs Anglois* can scarce get a kind look from them as it is.——The Marquis invited me to supper.

Mons. P***, the farmer-general, was just

* Plate, napkin, knife, fork, and spoon.

as inquisitive about our taxes.—They were very considerable, he heard.——If we knew but how to collect them, said I, making him a low bow.

I could never have been invited to Mons. P\*\*\*'s concerts upon any other terms.

I had been misrepresented to Madame de Q\*\*\* as an *esprit*.—Madame de Q\*\*\* was an *esprit* herself : she burnt with impatience to see me, and hear me talk. I had not taken my seat, before I saw she did not care a sous whether I had any wit or no—I was let in to be convinced she had.—I call Heaven to witness I never once open'd the door of my lips.

Madame de V\*\*\* vow'd to every creature she met, " She had never had a more improving conversation with a man in her life."

There are three epochas in the empire of a French woman :—She is coquette,—then Deist,—then *devote :* the empire during these is never lost ;—she only changes her subjects ; when thirty-five years and more have unpeopled her dominions of the slaves of love, she re-peoples it with the slaves of infidelity, and then with the slaves of the church.

Madame de V\*\*\* was vibrating betwixt the

first of these epochas : the colour of the rose was fading fast away ;—she ought to have been a Deist five years before the time I had the honor to pay my first visit.

She placed me upon the same sofa with her, for the sake of disputing the point of religion more closely.—In short, Madame de V*** told me she believed nothing.—I told Madame de V*** it might be her principle ; but I was sure it could not be her interest to level the outworks, without which I could not conceive how such a citadel as her's could be defended ; —that there was not a more dangerous thing in the world than for a beauty to be a Deist ; —that it was a debt I owed my creed, not to conceal it from her ;—that I had not been five minutes sat upon the sofa beside her, but I had began to form designs ;—and what is it but the sentiments of religion, and the persuasion they had excited in her breast, which could have check'd them as they rose up ? ——We are not adamant, said I, taking hold of her hand ;—and there is need of all restraints, till Age in her own time steals in and lays them on us.—But, my dear lady, said I, kissing her hand,—'tis too—too soon.—

I declare I had the credit all over Paris of unperverting Madame de V***.—She affirmed to Mons. D*** and the Abbé M*** that in one half hour I had said more for revealed religion than all their Encyclopedia had said against it,—I was lifted directly into Madame de V***'s *coterie ;*—and she put off the epocha of Deism for two years.

I remember it was in this *coterie*, in the middle of a discourse, in which I was shewing the necessity of a *first cause*, that the young Count de Faineant took me by the hand to the farthest corner of the room, to tell me my *solitaire* was pinn'd too strait about my neck.

——It should be *plus badinant*, said the Count, looking down upon his own ;—but a word, Mons. Yorick, *to the wise,*——

—And *from the wise*, Mons. le Count, replied I, making him a bow,—*is enough*.

The Count de Faineant embraced me with more ardour than ever I was embraced by mortal man.

For three weeks together, I was of every man's opinion I met,——*Pardi ! ce Mons. Yorick a autant d'esprit que nous autres.*——*Il raisonne bien*, said another.——*C'est un bon enfant,* said a third,—And at this price I could have eaten and drank and been merry all the days of my life at Paris ; but 'twas a dishonest *reckoning ;*—I grew ashamed of it.— It was the gain of a slave :—every sentiment of honor revolted against it ;—the higher I got, the more was I forced upon my *beggarly system ;*—the better the *coterie,*—the more children of Art,—I languish'd for those of Nature ; and one night, after a most vile prostitution of myself to half a dozen different people, I grew sick,—went to bed ;—ordered La Fleur to get me horses in the morning, to set out for Italy.

# MARIA

## MOULINES

I never felt what the distress of plenty was in any one shape till now,—to travel it through

the Bourbonnois, the sweetest part of France,—
in the hey-day of the vintage, when Nature is
pouring her abundance into every one's lap,
and every eye is lifted up,—a journey through
each step of which music beats time to *Labour*,
and all her children are rejoicing as they carry
in their clusters ;—to pass through this with
my affections flying out, and kindling at every
group before me,—and every one of them was
pregnant with adventures,—

Just Heaven !—it would fill up twenty
volumes ;—and alas ! I have but a few small
pages left of this to crowd it into,—and half
of these must be taken up with the poor Maria
my friend Mr. Shandy met with near Moulines.

The story he had told of that disordered
maid affected me not a little in the reading ;
but when I got within the neighbourhood
where she lived, it returned so strong into my
mind, that I could not resist an impulse which
prompted me to go half a league out of the
road, to the village where her parents dwelt,
to enquire after her.

'Tis going, I own, like the Knight of the
Woeful Countenance, in quest of melancholy
adventures ;—I know not how it is, but I

P                 203

am never so perfectly conscious of the existence of a soul within me, as when I am entangled in them.

The old mother came to the door ; her looks told me the story before she opened her mouth. —She had lost her husband ; he had died, she said, of anguish, for the loss of Maria's sense, about a month before.—She had feared at first, she added, that it would have plundered her poor girl of what little understanding was left ;—but, on the contrary, it had brought her more to herself ;—still she could not rest.— Her poor daughter, she said, crying, was wandering somewhere about the road.

—Why does my pulse beat languid as I write this ? and what made La Fleur, whose heart seem'd only to be tuned to joy, to pass the back of his hand twice across his eyes, as the woman stood and told it ? I beckoned to the postillion to turn back into the road.

When we had got within half a league of Moulines, at a little opening in the road, leading to a thicket, I discovered poor Maria sitting under a poplar.—She was sitting with her elbow in her lap, and her head leaning on one side within her hand :—a small brook ran at the foot of the tree.

I bid the postillion go on with the chaise to Moulines ;—and La Fleur to bespeak my supper ;—and that I would walk after him.

She was dressed in white, and much as my friend described her, except that her hair hung loose, which before was twisted with a silken net.—She had superadded likewise to her jacket, a pale green ribband, which fell across her shoulder to the waist ; at the end of which hung her pipe.—Her goat had been as faithless as her lover ; and she had got a little dog in lieu of him, which she kept tied by a string to her girdle. As I looked at her dog, she drew him towards her with the string.——" Thou shalt not leave me, Sylvio," said she. I looked in Maria's eyes, and saw she was thinking more of her father, than of her lover, or her little goat ; for as she uttered them, the tears trickled down her cheeks.

I sat down close by her ; and Maria let me wipe them away as they fell, with my handkerchief.—I then steeped it in my own,— and then in hers,—and then in mine,—and then I wiped hers again ;—and as I did it,

I felt such undescribable emotions within me, as I am sure could not be accounted for from any combinations of matter and motion.

I am positive I have a soul ; nor can all the books with which materialists have pestered the world, ever convince me to the contrary.

## MARIA

WHEN Maria had come a little to herself, I asked her if she remembered a pale thin person of a man, who had sat down betwixt her and her goat about two years before ?——— She said, she was unsettled much at that time, but remembered it upon two accounts :—— That, ill as she was, she saw the person pitied her ; and next, That her goat had stolen his handkerchief, and she had beat him for the theft ;—she had washed it, she said, in the brook, and kept it ever since in her pocket, to restore it to him, in case she should ever see him again ; which, she added, he had half-promised her. As she told me this, she took the handkerchief out of her pocket, to let me see it ; she had folded it up neatly in a couple of vine-leaves, tied round with a tendril.—On opening it, I saw an *S.* marked in one of the corners.

—She had since that, she told me, strayed as far as Rome, and walked round St. Peter's once,—and returned back :—that she found her way alone across the Apennines,—had travelled over all Lombardy without money,—and through the flinty roads of Savoy without shoes ;—how she had borne it, and how she had got supported, she could not tell ;—but *God tempers the winds,* said Maria, *to the shorn lamb.*

——Shorn indeed ! and to the quick, said I :—and wast thou in my own land, where I have a cottage, I would take thee to it, and shelter thee ; thou shouldst eat of my own bread, and drink of my own cup ;—I would be kind to thy Sylvio ;—in all thy weaknesses and wanderings I would seek after thee, and bring thee back ;—when the sun went down I would say

my prayers ; and when I had done, thou
shouldſt play thy evening-song upon thy
pipe : nor would the incense of my sacrifice be
worse accepted for entering Heaven along with
that of a broken heart !

Nature melted within me as I uttered this ;
and Maria observing, as I took out my handkerchief, that it was ſteeped too much already
to be of use, would needs go wash it in the
ſtream.——And where will you dry it, Maria ?
said I.——I'll dry it in my bosom, said she ;
—'twill do me good.

——And is your heart ſtill so warm,
Maria ? said I.

I touched upon the ſtring on which hung
all her sorrows ;—she looked with wiſtful
disorder for some time in my face ;—and
then, without saying any thing, took her
pipe, and played her service to the Virgin.——
The ſtring I had touched ceased to vibrate ;
—in a moment or two Maria returned to
herself,—let her pipe fall,—and rose up.

——And where are you going, Maria ?
said I.——She said, to Moulines.——Let us
go, said I, together.——Maria put her arm
within mine, and lengthening the ſtring to

let the dog follow,—in that order we entered
Moulines.

# MARIA

## MOULINES

Though I hate salutations and greetings
in the market-place, yet, when we got into the
middle of this, I stopped to take my last look
and last farewell of Maria.

Maria, though not tall, was nevertheless of
the first order of fine forms :—affliction had
touched her looks with something that was
scarce earthly ;—still she was feminine ;—
and so much was there about her of all that
the heart wishes, or the eye looks for in woman,
that could the traces be ever worn out of her
brain, and those of Eliza out of mine, she

should *not only eat of my bread and drink of my own cup*, but Maria should lie in my bosom, and be unto me as a daughter.

Adieu, poor luckless maiden !—Imbibe the oil and wine which the compassion of a stranger, as he journeyeth on his way, now pours into thy wounds ;—the Being who has twice bruised thee can only bind them up for ever.

## THE BOURBONNOIS

THERE was nothing from which I had painted out for myself so joyous a riot of the affections, as in this journey in the vintage, through this part of France ; but pressing through this gate of sorrow to it, my sufferings have totally unfitted me. In every scene of festivity I saw Maria in the back ground of the piece, sitting pensive under her poplar : and I had got almost to Lyons before I was able to cast a shade across her.

—Dear Sensibility ! source inexhausted of all that's precious in our joys, or costly in our sorrows !—thou chainest thy martyr down upon his bed of straw,—and 'tis thou who lift'st him up to Heaven !—Eternal fountain of our feeling !—'tis here I trace thee,—and this is thy " *divinity which stirs within me* " ;— not that, in some sad and sickening moments, " *my soul shrinks back upon herself, and startles at destruction !* "—mere pomp of words !— but that I feel some generous joys and generous cares beyond myself ;—all comes from thee, great,—great *Sensorium* of the world ! which vibrates, if a hair of our heads but falls upon the ground, in the remotest desert of thy creation. —Touch'd with thee, Eugenius draws my curtain when I languish,—hears my tale of symptoms, and blames the weather for the disorder of his nerves. Thou giv'st a portion of it sometimes to the roughest peasant who traverses the bleakest mountains :—he finds the lacerated lamb of another's flock.—This moment I behold him leaning with his head against his crook, with piteous inclination looking down upon it !—Oh ! had I come one moment sooner !—it bleeds to death !—his gentle heart bleeds with it !

Peace to thee, generous swain !—I see thou walkest off with anguish,—but thy joys shall balance it ;—for happy is thy cottage,—and happy is the sharer of it,—and happy are the lambs which sport about you.

# THE SUPPER

A shoe coming loose from the fore-foot of the thill-horse, at the beginning of the ascent of Mount Taurira, the postillion dismounted, twisted the shoe off, and put it in his pocket. As the ascent was of five or six miles, and that horse our main dependence, I made a point of having the shoe fasten'd on again as well as we could ; but the postillion had thrown away the nails ; and the hammer in the chaise-box being of no great use without them, I submitted to go on.

He had not mounted half a mile higher, when coming to a flinty piece of road, the poor Devil lost a second shoe, and from off his other fore-foot. I then got out of the chaise in good earnest ; and seeing a house about a quarter of a mile to the left hand, with a great deal to do I prevailed upon the postillion to turn up to it. The look of the house, and of every thing about it, as we drew nearer, soon reconciled me to the disaster.—It was a little farm-house, surrounded with about twenty acres of vineyard, about as much corn ;—and close to the house, on one side, was a *potagerie* of an acre and a half, full of every thing which could make plenty in a French peasant's house : —and, on the other side, was a little wood, which furnished wherewithal to dress it. It was about eight in the evening when I got to the house,—so I left the postillion to manage his point as he could ; and, for mine, I walk'd directly into the house.

The family consisted of an old grey-headed man and his wife, with five or six sons and sons-in-law, and their several wives, and a joyous genealogy out of them.

They were all sitting down together to their lentil-soup ; a large wheaten loaf was in the middle of the table ; and a flaggon of wine at each end of it promised joy through the stages of the repast :—'twas a feast of love.

The old man rose up to meet me, and, with a respectful cordiality, would have me sit down at the table ; my heart was set down the moment I entered the room : so I sat down at once, like a son of the family ; and, to invest myself in the character as speedily as I could, I instantly borrowed the old man's knife, and taking up the loaf, cut myself a hearty luncheon ; and, as I did it, I saw a testimony in every eye, not only of an honest welcome but of a welcome mix'd with thanks that I had not seem'd to doubt it.

Was it this ? or tell me, Nature, what else it was that made this morsel so sweet,—and to what magic I owe it, that the draught I took of their flaggon was so delicious with it, that they remain upon my palate to this hour ?

If the supper was to my taſte,—the grace which followed it was much more so.

## THE GRACE

WHEN supper was over, the old man gave a knock upon the table with the haft of his knife, to bid them prepare for the dance ; the moment the signal was given, the women and girls ran altogether into a back apartment to tie up their hair,—and the young men to the door to wash their faces, and change their *sabots* ; and, in three minutes, every soul was ready upon a little esplanade before the house to begin.—The old man and his wife came out laſt, and, placing me betwixt them, sat down upon a sofa of turf by the door.

The old man had some fifty years ago been

no mean performer upon the *vielle*,—and, at the age he was then of, touch'd it well enough for the purpose. His wife sung now and then a little to the tune,—then intermitted,—and join'd her old man again as their children and grand-children danced before them.

It was not till the middle of the second dance when, for some pauses in the movement wherein they all seem'd to look up, I fancied I could distinguish an elevation of spirit different from that which is the cause or the effect of simple jollity. In a word, I thought I beheld Religion mixing in the dance ;—but, as I had never seen her so engaged, I should have look'd upon it now as one of the illusions of an imagination which is eternally misleading me, had not the old man, as soon as the dance ended, said that this was their constant way ; and that all his life long he had made it a rule, after supper was over, to call out his family to dance and rejoice ; believing, he said, that a cheerful and contented mind was the best sort of thanks to Heaven that an illiterate peasant could pay——

——Or a learned prelate either, said I.

## THE CASE OF DELICACY

WHEN you have gain'd the top of Mount
Taurira, you run presently down to Lyons :
—adieu, then, to all rapid movements !—'tis
a journey of caution ; and it fares better with
sentiments, not to be in a hurry with them ;
so I contracted with a *voitu in* to take his time
with a couple of mules, and convey me in my
own chaise safe to Turin, through Savoy.

Poor, patient, quiet, honest people ! fear
not ; your poverty, the treasury of your simple
virtues, will not be envied you by the world,
nor will your vallies be invaded by it.—
Nature ! in the midst of thy disorders, thou
art still friendly to the scantiness thou hast
created : with all thy great works about thee,
little hast thou left to give, either to the scythe
or to the sickle—but to that little thou grantest
safety and protection ; and sweet are the
dwellings which stand so shelter'd !

Let the way-worn traveller vent his complaints upon the sudden turns and dangers of your roads, your rocks, your precipices ; the difficulties of getting up, the horrors of getting down, mountains impracticable,—and cataracts, which roll down great stones from their summits, and block up his road. The peasants had been all day at work in removing a fragment of this kind between St. Michael and Madane ; and, by the time my *voiturin* got to the place, it wanted full two hours of completing, before a passage could any how be gain'd. There was nothing but to wait with patience ;—'twas a wet and tempestuous night ; so that by the delay and that together, the *voiturin* found himself obliged to put up five miles short of his stage, at a little decent kind of an inn by the road-side.

I forthwith took possession of my bedchamber, got a good fire, order'd supper, and was thanking Heaven it was no worse,—when a *voiturin* arrived with a lady in it, and her servant-maid.

As there was no other bedchamber in the

house, the hostess, without much nicety, led them into mine, telling them, as she usher'd them in, that there was nobody in it but an English gentleman ;—that there were two good beds in it, and a closet within the room which held another. The accent in which she spoke of this third bed, did not say much for it ;—however, she said there were three beds, and but three people,—and she durst say the gentleman would do anything to accommodate matters.——I left not the lady a moment to make a conjecture about it, so instantly made a declaration that I would do any thing in my power.

As this did not amount to an absolute surrender of my bedchamber, I still felt myself so much the proprietor, as to have a right to do the honours of it ;—so I desired the lady to sit down, pressed her into the warmest seat, call'd for more wood, desired the hostess to enlarge the plan of the supper, and to favour us with the very best wine.

The lady had scarce warm'd herself five minutes at the fire, before she began to turn her head back, and to give a look at the beds; and the oftener she cast her eyes that way, the more they return'd perplex'd.—I felt for her —and for myself ; for in a few minutes, what by her looks, and the case itself, I found myself as much embarrassed as it was possible the lady could be herself.

That the beds we were to lie in were in one and the same room, was enough simply by itself to have excited all this ;—but the position of them (for they stood parallel, and so very close to each other, as only to allow a space for a small wicker-chair betwixt them) rendered the affair still more oppressive to us ; —they were fixed up moreover, near the fire, and the projection of the chimney on one side ; and a large beam which cross'd the room on the other, form'd a kind of recess for them that was no way favourable to the nicety of our sensations :—if any thing could have added to it, it was that the two beds were both of them so very small, as to cut us off from every idea of the lady and the maid lying together, which in either of them, could it have been feasible, my lying beside them, though a thing not to be wish'd, yet there was nothing in it so terrible which the imagination might not have pass'd over without torment.

As for the little room within, it offered little or no consolation to us : 'twas a damp, cold closet, with a half dismantled window-shutter, and with a window which had neither glass nor oil-paper in it to keep out the tempest of the night. I did not endeavour to stifle my cough when the lady gave a peep into it ; so it reduced the case in course to this alternative, —That the lady should sacrifice her health to her feelings, and take up with the closet herself, and abandon the bed next mine to her maid,—or, that the girl should take the closet, &c.

The lady was a Piedmontese of about thirty, with a glow of health in her cheeks. The maid was a Lyonoise of twenty, and as brisk and lively a French girl as ever moved. There were difficulties every way,—and the obstacle of the stone in the road, which brought us into the distress, great as it appeared whilst the peasants were removing it, was but a pebble to what lay in our way now.—I have only to add, that it did not lessen the weight which hung upon our spirits, that we were both too delicate to communicate what we felt to each other upon the occasion.

We sat down to supper ; and, had we not had more generous wine to it than a little inn in Savoy could have furnish'd, our tongues had been tied up till Necessity herself had set them at liberty ;—but the lady having a few bottles of Burgundy in her voiture, sent down her *fille de chambre* for a couple of them ; so that by the time supper was over, and we were left alone, we felt ourselves inspired with a strength of mind sufficient to talk, at least, without reserve upon our situation. We turn'd it every way, and debated and considered it in all kinds of lights in the course of a two hours' negociation; at the end of which the articles were settled finally betwixt us, and stipulated for in form and manner of a treaty of peace,—and, I believe, with as much religion and good faith on both sides, as in any treaty which has yet had the honor of being handed down to posterity.

They were as follow :—

First. As the right of the bedchamber is in Monsieur,—and he thinking the bed next to the fire to be warmest, he insists upon the concession on the lady's side of taking up with it.

Granted on the part of Madame ; with a proviso, That, as the curtains of that bed are of a flimsey transparent cotton, and appear likewise too scanty to draw close, that the *fille de chambre* shall fasten up the opening either by corking pins or needle and thread, in such manner as shall be deem'd a sufficient barrier on the side of Monsieur.

2dly, It is required on the part of Madame, that Monsieur shall lie the whole night through in his *robe de chambre*.

Rejected : in as much as Monsieur is not worth a *robe de chambre ;* he having nothing in his portmanteau but six shirts and a black silk pair of breeches.

The mentioning the silk pair of breeches made an entire change of the article,—for the breeches were accepted as an equivalent for the *robe de chambre* ; and so it was stipulated and agreed upon, that I should lie in my black silk breeches all night.

3dly, It was insisted upon, and stipulated for by the lady, that after Monsieur was got to bed, and the candle and fire extinguished, that Monsieur should not speak one single word the whole night.

Granted, provided Monsieur's saying his prayers might not be deem'd an infraction of the treaty.

There was but one point forgot in this treaty, and that was the manner in which the lady and myself should be obliged to undress and get to bed ;—there was one way of doing it, and that I leave to the reader to devise, protesting as I do it, that if it is not the most delicate in nature,—'tis the fault of his own imagination,—against which this is not my first complaint.

Now, when we were got to bed, whether it was the novelty of the situation, or what it was, I know not, but so it was, I could not shut my eyes; I tried this side and that, and turn'd and turn'd again, till a full hour after midnight, when Nature and Patience both wearing out,—O my God! said I.

——You have broke the treaty, Monsieur, said the lady, who had no more sleep than myself. I begg'd a thousand pardons; but insisted it was no more than an ejaculation,

——She maintained 'twas an entire infraction of the treaty.——I maintain'd it was provided for in the clause of the third article.

The lady would by no means give up the point, though she weaken'd her barrier by it; for, in the warmth of the dispute, I could hear two or three corking pins fall out of the curtain to the ground.

——Upon my word and honor, Madame, said I, stretching my arm out of bed by way of asseveration,—

(I was going to have added, that I would not have trespass'd against the remotest idea of decorum for the world)—

——But the *fille de chambre* hearing there were words between us, and fearing that hostilities would ensue in course, had crept silently out of her closet ; and it being totally dark, had stolen so close to our beds, that she had got herself into the narrow passage which separated them, and had advanced so far up as to be in a line betwixt her mistress and me ;—

So that, when I stretch'd out my hand, I caught hold of the *fille de chambre's*——.

# CONTENTS

50010

# INTRODUCTION

How many living writers are there from whose work could be gathered a group of stories comparable with those in the present volume?

I'll not even insist on the "living." For it happens that I have concentrated into the last two and a half years the reading of perhaps five thousand short stories, the majority classed as the finest examples of that art, in all times and countries; and I think the masters who produced those would be the first to invite some of these tales to a place beside their own.

Indeed, to one who was a reader in the 'nineties, it seems almost ludicrous to "introduce" Mary E. Wilkins. (Just a little like introducing Babe Ruth anywhere in the United States, in these latter days!) Her tales in *Harper's* were a part of the natural order of things, some better than others, but always providing a distinctive flavor in the menu. If you were an expatriated New Englander, it was almost equal to going back and listening to your own people, perhaps really understanding them for the first time; or if you chanced to be an unreconstructed Southerner, your delighted comprehension of these Yankees at home was probably spiced a bit by a titillating sense of superiority to some of the oddities and whimsicalities.

Certainly, should one wish to help a foreigner, say an intelligent transplanted Afghan Mussulman, to "get along" comfortably from the start in a New England community, little would be necessary except to get him to read a dozen or two of Mrs. Freeman's stories. For the very essence of her people is there.

Since Mr. George Moore's eye is not likely to fall upon this page, one may insist that "local color" like this is an expression of true literary art. It is completely different from the external tags, and cataloguish details whose cheap pretentiousness he excoriates with such savage contempt. The world is so full of a number of things—and each of the infinite number speaks so clearly in its own language—that no writer with a seeing eye can fail to express the particular local color of the scene and people he is describing; comprehendingly viewed, there's no such thing as an "insignificant" detail, whether of a butterfly's wing or a human being—as the Chinese painter has known for thousands of years, and Count Keyserling has recently discovered. These individual minutiæ grow from something inside. They flare with beauty and significance when they take their place in the pattern. Each one merely offers a fresh entrance for the mind, if the narrator himself has penetrated beneath the surface. And in the case of Mary Wilkins, one feels that she never had to penetrate, but that she is telling with childlike directness things she has always lived and known.

She was born at Randolph, Massachusetts, in 1862, but her family moved to Vermont when she was quite young, and she was brought up in a much more rural community than the suburban town south of Boston. Since a main strength of her work is its direct reflection of real people and scenes about her, it was perhaps fortunate that there were these years of contact with folk who preserved so much of the original character.

I asked her how she came to start writing:

"I did not want to write at all. I wanted to be an artist. But, for lack of paint, etc., and sufficiency of pens, ink, and paper, I wrote.

"I started with poems, religious. I took myself quite seriously then, also my Work. I showed these pious efforts to a Vermont clergyman, and he told me I was a genius, or to that effect. I thought he knew. Fortunately, I never offered those early poems for publication, and they are nonexistent.

"Then I wrote children's verses for a little Fall River magazine. It did not pay, but the editor was extremely kind: she wrote me encouraging letters which really meant more than dollars, though the family purse was very lean.

"Next I wrote verses and stories for the defunct *Wide Awake*, for $10 per. They were later collected in book form. The verses today sell better, comparatively, than any of my books. I do not know about the collection of stories, *The Pot of Gold*, for I never had royalty for that. I assume it circulates, from the number of letters which I have received about it, from both this country and abroad.

"I wrote my first adult story, a fifty-dollar-prize tale, for a Boston paper. It was called 'A Shadow Family,' and was a poor imitation of Dickens. I loaned that and it was never returned, and no copy exists.

"Then I wrote 'Two Old Lovers,' and Miss Booth accepted it for *Harper's Bazar*, and sent me a check for $25.

"She accepted it by the merest chance, for she thought at first sight it was written by a child—the writing was so unformed; she nearly tossed it away, but something arrested her attention: she read it and accepted it.

"After that very little was returned. 'A Humble Romance' was taken by Mr. Alden for *Harper's;* afterward he published my first novel, *Jane Field*, as a serial.

"I could not readily abandon my desire to be an artist. With a portion of that twenty-five dollars I bought paints, and started in to paint. I found I could mix colors, but could not paint, and had sense enough to relinquish art."

Nothing could be more unpretentious than the author's attitude, throughout the long list of novels and stories she has produced. There is no attempt at fine writing; she never challenges the attention with epigram or paradox or "daring" situations. Yet the most subtle French analyst might well be satisfied with the quiet certainty of artistic touch which builds up a convincing human character in the heroine of "A New England Nun"; as for humor—those who have once gotten the flavor of "Little-Girl-Afraid-of-a-Dog" or "The Revolt of Mother" need no asseveration on that point! And I think almost the final triumph is the way in which she makes truly interesting old worn-out drudges, and immature girls, and the "dull" round of everyday life under bitterly hard conditions.

To find the bright hues of romance amid such harshness of nature and human nature is perhaps to deserve better of one's fellows than to become a painter.

It is quite interesting to find so sophisticated a critic as Arthur Machen striving successfully to justify by his own formula his pleasure in Miss Wilkins's work. He lays down, first, the measuring rod of *ecstasy*—"rapture, beauty, adoration, wonder, awe, mystery, sense of the unknown, desire for the unknown"; "if ecstasy be present, then I say there is fine literature"; and, after eliminating Thackeray, Jane Austen, and Stevenson by this test, and placing at the summit *Pickwick, Don Quixote,* and *Pantagruel*—he finds Miss Wilkins almost unique among contemporaries. Not only are the tales "delightful," but he points out (with T. P. O'Connor) that there is no incongruity in finding "ecstasy" in these life episodes of reserved folk, for "passion does come through the reserve, and occasionally in the most volcanic manner." Also he discerns a remoteness and isola-

tion of soul, each human being living a life of his or her own,
—strong, full of character, tense with feeling, however restrained; and "literature proceeds" from this lonely reverie
and ecstasy.

All of which is sufficiently striking, from a cultivated Englishman of the modern school—which is often highly dis-
dainful of eternal simplicities.

And I think every thoughtful reader will agree that there
is truth in this attempt at analysis. Mrs. Freeman's work
offers just one more instance in the formidable list of proofs
that the writers who produce literature are apt to be those
who do not start out with any such intention, but are moved
to set down simply pictures of people and happenings which
have deeply stirred them.

It would be easy to dilate, and analyze, and point out
many special things in this collection. But writing about
writing is, after all, rather a second-hand business. The
stories which follow are their own best justification and
explanation.

Whether these are the "best" stories of Mrs. Freeman's
long list (nearly two hundred and fifty short tales), I do not
know. They are the ones I have liked best in re-reading the
mass of her work.

Far more important, they are characteristic examples of
her power. And that says enough to all who have made her
literary acquaintance.

H. W. L.

*October*, 1926

# BOOKS BY MARY E. WILKINS

## POEMS

DECORATIVE PLAQUES, *1883*
ONCE UPON A TIME, *and Other Child Verses, 1897*

## SHORT STORIES

THE ADVENTURES OF ANN, *1886*
A HUMBLE ROMANCE, *and Other Stories, 1887*
A NEW ENGLAND NUN, *and Other Stories, 1891*
YOUNG LUCRETIA, *and Other Stories, 1892*
THE POT OF GOLD *(Juvenile), 1892*
COMFORT PEASE, AND HER GOLD RING, *1895*
SILENCE, *and Other Stories, 1898*
PEOPLE OF OUR NEIGHBOURHOOD, *1898*
EVELINA'S GARDEN, *1899*
THE LOVE OF PARSON LORD, *and Other Stories, 1900*
UNDERSTUDIES, *1901*
SIX TREES, *1903*
THE WIND IN THE ROSE-BUSH, *and Other Stories, 1903*
THE GIVERS, *and Other Stories, 1904*
THE FAIR LAVINIA, *and Other Stories, 1907*
THE WINNING LADY, *and Other Stories, 1909*
THE COPY CAT, *and Other Stories, 1914*
EDGEWATER PEOPLE, *1918*

## NOVELS

JANE FIELD, *1892*
PEMBROKE, *1894*
MADELON, *1896*
JEROME, A POOR MAN, *1897*
THE JAMESONS, *1899*
THE HEART'S HIGHWAY, *1900*
THE PORTION OF LABOUR, *1901*
THE DEBTOR, *1905*
DOC GORDON, *1906*
BY THE LIGHT OF THE SOUL, *1906*

# BOOKS BY MARY E. WILKINS

## NOVELS—*Continued*

HYACINTHUS, *1906*
SHOULDERS OF ATLAS, *1908*
THE GREEN DOOR (*Novelette*), *1910*
BUTTERFLY HOUSE, *1912*
THE YATES PRIDE, a Romance (*Novelette*), *1912*

## IN COLLABORATION

THE LONG ARM (*with J. E. Chamberlin*), *1895*
LITTLE LASSIES, *1904*
AN ALABASTER BOX (*with Florence Morse Kingsley*), *1917*

## PLAY

GILES COREY, YEOMAN, *1893*

## MISCELLANEOUS

WHAT WOMEN CAN EARN, *1899*
IN COLONIAL TIMES, *1899*

(Note: An alphabetical list, by titles, of 227 stories by Mrs. Freeman will be found in "Index to Short Stories," Second and Enlarged Edition, Compiled by Ina Ten Eyck Firkins, H. W. Wilson Co., 1923—which can be consulted at any good library.)

# I. A HUMBLE ROMANCE[1]

She was stooping over the great kitchen sink, washing the breakfast dishes. Under fostering circumstances, her slenderness of build might have resulted in delicacy or daintiness; now the harmony between strength and task had been repeatedly broken, and the result was ugliness. Her finger joints and wrist bones were knotty and out of proportion, her elbows, which her rolled-up sleeves displayed, were pointed and knobby, her shoulders bent, her feet spread beyond their natural bounds—from head to foot she was a little discordant note. She had a pale, peaked face, her scanty fair hair was strained tightly back and twisted into a tiny knot, and her expression was at once passive and eager.

There came a ringing knock at the kitchen door, and a face of another description, large, strong-featured, and assured, peered out of the pantry, which was over against the sink.

"Who is it, Sally?"

"I don' know, Mis' King."

"Well, go to the door, can't you, an' not stan' thar gapin'. I can't; my hands are in the butter."

Sally shook the dish water off her red, sodden fingers and shuffled to the door.

A tall man with a scraggy sandy mustache stood there. He had some scales in his hand.

"Good mornin', marm," he said. "Hev you got any rags?"

"I'll see," said the girl. Then she went over to the pantry, and whispered to her mistress that it was the tin-peddler.

[1] Copyright, 1887, by Harper & Brothers. Copyright, 1915, by Mary E. Wilkins Freeman.

"Botheration!" cried Mrs. King, impatiently. "Why couldn't he hev come another day? Here I am right in the midst of butter, an' I've got lots of rags, an' I've got to hev some new milk-pails right away."

All of this reached the ears of the tin-peddler, but he merely stood waiting, the corners of his large mouth curving up good-naturedly, and scrutinized with pleasant blue eyes the belongings of the kitchen, and especially the slight, slouching figure at the sink, to which Sally had returned.

"I s'pose," said Mrs. King, approaching the peddler at length, with decision thinly veiled by doubt, "that I shall hev to trade with you, though I don't know how to stop this mornin' for I'm right in the midst of butter-making. I wish you'd 'a' happened along some other day."

"Wa'al," replied the peddler, laughing, "an' so I would, marm, ef I'd only known. But I don't see jest how I could hev, unless you'd 'a' pasted it up on the fences or had it put in the newspaper, or mebbe in the almanac."

He lounged smilingly against the door-casing, jingling his scales, and waiting for the woman to make up her mind.

She smiled unwillingly, with knitted brows.

"Well," said she, "of course you ain't to blame. I guess I'll go an' pick up my rags, up in the garret. There's quite a lot of 'em, an' it'll take some time. I don't know as you'll want to wait."

"Lor', I don't keer," answered the peddler. "I'd jest as soon rest a leetle as not. It's a powerful hot mornin' for this time o' year, an' I've got all day afore me."

He came in and seated himself, with a loose-jointed sprawl, on a chair near the door.

After Mrs. King had gone out, he sat a few minutes eyeing the girl at the sink intently. She kept steadily on with her work, though there was a little embarrassment and uncertainty in her face.

"Would it be too much trouble ef I should ask you to give me a tumbler of water, miss?"

She filled one of her hot, newly-washed glasses with water from a pail standing on a shelf at one end of the sink, and brought it over to him. "It's cold," she said. "I drawed it myself jest a few minutes ago, or I'd get some right out of the well for you."

"This is all right, an' thanky kindly, miss; it's proper good water."

He drained the glass, and carried it back to her at the sink, where she had returned. She did not seem to dare absent herself from her dish-washing task an instant.

He set the empty glass down beside the pail; then he caught hold of the girl by her slender shoulders and faced her round toward him. She turned pale and gave a smothered scream.

"Thar! thar! don't you go to being afeard of me," said the peddler. "I wouldn't hurt you for the whole world. I jest want to take a squar' look at you. You're the worst-off-lookin' little cretur I ever set my eyes on."

She looked up at him pitifully, still only half reassured. There were inflamed circles around her dilated blue eyes.

"You've been cryin', ain't you?"

The girl nodded meekly. "Please let me go," she said.

"Yes, I'll let you go; but I'm a-goin' to ask you a few questions first, an' I want you to answer 'em, for I'll be hanged ef I ever see— Ain't she good to you?"—indicating Mrs. King with a wave of his hand toward the door through which she had departed.

"Yes, she's good enough, I guess."

"Don't ever scold you, hey?"

"I don't know; I guess so, sometimes."

"Did this mornin', didn't she?"

"A little. I was kinder behind with the work."

"Keeps you workin' pretty stiddy, don't she?"

"Yes; thar's consider'ble to do this time o' year."

"Cookin' for hired men, I s'pose, and butter an' milk?"

"Yes."

"How long hev you been livin' here?"

"She took me when I was little."

"Do you do anything besides work?—go round like other gals?—hev any good times?"

"Sometimes." She said it doubtfully, as if casting about in her mind for reminiscences to prove the truth of it.

"Git good wages?"

"A dollar a week sence I was eighteen. I worked for my board an' clo'es afore."

"Got any folks?"

"I guess I've got some brothers and sisters somewhar. I don' know jest whar. Two of 'em went West, an' one is married somewhar in York State. We was scattered when father died. Thar was ten of us, an' we was awful poor. Mis' King took me. I was the youngest; 'bout four, they said I was. I ain't ever known any folks but Mis' King."

The peddler walked up and down the kitchen floor twice; Sally kept on with her dishes; then he came back to her.

"Look a-here," he said; "leave your dish washin' alone a minute. I want you to give me a good look in the face, an' tell me what you think of me."

She looked up shyly in his florid, freckled face, with its high cheek bones and scraggy sandy mustache; then she plunged her hands into the dish tub again.

"I don' know," she said, bashfully.

"Well, mebbe you do know, only you can't put it into words. Now jest take a look out the window at my tin-cart thar. That's all my own, a private consarn. I ain't runnin' for no company. I owns the cart an' horse, an' disposes of the rags, an' sells the tin, all on my own hook. An' I'm a-doin' pretty well at it; I'm a-layin' up a leetle money. I ain't got no family. Now this was what I was a-comin' at: s'pose you should jest leave the dishes, an' the scoldin' woman, an' the butter, an' everything, an' go a-ridin' off with me on my tin cart. I wouldn't know you, an' *she* wouldn't know you, an' you wouldn't know yourself, in a week. You wouldn't hev a bit of work to do, but jest set up thar like a queen, a-ridin' and seein' the country. For that's the way we'd live, you know. I wouldn't hev you keepin' house an' slavin'. We'd stop along the road for vittles, and bring up at taverns nights. What d'ye say to it?"

She stopped her dish washing now, and stood staring at him, her lips slightly parted and her cheeks flushed.

"I know I ain't much in the way of looks," the peddler went on, "an' I'm older than you—I'm near forty—an' I've been married afore. I don't s'pose you kin take a likin' to me right off, but you might arter a while. An' I'd take keer of you, you poor leetle thing. An' I don't b'lieve you know anything about how nice it is to be taken keer of, an' hev the hard, rough things kep' off by somebody that likes yer."

Still she said nothing, but stood staring at him.

"You ain't got no beau, hev you?" asked the peddler, as a sudden thought struck him.

"No." She shook her head, and her cheeks flushed redder.

"Well, what do you say to goin' with me? You'll hev to hurry up an' make up your mind, or the old lady'll be back."

The girl was almost foolishly ignorant of the world, but her instincts were as brave and innocent as an angel's. Tainted with the shiftless weariness and phlegm of her parents, in one direction she was vigorous enough.

Whether it was by the grace of God or an inheritance from some far-off Puritan ancestor, the fire in whose veins had not burned low, she could see, if she saw nothing else, the distinction between right and wrong with awful plainness. Nobody had ever called her anything but a *good* girl. It was said with a disparagement, maybe, but it was always "a good girl."

She looked up at the man before her, her cheeks burning painfully hot, her eyes at once drooping and searching. "I—don't know jest—how you mean," she stammered. "I wouldn't go with the king, if—it wasn't to—go honest—"

The peddler's face flushed as red as hers. "Now look a-here, little un," he said. "You jest listen, an' it's God's own truth; ef I hadn't 'a' meant all right I wouldn't 'a' come to you, but to some other gal, han'sumer, an' pearter, an'—but, O Lord! I ain't that kind, anyway. What I want is to merry you honest, an' take keer of you, an' git that look off your face. I know it's awful sudden, an' it's askin' a good deal of a gal to trust so much in a fellow she never set eyes on afore. Ef you can't do it, I'll never blame you; but ef you kin, well, I don't b'lieve you'll ever be sorry. Most folks would think I was a fool, too, an' mebbe I am, but I wanted to take keer on you the minute I set eyes on you; an' afore I know it the wantin' to take keer on you will be growin' into lovin' you. Now you hurry and make up your mind, or she will be back."

Sally had little imagination and a loving nature. In her heart, as in all girls' hearts, the shy, secret longing for a lover had strengthened with her growth, but she had never dreamed definitely of one. Now she surveyed the homely, scrawny, good-natured visage before her, and it filled well enough the longing nature had placed in her helpless heart. His appearance dispelled no previous illusion, for previous illusion there had been none. No one had ever spoken to her in this way. Rough and precipitate though it was, it was skillful wooing; for it made its sincerity felt, and a girl more sophisticated than this one could not have listened to it wholly untouched.

The erratic nature of the whole proceeding did not dismay her. She had no conscience for conventionalities; she was too simple; hers provided only for pure right and wrong. Strange to say, the possible injury she would do her mistress by leaving her in this way did not occur to her till afterward. Now she looked at her lover, and began to believe in him, and as soon as she began to believe in him—poor, unattractive, ignorant little thing that she was!—she began to love just like other girls. All over her crimson face flashed the signs of yielding. The peddler saw and understood them.

"You will—won't you, little un?" he cried. Then, as her eyes drooped more before his, and her mouth quivered between a sob and a smile, he took a step forward and stretched out his arms toward her. Then he stepped back, and his arms fell.

"No," he cried, "I won't; I'd like to give you a hug, but I won't; I won't so much as touch that little lean hand of yours till you're my wife. You shall see I mean honest. But come along now, little un, or she will be back. I declar' ef I don't more'n half believe she's fell in a fit, or she'd ha' been back afore now. Come now, dear, be spry!"

"Now?" said Sally, in turn.

"Now! Why, of course now! What's the use of waitin'? Mebbe you want to make some weddin' cake, but I reckon we'd better buy some over in Derby, for it might put the old lady out"; and the peddler chuckled. "Why, I'm jest a-goin' to stow you away in that 'ere tin cart of mine—there's plenty of room, for I've been on the road a-sellin' nigh a week. An' then I'm a-goin' to drive out of this yard, arter I've traded with your missis, as innocent as the very innocentest lamb you ever see, an' I'm a-goin' to drive along a piece till it's safe; an' then you're a-goin' to git out an' set up on the seat alongside of me, an' we're goin' to keep on till we git to Derby, an' then we'll git merried, jest as soon as we kin find a minister as wants to airn a ten-dollar bill."

"But," gasped Sally, "she'll ask whar I am."

"I'll fix that. You lay there in the cart an' hear what I say. Lor'! I'd jest as soon tell her to her face, myself, what we was goin' to do, an' set you right up on the seat aside of me, afore her eyes; but she'd talk hard, most likely, an' you look scared enough now, an' you'd cry, an' your eyes would git redder; an' she might sass you so you'd be ready to back out, too. Women kin say hard things to other women, an' they ain't likely to understan' any woman but themselves trustin' a man overmuch. I reckon this is the best way." He went toward the door, and motioned her to come.

"But I want my bonnet."

"Never mind the bunnit; I'll buy you one in Derby."

"But I don't want to ride into Derby bareheaded," said Sally, almost crying.

"Well, I don't know as you do, little un, that's a fact; but hurry an' git the bunnit, or she *will* be here. I thought I heard her a minute ago."

"Thar's a leetle money I've saved, too."

"Well, git that; we don't want to make the old lady vallyble presents, an' you kin buy yourself sugarplums with it. But be spry."

She gave him one more scared glance, and hastened out of the room, her limp calico accommodating itself to every ungraceful hitch of her thin limbs and sharp hips.

"I'll git her a gown with puckers in the back," mused the peddler, gazing after her. Then he hastened out to his tin cart, and arranged a vacant space in the body of it. He had a greatcoat, which he spread over the floor.

"Thar, little un, let me put you right in," he whispered, when Sally emerged, her bonnet on, a figured green delaine shawl over her shoulders, and her little hoard in an old stocking dangling from her hand.

She turned round and faced him once more, her eyes like a child's peering into a dark room. "You mean *honest?*"

"Before God, I do, little un. Now git in quick, for she *is* comin'!"

He had to lift her in, for her poor little limbs were too weak to support her. They were not a moment too soon, for Mrs. King stood in the kitchen door a second later.

"Here! you ain't goin', air you?" she called out.

"No, marm; I jest stepped out to look arter my hoss; he was a trifle uneasy with the flies, an' thar was a yaller wasp buzzin' round." And the peddler stepped up to the door with an open and artless visage.

"Well, I didn't know but you'd git tired waitin'. You spoke so about not bein' in a hurry that I stopped to pick my white rags out from the colored ones. I knew they'd bring more ef I did. I'd been meanin' to hev 'em all sorted out afore a peddler come along. I thought I'd hev Sally pick 'em over last week, but she was sick— Why, whar is Sally?"

"Who?"

"Sally—the girl that was washin' dishes when you come— she went to the door."

"Oh, the gal! I b'lieve I saw her go out the door a min- ute afore I went out to see to my hoss."

"Well, I'll call her, for she'll never git the dishes done, I guess, an' then we'll see about the rags."

Mrs. King strode toward the door, but the peddler stopped her.

"Now, marm, ef you please," said he, "I'd a leetle ray- ther you'd attend to business first, and call Sally afterward, ef it's jest the same to you, for I am gittin' in a leetle of a hurry and don't feel as ef I could afford to wait much longer."

"Well," said Mrs. King, reluctantly, "I don't suppose I orter ask you to, but I do hev such discouragin' times with help. I declare it don't seem to me as ef Sally ever would git them dishes done."

"Wa'al, it don't seem to me, from what I've seen, that she ever will, either," said the peddler, as he gathered up Mrs. King's rag bags and started for the car.

"Anybody wouldn't need to watch her for more'n two minutes to see how slow she was," assented Mrs. King, following. "She's a girl I took when she was a baby to bring up, an' I've wished more'n fifty times I hadn't. She's a good girl enough, but she's awful slow—no snap to her. How much is them milk pans?"

Mrs. King was reputedly a sharp woman at a bargain. To trade with her was ordinarily a long job for any peddler, but today it was shortened through skillful management. The tinman came down with astonishing alacrity from his first price, at the merest suggestion from his customer, and, in a much shorter time than usual, she bustled into the house, her arms full of pans, and the radiant and triumphant conviction of a good bargain in her face.

The peddler whirled rapidly into his seat and snatched up the lines; but even then he heard Mrs. King calling the girl as he rattled around the corner.

A quarter of a mile from Mrs. King's there was a house; a little beyond, the road ran through a considerable stretch of woods. This was a very thinly settled neighborhood. The peddler drove rapidly until he reached the woods; then he stopped, got down, and peered into the cart.

Sally's white face and round eyes peered piteously back at him.

"How're you gittin' along, little un?"

"Oh, let me git out an' go back!"

"Lor', no, little un, you don't want to go back now! Bless your heart, she's all primed for an awful sassin'. I tell you what 'tis, you shan't ride cooped up in thar any longer; you shall git out an' set up here with me. We'll keep our ears pricked up, an' ef we hear anybody comin', I'll stow you in the box under the seat afore you kin say Jack Robinson, an' thar ain't any houses for three mile."

He helped the poor shivering little thing out, and lifted her up to the high seat. When he had seated himself beside her and gathered up the lines, he looked down at her curiously. Her bonnet the severe taste of Mrs. King had regulated. It was a brown straw, trimmed with brown ribbon. He eyed it disapprovingly. "I'll git you a white bunnit, sich as brides wear, in Derby," said he.

She blushed a little at that, and glanced up at him, a little grateful light over her face.

"You poor little thing!" said the peddler, and put out his hand toward her, then drew it back again.

Derby was a town with the prestige of a city. It was the center of trade for a large circle of little country towns; its main street was crowded on a fair day, when the roads were good, with any quantity of nondescript and antediluvian-looking vehicles, and the owners thereof presented a wide variety of quaintness in person and attire.

So this eloping pair, the tall, bony, shambling man, and the thin, cowed-looking girl, her scant skirts slipping too far below her waist line in the back, and following the movements of her awkward heels, excited no particular attention.

After the tin cart had been put up in the hotel stable and the two had been legally pronounced man and wife, or, specifically, Mr. and Mrs. Jake Russell, they proceeded on foot down the principal street, in which all the shops were congregated, in search of some amendments to the bride's attire.

If it was comparatively unnoticed, Sally was fully alive to the unsuitableness of her costume. She turned around, and followed with wistful eyes the prettily dressed girls they met. There was a great regret in her heart over her best gown, a brown delaine, with a flounce on the bottom, and a shiny back. She had so confidently believed in its grandeur so long, that now, seen by her mental vision, it hardly paled before these splendors of pleating and draping. It compared advantageously, in her mind, with a brown velvet suit whose wearer looked with amusement in her eyes at Sally's forlorn figure. If she only had on her brown delaine, she felt that she could walk more confidently through this strangeness. But, nervously snatching her bonnet and her money, she had, in fact, heard Mrs. King's tread on the attic stairs, and had not dared to stop longer to secure it.

She knew they were out on a search for a new dress for her now, but she felt a sorrowful conviction that nothing could be found which could fully make up for the loss of her own beloved best gown. And then Sally was not very quick with her needle; she thought with dismay of the making up; the possibility of being aided by a dressmaker, or a ready-made costume, never entered her simple mind.

Jake shambled loosely down the street, and she followed meekly after him, a pace or two behind.

At length the peddler stopped before a large establishment, in whose windows some ready-made ladies' garments were displayed. "Here we air," said he, triumphantly.

Sally stepped weakly after him up the broad steps.

One particular dress in the window had excited the peddler's warm admiration. It was a trifle florid in design, with dashes of red here and there.

Sally eyed it a little doubtfully, when the clerk at Jake's request, had taken it down to show them. Untutored as her taste was, she turned as naturally to quiet plumage as a wood pigeon. The red slashes rather alarmed her. However, she said nothing against her husband's decision to purchase the dress. She turned pale at the price; it was nearly the whole of her precious store. But she took up her stocking purse determinedly when Jake began examining his pocketbook.

"I pays for this," said she to the clerk, lifting up her little face to him with scared resolve.

"Why, no, you don't, little un!" cried Jake, catching hold of her arm. "I'm a-goin' to pay for it, o' course. It's a pity ef I can't buy my own wife a dress."

Sally flushed all over her lean throat, but she resolutely held out the money.

"No," she said again, shaking her head obstinately, "I pays for it."

The peddler let her have her way then, though he bit his scraggy mustache with amaze and vexation as he watched her pay the bill and stare with a sort of frightened wistfulness after her beloved money as it disappeared in the clerk's grasp.

When they emerged from the store, the new dress under his arm, he burst out, "What on airth made you do that, little un?"

"Other folks does that way. When they gits merried they buys their own clo'es, ef they kin."

"But it took pretty nearly all you'd got, didn't it?"

"That ain't no matter."

The peddler stared at her, half in consternation, half in admiration.

"Well," said he, "I guess you've got a little will o' your own, arter all, little un, an' I'm glad on't. A woman'd orter hev a little will to back her sweetness; it's all too soft an' slushy otherways. But I'll git even with you about the dress."

Which he proceeded to do by ushering his startled bride into the next dry-goods establishment, and purchasing a dress pattern of robin's-egg blue silk, and a delicate white bonnet. Sally, however, insisted on buying a plain sun hat with the remainder of her own money. She was keenly alive to the absurdity and peril of that airy white structure on the top of a tin cart.

The pair remained in Derby about a week; then they started forth on their travels, the blue silk, which a Derby dressmaker had made up after the prevailing mode, and the white bonnet, stowed away in a little new trunk in the body of the cart.

The peddler, having only himself to consult as to his motions, struck a new route now. Sally wished to keep away from her late mistress's vicinity. She had always a nervous dread of meeting her in some unlikely fashion.

She wrote a curious little ill-spelled note to her, at the first town where they stopped after leaving Derby. Whether or not Mrs. King was consoled and mollified by it she never knew.

Their way still lay through a thinly settled country. The tin peddler found readier customers in those farmers' wives who were far from stores. It was late spring. Often they rode for a mile or two through the lovely fresh woods, without coming to a single house.

The girl had never heard of Arcadia, but, all unexpressed to herself, she was riding through it under gold-green bough, to the sweet, broken jangling of tinware.

When they stopped to trade at the farmhouses, how proudly she sat, a new erectness in her slender back, and held her husband's horse tightly while he talked with the woman of the house, with now and then a careful glance toward her to see if she were safe. They always contrived to bring up, on a Sabbath day, at some town where there was a place of worship. Then the blue silk and the white bonnet were taken reverently from their hiding place, and Sally, full of happy consciousness, went to church with her husband in all her bridal bravery.

These two simple pilgrims, with all the beauty and grace

in either of them turned only toward each other, and seen rightly only in each other's untutored, uncritical eyes, had journeyed together blissfully for about three months, when one afternoon Jake came out of a little country tavern, where they had proposed stopping for the night, with a pale face. Sally had been waiting on the cart outside until he should see if they could be accommodated. He jumped up beside her and took the lines.

"We'll go on to Ware," he said, in a dry voice; "it's only three mile further. They're full here."

Jake drove rapidly along, an awful look on his homely face, giving it the beauty of tragedy.

Sally kept looking up at him with pathetic wonder, but he never looked at her or spoke till they reached the last stretch of woods before Ware village. Then, just before they left the leafy cover, he slackened his speed a little, and threw his arm around her.

"See here, little un," he said, brokenly. "You've—got —consider'ble backbone, ain't you? Ef anything awful should happen, it wouldn't—kill you—you'd bear up?"

"Ef you told me to."

He caught at her words eagerly. "I would tell you to, little un—I do tell you to," he cried. "Ef anything awful ever should—happen—you'll remember that I told you to bear up."

"Yes, I'll bear up." Then she clung to him, trembling. "Oh, what is it, Jake?"

"Never mind now, little un," he answered; "p'rhaps nothin' awful's goin' to happen; I didn't say thar was. Chirk up an' give us a kiss, an' look at that 'ere sky thar, all pink an' yaller."

He tried to be cheerful, and comfort her with joking endearments then, but the awful lines in his face stayed rigid and unchanged under the smiles.

Sally, however, had not much discernment, and little of

the sensitiveness of temperament which takes impressions of coming evil. She soon recovered her spirits, and was unusually merry, for her, the whole evening, making, out of the excess of her innocence and happiness, several little jokes, which made Jake laugh loyally, and set his stricken face harder the next minute.

In the course of the evening he took out his pocketbook and displayed his money, and counted it jokingly. Then he spoke, in a careless, casual manner, of a certain sum he had deposited in a country bank, and how, if he were taken sick and needed it, Sally could draw it out as well as he. Then he spoke of the value of his stock in trade and horse and cart. When they went to bed that night he had told his wife, without her suspecting he was telling her, all about his affairs.

She fell asleep as easily as a child. Jake lay rigid and motionless till he had listened an hour to her regular breathing. Then he rose softly, lighted a candle, which he shaded from her face, and sat down at a little table with a pen and paper. He wrote painfully, with cramped muscles, his head bent on one side, following every movement of his pen, yet with a confident steadiness which seemed to show that all the subject matter had been learned by heart beforehand. Then he folded the paper carefully around a little book which he took from his pocket, and approached the bed, keeping his face turned away from his sleeping wife. He laid the little package on his vacant pillow, still keeping his face aside.

Then he got into his clothes quickly, his head turned persistently from the bed, and opened the door softly, and went out, never once looking back.

When Sally awoke the next morning she found her husband gone, and the little package on the pillow. She opened it, more curious than frightened. There was a note folded around a bank book. Sally spelled out the note laboriously, with whitening lips and dilating eyes. It was a singular composition, its deep feeling pricking through its illiterate stiffness.

DEAR WIFE,—I've got to go and leve you. It's the only way. Ef I kin ever come back, I will. I told you bout my bizness last night. You'd better drive the cart to Derby to that Mister Arms I told you bout, an' he'll help you sell it an' the hoss. Tell him your husband had to go away, an' left them orders. I've left you my bank book, so you can git the money out of the bank the way I told you, an' my watch an' pocketbook is under the pillow. I left you all the money, 'cept what little I couldn't git long without. You'd better git boarded somewhar in Derby. You'll hev enough money to keep you awhile, an' I'll send you some more when thet's gone, ef I hev to work my fingers to the bone. Don't ye go to worryin' an' workin' hard. An' bear up. Don't forgit thet you promised me to bear up. When you gits to feelin' awful bad, an' you will, jest say it over to yourself—"He told me to bear up, an' I said as I would bear up." Scuse poor writin' an' a bad pen.

Yours till death,      JAKE RUSSELL.

When Sally had read the letter quite through, she sat still a few minutes on the edge of the bed, her lean, round-shouldered figure showing painfully through her clinging nightdress, her eyes staring straight before her.

Then she rose, dressed herself, put the bank book, with the letter folded around it, and her husband's pocketbook, in her bosom, and went downstairs quietly. Just before she went out her room door she paused with her hand on the latch, and muttered to herself, "He told me to bear up, an' I said as I would bear up."

She sought the landlord to pay her bill, and found that it was already paid, and that her recreant husband had smoothed over matters in one direction for her by telling the landlord that he was called away on urgent business, and that his wife was to take the tin cart next morning, and meet him at a certain point.

So she drove away on her tin cart in solitary state without exciting any of the wondering comments which would have been agony to her.

When she gathered up the lines and went rattling down the country road, if ever there was a zealous disciple of a new religion, she was one. Her prophet was her raw-boned peddler husband, and her creed and whole confession of faith his parting words to her.

She did not take the road to Derby; she had made up her mind about that as she sat on the edge of the bed after reading the letter. She drove straight along the originally prescribed route, stopping at the farmhouses, taking rags and selling tin, just as she had seen her husband do. There were much astonishment and many curious questions among her customers. A woman running a tin cart was an unprecedented spectacle, but she explained matters, with meek dignity, to all who questioned her. Her husband had gone away, and she was to attend to his customers until he should return. She could not always quite allay the suspicion that there must needs be something wrong, but she managed the trading satisfactorily, and gave good bargains, and so went on her way unmolested. But not a farmyard did she enter or leave without the words sounding in her beating little heart, like a strong, encouraging chant, "He told me to bear up, an' I said as I would bear up."

When her stock ran low, she drove to Derby to replenish it. Here she had opposition from the dealers, but her almost abnormal persistence overcame it.

She showed Jake's letter to Mr. Arms, the tin dealer with whom she traded, and he urged her to take up with the advice in it, promising her a good bargain; but she was resolute.

Soon she found that she was doing as well as her husband had done, if not better. Her customers, after they had grown used to the novelty of a tin woman, instead of a tin man, liked her. In addition to the regular stock, she

carried various little notions needed frequently by house-
wives, such as pins, needles, thread, etc.

She oftener stayed at a farmhouse overnight than a tavern, and frequently stopped over at one a few days in severe
weather.

After her trip to Derby she always carried a little pistol,
probably more to guard Jake's watch and property than
herself.

Whatever money she did not absolutely require for cur-
rent expenses went to swell Jake's little hoard in the Derby
bank. During the three years she kept up her lonely travelling little remittances came directed to her from time to
time, in the care of Mr. Arms. When one came, Sally cried
pitifully, and put it into the bank with the rest.

She never gave up expecting her husband. She never
woke up one morning without the hope in her heart that
he would come that day. Every golden dawn showed a
fair possibility to her, and so did every red sunset. She
scanned every distant, approaching figure in the sweet country roads with the half conviction in her heart that it was
he, and when nearness dispelled the illusion, her heart
bounded bravely back from its momentary sinking, and she
looked ahead for another traveler.

Still he did not come for three years from the spring he
went away. Except through the money remittances, which
gave no clue but the New York postmark on the envelope,
she had not heard from him.

One June afternoon she, a poor lonely pilgrim, now without her beloved swain, driving through her old Arcadian soli-
tudes, whose enchanted meaning was lost to her, heard a
voice from behind calling to her, above the jangling of tin,
"Sally! Sally! Sally!"

She turned, and there he was, running after her. She
turned her head quickly, and, stopping the horse, sat per-

fectly still, her breath almost gone with suspense. She did not dare look again for fear she had not seen aright.

The hurrying steps came nearer and nearer; she looked when they came abreast the cart. It was he. It always seemed to her that she would have died if it had not been, that time.

"Jake! Jake!"

"Oh, Sally!"

He was up on the seat before she could breathe again, and his arms around her.

"Jake, I did—bear up—I did."

"I know you did, little un. Mr. Arms told me all about it. Oh, you dear little un, you poor little un, a-drivin' round on this cart all alone!"

Jake laid his cheek against Sally's and sobbed.

"Don't cry, Jake. I've airned money, I hev, an' it's in the bank for you."

"Oh, you blessed little un! Sally, they said hard things 'bout me to you in Derby, didn't they?"

She started violently at that. There was one thing which had been said to her in Derby, and the memory of it had been a repressed terror ever since.

"Yes; they said as how you'd run off with—another woman."

"What did you say?"

"I didn't believe it."

"I did, Sally."

"Well, you've come back."

"Afore I married you I'd been married before. By all that's good an' great, little un, I thought my wife was dead. Her folks said she was. When I come home from peddlin' one time, she was gone, an' they said she was off on a visit. I found out in a few weeks she'd run off with another fellow. I went off peddlin' ag'in without carin' much what become of me. 'Bout a year arterward I saw her death in a paper, an' I wrote to her folks, an' they said 'twas true. They were a bad lot, the whole of 'em. I got took in. But she had a mighty pretty face, an' a tongue like honey, an' I s'pose I was green. Three year ago, when I went into that 'ere tavern in Grover, thar she was in the kitchen a-cookin'. The fellow she ran off with had left her, an' she'd been trying to hunt me up. She was awful poor, an' had come across this place an' took it. She was allers a good cook, an' she suited the customers fust rate. I guess they liked to see her pretty face 'round too, confound her!

"Well, little un, she knew me right off, an' hung on to me, an' cried, an' begged me to forgive her; and when she spied you a-settin' thar on the cart, she tore. I hed to hold her to keep her from goin' out an' tellin' you the whole story. I thought you'd die ef she did. I didn't know then how you could bear up, little un. *Ef* you ain't got back-bone!"

"Jake, I did bear up."

"I know you did, you blessed little cretur. Well, she said ef I didn't leave you, an' go with her, she'd expose me. As soon as she found she'd got the weapons in her own hands, an' could hev me up for bigamy, she didn't cry so much, an' wa'n't quite so humble.

"Well, little un, then I run off an' left you. I couldn't stay with you ef you wa'n't my wife, an' 'twas all the way to stop her tongue. I met her that night, an' we went to New York. I got lodgin's for her; then I went to work in a box factory, an' supported her. I never went nigh her from one week's end to the other; I couldn't do it without hevin' murder in my heart; but I kep' her in money. Every scrap I could save I sent to you, but I used to lay awake nights, worryin' for fear you'd want things. Well, it's all over. She died a month ago, an' I saw her buried."

"I knowed she was dead when you begun to tell about her, because you'd come."

"Yes, she's dead this time, an' I'm glad. Don't you look scared, little un. I hope the Lord'll forgive me, but *I'm glad*. She was a bad un, you know, Sally."

"Was she sorry?"

"I don't know, little un."

Sally's head was resting peacefully on Jake's shoulder; golden flecks of light sifted down on them through the rustling maple and locust boughs; the horse, with bent head, was cropping the tender young grass at the side of the road.

"Now we'll start up the horse an' go to Derby an' git married over ag'in, Sally."

She raised her head suddenly, and looked up at him with eager eyes.

"Jake."

"Well, little un?"

"Oh, Jake, my blue silk dress an' the white bonnet is in the trunk in the cart jest the same, an' I can git 'em out, an' put 'em on under the trees thar, an' wear 'em to be married in!"

## II. *THE REVOLT OF "MOTHER"*[1]

"Father!"

"What is it?"

"What are them men diggin' over there in the field for?"

There was a sudden dropping and enlarging of the lower part of the old man's face, as if some heavy weight had settled therein; he shut his mouth tight, and went on harnessing the great bay mare. He hustled the collar on to her neck with a jerk.

"Father!"

The old man slapped the saddle upon the mare's back.

"Look here, father, I want to know what them men are diggin' over in the field for, an' I'm goin' to know."

"I wish you'd go into the house, mother, an' 'tend to your own affairs," the old man said then. He ran his words together, and his speech was almost as inarticulate as a growl.

But the woman understood; it was her most native tongue. "I ain't goin' into the house till you tell me what them men are doin' over there in the field," said she.

Then she stood waiting. She was a small woman, short and straight-waisted like a child in her brown cotton gown. Her forehead was mild and benevolent between the smooth curves of gray hair; there were meek downward lines about her nose and mouth; but her eyes, fixed upon the old man, looked as if the meekness had been the result of her own will, never of the will of another.

They were in the barn, standing before the wide-open doors. The spring air, full of the smell of growing grass

23

and unseen blossoms, came in their faces. The deep yard in front was littered with farm wagons and piles of wood; on the edges, close to the fence and the house, the grass was a vivid green, and there were some dandelions.

The old man glanced doggedly at his wife as he tightened the last buckles on the harness. She looked as immovable to him as one of the rocks in his pasture land, bound to the earth with generations of blackberry vines. He slapped the reins over the horse, and started forth from the barn.

*"Father!"* said she.

The old man pulled up. "What is it?"

"I want to know what them men are diggin' over there in that field for."

"They're diggin' a cellar, I s'pose, if you've got to know."

"A cellar for what?"

"A barn."

"A barn? You ain't goin' to build a barn over there where we was goin' to have a house, father?"

The old man said not another word. He hurried the horse into the farm wagon, and clattered out of the yard, jouncing as sturdily on his seat as a boy.

The woman stood a moment looking after him, then she went out of the barn across a corner of the yard to the house. The house, standing at right angles with the great barn and a long reach of sheds and outbuildings, was infinitesimal compared with them. It was scarcely as commodious for people as the little boxes under the barn eaves were for doves.

A pretty girl's face, pink and delicate as a flower, was looking out of one of the house windows. She was watching three men who were digging over in the field which bounded the yard near the road line. She turned quietly when the woman entered.

"What are they digging for, mother?" said she. "Did he tell you?"

"They're diggin' for—a cellar for a new barn."

"Oh, mother, he ain't going to build another barn?"

"That's what he says."

A boy stood before the kitchen glass combing his hair. He combed slowly and painstakingly, arranging his brown hair in a smooth hillock over his forehead. He did not seem to pay any attention to the conversation.

"Sammy, did you know father was going to build a new barn?" asked the girl.

The boy combed assiduously.

"Sammy!"

He turned, and showed a face like his father's under his smooth crest of hair. "Yes, I s'pose I did," he said, reluctantly.

"How long have you known it?" asked his mother.

"'Bout three months, I guess."

"Why didn't you tell of it?"

"Didn't think 'twould do no good."

"I don't see what father wants another barn for," said the girl, in her sweet, slow voice. She turned again to the window, and stared out at the digging men in the field. Her tender, sweet face was full of a gentle distress. Her forehead was as bald and innocent as a baby's, with the light hair strained back from it in a row of curl papers. She was quite large, but her soft curves did not look as if they covered muscles.

Her mother looked sternly at the boy. "Is he goin' to buy more cows?" said she.

The boy did not reply; he was tying his shoes.

"Sammy, I want you to tell me if he's goin' to buy more cows."

"I s'pose he is."

"How many?"

"Four, I guess."

His mother said nothing more. She went into the pantry, and there was a clatter of dishes. The boy got his cap from a nail behind the door, took an old arithmetic from the shelf, and started for school. He was lightly built, but clumsy. He went out of the yard with a curious spring in the hips that made his loose homemade jacket tilt up in the rear.

The girl went to the sink, and began to wash the dishes that were piled up there. Her mother came promptly out of the pantry, and shoved her aside. "You wipe 'em," said she; "I'll wash. There's a good many this mornin'."

The mother plunged her hands vigorously into the water, the girl wiped the plates slowly and dreamily. "Mother," said she, "don't you think it's too bad father's going to build that new barn, much as we need a decent house to live in?"

Her mother scrubbed a dish fiercely. "You ain't found out yet we're womenfolks, Nanny Penn," said she. "You ain't seen enough of menfolks yet to. One of these days you'll find it out, an' then you'll know that we know only what menfolks think we do, so far as any use of it goes, an' how we'd ought to reckon menfolks in with Providence, an' not complain of what they do any more than we do of the weather."

"I don't care; I don't believe George is anything like that, anyhow," said Nanny. Her delicate face flushed pink; her lips pouted softly, as if she were going to cry.

"You wait an' see. I guess George Eastman ain't no better than other men. You hadn't ought to judge father, though. He can't help it, 'cause he don't look at things jest the way we do. An' we've been pretty comfortable here, after all. The roof don't leak—ain't never but once—that's one thing. Father's kept it shingled right up."

"I do wish we had a parlor."

"I guess it won't hurt George Eastman any to come to see you in a nice clean kitchen. I guess a good many girls don't have as good a place as this. Nobody's ever heard me complain."

"I ain't complained either, mother."

"Well, I don't think you'd better, a good father an' a good home as you've got. S'pose your father made you go out an' work for your livin'? Lots of girls have to that ain't no stronger an' better able to than you be."

Sarah Penn washed the frying pan with a conclusive air. She scrubbed the outside of it as faithfully as the inside. She was a masterly keeper of her box of a house. Her one living room never seemed to have in it any of the dust which the friction of life with inanimate matter produces. She swept, and there seemed to be no dirt to go before the broom; she cleaned, and one could see no difference. She was like an artist so perfect that he has apparently no art. Today she got out a mixing bowl and a board, and rolled some pies, and there was no more flour upon her than upon her daughter who was doing finer work. Nanny was to be married in the fall, and she was sewing on some white cambric and embroidery. She sewed industriously while her mother cooked; her soft milk-white hands and wrists showed whiter than her delicate work.

"We must have the stove moved out in the shed before long," said Mrs. Penn. "Talk about not havin' things, it's been a real blessin' to be able to put a stove up in that shed in hot weather. Father did one good thing when he fixed that stove pipe out there."

Sarah Penn's face as she rolled her pies had that expression of meek vigor which might have characterized one of the New Testament saints. She was making mince pies. Her husband, Adoniram Penn, liked them better than any other kind. She baked twice a week. Adoniram often liked a piece of pie between meals. She hurried this morning. It had been later than usual when she began, and she wanted to have a pie baked for dinner. However deep a resentment she might be forced to hold against her husband, she would never fail in sedulous attention to his wants.

Nobility of character manifests itself at loopholes when it is not provided with large doors. Sarah Penn's showed itself today in flaky dishes of pastry. She made the pies faithfully, while across the table she could see, when she glanced up from her work, the sight that rankled in her patient and steadfast soul—the digging of the cellar of the new barn in the place where Adoniram forty years ago had promised her their new house should stand.

The pies were done for dinner. Adoniram and Sammy were home a few minutes after twelve o'clock. The dinner was eaten with serious haste. There was never much conversation at the table in the Penn family. Adoniram asked a blessing, and they ate promptly, then rose up and went about their work.

Sammy went back to school, taking soft sly lopes out of the yard like a rabbit. He wanted a game of marbles before school, and feared his father would give him some chores to do. Adoniram hastened to the door and called after him, but he was out of sight.

"I don't see what you let him go for, mother," said he. "I wanted him to help me unload that wood."

Adoniram went to work out in the yard unloading wood from the wagon. Sarah put away the dinner dishes, while Nanny took down her curl papers and changed her dress. She was going down to the store to buy some more embroidery and thread.

When Nanny was gone, Mrs. Penn went to the door. "Father!" she called.

"Well, what is it!"

"I want to see you jest a minute, father."

"I can't leave this wood nohow. I've got to git unloaded an' go for a load of gravel afore two o'clock. Sammy had ought to helped me. You hadn't ought to let him go to school so early."

"I want to see you jest a minute."

"I tell ye I can't, nohow, mother."

"Father, you come here." Sarah Penn stood in the door like a queen; she held her head as if it bore a crown; there was that patience which makes authority royal in her voice. Adoniram went.

Mrs. Penn led the way into the kitchen, and pointed to a chair. "Sit down, father," said she; "I've got somethin' I want to say to you."

He sat down heavily; his face was quite stolid, but he looked at her with restive eyes. "Well, what is it, mother?"

"I want to know what you're buildin' that new barn for, father?"

"I ain't got nothin' to say about it."

"It can't be you think you need another barn?"

"I tell ye I ain't got nothin' to say about it, mother; an' I ain't goin' to say nothin'."

"Be you goin' to buy more cows?"

Adoniram did not reply; he shut his mouth tight.

"I know you be, as well as I want to. Now, father, look here"—Sarah Penn had not sat down; she stood before her husband in the humble fashion of a Scripture woman— "I'm goin' to talk real plain to you; I never have sence I married you, but I'm goin' to now. I ain't never complained, an' I ain't goin' to complain now, but I'm goin' to talk plain. You see this room here, father; you look at it well. You see there ain't no carpet on the floor, an' you see the paper is all dirty an' droppin' off the walls. We ain't had no new paper on it for ten year, an' then I put it on myself, an' it didn't cost but ninepence a roll. You see this room, father; it's all the one I've had to work in an' eat in an' sit in sence we was married. There ain't another woman in the whole town whose husband ain't got half the means you have but

what's got better. It's all the room Nanny's got to have
her company in; an' there ain't one of her mates but what's
got better, an' their fathers not so able as hers is. It's all
the room she'll have to be married in. What would you
have thought, father, if we had had our weddin' in a room
no better than this? I was married in my mother's parlor,
with a carpet on the floor, an' stuffed furniture, an' a mahogany card table. An' this is all the room my daughter
will have to be married in. Look here, father!"

Sarah Penn went across the room as though it were a
tragic stage. She flung open a door and disclosed a tiny
bedroom, only large enough for a bed and bureau, with a
path between. "There, father," said she—"there's all the
room I've had to sleep in in forty year. All my children
were born there—the two that died an' the two that's livin'.
I was sick with a fever there."

She stepped to another door and opened it. It led into
the small, ill-lighted pantry. "Here," said she, "is all the
buttery I've got—every place I've got for my dishes, to set
away my victuals in, an' to keep my milk pans in. Father,
I've been takin' care of the milk of six cows in this place,
an' now you're goin' to build a new barn, an' keep more
cows, an' give me more to do in it."

She threw open another door. A narrow crooked flight
of stairs wound upward from it. "There, father," said she,
"I want you to look at the stairs that go up to them two
unfinished chambers that are all the places our son an'
daughter have had to sleep in all their lives. There ain't a
prettier girl in town nor a more ladylike one than Nanny,
an' that's the place she has to sleep in. It ain't so good as
your horse's stall; it ain't so warm an' tight."

Sarah Penn went back and stood before her husband.
"Now, father," said she, "I want to know if you think
you're doin' right an' accordin' to what you profess. Here,
where we was married, forty year ago, you promised me

faithful that we should have a new house built in that lot over in the field before the year was out. You said you had money enough, an' you wouldn't ask me to live in no such place as this. It is forty year now, an' you've been makin' more money, an' I've been savin' of it for you ever since, an' you ain't built no house yet. You've built sheds an' cow houses an' one new barn, an' now you're goin' to build another. Father, I want to know if you think it's right. You're lodgin' your dumb beasts better than you are your own flesh an' blood. I want to know if you think it's right."

"I ain't got nothin' to say."

"You can't say nothin' without ownin' it ain't right, father. An' there's another thing—I ain't complained; I've got along forty year, an' I s'pose I should forty more, if it wa'n't for that—if we don't have another house. Nanny, she can't live with us after she's married. She'll have to go somewheres else to live away from us, an' it don't seem as if I could have it so, noways, father. She wa'n't ever strong. She's got considerable color, but there wa'n't never any backbone to her. I've always took the heft of every-thing off her, an' she ain't fit to keep house an' do every-thing herself. She'll be all worn out inside of a year. Think of her doin' all the washin' an' ironin' an' bakin' with them soft white hands an' arms, an' sweepin'! I can't have it so, noways, father."

Mrs. Penn's face was burning; her mild eyes gleamed. She had pleaded her little cause like a Webster; she had ranged from severity to pathos; but her opponent employed that obstinate silence which makes eloquence futile with mocking echoes. Adoniram arose clumsily.

"Father, ain't you got nothin' to say?" said Mrs. Penn.

"I've got to go off after that load of gravel. I can't stan' here talkin' all day."

"Father, won't you think it over, an' have a house built there instead of a barn?"

"I ain't got nothin' to say."

Adoniram shuffled out. Mrs. Penn went into her bed-room. When she came out, her eyes were red. She had a roll of unbleached cotton cloth. She spread it out on the kitchen table, and began cutting out some shirts for her husband. The men over in the field had a team to help them this afternoon; she could hear their halloos. She had a scanty pattern for the shirts; she had to plan and piece the sleeves.

Nanny came home with her embroidery, and sat down with her needlework. She had taken down her curl papers, and there was a soft roll of fair hair like an aureole over her forehead; her face was as delicately fine and clear as porcelain. Suddenly she looked up, and the tender red flamed all over her face and neck. "Mother," said she.

"What say?"

"I've been thinking—I don't see how we're goin' to have any—wedding in this room. I'd be ashamed to have his folks come if we didn't have anybody else."

"Mebbe we can have some new paper before then; I can put it on. I guess you won't have no call to be ashamed of your belongin's."

"We might have the wedding in the new barn," said Nanny, with gentle pettishness. "Why, mother, what makes you look so?"

Mrs. Penn had started, and was staring at her with a curious expression. She turned again to her work, and spread out a pattern carefully on the cloth. "Nothin'," said she.

Presently Adoniram clattered out of the yard in his two-wheeled dump cart, standing as proudly upright as a Roman charioteer. Mrs. Penn opened the door and stood there a minute looking out; the halloos of the men sounded louder.

It seemed to her all through the spring months that she heard nothing but the halloos and the noises of saws and hammers. The new barn grew fast. It was a fine edifice for this little village. Men came on pleasant Sundays, in their meeting suits and clean shirt bosoms, and stood around it admiringly. Mrs. Penn did not speak of it, and Adoniram did not mention it to her, although sometimes, upon a return from inspecting it, he bore himself with injured dignity.

"It's a strange thing how your mother feels about the new barn," he said, confidentially, to Sammy one day.

Sammy only grunted after an odd fashion for a boy; he had learned it from his father.

The barn was all completed ready for use by the third week in July. Adoniram had planned to move his stock in on Wednesday; on Tuesday he received a letter which changed his plans. He came in with it early in the morning. "Sammy's been to the post office," said he, "an' I've got a letter from Hiram." Hiram was Mrs. Penn's brother, who lived in Vermont.

"Well," said Mrs. Penn, "what does he say about the folks?"

"I guess they're all right. He says he thinks if I come up country right off there's a chance to buy jest the kind of a horse I want." He stared reflectively out of the window at the new barn.

Mrs. Penn was making pies. She went on clapping the rolling pin into the crust, although she was very pale, and her heart beat loudly.

"I dun' know but what I'd better go," said Adoniram. "I hate to go off jest now, right in the midst of hayin', but the ten-acre lot's cut, an' I guess Rufus an' the others can git along without me three or four days. I can't get a horse round here to suit me, nohow, an' I've got to have another for all that wood haulin' in the fall. I told Hiram to watch out, an' if he got wind of a good horse to let me know. I guess I'd better go."

"I'll get out your clean shirt an' collar," said Mrs. Penn, calmly.

She laid out Adoniram's Sunday suit and his clean clothes on the bed in the little bedroom. She got his shaving water and razor ready. At last she buttoned on his collar and fastened his black cravat.

Adoniram never wore his collar and cravat except on extra occasions. He held his head high, with a rasped dignity. When he was all ready, with his coat and hat brushed, and a lunch of pie and cheese in a paper bag, he hesitated on the threshold of the door. He looked at his wife, and his manner was defiantly apologetic. "*If* them cows come today, Sammy can drive 'em into the new barn," said he; "an' when they bring the hay up, they can pitch it in there."

"Well," replied Mrs. Penn.

Adoniram set his shaven face ahead and started. When he had cleared the doorstep, he turned and looked back with a kind of nervous solemnity. "I shall be back by Saturday if nothin' happens," said he.

"Do be careful, father," returned his wife.

She stood in the door with Nanny at her elbow and watched him out of sight. Her eyes had a strange, doubtful expression in them; her peaceful forehead was contracted. She went in, and about her baking again. Nanny sat sewing. Her wedding day was drawing nearer, and she was getting pale and thin with her steady sewing. Her mother kept glancing at her.

"Have you got that pain in your side this mornin'?" she asked.

"A little."

Mrs. Penn's face, as she worked, changed; her perplexed forehead smoothed; her eyes were steady, her lips firmly set. She formed a maxim for herself, although incoherently with her unlettered thoughts. "Unsolicited opportunities are the guideposts of the Lord to the new roads of life," she repeated in effect, and she made up her mind to her course of action.

"S'posin' I *had* wrote to Hiram," she muttered once, when she was in the pantry—"s'posin' I had wrote, an' asked him if he knew of any horse? But I didn't, an' father's goin' wa'n't none of my doin'. It looks like a providence." Her voice rang out quite loud at the last.

"What you talkin' about, mother?" called Nanny.

"Nothin'."

Mrs. Penn hurried her baking; at eleven o'clock it was all done. The load of hay from the west field came slowly down the cart track and drew up at the new barn. Mrs. Penn ran out. "Stop!" she screamed—"stop!"

The men stopped and looked; Sammy upreared from the top of the load, and stared at his mother.

"Stop!" she cried out again. "Don't you put the hay in that barn; put it in the old one."

"Why, he said to put it in here," returned one of the hay-makers, wonderingly. He was a young man, a neighbor's son, whom Adoniram hired by the year to help on the farm.

"Don't you put the hay in the new barn; there's room enough in the old one, ain't there?" said Mrs. Penn.

"Room enough," returned the hired man, in his thick, rustic tones. "Didn't need the new barn, nohow, far as room's concerned. Well, I s'pose he changed his mind." He took hold of the horses' bridles.

Mrs. Penn went back to the house. Soon the kitchen windows were darkened, and a fragrance like warm honey came into the room.

Nanny laid down her work. "I thought father wanted them to put the hay into the new barn?" she said, wonderingly.

"It's all right," replied her mother.

Sammy slid down from the load of hay, and came in to see if dinner was ready.

"I ain't goin' to get a regular dinner today, as long as father's gone," said his mother. "I've let the fire go out. You can have some bread an' milk an' pie. I thought we could get along." She set out some bowls of milk, some bread, and a pie on the kitchen table. "You'd better eat your dinner now," said she. "You might jest as well get through with it. I want you to help me afterward."

Nanny and Sammy stared at each other. There was something strange in their mother's manner. Mrs. Penn did not eat anything herself. She went into the pantry, and they heard her moving dishes while they ate. Presently she came out with a pile of plates. She got the clothes basket out of the shed, and packed them in it. Nanny and Sammy watched. She brought out cups and saucers, and put them in with the plates.

"What you goin' to do, mother?" inquired Nanny, in a timid voice. A sense of something unusual made her tremble, as if it were a ghost. Sammy rolled his eyes over his pie.

"You'll see what I'm goin' to do," replied Mrs. Penn. "If you're through, Nanny, I want you to go upstairs an' pack up your things; an' I want you, Sammy, to help me take down the bed in the bedroom."

"Oh, mother, what for?" gasped Nanny.

"You'll see."

During the next few hours a feat was performed by this simple, pious New England mother which was equal in its way to Wolfe's storming of the Heights of Abraham. It took no more genius and audacity of bravery for Wolfe to cheer his wondering soldiers up those steep precipices, under the sleeping eyes of the enemy, than for Sarah Penn, at the head of her children, to move all their little household goods into the new barn while her husband was away.

Nanny and Sammy followed their mother's instructions without a murmur; indeed, they were overawed. There is a certain uncanny and superhuman quality about all such purely original undertakings as their mother's was to them. Nanny went back and forth with her light loads, and Sammy tugged with sober energy.

At five o'clock in the afternoon the little house in which the Penns had lived for forty years had emptied itself into the new barn.

Every builder builds somewhat for unknown purposes, and is in a measure a prophet. The architect of Adoniram Penn's barn, while he designed it for the comfort of four-footed animals, had planned better than he knew for the comfort of humans. Sarah Penn saw at a glance its possibilities. Those great box stalls, with quilts hung before them, would make better bedrooms than the one she had occupied for forty years, and there was a tight carriage room. The harness room, with its chimney and shelves, would make a kitchen of her dreams. The great middle space would make a parlor, by-and-by, fit for a palace. Upstairs there was as much room as down. With partitions and windows, what a house would there be! Sarah looked at the row of stanchions before the allotted space for cows, and reflected that she would have her front entry there.

At six o'clock the stove was up in the harness room, the kettle was boiling, and the table set for tea. It looked almost as homelike as the abandoned house across the yard had ever done. The young hired man milked, and Sarah directed him calmly to bring the milk to the new barn. He came gaping, dropping little blots of foam from the brimming pails on the grass. Before the next morning he had spread the story of Adoniram Penn's wife moving into the new barn all over the little village. Men assembled in the store and talked it over; women with shawls over their heads scuttled into each other's houses before their work was done. Any deviation from the ordinary course of life in this quiet town was enough to stop all progress in it. Everybody paused to look at the staid, independent figure on the side track. There was a difference of opinion with regard to her. Some held her to be insane; some, of a lawless and rebellious spirit.

Friday the minister went to see her. It was in the forenoon, and she was at the barn door shelling peas for dinner. She looked up and returned his salutation with dignity; then she went on with her work. She did not invite him in. The saintly expression of her face remained fixed, but there was an angry flush over it.

The minister stood awkwardly before her, and talked. She handled the peas as if they were bullets. At last she looked up, and her eyes showed the spirit that her meek front had covered for a lifetime.

"There ain't no use talkin', Mr. Hersey," said she. "I've thought it all over an' over, an' I believe I'm doin' what's right. I've made it the subject of prayer, an' it's betwixt me an' the Lord an' Adoniram. There ain't no call for nobody else to worry about it."

"Well, of course, if you have brought it to the Lord in prayer, and feel satisfied that you are doing right, Mrs. Penn," said the minister, helplessly. His thin gray-bearded face was pathetic. He was a sickly man; his youthful confidence had cooled; he had to scourge himself up to some of his pastoral duties as relentlessly as a Catholic ascetic, and then he was prostrated by the smart.

"I think it's right jest as much as I think it was right for our forefathers to come over from the old country 'cause they didn't have what belonged to 'em," said Mrs. Penn. She arose. The barn threshold might have been Plymouth Rock, from her bearing. "I don't doubt you mean well, Mr. Hersey," said she, "but there are things people hadn't ought to interfere with. I've been a member of the church for over forty year. I've got my own mind an' my own feet, an' I'm goin' to think my own thoughts an' go my own ways, an' nobody but the Lord is goin' to dictate to me unless I've a mind to have him. Won't you come in an' set down? How is Mis' Hersey?"

"She is well, I thank you," replied the minister. He added some more perplexed apologetic remarks; then he retreated.

He could expound the intricacies of every character study in the Scriptures; he was competent to grasp the Pilgrim Fathers and all historical innovators; but Sarah Penn was beyond him. He could deal with primal cases, but parallel ones worsted him. But, after all, although it was aside from his province, he wondered more how Adoniram Penn would deal with his wife than how the Lord would. Everybody shared the wonder. When Adoniram's four new cows arrived, Sarah ordered three to be put in the old barn, the other in the house shed where the cooking stove had stood. That added to the excitement. It was whispered that all four cows were domiciled in the house.

Toward sunset on Saturday, when Adoniram was expected home, there was a knot of men in the road near the new barn. The hired man had milked, but he still hung around the premises. Sarah Penn had supper all ready. There were brown bread and baked beans and a custard pie; it was the supper that Adoniram loved on a Saturday night. She had on a clean calico, and she bore herself imperturbably. Nanny and Sammy kept close at her heels. Their eyes were large, and Nanny was full of nervous tremors. Still there was to them more pleasant excitement than anything else. An inborn confidence in their mother over their father asserted itself.

Sammy looked out of the harness-room window. "There he is," he announced, in an awed whisper. He and Nanny peeped around the casing. Mrs. Penn kept on about her work. The children watched Adoniram leave the new horse standing in the drive while he went to the house-door. It was fastened. Then he went around to the shed. That door was seldom locked, even when the family was away. The thought how her father would be confronted by the cow flashed upon Nanny. There was a hysterical sob in her throat. Adoniram emerged from the shed and stood looking about in a dazed fashion. His lips moved; he was saying something, but they could not hear what it was. The hired man was peeping around a corner of the old barn, but nobody saw him.

Adoniram took the new horse by the bridle and led him across the yard to the new barn. Nanny and Sammy slunk close to their mother. The barn doors rolled back, and there stood Adoniram, with the long mild face of the great Canadian farm horse looking over his shoulder.

Nanny kept behind her mother, but Sammy stepped suddenly forward, and stood in front of her.

Adoniram stared at the group. "What on airth you all down here for?" said he. "What's the matter over to the house?"

"We've come here to live, father," said Sammy. His shrill voice quavered out bravely.

"What"—Adoniram sniffed—"what is it smells like cookin'?" said he. He stepped forward and looked in at the open door of the harness room. Then he turned to his wife. His old bristling face was pale and frightened. "What on airth does this mean, mother?" he gasped.

"You come in here, father," said Sarah. She led the way into the harness room and shut the door. "Now, father," said she, "you needn't be scared. I ain't crazy. There ain't nothin' to be upset over. But we've come here to live, an' we're goin' to live here. We've got jest as good a right here as new horses an' cows. The house wa'n't fit for us to live in any longer, an' I made up my mind I wa'n't goin' to stay there. I've done my duty by you forty year, an' I'm goin' to do it now; but I'm goin' to live here.

You've got to put in some windows and partitions; an' you'll have to buy some furniture."

"Why, mother!" the old man gasped.

"You'd better take your coat off an' get washed—there's the wash basin—an' then we'll have supper."

"Why, mother!"

Sammy went past the window, leading the new horse to the old barn. The old man saw him, and shook his head speechlessly. He tried to take off his coat, but his arms seemed to lack the power. His wife helped him. She poured some water into the tin basin, and put in a piece of soap. She got the comb and brush, and smoothed his thin gray hair after he had washed. Then she put the beans, hot bread, and tea on the table. Sammy came in, and the family drew up. Adoniram sat looking dazedly at his plate, and they waited.

"Ain't you goin' to ask a blessin', father?" said Sarah.

And the old man bent his head and mumbled.

All through the meal he stopped eating at intervals, and stared furtively at his wife; but he ate well. The home food tasted good to him, and his old frame was too sturdily healthy to be affected by his mind. But after supper he went out, and sat down on the step of the smaller door at the right of the barn, through which he had meant his Jerseys to pass in stately file, but which Sarah designed for her front house door, and he leaned his head on his hands.

After the supper dishes were cleared away and the milk pans washed, Sarah went out to him. The twilight was deepening. There was a clear green glow in the sky. Before them stretched the smooth level of field; in the distance was a cluster of haystacks like the huts of a village; the air was very cool and calm and sweet. The landscape might have been an ideal one of peace.

Sarah bent over and touched her husband on one of his thin, sinewy shoulders. "Father!"

The old man's shoulders heaved; he was weeping.

"Why, don't do so, father," said Sarah.

"I'll—put up the—partitions, an'—everything you—want, mother."

Sarah put her apron up to her face; she was overcome by her own triumph.

Adoniram was like a fortress whose walls had no active resistance, and went down the instant the right besieging tools were used. "Why, mother," he said, hoarsely, "I hadn't no idee you was so set on't as all this comes to."

## III. *LITTLE-GIRL-AFRAID-OF-A-DOG*[1]

"THE chickens are beginning to lay again," said Emmeline's aunt Martha, "and Emmeline can begin carrying eggs over to the poor Ticknors tomorrow." Martha, who was quite young and pretty, cast a glance of congratulation at Emmeline, as if she were proposing a great pleasure.

Emmeline's mother echoed her sister. "Yes, that is so," said she. "Sydney" (Sydney was the man) "said yesterday that the chickens were laying very well. Tomorrow Emmeline shall begin."

"Only think how nice it is going to be for those poor Ticknors, with all those children, to have half a dozen new-laid eggs every day," said Martha, again with that congratulatory glance at her little niece, who sat beside the window, holding her best doll.

"We shall be able to send more than that some days, I dare say," said Emmeline's mother. "Maybe, when I go to the store, I will buy a pretty new basket for you to carry the eggs in, dear."

"Yes'm," said Emmeline, in a low voice. She sat full in the glow of the setting wintry sun, and her whole little blond head and delicate face were gilded by it. It was impossible for her mother and her aunt to see that she had turned very pale. She kept her face turned toward the window, too, and when she said "Yes'm" infused a hypocritical tone of joy into the word, although she was a most honest and conscientious little girl. In fact, the joy was assumed because of a Jesuit-like issue of conscience in her inner dealings with herself.

[1] *Copyright, 1909, by Harper & Brothers.*

43

The Ticknors, the poor Ticknors, with the large brood of children, lived about half a mile down the road, and Emmeline's mother and aunt esteemed it a great delight for her to carry eggs to them when eggs were plentiful. Emmeline herself never denied the delight, but God alone knew how glad she was, how wickedly (she told herself that it was wickedly) glad she was, when about Thanksgiving time, when people naturally wished to use more eggs, the chickens, after the perverse nature of their race, laid fewer eggs, and there were only enough for the family. Then Emmeline had a respite. She grew plumper, and there was more color on her little, soft, curving cheeks. "Emmeline always seems so much better this time of the year," her mother often said; and she never dreamed why it was, although Emmeline could have told her, had it not been for her conscience, which pricked her on in spite of her pains.

The Ticknors had a dog—a very small dog, it is true, but with voice enough for a whole pack—and Emmeline was in mortal terror of him. He always barked at her when she went to carry the eggs, and he always sniffed ominously around her ankles. Sometimes he made bounds of vicious yelping joy at her, almost reaching her face, although he was a little dog. Emmeline was a little girl, small for her age, which was barely ten. She was very much under the dominion, the very loving dominion, of her mother and aunt. Her father was dead. The Ameses—Emmeline's last name was Ames—lived on a small farm, and Sydney managed it. They were regarded as quite rich people in the little village where they lived, and they looked at themselves in that light. Therefore they realized a sense of duty, of pleasurable duty, toward the less fortunate people around them. At that very moment both Aunt Martha and Mrs. Ames were sewing upon garments for poor people—some strong and durable flannelette petticoats of soft pink and blue. Sometimes Emmeline herself was asked to sew a seam on these soft garments, and she always obeyed with the utmost docility, although she did not like to sew very well. She was a sober, reflective little girl, not exactly indolent, but inclined to sit quite still, while her young mind indulged in pryings into the future and conceptions of life and her own little niche in the universal scheme of things, which would have quite astounded her mother and her aunt Martha had they known of it. They saw in Emmeline only a darling, obedient, sweet little girl holding her doll baby; not as she really was—lit into flame by her own imaginings and the sun. Neither dreamed that, as she sat there and said "Yes'm" so prettily, she was shuddering in her very soul from a most exaggerated fear, stimulated by an imagination entirely beyond theirs, of the Ticknors' little dog.

Soon the copper-gilt glow faded from Emmeline's head and face, and she sat, a pale little shadow in the dusk, until her mother lighted the lamp, and Annie, the maid, came in to announce supper. Emmeline had not much appetite that night, although there were her favorite fried oysters and waffles. It seemed as if the subject of the eggs and the Ticknors, which caused her to project more plainly her vision of fear concerning the little dog, could not be let alone. They had hardly seated themselves at the table before Annie spoke of the large number of eggs which had been brought in that day. Annie had been with the Ameses a long time, and was considered quite a member of the family. "I think you can carry a dozen eggs tomorrow morning, dear," Emmeline's mother said, happily.

"Yes'm," replied Emmeline.

"Only think what it will mean to those poor Ticknors," said Aunt Martha.

"Yes'm," said Emmeline.

Then Emmeline's mother noticed that the child was not eating as usual. "Why, Emmeline," she said, "you have not half finished your oysters!"

Emmeline looked helplessly at her plate, and said that she was not very hungry. She felt that she was wicked because she was not hungry, since she was so afraid of the Ticknors' little dog that she did not want to carry the eggs to them the next morning, when they were so poor and needed the eggs so much.

"If you don't eat your oysters, you must swallow two raw eggs," said Emmeline's mother, suddenly. "Annie, beat up two eggs with a little sugar and nutmeg and a little milk."

Emmeline felt just then more than a physical loathing: she felt a moral loathing for anything in the shape of an egg; but she swallowed the mixture, which Annie presently brought to her, with her usual docility.

"That will be just as nourishing as the oysters," said Aunt Martha. Aunt Martha had on her pretty blue gown. She was expecting Mr. John Adams that evening. It was Wednesday, and Mr. John always came on Wednesday and Sunday evenings. Emmeline knew why. She knew with a shy and secret admiration, and a forecast of Wednesday and Sunday evenings yet to be when some young man should come to see her. She made up her mind that she would wear red on those interesting occasions, which filled her, young as she was, with a sweet sense of mystery and pre-science. She gazed at pretty Aunt Martha, in her gown of soft blue, cut out in a tiny square at the neck, revealing her long white throat. She forgot for a second the Ticknors and the Ticknor dog, which represented the genuine bugbear of her childhood. Then the old fear overcame her again. Her mother regarded her, and Aunt Martha regarded her; then the two women exchanged glances. After supper, when they were all on their way back to the sitting room, Emme-line's mother whispered anxiously in Martha's ear, "She doesn't look well."

Martha nodded assent. "I don't think she has had enough

fresh air lately," she said, in a low voice. "It will do her good to take that morning run to the Ticknors'."

"That is so," assented Emmeline's mother. "I'll have her go to bed early tonight; then right after breakfast tomorrow morning, when the air is fresh, she can take the eggs to the Ticknors."

Emmeline went to bed before Mr. John Adams arrived. Her mother tucked her in and kissed her, then blew out the lamp and went downstairs. Emmeline had said her prayers, introducing, mentally, a little clause with regard to the Ticknor dog. It was a piteous little child codicil to the Lord's Prayer and "Now I lay me," which she always said.

After her mother had gone downstairs Emmeline lay awake staring at the darkness. The darkness very soon seemed to flicker with wildfire; grotesque faces grinned at her from the midst of this fire, which was and was not. A terrible horror, of which the little bugbear dog was the keystone, was over her. She wanted so to call her mother, to get up and run downstairs into the lamp-lit sitting room; but she lay still, stiff and rigid. She had too much self-control for her own good, young as she was. Presently she heard the distant tinkle of the front-door bell, and heard Aunt Martha open the door and greet Mr. John Adams. Again, for a second, her own spirit of joyous prophecy was over her; but after Mr. John Adams and Aunt Martha had gone into the parlor, and she could only hear the faint hum of their voices, she returned to her former state. However, it was not very long before her attention was again diverted. Mr. John Adams had a very deep bass voice. All of a sudden this great bass was raised. Emmeline could not distinguish one word, but it sounded like a roar to her. Then, also, she heard her Aunt Martha's sweet, shrill voice, almost loud enough for the words to be audible. Then she heard doors opening, and shutting with almost a slam; then she was certain she heard a sob from the front entry. Then she heard the sitting-room door opened with a fling, then a continuous agitated hum of conversation between her mother and aunt. Emmeline wondered why Mr. John Adams had gone so soon, and why he had almost slammed the door, and what her aunt and mother were talking about so excitedly. Then, as she had not much curiosity, her mind reverted to her own affairs, and again the wildfire of the darkness flickered and the grotesque faces grinned at her, and all her pleasant gates of sleep and dreams were guarded against her by the Ticknors' little dog.

Emmeline slept very little that night. When she did sleep, she had horrible dreams. Once she woke crying out, and her mother was standing over her with a lighted lamp. "What is the matter? Are you ill?" asked her mother. Her mother was much older than Aunt Martha, but she looked very pretty in her long, trailing white robe, with the lamplight shining upon her loving, anxious face.

"I had a dream," said Emmeline, faintly.

"I guess you were lying on your back," said her mother. "Turn over on your side, darling, and try to go to sleep again. Don't think about the dream. Remember how you are going to carry eggs to those poor Ticknor children tomorrow morning. Then, I know, you will go to sleep."

"Yes'm," said Emmeline; and she turned obediently on her side, and her mother went out.

Emmeline slept no more that night. It was about four o'clock in the morning. The Ameses had quite an early breakfast, at seven o'clock. Emmeline reflected that in three hours she should be up and dressed and at the breakfast table; that breakfast would take about half an hour; that in about three hours and a half she would be on her way to the Ticknors'. She felt almost as a condemned criminal might have felt on the morning of his execution.

When she went laggingly downstairs, as Annie played a discordant chime on the string of Japanese bells, she felt weak and was very pale. Her mother and Martha, who herself looked wretched, as if she had been weeping all night, glanced at her, then again at each other. "It will do her good to get out in the fresh air," said Martha, stifling a heavy sigh.

Emmeline's mother looked commiseratingly at her sister. "Why don't you slip on your brown gown and go with her, dear?" she said. "You look as if the air would do you good, too."

Annie, coming in with the eggs, cast a sharp glance of mingled indignation and sympathy at Miss Martha. She knew perfectly well what the matter was. She had abnormally good ears, and had been in the dining room, the evening before, when Mr. John Adams was in the parlor with Miss Martha, and there was a door between, a badly hung door, with cracks in it, and she had heard. She had not meant to listen, although she felt that all the affairs of the Ames family were her own, and she had a perfect right to know about them. She knew that Mr. John Adams had been talking about where he and Miss Martha should live after they were married, and had insisted upon her going to live in the old Adams homestead with his mother and elder brother and two sisters, instead of living right along with Emmeline and her mother and herself (Annie). She considered that Miss Martha had done exactly right to stand out as she had done. Everybody knew what old Mrs. Adams was, and one of the sisters was called quick-tempered, and the elder brother was unmarried, and there was therefore no possible reason why Mr. John Adams should feel obliged to remain at home after his marriage. On the other side, it would obviously be very hard for Emmeline's mother to part with her sister and live alone in her big house with Emmeline and Annie. It was a very large house, and there was plenty of room; whereas the Adams house was small. There could be no question, so Annie thought, and so Emmeline's mother thought, and so Martha herself thought, but she had done right. Martha reasoned it out in her own mind that John Adams could not care so very much for her, or he would not insist upon subjecting her to such discomfort and annoyance as she would evidently experience if she were to live in the Adams house after her marriage.

John had always been frank about his mother's difficult temper and his sister's, although he was a devoted son and brother. He knew, too, that Martha could not have a sitting room to herself in which to display her wedding treasures, and she could have that in the Ames house. She considered within herself that he could not possibly love her as much as she had supposed, because he had given no reason whatever for his insistence that she should comply with his wishes except that they were his wishes. Martha had a pretty spirit of her own, and she resented anything like tyranny, even in those whom she loved. So she held her head high, although her eyes were red, and said, in reply to her sister's suggestion, that she rather thought she would not. She thought she would take the ten-thirty train for Bolton and do a little shopping. She wanted to see about a spring suit, and the sooner she got the material to the dressmaker's the better. She said it exactly as if she had not planned to have that same spring suit her going-away costume when she was married. Martha had expected to be married the first of June. It was now March. When she said that about going to Bolton her sister's face brightened, and she gave her a look of pride in her spirit. "So I would," said she.

She did not notice at all how Emmeline's face fell. For a second the thought of her aunt's going with her to the Ticknors' and shooing away with her superior courage and strength that dreadful little dog had caused her heart to leap exultantly. But now that chance of respite was gone. She took a spoonful of her cereal, puckering her little mouth most pathetically after she had swallowed it. She did not care for cereal, and ate it only because her mother and aunt said that it was good for her. Emmeline had begun to wonder why so many things which she disliked, and so many things which she more than disliked, were so good for her. She acquiesced in the wisdom of her elders, but she wondered.

She ate her cereal, then her soft-boiled egg on toast. She hated eggs that morning, although usually she liked them. She felt as if she was fairly eating her terror and dread of what lay before her: eggs were so intimately associated with it. It seemed to her that the fear in her heart was enough, without being obliged to have it in her stomach also.

After breakfast Emmeline put on her red coat and hat (she was still wearing her winter garments), and her mother gave the basket of eggs to her and kissed her. "Don't walk too fast and get all tired out, dear," she said.

She and Martha stood at the window watching the gay little figure move slowly down the road. They need not have cautioned her against speed. She did not feel in the least inclined to hurry.

"The child does not look very well this morning," said Mrs. Ames. "She has that old anxious expression again, and she is pale, and she ate her breakfast as if she did not want it."

"Ate it just as if she was swallowing pills," said Annie.

"Yes, she did," Mrs. Ames agreed, anxiously.

"Well, the walk in the fresh morning air will do her good," said Martha. "I must make a start if I am going to catch that ten-thirty train. I must mend my gloves. I think I will wear my brown taffeta. I may call at the Robinses' while I am in Bolton."

"I would," said Mrs. Ames. It was tacitly understood between them that nothing more was to be said about Mr.

John Adams, that the whole subject was to be left out of sight and hearing, and everything was to go on as before. However, as the last glimpse of red disappeared down the street, and Martha's step was heard overhead, her sister thought how glad she was that she had proposed going to Bolton. "It will take her mind up," she thought, but she would not have said it to Martha for the world.

Meantime, Emmeline continued slowly but none the less surely on her road to the Ticknors'. It was a perfectly straight road for a quarter of a mile, then it curved. It was not until one passed this curve that one could see the Ticknors' ragged, squalid residence. Then one saw it as a blur on the landscape. How Emmeline dreaded rounding that curve! She walked very slowly, toeing in a little, as was her wont when she was nervously intent. She prayed incessantly, and her poor little prayer ran in this wise: "Oh, Father in Heaven, please take care of me, and don't let Spotty come near me nor hurt me nor bark at me."

Emmeline repeated this prayer over and over in a sort of rhythmic cadence. She fairly kept step with it, and yet she had not the slightest faith in the prayer. She could not really see why she should have. She had always prayed in such wise while carrying eggs to the Ticknors, and Spotty had never failed to race barking out to meet her, and sniff at her nervous, twitching little ankles and try little nips and tugs at her skirts. The prayer had never, so far as she could see, been answered, and why should she expect it to be now? Emmeline was a very honest little girl. She was reverent, and she believed God could keep Spotty from barking at her; but she did not believe that He would. Moreover, she was Christian enough to hope and trust, somehow, that these agonies of terror which she was called upon to undergo were in the end for her spiritual good. She did not complain, but she knew that she suffered, and she knew that Spotty would not fail to bark.

Presently she turned that dreaded curve of the road, and she could see the wretched place where the Ticknors lived. The dwelling itself was an unpainted, out-of-drawing shanty, leaning so far to one side that it seemed it must topple over, but saving itself by a lurch in another direction. It was a very drunkard of a house, a habitation which had taken upon itself the character of its inmates. It was degenerate, miserable, and oblivious to its misery. Beside this main shanty was a stable, far out of the perpendicular, out of which looked a high-hipped cow. Sometimes Emmeline was afraid of the cow, which was often at large, but never as of the dog. There was also a pigsty and various other horrible little adjuncts of the main whole. Emmeline shuddered as she came in sight of it. The mere aspect of the place would have gotten on her sensitive nerves even if Spotty had not been there. But immediately, breaking upon her prayer, came the well-known vicious little yelp.

Spotty was a mongrel, but he had wondrous ears. Emmeline espied the little animal coming for her so fast that he seemed a mere line of speed, but never ceasing that wild yelp. Emmeline prayed on, and walked on. It was strange that she never at such times thought of turning round and running. It never occurred to her to disobey her mother and not take the eggs to the Ticknors. She walked along, praying, her heart beating heavily, her limbs shaking. The little dog reached her. He was a little dog, and it was a sheer absurdity for her to feel such fear of him. He danced around in circles, a regular dog war dance, as she advanced. His yelps became louder and louder. It seemed inconceivable that such a small animal could have such a terrific bark. Emmeline went steadily on, toeing in, holding her basket of eggs in a hand which did not feel as if it belonged to her. It did not seem that her whole body belonged to her in any other sense than as a machine which bore her conscience, her obedience, her fear, and the basket of eggs.

When she reached the Ticknor house she was blue-white, trembling with a curious rigid tremor. She knocked, and the little dog gave a furious, a frantic yelp, and tugged at her skirt. Then the second of her deliverance came. The door opened. An enormous slatternly woman, a mountain of inert flesh appeared. She bade the dog be quiet. He did not obey, but Emmeline had a sense of protection. It had occurred to her more than once that perhaps Mrs. Ticknor, in consideration of the eggs, would, if Spotty actually attacked her, sit upon him; that she would not actually let her be bitten. Behind Mrs. Ticknor the close room swarmed with children—children with gaping, grinning faces, some of them with impudent faces, but most of them placidly inert like their mother. The Ticknors represented the very doldrums of humanity. None of them worked nor progressed, except the father, who occasionally could be induced to do a little work for the neighbors when the supplies ran too low and actual starvation became a temporary goad. Today he was plowing for a farmer, plodding lazily along behind a heavy old horse. He could scarcely be said to be working. Emmeline was glad that he was not at home. Sometimes he had been drinking considerable hard cider, and although he never spoke to her, the hard red in his face disturbed her; also the glassy stare of his stupid eyes.

"Mother sent these eggs," said Emmeline in a small, weak voice. Mrs. Ticknor took them with an inarticulate note of thanks, like a dumb beast. The children stared and grinned and gaped. All the dingy room seemed full of staring eyes and gaping, grinning mouths. The little dog yelped viciously, louder and louder. It was incredible of what a crescendo that small dog was capable. Emmeline pinned her faith on Mrs. Ticknor's coming to her rescue in case of an actual assault, but every minute she expected to feel the needlelike teeth in her ankle. All her flesh shrank and quivered. It seemed as if Mrs. Ticknor would never find a dish in which to deposit the eggs. Finally she did, however, and Emmeline took her basket. The little dog followed, with his circling war dance and his crescendo of yelps, to the curve of the road. Then, as was invariably the case, he turned suddenly and ran home, as if with a sudden conviction that the game was not worth the candle.

Then Emmeline toed out, and walked on briskly, her head up; her trial for that day was over.

When she reached home her mother looked at her and her face brightened. "You look so much better for your walk, darling," she said. Then she asked if the Ticknors seemed pleased with the eggs. Emmeline was in a little doubt as to the amount of actual pleasure which the Ticknors had displayed, but she said, "Yes'm."

"It means a great deal to them, poor things," said her mother. "I am so glad we can help them a little, and so glad you can do your part."

"Yes'm," said Emmeline.

The next morning the torture was repeated. It was like a historical promenade between two rows of Indians armed with cruel weapons. However, she survived it, and when she came home both her mother and aunt remarked upon her improved appearance. That was what so misled them. Every morning Emmeline returned from her charitable trip with such a sense of momentary relief that her face was naturally brighter than when she started, but all the while she steadily lost ground under the strain. Finally the doctor was called in and a tonic prescribed, and when school began, after the spring vacation, it was decided that Emmeline should remain at home, but try to go on with her class with Aunt Martha's assistance.

"I think nothing except that morning walk to the Ticknors', to carry eggs, keeps the poor child up, anyway," said

Emmeline's mother, who had followed the doctor to the door.

"I dare say," he replied. "Keep her out in the fresh air all you can, and send her on errands that interest her."

"That does interest her," said Mrs. Ames. "She is so pleased to think she is helping those poor Ticknors, dear little thing."

Emmeline overheard what was said; the door was slightly ajar. There was a curious little twitch about her sensitive mouth. Troubled as she was, she saw the humor in the situation. The very thing which was making her ill her mother regarded as her chief medicine.

It seemed strange that Emmeline did not tell her mother of her true state of mind. The expeditions would have been at once stopped. She did not tell her, however, and probably for reasons which she did not herself understand. There is in every complete personality a side which is dark except toward its own self and God, and Emmeline realized this dark side in herself, although vaguely. She knew perfectly well that nobody, not even her mother, who loved her, could understand rightly this dark side, which was sacred to herself. She knew that if she told her mother how afraid she was of that little Ticknor dog she would be petted and comforted, and would never have to face the terror again; and yet she knew that her mother would secretly laugh over her and not comprehend how she felt, and it seemed to her that she could not face that. She would rather face the dog.

So she continued carrying the eggs and praying, and the little dog continued barking at her and snapping at her heels and tugging at her dress, and she took the doctor's medicine, and yet she grew paler and thinner, and slept less, and ate less, and her mother and aunt thought that the daily walk in the open was all that kept the child up. Then, three weeks after she first began her charitable trips, something happened.

It was almost the 1st of April, but the spring was very late, and that Wednesday morning had seemed to suffer an actual relapse into winter. The northwest wind blew cold, as if from northern snow and ice fields; the ground was frozen hard, and the farmers had been obliged to quit their plowing, which they had begun on mild days. The long furrows in a field which Emmeline had to pass before she reached the curve in the road lay stretched out stiff and rigid like dead men. In the midst of that field stood a little corn house, the door of which was open. Emmeline glanced casually across the field as she lagged along. She still wore her little red coat and hat, under which her soft fleece of blond hair flew before the wind like a flag. She glanced casually; then her heart gave a great leap and seemed to stand still.

Over that rigid field she had seen a little live object scamper and make straight for that corn house, which he entered, doubtless in pursuit of some smaller, swifter thing which she could not see, possibly a field mouse or a mole. Emmeline knew the pursuer to be the Ticknor dog. A thought leaped into her brain—a thought so wild and audacious that she could not entirely harbor it for a second. Then all her faculties rose to action. Down on the ground she set her basket of eggs. Over the fence, with its tangle of leafless vines, she went, and across the field she raced, her little feet skipping from furrow to furrow, her hair streaming. She reached the corn house, and grasped the door, swinging outward and creaking in the cold wind, with a grasp of despair. She slammed it to, and fastened it. Emmeline at last had her enemy safe in prison. An angry bark and a scratching assailed her ears as she sped back to the road, but Spotty could not get loose. She was sure of that. It was a strong little house.

Emmeline took up her basket of eggs and went on. Nobody had seen her. This was a lonely spot in the road. A mad exultation filled her heart. For the first time she was going to the Ticknors' without fear clutching her, body and soul. When she rounded the curve in the road and came in sight of the squalid little group of buildings they looked almost beautiful to her. She fairly laughed to herself. She almost danced as she went on. When she reached the house and Mrs. Ticknor opened the door as usual she saw for the first time what a really lovely little face the next little girl to the baby had, in spite of dirt. She smiled as she delivered the eggs, and stood beaming while Mrs. Ticknor emptied the basket and returned it. She had no need to look about or listen for any little spiteful animal now. She was quite safe. She went home light-footed. She was quite rosy when she reached there.

"The dear child is really better," her aunt said to her mother when Emmeline had gone to put away her outdoor wraps.

"Yes," said Mrs. Ames, "she certainly does look better, and I do believe it is nothing but that walk every morning in the fresh air has done her good."

"I think so, too," said Martha. "I think it has done her much more good than the doctor's medicine."

Poor Martha herself looked, in spite of her pride and her high carriage of head, as if she needed some helpful tonic for either soul or body, or both. She had grown thinner, and although she smiled, the smile did not look spontaneous. In these days Martha smiled mechanically and only with her lips. Her lips curved prettily, but her eyes remained serious and thoughtful, even while she spoke about Emmeline's looking better.

Emmeline did, in reality, seem better all that day. She even asked for luncheon between breakfast and noon. She slept well that night. She ate her breakfast with an appetite the next morning, and set out even merrily on her errand to the Ticknors'. It was still cold, and the northwest wind had not gone down. It had raged all night. When she came to the field in which the corn house stood the door was closed fast; no one was at work, and the plow ridges which later on would be green with waving flags of corn lay stiffly like dead men, as they had done the day before. Emmeline looked at the corn house. She thought, but she was not quite sure, that she heard a little plaintive sound, something between a whine and yelp. When she returned she was quite sure. She knew that she heard it. Her face sobered. When she reached home her mother and aunt exchanged glances, and her mother went into the kitchen to tell Annie to make some beef tea. Emmeline had to drink a cup of it when it was made. Her mother and aunt had agreed, with dismay, that she did not look so well as she had done the day before.

She looked still worse as the day wore on and the days wore on. During three days Emmeline suffered tortures of remorse with regards to the little dog shut up in the corn house and perhaps starving to death, unless there might be some scattered corn left over from the year before, or rats. Emmeline was not quite sure as to whether Spotty would eat rats, even if reduced to starvation. She astonished her mother on the evening of the second day by inquiring, apropos of nothing at all, "Mother, do dogs ever eat rats?" And when both her mother and aunt seemed unable to answer positively in the affirmative, her little face took on an expression of white misery which amazed them. After Emmeline had gone to bed that night her mother told her aunt that if the child was not better before long she should call in another doctor.

It was horrible for Emmeline during those mornings to pass that corn house, with its shut door and desolate field. She felt like a murderess. She was not quite sure whether she heard Spotty's plaintive whine. She wondered if he were dead and she had killed him.

It was the evening of the third day that Emmeline made up her mind. Chance favored her. Annie had forgotten to order a yeast-cake, and the fact was mentioned in her presence just before supper. Annie said that she would go to the store after supper and get it, for she must mix bread that night. Then Emmeline spoke eagerly:

"Mother, can't I go? There is plenty of time before supper. Please let me go."

Her aunt abetted her. "I would let her go if I were you," she said. "She will sleep better. The air is lovely, although it is frosty for this time of year." Martha had just come from a walk to the post office. "There I have been right in the store, and could have got it if I had known," she said; "but I do think it will do Emmeline good to run out, and it will not be dark until after she gets back."

So Emmeline went. She had mysteriously tucked up the sleeve of her red coat a little parcel which contained two chicken bones. They were nice little chicken bones, wrapped in white paper. She carried also her little purse, in which she had some money of her own besides the pennies which her mother had given her to buy the yeast with.

Emmeline flashed out of sight of the house windows, a swift little figure in red.

"I can't make her out at all," Emmeline's mother said. "There she has seemed all down in the dumps for two days and a half, and all of a sudden she is as eager to go to the store as I ever saw her about anything in her life. Her eyes looked as bright as stars."

"If she were grown up, I should think she had something on her mind," Martha said, reflectively.

"Now, Martha, what nonsense! What can that baby, with everything done for her, have on her mind?"

"Of course she cannot," said Martha, but her eyes were reflective.

Meantime, Emmeline sped on her way. The store was on a street at right angles to the one leading to the Ticknors', which opened just before the field with the corn house was reached. Emmeline hurried to the store, bought the yeast-cake, and also with her own money a little paper bag of sweet crackers. Then swiftly, without a moment's hesitation, she ran back to the other road and across the field to the corn house. She listened for just one second before opening the door. She heard a little whine—not a bark, but a whine. Then she opened the door, and no soldier charging the enemy ever required more spirit than she; but open it she did. She held out the chicken bones. Then she flung them at poor Spotty, emerging trailingly from the dusty interior. Spotty caught at the little bones and crunched them down. Then Emmeline fed him with the sweet crackers. She put one on the ground. Then, as the little animal caught it up, a feeling of great love and pity overcame her. All at once she loved that which she had feared. She fed Spotty the rest of the sweet crackers from her little red-mittened hand, and did not have the slightest quiver of terror, even when the sharp little teeth were so near her fingers.

After the crackers were all gone, Emmeline started homeward, and Spotty followed her. He bounded around her, leaping up, barking with joy. He was a poor little mongrel, and from heredity and poor training he had lacked the better traits of his kind. He had been mischievous, cowardly, and malicious. He had loved nobody. But now he loved Emmeline for setting him free and giving him food. He knew nothing of the injury which she had done him. He was conscious only of the benefit. So he followed her, as he had never followed any of the Ticknors. They, in truth, had never cared for him. They had simply been too indolent and too indifferent to turn him adrift when, a poor canine wanderer, he had located himself with them uninvited. But this was different. He loved this little girl, who had opened his prison door and fed him with nice chicken bones and sweet crackers. He had suffered, and she had come to his aid. He was still thirsty, but thirst also would be satisfied by her. He followed her with joyful faith across the field. When they reached the road leading to the store a man emerged thence, walking hurriedly. Emmeline knew him at once. He was Mr. John Adams.

John spoke to Emmeline in a confused sort of way. "Oh, it is you, Emmeline!" he said.

"Yes, sir," replied Emmeline.

"How are your mother and aunt?"

"Pretty well, I thank you."

"Have you been to supper?"

"No, sir."

Mr. John Adams hesitated still more. "Well," he said, "I had my supper early, and so, and so—"

Emmeline glanced up at him, and saw to her amazement that his face was burning red, and he was smiling foolishly.

"I thought," he said, finally, "that I would run up to your house this evening and—I thought I would go early, because —I happened to think it was the evening for prayer meeting, and I didn't know but she—your mother and aunt might be going, and—I thought if they were—if I went early, I would go along with them."

"Mother and Aunt Martha aren't going to meeting. I heard them say so," said Emmeline. Then she added, out of the innocence of her soul: "I know Aunt Martha will be real glad to see you."

"Do you think she will?" asked Mr. John Adams, eagerly.

"Yes, sir."

"I wonder how you would like it if I should come and

live in your house, with you and your mother and aunt?"
said John Adams.

Emmeline slipped her little hand into his. "I think it
would be real nice," she said.

"You dear little soul!" said Mr. John Adams. He
squeezed her hand in his big strong one. "Is that your dog,
little one?" he asked.

"No, sir."

"I didn't know but you had been getting a pet dog since
I was at your house."

"That is the Ticknor dog; he followed me." Just then
the dog leaped up, and Emmeline patted his head, laughing.

"He is a mongrel, but he seems a bright little dog," said
Mr. John Adams. "I should think you would keep him.
He can't have a very good home at the Ticknors'."

"I am going to if mother will let me," said Emmeline,
with sudden resolve.

The little triumphal procession went on its way. The west
was a clear cold red. They passed a field in which stood
scattered stacks of last year's corn. In the shadow the
withered blades had a curious vivid crudeness of something
which was rather tone than color. They gleamed out like
newly cut wood, like naked flesh. They were elemental,
belonging to the first: dry death, for which there are no
paints on the palette, any more than for light and air and
sentient life. But where the red western glow struck these
blades of corn they were lit with brilliant reflections, and
seemed to leap into flames of red gold.

In the sky was faintly visible a filmy arc of new moon.
A great star was slowly gathering light near it. Emmeline
danced along, holding to Mr. John Adams' hand. Her head
was up. Her whole face laughed. The little dog raced
ahead; he ran back; he leaped and barked short joyous
barks. They were all conquerors, by that might of spiritual
panoply of love with which they had been born equipped.

There was the dog, in whom love had conquered brute spite and maliciousness; the man in whom love had conquered self-will. But the child was the greatest conqueror of the three, for in her love had conquered fear, which is in all creation its greatest foe, being love's own antithesis.

# IV. *A NEW ENGLAND NUN* [1]

IT was late in the afternoon, and the light was waning. There was a difference in the look of the tree shadows out in the yard. Somewhere in the distance cows were lowing and a little bell was tinkling; now and then a farm wagon tilted by, and the dust flew; some blue-shirted laborers with shovels over their shoulders plodded past; little swarms of flies were dancing up and down before the people's faces in the soft air. There seemed to be a gentle stir arising over everything for the mere sake of subsidence—a very premonition of rest and hush and night.

This soft diurnal commotion was over Louisa Ellis also. She had been peacefully sewing at her sitting-room window all the afternoon. Now she quilted her needle carefully into her work, which she folded precisely, and laid in a basket with her thimble and thread and scissors. Louisa Ellis could not remember that ever in her life she had mislaid one of these little feminine appurtenances, which had become, from long use and constant association, a very part of her personality.

Louisa tied a green apron round her waist, and got out a flat straw hat with a green ribbon. Then she went into the garden with a little blue crockery bowl, to pick some currants for her tea. After the currants were picked she sat on the back doorstep and stemmed them, collecting the stems carefully in her apron and afterward throwing them into the hencoop. She looked sharply at the grass beside the step to see if any had fallen there.

Louisa was slow and still in her movements; it took her a long time to prepare her tea; but when ready it was set forth with as much grace as if she had been a veritable guest to her own self. The little square table stood exactly in the center of the kitchen, and was covered with a starched linen cloth whose border pattern of flowers glistened. Louisa had a damask napkin on her tea tray, where were arranged a cut-glass tumbler full of teaspoons, a silver cream pitcher, a china sugar bowl, and one pink china cup and saucer. Louisa used china every day—something which none of her neighbors did. They whispered about it among themselves. Their daily tables were laid with common crockery, their sets of best china stayed in the parlor closet, and Louisa Ellis was no richer nor better bred than they. Still she would use the china. She had for her supper a glass dish full of sugared currants, a plate of little cakes, and one of light white biscuits. Also a leaf or two of lettuce, which she cut up daintily. Louisa was very fond of lettuce, which she raised to perfection in her little garden. She ate quite heartily, though in a delicate, pecking way; it seemed almost surprising that any considerable bulk of the food should vanish.

After tea she filled a plate with nicely baked thin corn cakes, and carried them out into the back yard.

"Cæsar!" she called. "Cæsar! Cæsar!"

There was a little rush, and the clank of a chain, and a large yellow-and-white dog appeared at the door of his tiny hut, which was half hidden among the tall grasses and flowers. Louisa patted him and gave him the corn cakes. Then she returned to the house and washed the tea things, polishing the china carefully. The twilight had deepened; the chorus of the frogs floated in at the open window wonderfully loud and shrill, and once in a while a long sharp drone from a tree toad pierced it. Louisa took off her green gingham apron, disclosing a shorter one of pink-

and-white print. She lighted her lamp, and sat down again with her sewing.

In about half an hour Joe Dagget came. She heard his heavy step on the walk, and rose and took off her pink-and-white apron. Under that was still another—white linen with a little cambric edging on the bottom; that was Louisa's company apron. She never wore it without her calico sewing apron over it unless she had a guest. She had barely folded the pink-and-white one with methodical haste and laid it in a table drawer when the door opened and Joe Dagget entered.

He seemed to fill up the whole room. A little yellow canary that had been asleep in his green cage at the south window woke up and fluttered wildly, beating his little yellow wings against the wires. He always did so when Joe Dagget came into the room.

"Good evening," said Louisa. She extended her hand with a kind of solemn cordiality.

"Good evening, Louisa," returned the man, in a loud voice.

She placed a chair for him, and they sat facing each other, with the table between them. He sat bolt upright, toeing out his heavy feet squarely, glancing with a good-humored uneasiness around the room. She sat gently erect, folding her slender hands in her white-linen lap.

"Been a pleasant day," remarked Dagget.

"Real pleasant," Louisa assented, softly. "Have you been haying?" she asked, after a little while.

"Yes, I've been haying all day, down in the ten-acre lot. Pretty hot work."

"It must be."

"Yes, it's pretty hot work in the sun."

"Is your mother well today?"

"Yes, mother's pretty well."

"I suppose Lily Dyer's with her now?"

Dagget colored. "Yes, she's with her," he answered, slowly.

He was not very young, but there was a boyish look about his large face. Louisa was not quite so old as he, her face was fairer and smoother, but she gave people the impression of being older.

"I suppose she's a good deal of help to your mother," she said, further.

"I guess she is; I don't know how mother'd get along without her," said Dagget, with a sort of embarrassed warmth.

"She looks like a real capable girl. She's pretty-looking too," remarked Louisa.

"Yes, she is pretty fair looking."

Presently Dagget began fingering the books on the table. There was a square red autograph album, and a Young Lady's Gift Book which had belonged to Louisa's mother. He took them up one after the other and opened them; then laid them down again, the album on the Gift Book.

Louisa kept eyeing them with mild uneasiness. Finally she rose and changed the position of the books, putting the album underneath. That was the way they had been arranged in the first place.

Dagget gave an awkward little laugh. "Now what difference did it make which book was on top?" said he.

Louisa looked at him with a deprecating smile. "I always keep them that way," murmured she.

"You do beat everything," said Dagget, trying to laugh again. His large face was flushed.

He remained about an hour longer, then rose to take leave. Going out, he stumbled over a rug, and trying to recover himself, hit Louisa's work basket on the table, and knocked it on the floor.

He looked at Louisa, then at the rolling spools; he ducked himself awkwardly toward them, but she stopped him. "Never mind," said she; "I'll pick them up after you're gone."

She spoke with a mild stiffness. Either she was a little disturbed, or his nervousness affected her and made her seem constrained in her effort to reassure him.

When Joe Dagget was outside he drew in the sweet evening air with a sigh, and felt much as an innocent and perfectly well-intentioned bear might after his exit from a china shop.

Louisa, on her part, felt much as the kind-hearted, long-suffering owner of the china shop might have done after the exit of the bear.

She tied on the pink, then the green apron, picked up all the scattered treasures and replaced them in her work basket, and straightened the rug. Then she set the lamp on the floor and began sharply examining the carpet. She even rubbed her fingers over it, and looked at them.

"He's tracked in a good deal of dust," she murmured. "I thought he must have."

Louisa got a dustpan and brush, and swept Joe Dagget's track carefully.

If he could have known it, it would have increased his perplexity and uneasiness, although it would not have disturbed his loyalty in the least. He came twice a week to see Louisa Ellis, and every time, sitting there in her delicately sweet room, he felt as if surrounded by a hedge of lace. He was afraid to stir lest he should put a clumsy foot or hand through the fairy web, and he had always the consciousness that Louisa was watching fearfully lest he should.

Still the lace and Louisa commanded perforce his perfect respect and patience and loyalty. They were to be married in a month, after a singular courtship which had lasted for a matter of fifteen years. For fourteen out of the fifteen years the two had not once seen each other, and they had seldom exchanged letters. Joe had been all those years in Australia, where he had gone to make his fortune, and where he had stayed until he made it. He would have stayed fifty years if it had taken so long, and come home feeble and tottering, or never come home at all, to marry Louisa.

But the fortune had been made in the fourteen years, and he had come home now to marry the woman who had been patiently and unquestioningly waiting for him all that time.

Shortly after they were engaged he had announced to Louisa his determination to strike out into new fields and secure a competency before they should be married. She had listened and assented with the sweet serenity which never failed her, not even when her lover set forth on that long and uncertain journey. Joe, buoyed up as he was by his study determination, broke down a little at the last, but Louisa kissed him with a mild blush, and said good-by.

"It won't be for long," poor Joe had said, huskily; but it was for fourteen years.

In that length of time much had happened. Louisa's mother and brother had died, and she was all alone in the world. But greatest happening of all—a subtle happening which both were too simple to understand—Louisa's feet had turned into a path, smooth maybe under a calm, serene sky, but so straight and unswerving that it could only meet a check at her grave, and so narrow that there was no room for anyone at her side.

Louisa's first emotion when Joe Dagget came home (he had not apprised her of his coming) was consternation, although she would not admit it to herself, and he never dreamed of it. Fifteen years ago she had been in love with him—at least she considered herself to be. Just at that time, gently acquiescing with and falling into the natural drift of girlhood, she had seen marriage ahead as a reasonable feature and a probable desirability of life. She had listened with calm docility to her mother's views upon the subject. Her mother was remarkable for her cool sense and sweet, even temperament. She talked wisely to her daughter when Joe Dagget presented himself, and Louisa accepted him with no hesitation. He was the first lover she had ever had.

She had been faithful to him all these years. She had never dreamed of the possibility of marrying anyone else. Her life, especially for the last seven years, had been full of a pleasant peace; she had never felt discontented nor impatient over her lover's absence; still, she had always looked forward to his return and their marriage as the inevitable conclusion of things. However, she had fallen into a way of placing it so far in the future that it was almost equal to placing it over the boundaries of another life.

When Joe came she had been expecting him, and expecting to be married for fourteen years, but she was as much surprised and taken aback as if she had never thought of it.

Joe's consternation came later. He eyed Louisa with an instant confirmation of his old admiration. She had changed but little. She still kept her pretty manner and soft grace, and was, he considered, every whit as attractive as ever. As for himself, his stent was done; he had turned his face away from fortune seeking, and the old winds of romance whistled as loud and sweet as ever through his ears. All the song which he had been wont to hear in them was Louisa; he had for a long time a loyal belief that he heard it still, but finally it seemed to him that although the winds sang always that one song, it had another name. But for Louisa the wind had never more than murmured; now it had gone down, and everything was still. She listened for a little while with half-wistful attention;

then she turned quietly away and went to work on her wedding clothes.

Joe had made some extensive and quite magnificent altera-tions in his house. It was the old homestead; the newly-married couple would live there, for Joe could not desert his mother, who refused to leave her old home. So Louisa must leave hers. Every morning, rising and going about among her neat maidenly possessions, she felt as one look-ing her last upon the faces of dear friends. It was true that in a measure she could take them with her, but, robbed of their old environments, they would appear in such new guises that they would almost cease to be themselves.

Then there were some peculiar features of her happy soli-tary life which she would probably be obliged to relinquish altogether. Sterner tasks than these graceful but half-need-less ones would probably devolve upon her. There would be a large house to care for; there would be company to entertain; there would be Joe's rigorous and feeble old mother to wait upon; and it would be contrary to all thrifty village traditions for her to keep more than one servant.

Louisa had a little still, and she used to occupy herself pleasantly in summer weather with distilling the sweet and aromatic essences from roses and peppermint and spearmint. By-and-by her still must be laid away. Her store of es-sences was already considerable, and there would be no time for her to distill for the mere pleasure of it. Then Joe's mother would think it foolishness; she had already hinted her opinion in the matter.

Louisa dearly loved to sew a linen seam, not always for use, but for the simple, mild pleasure which she took in it. She would have been loath to confess how more than once she had ripped a seam for the mere delight of sewing it together again. Sitting at her window during long sweet afternoons, drawing her needle gently through the dainty fabric, she was peace itself. But there was small chance of such foolish comfort in the future. Joe's mother, domineering, shrewd old matron that she was even in her old age, and very likely even Joe himself, with his honest masculine rudeness, would laugh and frown down all these pretty but senseless old maiden ways.

Louisa had almost the enthusiasm of an artist over the mere order and cleanliness of her solitary home. She had throbs of genuine triumph at the sight of the windowpanes which she had polished until they shone like jewels. She gloated gently over her orderly bureau drawers, with their exquisitely folded contents redolent with lavender and sweet clover and very purity. Could she be sure of the endurance of even this? She had visions, so startling that she half repudiated them as indelicate, of coarse masculine belongings strewn about in endless litter; of dust and disorder arising necessarily from a coarse masculine presence in the midst of all this delicate harmony.

Among her forebodings of disturbance, not the least was with regard to Cæsar. Cæsar was a veritable hermit of a dog. For the greater part of his life he had dwelt in his secluded hut, shut out from the society of his kind and all innocent canine joys. Never had Cæsar since his early youth watched at a woodchuck's hole; never had he known the delights of a stray bone at a neighbor's kitchen door. And it was all on account of a sin committed when hardly out of his puppyhood. No one knew the possible depth of remorse of which this mild-visaged, altogether innocent-looking old dog might be capable; but whether or not he had encountered remorse, he had encountered a full measure of righteous retribution. Old Cæsar seldom lifted up his voice in a growl or a bark; he was fat and sleepy; there were yellow rings which looked like spectacles around his dim old eyes; but there was a neighbor who bore on his hand the imprint of several of Cæsar's sharp white youthful teeth, and for that he had lived at the end of a chain, all alone in a little hut, for fourteen years. The neighbor, who was choleric and smarting with the pain of his wound, had demanded either Cæsar's death or complete ostracism. So Louisa's brother, to whom the dog had belonged, had built him his little kennel and tied him up. It was now fourteen years since, in a flood of youthful spirits, he had inflicted that memorable bite, and with the exception of short excursions, always at the end of the chain, under the strict guardianship of his master or Louisa, the old dog had remained a close prisoner. It is doubtful if, with his limited ambition, he took much pride in the fact, but it is certain that he was possessed of considerable cheap fame. He was regarded by all the children in the village and by many adults as a very monster of ferocity. St. George's dragon could hardly have surpassed in evil repute Louisa Ellis's old yellow dog. Mothers charged their children with solemn emphasis not to go too near to him, and the children listened and believed greedily, with a fascinated appetite for terror, and ran by Louisa's house stealthily, with many sidelong and backward glances at the terrible dog. If perchance he sounded a hoarse bark, there was a panic. Wayfarers chancing into Louisa's yard eyed him with respect, and inquired if the chain were stout. Cæsar at large might have seemed a very ordinary dog and excited no comment whatever; chained, his reputation overshadowed him, so that he lost his own proper outlines and looked darkly vague and enormous. Joe Dagget, however, with his good-humored sense and shrewdness, saw him as he was. He strode valiantly up to him and patted him on the head, in spite of Louisa's soft clamor of warning, and even attempted to set him loose. Louisa grew so alarmed that he desisted, but kept announcing his opinion in the matter quite forcibly at intervals. "There ain't a better-natured dog in town," he would say, "and it's downright cruel to keep him tied up there. Some day I'm going to take him out."

Louisa had very little hope that he would not, one of these days, when their interests and possessions should be more completely fused in one. She pictured to herself Cæsar on the rampage through the quiet and unguarded village. She saw innocent children bleeding in his path. She was herself very fond of the old dog, because he had belonged to her dead brother, and he was always very gentle with her; still she had great faith in his ferocity. She always warned people not to go too near him. She fed him on ascetic fare of corn mush and cakes, and never fired his dangerous temper with heating and sanguinary diet of flesh and bones. Louisa looked at the old dog munching his simple fare, and thought of her approaching marriage and trembled. Still no anticipation of disorder and confusion in lieu of sweet peace and harmony, no forebodings of Cæsar on the rampage, no wild fluttering of her little yellow canary, were sufficient to turn her a hair's-breadth. Joe Dagget had been fond of her and working for her all these years. It was not for her, whatever came to pass, to prove untrue and break his heart. She put the exquisite little stitches into her wedding garments, and the time went on until it was only a week before her wedding day. It was a Tuesday evening, and the wedding was to be a week from Wednesday.

There was a full moon that night. About nine o'clock Louisa strolled down the road a little way. There were harvest fields on either hand, bordered by low stone walls. Luxuriant clumps of bushes grew beside the wall, and trees —wild cherry and old apple trees—at intervals. Presently Louisa sat down on the wall and looked about her with mildly sorrowful reflectiveness. Tall shrubs of blueberry and meadow-sweet, all woven together and tangled with backberry vines and horsebriers, shut her in on either side.

She had a little clear space between them. Opposite her, on the other side of the road, was a spreading tree; the moon shone between its boughs, and the leaves twinkled like silver. The road was bespread with a beautiful shifting dapple of silver and shadow; the air was full of a mysterious sweetness. "I wonder if it's wild grapes?" murmured Louisa. She sat there some time. She was just thinking of rising, when she heard footsteps and low voices, and remained quiet. It was a lonely place, and she felt a little timid. She thought she would keep still in the shadow and let the persons, whoever they might be, pass her.

But just before they reached her the voices ceased, and the footsteps. She understood that their owners had also found seats upon the stone wall. She was wondering if she could not steal away unobserved, when the voice broke the stillness. It was Joe Dagget's. She sat still and listened.

The voice was announced by a loud sigh, which was as familiar as itself. "Well," said Dagget, "you've made up your mind, then, I suppose?"

"Yes," returned another voice; "I'm going day after tomorrow."

"That's Lily Dyer," thought Louisa to herself. The voice embodied itself in her mind. She saw a girl tall and full-figured, with a firm, fair face, looking fairer and firmer in the moonlight, her strong yellow hair braided in a close knot. A girl full of a calm rustic strength and bloom, with a masterful way which might have beseemed a princess. Lily Dyer was a favorite with the village folk; she had just the qualities to arouse the admiration. She was good and handsome and smart. Louisa had often heard her praises sounded.

"Well," said Joe Dagget, "I ain't got a word to say."

"I don't know what you could say," returned Lily Dyer.

"Not a word to say," repeated Joe, drawing out the words heavily. Then there was a silence. "I ain't sorry," he began at last, "that that happened yesterday—that we kind of let on how we felt to each other. I guess it's just as well we knew. Of course I can't do anything any different. I'm going right on an' get married next week. I ain't going back on a woman that's waited for me fourteen years, an' break her heart."

"If you should jilt her tomorrow, I wouldn't have you," spoke up the girl, with sudden vehemence.

"Well, I ain't going to give you the chance," said he; "but I don't believe you would, either."

"You'd see I wouldn't. Honor's honor, an' right's right. An' I'd never think anything of any man that went against 'em for me or any other girl; you'd find that out, Joe Dagget."

"Well, you'll find out fast enough that I ain't going against 'em for you or any other girl," returned he. Their voices sounded almost as if they were angry with each other. Louisa was listening eagerly.

"I'm sorry you feel as if you must go away," said Joe, "but I don't know but it's best."

"Of course it's best. I hope you and I have got common sense."

"Well, I suppose you're right." Suddenly Joe's voice got an undertone of tenderness. "Say, Lily," said he, "I'll get along well enough myself, but I can't bear to think— You don't suppose you're going to fret much over it?"

"I guess you'll find out I shan't fret much over a married man."

"Well, I hope you won't—I hope you won't, Lily. God knows I do. And—I hope—one of these days—you'll— come across somebody else—"

"I don't see any reason why I shouldn't." Suddenly her tone changed. She spoke in a sweet, clear voice, so loud that she could have been heard across the street. "No, Joe Dagget," said she, "I'll never marry any other man as long as I live. I've got good sense, an' I ain't going to break my heart nor make a fool of myself; but I'm never going to be married, you can be sure of that. I ain't that sort of a girl to feel this way twice."

Louisa heard an exclamation and a soft commotion behind the bushes; then Lily spoke again—the voice sounded as if she had risen. "This must be put a stop to," said she. "We've stayed here long enough. I'm going home."

Louisa sat there in a daze, listening to their retreating steps. After a while she got up and slunk softly home herself. The next day she did her housework methodically; that was as much a matter of course as breathing; but she did not sew on her wedding clothes. She sat at her window and meditated. In the evening Joe came. Louisa Ellis had never known that she had any diplomacy in her, but when she came to look for it that night she found it, although meek of its kind, among her little feminine weapons. Even now she could hardly believe that she had heard aright, and that she would not do Joe a terrible injury should she break her troth plight. She wanted to sound him without betraying too soon her own inclinations in the matter. She did it successfully, and they finally came to an understanding; but it was a difficult thing, for he was as afraid of betraying himself as she.

She never mentioned Lily Dyer. She simply said that while she had no cause of complaint against him, she had lived so long in one way that she shrank from making a change.

"Well, I never shrank, Louisa," said Dagget. "I'm going to be honest enough to say that I think maybe it's better this way; but if you'd wanted to keep on, I'd have stuck to you till my dying day. I hope you know that."

"Yes, I do," said she.

That night she and Joe parted more tenderly than they had done for a long time. Standing in the door, holding each other's hands, a last great wave of regretful memory swept over them.

"Well, this ain't the way we've thought it was all going to end, is it, Louisa?" said Joe.

She shook her head. There was a little quiver on her placid face.

"You let me know if there's ever anything I can do for you," said he. "I ain't ever going to forget you, Louisa." Then he kissed her, and went down the path.

Louisa, all alone by herself that night, wept a little, she hardly knew why; but the next morning, on waking, she felt like a queen who, after fearing lest her domain be wrested away from her, sees it firmly insured in her possession.

Now the tall weeds and grasses might cluster around Cæsar's little hermit hut, the snow might fall on its roof year in and year out, but he never would go on a rampage through the unguarded village. Now the little canary might turn itself into a peaceful yellow ball night after night, and have no need to wake and flutter with wild terror against its bars. Louisa could sew linen seams, and distill roses, and dust and polish and fold away in lavender, as long as she listed. That afternoon she sat with her needlework at the window, and felt fairly steeped in peace. Lily Dyer, tall and erect and blooming, went past; but she felt no qualm. If Louisa Ellis had sold her birthright she did not know it; the taste of the pottage was so delicious, and had been her sole satisfaction for so long. Serenity and placid narrowness had become to her as the birthright itself. She gazed ahead through a long reach of future days strung together like pearls in a rosary, every one like the others, and all smooth and flawless and innocent, and her heart went up in thankfulness. Outside was the fervid summer afternoon; the air was filled with the sounds of the busy harvest of men and birds and bees; there were halloos, metallic clatterings, sweet calls, and long hummings. Louisa sat, prayerfully numbering her days, like an uncloistered nun.

# V. ONE GOOD TIME[1]

RICHARD STONE was nearly seventy-five years old when he died; his wife was over sixty, and his daughter Narcissa past middle age. Narcissa Stone had been very pretty, and would have been pretty still had it not been for those lines, as distinctly garrulous of discontent and worry as any words of mouth, which come so easily in the face of a nervous, delicate-skinned woman. They were around Narcissa's blue eyes, her firmly closed lips, her thin nose; a frown like a crying repetition of some old anxiety and indecision was on her forehead; and she had turned her long neck so much to look over her shoulder for new troubles on her track that the lines of fearful expectation had settled there. Narcissa had yet her beautiful thick hair, which the people in the village had never quite liked because it was red; her cheeks were still pink, and she stooped only a little from her slender height when she walked. Some people said that Narcissa Stone would be quite good-looking now if she had a decent dress and bonnet. Neither she nor her mother had any clothes which were not deemed shabby, even by the humbly attired women in the little mountain village. "Mis' Richard Stone, she ain't had a new silk dress since Narcissa was born," they said; "and as for Narcissa, she ain't never had anything that looked fit to wear to meeting."

When Richard Stone died, people wondered if his widow and Narcissa would not have something new. Mrs. Nathan Wheat, who was a third cousin to Richard Stone, went, the day before the funeral, a half mile down the brook road to see Hannah Turbin, the dressmaker. The road was little

[1] *Copyright, 1900, by Mary E. Wilkins.*

traveled; she walked through an undergrowth of late autumn flowers, and when she reached the Turbins' house her black Thibet gown was gold-powdered and white-flecked to the knees with pollen and winged seeds of passed flowers.

Hannah Turbin's arm, brown and wrinkled like a monkey's, in its woolen sleeve, described arcs of jerky energy past the window, and never ceased when Mrs. Wheat came up the path and entered the house. Hannah herself scarcely raised her seamy brown face from her work.

"Good afternoon," said Mrs. Wheat.

Hannah nodded. "Good afternoon," she responded then, as if words were an after-thought.

Mrs. Wheat shook her black skirts vigorously. "I'm all over dust from them yaller weeds," said she. "Well, I don't care about this old Thibet." She pulled a rocking-chair forward and seated herself. "Warm for this time of year," said she.

Hannah drew her thread through her work. "Yes, 'tis," she returned, with a certain pucker of scorn, as if the utter foolishness of allusions to obvious conditions of nature struck her. Hannah Turbin was not a favorite in the village, but she was credited with having much common sense, and people held her in somewhat distant respect.

"Guess it's Injun summer," remarked Mrs. Wheat.

Hannah Turbin said nothing at all to that. Mrs. Wheat cast furtive glances around the room as she swayed in her rocking-chair. Everything was very tidy and there were few indications of its owner's calling. A number of fashion papers were neatly piled on a bureau in the corner, and some nicely folded breadths of silk lay beside them. There was not a scrap or shred of cloth upon the floor; not a thread, even. Hannah was basting a brown silk basque. Mrs. Wheat could see nowhere the slightest evidence of what she had come to ascertain, so was finally driven to inquiry, still, however, by devious windings.

"Seems sad about Richard," she said.

"Yes," returned Hannah, with a sudden contraction of her brown face, which seemed to flash a light over a recollection in Mrs. Wheat's mind. She remembered that there was a time, years ago, when Richard Stone had paid some attention to Hannah Turbin, and people had thought he might marry her instead of Jane Basset. However, it had happened so long ago that she did not really believe that Hannah dwelt upon it, and it faded immediately from her own mind.

"Well," said she, with a sigh, "it is a happy release, after all; he's been such a sufferer so long. It's better for him, and it's better for Jane and Narcissa. He's left 'em comfortable; they've got the farm, and his life's insured, you know. Besides, I suppose Narcissa'll marry William Crane now. Most likely they'll rent the farm, and Jane will go and live with Narcissa when she's married. I want to know—"

Hannah Turbin sewed.

"I was wondering," continued Mrs. Wheat, "if Jane and Narcissa wasn't going to have some new black dresses for the funeral. They ain't got a thing that's fit to wear, I know. I don't suppose they've got much money on hand now except what little Richard saved up for his funeral expenses. I know he had a little for that because he told me so, but the life insurance is coming in, and anybody would trust them. There's a nice piece of black cashmere down to the store, a dollar a yard. I didn't know but they'd get dresses off it; but Jane she never tells me anything—anybody'd think she might, seeing as I was poor Richard's cousin; and as for Narcissa, she's as close as her mother."

Hannah Turbin sewed.

"Ain't Jane and Narcissa said anything to you about making them any new black dresses to wear to the funeral?" asked Mrs. Wheat, with desperate directness.

"No, they ain't," replied Hannah Turbin.

"Well, then, all I've got to say is they'd ought to be ashamed of themselves. There they've got fourteen if not fifteen hundred dollars coming in from poor Richard's insurance money, and they ain't even going to get decent clothes to wear to his funeral out of it. They ain't made any plans for new bonnets, I know. It ain't showing proper respect to the poor man. Don't you say so?"

"I suppose folks are their own best judges," said Hannah Turbin, in her conclusive, half-surly fashion, which intimidated most of their neighbors. Mrs. Wheat did not stay much longer. When she went home through the ghostly weeds and grasses of the country road she was almost as indignant with Hannah Turbin as with Jane Stone and Narcissa. "Never saw anybody so close in my life," said she to herself. "Needn't talk if she don't want to. Dun'no' as thar's any harm in my wanting to know if my own third cousin is going to have mourning wore for him."

Mrs. Wheat, when she reached home, got a black shawl which had belonged to her mother out of the chest, where it had lain in camphor, and hung it on the clothesline to air. She also removed a spray of bright velvet flowers from her bonnet, and sewed in its place a black ostrich feather. She found an old crêpe veil, too, and steamed it into stiffness. "I'm going to go to that funeral looking decent, if his own wife and daughter ain't," she told her husband.

"If I wa'n't along, folks would take you for the widder," said Nathan Wheat with a chuckle. Nathan Wheat was rather inclined to be facetious with his wife.

However, Mrs. Wheat was not the only person who attended poor Richard Stone's funeral in suitable attire. Hannah Turbin was black from head to foot; the material, it is true, was not of the conventional mourning kind, but the color was. She wore a black silk gown, a black ladies'-cloth mantle, a black velvet bonnet trimmed with black flowers, and a black lace veil.

"Hannah Turbin looked as if she was dressed in second mourning," Mrs. Wheat said to her husband after the funeral. "I should have thought she'd most have worn some color, seeing as some folks might remember she was disappointed about Richard Stone; but, anyway, it was better than to go looking the way Jane and Narcissa did. There was Jane in that old brown dress, and Narcissa in her green, with a blue flower in her bonnet. I think it was dreadful, and poor Richard leaving them all that money through his dying, too."

In truth, all the village was scandalized at the strange attire of the widow and daughter of Richard Stone at his funeral, except William Crane. He could not have told what Mrs. Stone wore, through scarcely admitting her in any guise into his inmost consciousness, and as for Narcissa, he admitted her so fully that he could not see her robes at all in such a dazzlement of vision.

"William Crane never took his eyes off Narcissa Stone all through the funeral; shouldn't be surprised if he married her in a month or six weeks," people said.

William Crane took Jane and Narcissa to the grave in his covered wagon, keeping his old white horse at a decorous jog behind the hearse in the little funeral procession, and people noted that. They wondered if he would go over to the Stones' that evening, and watched, but he did not. He left the mother and daughter to their closer communion of grief that night, but the next the neighbors saw him in his best suit going down the road before dark. "Must have done up his chores early to get started soon as this," they said.

William Crane was about Narcissa's age but he looked older. His gait was shuffling, his hair scanty and gray, and, moreover, he had that expression of patience which comes only from long abiding, both of body and of soul. He went through the south yard to the side door of the house, stepping between the rocks. The yard abounded in mossy slopes of half-sunken rocks, as did the entire farm. Folks often remarked of Richard Stone's place, as well as himself, "Stone by name, and stone by nature." Underneath nearly all his fields, cropping plentifully to the surface, were rock ledges. The grass could be mown only by hand. As for this south yard, it required skilful maneuvering to drive a team through it. When William Crane knocked that evening, Narcissa opened the door. "Oh, it's you!" she said. "How do you do?"

"How do you do, Narcissa?" William responded, and walked in. He could have kissed his old love in the gloom of the little entry, but he did not think of that. He looked at her anxiously with his soft, patient eyes. "How are you gettin' on?" he asked.

"Well as can be expected," replied Narcissa.

"How's your mother?"

"She's as well as can be expected."

William followed Narcissa, who led the way, not into the parlor as he had hoped, but into the kitchen. The kitchen's great interior of smoky gloom was very familiar to him, but tonight it looked strange. For one thing, the armchair to which Richard Stone had been bound with his rheumatism for the last fifteen years was vacant, and pushed away into a corner. William looked at it, and it seemed to him that he must see the crooked, stern old figure in it, and hear again the peremptory tap of the stick which he kept always at his side to summon assistance. After his first involuntary glance at the dead man's chair, William saw his widow coming forward out of her bedroom with a great quilt over her arm.

"Good evenin', William," she said, with faint melancholy, then lapsed into feeble weeping.

"Now, mother, you said you wouldn't; you know it don't do any good, and you'll be sick," Narcissa cried out, impatiently.

"I know it, Narcissa, but I can't help it, I can't. I'm dreadful upset! Oh, William, I'm dreadful upset! It ain't his death alone—it's——"

"Mother, I'd rather tell him myself," interrupted Narcissa. She took the quilt from her mother, and drew the rocking chair toward her. "Do sit down and keep calm, mother," said she.

But it was not easy for the older woman, in her bewilderment of grief and change, to keep calm.

"Oh, William, do you know what we're goin' to do?" she wailed, yet seating herself obediently in the rocking chair. "We're goin' to New York. Narcissa says so. We're goin' to take the insurance money, when we get it, an' we're goin' to New York. I tell her we hadn't ought to, but she won't listen to it! There's the trunk. Look at there, William! She dragged it down from the garret this forenoon. Look at there, William!"

William's startled eyes followed the direction of Mrs. Stone's wavering index finger, and saw a great ancient trunk lined with blue-and-white wall paper, standing open against the opposite wall.

"She dragged it down from the garret this forenoon," continued Mrs. Stone, in the same tone of unfaltering tragedy, while Narcissa, her delicate lips pursed tightly, folded up the bed quilt which her mother had brought. "It bumped so hard on those garret stairs I thought she'd break it, or fall herself, but she wouldn't let me help her. Then she cleaned it, an' made some paste, an' lined it with some of the parlor paper. There ain't any key to it—I never remember none. The trunk was in this house when I come here. Richard had it when he went West before we were married. Narcissa she says she is goin' to tie it up with the clothesline. William, can't you talk to her? Seems to me I can't go to New York, nohow."

William turned then to Narcissa, who was laying the folded bed quilt in the trunk. He looked pale and bewildered, and his voice trembled when he spoke. "This ain't true, is it, Narcissa?" he said.

"Yes, it is," she replied, shortly, still bending over the trunk.

"We ain't goin' for a month," interposed her mother again; "we can't get the insurance money before then, Lawyer Maxham says; but she says she's goin' to have the trunk standin' there, an' put things in when she thinks of it, so she won't forgit nothin'. She says we'd better take one bed quilt with us, in case they don't have 'nough clothes on the bed. We've got to stay to a hotel. Oh, William, can't you say anything to stop her?"

"This ain't true, Narcissa?" William repeated, helplessly.

Narcissa raised herself and faced him. Her cheeks were red, her blue eyes glowing, her hair tossing over her temples in loose waves. She looked as she had when he first courted her. "Yes, it is, William Crane," she cried. "Yes, it is."

William looked at her so strangely and piteously that she softened a little. "I've got my reasons," said she. "Maybe I owe it to you to tell them. I suppose you were expecting something different." She hesitated a minute, looking at her mother, who cried out again:

"Oh, William, say somethin' to stop her! Can't you say somethin' to stop her?"

Then Narcissa motioned to him resolutely. "Come into the parlor, William," said she, and he followed her out across the entry. The parlor was chilly; the chairs stood as they had done at the funeral, primly against the walls glimmering faintly in the dusk with blue and white paper like the trunk lining. Narcissa stood before William and talked with feverish haste. "I'm going," said she—"I'm going to take that money and go with mother to New York, and you mustn't try to stop me, William. I know what you've been expecting. I know, now father's gone, you think there ain't anything to hinder our getting married; you think we'll rent this house, and mother and me will settle down in yours for the rest of our lives. I know you ain't counting on that insurance money; it ain't like you."

"The Lord knows it ain't, Narcissa," William broke out with pathetic pride.

"I know that as well as you do. You thought we'd put it in the bank for a rainy day, in case mother got feeble, or anything, and that is all you did think. Maybe I'd ought to. I s'pose I had, but I ain't going to. I ain't never done anything my whole life that I thought I ought not to do, but now I'm going to. I'm going to if it's wicked. I've made up my mind. I ain't never had one good time in my whole life, and now I'm going to even if I have to suffer for it afterward.

"I ain't never had anything like other women. I've never had any clothes nor gone anywhere. I've just stayed at home here and drudged. I've done a man's work on the farm. I've milked and made butter and cheese; I've waited on father; I've got up early and gone to bed late. I've just drudged, drudged, ever since I can remember. I don't know anything about the world nor life. I don't know anything but my own old tracks, and—I'm going to get out of them for a while, whether or no."

"How long are you calculating to stay?"

"I don't know."

"I've been thinking," said William, "I'd have some new gilt paper on the sitting room at my house, and a new stove in the kitchen. I thought——"

"I know what you thought," interrupted Narcissa, still

trembling and glowing with nervous fervor. "And you're real good, William. It ain't many men would have waited for me as you've done, when father wouldn't let me get married as long as he lived. I know by good rights I hadn't ought to keep you waiting, but I'm going to, and it ain't because I don't think enough of you— it ain't that; I can't help it. If you give up having me at all, if you think you'd rather marry somebody else, I can't help it; I won't blame you——"

"Maybe you want me to, Narcissa," said William, with a sad dignity. "If you do, if you want to get rid of me, if that's it——"

Narcissa started. "That ain't it," said she. She hesitated, and added, with formal embarrassment—she had the usual reticence of a New England village woman about expressions of affection, and had never even told her lover in actual words that she loved him—"My feelings toward you are the same as they have always been, William."

It was almost dark in the parlor. They could see only each other's faces gleaming as with pale light. "It would be a blow to me if I thought they wa'n't, Narcissa," William returned, simply.

"They are."

William put his arm around her waist, and they stood close together for a moment. He stroked back her tumbled red hair with clumsy tenderness. "You have had a hard time, Narcissa," he whispered, brokenly. "If you want to go, I ain't going to say anything against it. I ain't going to deny I'm kind of disappointed. I've been living alone so long, and I feel kind of sore sometimes with waitin' but——"

"I shouldn't make you any kind of a wife if I married you now, without waiting," Narcissa said, in a voice at once stern and tender. She stood apart from him, and put up her hand with a sort of involuntary maiden primness to smooth her hair where his had stroked it awry. "If," she went on, "I had to settle down in your house, as I have done in father's, and see the years stretching ahead like a long road without any turn, and nothing but the same old dog trot of washing and ironing and scrubbing and cooking and sewing and washing dishes till I drop into my grave, I should hate you, William Crane."

"I could fetch an' carry all the water for the washin', Narcissa, and I could wash the dishes," said William, with humble beseeching.

"It ain't that. I know you'd do all you could. It's—Oh, William! I've got to have a break; I've got to have one good time. I—like you, and—I liked father; but love ain't enough sometimes when it ties anybody. Everybody has got their own feet and their own wanting to use 'em, and sometimes when love comes in the way of that, it ain't anything but a dead wall. Once we had a black heifer that would jump all the walls; we had to sell her. She always made me think of myself. I tell you, William, I've got to jump my wall, and I've got to have one good time."

William Crane nodded his gray head in patient acquiescence. His forehead was knitted helplessly; he could not in the least understand what his sweetheart meant; in her present mood she was in altogether a foreign language for him, but still the unintelligible sound of her was sweet as a song to his ears. This poor village lover had at least gained the crown of absolute faith through his weary years of waiting; the woman he loved was still a star, and her rays not yet resolved into human reachings and graspings.

"How long do you calculate to be gone, Narcissa?" he asked again.

"I don't know," she replied. "Fifteen hundred dollars is a good deal of money. I s'pose it'll take us quite a while to spend it, even if we ain't very saving."

"You ain't goin' to spend it all, Narcissa!" William gave a little dismayed gasp in spite of himself.

"Land, no! we couldn't, unless we stayed three years, an' I ain't calculating to be gone as long as that. I'm going to bring home what we don't want, and put it in the bank; but—I shouldn't be surprised if it took 'most a year to spend what I've laid out to."

" 'Most a year!"

"Yes; I've got to buy us both new clothes, for one thing. We ain't neither of us got anything fit to wear, and ain't had for years. We didn't go to the funeral lookin' decent, and I know folks talked. Mother felt bad about it, but I couldn't help it. I wa'n't goin' to lay out money foolish and get things here when I was going to New York and could have others the way they ought to be. I'm going to buy us some jewelry, too; I ain't never had a good breastpin even; and as for mother, father never even bought her a ring when they were married. I ain't saying anything against him; it wa'n't the fashion so much in those days."

"I was calculatin'—" William stammered, blushing. "I always meant to, Narcissa."

"Yes, I know you have; but you mustn't lay out too much on it, and I don't care anything about a stone ring—just a plain gold one. There's another thing I'm going to have, too, an' that's a gold watch. I've wanted one all my life."

"Mebbe—" began William, painfully.

"No!" cried Narcissa, peremptorily. "I don't want you to buy me one. I ain't ever thought of it. I'm going to buy it myself. I'm going to buy mother a real cashmere shawl, too, like the one that New York lady had that came to visit Lawyer Maxham's wife. I've got a list of things written down on paper. I guess I'll have to buy another trunk in New York to put them in."

"Well," said William, with a great sigh, "I guess I'd

better be goin'. I hope you'll have as good a time as you're countin' on, Narcissa."

"It's the first good time I ever did count on, and I'd ought to," said Narcissa. "I'm going to take mother to the theater, too. I don't know but it's wicked, but I'm going to." Narcissa fluttered out of the parlor and William shuffled after her. He would not go into the kitchen again.

"Well, good night," said Narcissa, and William also said good night, with another heavy sigh. "Look out for them rocks going out of the yard, an' don't tumble over 'em," she called after him.

"I'm used to 'em," he answered back, sadly, from the darkness.

Narcissa shut and bolted the door. "He don't like it; he feels real bad about it; but I can't help it—I'm going."

Through the next few weeks Narcissa Stone's face looked strange to those who had known her from childhood. While the features were the same, her soul informed them with a new purpose, which overlighted all the old ones of her life, and even the simple village folks saw the effect, though with no understanding. Soon the news that Narcissa and her mother were going to New York was abroad. On the morning they started, in the three-seated open wagon which served as stage to connect the little village with the railroad ten miles away, all the windows were set with furtively peering faces.

"There they go," the women told one another. "Narcissa an' her mother an' the trunk. Wonder if Narcissa's got that money put away safe? They're wearin' the same old clothes. S'pose we shan't know 'em when they get back. Heard they was goin' to stay a year. Guess old Mr. Stone would rise up in his grave if he knew it. Lizzy saw William Crane a-helpin' Narcissa h'ist the trunk out ready for the stage. I wouldn't stan' it if I was him. Ten chances to one Narcissa'll pick up somebody down to

New York, with all that money. She's good-lookin', and she looks better since her father died."

Narcissa, riding out of her native village to those unknown fields in which her imagination had laid the scene of the one good time of her life, regarded nothing around her. She sat straight, her slender body resisting stiffly the jolt of the stage. She said not a word, but looked ahead with shining eyes. Her mother wept, a fold of her old shawl before her face. Now and then she lamented aloud, but softly, lest the driver hear. "Goin' away from the place where I was born an' married an' have lived ever since I knew anything, to stay a year. I can't stan' it, I can't."

"Hush, mother! You'll have a real good time."

"No, I shan't, I shan't. Goin'—to stay a whole—year. I —can't, nohow."

"S'pose we shan't see you back in these parts for some time," the stage driver said, when he helped them out at the railroad station. He was an old man, and had known Narcissa since her childhood.

"Most likely not," she replied. Her mother's face was quite stiff with repressed emotion when the stage driver lifted her out. She did not want him to report in the village that she was crying when she started for New York. She had some pride in spite of her distress.

"Well, I'll be on the lookout for ye a year from today," said the stage driver, with a jocular twist of his face. There were no passengers for his village on the in-coming train, so he had to drive home alone through the melancholy autumn woods. The sky hung low with pale, freezing clouds; over everything was that strange hush which prevails before snow. The stage driver, holding the reins loosely over his tramping team, settled forward with elbows on his knees, and old brows bent with aimless brooding. Over and over again his brain worked the thought, like a peaceful cud of contemplation. "They're goin' to be gone a year. Narcissa Stone an' her mother are goin' to be gone a year afore I'll drive 'em home."

So little imagination had the routine of his life fostered that he speculated not, even upon the possible weather of that far-off day, or the chances of his living to see it. It was simply, "They're goin' to be gone a year afore I'll drive 'em home."

So fixed was his mind upon that one outcome of the situation that when Narcissa and her mother reappeared in less than one week—in six days—he could not for a moment bring his mind intelligently to bear upon it. The old stage driver may have grown something like his own horses through his long sojourn in their company, and his intelligence, like theirs, been given to only the halts and gaits of its first breaking.

For a second he had a bewildered feeling that time had flown fast, that a week was a year. Everybody in the village had said the travelers would not return for a year. He hoisted the ancient paper-lined trunk into his stage, then a fine new one, nailed and clamped with shining brass, then a number of packages, all the time with puzzled eyes askant upon Narcissa and her mother. He would scarcely have known them, as far as their dress was concerned. Mrs. Stone wore a fine black satin gown; her perturbed old face looked out of luxurious environments of fur and lace and rich black plumage. As for Narcissa, she was almost regal. The old stage driver backed and ducked awkwardly, as if she were a stranger, when she approached. Her fine skirts flared imposingly and rustled with unseen silk; her slender shoulders were made shapely by the graceful spread of rich fur; her red hair shone under a hat fit for a princess, and there was about her a faint perfume of violets which made the stage driver gaze confusedly at the snowy ground under the trees when they had started on the homeward road.

"Seems as if I smelt posies, but I know there ain't none hereabouts this time of year," he remarked, finally, in a tone of mild ingratiation, as if more to himself than to his passengers.

"It's some perfumery Narcissa's got on her pocket handkerchief that she bought in New York," said Mrs. Stone, with a sort of sad pride. She looked worn and bewildered, ready to weep at the sight of familiar things, and yet distinctly superior to all such weakness. As for Narcissa, she looked like a child thrilled with scared triumph at getting its own way, who rejoices even in the midst of correction at its own assertion of freedom.

"That so?" said the stage driver, admiringly. Then he added, doubtfully, bringing one white-browed eye to bear over his shoulder, "Didn't stay quite so long as you calcu- lated on?"

"No, we didn't," replied Narcissa, calmly. She nudged her mother with a stealthy, firm elbow, and her mother understood well that she was to maintain silence.

"I ain't going to tell a living soul about it but William Crane; I owe it to him," Narcissa had said to her mother before they started on their homeward journey. "The other folks shan't know. They can guess and surmise all they want to, but they shan't know. I shan't tell; and William, he's as close-mouthed as a rock; and as for you, mother, you always did know enough to hold your tongue when you made up your mind to it."

Mrs. Stone had compressed her mouth until it looked like her daughter's. She nodded. "Yes," said she; "I know some things that I ain't never told you, Narcissa."

The stage passed William Crane's house. He was shuf- fling around to the side door from the barn, with a milk pail in each hand, when they reached it.

"Stop a minute," Narcissa said to the driver. She beck- oned to William, who stared, standing stockstill, holding his pails. Narcissa beckoned again imperatively. Then William set the pails down on the snowy ground and came to the fence. He looked over it, quite pale, and gaping.

"We've got home," said Narcissa.

William nodded; he could not speak.

"Come over by-and-by," said Narcissa.

William nodded.

"I'm ready to go now," Narcissa said to the stage driver. "That's all."

That evening, when William Crane reached his sweetheart's house, a bright light shone on the road from the parlor windows. Narcissa opened the door. He stared at her open-mouthed. She wore a gown the like of which he had never seen before—soft lengths of blue silk and lace trailed about her; blue ribbons fluttered.

"How do you do?" said she.

William nodded solemnly.

"Come in."

William followed her into the parlor, with a wary eye upon his feet, lest they trample her trailing draperies. Narcissa settled gracefully into the rocking chair; William sat opposite and looked at her. Narcissa was a little pale, still her face wore that look of insistent triumph.

"Home quicker'n you expected," William said, at length.

"Yes," said Narcissa. There was a wonderful twist on her red hair, and she wore a high shell comb. William's dazzled eyes noted something sparkling in the laces at her throat; she moved her hand, and something on that flashed like a point of white flame. William remembered vaguely how, often in the summertime when he had opened his house door in the sunny morning, the dewdrops on the grass had flashed in his eyes. He had never seen diamonds.

"What started you home so much sooner than you expected?" he asked, after a little.

"I spent—all the money—"

"All—that money."

"Yes."

"Fifteen hundred dollars in less'n a week?"

"I spent more'n that."

"More'n that?" William could scarcely bring out the words. He was very white.

"Yes," said Narcissa. She was paler than when he had entered, but she spoke quite decidedly. "I'm going to tell you all about it, William. I ain't going to make a long story of it. If after you've heard it you think you'd rather not marry me, I shan't blame you. I shan't have anything to say against it. I'm going to tell you just what I've been doing; then you can make up your mind.

"Today's Tuesday, and we went away last Thursday. We've been gone just six days. Mother an' me got to New York Thursday night, an' when we got out of the cars the men come round hollering this hotel an' that hotel. I picked out a man that looked as if he didn't drink and would drive straight, an' he took us to an elegant carriage, an' mother an' me got in. Then we waited till he got the trunk an' put it up on the seat with him where he drove. Mother, she hollered to him not to let it fall off.

"We went to a beautiful hotel. There was a parlor with a red velvet carpet and red stuffed furniture, and a green sitting room and a blue one. The ceilin' had pictures on it. There was a handsome young gentleman downstairs at a counter in the room where we went first, and mother asked him, before I could stop her, if the folks in the hotel was all honest. She'd been worrying all the way for fear somebody'd steal the money.

"The gentleman said—he was real polite—if we had any money or valuables, we had better leave them with him, and he would put them in the safe. So we did. Then a young man with brass buttons on his coat took us to the elevator and showed us our rooms. We had a parlor with a velvet carpet an' stuffed furniture and a gilt clock on the mantel shelf, two bedrooms, and a bathroom. There ain't anything in town equal to it. Lawyer Maxham ain't got anything to come up to it. The young man offered to untie the rope on the trunk, so I let him. He seemed real kind about it.

"Soon's the young man went I says to mother, 'We ain't going down to get any tea tonight.'

" 'Why not?' says she.

" 'I ain't going down a step in this old dress,' says I, 'an' you ain't going in yours.'

"Mother didn't like it very well. She said she was faint to her stomach, and wanted some tea, but I made her eat some gingerbread we'd brought from home, an' get along. The young man with the brass buttons come again after a while an' asked if there was anything we wanted, but I thanked him an' told him there wasn't.

"I would have asked him to bring up mother some tea and a hot biscuit, but I didn't know but what it would put 'em out; it was after seven o'clock then. So we got along till morning.

"The next morning mother an' me went out real early, an' went into a bakery an' bought some cookies. We ate 'em as we went down the street, just to stay our stomachs; then we went to buying. I'd taken some of the money in my purse, an' I got mother an' me, first of all, two handsome black silk dresses, and we put 'em on as soon as we got back to the hotel, and went down to breakfast.

"You never see anythin' like the dining room, and the kinds of things to eat. We couldn't begin to eat 'em all. There were men standin' behind our chairs to wait on us all the time.

"Right after breakfast mother an' me put our rooms to rights; then we went out again and bought things at the stores. Everybody was buying Christmas presents, an' the stores were all trimmed with evergreen—you never see anything like it. Mother an' me never had any Christmas presents, an' I told her we'd begin, an' buy 'em for each other. When the money I'd taken with us was gone, I sent things to the hotel for the gentleman at the counter to pay, the way he'd told me to. That day we bought our breastpins and this ring, an' mother's and my gold watches, an'—I got one for you, too, William. Don't you say anything—it's your Christmas present. That afternoon we went to Central Park, an' that evenin' we went to the theater. The next day we went to the stores again, an' I bought mother a black satin dress, and me a green one. I got this I've got on, too. It's what they call a tea gown. I always wore it to tea in the hotel after I got it. I got a hat, too, an' mother a bonnet; an' I got a fur cape, and mother a cloak with fur on the neck an' all around it. That evening mother an' me went to the opera; we sat in something they call a box. I wore my new green silk and breastpin, an' mother wore her black satin. We both of us took our bonnets off. The music was splendid; but I wouldn't have young folks go to it much.

"The next day was Sunday. Mother an' me went to meeting in a splendid church, and wore our new black silks. They gave us seats way up in front, an' there was a real good sermon, though mother thought it wa'n't very practical, an' folks got up an' sat down more'n we do. Mother an' me set still, for fear we'd get up an' down in the wrong place. That evening we went to a sacred concert. Everywhere we went we rode in a carriage. They invited us to at the hotel, an' I s'posed it was free, but it wa'n't, I found out afterward.

"The next day was Monday—that's yesterday. Mother an' me went out to the stores again. I bought a silk bed quilt, an' some handsome vases, an' some green-an'-gilt teacups setting in a tray to match. I've got 'em home without breaking. We got some silk stockings, too, an' some shoes, an' some gold-bowed spectacles for mother, an' two more silk dresses, an' mother a real Cashmere shawl. Then we went to see some waxworks, and the pictures and curiosities in the Art Museum; then in the afternoon we went to ride again, and we were goin' to the theater in the evening; but the gentleman at the counter called out to me when I was going past an' said he wanted to speak to me a minute.

"Then I found out we'd spent all that fifteen hundred dollars, an' more, too. We owed 'em 'most ten dollars at the hotel; an' that wa'n't the worst of it—we didn't have enough money to take us home.

"Mother, she broke right down an' cried, an' said it was all we had in the world besides the farm, an' it was poor father's insurance money, an' we couldn't get home, an' we'd have to go to prison.

"Folks come crowding round, an' I couldn't stop her. I don't know what I did do myself; I felt kind of dizzy, an' things looked dark. A lady come an' held a smelling bottle to my nose, an' the gentleman at the counter sent a man with brass buttons for some wine.

"After I felt better an' could talk steady they questioned me up pretty sharp, an' I told 'em the whole story—about father an' his rheumatism, an' everything, just how I was situated, an' I must say they treated us like Christian folks, though, after all, I don't know as we were much beholden to 'em. We never begun to eat all there was on the list, an' we were real careful of the furniture; we didn't really get our money's worth after all was said. But they said the rest of our bill to them was no matter, an' they gave us our tickets to come home."

There was a pause. William looked at Narcissa in her blue gown as if she were a riddle whose answer was lost in his memory. His honest eyes were fairly pitiful from excess of questioning.

"Well," said Narcissa, "I've come back, an' I've spent all that money. I've been wasteful an' extravagant an'— There was a gentleman beautifully dressed who sat at our table, an' he talked real pleasant about the weather, an'— I got to thinking about him a little. Of course I didn't like him as well as you, William, for what comes first comes last with all our folks, but somehow he seemed to be kind of a part of the good time. I shan't never see him again, an' all there was betwixt us was his saying twice it was a pleasant day, an' once it was cold, an' me saying yes; but I'm going to tell you the whole. I've been an' wasted fifteen hundred dollars; I've let my thoughts wander from you; an' that ain't all. I've had a good time an' I can't say I ain't. I've had one good time, an'—I ain't sorry. You can—do just what you think best, William, an'—I won't blame you."

William Crane went over to the window. When he turned round and looked at Narcissa his eyes were full of tears and his wide mouth was trembling. "Do you think you can be contented to—stay on my side of the wall now, Narcissa?" he said, with a sweet and pathetic dignity.

Narcissa in her blue robes went over to him and put, for the first time of her own accord, an arm around his faithful neck. "I wouldn't go out again if the bars were down," said she.

## VI. *THE LAST GIFT*[1]

ROBINSON CARNES pilgrimed along the country road between Sanderson and Elmville. He wore a shabby clerical suit, and he carried a rusty black bag which might have contained sermons. It did actually hold one sermon, a favorite which he had delivered many times in many pulpits, and in which he felt a certain covert pride of authorship.

The bag contained, besides the sermon, two old shirts with frayed cuffs, three collars, one pocket handkerchief, a Bible, and a few ancient toilet articles. These were all his worldly goods, except the clothes he wore, and a matter of forty-odd cents in his old wallet. Robinson Carnes subsisted after a curious parasitical fashion. He traveled about the country with his rusty black bag, journeying from place to place—no matter what place, so long as it held an evangelical church. Straight to the parson of this church he went, stated his name and calling, produced certain vouchers in proof of the same, and inquired if he knew of any opening for a clergyman out of employment, if he had heard of any country pulpit in which an itinerant preacher might find humble harbor. He never obtained any permanent situation; he sometimes supplied a pulpit for a day, or officiated at a funeral or wedding, but that was all. But he never failed to receive hospitality, some sufficient meals, and lodging for one night at least in the parsonage guest chamber.

Although Carnes's living was so precarious, he looked neither forlorn nor hungry. He had, in fact, had at noon an excellent dinner of roast beef at the home of the Pres-

byterian minister in Sanderson. It was the day before
Christmas, and a certain subtle stir of festive significance
was in the very air. Every now and then a wagon laden
with young hemlocks and trailing with greens passed him.
The road was strewn with evergreen sprigs and stray
branches, with an occasional jewellike sprinkle of holly berries. Often he heard a silvery burst of laughter and chat-
ter, and boys and girls appeared from a skirting wood with
their arms laden with green vines and branches. He also
met country carriages whose occupants had their laps heaped
with parcels of Christmas presents. These last gave the
tramp preacher a feeling of melancholy so intense that it
amounted to pain. It was to him like the sight of a tavern
to a drunkard when his pockets are empty and his thirst is
great. It touched Robinson Carnes in his tenderest point.

He had fallen a victim in early youth to a singular species
of spiritual dissipation. Possessed by nature of a most
unselfish love for his kind, and an involuntary generosity,
this tendency, laudable in itself, had become in time like a
flower run wild until it was a weed. His love of giving
amounted to a pure and innocent but unruly passion. It
had at one time assumed such proportions that it barely
escaped being recognized as actual mania. As it was, people, even those who had benefited by his reckless generosity,
spoke of him as a mild idiot.

There had been a day of plenty with him, for he had
fallen joint heir to a large and reasonably profitable New
England farm and a small sum in bank. The other heir
was his younger brother. His brother had just married.
Robinson told him to live on the farm and give him a small
percentage of the profits yearly. When the crops failed
through bad weather and mismanagement, he said easily,
without the slightest sense of self-sacrifice, that the brother
need not pay him the percentage that year. The brother
did not pay it, as a matter of course, the next year, and

in fact never did. In three years the brother's wife was ailing and the family increasing, and he was in debt for the taxes. Robinson paid them all, and he continued paying them as long as his money in the bank lasted. He wished his brother to keep his share intact on account of his family. Then he gave from his poor salary to everything and everybody. Then he was in debt for his board. He rented a small room, and lived, it was said, on oatmeal porridge until the debt was paid.

Robinson Carnes had a fierce honesty. When he was in debt, he felt, for the first time in his life, disgraced, and like hiding his head. He often reflected with the greatest shame upon that period of his life when he had an impulse to go out of his way to avoid the woman whom he owed. He felt nothing like it, now, although to some his present mode of existence might savor of beggary. He considered that in some fashion he generally rendered an equivalent for the hospitality which kept the breath of life in him. Sometimes the minister who entertained him was ailing, and he preached the sermon in his black bag in his stead. Sometimes he did some copying for him; often he had toiled to good purpose at his woodpile or in his garden; he had even assisted the minister's wife with her carpet beating in her spring cleaning. He had now nothing to be ashamed of, but he felt his very memory burn with shame when he remembered that time of debt. That had been the end of his career as a regularly settled minister. People might have forgiven the debt, but they could not forgive nor overlook the fact that while in such dire straits he had given away the only decent coat which he owned to wear in the pulpit, and also that he had given away to a needy family, swarming with half-fed children, the cakes and pies with which some female members of his parish had presented him to alleviate his oatmeal diet. That last had in reality decided the matter. He was requested to resign.

So Robinson Carnes resigned his pastorate and had never been successful in obtaining another. He went out of the village on foot. He had given away every dollar of the last installment of his meager salary to a woman in sore straits. He had given away his trunk years ago to a young man about to be married and settle in the West. He regretted leaving his sermons behind because of the lack of a trunk. He stored them in a barrel in the garret of one of the deacons' houses. He stowed away what he could of his poor little possessions in his black bag, feeling thankful that no one had seemed to need that also. Since he had given away his best coat, he had only his old one, which was very shabby. When he shook hands with his half-hearted friends at parting, he was careful not to raise his right arm too high, lest he reveal a sad rip in the underarm seam. Since, he had had several coats bestowed upon him by his clerical friends, when an old one was on the verge of total disruption, but the new coat was always at variance as to its right underarm seams. Robinson Carnes had thereby acquired such an exceedingly cautious habit of extending his right arm as to give rise to frequent inquiries whether he had put his shoulder out of joint or had rheumatism. Now the ripped seam was concealed by an old but very respectable and warm overcoat which the Presbyterian minister in Sanderson had bestowed upon him and which he had requited by an interpretation of the original Greek of one of the Gospels, which aided the minister materially in the composition of his Christmas sermons. Carnes was an excellent Hebrew and Greek scholar, and his entertainer was rusty and had never been very proficient. Robinson had been in the theological seminary with this man, and had often come to his aid when there. Robinson had also set up the Christmas tree for the Sunday school in the church vestry. He was exceedingly skillful with his hands. The Christmas tree had awakened in him the old passion, and his face saddened as he looked at the inviting spread of branches.

"I wish I had something to hang on the tree for your children and the Sunday school," he said, wistfully, to the minister; and the other man, who knew his history, received his speech in meaning silence. But when Carnes repeated his remark, being anxious that his poor little gift of a Christmas wish, which was all that he had to offer, might at least be accepted, the other replied, coldly, that one's first duty was to oneself, and unjustified giving was pauperizing to the giver and the recipient.

Then poor Robinson Carnes, abashed, for he understood the purpose of the speech, bade the minister good-by meekly and went his way. When he saw the other Christmas trees on the road to Elmville his wistful sadness became intensified. He felt the full bitterness of having absolutely nothing to give, of having even a kindly wish scorned when the wish was his last coin. He felt utterly bankrupt as to benefits toward his fellow creatures, that sorest bankruptcy for him who can understand it.

Carnes had just watched a wagon loaded with Christmas greens pass slowly out of sight around a bend in the road, when he came unexpectedly upon a forlorn company. They were so forlorn, and so unusual in the heart of a prosperous State, that he could hardly believe his eyes at first. They seemed impossible. There were six of them in all: a man, two women—one young and one old—and three children, one a baby two years old, the others five and eight. The man stood bolt upright, staring straight ahead with blank eyes; the women were seated on the low stone wall which bordered the road. The younger, the mother, held the five-year-old child; the older, evidently the grandmother, held the youngest; the eldest—all were girls—sat apart, huddled upon herself, her small back hooped, hugging herself with her thin arms in an effort to keep warm. As Carnes drew near she looked at him, and an impulse of flight was evident in her eyes. The younger of the two women surveyed him with a sort of apathy which partook of anger. The youngest child, in the old woman's lap, was wailing aloud. The grandmother did not try to hush it. Her face, full of a dumb appeal to and questioning of something which Carnes felt dimly was beyond him, gazed over the small head in a soiled white hood which beat wrathfully against her withered bosom. The woman wore an old shawl which was warm; she kept a corner well wrapped about the crying child. The younger woman was very thinly clad. Her hat had a pathetic last summer's rose in it. Now and then a long rigor of chill passed over her; at such times her meager body seemed to elongate; her arms held the little girl on her lap like two clamps. The man, standing still, with face turned toward the sky over the distant horizon line, gave a glance at Carnes with eyes which bore no curiosity or interest, but were simply indifferent. He looked away again, and Carnes felt that he was forgotten, while his shadow and the man's still intermingled.

Then Carnes broke the silence. He stepped in front of the man. "See here, friend," he said, "what's the matter?"

The man looked at him perforce. He was past words. He had come to that pass where speech as a means of expression seemed superfluous. His look said as much to his questioner. "You ask me what is the matter?" the look said. "Are you *blind*?" But the question in the man's dull eyes was not resentful. He was not one in whom misery arouses resentment against others or Providence. Fate seemed to have paralyzed him, as the clutch of a carnivorous animal is said to paralyze a victim.

"What is it?" Carnes inquired again. "What is the matter?"

Still the man did not answer, but the younger of the

two women did. She spoke with great force, but her lips were stiff and apparently not a muscle of her face moved. "I'll tell you what the matter is," said she. "He's good for nuthin'. He's a no-account man. He ain't fit to take care of a family. That's what's the matter." Then the other woman bore her testimony, which was horrible from its intensity and its triviality. It was the tragedy of a pin prick in a meager soul.

"He's left my hair sofy an' my feather bed," said she, in a high, shrill plaint.

Then the forlorn male, badgered betwixt the two females of his species, who were, as it often happens with birds, of a finer, fiercer sort than he, broke silence with a feeble note of expostulation. "Now don't, mother," said he. "You shall hev that sofy and that feather bed again."

The younger woman rose, setting the little girl on the frozen ground so hard that she began to cry. "Have 'em back? How is she goin' to have 'em back?" she demanded. "There's the haircloth sofy she earned and set her eyes by, and there's the feather bed she's always slept on, left over there in Sanderson, stored away in a dirty old barn. How's she goin' to ever git 'em again? What's the poor old woman goin' to sit on an' sleep on?"

"We'll go back an' git 'em," muttered the man. "Don't, Emmy."

"Yes, I will! I'll tell the truth, and I don't care who knows it. You're a no-account man. How are we goin' to git 'em back, I'd like to know? You hain't a cent and you can't get work. If I was a man, I'd git work if it killed me. How is your mother goin' to git that sofy and feather bed again as long as she lives? And that ain't all— there's all my nice furniture that I worked for and earned before I was married; you didn't earn none of it except jest that one bedstead and bureau that you bought. I earned all the other things workin' in the shop myself, and

there they all be stored in that dirty old barn to be eaten
up by rats and covered with dust."

"We will git 'em back. Don't, Emmy."

"How'll we git 'em back? You're a good-for-nuthin'
man. You ain't fit to support a family."

"He's left my sofy an' feather bed," reiterated the old
woman.

The man looked helplessly from one to the other; then
he cast a glance at Carnes—that look full of agony and
appeal which one man gives another in such a crisis when
he is set upon by those whom he cannot fight.

Carnes, when he met his fellow man's piteous look, felt
at once an impulse of partisanship. He stepped close to
him and laid a hand on the thin shoulder in the thin coat.
"See here, friend," he said, "tell me all about it." The
compassion in Carnes's voice was a power in itself; he had,
moreover, a great deal of the clergyman evident, as well in
his manner as in the cut of his clothes.

The man hesitated a moment, then he began, and the
story of his woes flowed like a stream. It was a simple
story enough. The man was evidently one of those who
work well and faithfully while in harness, like a horse.
Taken out, he was naked and helpless and ashamed, without spirit enough to leave his old hitching posts and beaten
roads of life and gallop in new pastures unbridled. He
became a poor nondescript, not knowing what he knew.
The man, whose name was William Jarvis, had worked in
a shoe factory ever since he was a boy. He had been an
industrious and skilled workman, but had met with many
vicissitudes. He had left a poor position for an exceedingly lucrative one in a large factory in Sanderson, and
had moved there with his family. Then the factory had
been closed through the bankruptcy of the owner. Since
then he had had a hard time. He had left his family in
Sanderson in their little rented house, and he had been

about the country seeking in vain for employment. Then he had returned, to find that the old factory was to be re-opened in a month's time, and then he could have a job; but every cent of his money was gone and he was in debt. Not only Jarvis's money was gone, but his credit. The tradesmen had learned to be wary about trusting the shifting factory population.

The rent was due on the house; Jarvis paid that and was literally penniless. He packed his humble furniture, and stored it in a neighbor's barn, on condition that it should be taken for storage if he did not claim it within a year.

Then he and his family set forth. It was the hopeless, senseless sort of exodus which might have been expected of people like these, who deal only with the present, being incapacitated, like some insects, from any but a limited vision in one direction. Carnes received a confused impression, from a confused statement of the man, that they had a hope of being able to reach a town in the northern part of the State, where the wife had some distant relatives, and the others of this poor clan might possibly come to their rescue. They had had a hope of friendly lifts in northward-journeying wagons. But there had been no lifts, and they had advanced only about five miles toward their forlorn Mecca on the day before Christmas. The children were unable to walk farther, and the parents were unable to carry them. The grandmother, too, was at the end of her strength. The weather was very cold, and snow threatened. They were none too warmly clad. They had only the small luggage which they could carry—an old valise and a bundle tied up in an old shawl. The middle child had an old doll that had lost one arm, her blond wig, and an eye, but was going on her travels in her best, faded pink muslin dress and a bit of blue sash. The child stood sobbing wearily, but she still held fast to the doll. The

eldest girl eyed her with tender solicitude. She had out-
grown dolls. She got a dingy little handkerchief from
her pocket and folded it cornerwise for a shawl; then she
got down from the wall and pinned it closely around the
doll. "There," she said, "that is better." After that the
children themselves felt warmer.

Carnes saw everything—the people, the doll, their poor
little possessions—and an agony of pity, which from the
nature of the man and its futility became actual torture,
seized him. He looked at the other man who had con-
fided in him, at the women who now seemed to watch
him with a lingering hope of assistance. He opened his
mouth to speak, but he said nothing. What could he say?

Then the man, William Jarvis, added something to this
poor story. Two weeks before he had slipped on the ice
and injured his shoulder; he had strained it with moving,
and it was causing him much distress. Indeed, his face,
which was strained with pain as well as misery, bore witness to the truth of that.

The wife had eyed her husband with growing concentration during this last. When he had finished, her face
brightened with tenderness; she made a sudden move forward and threw her arms around him and began to weep
in a sort of rage of pity and love and remorse. "Poor
Willy! Poor Willy!" she sobbed. "Here we've been abusin'
you when you've worked like a dog with your shoulder
'most killin' you. You've always done the best you could.
I don't care who says you haven't. I'd like to hear anybody say you haven't. I guess they wouldn't darse say it
twice to me." She turned on the old woman with unrea-
soning fury. "Hold your tongue about your old haircloth
sofy an' your feather bed, grandma!" said she. "Ain't he
your own son? I guess you won't die if you lose your old
haircloth sofy an' your feather bed! The stuffin's all comin'

out of your old sofy, anyhow! You ought to be ashamed of yourself, grandma! Ain't he your own son?"

"I guess he was my son afore he was your husband," returned the old woman, with spirit. "I ain't pesterin' of him any more'n you be, Emmy Jarvis." With that she began to weep shrilly like a child, leaning her face against the head of the crying child in her lap. The little girl with the doll set up a fresh pipe of woe; the doll slipped to the ground. The elder sister got down from the stone wall and gathered it up and fondled it. "You've dropped poor Angelina and hurt her, Nannie," said she, reproachfully.

"Poor Willy!" again sobbed his wife. "You've been treated like a dog by them you had a right to expect something better of, an' I don't care if I do say so."

Again the man's eyes, overlooking his wife's head, sought the other man's for an understanding of this peculiar masculine distress.

Carnes returned the look with such utter comprehension and perfect compassion as would have lifted the other's burden for all time could it have taken practical form. In reality, Carnes, at this juncture, suffered more than the man. Here was a whole family penniless, suffering. Here was a man with the impulse of a thousand Samaritans to bring succor, but positively helpless to lift a finger toward any alleviation of their misery. It became evident to him in a flash what the outside view of the situation would be: that the only course for a man of ordinary sense and reason was to return to Sanderson and notify the authorities of this suicidal venture; that it was his duty for the sake of the helpless children to have them cared for by force, if there was no other way. But still, this course he could not bring himself to follow. It seemed an infringement upon all the poor souls had left in the world—their individual freedom. He could not do it, and yet what else was there to do? He thought of his forty cents, his only available asset against this heavy arrear of pity and generosity, with fury. At that moment the philanthropist without resources, the Samaritan without his flask of oil, was fairly dangerous to himself from this terrible blocking of almost abnormal impulses for good. It seemed to him that he must die or go mad if he could not do something for these people. He cast about his eyes, like a drowning man, and he saw in a field on the left, quite a distance away, a small house; only its chimneys were visible above a gentle slope. A thought struck him. "Wait a moment," he ordered, and leaped the stone wall and ran across the field, crunching the frozen herbage until his footsteps echoed loudly. The forlorn family watched him. It was only a short time before he returned. He caught up the second little girl from the ground. "Come!" cried Carnes in an excited voice. "Come! Nobody lives in that house over there! I can get in! There is a shed with hay in it! There's a fireplace! There's plenty of wood to pick up in the grove behind it! Come!"

His tone was wild with elation. Here was something which could be done. It was small, but something. The others were moved by his enthusiasm. Their faces lightened. The father caught the youngest child from the grandmother; the mother took the eldest by the hand. They all started, the old grandmother outracing them with a quick, short-stepped toddle like a child. "See your mother go," said the wife, and she fairly laughed. In fact, the old woman was almost at her last gasp, and it was an extreme effort of nature, a final spurt of nerve and will.

The house was a substantial cottage, in fair repair. The door at the back was unlocked. Carnes threw it open and ushered in the people as if they had been his guests. A frightful chill struck them as they entered. It was much colder than outside, with a concentration of chill which overwhelmed like an actual presence of wintry death. The children, all except the eldest girl, who hugged the doll tightly, and whispered to her not to mind, it would be warm pretty soon, began to cry again. This was a new deprivation added to the old. They had expected something from the stranger, and he had betrayed them. The grandmother leaned exhausted against the wall; her lips moved, but nothing could be heard. The wife caught up the youngest crying child and shook her.

"Be still, will you?" she said, in a furious voice. "We've got enough to put up with without your bawling." Then she kissed and fondled it, and her own tears dropped fast on its wet face.

But not one whit of Carnes's enthusiasm abated. He beckoned the man, who sprang to his bidding. They brought wood from the grove behind the house. Carnes built a fire on the old hearth, and he found some old boxes in the little barn. He rigged up some seats with boards, and barrels for backs; he spread hay on the boards for cushions. The warmth and light of the fire filled the room. All of a sudden it was furnished and inhabited. Their faces began to relax and lighten. The awful blue tints of cold gave place to soft rose and white. The children began to laugh.

"What did I tell you?" the eldest girl asked the doll, and she danced it before the ruddy glow. The wife bade her husband sit with his lame shoulder next the fire. The youngest child climbed into her grandmother's lap again, and sat with her thumb in her mouth surveying the fire. She was hungry, but she sucked her own thumb, and she was warm. The old woman nodded peacefully. She had taken off her bonnet, and her white head gleamed with a rosy tint in the firelight.

Carnes was radiant for a few minutes. He stood surveying the transformation he had wrought. "Well, now, this is better," he said, and he laughed like a child. Then

suddenly his face fell again. This was not a solution of
the problem. He had simply stated it. There was no
food; there was no permanent shelter. Then the second
little girl, who was the most delicate and nervous of them all,
began to cry again. "I want somefin to eat," she wailed.
Her father, who had been watching them with as much
delight as Carnes, also experienced a revulsion. Again he
looked at Carnes.

"Yes," said the wife in a bitter tone, "here is a fire and
a roof over us, but we may get turned out any minute if
anybody sees the smoke comin' out of the chimney; and
there's nothing to eat."

The eldest little girl's lip quivered. She hugged the doll
more closely.

"Don't cry, and you shall have a piece of cake pretty
soon," she whispered. The man continued to look at
Carnes, who suddenly stood straight and threw up his head
with a resolute look. "I'm going, but I will come back very
soon," said he, "and then we'll have supper. Don't worry.
Put enough wood on the fire to keep warm." Then he
went out.

He hurried across the field to the road under the lower-
ing quiet of the gray sky. His resolve was stanch, but
his heart failed him. Again the agony of balked compassion was over him. He looked ahead over the reach of
frozen highway without a traveler in sight, he looked up
at the awful winter sky threatening with storm, and he was
in a mood of blasphemy. There was that misery; there
was he with the willingness to relieve, and—forty cents. It
was a time when money reached a value beyond itself,
when it represented the treasure of heaven. This poor forty
cents would buy bread, at least, and a little milk. It would
keep them alive a few hours, but that was only a part of
the difficulty solved. The cold was intense, and they were
not adequately protected against it. There were an old

woman and three children. He was giving them only the most ephemeral aid, and what would come next?

Carnes, standing there in the road all alone, mechanically thrust his hand in his pocket for the feel of his forty cents; but instead of putting his hand in his own coat pocket, he thrust it in the pocket of the overcoat which the minister in Sanderson had given him. He pulled out, instead of his own poor old wallet, a prosperous portly one of black sealskin. He did not at first realize what it meant. He stood staring vacuously. Then he knew. The minister in Sanderson had left his own wallet in the overcoat pocket. The coat was one which he had been wearing until his new one had come from the tailor's the day before.

Carnes stood gazing at this pocketbook; then he slowly, with shaking fingers, opened it. There were papers, which he saw at a glance were valuable, and there was a large roll of bills. Carnes began counting them slowly. He sat down on the stone wall the while. His legs trembled so that he could scarcely stand. There was over two hundred dollars in bills in the wallet. Carnes sat awhile regarding the bills. A strange expression was coming over his gentle, scholarly, somewhat weak face—an expression evil and unworthy in its original meaning, but, as it were, glorified by the motive which actuated it. The man's face became full of a most angelic greed of money. He was thinking what he could do with only a hundred dollars of that other man's money. He knew with no hesitation that he would run to Elmville, hire a carriage, take the distressed family back to Sanderson to their old house, pay the rent a month in advance, pay their debts, get the stored furniture, help them set it up, give them money to buy fuel and provisions for the month before the factory opened. A hundred dollars of that money in his hand, which did not belong to him, meant respite for distress, which would be like a taste of heaven; it meant perhaps life instead of death; it meant perhaps more than earthly life, perhaps spiritual life, to save this family from the awful test of despair.

Carnes separated a hundred dollars from the rest. He put it in his own old wallet. He replaced the remainder in the minister's, and he went on to Elmville.

It was ten o'clock on Christmas Eve before Robinson Carnes, having left the Jarvis family reinstated in their old home, warmed and fed, and happier perhaps than they had ever been or perhaps ever would be, went to the vestry blazing with light in which the Christmas tree was being held. He stood in the door and saw the minister, portly and smiling, seated well forward. As he watched, the minister's name was called, and he received a package. The minister was a man with a wealthy parish; he had, moreover, money of his own, and not a large reputation for giving. Carnes reflected upon this as he stood there. It seemed to him that with such a man his chances of mercy were small. He had his mind steeled for the worst. He considered, as he stood there, his every good chance of arraignment, of imprisonment. "It may mean State prison for me," he thought. Then a wave of happiness came over him. "Anyway," he told himself, "they have the money." He did not conceive the possibility of the minister taking away the money from that poverty and distress; that was past his imagination. "They have the money," he kept repeating. It also occurred to him, for he was strong in the doctrines of his church creed, that he had possibly incurred a heavier than earthly justice for his deed; and then he told himself again, "Well, they have it."

A mental picture of the family in warmth and comfort in their home came before him, and while he reflected upon theft and its penalty, he smiled like an angel. Presently he called a little boy near by and sent him to the minister.

"Ask Mr. Abbot if he will please see Mr. Carnes a

moment," he said. "Say he has something important to tell him."

Soon the boy returned, and his manner unconsciously aped Mr. Abbot.

"Mr. Abbot says he is sorry, but he cannot leave just now," he said. It was evident that the minister wished to shake off the mendicant of his holy profession.

Carnes took the rebuff meekly, but he bade the boy wait a moment. He took a pencil from his pocket and wrote something on a scrap of paper. He wrote this:

"I found this wallet in your pocket in the coat which you gave me. I have stolen one hundred dollars to relieve the necessities of a poor family. I await your pleasure, Robinson Carnes."

The boy passed up the aisle with the pocketbook and the note. Carnes, watching, saw a sudden convulsive motion of the minister's shoulders in his direction, but he did not turn his head. His name was called again for a present as the boy passed down the aisle, returning to Carnes.

Again the boy unconsciously aped Mr. Abbot's manner as he addressed Carnes. It was conclusive, coldly disapproving, non-retaliative, dismissing. Carnes knew the minister, and he had no doubt. "Mr. Abbot says that he has no need to see you, that you can go when you wish," said the boy. Carnes knew that he was quite free, that no penalty would attach to his theft.

The snow had begun to fall as Robinson Carnes took his way out of Sanderson on the road to Elmville, but the earth had come into a sort of celestial atmosphere which obliterated the storm for human hearts. All around were innocent happiness and festivity, and the display of love by loving gifts. The poor minister was alone on a stormy road on Christmas Eve. He had no presentiment of anything bright in his future: he did not know that he was to find an asylum and a friend for life in the clergyman in the town toward which his face was set. He traveled on, bending his shoulders before the sleety wind. His heart was heavier and heavier before the sense of his own guilt. He felt to the full that he had done a great wrong. He had stolen, and stolen from his benefactor. He had taken off the minister's coat and laid it gently over the back of a settee in the vestry before he left, but that made no difference. If only he had not stolen from the man who had given him his coat. And yet he always had, along with the remorse, that light of great joy which could not be wholly darkened by any thought of self, when he reflected upon the poor family who were happy. He thought that possibly the minister had in reality been glad, although he condemned him. He began to love him and thank him for his generosity. He pulled his thin coat closely around him and went on. He had given the last gift which he had to give—his own honesty.

## VII. *A NEW ENGLAND PROPHET*[1]

AT half-past six o'clock a little company of people passed down the village street in the direction of the Lennox farmhouse.

They passed in silence, stepping along the frozen ridges of the road. It was cold, but there was no snow. There was a young moon shining through thin white clouds like nebulæ.

Now and then, as the company went on, new recruits were gathered from the scattered houses. A man would emerge darkly from a creaking gate, with maybe a second and third dark figure following, with a flirt of feminine draperies. "There's Deacon Scranton," or "There's Thomas Jennings and his wife and Ellen," the people would murmur to one another.

Once a gleam of candlelight from an open door lay across the road in advance, and wavered into darkness with a slam of the door when the company drew near. Then a solitary woman came ponderously down the front walk, seeming to jar the frozen earth with the jolt of her great feminine bulk. "There's Abby Mosely," somebody muttered. Sometimes two young girls fluttered out of a dooryard, clinging together with nervous giggles and outcries, which were soon hushed. They moved along with the others, their little cold fingers clinging together with a rigid clutch. It was as if a strange, solemn atmosphere surrounded this group moving along the country road in the starlit night. Whoever came into their midst felt it, and

[1] *Copyright, 1898, by Harper & Brothers. Copyright, 1926, by Mary E. Wilkins Freeman.*

his emotions changed involuntarily as respiration changes on a mountaintop.

When the party reached a windy hilltop in sight of the lighted windows of the Lennox house in the valley below, it numbered nearly twenty. Halfway down the hill somebody else joined them. He had been standing ahead of them, waiting in the long shadow of a poplar, and they had not discerned him until they were close to him. Then he stepped forward and the shadow of the tree was left motionless. The young girls half screamed, he appeared so suddenly, and their nerves were strained. The elders made a solemn hushed murmur of greeting. They knew as soon as he moved that he was Isaac Penfield. He had a martial carriage of his shoulders, he was a captain in the militia, and he wore an ash-colored cloak which distinguished him.

The young girls cast glances, bolder from the darkness, toward his stately ash-colored shoulders and the pale gleam of his face. Not one of them who had not her own lover but had her innocent secret dreams about this Isaac Penfield. Now, had a light shone out suddenly in the darkness, their dreams would have shown in their faces.

One slender girl slunk softly around in the rear darkness and crept so close to Isaac Penfield that his ash-colored cloak, swinging out in the wind, brushed her cheek. He did not notice her; indeed, after his first murmur of salutation, he did not speak to anyone.

They all went in silence down the hill and flocked into the yard of the Lennox house. There was a red flicker of light in the kitchen windows from the great hearth fire, but a circle of dark heads and shoulders hid the fire itself from the newcomers. There were evidently a number of people inside.

Deacon Scranton raised the knocker, and the door was opened immediately. Melissa Lennox stood there holding a candle in a brass candlestick, with the soft light streaming up on her fair face. She looked through it with innocent, anxious blue eyes at the company. "Won't you walk in?" she said, tremulously, and the people passed into the south entry, and through the door on the left into the great Lennox kitchen. Some dozen persons who had come from the other end of the village were already there.

Isaac Penfield entered last. Melissa did not see him until he stepped suddenly within her radius of candlelight. Then she started, and bent her head before him, blushing. The candle shook in her outstretched hand.

Isaac Penfield took the candle without a word and set it on the stairs. Then he took Melissa's slim right hand in his and stood a moment looking down at her bent head with its parted gloss of hair. His forehead was frowning, and yet he half smiled with tender triumph.

"Come out in the front yard with me a moment," he whispered. He pulled her with gentle force toward the door, and the girl yielded, after a faint murmur of expostulation.

Out in the front yard Isaac Penfield folded a corner of his ash-colored cloak around Melissa's slender shoulders.

"Now I want you to tell me, Melissa," he whispered. "You are not still carried away by all this?" He jerked his head toward the kitchen windows.

Melissa trembled against the young man's side under the folds of his cloak.

"You are not, after all I said to you, Melissa?"

She nodded against his breast, with a faint sob.

"I hoped you would do as I asked you, and cut loose from this folly," Isaac Penfield said, sternly.

"Father—says—it's true. Oh, I am afraid—I am afraid! My sins are so great, and I cannot hide from the eyes of the Lord. I am afraid!"

Isaac Penfield tightened his clasp of the girl's trembling

figure, and bent his head low down over hers. "Melissa dear, can't you listen to me?" he whispered.

Suddenly the kitchen door opened and a new light streamed across the entry.

"Melissa, where be you?" called a woman's voice, high pitched and melancholy.

"There's mother calling," Melissa said in a frightened whisper, and she broke away and ran into the house.

Her mother stood in the kitchen door. "Where have you been?" she began. Then she stopped, and looked at Isaac Penfield with a half-shrinking, half-antagonistic air. This stalwart young man, radiant with the knowledge of his own strength, represented to this delicate woman, who was held to the earth more by the tension of nerves than the weight of matter, the very pride of life, the material power which she was to fear and fight for herself and for her daughter.

"I thought I would step into your meeting tonight, if I were permitted," Isaac Penfield said.

Mrs. Lennox looked at him with deep-blue eyes under high, thin temples. "All are permitted who listen to the truth with the right spirit," said she, and turned shortly and glided into the kitchen. Melissa and Isaac followed.

The company sat in wide semicircles, three deep, before the fire. In the open space between the first semicircle and the fire, his wide armchair on the bricks of the broad hearth, half facing the company, sat Solomon Lennox. Near him sat his deaf-and-dumb son Alonzo. He held up a large slate so the firelight fell upon it, and marked upon it with a grating pencil. He screwed his face with every stroke, so it seemed that one watching attentively might discern the picture itself from his changing features.

Alonzo Lennox was fourteen years old, but he looked no more than ten, and he had been deaf and dumb from his birth. The firelight gave a reddish tinge to his silvery blond hair, spreading out stiffly from the top of his head over his ears like the thatch of a hut. His delicate irregular profile bent over the slate; now and then a spasm of silent merriment shook his narrow chest, and the surrounding people looked at him with awe. They regarded it as the mystic ecstasy of a seer.

Melissa and her mother had slid softly through the semicircles to the chairs they had left. Isaac Penfield stood on the outskirts, towering over all the people, refusing a seat which somebody offered him. He threw off his ash-colored cloak and held it on his arm. His costume of fine broadcloth and flowered satin and glittering buttons surpassed any there, as did his face and his height and his carriage; and, more than all, he stood among the others raised upon a spiritual eminence, unseen, but none the less real, which his ancestors had reared for him before his birth. The Penfield name had been a great one in that vicinity for three generations. Once Penfields had owned the larger part of the township. Isaac's father, and his grandfather before him, had been esquires, and held as nearly the position of lords of this little village as was possible in New England. Now this young man was the last of his race, living, with his housekeeper and an old servant, in the Penfield homestead; and the village adulation which had been accorded to his ancestors was his also in a large measure.

Tonight, as he entered, people glanced at him, away from Alonzo and his slate, but only for a moment. The matter under discussion that night was too solemn and terrible to be lost sight of long.

In about ten minutes after Isaac Penfield entered, the boy gave a shout, grating and hideous, with a discord of human thoughts and senses in it. A shudder passed over the company like a wind.

Alonzo Lennox sprang up and waved the slate, and his

father reached out for it. "Give it to me," he demanded, sternly, as if the boy could hear. But Alonzo gave another shout, and leaped aside, and waved the slate out of his father's reach. Then he danced lightly up and down on the tips of his toes, shaking his head and flinging out fantastic heels. His shock of hair flew out wildly and looked like a luminous crown; the firelight struck his dilated eyes, and they gleamed red.

The people watched him with sobbing breaths and pale faces, all except Isaac Penfield and one other. Isaac stood looking at him, with his mouth curling in a scornful smile. Solomon Lennox stood aside with a startled air; then he caught the boy firmly by the arm and grasped the slate.

Alonzo grinned impishly in his father's face; then he let go the slate and sank down on his stool in the chimney corner. There he sat submissive and inactive, except for the cunning, sharp flash of his blue eyes under his thatch of hair.

Solomon Lennox held the slate to the light and looked at it, while the people waited breathless, their pale intent faces bent forward. Then he handed the slate, without a word, to the man at the end of the first semicircle, and it was circulated through the entire company. As one passed the slate to another a shuddering thrill like an electric shock seemed to be passed with it, and there was a faint murmur of horror.

Isaac Penfield held the slate longest, and examined it closely. Drawn with a free hand, which certainly gave evidence of some inborn artistic skill aside from aught else, were great sweeping curves of wings upbearing an angel with a trumpet at his mouth. Under his feet were lashing tongues as of flames, with upturned faces of agony in the midst of them. And everywhere, between the wings and the angel and the flames and the faces, were, in groups of five, those grotesque little symbols of the sun, a disk with human features therein, which one sees in the almanacs.

After Isaac Penfield had finished looking at the mystic slate he passed it to Solomon Lennox's elder brother, Simeon, who sat at his right. The old man's hard shaven jaws widened in a sardonic grin; his small black eyes twinkled derisively over the drawings. "Pretty pictures," he said, half aloud. Then he passed the slate along with a contemptuous chuckle which was heard in the solemn stillness all over the room.

Solomon Lennox gave a furious glance in his brother's direction. "This is no time nor season for scoffer!" cried he. And his voice seemed to shock the air like a musket shot.

Simeon Lennox chuckled again. Solomon's right hand clinched. He arose; then sat down again, with his mouth compressed. He sat still until the slate had gone its rounds and returned to the boy, who sat contemplating it with uncouth delight; then he stood up, and the words flowed from his mouth in torrents. Never at a loss for subject matter of speech was Solomon Lennox. By the fluency of his discourse he might well have been thought inspired. He spoke of visions of wings and holy candlesticks and beasts and cups of abomination as if he had with his own eyes seen them like the prophet of old. He expounded strange and subtle calculations and erratic interpretations of history as applied to revelation with a fervor which brought conviction to his audience. He caught the slate from his deaf-and-dumb son, and explained the weird characters thereon. The five suns were five days. Five times the sun should arise in the east, as it had done from the creation; then should the angel, upborne on those great white wings, sound his trumpet, and the flames burst forth from the lower pit, and those upturned faces in the midst of them gnash with despair.

"Repent, for the day of the Lord is at hand!" shouted

Solomon Lennox at the close of his arguments, and his voice itself rang like a trumpet full of all intonations and reverberations, of awe and dread. "Repent, for the great and dreadful day of the Lord is at hand! Repent while there is yet time, while there is yet a foothold on the shore of the lake of fire! Repent! Repent! Prepare your ascension robes! Renounce the world and all the lust and the vanity thereof! Repent, for the Day of Judgment is here! Soon shall ye choke with the smoke of the everlasting burning, soon shall your eyes be scorched with the fiery scroll of the heavens, your ears be deafened with the blast of the trumpet of wrath, and the cry against you of your own sins! Repent! Repent! Repent!"

Solomon Lennox's slight figure writhed with his own emotion as with internal fire; the veins swelled out on his high bald forehead; his eyes blazed with fanatical light. Aside from the startling nature of his discourse, he himself was a marvel and a terror to his neighbors. His complete deviation from a former line of life produced among them the horror of the supernatural. He affected them like his own ghost. He had always been a man of few and quiet words, who had never expressed his own emotions in public beyond an inaudible, muttered prayer at conference meeting, and now this flood of fiery eloquence from him seemed like a very convulsion of human nature.

When a great physical malady is epidemic there are often isolated cases in remote localities whose connection with the main disturbance cannot be established. So in this little New England village, far from a railroad, scarcely reached by the news of the day, Solomon Lennox had developed within himself, with seeming spontaneity, some of the startling tenets of Joseph Miller, and had established his own small circle of devoted disciples and followers. It was as if some germs of a great spiritual disturbance had sought, through some unknown medium, this man's mind as their best ripening place.

After Solomon had arisen one night in conference meeting and poured forth his soul to his startled neighbors in a strain of fiery prophecy, Millerite publications had been sent for, and he had strengthened his own theories with those of the original leader, although in many respects his maintained a distinct variance.

The effect of Solomon's prophecies had been greatly enhanced by the drawings of his deaf-and-dumb son. Alonzo Lennox's slate, covered with rude representations of beasts and trumpets and winged creatures—the weird symbolic figures of the prophet Daniel—had aroused a tumult of awe and terror in the village. And the more so because the boy had never learned the language of the deaf and dumb, and had no ordinary and comprehensible means of acquiring information upon such topics.

Tonight, as his father spoke, he kept his blue eyes upon his face with such a keen look that it seemed almost impossible that he did not hear and comprehend every word. Unbelievers in this new movement were divided between the opinion that Lonny Lennox had heard more than folks had given him credit for right along, and the one that he understood by some strange power which the loss of his other faculties had sharpened.

"The boy has developed the sixth sense," Isaac Penfield thought as he watched his intent face upturned toward his father's; and he also thought impatiently that he should be cuffed and sent to bed for his uncanny sharpness. He grew more and more indignant as the time went on and the excitement deepened. He watched Melissa grow paler and paler and finally press her slender hands over her face and shake with sobs, and made a sudden motion as if he would go to her. Then he restrained himself and muttered something between his teeth.

mill, afore you got at the meanin' you wanted," returned his brother, contemptuously. "That ain't the kind of passage I'm after. There's too much two-facedness an' double-dealin' about the Scripturs anyway, judgin' by some of you folks. What I want is a square up-an'-down passage that says, without no chance of its meanin' anything else, 'The world is comin' to an end next week Thursday.' I stump ye to show me sech a passage as that. *Ye can't do it!*"

The habits of a lifetime are strong even in strained and exalted states, acting like the lash of a familiar whip. Solomon Lennox was the younger brother; all his life he had borne a certain docility of attitude toward Simeon, which asserted itself now.

The fervid orator stood for a moment silent before this sceptical, sneering elder brother. "I'd like to know how you account for Lonny's drawin's," he said at length, in a tone which he might have used when bullied by Simeon in their boyhood.

"Drawin's," drawled Simeon, and sarcasm itself seemed to hiss in the final s—"dr-r-awin's! The little scamp is sharp as steel, an' he's watched an' he's eyed till he's put two an' two together. It's easy enough to account for the drawin's. The air here has been so thick lately with wings an' wheels an' horns an' trumpets an' everlastin' fire that anybody that wa'n't an idgit could breathe it in. An' I miss my guess if his mother ain't showed him the picturs in the big Bible more'n once when you've been talkin', an' pointed out the hearth fire an' the candlesticks an' the powderhorn. Sophy Anne's sharp, an' she's done more to learn that boy than anybody knows of, though I've got my doubts now as to how straight he's really got it in his mind. Lord! them drawin's ain't nothin'. Solomon Lennox, you can't look me in the face an' say that you actilly believe all this darned tomfoolery!"

Solomon for these few minutes had been on the old

level of a brotherly argument, but now he arose suddenly to his latter heights.

"I believe that the end of the world is near, that the great and dreadful day of the Lord is at hand, accordin' to prophecy and revelation," he proclaimed, and his eyes shone under his high forehead as under a majestic dome of thought and inspiration.

Simeon whistled. "Ye don't, though. Look at here, Solomon; tell ye what I'll do. I'll put ye to the test. Look at here, you say the world's comin' to an end next Thursday. Well, it stands to reason if it is, that you ain't got no more need of temporal goods. S'pose—you give me a deed of this 'ere farm?"

Solomon stared at his brother.

Simeon shook his fist at him slowly. *"Ye won't do it,"* he said, with a triumphant chuckle.

"I *will* do it."

"Git Lawyer Bascombe to draw up the papers tomorrow?"

*"I will."*

"Me to take possession by daylight next Friday mornin', if the world don't come to an end Thursday night?"

*"Yes,"* replied Solomon, hurling the word at his brother like a stone.

Simeon got up and buttoned his coat over his lean chest. "Well," said he, "I've had pretty hard luck. I've lost three wives, and I've been burnt out twice, an' the last house ain't none too tight. I'll move right in here next Friday mornin' at daylight. Mebbe I'll get married again."

"Much good will the heaping up of barns an' storehouses do when you hear the voice of the Lord saying, 'Thou fool, this night shall thy soul be required of thee,'" returned his brother; but he spoke the fervid words with a certain feebleness. All his life since he was a boy had Solomon Lennox toiled and saved to own this noble farm. The bare imagination of giving it up to another cost him much, although he firmly believed that in a week's space it would be only a modicum of the blackened ashes of a world. He stood the test of his faith, but he felt the scorch of sacrificial flame.

"It ain't me that's the fool," said Simeon, shrugging himself into his greatcoat. "I ain't goin' to hang back with my soul when it's required of me, but I ain't goin' to keep chuckin' of it in the face of the Lord afore He's ready for it, like some folks I know. Them's the fools. When'll you be down to Lawyer Bascombe's tomorrow, Solomon, to deed away these barns an' storehouses that you ain't no more use for?"

"I'll be down there at nine o'clock tomorrow mornin'."

"All right; you can count on me," said Simeon. He went out, and Solomon bolted the door after him promptly. But he had no sooner returned to the kitchen than there came a sharp tap on the window, and there was Simeon's hard leering old face pressed against the pane. "You'll—have—to—fetch Sophy Anne down there tomorrow," he called. "She'll—have to sign that deed, too, or it won't stan'."

"All right," shouted Solomon, and the face at the window, with a parting nod, disappeared.

Lawyer Bascombe's office was in the center of the village, over the store. A steep flight of stairs at the right of the store led to it. Up these stairs, at nine o'clock the next morning, climbed Solomon Lennox and his wife Sophia Anne, with pale devoted faces, and signed away all their earthly goods as an evidence of their faith.

In some way the matter had become known in the village. When Solomon and Sophia Anne came down the stairs there was quite a crowd before the door, standing back with awed curiosity to let them pass. Simeon Lennox did not leave at once after the signing of the deed. When he appeared in the doorway with a roll of paper in his hand the crowd had dispersed.

Without any doubt this act of Solomon Lennox and his wife materially strengthened their cause. When it became known that they had actually signed away their property in their confidence that days of property holding were over, even scoffers began to look serious. That evening the meeting at Solomon Lennox's house numbered a third more than usual. The next evening it was doubled, and the best room as well as the kitchen was filled. Solomon stood at the foot of the stairs in the entry between the rooms and exhorted, while the deaf-and-dumb boy's slate circulated among the awe-stricken people.

Isaac Penfield came to no more meetings, and he did not see Melissa again until Tuesday. Late Tuesday afternoon she went up to the village store with a basket of eggs. The days of barter were nearly over, as she had been taught to believe, but there was no molasses in the house, and the poor deaf-and-dumb boy was weeping for it with uncouth grief and could not be comforted by the prospect of eternal joys. When Melissa came out of the store with the bottle of molasses in her basket, Isaac Penfield's bay mare and chaise were drawn up before the platform, and Isaac stood waiting. Melissa started and colored when she saw him.

"Get in, please," he said, motioning her toward the chaise. She looked at him falteringly.

"Get in, please, Melissa. I want to speak to you."

The bay mare was restive, tossing her head and pawing with one delicate forefoot. Isaac could scarcely keep her quiet until Melissa got in. When he took the reins she gave a leap forward, and the chaise swung about with a lurch. Isaac threw himself back and held the reins taut; the mare flew down the road, pulling hard on her bit; the chaise rocked high on the frozen road. Melissa sat still, her delicate face retired within the dark depths of her silk hood.

Isaac did not speak to her until they reached the foot of

a long hill. "I want to ask you something," he said then, with a wary eye still on the straining shoulders of the mare. "I want to ask you again to give this up."

Melissa did not speak.

"Won't you promise me?"

"I can't," she said, faintly.

"You can if you will." Suddenly Isaac leaned over her. "Won't you promise *me*, Melissa?"

She shrank away from him. "I—can't. I believe father."

"Melissa, you don't."

"I do," said she, with a despairing sob.

Isaac Penfield bent his face down close to hers. "Can't you believe me as well as your father? Melissa, look at me."

Melissa bent her head down over her hands.

"Look at me, Melissa."

She raised her head slowly as if there were a constraining hand under her chin, and her eyes met his.

"Can't you, Melissa?"

Fair locks of hair fell over the girl's gentle cheeks; her soft mouth quivered. It seemed as if her piteous blue eyes were upheld only by the look in the young man's, and as if all the individual thought and purpose in her face and her whole soul were being overcast by his imperious will, but she shook her head.

"Can't you, Melissa?"

She shook her head again.

Isaac Penfield's face turned white. He touched the whip to the mare and she gave a sharp bound forward. They had not much farther to go. Neither of them spoke again until Isaac assisted Melissa out of the chaise at her own gate.

"Good-by," he said, then, shortly.

Melissa looked up at him and caught her breath. She could not speak. Isaac sprang into his chaise, and was out of the yard with a sharp grate of wheels, and she went into the house.

Her mother was setting chairs in order for the evening meeting. She looked up sharply as Melissa entered.

"Who was that brought you home?" said she.

"Isaac Penfield," replied Melissa, turning her face from her mother's eyes.

"I hope you ain't letting your thoughts dwell on anything of that kind now," said her mother.

"I met him as I was coming out of the store, and he asked me to ride. I shan't ever see him again," Melissa returned faintly.

The deaf-and-dumb boy had been dozing with gaping mouth in his chimney corner. Now he waked and caught sight of his sister and the basket, and hastened to her with a cry of uncouth hunger and greediness.

"In a minute, sonny," Melissa said, in a sobbing voice. "Wait a minute." She held the basket aloof while she removed her hood and shawl.

"You may see him on his way to the outer darkness," said her mother with solemn vindictiveness.

"Mother, he has repented; he is a member of the church," Melissa cried out, with sudden sharpness.

"Repentance avails nothing without faith," returned her mother, setting down a chair so heavily that the deaf-and-dumb boy started at the concussion and looked about him wonderingly.

"He has repented; he is a member of the church; he is safe," Melissa cried again.

"I tell you he is not," said her mother.

Melissa went into the pantry, with her brother at her elbow, and prepared for him a plate of bread and molasses. The tears fell over her cheeks, but Alonzo noticed nothing. His greedy eyes were fixed on the food. When it was ready for him he sat down on his stool in the chimney corner and devoured it with loud smacks of his lips. That was all the evening meal prepared in the Lennox house that night. After the chairs were set in order for the meeting, Melissa and her mother sat down close to the fire and sewed on some white stuff which flowed in voluminous folds over their knees to the floor. Solomon came in presently, and seated himself with the great Bible on his knees. He read silently, but now and then gesticulated fiercely, as if he read aloud.

The meeting began at half-past six. About a quarter of an hour before, the outer door was heard opening, and there was a shuffling step and a clearing cough in the entry.

"It's your uncle Simeon," whispered Mrs. Lennox to Melissa, and her mouth took on a severer tension.

Solomon frowned over the Holy Writ on his knee.

Simeon advanced into the room, his heavy boots clapping the floor with a dull clatter as of wood, dispelling the solemn stillness. His grinning old face, blue with the cold, was sunk in the collar of his greatcoat. He rubbed his hands together as he approached the fire.

"Well, how are ye all?" he remarked, with a chuckle, as if there were a joke in the speech.

Nobody replied. Simeon pulled a chair up close to the fire and sat down.

"It's 'tarnal cold," said he, leaning over and spreading out his old hands to the blaze.

"The brands are all ready for the burning," said his sister-in-law, in a hollow, trembling voice. She drew a long thread through the white stuff on her knee.

Simeon turned suddenly and looked at her with a flash of small bright eyes. Then he laughed. "Lord bless ye, Sophy Anne, I forgot how 'tarnal hot you folks are calculatin' to have it day after tomorrow," said he. "Well, if you fail in your calculations, an' the cold continues, I shall be mighty glad to come in here. My house is darned cold this weather, and Abby Mosely ain't particular 'bout the doors; seems to me sometimes as if I was settin' in a hurricane the heft of the time, and as if my idees were gettin' on aslant. Abby thinks she's goin' up Thursday, and I wish in thunder she would. I wouldn't have her another day if she wa'n't a lone woman and nowheres to go. She ain't no kind of a cook. Look at here, Sophy Anne—"

Mrs. Lennox sewed on with compressed lips.

"Sophy Anne, look at here. You ain't got no mince pies on hand now, have you?"

"No, I ain't."

"Well, I didn't much s'pose you'd made any, you've been so busy gettin' ready to fly lately. Look at here, Sophy Anne, don't you feel as if you could roll me out a few mince pies tomorrow, hey?"

Mrs. Lennox looked at him.

"I dun'no' when I've eat a decent mince pie," pursued Simeon. "Abby Mosely keeps the Commandments, but she can't make pies that's fit to eat. I ain't had a mince pie I could eat since my last wife died. I wish you'd contrive an' roll me out a few, Sophy Anne. Your mince pies used to go ahead of Maria's; she always said they did. If the world don't come to an end day after tomorrow, I'd take a sight of comfort with 'em, and I'll be darned, if it does come to an end, if I don't think I'll have a chance to eat one or two of 'em before the fire got round to me. Can't ye do it, Sophy Anne, nohow?"

"No, I can't."

"Can't ye roll me out just half a dozen mince pies?"

"I will never roll out a mince pie for you, Simeon Lennox," said Sophia Anne, with icy fervor.

"Ye never will?"

"No, I never will." Sophia Anne's stern eyes in their hollow blue orbits met his.

Simeon chuckled; then he turned to his brother. "Well, Sol'mon, s'pose you're flappin' all ready to fly?" he said.

Solomon made no reply. He frowned over the great volume on his knees. The deaf-and-dumb boy had set his empty plate on the hearth and fallen asleep again, with his head tilted against the jamb. Melissa sewed, her pale face bent closely over her work.

"Hear ye are goin' to fly from Penfield's hill?" said Simeon.

Still Solomon said nothing.

"Well, I s'pose that's as good a place as any," said Simeon, "though 'tain't a very high hill. I should 'most think you'd want a higher hill than Penfield's. I s'pose you'll be kind of unhandy with your wings at first, an' start off something like hens. But then I s'pose a few feet more or less won't made no odds when they get fairly to workin'. I heard the women was makin' flyin' petticoats. Them what you're to work on, Sophy Anne, you and Melissy?"

Sophia Anne gave one look at him, then she took a stitch.

"Abby Mosely's to work on one, I guess," said Simeon. "She's b'en a-settin' in a heap of white cloth a-sewin' for three days. I came in once, an' she was tryin' of it on, an' she slipped out of it mighty sudden. All I've got to say is she'll cut a queer figure flyin'. She's pretty hefty. I miss my guess if she don't find it a job to strike out at first. Now I should think you might take to flyin' pretty natural, Sophy Anne."

Mrs. Lennox's pale face was flushed with anger, but she sewed on steadily.

"As for Melissy," said Simeon, in his chuckling drawl, "I ruther guess she could fly without much practice, too. She's built light; but it strikes me she'd better have a weddin' gown than a flyin' petticoat. Young Penfield goin' to fly with you, Melissy?"

Solomon Lennox closed the Bible with a great clap. "I'll have no more of this!" he said, with a shout of long-repressed fury.

"Now, Solomon, don't ye get r'iled so near the end of the world," drawled his brother, getting up slowly. "I'm goin'. I ain't goin' to be the means of makin' you backslide when ye're so nigh the top of Zion's Hill. I'm a-goin' home. I don't s'pose I shall get no supper on account of Abby's hurryin' up on her flyin' petticoat. Sure you ain't goin' to make them mince pies for me, Sophy Anne?"

"Yes, I be sure."

The brother-in-law thrust his sharp old face down close to Sophia Anne's. "Sure?" he repeated.

Sophia Anne started back and stared at him. There was something strange in his manner.

The old man laughed and straightened himself. "Well, I'm a-goin'," said he. "Good-by. Mebbe I shan't see ye again before ye fly. Hope ye'll 'light easy. Good-by."

After Simeon had closed the door, he opened it again and thrust his sharp features through a narrow aperture. "Look at here, Solomon," said he. "Mind ye leave the key in the door when ye go out to fly Thursday night. I want to come right in." Then Simeon shut the door again, but his malicious laugh could be plainly heard in the entry.

He did not go straight home as he had said, but up the road to Lawyer Bascombe's office. When he returned, the meeting in his brother's house was in session and the windows were dark with heads against the red firelight. Old Simeon stared up at them, and laughed aloud to himself as he went by. "Sophy Anne won't make me no mince pies. She's sure on't," he said, and laughed again.

The next day all the ordinary routine of life seemed at a standstill in the village. The storekeeper had become a convert; the store was closed, and the green inside shutters were fastened. Now and then a village loafer lounged disconsolately up, shook the door on its rattling lock, stared at the shuttered windows, then lounged away, muttering. The summer resting place of his kind, the long, bewhittled wooden bench on the store platform, could not be occupied that wintry day. The air was clear, and the dry pastures were white and stiff with the hoarfrost; the slants of the roofs glistened with it in the sun. The breaths of the people going to and from Solomon Lennox's house were like white smoke. The meeting began at dawn. Children were dragged hither at their parents' heels, cold and breakfastless. Not a meal was cooked that day in the houses of Solomon Lennox's followers. All the precious hours were spent in fasting and prayer. Toward night the excitement deepened. There was present within the village a spiritual convulsion as real as any other convulsion of nature, and as truly although more subtly felt. Even they who had scoffed and laughed at this new movement from the first, and were now practically untouched by it, grew nervous and ill at ease toward night, as from the gathering of a storm. The air seemed charged with electricity generated by the touch of human thought and faith with the Unknown. The unbelievers pressed their faces against the windowpanes, shading their eyes from the light within as the dusk deepened, or stood out in their yards watching the sky, half fearful they should indeed see some sign or marvel therein.

But the night came on and the stars shone out in their order as they had done from the first, and there was no sign but the old one of eternal love and beauty in the sky. The moon arose at nine o'clock, nearly at her full. That, from some interpretation of symbolical characters on the deaf-and-dumb boy's slate, had been fixed upon as the hour of meeting upon Penfield's hill. The solemn and dreadful moment which was to mark the climax of all creation was expected between that hour and dawn.

At half-past eight white-robed figures began to move along the road. People peeped around their curtains to see them pass; now and then belated children ran shrieking with terror into the houses at sight of them.

Beside the road, close to the gate which led to the wide field at the foot of Penfield's hill, under the shadow of a clump of hemlocks, Isaac Penfield had been waiting since quarter past eight o'clock. When the white company came in sight he drew farther back within the shadow, scanning the people eagerly as they passed.

Solomon Lennox and Deacon Scranton let down the bars, and the people passed through silently, crowding one another whitely like a flock of sheep. Sophia Anne, the deaf-and-dumb boy holding fast to her hand, was among the first.

Isaac had expected to see Melissa close to her mother; but she had become separated from her and came among the last.

Her slender figure was hidden in her flowing white robes, but there was no mistaking her gentle faltering gait and the delicate bend of her fair uncovered head.

Isaac stepped forward suddenly, threw his arms around Melissa, and drew her back with him within the shadow of the hemlocks. Nobody saw it but Abby Mosely, Simeon Lennox's housekeeper, and she was too panic-stricken to heed it intelligently; she went panting on after the others in her voluminous white robe, and left Melissa alone with Isaac Penfield.

Isaac pressed Melissa's head close to his breast, leaned his face down to hers, and whispered long in her ear. She listened trembling and unresisting; then she broke away from him weakly. "I can't, I can't!" she moaned. But he caught her again, and whispered again with his lips close to her soft pale cheek, and frequent kisses between the words.

"Come, now, sweetheart," he said at length, and attempted to draw her with him into the road; but she pulled herself away from him again, and stood warding him off with her white-draped arms.

"I can't, I can't!" she moaned again. "I must go with father and mother."

"I tell you they are wrong. Can't you believe me?"

"I—must—go with them."

"No; come with me, Melissa."

Melissa, still with her arms raised against him, looked away over the meadow, full of moving white figures. The moon shone out over it, and it gleamed like a field of Paradise peopled with angels. Then she looked up in her lover's face, and suddenly it was to her as if she saw therein the new earth of all her dreams.

Solomon Lennox and his followers kept on to Penfield's hill, which arose before them crowned with silver, and Isaac Penfield hastened down the road to the village, half carrying Melissa's little white-clad figure, wrapped against the cold in his own gray cloak.

Early the next morning a small company of pallid shivering people crept through the village to their homes. Many had weakened and deserted long before dawn, chilled to their very thoughts and fancies by their long vigil on the hilltop. Young girls ran home, crying aloud like children, and men half dragged hysterical wives rigid with chills. Solomon Lennox and his wife remained until the dawn light shone; then he beckoned to her and the whimpering deaf-and-dumb boy, and led the way down the hill without a word. He never looked at the rest of the company, but they followed silently.

The Penfield house was about a quarter of a mile from the pasture bars. When they reached it, Isaac stood waiting at the gate. He went up to Solomon, who was passing without a look, and touched his arm with an impatient yet respectful gesture. "You and Mrs. Lennox and Lonny had better come in here, I think," he said.

Solomon was moving on with dull obstinacy, but Isaac laid his hand on his arm. "I—think you have—forgotten," he said. "I am sorry, but—your brother Simeon has—taken possession of your house."

Solomon stared at him dully. He did not seem to comprehend. Sophia Anne looked as blue and bloodless in her white robe as if she were dead. She had scarce more control of her trembling tongue than if it were paralyzed, but her highly strung feminine nerves gave out vibrations still.

"Has Simeon took possession?" she demanded, fiercely.

Isaac Penfield nodded. "I think it would be pleasanter for you to come in here now," he said. Then he hesitated and colored suddenly. "Your daughter is in here," he added.

Sophia Anne gave a keen glance at him. Then she turned in at the gate with a sharp twitch at the arm of the deaf-and-dumb boy, who was making strange cries and moans, like a distressed animal. "Come, father," she called, impatiently; and Solomon also entered the Penfield gate with a piteous, dazed air.

In the great south room of the Penfield house were Melissa and Mrs. Martha Joyce, the housekeeper. Mrs. Joyce was mixing something in a steaming bowl; Melissa sat still, gazing at the fire. She was dressed in a blue satin gown and fine lace tucker, which had belonged to Isaac Penfield's mother. Madam Penfield had been nearly Melissa's size, and the gown fitted her slender figure daintily. She sat with her fair head bent, the color coming and going in her soft cheeks, as if from her own thoughts. Her little hands were folded in her blue satin lap, and on one finger gleamed a great pearl which Madam Penfield had used to wear.

When the door opened and her parents entered, she half started up, with a great blush; then she sank back, trembling and pale.

Isaac Penfield crossed over to her and laid his hand on

her shoulder. "She is my wife," he said. "We were married last night."

Sophia Anne made a faint gesture, which might have expressed anything. Solomon staggered to a chair without a look. In truth, when they entered the warm room, and the long strain of resistance against cold and fatigue ceased, exhaustion overcame them. Mrs. Joyce administered hot porridge and cordials, and Melissa knelt down in her blue satin and rubbed her mother's benumbed hands.

Solomon took whatever was offered him, meekly, like a child. His face was changed; the look which it had worn during the greater part of his life, the expression of himself within his old worn channel, had returned.

He was sitting by the fire, sipping cordial, when his brother Simeon came in; he had not even noticed the brazen clang of the knocker.

Simeon came tiptoeing around in front of his brother, thrust down his face on a level with his, and peered at him with a sharp twinkle of black eyes. Then he looked at Sophia Anne and chuckled. " 'Pears to me wings didn't work very well," said he.

Simeon had a roll of paper in his hand. He went to the desk and spread it out ostentatiously. Then he began to read in a high, solemn voice, with an undertone of merriment in it. "Know all men by these presents," began Simeon Lennox, and read straight through the deed, with all its strange legal formalities, by which his brother Solomon had conveyed his worldly goods to him.

Sophia Anne writhed in her chair as Simeon read. She was on a rack of torture, and every new word was a turn of the screw. Solomon set his tumbler of cordial on the hearth, and rested his head on his hands.

After Simeon had finished reading the deed, he paused for a moment. Sophia Anne gave a dry sob.

Simeon cleared his throat, and continued: "The foregoing

I do hereby declare null and void, and I do hereby remise, release, sell, and forever quitclaim, for myself and my heirs, by these presents, the aforementioned premises, with all the privileges and appurtenances thereunto belonging, to the said Solomon Lennox, his heirs and assigns forever, in consideration that Sophia Anne, the wife of said Solomon Lennox, shall, during the term of her natural life, unless she be prevented by sickness from so doing, make, mix, season, and bake for me with her own hands, with her best skill, according to her own conscience, seven mince pies during every week of the year, with one extra for every Independence and Thanksgiving day, and that the said Sophia Anne, the wife of the said Solomon Lennox, shall hereunto set her hand and seal."

Simeon looked at Sophia Anne. She stared back at him, speechless.

"Well, what ye goin' to do about it, Sophy Anne?" said Simeon.

Sophia Anne still looked at him as if he were a blank wall against which her very spirit had been brought to a standstill.

"Goin' to sign it, Sophy Anne?"

Sophia Anne got up. Her knees trembled, but she motioned back Isaac Penfield's proffered arm. She went to the desk, sat down, took the quill, dipped it carefully in the inkstand, and shook it lest it blot. Her lean arm crooked as stiffly as a stick, her lips were a blue line, but she wrote her name with sharply rippling strokes, and laid the pen down.

"Sure ye won't make them mince pies, Sophy Anne?" said Simeon.

Sophia Anne made no reply. She put her elbow on the desk, and leaned her head on her hand. Simeon looked at her a moment, then he gave her a rough pat on her shoulder and turned and went to the window, and stood there, staring out.

Melissa was weeping softly; Isaac stood beside her, smoothing her hair tenderly. The deaf-and-dumb boy's fair head hung helplessly over his shoulder. He had fallen asleep with the tears on his cheeks.

The morning sunlight shone broadly into the room over them all, but Solomon Lennox did not seem to heed that or anything that was around him, sitting sadly within himself: a prophet brooding over the ashes of his own prophetic fire.

# VIII. *A VILLAGE SINGER*[1]

THE trees were in full leaf, a heavy south wind was blowing, and there was a loud murmur among the new leaves. The people noticed it, for it was the first time that year that the trees had so murmured in the wind. The spring had come with a rush during the last few days.

The murmur of the trees sounded loud in the village church, where the people sat waiting for the service to begin. The windows were open; it was a very warm Sunday for May.

The church was already filled with this soft sylvan music —the tender harmony of the leaves and the south wind, and the sweet, desultory whistles of birds—when the choir arose and began to sing.

In the center of the row of women singers stood Alma Way. All the people stared at her, and turned their ears critically. She was the new leading soprano. Candace Whitcomb, the old one, who had sung in the choir for forty years, had lately been given her dismissal. The audience considered that her voice had grown too cracked and uncertain on the upper notes. There had been much complaint, and after long deliberation the church officers had made known their decision as mildly as possible to the old singer. She had sung for the last time the Sunday before, and Alma Way had been engaged to take her place. With the exception of the organist, the leading soprano was the only paid musician in the large choir. The salary was very modest; still, the village people considered it large for a

[1] *Copyright, 1891, by Harper & Brothers. Copyright, 1919, by Mary E. Wilkins Freeman.*

young woman. Alma was from the adjoining village of East Derby; she had quite a local reputation as a singer.

Now she fixed her large solemn blue eyes; her long, delicate face, which had been pretty, turned paler; the blue flowers on her bonnet trembled; her little thin gloved hands, clutching the singing book, shook perceptibly; but she sang out bravely. The most formidable mountain height of the world, self-distrust and timidity, arose before her, but her nerves were braced for its ascent. In the midst of the hymn she had a solo; her voice rang out piercingly sweet; the people nodded admiringly at one another; but suddenly there was a stir; all the faces turned toward the windows on the south side of the church. Above the din of the wind and the birds, above Alma Way's sweetly straining tones, arose another female voice, singing another hymn to another tune.

"It's her," the women whispered to each other; they were half aghast, half smiling.

Candace Whitcomb's cottage stood close to the south side of the church. She was playing on her parlor organ, and singing, to drown out the voice of her rival.

Alma caught her breath; she almost stopped; the hymn book waved like a fan; then she went on. But the long husky drone of the parlor organ and the shrill clamor of the other voice seemed louder than anything else.

When the hymn was finished, Alma sat down. She felt faint; the woman next her slipped a peppermint into her hand. "It ain't worth minding," she whispered, vigorously. Alma tried to smile; down in the audience a young man was watching her with a kind of fierce pity.

In the last hymn Alma had another solo. Again the parlor organ droned above the carefully delicate accompaniment of the church organ, and again Candace Whitcomb's voice clamored forth in another tune.

After the benediction, the other singers pressed around

Alma. She did not say much in return for their expressions of indignation and sympathy. She wiped her eyes furtively once or twice, and tried to smile. William Emmons, the choir leader, elderly, stout, and smooth-faced, stood over her and raised his voice. He was the old musical dignitary of the village, the leader of the choral club and the singing schools. "A most outrageous proceeding," he said. People had coupled his name with Candace Whitcomb's. The old bachelor tenor and old maiden soprano had been wont to walk together to her home next door after the Saturday-night rehearsals, and they had sung duets to the parlor organ. People had watched sharply her old face, on which the blushes of youth sat pitifully, when William Emmons entered the singing seats. They wondered if he would ever ask her to marry him.

And now he said further to Alma Way that Candace Whitcomb's voice had failed utterly of late, that she sang shockingly, and ought to have had sense enough to know it.

When Alma went down into the audience room, in the midst of the chattering singers, who seemed to have descended, like birds, from song flights to chirps, the minister approached her. He had been waiting to speak to her. He was a steady-faced, fleshy old man, who had preached from that one pulpit over forty years. He told Alma, in his slow way, how much he regretted the annoyance to which she had been subjected, and intimated that he would endeavor to prevent a recurrence of it. "Miss Whitcomb—must be— reasoned with," said he; he had a slight hesitation of speech, not an impediment. It was as if his thoughts did not slide readily into his words, although both were present. He walked down the aisle with Alma, and bade her good morning when he saw Wilson Ford waiting for her in the doorway. Everybody knew that Wilson Ford and Alma were lovers; they had been for the last ten years.

Alma colored softly and made a little imperceptible motion with her head; her silk dress and the lace on her mantle fluttered, but she did not speak. Neither did Wilson, although they had not met before that day. They did not look at each other's faces—they seemed to see each other without that—and they walked along side by side.

They reached the gate before Candace Whitcomb's little house. Wilson looked past the front yard, full of pink and white spikes on flowering bushes, at the lace-curtained windows; a thin white profile, stiffly inclined, apparently over a book, was visible at one of them. Wilson gave his head a shake. He was a stout man, with features so strong that they overcame his flesh. "I'm going up home with you, Alma," said he; "and then—I'm just coming back, to give Aunt Candace one blowing up."

"Oh, don't, Wilson."

"Yes, I shall. If you want to stand this kind of a thing you may; I shan't."

"There's no need of your talking to her. Mr. Pollard's going to."

"Did he say he was?"

"Yes. I think he's going in before the afternoon meeting, from what he said."

"Well, there's one thing about it, if she does that thing again this afternoon, I'll go in there and break that old organ up into kindling wood." Wilson set his mouth hard and shook his head again.

Alma gave little side glances up at him; her tone was deprecatory, but her face was full of soft smiles. "I suppose she does feel dreadfully about it," said she. "I can't help feeling kind of guilty, taking her place."

"I don't see how you're to blame. It's outrageous, her acting so."

"The choir gave her a photograph album last week, didn't they?"

"Yes. They went there last Thursday night, and gave her

an album and a surprise party. She ought to behave herself."

"Well, she's sung there so long, I suppose it must be dreadful hard for her to give it up."

Other people going home from church were very near Wilson and Alma. She spoke softly that they might not hear; he did not lower his voice in the least. Presently Alma stopped before a gate.

"What are you stopping here for?" asked Wilson.

"Minnie Lansing wanted me to come and stay with her this noon."

"You're going home with me."

"I'm afraid I'll put your mother out."

"Put mother out! I told her you were coming, this morning. She's got all ready for you. Come along; don't stand here."

He did not tell Alma of the pugnacious spirit with which his mother had received the announcement of her coming, and how she had stayed at home to prepare the dinner and make a parade of her hard work and her injury.

Wilson's mother was the reason why he did not marry Alma. He would not take his wife home to live with her, and was unable to support separate establishments. Alma was willing enough to be married and put up with Wilson's mother, but she did not complain of his decision. Her delicate blond features grew sharper, and her blue eyes more hollow. She had had a certain fine prettiness, but now she was losing it and beginning to look old, and there was a prim, angular, old-maiden carriage about her narrow shoulders.

Wilson never noticed it, and never thought of Alma as not possessed of eternal youth, or capable of losing or regretting it.

"Come along, Alma," said he; and she followed meekly after him down the street.

Soon after they passed Candace Whitcomb's house, the

minister went up the front walk and rang the bell. The pale profile at the window had never stirred as he opened the gate and came up the walk. However, the door was promptly opened, in response to his ring. "Good morning, Miss Whitcomb," said the minister.

"*Good* morning." Candace gave a sweeping toss of her head as she spoke. There was a fierce upward curl to her thin nostrils and her lips, as if she scented an adversary. Her black eyes had two tiny cold sparks of fury in them, like an enraged bird's. She did not ask the minister to enter, but he stepped lumberingly into the entry, and she retreated rather than led the way into her little parlor. He settled into the great rocking-chair and wiped his face. Candace sat down again in her old place by the window. She was a tall woman, but very slender and full of pliable motions, like a blade of grass.

"It's a—very pleasant day," said the minister.

Candace made no reply. She sat still, with her head drooping. The wind stirred the looped lace curtains; a tall rose tree outside the window waved; soft shadows floated through the room. Candace's parlor organ stood in front of an open window that faced the church; on the corner was a pitcher with a bunch of white lilacs. The whole room was scented with them. Presently the minister looked over at them and sniffed pleasantly.

"You have—some beautiful—lilacs there."

Candace did not speak. Every line of her slender figure looked flexible, but it was a flexibility more resistant than rigor.

The minister looked at her. He filled up the great rocking-chair; his arms in his shiny black coat sleeves rested squarely and comfortably upon the haircloth arms of the chair.

"Well, Miss Whitcomb, I suppose I—may as well come to—the point. There was—a little—matter I wished to speak to you about. I don't suppose you were—at least I can't suppose you were—aware of it, but—this morning, during the singing by the choir, you played and—sung a little too—loud. That is, with—the windows open. It—disturbed us—a little. I hope you won't feel hurt—my dear Miss Candace, but I knew you would rather I would speak of it, for I knew—you would be more disturbed than anybody else at the idea of such a thing."

Candace did not raise her eyes; she looked as if his words might sway her through the window. "I ain't disturbed at it," said she. "I did it on purpose; I meant to."

The minister looked at her.

"You needn't look at me. I know jest what I'm about. I sung the way I did on purpose, an' I'm goin' to do it again, an' I'd like to see you stop me. I guess I've got a right to set down to my own organ, an' sing a psalm tune on a Sabbath day, 'f I want to; an' there ain't no amount of talkin' an' palaverin' a-goin' to stop me. See there!" Candace swung aside her skirts a little. "Look at that!"

The minister looked. Candace's feet were resting on a large red-plush photograph album.

"Makes a nice footstool, don't it?" said she.

The minister looked at the album, then at her; there was a slowly gathering alarm in his face; he began to think she was losing her reason.

Candace had her eyes full upon him now, and her head up. She laughed, and her laugh was almost a snarl. "Yes; I thought it would make a beautiful footstool," said she. "I've been wantin' one for some time." Her tone was full of vicious irony.

"Why, Miss—" began the minister; but she interrupted him:

"I know what you're a-goin' to say, Mr. Pollard, an' now I'm goin' to have my say; I'm a-goin' to speak. I want to know what you think of folks that pretend to be Christians treatin' anybody the way they've treated me? Here I've sung in those singin' seats forty year. I ain't never missed a Sunday, except when I've been sick, an' I've gone an' sung a good many times when I'd better been in bed, an' now I'm turned out without a word of warnin'. My voice is jest as good as ever 'twas; there can't anybody say it ain't. It wa'n't ever quite so high pitched as that Way girl's, mebbe; but she flats the whole durin' time. My voice is as good an' high today as it was twenty year ago; an' if it wa'n't, I'd like to know where the Christianity comes in. I'd like to know if it wouldn't be more to the credit of folks in a church to keep an old singer an' an old minister, if they didn't sing an' hold forth quite so smart as they used to, ruther than turn 'em off an' hurt their feelin's. I guess it would be full as much to the glory of God. S'pose the singin' an' the preachin' wa'n't quite so good, what difference would it make? Salvation don't hang on anybody's hittin' a high note, that I ever heard of. Folks are gettin' as high steppin' an' fussy in a meetin' house as they are in a tavern, nowadays. S'pose they should turn you off, Mr. Pollard, come an' give you a photograph album, an' tell you to clear out, how'd you like it? I ain't findin' any fault with your preachin'; it was always good enough to suit me; but it don't stand to reason folks'll be as took up with your sermons as when you was a young man. You can't expect it. S'pose they should turn you out in your old age, an' call in some young bob squirt, how'd you feel? There's William Emmons, too; he's three years older'n I am, if he does lead the choir an' run all the singin' in town. If my voice has gi'en out, it stan's to reason his has. It ain't, though. William Emmons sings jest as well as he ever did. Why don't they turn him out the way they have me, an' give him a photograph album? I dunno' but it would be a good idea to send everybody, as soon as they get a little old an' gone by, an' young folks begin to push, on to some desert island, an' give 'em each a photograph album. Then they can sit down an' look at pictures the rest of their days. Mebbe government'll take it up.

"There they come here last week Thursday, all the choir, jest about eight o'clock in the evenin', an' pretended they'd come to give me a nice little surprise. Surprise! h'm! Brought cake an' oranges, an' was jest as nice as they could be, an' I was real tickled. I never had a surprise party before in my life. Jenny Carr she played, an' they wanted me to sing alone, an' I never suspected a thing. I've been mad ever since to think what a fool I was, an' how they must have laughed in their sleeves.

"When they'd gone I found this photograph album on the table, all done up as nice as you please, an' directed to Miss Candace Whitcomb from her many friends, an' I opened it, an' there was the letter inside givin' me notice to quit.

"If they'd gone about it any decent way, told me right out honest that they'd got tired of me an' wanted Alma Way to sing instead of me, I wouldn't minded so much. I should have been hurt 'nough, for I'd felt as if some that had pretended to be my friends wa'n't; but it wouldn't have been as bad as this. They said in the letter that they'd always set great value on my services, an' it wa'n't from any lack of appreciation that they turned me off, but they thought the duty was gettin' a little too arduous for me. H'm! I hadn't complained. If they'd turned me right out fair an' square, showed me the door, an' said, 'Here, you get out,' but to go an' spill molasses, as it were, all over the threshold, tryin' to make me think it's all nice an' sweet—

"I'd sent that photograph album back quick's I could pack it, but I didn't know who started it, so I've used it for a footstool. It's all it's good for, 'cordin' to my way of thinkin'. An' I ain't been particular to get the dust off my shoes before I used it, neither."

Mr. Pollard, the minister, sat staring. He did not look

at Candace; his eyes were fastened upon a point straight ahead. He had a look of helpless solidity, like a block of granite. This country minister, with his steady, even temperament, treading with heavy precision his one track for over forty years, having nothing new in his life except the new sameness of the seasons, and desiring nothing new, was incapable of understanding a woman like this, who had lived as quietly as he, and all the time held within herself the elements of revolution. He could not account for such violence, such extremes, except in a loss of reason. He had a conviction that Candace was getting beyond herself. He himself was not a typical New Englander; the national elements of character were not pronounced in him. He was aghast and bewildered at this outbreak, which was tropical, and more than tropical, for a New England nature has a floodgate, and the power which it releases is an accumulation. Candace Whitcomb had been a quiet woman, so delicately resolute that the quality had been scarcely noticed in her, and her ambition had been unsuspected. Now the resolution and the ambition appeared raging over her whole self.

She began to talk again. "I've made up my mind that I'm goin' to sing Sundays the way I did this mornin', an' I don't care what folks say," said she. "I've made up my mind that I'm goin' to take matters into my own hands. I'm goin' to let folks see that I ain't trod down quite flat, that there's a little rise left in me. I ain't goin' to give up beat yet a while; an' I'd like to see anybody stop me. If I ain't got a right to play a psalm tune on my organ an' sing, I'd like to know. If you don't like it, you can move the meetin' house."

Candace had had an inborn reverence for clergymen. She had always treated Mr. Pollard with the utmost deference. Indeed, her manner toward all men had been marked by a certain delicate stiffness and dignity. Now she was talking to the old minister with the homely freedom with which she might have addressed a female gossip over the back fence. He could not say much in return. He did not feel competent to make headway against any such tide of passion; all he could do was to let it beat against him. He made a few expostulations, which increased Candace's vehemence; he expressed his regret over the whole affair, and suggested that they should kneel and ask the guidance of the Lord in the matter, that she might be led to see it all in a different light.

Candace refused flatly. "I don't see any use prayin' about it," said she. "I don't think the Lord's got much to do with it, anyhow."

It was almost time for the afternoon service when the minister left. He had missed his comfortable noontide rest, through this encounter with his revolutionary parishioner. After the minister had gone, Candace sat by the window and waited. The bell rang, and she watched the people file past. When her nephew, Wilson Ford, with Alma appeared, she grunted to herself. "She's thin as a rail," said she; "guess there won't be much left of her by the time Wilson gets her. Little soft spoken nippin' thing, she wouldn't make him no kind of a wife, anyway. Guess it's jest as well."

When the bell had stopped tolling, and all the people entered the church, Candace went over to her organ and seated herself. She arranged a singing book before her, and sat still, waiting. Her thin, colorless neck and temples were full of beating pulses; her black eyes were bright and eager; she leaned stiffly over toward the music rack, to hear better. When the church organ sounded out she straightened herself; her long skinny fingers pressed her own organ keys with nervous energy. She worked the pedals with all her strength; all her slender body was in motion. When the first notes of Alma's solo began, Candace sang. She had really possessed a fine voice, and it was wonderful how little she had lost it. Straining her throat with jealous fury, her notes were still for the main part true. Her voice filled the whole room; she sang with wonderful fire and expression. That, at least, mild little Alma Way could never emulate. She was full of steadfastness and unquestioning constancy, but there were in her no smoldering fires of ambition and resolution. Music was not to her what it had been to her older rival. To this obscure woman, kept relentlessly by circumstances in a narrow track, singing in the village choir had been as much as Italy was to Napoleon —and now on her island of exile she was still showing fight.

After the church service was done, Candace left the organ and went over to her old chair by the window. Her knees felt weak and shook under her. She sat down and leaned back her head. There were red spots on her cheeks. Pretty soon she heard a quick slam of her gate and an impetuous tread on the gravel walk. She looked up, and there was her nephew, Wilson Ford, hurrying up to the door. She cringed a little; then she settled herself more firmly in her chair.

Wilson came into the room with a rush. He left the door open, and the wind slammed it to after him.

"Aunt Candace, where are you?" he called out, in a loud voice.

She made no reply. He looked around fiercely, and his eyes seemed to pounce upon her.

"Look here, Aunt Candace," said he, "are you crazy?" Candace said nothing. "Aunt Candace!" She did not seem to see him. "If you don't answer me," said Wilson, "I'll just go over there and pitch that old organ out of the window!"

"Wilson Ford!" said Candace, in a voice that was almost a scream.

"Well, what say! What have you got to say for yourself, acting the way you have? I tell you what 'tis, Aunt Candace, I won't stand it."

"I'd like to see you help yourself."

"I will help myself. I'll pitch that old organ out of the window, and then I'll board up the window on that side of your house. Then we'll see."

"It ain't your house, and it won't never be."

"Who said it was my house? You're my aunt, and I've got a little lookout for the credit of the family. Aunt Candace, what are you doing this way for?"

"It don't make no odds what I'm doin' so for. I ain't bound to give my reasons to a young fellar like you, if you do act so mighty toppin'. But I'll tell you one thing, Wilson Ford, after the way you've spoke today, you sha'n't never have one cent of my money, an' you can't never marry that Way girl if you don't have it. You can't never take her home to live with your mother, an' this house would have been mighty nice an' convenient for you some day. Now you won't get it. I'm goin' to make another will. I'd made one, if you did but know it. Now you won't get a cent of my money, you nor your mother, neither. An' I ain't goin' to live a dreadful while longer, neither. Now I wish you'd go home; I want to lay down. I'm 'bout sick."

Wilson could not get another word from his aunt. His indignation had not in the least cooled. Her threat of disinheriting him did not cow him at all; he had too much rough independence, and indeed his aunt Candace's house had always been too much of an air castle for him to contemplate seriously. Wilson, with his burly frame and his headlong common sense, could have little to do with air castles, had he been hard enough to build them over graves. Still he had not admitted that he never could marry Alma. All his hopes were based upon a rise in his own fortunes, not by some sudden convulsion, but by his own long and

steady labor. Sometime, he thought, he should have saved
enough for the two homes.

He went out of his aunt's house still storming. She
arose after the door had shut behind him, and got out into
the kitchen. She thought that she would start a fire and
make a cup of tea. She had not eaten anything all day.
She put some kindling wood into the stove and touched a
match to it; then she went back to the sitting room, and settled down again into the chair by the window. The fire in
the kitchen stove roared, and the light wood was soon burned
out. She thought no more about it. She had not put on
the teakettle. Her head ached, and once in a while she
shivered. She sat at the window while the afternoon waned
and the dusk came on. At seven o'clock the meeting bell
rang again, and the people flocked by. This time she did
not stir. She had shut her parlor organ. She did not need
to outsing her rival this evening; there was only congregational singing at the Sunday-night prayer meeting.

She sat still until it was nearly time for meeting to be
done; her head ached harder and harder, and she shivered
more. Finally she arose. "Guess I'll go to bed," she muttered. She went about the house, bent over and shaking, to
lock the doors. She stood a minute in the back door, looking over the fields to the woods. There was a red light over
there. "The woods are on fire," said Candace. She watched
with a dull interest the flames roll up, withering and destroy-
ing the tender green spring foliage. The air was full of
smoke, although the fire was half a mile away.

Candace locked the door and went in. The trees with
their delicate garlands of new leaves, with the new nests of
song birds, might fall; she was in the roar of an intenser
fire; the growths of all her springs and the delicate wonted-
ness of her whole life was going down in it. Candace went
to bed in her little room off the parlor, but she could not
sleep. She lay awake all night. In the morning she crawled

to the door and hailed a little boy who was passing. She bade him go for the doctor as quickly as he could, then to Mrs. Ford's, and ask her to come over. She held on to the door while she was talking. The boy stood staring wonderingly at her. The spring wind fanned her face. She had drawn on a dress skirt and put her shawl over her shoulders, and her gray hair was blowing over her red cheeks.

She shut the door and went back to her bed. She never arose from it again. The doctor and Mrs. Ford came and looked after her, and she lived a week. Nobody but herself thought until the very last that she would die; the doctor called her illness merely a light run of fever; she had her senses fully.

But Candace gave up at the first. "It's my last sickness," she said to Mrs. Ford that morning when she first entered; and Mrs. Ford had laughed at the notion; but the sick woman held to it. She did not seem to suffer much physical pain; she only grew weaker and weaker, but she was distressed mentally. She did not talk much, but her eyes followed everybody with an agonized expression.

On Wednesday William Emmons came to inquire for her. Candace heard him out in the parlor. She tried to raise herself on one elbow that she might listen better to his voice.

"William Emmons come in to ask how you was," Mrs. Ford said, after he was gone.

"I—heard him," replied Candace. Presently she spoke again. "Nancy," said she, "where's that photograph album?"

"On the table," replied her sister, hesitatingly.

"Mebbe—you'd better—brush it up a little."

"Well."

Sunday morning Candace wished that the minister should be asked to come in at the noon intermission. She had refused to see him before. He came and prayed with her, and she asked his forgiveness for the way she had spoken the Sunday before. "I—hadn't ought to—spoke so," said she. "I was—dreadful wrought up."

"Perhaps it was your sickness coming on," said the minister, soothingly.

Candace shook her head. "No—it wa'n't. I hope the Lord will—forgive me."

After the minister had gone, Candace still appeared unhappy. Her pitiful eyes followed her sister everywhere with the mechanical persistency of a portrait.

"What is it you want, Candace?" Mrs. Ford said at last. She had nursed her sister faithfully, but once in a while her impatience showed itself.

"Nancy!"

"What say?"

"I wish—you'd go out when—meetin's done, an'—head off Alma an' Wilson, an'—ask 'em to come in. I feel as if—I'd like to—hear her sing."

Mrs. Ford stared. "Well," said she.

The meeting was now in session. The windows were all open, for it was another warm Sunday. Candace lay listening to the music when it began, and a look of peace came over her face. Her sister had smoothed her hair back and put on a clean cap. The white curtain in the bedroom window waved in the wind like a white sail. Candace almost felt as if she were better, but the thought of death seemed easy.

Mrs. Ford at the parlor window watched for the meeting to be out. When the people appeared, she ran down the walk and waited for Alma and Wilson. When they came she told them what Candace wanted, and they all went in together.

"Here's Alma an' Wilson, Candace," said Mrs. Ford, leading them to the bedroom door.

Candace smiled. "Come in," she said, feebly. And Alma and Wilson entered and stood beside the bed. Candace continued to look at them, the smile straining her lips.

"Wilson!"

"What is it, Aunt Candace?"

"I ain't altered that—will. You an' Alma can—come here an'—live—when I'm—gone. Your mother won't mind livin' alone. Alma can have—all—my things."

"Don't, Aunt Candace." Tears were running over Wilson's cheeks, and Alma's delicate face was all of a quiver.

"I thought—maybe—Alma'd be willin' to—sing for me," said Candace.

"What do you want me to sing?" Alma asked, in a trembling voice.

" 'Jesus, lover of my soul.' "

Alma, standing there beside Wilson, began to sing. At first she could hardly control her voice; then she sang sweetly and clearly.

Candace lay and listened. Her face had a holy and radiant expression. When Alma stopped singing it did not disappear, but she looked up and spoke, and it was like a secondary glimpse of the old shape of a forest tree through the smoke and flame of the transfiguring fire the instant before it falls. "You flatted a little on—soul," said Candace.

## IX. OLD WOMAN MAGOUN[1]

THE hamlet of Barry's Ford is situated in a sort of high valley among the mountains. Below it the hills lie in moveless curves like a petrified ocean; above it they rise in green-cresting waves which never break. It is *Barry's* Ford because one time the Barry family was the most important in the place; and *Ford* because just at the beginning of the hamlet the little turbulent Barry River is fordable. There is, however, now a rude bridge across the river.

Old Woman Magoun was largely instrumental in bringing the bridge to pass. She haunted the miserable little grocery, wherein whisky and hands of tobacco were the most salient features of the stock in trade, and she talked much. She would elbow herself into the midst of a knot of idlers and talk.

"That bridge ought to be built this very summer," said Old Woman Magoun. She spread her strong arms like wings, and sent the loafers, half laughing, half angry, flying in every direction. "If I were a *man*," said she, "I'd go out this very minute and lay the fust log. If I were a passel of lazy men layin' round, I'd start up for once in my life, I would." The men cowered visibly—all except Nelson Barry; he swore under his breath and strode over to the counter.

Old Woman Magoun looked after him majestically. "You can cuss all you want to, Nelson Barry," said she; "I ain't afraid of you. I don't expect you to lay ary log of the bridge, but I'm goin' to have it built this very summer." She did. The weakness of the masculine element in Barry's Ford was laid low before such strenuous feminine assertion.

Old Woman Magoun and some other women planned a treat—two sucking pigs, and pies, and sweet cake—for a reward after the bridge should be finished. They even viewed leniently the increased consumption of ardent spirits.

"It seems queer to me," Old Woman Magoun said to Sally Jinks, "that men can't do nothin' without havin' to drink and chew to keep their sperits up. Lord! I've worked all my life and never done nuther."

"Men is different," said Sally Jinks.

"Yes, they be," assented Old Woman Magoun, with open contempt.

The two women sat on a bench in front of Old Woman Magoun's house, and little Lily Barry, her granddaughter, sat holding her doll on a small mossy stone near by. From where they sat they could see the men at work on the new bridge. It was the last day of the work.

Lily clasped her doll—a poor old rag thing—close to her childish bosom, like a little mother, and her face, round which curled her long yellow hair, was fixed upon the men at work. Little Lily had never been allowed to run with the other children at Barry's Ford. Her grandmother had taught her everything she knew—which was not much, but tending at least to a certain measure of spiritual growth—for she, as it were, poured the goodness of her own soul into this little receptive vase of another. Lily was firmly grounded in her knowledge that it was wrong to lie or steal or disobey her grandmother. She had also learned that one should be very industrious. It was seldom that Lily sat idly holding her doll baby, but this was a holiday because of the bridge. She looked only a child, although she was nearly fourteen; her mother had been married at sixteen. That is, Old Woman Magoun said that her daughter, Lily's mother, had married at sixteen; there had been rumors, but no one had dared openly gainsay the old woman. She said that her daughter had married Nelson Barry and he had deserted her. She had lived in her mother's house, and Lily had been born there, and she had died when the baby was only a week old.

Lily's father, Nelson Barry, was the fairly dangerous degenerate of a good old family. Nelson's father before him had been bad. He was now the last of the family, with the exception of a sister of feeble intellect, with whom he lived in the old Barry house. He was a middle-aged man, still handsome. The shiftless population of Barry's Ford looked up to him as to an evil deity. They wondered how Old Woman Magoun dared brave him as she did. But Old Woman Magoun had within her a mighty sense of reliance upon herself as being on the right track in the midst of a maze of evil, which gave her courage. Nelson Barry had manifested no interest whatever in his daughter. Lily seldom saw her father. She did not often go to the store which was his favorite haunt. Her grandmother took care that she should not do so.

However, that afternoon she departed from her usual custom and sent Lily to the store.

She came in from the kitchen, whither she had been to baste the roasting pig. "There's no use talkin'," said she, "I've got to have some more salt. I've jest used the very last I had to dredge over that pig. I've got to go to the store."

Sally Jinks looked at Lily. "Why don't you send her?" she asked.

Old Woman Magoun gazed irresolutely at the girl. She was herself very tired. It did not seem to her that she could drag herself up the dusty hill to the store. She glanced with covert resentment at Sally Jinks. She thought that she might offer to go. But Sally Jinks said again, "Why don't you let her go?" and looked with a languid eye at Lily holding her doll on the stone.

Lily was watching the men at work on the bridge, with her childish delight in a spectacle of any kind, when her grandmother addressed her.

"Guess I'll let you go down to the store an' git some salt, Lily," said she.

The girl turned uncomprehending eyes upon her grandmother at the sound of her voice. She had been filled with one of the innocent reveries of childhood. Lily had in her the making of an artist or a poet. Her prolonged childhood went to prove it, and also her retrospective eyes, as clear and blue as blue light itself, which seemed to see past all that she looked upon. She had not come of the old Barry family for nothing. The best of the strain was in her, along with the splendid stanchness in humble lines which she had acquired from her grandmother.

"Put on your hat," said Old Woman Magoun; "the sun is hot and you might git a headache." She called the girl to her, and put back the shower of fair curls under the rubber band which confined the hat. She gave Lily some money, and watched her knot it into a corner of her little cotton handkerchief. "Be careful you don't lose it," said she, "and don't stop to talk to anybody, for I am in a hurry for that salt. Of course, if anybody speaks to you answer them polite, and then come right along."

Lily started, her pocket handkerchief weighted with the small silver dangling from one hand, and her rag doll carried over her shoulder like a baby. The absurd travesty of a face peeped forth from Lily's yellow curls. Sally Jinks looked after her with a sniff.

"She ain't goin' to carry that rag doll to the store?" said she.

"She likes to," replied Old Woman Magoun, in a half-shamed yet defiantly extenuating voice.

"Some girls at her age is thinkin' about beaux instead of rag dolls," said Sally Jinks.

The grandmother bristled, "Lily ain't big nor old for her age," said she. "I ain't in any hurry to have her git married. She ain't none too strong."

"She's got a good color," said Sally Jinks. She was crocheting white cotton lace, making her thick fingers fly. She really knew how to do scarcely anything except to crochet that coarse lace; somehow her heavy brain or her fingers had mastered that.

"I know she's got a beautiful color," replied Old Woman Magoun, with an odd mixture of pride and anxiety, "but it comes an' goes."

"I've heard that was a bad sign," remarked Sally Jinks, loosening some thread from her spool.

"Yes, it is," said the grandmother. "She's nothin' but a baby, though she's quicker than most to learn."

Lily Barry went on her way to the store. She was clad in a scanty short frock of blue cotton; her hat was tipped back, forming an oval frame for her innocent face. She was very small, and walked like a child, with the clap-clap of little feet of babyhood. She might have been considered, from her looks, under ten.

Presently she heard footsteps behind her; she turned around a little timidly to see who was coming. When she saw a handsome well-dressed man, she felt reassured. The man came alongside and glanced down carelessly at first; then his look deepened. He smiled, and Lily saw he was very handsome indeed, and that his smile was not only reassuring but wonderfully sweet and compelling.

"Well, little one," said the man, "where are you bound, you and your dolly?"

"I am going to the store to buy some salt for grandma," replied Lily, in her sweet treble. She looked up in the man's face, and he fairly started at the revelation of its innocent beauty. He regulated his pace by hers, and the two went on together. The man did not speak again at once. Lily kept glancing timidly up at him, and every time that she did so the man smiled and her confidence increased. Presently when the man's hand grasped her little childish one hanging by her side, she felt a complete trust in him. Then she smiled up at him. She felt glad that this nice man had come along, for just here the road was lonely.

After a while the man spoke. "What is your name, little one?" he asked, caressingly.

"Lily Barry."

The man started. "What is your father's name?"

"Nelson Barry," replied Lily.

The man whistled. "Is your mother dead?"

"Yes, sir."

"How old are you, my dear?"

"Fourteen," replied Lily.

The man looked at her with surprise. "As old as that?"

Lily suddenly shrank from the man. She could not have told why. She pulled her little hand from his, and he let it go with no remonstrance. She clasped both her arms around her rag doll, in order that her hand should not be free for him to grasp again.

She walked a little farther away from the man, and he looked amused.

"You still play with your doll?" he said, in a soft voice.

"Yes, sir," replied Lily. She quickened her pace and reached the store.

When Lily entered the store, Hiram Gates, the owner, was behind the counter. The only man besides in the store was Nelson Barry. He sat tipping his chair back against the wall; he was half asleep, and his handsome face was bristling with a beard of several days' growth and darkly flushed. He opened his eyes when Lily entered, the strange man following. He brought his chair down on all fours, and he looked at the man—not noticing Lily at all—with a look compounded of defiance and uneasiness.

"Hullo, Jim!" he said.

"Hullo, old man!" returned the stranger.

Lily went over to the counter and asked for the salt, in her pretty little voice. When she had paid for it and was crossing the store, Nelson Barry was on his feet.

"Well, how are you, Lily? It is Lily, isn't it?" he said.

"Yes, sir," replied Lily, faintly.

Her father bent down and, for the first time in her life, kissed her, and the whisky odor of his breath came into her face.

Lily involuntarily started, and shrank away from him. Then she rubbed her mouth violently with her little cotton handkerchief, which she held gathered up with the rag doll.

"Damn it all! I believe she is afraid of me," said Nelson Barry, in a thick voice.

"Looks a little like it," said the other man, laughing.

"It's that damned old woman," said Nelson Barry. Then he smiled again at Lily. "I didn't know what a pretty little daughter I was blessed with," said he, and he softly stroked Lily's pink cheek under her hat.

Now Lily did not shrink from him. Heredity instincts and nature itself were asserting themselves in the child's innocent, receptive breast.

Nelson Barry looked curiously at Lily. "How old are you, anyway, child?" he asked.

"I'll be fourteen in September," replied Lily.

"But you still play with your doll?" said Barry, laughing kindly down at her.

Lily hugged her doll more tightly, in spite of her father's kind voice. "Yes, sir," she replied.

Nelson glanced across at some glass jars filled with sticks of candy. "See here, little Lily, do you like candy?" said he.

"Yes, sir."

"Wait a minute."

Lily waited while her father went over to the counter. Soon he returned with a package of the candy.

"I don't see how you are going to carry so much," he said, smiling. "Suppose you throw away your doll?"

Lily gazed at her father and hugged the doll tightly, and there was all at once in the child's expression something mature. It became the reproach of a woman. Nelson's face sobered.

"Oh, it's all right, Lily," he said; "keep your doll. Here, I guess you can carry this candy under your arm."

Lily could not resist the candy. She obeyed Nelson's instructions for carrying it, and left the store laden. The two men also left, and walked in the opposite direction, talking busily.

When Lily reached home, her grandmother, who was watching for her, spied at once the package of candy.

"What's that?" she asked, sharply.

"My father gave it to me," answered Lily, in a faltering voice. Sally regarded her with something like alertness.

"Your father?"

"Yes, ma'am."

"Where did you see him?"

"In the store."

"He gave you this candy?"

"Yes, ma'am."

"What did he say?"

"He asked me how old I was, and—"

"And what?"

"I don't know," replied Lily; and it really seemed to her that she did not know, she was so frightened and bewildered by it all, and, more than anything else, by her grandmother's face as she questioned her.

Old Woman Magoun's face was that of one upon whom a long-anticipated blow had fallen. Sally Jinks gazed at her with a sort of stupid alarm.

Old Woman Magoun continued to gaze at her grand-child with that look of terrible solicitude, as if she saw the girl in the clutch of a tiger. "You can't remember what else he said?" she asked, fiercely, and the child began to whimper softly.

"No, ma'am," she sobbed. "I—don't know, and—"

"And what? Answer me."

"There was another man there. A real handsome man."

"Did he speak to you?" asked Old Woman Magoun.

"Yes, ma'am; he walked along with me a piece," confessed Lily, with a sob of terror and bewilderment.

"What did *he* say to you?" asked Old Woman Magoun, with a sort of despair.

Lily told, in her little, faltering, frightened voice, all of the conversation which she could recall. It sounded harmless enough, but the look of the realization of a long-expected blow never left her grandmother's face.

The sun was getting low and the bridge was nearing completion. Soon the workmen would be crowding into the cabin for their promised supper. There became visible in the distance, far up the road, the heavily plodding figure of another woman who had agreed to come and help. Old Woman Magoun turned again to Lily.

"You go right upstairs to your own chamber now," said she.

"Good land! ain't you goin' to let that poor child stay up and see the fun?" said Sally Jinks.

"You jest mind your own business," said Old Woman Magoun, forcibly, and Sally Jinks shrank. "You go right up there now, Lily," said the grandmother, in a softer tone, "and grandma will bring you up a nice plate of supper."

"When be you goin' to let that girl grow up?" asked Sally Jinks when Lily had disappeared.

"She'll grow up in the Lord's good time," replied Old Woman Magoun, and there was in her voice something both sad and threatening. Sally Jinks again shrank a little.

Soon the workmen came flocking noisily into the house. Old Woman Magoun and her two helpers served the bountiful supper. Most of the men had drunk as much as, and more than, was good for them, and Old Woman Magoun had stipulated that there was to be no drinking of anything except coffee during supper.

"I'll git you as good a meal as I know how," she said, "but if I see ary one of you drinkin' a drop, I'll run you all out. If you want anything to drink, you can go up to the store afterward. That's the place for you to go to, if you've got to make hogs of yourselves. I ain't goin' to have no hogs in my house."

Old Woman Magoun was implicitly obeyed. She had a curious authority over most people when she chose to exercise it. When the supper was in full swing, she quietly stole upstairs and carried some food to Lily. She found the girl, with the rag doll in her arms, crouching by the window in her little rocking-chair—a relic of her infancy, which she still used.

"What a noise they are makin', grandma!" she said, in a terrified whisper, as her grandmother placed the plate before her on a chair.

"They've 'most all of 'em been drinkin'. They air a passel of hogs," replied the old woman.

"Is the man that was with—with my father down there?" asked Lily, in a timid fashion. Then she fairly cowered before the look in her grandmother's eyes.

"No, he ain't, and what's more, he never will be down

there if I can help it," said Old Woman Magoun, in a fierce whisper. "I know who he is. They can't cheat me. He's one of them Willises—that family the Barrys married into. They're worse than the Barrys, ef they *have* got money. Eat your supper, and put him out of your mind, child."

It was after Lily was asleep, when Old Woman Magoun was alone, clearing away her supper dishes, that Lily's father came. The door was closed, and he knocked, and the old woman knew at once who was there. The sound of that knock meant as much to her as the whir of a bomb to the defender of a fortress. She opened the door, and Nelson Barry stood there.

"Good evening, Mrs. Magoun," he said.

Old Woman Magoun stood before him, filling up the doorway with her firm bulk.

"Good evening, Mrs. Magoun," said Nelson Barry again.

"I ain't got no time to waste," replied the old woman, harshly. "I've got my supper dishes to clean up after them men."

She stood there and looked at him as she might have looked at a rebellious animal which she was trying to tame. The man laughed.

"It's no use," said he. "You know me of old. No human being can turn me from my way when I am once started in it. You may as well let me come in."

Old Woman Magoun entered the house, and Barry followed her.

Barry began without any preface. "Where is the child?" asked he.

"Upstairs. She has gone to bed."

"She goes to bed early."

"Children ought to," returned the old woman, polishing a plate.

Barry laughed. "You are keeping her a child a long

while," he remarked, in a soft voice which had a sting in it.

"She *is* a child," returned the old woman, defiantly.

"Her mother was only three years older when Lily was born."

The old woman made a sudden motion toward the man which seemed fairly menacing. Then she turned again to her dish washing.

"I want her," said Barry.

"You can't have her," replied the old woman, in a still stern voice.

"I don't see how you can help yourself. You have always acknowledged that she was my child."

The old woman continued her task, but her strong back heaved. Barry regarded her with an entirely pitiless expression.

"I am going to have the girl, that is the long and short of it," he said, "and it is for her best good, too. You are a fool, or you would see it."

"Her best good?" muttered the old woman.

"Yes, her best good. What are you going to do with her, anyway? The girl is a beauty, and almost a woman grown, although you try to make out that she is a baby. You can't live forever."

"The Lord will take care of her," replied the old woman, and again she turned and faced him, and her expression was that of a prophetess.

"Very well, let Him," said Barry, easily. "All the same I'm going to have her, and I tell you it is for her best good. Jim Willis saw her this afternoon, and—"

Old Woman Magoun looked at him. "Jim Willis!" she fairly shrieked.

"Well, what of it?"

"One of them Willises!" repeated the old woman, and this time her voice was thick. It seemed almost as if she were stricken with paralysis. She did not enunciate clearly.

The man shrank a little. "Now what is the need of your making such a fuss?" he said. "I will take her, and Isabel will look out for her."

"Your half-witted sister?" said Old Woman Magoun.

"Yes, my half-witted sister. She knows more than you think."

"More wickedness."

"Perhaps. Well, a knowledge of evil is a useful thing. How are you going to avoid evil if you don't know what it is like? My sister and I will take care of my daughter."

The old woman continued to look at the man, but his eyes never fell. Suddenly her gaze grew inconceivably keen. It was as if she saw through all externals.

"I know what it is!" she cried. "You have been playing cards and you lost, and this is the way you will pay him."

Then the man's face reddened, and he swore under his breath.

"Oh, my God!" said the old woman; and she really spoke with her eyes aloft as if addressing something outside of them both. Then she turned again to her dish washing.

The man cast a dogged look at her back. "Well, there is no use talking. I have made up my mind," said he, "and you know me and what that means. I am going to have the girl."

"When?" said the old woman, without turning around.

"Well, I am willing to give you a week. Put her clothes in good order before she comes."

The old woman made no reply. She continued washing dishes. She even handled them so carefully they did not rattle.

"You understand," said Barry. "Have her ready a week from today."

"Yes," said Old Woman Magoun, "I understand."

Nelson Barry, going up the mountain road, reflected that Old Woman Magoun had a strong character, that she understood much better than her sex in general the futility of withstanding the inevitable.

"Well," he said to Jim Willis when he reached home, "the old woman did not make such a fuss as I expected."

"Are you going to have the girl?"

"Yes; a week from today. Look here, Jim; you've got to stick to your promise."

"All right," said Willis. "Go you one better."

The two were playing at cards in the old parlor, once magnificent, now squalid, of the Barry house. Isabel, the half-witted sister, entered, bringing some glasses on a tray. She had learned with her feeble intellect some tricks, like a dog. One of them was the mixing of sundry drinks. She set the tray on a little stand near the two men, and watched them with her silly simper.

"Clear out now and go to bed," her brother said to her, and she obeyed.

Early the next morning Old Woman Magoun went up to Lily's little sleeping chamber, and watched her a second as she lay asleep, with her yellow locks spread over the pillow. Then she spoke. "Lily," said she—"Lily, wake up. I am going to Greenham across the new bridge, and you can go with me."

Lily immediately sat up in bed and smiled at her grandmother. Her eyes were still misty, but the light of awakening was in them.

"Get right up," said the old woman. "You can wear your new dress if you want to."

Lily gurgled with pleasure like a baby. "And my new hat?" said she.

"I don't care."

Old Woman Magoun and Lily started for Greenham before Barry's Ford, which kept late hours, was fairly awake. It was three miles to Greenham. The old woman said that, since the horse was a little lame, they would walk. It was a beautiful morning, with a diamond radiance of dew over everything. Her grandmother had curled Lily's hair more punctiliously than usual. The little face peeped like a rose out of two rows of golden spirals. Lily wore her new muslin dress with a pink sash, and her best hat of a fine white straw trimmed with a wreath of rosebuds; also the neatest black openwork stockings and pretty shoes. She even had white cotton gloves. When they set out, the old, heavily stepping woman, in her black gown and cape and bonnet, looked down at the little pink fluttering figure. Her face was full of the tenderest love and admiration, and yet there was something terrible about it. They crossed the new bridge—a primitive structure built of logs in a slovenly fashion. Old Woman Magoun pointed to a gap.

"Jest see that," said she. "That's the way men work."

"Men ain't very nice, be they?" said Lily, in her sweet little voice.

"No, they ain't, take them all together," replied her grandmother.

"That man that walked to the store with me was nicer than some, I guess," Lily said, in a wishful fashion. Her grandmother reached down and took the child's hand in its small cotton glove. "You hurt me, holding my hand so tight," Lily said presently, in a deprecatory little voice.

The old woman loosened her grasp. "Grandma didn't know how tight she was holding your hand," said she. "She wouldn't hurt you for nothin', except it was to save your life, or somethin' like that." She spoke with an undertone of tremendous meaning which the girl was too childish to grasp. They walked along the country road. Just before they reached Greenham they passed a stone wall overgrown with blackberry vines, and, an unusual thing in that vicinity, a lusty spread of deadly nightshade full of berries.

"Those berries look good to eat, grandma," Lily said.

At that instant the old woman's face became something

terrible to see. "You can't have any now," she said, and hurried Lily along.

"They look real nice," said Lily.

When they reached Greenham, Old Woman Magoun took her way straight to the most pretentious house there, the residence of the lawyer, whose name was Mason. Old Woman Magoun bade Lily wait in the yard for a few moments, and Lily ventured to seat herself on a bench beneath an oak tree; then she watched with some wonder her grandmother enter the lawyer's office door at the right of the house. Presently the lawyer's wife came out and spoke to Lily under the tree. She had in her hand a little tray containing a plate of cake, a glass of milk, and an early apple. She spoke very kindly to Lily; she even kissed her, and offered her the tray of refreshments, which Lily accepted gratefully. She sat eating, with Mrs. Mason watching her, when Old Woman Magoun came out of the lawyer's office with a ghastly face.

"What are you eatin'?" she asked Lily, sharply. "Is that a sour apple?"

"I thought she might be hungry," said the lawyer's wife, with loving, melancholy eyes upon the girl.

Lily had almost finished the apple. "It's real sour, but I like it; it's real nice, grandma," she said.

"You ain't been drinkin' milk with a sour apple?"

"It was real nice milk, grandma."

"You ought never to have drunk milk and eat a sour apple," said her grandmother. "Your stomach was all out of order this mornin', an' sour apples and milk is always apt to hurt anybody."

"I don't know but they are," Mrs. Mason said, apologetically, as she stood on the green lawn with her lavender muslin sweeping around her. "I am real sorry, Mrs. Magoun. I ought to have thought. Let me get some soda for her."

"Soda never agrees with her," replied the old woman, in a harsh voice. "Come," she said to Lily, "it's time we were goin' home."

After Lily and her grandmother had disappeared down the road, Lawyer Mason came out of his office and joined his wife, who had seated herself on the bench beneath the tree. She was idle, and her face wore the expression of those who review joys forever past. She had lost a little girl, her only child, years ago, and her husband always knew when she was thinking about her. Lawyer Mason looked older than his wife; he had a dry, shrewd, slightly one-sided face.

"What do you think, Maria?" he said. "That old woman came to me with the most pressing entreaty to adopt that little girl."

"She is a beautiful little girl," said Mrs. Mason, in a slightly husky voice.

"Yes, she is a pretty child," assented the lawyer, looking pityingly at his wife; "but it is out of the question, my dear. Adopting a child is a serious measure, and in this case a child who comes from Barry's Ford!"

"But the grandmother seems a very good woman," said Mrs. Mason.

"I rather think she is. I never heard a word against her. But the father! No, Maria, we cannot take a child with Barry blood in her veins. The stock has run out; it is vitiated physically and morally. It won't do, my dear."

"Her grandmother had her dressed up as pretty as a little girl could be," said Mrs. Mason, and this time the tears welled into her faithful, wistful eyes.

"Well, we can't help that," said the lawyer, as he went back to his office.

Old Woman Magoun and Lily returned, going slowly along the road to Barry's Ford. When they came to the stone wall where the blackberry vines and the deadly nightshade grew, Lily said she was tired, and asked if she could not sit down for a few minutes. The strange look on her grandmother's face had deepened. Now and then Lily glanced at her and had a feeling as if she were looking at a stranger.

"Yes, you can set down if you want to," said Old Woman Magoun, deeply and harshly.

Lily started and looked at her, as if to make sure that it was her grandmother who spoke. Then she sat down on a stone which was comparatively free of the vines.

"Ain't you goin' to set down, grandma?" Lily asked, timidly.

"No; I don't want to get into that mess," replied her grandmother. "I ain't tired. I'll stand here."

Lily sat still; her delicate little face was flushed with heat. She extended her tiny feet in her best shoes and gazed at them. "My shoes are all over dust," said she.

"It will brush off," said her grandmother, still in that strange voice.

Lily looked around. An elm tree in the field behind her cast a spray of branches over her head; a little cool puff of wind came on her face. She gazed at the low mountains on the horizon, in the midst of which she lived, and she sighed, for no reason that she knew. She began idly picking at the blackberry vines; there were no berries on them; then she put her little fingers on the berries of the deadly nightshade. "These look like nice berries," she said.

Old Woman Magoun, standing stiff and straight in the road, said nothing.

"They look good to eat," said Lily.

Old Woman Magoun still said nothing, but she looked up into the ineffable blue of the sky, over which spread at intervals great white clouds shaped like wings.

Lily picked some of the deadly nightshade berries and ate them. "Why, they are real sweet," said she. "They are nice." She picked some more and ate them.

Presently her grandmother spoke. "Come," she said, "it is time we were going. I guess you have set long enough."

Lily was still eating the berries when she slipped down from the wall and followed her grandmother obediently up the road.

Before they reached home, Lily complained of being very thirsty. She stopped and made a little cup of a leaf and drank long at a mountain brook. "I am dreadful dry, but it hurts me to swallow," she said to her grandmother when she stopped drinking and joined the old woman waiting for her in the road. Her grandmother's face seemed strangely dim to her. She took hold of Lily's hand as they went on. "My stomach burns," said Lily, presently. "I want some more water."

"There is another brook a little farther on," said Old Woman Magoun, in a dull voice.

When they reached that brook, Lily stopped and drank again, but she whimpered a little over her difficulty in swallowing. "My stomach burns, too," she said, walking on, "and my throat is so dry, grandma." Old Woman Magoun held Lily's hand more tightly. "You hurt me, holding my hand so tight, grandma," said Lily, looking up at her grandmother, whose face she seemed to see through a mist, and the old woman loosened her grasp.

When at last they reached home, Lily was very ill. Old Woman Magoun put her on her own bed in the little bedroom out of the kitchen. Lily lay there and moaned, and Sally Jinks came in.

"Why, what ails her?" she asked. "She looks feverish."

Lily unexpectedly answered for herself. "I ate some sour apples and drank some milk," she moaned.

"Sour apples and milk are dreadful apt to hurt anybody," said Sally Jinks. She told several people on her way home that Old Woman Magoun was dreadful careless to let Lily eat such things.

Meanwhile Lily grew worse. She suffered cruelly from the burning in her stomach, the vertigo, and the deadly nausea. "I am so sick, I am so sick, grandma," she kept moaning. She could no longer see her grandmother as she bent over her, but she could hear her talk.

Old Woman Magoun talked as Lily had never heard her talk before, as nobody had ever heard her talk before. She spoke from the depths of her soul; her voice was as tender as the coo of a dove, and it was grand and exalted. "You'll feel better very soon, little Lily," said she.

"I am so sick, grandma."

"You will feel better very soon, and then—"

"I am sick."

"You shall go to a beautiful place."

Lily moaned.

"You shall go to a beautiful place," the old woman went on.

"Where?" asked Lily, groping feebly with her cold little hands. Then she moaned again.

"A beautiful place, where the flowers grow tall."

"What color? Oh, grandma, I am so sick."

"A blue color," replied the old woman. Blue was Lily's favorite color. "A beautiful blue color, and as tall as your knees, and the flowers always stay there, and they never fade."

"Not if you pick them, Grandma? Oh!"

"No, not if you pick them; they never fade, and they are so sweet you can smell them a mile off; and there are birds that sing, and all the roads have gold stones in them, and the stone walls are made of gold."

"Like the ring grandpa gave you? I am so sick, grandma."

"Yes, gold like that. And all the houses are built of silver and gold, and the people all have wings, so when they get tired walking they can fly, and—"

"I am so sick, grandma."

"And all the dolls are alive," said Old Woman Magoun. "Dolls like yours can run, and talk, and love you back again."

Lily had her poor old rag doll in bed with her, clasped close to her agonized little heart. She tried very hard with her eyes, whose pupils were so dilated that they looked black, to see her grandmother's face when she said that, but she could not. "It is dark," she moaned, feebly.

"There where you are going it is always light," said the grandmother, "and the commonest things shine like that breastpin Mrs. Lawyer Mason had on today."

Lily moaned pitifully, and said something incoherent. Delirium was commencing. Presently she sat straight up in bed and raved; but even then her grandmother's wonderful compelling voice had an influence over her.

"You will come to a gate with all the colors of the rainbow," said her grandmother; "and it will open, and you will go right in and walk up the gold street, and cross the field where the blue flowers come up to your knees, until you find your mother, and she will take you home where you are going to live. She has a little white room all ready for you, white curtains at the windows, and a little white looking-glass, and when you look in it you will see—"

"What will I see? I am so sick, grandma."

"You will see a face like yours, only it's an angel's; and there will be a little white bed, and you can lay down an' rest."

"Won't I be sick, grandma?" asked Lily. Then she moaned and babbled wildly, although she seemed to understand through it all what her grandmother said.

"No, you will never be sick any more. Talkin' about sickness won't mean anything to you."

It continued. Lily talked on wildly, and her grandmother's great voice of soothing never ceased, until the child fell into a deep sleep, or what resembled sleep; but she lay stiffly in that sleep, and a candle flashed before her eyes made no impression on them.

Then it was that Nelson Barry came. Jim Willis waited outside the door. When Nelson entered he found Old Woman Magoun on her knees beside the bed, weeping with dry eyes and a might of agony which fairly shook Nelson Barry, the degenerate of a fine old race.

"Is she sick?" he asked, in a hushed voice.

Old Woman Magoun gave another terrible sob, which sounded like the gasp of one dying.

"Sally Jinks said that Lily was sick from eating milk and sour apples," said Barry, in a tremulous voice. "I remember that her mother was very sick once from eating them."

Lily lay still, and her grandmother on her knees shook with her terrible sobs.

Suddenly Nelson Barry started. "I guess I had better go to Greenham for a doctor if she's as bad as that," he said. He went close to the bed and looked at the sick child. He gave a great start. Then he felt of her hands and reached down under the bedclothes for her little feet. "Her hands and feet are like ice," he cried out. "Good God! why didn't you send for some one—for me—before? Why, she's dying; she's almost gone!"

Barry rushed out and spoke to Jim Willis, who turned pale and came in and stood by the bedside.

"She's almost gone," he said, in a hushed whisper.

"There's no use going for the doctor; she'd be dead before he got here," said Nelson, and he stood regarding the passing child with a strange, sad face—unutterably sad, because of his incapability of the truest sadness.

"Poor little thing, she's past suffering, anyhow," said the other man, and his own face also was sad with a puzzled, mystified sadness.

Lily died that night. There was quite a commotion in Barry's Ford until after the funeral, it was all so sudden, and then everything went on as usual. Old Woman Magoun continued to live as she had done before. She supported herself by the produce of her tiny farm; she was very industrious, but people said that she was a trifle touched, since every time she went over the log bridge with her eggs or her garden vegetables to sell in Greenham, she carried with her, as one might have carried an infant, Lily's old rag doll.

## X. THE JOY OF YOUTH [1]

EMMELINE AMES, going down the village street that winter
afternoon, was conscious of a little uncomfortable lump in
her right shoe. She was also conscious of an innocent
bravado of shame as the lump worked from the hollow of
her instep toward her toes. A soft red, and a delicious, silly
smile, overspread her face. The lump was composed of
some dried sprigs of the plant called boys'-love, or southernwood. Emmeline believed firmly in the superstition concerning it. She was sure that a girl with a sprig of boys'-
love in her shoe would marry the first boy whom she met.
In summer, when the plant with its long, gray-green,
aromatic leaves flourished in the garden, she often wore a
sprig in her shoe, and she had secretly pressed some in her
own particular books, in order that she might be able to
try the charm in the wintertime. Emmeline had too much
credulity and imagination to be in a perfectly normal state;
or, on the contrary, she may have been too normal, with all
her human instincts dangerously near the surface, and as
prone to injury as her great-grandmother's eggshell china
teacups.

There was a cousin of Mr. John Adams's, whom her aunt
Martha had married, who visited often at the Ames house.
The cousin's name was Miss Abby Jennison; she was a pro-
fessor in a girls' college, and rather uncomfortably analyti-
cal. One day she told Emmeline's anxious mother that
Emmeline was a good example of overgrowth induced by
the strain of civilization, and when Emmeline's mother had
rejoined that she was such a simple, even primitive, child,

Miss Jennison had triumphantly declared that that only confirmed her in her opinion. Emmeline had reverted to an original type. "How long can you keep a pansy from returning to a little heartsease if it blooms season after season in the same garden?" inquired Miss Jennison. "Emmeline is a First Principle, bless her. I adore First Principles."

Emmeline's mother inferred that it must be desirable for a little girl to be a First Principle; still, she felt a little uneasy. One day, after Miss Jennison had returned to her college, she asked her sister Martha, Mrs. John Adams, what she supposed Abby Jennison had meant. Martha was rocking comfortably with her second little girl in her lap. The first little girl was playing on the floor at her feet with six dolls, a very small horse, and a very large woolly lamb. Martha looked smilingly over the golden downy ball of the baby's head. "She meant what most people mean who live on paper and in words," said Martha Adams.

"You don't think she meant that Emmeline was not healthy—too nervous or anything?"

"Of course she is a little too nervous," said Martha. "But what would one give for a child without nerves? Emmeline never begun to have the nerves that my children have." She spoke as if nerves were a distinction, and her sister said no more. She had imbibed a hazy idea that being a First Principle meant being nervous, and that being nervous might be desirable; still, she remained somewhat uneasy. Had she begun to know what went on within Emmeline's little blossoming mind she would have been distracted. Her own child was to her as a sealed casket filled with mysterious processes which were quite beyond her scope. Emmeline reflected much upon topics which her elders considered as being remote from her furthest imaginings. For instance, that sprig of dried southernwood in her shoe would have been incredible to her mother and aunt.

Emmeline walked along, gazing hopefully ahead. She

was slight and straight, and carried her delicate chin high. She was very pretty, and she was glad on account of the Boy. She stepped daintily, carefully pointing her toes out. She had a tendency to toe in, which she was trying to overcome. She was going to the store. She had a number of commissions for her mother and aunt.

It was very cold, and the snow, which was trodden hard, gave out silvery creaks underfoot. The fields lay in wide frozen levels of a uniform pearl gray. There were no blue lights; the sky was clouded. The trees stretched out their limbs with a curious stiffness. The bushes, in which were still tangled a few dry leaves, looked brittle. Emmeline came to a large bush, and a swarm of sparrows flew out of it, as if the dead leaves had been assailed by a sudden wind. She walked on, gazing ahead for the Boy whom she should know for her future husband by virtue of that sprig of dry southernwood in her shoe.

Emmeline, as she went on, became very much afraid that this test would end as had former ones. She had been singularly unfortunate in her experiments with boys'-love. Her most intimate friend, Anita Lord, had met Johnny Woodfield while trying the charm, and Emmeline, who had included Johnny in her own list of possibilities, had straightway loyally eliminated him. After that it had seemed as if she were fated to meet Johnny Woodfield when she herself was afield with southernwood aromatically crushed underfoot. Now she saw him approaching, and sighed. It did seem hard that she should inevitably meet a boy who was destined to become the husband of her dearest friend. She spoke rather stiffly to him and was passing on, but Johnny stopped her.

"What's your hurry?" he inquired, affably.

"I have some errands at the store, and I must get home before dark."

"Shucks! loads of time! Say, Emmeline—"

"Well?"

Johnny, who was rather large and stout for his age, hesitated. He shifted his weight from one foot to the other. His cheeks were already crimson with the cold, but a warmer glow of young blood deepened the tint.

"It's a corking cold day, ain't it?" he said at length.

"Awful," returned Emmeline. She looked up in Johnny Woodfield's face. It was a handsome boy face. She realized that had it not been for Anita, she might—but she shook her head impatiently. She made a motion to pass, then Johnny spoke to the point.

"Say, Emmeline," he blurted out, "don't you want to go to the concert with me tomorrow night?" It was the first time that Johnny Woodfield had ever invited a girl to go anywhere with him, and it was the first time that Emmeline had been invited. It was a tremendous moment for both of them. Emmeline, however, was a girl, and she had her wits about her. She knew exactly what to say, and she said it beautifully.

"Thank you," she said; "you are very kind, but I have a previous engagement."

Johnny Woodfield realized the dignity and finality of the reply. He jerked his cap from his head, which looked pathetically curly. His cheeks blazed. He stood aside for Emmeline to pass. Then the little girl's pitiful heart misgave her. She looked at him, and her pretty mouth quivered.

"You aren't mad, are you, Johnny?" she said.

"Of course I ain't," replied Johnny, manfully. "If you have a previous engagement, that settles it."

"I don't think Anita has any engagement."

"Oh, well, I may not go to the concert, anyway," returned Johnny. "Good evening, Emmeline."

"Good evening," returned Emmeline. She walked on rather sadly. She had no regrets concerning Johnny, since she firmly believed him to be Anita's property, but she was, of course, facing an irony of fate.

It was not long before she faced another. She saw some one approaching, and her heart leaped. Was it—? A young man jauntily swinging a tightly rolled umbrella came toward her. Emmeline did not raise her eyes until she met him. She was almost sure. When she did look up she encountered the handsome, patronizing eyes of Mr. Lionel Bates, who was going to be married in the spring to Miss Ellen Sylvester. Emmeline knew Mr. Bates. He was a lawyer and had had business dealings with her mother.

"How do you do, little one?" said Mr. Bates as he passed. He did not even consider it worth his while to raise his hat. Emmeline passed on. She reflected that if a grown-up young man could know what a girl of fourteen really thought of him, he perhaps would not swing his umbrella quite so airily.

Then she saw old Mr. Henry T. Meredith, who was eighty and had had three wives, approaching. Emmeline shuddered at the thought that the southernwood might point to him. Mr. Meredith was fond of little girls, and he was perpetually mistaking a little girl for one of his own descendants. He had grandchildren and great-grandchildren, and his memory had begun to fail. He stopped and rested on his stick when he met Emmeline, and felt in his overcoat pocket, from which he drew a sticky molasses drop. Then he thrust the sweet into Emmeline's mouth with a loud cackle of intense enjoyment.

"Didn't think ye was goin' to meet grandpa, did ye?" said he. "How be ye, grandpa's little Lizzie? How's your ma?"

Emmeline's disgust and indignation struggled with her native politeness and veneration for age. She spoke as well as she could on account of the sticky sweetmeat in her mouth.

"I am not Lizzie," said she. "You have made a mistake, Mr. Meredith. I am Emmeline Ames."

It was all thrown away on Mr. Meredith. He did not hear one word. He thrust another molasses drop into Emmeline's hand, and he cackled again. "Here's another for ye," said he. "Now run right home to your ma, Lizzie, or you'll ketch cold."

Old Mr. Meredith went his way and Emmeline went hers. As soon as she was quite sure she was unobserved she disposed of the two molasses drops. This time the irony of fate had almost cuffed her ears.

She walked on a little farther. She had almost given up when she saw the Boy advancing. This time she *knew*. When they met she glanced quickly at him, disclosing a flash of brilliant blue under gold-fringed lids which immediately dropped upon paling cheeks. She was *sure* the Boy's eyes had met hers, but he did not look away so quickly. She could feel his earnest gaze upon her face. She knew that he turned and looked after her. She wondered if she were walking straight. She felt the boys'-love in her shoe. Her heart beat so loud that she did not hear the resonant creak of the snow. She did not feel the bite of the winter wind upon her face. A sleigh passed with a loud jangle of bells. She did not notice it. She had met the Boy. She had no doubt. She did not know who he was. He was a beautiful boy. He was tall and straight and slender, and he had a handsome dark face. Emmeline had met him with a sprig of southernwood in her shoe, and she *knew*. It made no difference to her that the superstition was to the effect that a girl would marry the *first* one whom she met. She obviously could not marry a boy who was the property of her dearest friend, or an engaged young man, or an old gentleman who could not tell her from one of his own great-grandchildren.

In her agitation, Emmeline walked nearly a quarter of a

mile past the store. Then she met Anita, who asked her where she was going, and she remembered.

"To the store?" repeated Anita. "Why, Emmeline Ames, you have walked 'way past it! It is freezing cold, too."

Anita was very fat, and there was a curious unfinished effect about her nose and mouth. She had a quantity of black hair, and she had just begun to do it up. A great knot of it wobbled about her neck as she spoke.

"I don't feel a bit cold," replied Emmeline.

"It is cold—the coldest day of the year. Well, turn round and walk back with me. I am going to the store, too. Aunt Rachel wants some knitting cotton—she is out of it—for those everlasting face cloths she is always knitting."

"I suppose she likes to knit them," Emmeline remarked, dreamily, as she walked back with Anita.

"I suppose she does, or she knits them because she hasn't anything she *does* like to do."

Emmeline did not hear what Anita said. She was thinking of the Boy. Then suddenly she thought she must say something to her friend. "I met Johnny just now," she said.

The color flew into Anita's face. She tossed her head, and the great knot of black hair wobbled dangerously.

"Huh!" said she, "I don't know as I think so very much of Johnny Woodfield, after all."

"But, Anita," Emmeline said, wonderingly, "you remember how you met him last summer when you had that sprig of boys'-love in your shoe."

"Huh!" said Anita, quite violently, "I don't know as I have much faith in that sign, anyway. Johnny Woodfield isn't the only boy in this town, and I don't waste my thoughts on any boy myself. I am going to begin to study French with Miss Laselle next week. Grandmother says perhaps I can go to Europe for a year after I am through the high school, and if I can't speak French nobody can understand a word I say. I might just as well be a cat traveling!"

Emmeline stared at Anita.

"Grandmother says she thinks I shall need a year's rest before I go to college," said Anita, proudly. "I am not very strong."

Emmeline, little, slender, high-browed girl, looked at her with surprise. "Why, Anita, you look real strong!" said she.

"I know I weigh more than you do, Emmeline," Anita returned, severely, "but weight does not always mean health. I am *very* delicate."

Then they entered the store. Emmeline made her purchases, and Anita bought white knitting cotton. Then she and Anita said good-by to each other and parted. Emmeline walked home through the deepening winter twilight. She gazed ahead with her innocent, serious blue eyes. She had a listening air, as if she heard music. She was very happy.

When she reached home she went into the sitting room, where her mother and Aunt Martha and the children and her little dog Spotty were all grouped before the hearth fire. Spotty sprang at her, yelping with delight. He tried to reach her beloved little face with his affectionate, quivering tongue.

"Have you almost perished with the cold, dear?" asked Emmeline's mother.

"I am not a bit cold," replied Emmeline.

She removed her wraps, and sat down with the others before the fire, which cast a strange crimson glow upon her head. Emmeline sat still, smiling a strange, inscrutable smile. Her eyes, very blue and bright, seemed gazing within herself into long vistas of joy. Little Sally was fast asleep on the bearskin rug. The firelight was playing over her, and she also was smiling, in her sleep, with ineffable mystery. The baby in Aunt Martha's arms laughed and crowed, and held out little imploring arms to Emmeline, who immediately arose and took her carefully, with tender kisses. The baby cuddled up against her shoulder when she sat down again, and Emmeline smiled over the little head, that same smile of inscrutable joy.

Mr. John Adams, Aunt Martha's husband, came in. "Whew! but it is a cold night! It seems mighty good to get home," he said. He kissed Martha, and patted the children's and Emmeline's heads.

Then Annie came to the door and said that dinner was ready. After dinner Emmeline read a little while, then went to bed. When she had left the room after her good-night kisses, Mr. John Adams looked across his evening paper at his wife and sister-in-law.

"That girl is going to make havoc with young men's hearts before very long," said he.

"She is growing prettier every day," assented Martha.

Mrs. Ames smiled proudly but a little uneasily. "Don't put such ideas into the child's head, John," she said.

"There is no need of putting in things which are there already," said John, shrewdly. Then the door bell rang, and he had to go into another room to see a man on business.

Mrs. Ames regarded her sister with a troubled expression. "You don't think that *baby* has begun to even think of such things?" she said, piteously.

"Of course not, dear," replied Martha. "It is only John's nonsense."

"She always tells me everything," said Mrs. Ames, looking somewhat consoled, "and I have never allowed her to read novels."

"I think you have been very wise about that," said Martha. "I don't mean that Sally and Rosamond shall read a page of a novel before they are eighteen."

Neither woman dreamed how the girl in her dainty nest overhead was lying awake and reading that novel of her own heart, which the most loving and watchful of guardians cannot close from the eyes of youth. Emmeline, curled up

in her little white bed, was thinking of the Boy. An innocent rapture permeated every nerve when his face came
before her mental vision. Such a beautiful boy, and she had
not a doubt about the linking of his future with her own.

The next morning, when she woke, her first thought was
of the Boy, and a great ecstasy followed the thought. She
looked at her window and saw the snow drifting past it like
a white veil. If it had been pleasant she might have gone
to the post office for the morning mail and she might have
met the Boy; now Sydney would go. However, she was
not troubled; the thought of the Boy was enough to fill
her with strange content.

She was very happy all day. She sat beside a window,
looking out often at the white storm. She had some embroidery in her lap, but she did not work much. She
watched the snow fall and thought of the Boy. It was a
very severe storm. The wind blew and the snow drifted in
the yard with curling crests like waves. The trees stood
as if knee-deep in eddying hollows of snow. It was strange,
but the fiercer the storm became the greater became the
spiritual exaltation of the little girl with first love blossoming in her heart. The storm and her happiness increased
by a similar ratio. She would not have been as happy on a
day when the weather was commonplace. She hardly spoke
from morning until night. She had never, in all her life,
been so happy. Even the baby's crying when the light began to wane did not disturb her. The baby was cutting teeth.
Usually Emmeline was troubled when the baby, of whom
she was very fond, cried. Now cutting teeth seemed a part
of the universal joyous scheme of things. Emmeline took
the baby, and danced her up and down and comforted her.
When the child finally fell asleep on her shoulder the sleep
also seemed a part of joy.

The storm continued all night and during the next day

until noon. Then the sky cleared and the world was a great blue dazzle, sparkling as if with diamonds.

Emmeline watched the men clearing the road and Sydney heaping up the snow in great ridges on either side of the front walk. She did not go out that day, and missed more chances of seeing the Boy; still, the thought of him was entirely sufficient to content her.

The thought of him was sufficient to content her as days and weeks and months passed and she did not see him again. She was even curiously afraid that somebody might mention him to her and she might discover who he was. She felt instinctively that any mention of the Boy might disturb the beautiful crystalline isolation in which she dwelt with him.

The winter was over, then the spring school term when Emmeline graduated at the village high school, then the long summer vacation began. All this time Emmeline was very happy with her remembrance and her dream and her blossoming hopes, although she never saw the Boy. She grew taller, and people said she was fast becoming a beauty. Emmeline herself did not realize any difference. She had always considered herself pretty, and loved, very innocently, her face in her looking-glass. She lived so in her dream that she could not realize what changes the dream was working within herself.

Toward twilight one summer day Emmeline started to spend the night at Anita Lord's. Anita was to have a little party, and Emmeline was invited to remain all night with her. Emmeline wore her new white dress trimmed with lace and embroidery, and a white hat trimmed with white ribbon and roses. She carried a bag containing her night-gown and toilet things.

She walked fast, for there was a cloud in the northwest which might mean a thundershower, the light was waning fast, and she wanted to reach Anita's house. She had come to an unsettled place bordered by fields when she heard a hoarse, drunken shout behind her which filled her with panic. She ran, but as she ran she glanced back. She saw a huge figure coming after her at a staggering run. She knew immediately who it was—Mr. Ticknor. He shouted again, and she understood. "Violetty! Violetty!" shouted Mr. Ticknor. Emmeline knew that he was mistaking her for his daughter Violetta.

She had heard a great deal about Mr. Ticknor's brutal treatment of his family. She reflected that since Mr. Ticknor mistook her for his daughter Violetta he might, if he caught her, be brutal to her. She ran on. The hoarse shouts gained in intensity. She heard the name of Violetta coupled with alarming threats. She made out that she was to be beaten within an inch of her life. Her slim legs skimmed the ground as lightly as a bird's, but, alas! Mr. Ticknor could cover twice as much at a jump as she. He would certainly have caught her had it not been for his frequent departures from a straight course. As it was, Emmeline heard the heavy, padding footsteps nearer and nearer. She saw at a quick glance what might be her only chance. She had reached the field in which stood the little corn house where she had fastened Spotty four years ago.

She turned abruptly, and made for the little structure. She flashed through the ranks of fodder corn like a frightened bird. She heard a louder shout of rage from Mr. Ticknor. She did not look around. She wondered, as she ran, if she remembered correctly that, besides the wooden bolt on the outside of the corn-house door, there was a lock and key. If she were mistaken, and it was a padlock to be fastened only from the outside, she was lost. She hoped that she remembered rightly and that there was a lock, although it was unusual in such a place. When she reached the corn house she saw that it had an old house door which was equipped with a heavy lock and key. Emmeline dashed in. She slammed the door. She laid her hand on the key which was in the lock.

There was a moment of breathless agony; the key turned very hard. But at last it clicked, and Emmeline sank down on the dusty floor. She realized that she was faint. There was a singing in her ears, but through the singing she heard Mr. Ticknor's raging voice. Then suddenly it ceased. After a while Emmeline got strength enough to rise and stand on tiptoe and push the little sliding window a crack aside. No one was in sight. She tried to turn the key back, but she could not move it at all. It was hampered. Then she knew that she was a prisoner in the corn house until some chance rescuer should arrive. The one window was high in the wall, and too small for even a girl of Emmeline's proportions to crawl through. Emmeline tugged again at the key. She blistered one hand, but it was all useless. Then she stood on tiptoe again and peeped out of the window. Presently a buggy drawn by a white horse passed, and she did make a dismal little outcry, but the buggy rattled rapidly past. Emmeline sat down on a pile of last year's corn. She did not weep. The situation was beyond tears.

She could not sit still long. She was at the window again. She saw in the dim light a figure pass along the road. Then she realized that she could not possibly know who it was, that she might be rushing from one danger to another. She realized that she must remain where she was all night!— that she must make up her mind to it. She thought of the party at Anita's. She knew that her relatives would have no occasion to worry because she did not come home; that Anita would only think that something had detained her, and would not worry, either; that nobody would institute a search for her until the next day. Then she heard a familiar little sound which revived her. It was Spotty's small, far-reaching bark. The little dog came across the field like a flying shadow. First he leaped at the window, which he could not reach.  He whined; he called his consternation, his sympathy, with all the tones in his faithful dog voice. All night long he barked and howled at intervals.  If it had not been for Spotty, Emmeline considered that she could never have endured such a night.  The little dog's scratchings on the door and his commiserating cries were all she had to sustain her.  She sat miserably on the pile of corn, and waited for morning.  She soon realized that there were mice, if not rats, in the corn house.  She had frequently to move about to keep them quiet.

Finally the sun rose.  Then she took up her station at the window.  People began to pass, on the road, walking and driving.  Emmeline, whenever she thought she was safe in so doing, cried out, but her voice did not carry well and nobody heard her.  Spotty also made frantic dashes at everybody, but he was simply shooed away.  Nobody understood his dog language.  It was ten o'clock before help came.  Emmeline saw a slim, straight young figure swinging along the road.  Spotty made one of his desperate dashes.  The figure stopped.  Then Emmeline saw the dog, mad with joy, careering back to her prison, and running in his wake the Boy.  When the Boy reached the corn house he saw, in a little window high in the wall, a beautiful little pale face fluffed around with yellow hair against a background of amber dusk.

"What *is* the matter?" said the Boy.

Emmeline explained in little gasps as well as she was able.  The Boy immediately rose to the situation.  He was a strong Boy.  He put knee and shoulder against the corn-house door and Emmeline was free.  "You poor little soul!" said the Boy.  Emmeline was so weak she could hardly stand.  "Here, take my arm," said the Boy.  He was not at all awkward with a girl, although he was a boy.  Emmeline took his arm, and the two went through the corn, every blade of which was strung with a row of

dewdrops, like a lily-of-the-valley, and Spotty raced ahead
with joyous yelps, and returned to circle with leaping bounds
around the two. "That's a nice little dog," said the Boy,
when a lull in the explanations of the situation came.

"Yes," said Emmeline. "I don't know how I could ever
have lived through the night if it hadn't been for Spotty."

"Poor little soul!" said the Boy, again.

Emmeline felt a thrill of something which seemed like
the light of the dewy morning.

"I don't know what your name is," said the Boy.

"Emmeline Ames. I don't know what your name is,
either."

"My name is Guy Russell. I am Mrs. Elizabeth Russell's nephew. My father and mother died when I was a
baby. When I haven't been at school I have lived with
my aunt Edith, but she died last winter, and now I suppose I shall be here with Aunt Elizabeth a good deal. I
enter Yale next fall, and next summer I am going abroad."

Emmeline felt a sinking at her heart.

"Are you?" she said.

"Yes. I shall be gone only six weeks. I shall be here
with Aunt Elizabeth the rest of the time when I am at
college. I am to stay here the rest of this summer."

"I am sorry your aunt Edith died," said Emmeline.

"She was just like a mother to me," said the Boy, simply.

Emmeline felt very sorry for him. It seemed to her
that she had never felt so sorry for anyone before. She
gave the Boy's arm the most delicate little pressure with
her hand, and he immediately pressed the arm closer against
his side.

"But Aunt Elizabeth is all right," said the Boy. "Do you
know her?"

"By sight," replied Emmeline, and she spoke with a little awe. Mrs. Elizabeth Russell was a very wealthy woman,
the only really wealthy woman in the village. She lived in

a most beautiful house. She had traveled. She had wonderful guests from cities during the summer. She mingled very little with the village people. She was popularly
supposed to be very proud, although she was said to be
charitable, and very pleasant "when you knew her." She
had once called on Emmeline's mother, and Mrs. Ames,
very particularly dressed, had returned the call, but that
was when Emmeline was very young. She had seen Mrs.
Russell only across the church or driving, but she had always regarded her with a sort of feudal admiration. "I
think your aunt Elizabeth is beautiful," she said, warmly.

"Yes, she is," assented the Boy.

Then they had reached Emmeline's house, and Emmeline was trembling with irresolution as to whether she
ought or ought not to invite the Boy in. Her mother and
Aunt Martha solved the question by rushing out with
exclamations and questions. They had just heard that
Emmeline had not been at Anita's party, and Mr. John
Adams was even then on another road with some men
searching for her.

While Mrs. Ames and Aunt Martha hugged Emmeline
and exclaimed over her, she and the Boy, between them,
told the story. Then Emmeline and the Boy were in the
house at the breakfast table. It seemed that, although the
Boy had already eaten one breakfast, there was something
about Annie's waffles and coffee and omelette which surpassed his aunt's French cook's efforts. Emmeline was
blissfully watchful of the Boy while he ate. She herself
ate, but did not seem to taste anything except what the
Boy ate.

"I wonder the dear child looks so well after such an
awful night," Aunt Martha said to Emmeline's mother.

Mrs. Ames looked happily at Emmeline's pink cheeks
and the blue delight of her eyes. "I wonder she isn't down
sick," said she. The two women looked approvingly at

young Guy Russell. After he had gone and Emmeline had been put to bed, they agreed that he looked as if he might grow to be a splendid man.

"I suppose he will have all his aunt's money, too," said Mrs. Ames. Then she looked ashamed of herself. "But that is nothing compared with his being such a good, honest, innocent boy," she said.

"His aunt Edith Sloan was a splendid woman, from everything I have heard of her. It is easy to see that the boy has been brought up by a good woman. He shows it." Mrs. Ames had a dreamy look in her eyes. Her sister smiled a little furtive smile.

They both thought Emmeline, upstairs in her little room, was asleep, but she was not. She was too happy to sleep. She was one of the very few on the face of this earth who dream and keep the precious crystal of the dream unshattered by the shock with reality.

It was a week after that that Mrs. Elizabeth Russell gave a party for her nephew, and Emmeline was invited. Mrs. Russell sent her carriage for her. Emmeline had her first silk dress to wear. It was made over from one her mother had worn when a girl. It was white silk sprinkled with little silver dots. Emmeline's hair was tied with a great white bow, and she had white shoes, and she looked, her mother and aunt thought, the prettiest thing in the world. "I am glad the dear child doesn't know what a beauty she is," said Mrs. Ames, after the carriage had rolled away.

"She hasn't an idea," said Martha.

Neither dreamed that Emmeline knew perfectly well how she looked, and that an innocent rapture because of her beauty in her silver-dotted gown seemed to perfume her very soul. It is more beautiful than beauty itself to be innocently conscious of it, and to value it more for the sake of the love of another than for self-love. Emmeline reflected how pleased the Boy would be with her appearance and she tasted that pleasure instead of her own, exactly as she had tasted the breakfast the morning after he had rescued her from her prison.

There was a palm room in Mrs. Elizabeth Russell's house. An hour later Emmeline and the Boy were in there. They stood under some great spreading fronds and looked out of a wide window at a wonderful sight. The lawn was all dotted with swinging Japanese lanterns, and electric lights made strange shadows which seemed alive. The night looked like another world, full of mysteries of beauty unfolding upon beauty, and joy upon joy. Each saw more than there really was, because each saw with the other's eyes. They looked out at the fairy night; then they looked at each other.

"You are the most beautiful girl I ever saw in my whole life," said the Boy, with blunt fervor. He spoke as if he had lived ages. The girl made no disclaimer. She believed him. She gazed back at him with radiant delight in his appreciation of her.

The window opened like a door. The Boy threw it wide, and took Emmeline's hand with a caressing touch in his hard, boyish one. "Let's walk out there," he said, stammeringly. He and Emmeline went out. They strolled arm in arm along a broad gravel walk, and finally sat down under a tree swarming with brilliant lanterns like butterflies. They were quite alone. Most of the guests were on the other side of the lawn, where refreshments were being served and where the orchestra played behind some flowering bushes. The Boy put his arm around the girl. "I love you," he whispered. Emmeline said nothing. She felt as if some divine fluid were coursing through all her veins.

"Don't you love me?" said the Boy.

"Yes," replied Emmeline.

She and the Boy kissed each other.

"Then we are engaged," said the Boy. Emmeline nodded. She looked at him, and her face of love, and ignorance of love was fairly dazzling. The Boy kissed her again. Then they sat still. The Boy's arm was around the girl and her head on his shoulder. Both tasted the uttermost joy of the present. Happiness stood still in their heaven.

## XI. *BILLY AND SUSY*[1]

For years the sisters, Miss Melissa Abbot and Mrs. Sarah Drew, had lived in peace and concord, not in the same house, but in adjoining ones. Mrs. Drew had married when very young, and her husband had lived only a year. At that time the old Abbot homestead had been filled with unmarried sons and daughters, and the young widow had continued to reside in the pretty little cottage which her husband had built for her. Now Miss Melissa had been living alone for some years, and so had Mrs. Drew, and people wondered why they did not keep house together, but both were women of habit, and did not relish any change. Moreover, the two houses, the square old homestead and the little cottage with its piazza under the overhang of the roof, were so near that the sisters could talk from open windows. They were devoted to each other; in fact, they were considered an example of sisterly affection for the whole village, until they were both old women and the advent of Billy and Susy. Billy and Susy were two remarkably pretty yellow kittens; young Mira Holmes had brought them over one afternoon in May, in a covered basket. She stopped at Mrs. Drew's. Miss Melissa was spending the afternoon there. She could see both elderly heads at the sitting-room windows. She knocked, and then ran in. She was quite at home there. She kissed both sisters; then she opened the basket, and two little yellow balls of fur flew out. "Our cat had five," said Mira, "and they were so pretty we could not bear to have them drowned. So we thought maybe you would like these. Nellie Stowe

[1] *Copyright, 1909, by Harper & Brothers.*

has two, and we are going to keep one ourselves. Would you like them?" Mira Holmes was a very pretty, slight girl, and she had a wistful, affectionate way of speaking, and a little pathetic expression. Mira had been as good as engaged to Harry Ayres, but he had ceased to visit her some six months before. Mira went her way patiently, but she was thinner, and pathetic, in spite of everything. She laughed with the old ladies when the yellow kittens flew out of the basket, but the laugh was as sad as a sob. The sisters were enthusiastic over the gift.

"It was only yesterday that sister and I were saying that we really must have some cats; we are both overrun with mice," declared Mrs. Sarah Drew, and she appropriated directly one of the kittens, and folded it under her soft double chin. "I will call him Billy, after the cat I had when I first came to live here," said she. "That was a yellow cat, too."

Miss Melissa gathered up the other kitten lovingly. "I will call her Susy," she announced. "You remember I had a yellow cat named Susy, once, sister?"

Mira did not remain very long. She went her way with her empty basket on her arm. As she went out of the yard between the bridal-wreath bushes, and the flowering almond, and the striped grass, her head drooped wearily under her spring hat trimmed with rosebuds.

"Poor little thing!" said Mrs. Drew, pityingly.

Miss Melissa tossed her head. "Good land!" said she. "I guess she will get another beau, a girl as pretty as Mira Holmes, and if she doesn't it is no matter; beaux are not everything in the world. Girls are silly."

Then Miss Melissa turned toward her yellow kitten, but both sisters had put the kittens on the floor when they bade farewell to Mira, and now came disaster; their first quarrel. Miss Melissa gathered up a kitten lovingly, but

Mrs. Drew interposed. "Stop, Melissa," said she; "that is my kitten; that is my yellow kitten, that is Billy."

"Why, Sarah Drew," cried Miss Melissa, "you know better! You know this is Susy."

Mrs. Drew caught up the other yellow kitten, and both sisters glared over the little, soft, yellow, wriggling things. "This is Susy," declared Melissa.

"This is Susy. You have got my cat," insisted Sarah.

The kittens were exactly alike to the ordinary observer, but not to the sisters. "I know I have my Susy," said Melissa. "I noticed particularly her expression."

"Cat's hind leg!" said Sarah, contemptuously. It was a sarcastic expletive peculiar to her herself, and in this case more appropriate than usual. "Talk about a cat having expression," she added. Then she laughed a disagreeable laugh. Sarah had a temper.

Miss Melissa also had a temper, but hers was of the tearful variety. Tears streamed over her faded blond cheeks —tears of rage and hurt sentiment. "Cats have expression," she declared, in a hysterical voice. "You can talk all you want. My Susy had the most innocent expression, and this one looks just like her. Precious little Susy cat!" she crooned to the yellow kitten.

"Susy nothing," said Sarah. "That cat is my Billy, and this is your precious Susy. I wouldn't have this kind of a cat, anyway. They keep you always drowning kittens or trying to give them away. Give me Billy!"

"You have got Billy now," said Miss Melissa, tearfully. "Precious little Susy cat!"

"That cat you *have is Billy,*" said Sarah Drew, with awful firmness.

"You have Billy, and this precious is Susy," returned Melissa, with more sentiment but equal obstinacy.

Neither would yield. Melissa, grasping the yellow cat which she claimed so tightly that it clawed and mewed, went home. Sarah Drew thrust the remaining cat viciously into the kitchen. "Here, Abby," she said to the old woman who had worked for her ever since her marriage, "take this miserable cat! Miss Mira brought it, but I don't want it."

Abby had heard every word of the discussion. She always heard: she considered it her duty. She gathered up the kitten, and presently she came to the sitting-room door.

"Miss Sarah," said she.

"I don't want to hear a word," replied Sarah, shortly and haughtily.

"But—"

"I don't want to hear a word. I know you were listening, and you always take everybody's part against me. Now, you can either keep that miserable cat in the kitchen or drown it, I don't care which, but if you do keep it, you must dispose of the kittens. Now, I don't want to hear another word."

Abby, who was as tall and angular as a man, went out.

Later in the afternoon she and Miss Melissa's girl, who was also an old woman, had a conference out in the garden, over the fence. Each held a yellow kitten. They parted after a while, because Mrs. Drew was seen standing in the kitchen door watching them. But Maria, Miss Melissa's maid, said, in a whisper, "Both of them were always awful set," and Abby nodded assent.

Neither of the women was a gossip. It was nearly a month before it leaked out that Melissa Abbot and Sarah Drew had had a quarrel and were not on speaking terms. The two led a sad life. Melissa got no comfort from fondling her yellow cat, which grew in size and beauty. Abby kept the other carefully from her mistress' sight, and tried to cook things to tempt her appetite. Both sisters were very unhappy. They had always been of a sociable disposition, and each was afraid to accept an invitation lest she should meet her sister. They stayed at home and moped. The curtains were drawn over the opposite windows in the cottage and homestead. Mrs. Drew was constantly on the alert, and never stirred out-of-doors unless she was quite sure that her sister was at home and there was no danger of meeting her upon the street. Each became afraid of venturing abroad unless the other was housed. Sarah Drew watched. Melissa Abbot watched. Each knew that the other watched. Each knew the other so well that she could judge exactly of her sister's state of mind from her own. Thus each suffered doubly.

Mira Holmes heard of the estrangement, and came to see Mrs. Drew about it. "I am so sorry," said she, and the tears, always in her heart for her own trouble, welled into her patient blue eyes.

"It is nothing you are to blame for, child," replied Sarah Drew with dignity. Both sisters were too proud to say anything to each other's detriment. "It is unfortunate that the cats looked *so* much alike, but I can't see how you are responsible for that."

"Maybe not," admitted Mira. Then she broke down, and wept. "I am so sorry to have been the means of parting two sisters like you," she sobbed. Her own grief stung her afresh as she wept for that of the sisters.

"You didn't part us," replied Sarah Drew. "It was two yellow cats that looked exactly alike." She called to Abby to make some tea and cut some sponge cake. When the tea and cake arrived she served them as calmly as if there were no yellow cats of confused identity in the world. "Drink this tea and eat some cake," said she. "There is no sense in making yourself sick. This is a personal matter between my sister and myself."

"I wish they didn't look so much alike," sobbed Mira, trying to sip the tea.

"I can't see how you are to blame for that," Sarah Drew said again.

"If I had only brought one tiger cat and one yellow! There were two lovely tigers that I gave Nellie Stowe," said Mira, pitifully.

"I never liked tiger cats; I prefer yellow cats, but not one of this kind," said Sarah Drew. Then she changed the subject. "It's a beautiful day," said she, "though it is pretty warm for so early in the season." She talked at length about the weather, and how the apple trees were blooming; then she talked about the fair which the ladies of the Mission Circle were to give. Whenever poor young Mira Holmes essayed to bring up the subject of the yellow cats, Sarah gently, but firmly, swerved her aside.

When Mira left, she went to make a call upon Melissa, but her call was just as devoid of good results. Miss Melissa was much more reserved than her sister upon the subject. She even refused to justify herself in her conduct. The only thing she did was to call Maria and ask her to take Susy out of the room. The kitten had been curled up in a little coil of yellow fur upon the sofa when Mira entered. Poor Mira had to drink another cup of tea, and eat more sponge cake made from the identical recipe of the other; then she went home. On her way home she met Harry Ayres, the young man to whom she had been engaged, and he hardly noticed her, simply raising his hat without a smile, as if she had been a stranger. Mira scarcely inclined her pretty head. When she reached home, however, she found a certain comfort in throwing herself openly into a chair and weeping, and sobbing out to her mother how bad she felt about Mrs. Drew and Miss Melissa and the two yellow cats. She had felt obliged to conceal her tears heretofore from her mother. Now it was a comfort to weep before her for something for which she need not be ashamed, and at the same time weep for her own private misery.

If Mira's mother knew that the girl was weeping for something besides the complication of the cats, she did not show it. She was a very gentle, soft-voiced woman, with beautiful rippling folds of yellow hair over her ears. She stroked Mira's head. "Don't, dear," said she. "You are not to blame."

"I thought they would—like the—cats," sobbed Mira.

"Of course you did, dear. Don't feel so. I will go over and see them myself tomorrow afternoon. I have an errand about the fair, and I will see if I can't do something."

"Miss Melissa may be mistaken, and Mrs. Drew may be mistaken; nobody knows," said Mira.

"If they are, it will be very hard for them to give in," said Mrs. Holmes. "They are nice women, but they were always very set. They were when I used to go to school with them. But I will see what I can do."

It ended in Mrs. Holmes drinking tea and eating sponge cake in both houses, and coming away exactly as Mira had done. It ended in the same way for many others. Many good women called, and drank tea and ate sponge cake and tried to make peace between the sisters, and came away realizing that their effort had been fruitless. Even the minister's wife drank tea and ate sponge cake, and the minister himself drank, and ate, and offered prayer in vain. After his call the sisters did not attend church at all. Previously they had gone to church, but had sat in different pews, leaving the old Abbot pew quite unoccupied. Both Miss Melissa and Mrs. Drew, on the Sunday after the minister's call, watched with secret pride and approved each other's staying at home from church. Although at bitter enmity with her, each sister felt that she should have been personally mortified had she seen the other emerge from her front door, clad in her Sabbath best, after the minister's call and his direct importunities at the throne of grace that they of the Abbot family should see the error of their ways.

Miss Melissa caressed her yellow cat, and said, aloud: "Well, I am glad she has some pride, if she hasn't anything else"; and Mrs. Drew told Abby, after the church bell had done ringing, if she had made up her mind to keep that miserable cat, to be sure it had plenty of milk and no meat until it was older, for fear of fits, and added that if she had to keep animals that belonged to other folks she did not want them neglected under her roof anyway.

That Sunday there was almost a rift in the cloud of dissension between the sisters, a rift based upon common pride and resentment of interference: an unworthy rift of unnatural sunlight of forgiveness caused by anger against another. But it did not last. By the next Sunday, neither expecting the other to go to church, each realized a complete return of the old bitterness. And the bitterness, as the days and weeks went on, caused more and more unhappiness. The two old women were fighting with two-edged swords, which they who love and fight must always use, and every time one inflicted a wound upon the other she hurt herself. People began to say that the sisters were aging terribly. Finally the doctor was seen stopping every day at both houses; then the news was spread abroad that the sisters had been told that they must have a change of scene. They were not wealthy enough to have a change of scene, unless it took the form of a visit. Then Miss Melissa went to pay her married brother, Thomas Abbot, who lived in Springfield, a visit, and Mrs. Drew went to pay her married sister Eliza, who lived in New York State, a visit, and Abby and Maria took care of their houses and the two yellow cats. Now and then they had letters from the sisters, which stated that they were improving in health, but one day the two old servants, knee-deep in catnip and with their skirts catching in a tangle of sweetbrier, talking over the back fence, agreed that their mistresses did not write as if they were happy.

"I know Mis' Drew," said Abby. "She can set up as stiff as she's a mind to, but she can't cheat me. She'll never be herself ag'in till she and her sister make up. When two women have lived as many years as they have, and thought so much of each other, it's goin' to take somethin' more'n a quarrel over two yeller cats to make them live this way and be jest as chipper as if nothin' had happened."

"I know Miss Melissa never will be the same," said Maria. "She's tried to make out as if she set the earth by that cat, but I've seen her look as if she'd like to pitch it out of the winder."

"It's a pity they wouldn't neither of them let us tell them," said Abby.

"Well, they wouldn't. The minute I begun to speak I was hushed up, and so was you," said Maria.

"Yes, that's so," said Abby. "Guess I'll take in some of this catnip for the cat. It won't last much longer, and I guess I'll dry some."

"I guess I will, too," said Maria. "It looks something like frost tonight."

"There won't be a frost unless the wind goes down," returned Abby. Her gray hair whipped about her face as she picked a great bunch of catnip.

"It does blow. When do you expect *her* home?"

"She hasn't said anything about coming. I shouldn't wonder if she didn't come before Thanksgiving. When do you expect *her*?"

"I don't know any more than you do. Good land! It will be a queer Thanksgiving if they don't make up first!"

"Maybe they will."

"They're awful set, both of them."

"Well," said Abby, "they may hate each other like poison for the rest of their natural lives. They may be set about that, but there's some things they can't be set about, nohow."

Both women laughed as they parted, and went their ways with bundles of catnip.

It was a week before Thanksgiving when Miss Melissa came home, and Mrs. Drew arrived the next day. It was four o'clock in the afternoon when Melissa, with her white hood over her head, muffled against the bitter wind in her soft gray shawl, entered the south door, just as she had been accustomed to. "So you've got home, Sarah?" said she. She was pale and red by turns. She looked afraid and troubled, and yet as if she wanted to laugh. Mrs. Drew had much the same shift of expression.

"Yes," she said. "I came on the half-past-three train. Sit down."

Melissa sat down.

"Take your things off and stay to supper. Abby's making cream-of-tartar biscuits. Did you have a pleasant visit at Thomas's?"

"Very pleasant, thank you."

"How are they all? How is Thomas's wife? Is Grace well?"

"They both seem real well. Did you have a pleasant visit at Eliza's?"

"Very pleasant, thank you."

"How is Eliza? Is Henry getting on well in his law office, and how is Lizzie?"

"They all seem real well, and Henry is smart as a whip. Eliza has a beautiful new winter cloak."

There was a silence. Miss Melissa's face reddened and paled, then reddened. She laughed nervously. "Oh," said she, "I have something to say to you, Sarah."

"Well?"

"It's nothing, only—I feel as if I must tell you, I—was right—Billy is Susy, and she's got five kittens. They haven't got their eyes open yet."

Mrs. Drew laughed. "Susy, is she?"

"Yes. You must have been mistaken."

"Well, I guess I was; but as for Billy's being Susy, well—" Mrs. Drew gave a long sigh. Then she laughed again, a sharp cackle of nervous mirth.

Miss Melissa stared at her. She looked relieved, but a little alarmed. "I'm glad you don't lay it up," said she, "but—"

"Just wait a minute. Abby!"

Abby opened the door.

"Bring in that basket, please, Abby," said Mrs. Drew.

Melissa looked at her sister with such curiosity that her face assumed a vacant expression. Mrs. Drew continued to laugh. Finally Melissa joined in, although unwillingly. "What in the world we are laughing at I don't see," she tittered.

"Because we've been a pair of fools," said Mrs. Drew, as Abby returned. She set down on the floor before the two old women a basket in which lay curled up a yellow mother cat luxuriously purring love to some yellow kittens.

"There are four of them," said Mrs. Drew, "all yellow, and they have had their eyes open some time."

Miss Melissa stared at the cat and kittens, then at her sister.

"Then—" she began.

"They were both Susy," said Mrs. Drew, "and we quarreled over nothing at all."

"Sarah—"

"Well?"

"I had made up my mind, anyway, to come over here

and ask you to forgive me, and take my Susy if you thought she was Billy."

"And I had made up my mind to go over to your house, anyway, and ask you to forgive me, and keep Billy if you thought he was Susy," said Mrs. Drew.

Then the two women laughed in chorus. "No Billy at all," said Miss Melissa, giggling like a girl.

"And two old women making themselves ridiculous, fighting over two yellow cats," said Mrs. Drew.

Out in the kitchen Abby echoed their mirth with an irrestrainable peal of laughter.

"Mira Holmes and Harry Ayres have made up and are going to be married, Abby tells me," said Mrs. Drew. "I mean she shall have two of those yellow kittens."

"I hate to have my Susy's drowned," said Melissa. "Maria says she thinks we can give them away. They are beautiful kittens: all yellow, just like these. Of course, you are coming over to dinner tomorrow, Sarah. Maria has the Thanksgiving cooking all done."

"I'd like to see myself doing anything else," said Mrs. Drew.

"I'll tell you what I'll do," said Melissa.

"What?"

"I'll send over and ask Mira and her mother and Harry to supper tomorrow night. I suppose they'll go to his folks to dinner, but maybe they'll like to come to supper. Maria has made some chicken pies."

"I think that is a real good idea," said Sarah Drew, warmly.

So it happened that Thanksgiving evening the old Abbot house was brightly lighted, and after supper the sisters, Mira and her mother, and Harry Ayres all sat in the best parlor in the old Abbot house, before the hearth fire. It was so pleasant that Mira had begged not to have the lamp lighted. She wore a red gown, and the firelight played over her pretty face and over her lover's, and the two held hands under a fold of the red gown, and trusted that nobody saw in the uncertain light.

"I thought maybe you would like to have two of the kittens when you begin housekeeping," Mrs. Drew was saying.

"That house your father has bought for you is the handsomest in the village," Miss Melissa said to Harry; "but it is old, and I never saw an old house yet where there weren't mice."

"That is true," said Mira's mother, in her soft voice.

"I think that is a grand idea, thank you, Mrs. Drew," Harry said, in his pleasant, happy, boyish voice.

"I should love to have them, thank you, Mrs. Drew," said Mira.

Neither she nor her young lover dreamed that the love in the hearts of the two old sisters struck, albeit free from all romance, a note which chorded with their own into a true harmony of thanksgiving.

## XII. *THE BUTTERFLY*[1]

"It's time for Vilola to come home again, and B. F. Brown is havin' paintin' and paperin' done," said Mrs. Abner Wells to her sister. Her sister's name was Mrs. Francis Baker, and she had come over with her work and her baby to spend the afternoon.

"Well, I thought there was something goin' on there when I came past," responded Mrs. Baker. "I noticed that the front chamber windows were open, and I saw some old room paper flyin' round the yard."

"The man just finished it—went away since dinner."

"That front room is Vilola's, ain't it?"

"Yes, of course it is. Didn't you know it?"

"Why, when did he have that room papered before?"

"He had it papered only the last time she came," said Mrs. Wells, impressively.

"Why, that couldn't have been more'n a year ago."

"Of course it couldn't. Don't Vilola Brown always come once a year and spend six months with her father, and then go back to Jefferson and spend six months with her mother? Ain't she done that ever since her father and mother separated when she was a baby? I should think you might know that as well as I do, Elmira Baker."

"Oh, of course I do," said Mrs. Baker. "I was only talking at random. I was only wondering what he was having that room papered for if it was done only a year ago."

"Well, I can tell you," said Mrs. Wells, with asperity.

[1] *Copyright, 1902, 1903, 1904, by Harper & Brothers.*

"Some folks have money to throw away for nothing, or think they do. They may find out they don't have any more than some other folks in the long run. I can tell you why. When we had that heavy spell of rain last fall it leaked in that room around the chimney and there was a place about as big as a saucer stained, that's why."

"Was that all?"

"Yes, that was all. B. F. Brown ain't goin' to have his precious Vilola comin' home to sleep in a room that's got a spot on the paper, if it ain't any bigger than the head of a *pin*. I don't know what he thinks that girl is."

"Couldn't he have had the paper pieced?"

"Oh no. It was faded just a little. He wouldn't have *Vilola* sleep in a room with a patch of paper showin'. I *guess* he wouldn't."

"Now, Susan, you don't mean he's so silly as that?"

"Yes, I do. I had it from the woman he's been having to clean the house. I tell you that house has been cleaned from attic to cellar. Every carpet has been up. Well, it needed it bad enough. I don't believe it had been swept since Vilola went away last July."

"I wonder if B. F. Brown makes much money in his store?" said Mrs. Baker.

"I don't believe he makes much," said Mrs. Wells, with angry exultation. "I know lots of folks that won't trade there. They say he never has just what they want. They say Deering, and Lawton, or Hapgood & Lewis have a great deal better assortment. I ain't been inside the door since I bought my brown cashmere there, and it faded so after I'd only wore it six months, and he wouldn't allow me anything for it. I told him then it was the last trading I'd do in his store, and it *was* the last."

"I wonder if she's comin' to-night?" said Mrs. Baker.

"No, she ain't comin' to-night. The six months with

her mother ain't up till next-week Thursday. I've kept account."

"It's a queer way for folks to live, ain't it?" said Mrs. Baker. "I rather *think* it's queer."

"How long is it since they've lived together? I declare, I've forgot."

"*I* ain't forgot. Vilola Brown is just seven years younger than I be. She's nineteen, and her father and mother ain't lived together since she was three years old. That makes sixteen years. I was ten years old when they separated and her mother went to Jefferson to live, and he stayed here, and one had Vilola six months and the other six months, turn and turn about, ever since, and he's paid his wife ten dollars a week all this time, and nobody knows how much Vilola has cost him. She's had everything, and she's never raised her finger to earn a penny herself."

"What do you s'pose the trouble was?"

"Well, they were dreadful close-mouthed, but I guess it was pretty well known at the time what the matter was. I've heard mother talk about it with the neighbors. Mrs. B. F. Brown had an awful temper, and so has B. F. They couldn't get along together."

"There wasn't anything against her, was there?" ·

"No, I never heard a word against her. She was a dreadful pretty woman. I can just remember how she looked. It was when they used to wear curls, and she had real feathery light ones, and the pinkest cheeks, and used to dress real tasty, too. I guess folks sided with her pretty generally. I don't believe B. F. Brown has ever stood quite so well here as he did before."

"Vilola don't take much after her mother, does she?"

"No, she don't. There ain't a homelier girl anywheres around than Vilola Brown, and she hasn't got a mite of style about her, either."

B. F. Brown was rather laboriously making milk toast for supper. By dint of long practice he could make milk toast, griddle cakes, and fry a slice of meat or fish and boil a potato. He was not an expert at any household tasks, though he had served long, having an unusual measure of masculine clumsiness. Although he was not a large man, his fingers were large, with blunt, round ends. He had no deftness of touch. He burned himself sceing if the toast was brown, and finally burned the toast. When the meal was ready he called the cat, which was asleep in a round, yellow ring of luxurious comfort beside the stove. The cat rose lazily at his summons, rounding its back and stretching. The cat belonged to Vilola, and he cherished it like a child during the six months of her absence with her mother. "If anything happened to that cat, I don't know what my daughter would say," he told his clerk, John Bartlett. B. F. Brown kept a small dry-goods store on the village Main Street, and John Bartlett, who was as old as himself and had been with him ever since he was in business, and a boy constituted his entire force of trade.

"I should think she would have to take the cat with her when she goes to stay with her mother, she thinks so much of her," replied John Bartlett. The conversation had taken place upon the occasion of a temporary loss and recovery of the cat.

"Oh, she has another cat she keeps there—a tiger," said B. F. Brown. "She leaves him there when she comes here; but she don't think near so much of him as she does of this yellow one."

Tonight, as B. F. Brown placed a saucer filled with a share of his own supper on the floor beside the stove for the cat, he talked to it with a pitiful, clumsy, masculine crooning: "Poor kitty, poor kitty! There now; eat your supper, kitty."

"Guess that pussy cat will be glad to see her," he muttered, as he sat down to his own supper. Every now and then as he ate he paused, with his fork suspended halfway to his mouth with a bit of toast, and looked upward with an ecstatic expression. His soul was tasting to the full such a savor of anticipatory happiness that he had small comprehension of physical sensations. After he had finished supper he washed his dishes with painful care. He was particular to put every dish in its place on the pantry shelves. He had had the pantry thoroughly cleaned and all the dishes washed and rearranged, and he was fearful lest he disorder them before his daughter arrived. Then he went back to the kitchen and surveyed the clean, shining, yellow surface of the floor anxiously. He had had that newly painted, and he was desperately afraid of marring it before his daughter saw it. He took off his shoes and put on slippers before stepping on it. He kept his slippers in the shed for that purpose and entered through the shed door. He spied a few crumbs on the floor, which he carefully gathered up with his blunted fingers; then he saw a dusty place, which he wiped over with his pocket handkerchief.

He had planned many surprises for his daughter, as he always did on her homecoming. This time he had one which was, in his estimation, almost stupendous. He had purchased a sideboard. Vilola had always talked about a sideboard for the dining room some time when they got rich. She had never asked for one. That was not Vilola's way. She had seldom asked for anything in her whole life, but her father had taken note and remembered. The week before he had gone about anxiously pricing sideboards. He had saved up a certain amount for one. When he found that he could not only purchase a sideboard with his hoard, but a nice little rocking-chair for Vilola's room as well, he was jubilant.

He went home whistling under his breath like a boy. He

had an idea that there should be a rich display of some sort on a sideboard, and he searched the house for suitable ornaments. He found an old-fashioned glass preserve dish on a standard, a little painted mug which had been his in babyhood, and a large cup and saucer with "Gift of Friendship" on the front in gold letters. He arranged these in a row on the sideboard with the tall glass dish in the center. Then he stood off and surveyed the cheap oak piece with its mirror and gaudily carved doors and its decorations doubtfully, not being entirely satisfied.

Then all at once his face lit up. He hastened into his own bedroom out of the sitting room, and brought forth in triumph his last year's Christmas present from Vilola. It was a brush-and-comb tray decorated with blue roses. He dusted it carefully with his pocket handkerchief and placed it on the sideboard to the right of the cup and saucer. In the tray were the nice new brush and comb which had been a part of the present. He had never used them. He thought too much of them for that. He removed the brush and comb and stood for a minute with them in his hand, with his head on one side, surveying the effect of the sideboard without them.

Then he replaced the brush and comb in the tray. He was fully satisfied.

"She'll be tickled 'most to death," he said. He whistled again as he went upstairs to see Vilola's room. He whistled "Annie Laurie," and the words of the old song floated through his mind in company with the air:

> "Her brow is like the snaw-drift,
> Her throat is like the swan, . . .
> And for bonnie Annie Laurie
> I'd lay me doun and dee."

His dear daughter Vilola was in his fancy as Annie Laurie. All the romance of his nature, purified and spiritualized, was represented by his daughter.

When he reached her room, the best chamber in the house, the front one with two windows, he set the little lamp which he carried on the shelf and looked about with delight. The new paper was all on. It was a pretty paper —a white ground with a luster of satin, covered with garlands of blue violets. There was a deep border and a little white-and-gold picture molding. This last was something quite new; Vilola had never had a picture molding in her room. "I guess she'll like that," he chuckled. He joyously anticipated hanging the pictures the next evening. That evening he had to be in his store. The next day the woman was to put down the carpet in the room and clean the paint and windows. The next evening he himself would give the finishing touches. Never had he looked forward to any treat as he did to this simple service for the sake of his daughter. Vilola was coming in two days. The day after tomorrow was to be devoted by the woman to cooking. When Vilola was at home the fare was very different from his when alone. Anything was good enough for him, nothing good enough for Vilola.

Tonight he stood in the dining room door and surveyed the sideboard again. It looked more beautiful to him than ever. "It's a grand piece of furniture, and no mistake," he said. Then he sat happily down by the kitchen stove and the cat jumped up in his lap. Suddenly he reflected that a ribbon around the cat's neck would be an appropriate attention. "Want a ribbon bow on your neck when she comes home?" he asked the cat. He stroked the cat, who purred, and the man would have purred had his state of mind been the only essential.

The next morning he bought a great turkey. In the afternoon the house was redolent with savory odors of cooking. The woman who had cleaned the house had come in the morning to put Vilola's room in order, in the afternoon to do the cooking. B. F. had a great store of cakes and pies prepared, and the turkey also was cooked.

He consulted with the woman, and it was agreed that it could be warmed over the next day and be just as good. "I don't want her to have to go right to hard cookin'," he said.

After the woman had gone that night B. F. went about the house viewing the improvements. He gazed blissfully at the loaded pantry shelves. He had refused to touch one of the new pies or cakes for his supper. He and the cat had fared as usual on milk toast.

Then he went up to Vilola's room. The carpet was now down in the room; he had hung the simple pictures, a few photographs, and two or three flower pieces which had come as prizes with periodicals. Everything was in order. The delicate blue-and-white paper was charming. The curtains had been washed and ironed, and hung crisply in ruffling folds of muslin; there was a fresh white cover on the bureau; Vilola's blue pincushion had been taken from the top drawer; her father had bought a bottle of violet water, and that stood beside it. There was a clean white counterpane on the bed, and the pillowshams were stiff surfaces of shiny whiteness. B. F. looked about, and there was something childish in his expression. His joy over his daughter's prospective joy was at once simple, puerile, and almost heavenly in its innocence.

"I guess she'll be pretty pleased," he said, and he whistled going downstairs.

Vilola was to arrive the next afternoon. B. F. came home from the store about eleven o'clock in the morning. He made a slow fire in the kitchen stove. He put the turkey in the oven. He laboriously prepared the vegetables himself and put them on to boil. He set the table, putting on a clean tablecloth, awry and wrong side out, and, as a crowning glory, he had bought a dozen carnation pinks.

These hung sprawling from a tumbler in the center of the table. He had also bought four pots of geraniums, all in bloom, and these were on a light stand in the sitting-room window. Then he got ready to go to the station to meet Vilola. He shaved, and put on a clean shirt and collar and black tie. He brushed his clothes carefully. His clothes were all that worried him. He really needed a new suit and a new overcoat, but if he had bought them the sideboard and the new paper could not have been bought, unless he had run in debt. B. F. had a horror of debt, even for the gratification of Vilola. He brushed his clothes very carefully, and hoped that Vilola would not feel ashamed of him. The collar of the overcoat troubled him the most, for there were worn places quite white on the velvet. But just before he set out a lucky expedient occurred to him. He got the ink bottle and smeared the white places with ink. Then he put on the coat and was quite easy in his mind. He did not know that his face and his white collar were smeared with the ink.

He hurried down the street to the railroad station. It was about half a mile away. The air was raw and the sky overcast, and snow threatened. He noticed that and his joy was enhanced. It would snow, and he and Vilola would be so snug in the warm house, with the flowers and all that good fare. Before his eyes moved ever in advance, as he walked, a little picture of home and innocent love and happiness, projected upon the wintry landscape from the inward light of his soul. He bowed radiantly to everybody whom he met. "Hullo, B. F.! Have you struck oil?" one man asked, jocosely.

"No," replied B. F.; "my daughter is coming on the one-six train."

"Oh!" returned the man, who was on his way home to dinner. When he saw his own daughter, a plump school-girl, he looked at her with a new wonder of tenderness in his eyes. "It would come pretty hard not to see Nellie for six months at a time," he reflected. He knew B. F.'s story—or as much as anybody knew of it.

B. F. reached the station twenty minutes before the arrival of the train. He went into the waiting room and sat down on a settee, but he did not remain long. He went out on the platform and paced up and down, his overcoat buttoned tightly. The air had the snow chill. "I hope she's dressed warm," he thought. Every time he reached the forward end of the platform he peered down the track for a first glimpse of the train. "Train ain't due for fifteen minutes," said the village expressman, with friendly importance. "I know it," responded B. F., but he continued to peer down the track. He got a certain pleasure from so doing; he seemed in that manner to be prolonging the delight of seeing the first approach of the train. He was drawing out the sweetness of a passing moment to its full length.

At last the train came in sight. B. F. saw quite distinctly the puff of smoke from the locomotive. He heard the deep panting like the respiration of a giant. His heart leaped; he felt almost a hysterical impulse to tears. Then all at once a terror gripped him. Suppose she had not come—suppose anything had happened? The terror was so convincing that he felt for a second all the pangs of disappointment. The train came to a stop before the station. The people began streaming out. B. F. drew timidly near, incalculable anxiety and suspense in his face superseding joyous expectation. He felt sure that she had not come. Then he saw her coming rather clumsily down the steps of a car, holding her heavy satchel before her. Vilola was inclined to stoutness, although a young girl, and she had not much muscle. B. F. felt that revulsion of spirits which comes from the realization of a longed-for happiness after the dread of disappointment. He sprang forward. "Here you be," he said, in a hoarse voice. He clutched Vilola's satchel; he helped her down the steps. He did not look at her, for he felt his face working, but he felt her pleasant, loving, blue eyes on him.

"Well, I am glad to get here," said she, in a sweet, low, droning voice. "I was afraid the snow would come and delay the train. It has been spitting snow half the way. How are you, father?"

"Well—well," replied B. F., in a sort of ecstatic gasp. He seized Vilola by the arm with a sort of fierceness. "She's here," he told himself, defiantly. "She's here; nothing can alter that now. She's here."

When he and Vilola were in the stagecoach—an old-fashioned stagecoach ran to the railroad station—he kept glancing at her with the same exaltation, which had in it something challenging. It was as if he said to a hard fate which had hitherto oftener than not pressed him against the wall, "This joy I have, and it cannot be otherwise."

Suddenly Vilola, looking at him, began to laugh. "What *have* you got on your face, father?" said she. "A great, black smirch. Your collar, too." It was the ink. She took her handkerchief and rubbed his face hard. B. F. shut his eyes tightly. She hurt him, but he was blissful. "It won't come off," said she. "We shall have to wait till we get home. You are a sight!" But she looked at him with the tenderest admiration, even as she laughed.

Vilola chattered pleasantly all the way home. She looked out at her father's little dry-goods store on the Main Street with interest. She asked about business. She asked for one and another of the neighbors. "Oh, how glad I am to be home!" she kept repeating, in a heartfelt tone like a refrain.

"How did you leave your mother?" B. F. asked, in a peculiar tone—the one he always used on these occasions when inquiring for his wife.

"Oh, mother's real well," replied Vilola, "and she looks younger than ever. She looks young enough to be my daughter. She's as pretty as a picture this winter; she's got a lovely new dress with brown fur on it, and a black hat. Mr. Anderson was in last evening, and he told her she ought to have her picture painted in it. She wore it to church last Sunday. I saw Mr. Anderson looking at her."

"You say Mr. Anderson came in last evening?" asked B. F., quickly.

"Yes," replied Vilola, looking at him with wonder.

"What did he come for?"

"He brought home a magazine that mother had lent Mrs. Anderson. She had kept it 'most a month, and mother hadn't read it herself. Why, what makes you look so, father?"

B. F.'s face had sobered as they jolted along in the stagecoach. Vilola looked at him uneasily. "Why, what's the matter, father?" she asked. "What's come over you? Ain't you glad I've come home?"

Then B. F. pulled himself together. He laughed tenderly, and looked at the girl with a beaming face.

"So you think father ain't glad to get you home?" he said. "Well!"

Vilola laughed too. "Well, you looked so solemncholy all at once. I didn't know," said she, with the pretty little pout of a petted creature who can estimate her power with mathematical accuracy. Vilola had been petted by her mother as well as her father. She was a plain girl who gave the effect of prettiness. Her features were not regular; she had a rippling profile and a wide mouth, but her color was beautiful, and so was her thick, soft, light hair puffing over her broad forehead, and she had an expression of arch amiability which was charming. She was rather stout, but daintily built, and dimpled. She had pulled off her gloves, and she had hold of her father's arm with one little plump hand, dented over the knuckles. On one finger shone a small turquoise ring which her father had given her. He looked at it with proprietary delight.

"Haven't lost your ring, have you?"

"No; and everybody admires it. They ask me where I got my ring. They think some fellow gave it to me, and when they say so I laugh and say, 'Yes, the nicest fellow in the whole world gave me that ring,' and then they wonder. Why, it got all around Jefferson that I was engaged, and even mother came to me and asked what it meant. She laughed when I told her. Mother wanted to be remembered to you, father."

"I'm much obliged to her," replied B. F., with gravity.

"How long is it since you've seen mother?" said Vilola.

"Oh, about sixteen years next spring, I guess."

"I guess you'd know her anywhere if you were to see her," said Vilola. "I don't believe she can be changed a mite. She is just as pretty. She looks like a girl."

Vilola spoke with a certain wistfulness. She looked at her father with an unspoken plea and question in her eyes. He knew what it was— "Oh, father, why don't you go to see mother? Why don't you live together, and let me live with you both, instead of having these partings? Why, father?"

Once she had put her question into words, and her father had answered with a decision and dignity which she had never seen in him before. "Never, as long as you live, ask me that again, Vilola," he had said. "I have done the best I can do for us all." That ended it. Vilola had never spoken on the subject again, but she often looked at him with the question in her eyes.

When the stagecoach drew up in front of B. F.'s little story-and-half cottage where Vilola had been born, and which was more like home to her than any other, more like home than her mother's house inherited from her grandmother, which was more pretentious, the girl dimpled with delight at the sight of the little familiar place. "Oh, how good it looks!" said she. "I am so glad to get back!" She jumped out of the stage and ran up the path to the door. She danced up and down like a child. She could not wait for her father to unlock the door. "Hurry! hurry!" said she. "I want to get in! I want to see how it looks!"

B. F., looking fairly foolish with rapture, fumbled with the key. He cast a blissfully confidential glance at the man bringing in the trunk, when he straightened himself up and flung open the door, and Vilola flew in before them.

Vilola was in the kitchen doorway, dancing and sniffing. "Oh, I smell something awful good—awful good!" she proclaimed. "I know what it is. You can't cheat me." She raced into the kitchen and opened the oven door. "I knew, I knew!" cried she, with a shout of exultant laughter. "Oh, isn't it great—isn't it great! I'm home, and I'm going to have roast turkey for dinner!"

"I thought you would like it," returned B. F., with a queer little embarrassed pucker of his mouth. He was so happy, so enraptured at the success of his preparations, that he was fairly shamefaced. When he had shut the front door after the man, Vilola had penetrated the dining room and discovered the new sideboard. She stood with the cat in her arms, gazing at it, then at him, alternately, speechless. He laughed; at the same time he felt the tears in his eyes. "Well," he said, "well!"

Then Vilola spoke. "*Father!*" said she. "Father Brown— If you aren't— I never—a new—" It was disjointed, but the more expressive. Joy at its extreme is not sequential.

"I thought you would like it," said B. F.

"Like it!"

"Do you think it is a pretty one?" asked B. F., anxiously.

"Pretty? Why, father, it is the most beautiful side-board I ever saw! It is magnificent—just magnificent!"

"I don't know what you'd like on it," said B. F., radiantly. "So I thought I would put a few things on it, and you could fix 'em up when you came. Take 'em off if you don't like 'em."

Vilola's eyes at that moment rested full on the brush-and-comb tray and the brush and comb, but she smiled like an angel at her father—a smile of grateful tenderness which had in it something protecting. "It is all beautiful," said she—"beautiful!"

When Vilola saw her own room and the new paper she was wild with delight. "Oh, it is lovely!" said she. "Lovely! It is prettier than the paper on my room at mother's, and I thought that was lovely."

"I'm real glad it suits you," said B. F.

"It is perfectly lovely, but I didn't need it. Why, the paper on my room at mother's is new, too, and the other in this room was on only six months. You're extravagant, father."

"Oh, it don't cost much," said B. F., "and the other paper was stained pretty bad. It leaked in when it rained."

"The way you and mother spoil me!" said Vilola. "Here both of you have got new paper for my room twice in one year."

"Guess ther ain't much spoiling," said B. F. He did not tell her that it was at his instance that the new paper had been put upon her room at her mother's, and that he had paid for it. Neither did he tell her that the pretty, new suit that she wore had been purchased with money provided by him. Vilola believed that her mother had furnished it from her own income. She had a little income besides the ten dollars a week paid her by her husband.

B. F. Brown had guarded all along his wife's good name

so carefully that people, generally speaking, believed in it. There had never been any scandal. People opined that she was a good woman as well as a very pretty one.

B. F.'s wife had been quite a favorite, particularly with men, though there had never been a whisper against her in consequence. Other women never accused her of any indiscretion, though they made insinuations against her temper. B. F. had not so strenuously defended her temper, though he never made voluntary mention of it. Vilola supposed that her mother's temper was the reason of the separation. That day, when she and her father were happily seated at dinner with the turkey and the bouquet of pinks between them, Vilola, when there came a lull in the conversation, said, with an expression which showed that she had had it on her mind to say, "Mother and I have been getting on real nice together lately, father."

"I'm glad you have," said B. F.

"I have never seen that mother's temper was so very bad," said Vilola. "Maybe it's better than it was when I was very young."

"Maybe it is," said B. F.

Then he helped Vilola to some turkey, and nothing more was said about the subject. Vilola had had her girlish dreams of bringing about a reconciliation between her parents, but she had always been baffled by both. Her mother had answered her always as her father had done, though with a certain haste and terror instead of his dignified decision. "It ain't best," said she. "It ain't best for us ever to live together. Don't talk any more about it."

Vilola had spent many anxious and speculative hours over the whole situation. She was a girl of strongly developed affections, and she adored both her parents. She had never had a lover. She was not that sort of girl, people said. Vilola never considered the matter much herself.

"The girls say I am going to be an old maid," she told her father. "And I don't know but I am."

"Well, I hope it will turn out the way that is best for you," said B. F.

"It looks to me now as if I would full as soon keep house for you and mother as get married," said Vilola. "I don't know as I care anything about getting married. It looks to me like quite an undertaking."

"Yes, it's apt to be," said B. F., soberly.

Vilola was a good housekeeper; she took genuine delight in it. She and her father lived together very happily during the six months. Occasionally Vilola had a tea party. The day before she was to leave, the last day of June, when her six months with her father were up, she invited Mrs. Abner Wells and her sister, Mrs. Francis Baker, to tea. It was a beautiful tea, and Vilola had cooked everything herself. The house also, as the visitors said, looked like wax. Mrs. Baker told B. F. Brown that his daughter was a wonderful housekeeper and she had never eaten such biscuits. Brown was radiant with pride and affection. Mrs. Wells had been covertly questioning Vilola all the afternoon; now she turned on her father.

"I guess your daughter takes after her mother," said she, in a sour-sweet voice. "Her mother was a splendid housekeeper, wasn't she?"

"Yes," said B. F., "Vilola's mother *was* a splendid housekeeper. I guess Vilola *did* take it from her."

"Her mother must have spent a good deal of time teaching her," said Mrs. Wells. This was while Vilola was in the kitchen putting away the tea dishes.

"Yes," said B. F., "she did take a sight of pains with her."

"I just remember your wife," said Mrs. Wells, "and I used to think she was about the prettiest woman. She *was* a real pretty woman, wasn't she?"

"Yes, she was, real pretty," said B. F.

Vilola came in then with some dishes to be put in the parlor china closet. "Mother's just as handsome now as ever she was," said she, proudly.

"Yes," said B. F., "I'm sure she is."

"She was real tasty, wasn't she, too?" said Mrs. Wells.

"Yes," said B. F., patiently.

"And real pretty spoken?"

"Yes."

"Oh," said Vilola, "mother has got the prettiest ways. Everybody is taken with mother."

"It was always so," said B. F., with a certain fervor.

He even smiled, as if at the contemplation of something pleasant which was before his eyes.

"And she was real kind-hearted, too; I've heard my mother say so," continued Mrs. Wells. "She used to say that Mis' B. F. Brown was always ready to do any little thing for a neighbor when they needed it. She'd lend her tablecloths and napkins when they had company, or her spoons, and if they was short of victuals and company came unexpected, she'd send over cake or pie just as free. And she was always ready to sit up when anybody was sick. Mother said that she was about the kindest-hearted woman and the most generous she ever saw."

"Yes," assented B. F., with a joyous expression. "Yes, she *was* real kind-hearted and always ready to help anybody."

"She is now," said Vilola, setting away the best cups and saucers in the parlor china closet.

Mrs. Wells was baffled; she smiled aimlessly, and repeated that she had heard her mother say so. She was relieved when her sister, Mrs. Baker, gave a sudden cry and diverted attention from the subject.

"For goodness' sake, just look at that, will you!" cried Mrs. Baker.

And they all looked at a gorgeous black-and-gold butterfly sailing about the room and finally pausing over a vase of June roses on the parlor shelf. "Isn't he a beauty?" said Vilola. "I don't know as I ever saw a butterfly in the house before."

"It's a dreadful bad sign, I've always heard," said Mrs. Wells, presagefully.

"A sign of what?" asked Vilola, rather anxiously. She had a vein of superstition.

"I don't know," replied Mrs. Wells; "something dreadful. Mother always used to say it was. It's worse than a bird." She gave a glance at B. F., as if she was rather pleased that a misfortune was on his track. Going home that night she told her sister that she had never seen such a double-faced man as B. F. Brown, treating his poor wife the way he did and yet praising her.

After the guests had left, Vilola sat down beside the open window and looked out on the moonlit night, full of soft, waving shadows and breathing with sweet flower scents. Her father sat at the other front window, also looking out. Finally, Vilola turned to him.

"Father," said she.

B. F. looked up. "Well?" he replied.

"I can't get something through my head."

"What?"

"I can't get it through my head," said Vilola, quite boldly and simply, "why, when you don't live with mother, and when, of course, you don't think so very much of her, you should say all those nice things about her that you did this evening."

"They were true," said B. F.

"Well, I know that; of course they were true, but—you acted as if you were glad they were true."

B. F. looked out at the moonlit night, and he had an exalted, far-away expression. "Well," he said, "as near as

I can tell you, it's something like this: You know about butterflies, don't you, how there's always a butterfly comin' out of the worm and that little case they crawl into?"

"Why, yes," replied Vilola, wonderingly.

"Well," said B. F., in a tone at once shamed and sublime, "I've about come to the conclusion that there's always a butterfly, or something that's got wings, that comes from everything, and if you look sharp you'll see it, and there can't anything hinder your havin' that, anyhow, and— mebbe that's worth more than all the rest."

"Oh," said Vilola.

B. F. said no more. He gazed out of the window again, and his face shone in the moonlight. Vilola kept glancing at him. Her forehead was knitted perplexedly; her eyes showed a furtive alarm. This speech of B. F.'s was at variance with anything which her New England training had led her to expect. A vague terror of and admiration for her father seized her. "What made him say that?" she kept repeating to herself, even after she was in bed. Her trunk was all packed, for she was going in the morning. She was sorry to go, and her heart was sore with pity for her father to be left alone, but she reflected with joy upon the prospect of seeing her mother. She was going on an earlier train than usual; she usually did not leave until night, arriving in Jefferson the next morning. This time she would travel part of the way by day, and reach her destination about midnight. She had not advised her mother of her change of plan. "I guess mother will be surprised," she told her father, when he was seeing her off at the station the next day.

"Now, I don't feel very easy about your getting there at midnight and nobody there to meet you," said B. F. "Hadn't I better send a telegram to your mother?"

"If you do I shall be dreadfully disappointed," said Vilola. "I've set my heart on surprising mother. There's always a carriage at the midnight train; and it isn't five minutes from the station. Promise you won't telegraph, father."

"Well," said B. F., and then the train came.

B. F.'s heart was heavy going home alone. It was noon, and he had not had any dinner. He had a vague idea of eating something before he went to the store, but he sat down beside the kitchen window and remained there a half hour. It was cool for July. He gazed out at the green yard. There was a cherry tree full of red fruit, and the robins were clamoring in it. Vilola was fond of the cherries. Yesterday afternoon he had had some picked for her, and she had carried a basketful away. B. F. gazed at the cherry tree. He could not bear to look at the empty room behind him. He could hear the tick of the clock, and it sounded like the very voice of loneliness. He took out his handkerchief and put it to his eyes, and bent his head, and his narrow, elderly shoulders shook a little. His bowed gray head looked patient and pathetic. Presently he rose and went to the store without eating anything.

The next day, about six o'clock in the afternoon, a thunderstorm was gathering in the northwest. B. F. started for home, and he walked rather quickly in order to reach shelter before the storm broke. The northwest was a livid black with copper lights. There was a confluent mutter of thunder. B. F. came in sight of his house, and saw, to his amazement, that the front chamber windows were open. He had thought they were closed as usual when Vilola went away. He smelled smoke, and, looking up, saw a thin spiral of blue curling out of the kitchen chimney. A sudden alarm seized him. His knees trembled as he hurried around to the kitchen door. The door stood open. There was an odor of tea. B. F. gasped. He entered tremulously. As he did so there was a blue flash of lightning in the room, then there was a sharp fusillade of thunder. Vilola came running out of the dining room. "Oh, I'm so glad you've come," said she. "It's going to be a terrible tempest."

B. F. gazed at her. He strove to speak, but he only stammered.

Vilola looked at him quite firmly, though she was very pale, and there was a curious, shocked expression in her blue eyes. "Yes," said she, "I've come back."

B. F. continued to look at her.

"Yes," said Vilola, "I'm never going to live with mother again."

Suddenly, as she said mother, a burning, painful red flushed her face and neck.

"Yes, I guess you had better live with me all the time now," said B. F. There came another blue flash of blinding light, a tremendous jar of thunder, then the rain roared past the windows. "I've left my chamber windows open, and my new paper will be wet!" cried Vilola, as she ran. The tea-kettle on the stove boiled over with a furious sputter. B. F. rose and set it back. Then he stood staring absently out of the window at the flooding of the rain which was washing off some of the dust of the world.

## XIII. *BOTH CHEEKS*[1]

"I THINK you ought to present that demand note of Uncle Abel's for collection," said James Lord.

His old uncle Zenas sighed heavily.

"I think we have talked that matter over enough, don't you?" he returned.

The square old room in the low light of the gathering night was lovely, lovelier than in broad daylight, when its shabbiness, which was almost sordid, offended. Now soft shadows lay over it, and there were little pools of dim radiance here and there from polished surfaces of old furniture; an engraving over the mantel gleamed out like a sheet of silver, and right across the floor lay a mysterious beam of reflection beyond tracing. James saw that every night before the lamp was lit, and had never been able to trace its source. The glass over the engraving showing silver was simple enough. The street light caused that. The beam across the floor defied him. He gazed at it now as he talked with his uncle. Zenas was his paternal uncle. The Abel to whom he referred was on his mother's side of the family, Abel Carson. He was a rich old man and Zenas held his demand note, but would not make any effort to collect it.

"No, Uncle Zenas, I don't think we have talked enough until we have talked to some purpose," said James Lord. "If you had that money I could enlist."

"Do you think that is a reason for me to collect?"

Suddenly the boy rose and was across the room. His wiry young figure stood over the old man in the chair.

[1] *Copyright, 1918, by Harper & Brothers.*

244

"Yes, I do," he said, vehemently. "I do, and you ought to think so. You are an old man, Uncle Zenas, but I am ashamed for you. God knows, in time of peace I would be willing to stay here in Leicester and work in the Sylvesters' antique-store till I died, to support you; but this is different. If you had the money which that note represents you would have plenty if the war continued four years, and I could save a little out of my pay for you; but now here I am tied hand and foot. I see all the others going, and I am pinned down here because I am your sole support when you could get enough money tomorrow to set me free."

"You know how I feel about this war," said the old man, and there was a terrible inflexibility in his voice.

"Know how you feel! I should think so! I know to my shame and disgrace, and all the town knows. But I would go, for all that, Uncle Zenas, and I would feel right about going if you had enough money to live on."

"You really mean that you would go to war when you know how I feel about the wickedness of war and how I am convinced that love and peace would take its place?"

"I love peace enough to fight for it," the young voice rang out. "I don't love it enough to stay in a safe place and talk about it while the other fellows are getting hit. Uncle Zenas, for God's sake, why won't you collect that note? Uncle Abel has plenty of money. He is just laughing in his sleeve because you don't."

"I have never had any quarrel with your uncle Abel," said the old voice, inexorably.

"And you won't try to collect because Uncle Abel has such a devilish temper and hates to pay out money like poison."

"I cannot have a quarrel, James."

"Uncle Zenas——"

The old man said nothing.

"Look here, Uncle Zenas, could you get on with what I could save from my pay if I did enlist? Have you got anything besides that note?"

The old man was silent.

"Is this house mortgaged?"

There was no reply.

"You could mortgage the house and set me free," said the young voice, with a burst of courage.

"Mortgage the house where your grandfather was born!"

"Well, I suppose that would come sort of hard for you, but I would pay it as soon as I could after the war."

"Young men often never return from war, and often when they do return it is to be burdens rather than agents to remove them. You can't guarantee anything when you go to war—you know that, James Lord."

"Uncle Zenas, haven't you anything besides?"

Then the old man spoke with cold fury:

"If I had a million in banknotes here this minute I would put it in the fire and make you stay at home and support me. You shall not go to war, James Lord!"

"Uncle Zenas, if you were young and able-bodied, do you mean to say you would not go?"

"I would not! I would settle the whole peaceably."

"No man can settle matters peaceably when there is no peace."

The boy's voice rang high; then he hushed suddenly. He struck a match and lit the lamp on the table and made for the door.

"Where are you going?" asked Zenas.

"Over to the Sylvesters'. I see Thomas Dodd coming in here, and I don't want to stay and hear the old argument, when I am on Dodd's side and can't say so because you are my uncle. I don't like Dodd, either."

James went out of the room, and at the same time the

knocker clanged and a dog barked. The dog barked with
a volley of shrill yelps.

Zenas rose and went to the front door. A large stout
man stood there and a fox terrier was snapping at his
heels. The large man kicked out at the dog, but did not hit
him, and entered.

"Why in the name of common sense don't you tell Sam
Buzzy to keep that nasty little cur of his at home?" he
demanded. "He always hangs round your door, don't he?"

"I think he does a good deal," admitted Zenas.

"Why don't you tell Buzzy to tie him up?"

"I like to live on good terms with my neighbors."

"Oh, my Lord!" snarled the stout man. "And so you
let your friends take chances of being bitten by mad dogs
rather than have a row with a neighbor!" The man seated
himself and the chair creaked. "This old relic won't let
me down with a broken bone, will it?" he growled.

"I think it is fairly strong."

"It isn't as if you had steam heat. Steam heat is the
very dickens for old furniture. You ought to have it,
though. Only thing for a house as big as this. Hot-air
furnace don't begin to heat it."

"It does, except when the wind is in certain directions."

"Strange the wind ain't as accommodating as you peace
folks. Sort of queer nature seems to go on such strikes."

Zenas flushed. He was a handsome, small old man,
with delicate but strong features and a small, closely set
mouth.

"When are you going to start your peace delegation?"
said the other. His voice hissed with aggravation.

Zenas said nothing.

"Ain't you going to send a peace delegation to Europe
pretty soon?" demanded Thomas Dodd.

Zenas spoke sharply.

"Would to God I could do that very thing and stop this frightful slaughter!" said he.

"H'm! Suppose you think a peace delegation, with the women wearing stuffed doves on their hats, and the men with olive sprigs in their buttonholes, and the whole lot preaching and praying, could do more than the armies of the Allies and the United States, now we are in it. H'm!"

"I certainly do," said Zenas, firmly.

The argument was on.

Thomas rose and towered over Zenas ponderously. He shook the index finger of his right hand in his face:

"You believe that right against Scripture?"

Zenas looked at Thomas and his small face seemed as hard as flint.

"I think that is Scripture."

"What do you make of this saying from the Gospel, 'I came not to send peace, but a sword'? What do you think of that, eh?"

Zenas spoke with tense firmness:

"'If any man strike you on one cheek I say unto you turn the other also.'"

Thomas Dodd openly sneered. "If I were you I would quote Scripture correctly," said he. Then he fairly shouted, "'But whosoever shall smite thee on thy right cheek, turn to him the other also.'"

"The meaning is the same," returned Zenas, firmly.

"You know what is said if anybody changes just one word in the Bible, I suppose," sneered Thomas Dodd.

Zenas did not answer. He was a gentleman, and Dodd lacked some of the traits of one. That gave Zenas a certain dignity.

Thomas dimly recognized the fact. His great face blazed red. He shook his finger in the other man's face.

"You traitor, you!" he shouted. "That's what you are, a damn traitor!"

"If believing in saving the sons of my country from quarrel and bloodshed is treachery, then I am a traitor," replied Zenas.

He gazed straight at the index finger, which nearly touched his delicate nose. Zenas looked more high-bred than usual in contrast with Thomas Dodd. His face did not flush. It was slightly paler and his features stood out more distinctly.

"Damn traitor!" said Thomas Dodd.

Zenas said nothing.

"You really mean you would be content to let those crowing fools—for they are fools, and history is going to show it—sink our ships, and murder Americans, and make plots against our government, and try to get us into war with other nations, and into civil war, and blow up our factories and our bridges—and not fight?"

"I believe in peace."

"Hang peace! Why, there isn't any peace! How in Sam Hill can you want to keep what isn't in existence? There hasn't been any peace in this happy-go-lucky country, bless it, since those doggoned Germans goose stepped over the Belgian frontier! Peace! Huh!"

"I do not defend the invasion of Belgium," stated Zenas, mildly. "I admit I feel that the principle is wrong and——"

"Who cares a cat's hind leg about principle, now the United States has finally reared and is shaking all her flags out, and getting her men and her guns and her ships into the ring?" shouted Thomas Dodd. He fairly danced up and down. "Don't I know that principle is behind the whole devilish mess? But now we have taken our stand on principle for granted, and are saying, 'Look here, Bill Hohenzollern, you have hit us; now we hit you.' Lord-a-mighty, it was all well enough to talk principle and high-mindedness when we begun, but now it is hit back, and sit on the whole crew like our fathers sat on the Indians.

I tell you now, Zenas Lord, it is hit! Do ye hear me? Hit! Hit!"

"I believe in peace," said Zenas.

"Do you actually sit there and say, you whose folks did some tall fighting in the little baby wars we used to have, that you would stand for that usage any longer, and let them go on hitting us and turn the other cheek?"

"I believe in following the lead of Scripture," said Zenas.

"Well, here goes!" shouted Thomas Dodd. "I'll give you one chance to practise what you preach!" With that Thomas Dodd gave the man in the chair a mighty slap on his right cheek. Directly over its delicate pallor red finger marks blazed out. Zenas said nothing. Slowly and with dignity he turned the other cheek. Thomas Dodd nearly knocked him out of his chair with a blow on the left jaw.

Then there was a crash. Zenas Lord's chair fell over backward and he was fighting Thomas Dodd. Zenas landed a terrible blow on the right cheek of Thomas, then on the left, with little fists that seemed as hard as steel. Zenas was a small man, but small men sometimes make mighty fighters. Zenas had always known he could fight. He would not, perhaps, have been a pacifist if he had not known that. Deep in his mind had lurked the knowledge of restrained power. For an old man he was amazing. He fairly seemed a blur of motion, so fast he rained blow after blow upon the other man.

Thomas Dodd was no coward. He had been taken by surprise. It was as if a dove had attacked him like a tiger; but he soon began to defend himself. Nothing except defense, and that only to a limited extent, was possible. As well attack a buzz saw as that fierce old man who had turned from his precepts of peace.

Zenas simply could not be hit. When the blow landed he was not there, and immediately Thomas received one.

The two were all over the room. The table and the lamp and a vase of flowers went over, and water and oil trickled over the carpet.

The fighters collided against the silver-gleaming picture over the low mantel, and that crashed down. Zenas pushed Thomas against a gilt-framed mirror, and it cracked, and stars and fissures appeared with noises of explosions.

Always Thomas was on the defense, trying to dodge those blows off the steely little fists of the peaceful man, and never got in one blow himself. Thomas's nose was bleeding; his mouth was puffing; his eyes were closing. He was panting terribly. He was game withal. Never once did he whimper, but he was being worsted.

At last both men crashed down on the floor, and Zenas was sitting on Thomas and pounding the floor with Thomas's great head. Zenas was now beyond himself. The blood which had been held so long in check by laws of peace was over the dam, in flood tide. He was dangerous and terrible.

Zenas pounded the floor with the head of Thomas, and Thomas was gasping when the two old Sylvester brothers, who lived next door, came rushing in. With them was their niece Adeline and her husband, Marion Leicester.

For a moment not one trusted vision. The whole was monstrous and incredible. That little old Zenas Lord, who had antagonized everybody in Leicester and the Barrs by his peaceful attitude when the world was at fighting point, was himself fighting and, it seemed, ready to murder another man, was unbelievable.

Marion Leicester, who wore the khaki and was home on furlough, stared. They all stared. Then Marion made a spring.

"You'll kill him if you don't stop that!" he called, and grasped Zenas's shoulders. They felt like shoulders of steel. Marion was strong, but he could not move those dreadful shoulders of rage. "Let up, for God's sake, man! You don't want to kill him!" he shouted.

Old Zenas twisted round a terrible face of white wrath. "That is just what I want to do," said he. "I want to kill him!"

Zenas made as if to give the floor another pound with the head of Thomas, but Adeline Leicester was before him. Thomas's head came down upon a very large feather cushion which Adeline had snatched from the sofa.

"Take away that damned thing!" screamed Zenas.

He snatched it away himself, and again raised the head. The two Sylvesters and Marion Leicester tugged at Zenas, but all three were not sufficient to prevent another thud.

"He'll kill him!" cried Adeline. She was sobbing and poising the sofa cushion when James Lord came in at a run.

"What in time——" he began.

"James! James!" gasped Adeline. "Your uncle has gone crazy! He's killing Mr. Dodd!"

Zenas unexpectedly spoke in a collected voice.

"I am not killing Thomas Dodd. I am killing war," said he.

"For Heaven's sake, give us a hand, Jim," gasped Marion Leicester, "or I believe in my soul your uncle will kill him! He's like a man made of steel."

As he spoke he again endeavored to get a hold on the old man's shoulders, but such awful tenacity of nerve and will was beyond his strength to overcome.

James was as small as his uncle and of about the same build, and he was young. Finally the four men forced Zenas into a chair, and Marion and James held him while the Sylvesters and Adeline attended to Thomas Dodd.

Presently Thomas Dodd was lying on the sofa, the blood washed from his face, a bandage soaked with liniment on his left jaw and another wet with ice water on his eye. He was still game. As soon as he could speak he turned his right eye in the direction of old Zenas, held in his chair like a restrained charge of dynamite.

"What in tunket possessed you?" he demanded.

Zenas glared at him.

"You're licked!" he proclaimed, in a high voice of triumph.

James stared at him. He really thought his uncle had gone stark mad.

"What made you fly in the face of Scripture?" snarled the old man on the sofa.

"Scripture doesn't say what's to be done when the second cheek is hit," declared Zenas.

"Hum!" demanded the old man on the sofa. "Do you mean to say the second cheek of your own country wasn't hit when Germany tried her devilish plots and blew up our factories and more ships, after the *Lusitania?*"

Zenas was silent.

"And wasn't more than both cheeks of every decent country on the face of the earth hit after Belgium, anyhow?" demanded Thomas Dodd. "Wasn't all humanity hit? Wasn't—God Almighty himself hit?"

After another silence Zenas spoke in a queer, shocked voice.

"Maybe you are right," he said.

"Of course I'm right! But you had to have both your own cheeks hammered, and behave like Germany yourself, making out you were the injured one and pitching into your friend, before you could get it into your hard head. Yes, sir, the United States of America had both cheeks hit, and her heart hit, and the God in whom she believes hit, before she sailed in. Now she's going to hit, and I guess Germany will be on the sofa before long about as beat out as I am. Well, it was worth it. If you hadn't owned up you could have used my head for a tack hammer till you were convinced I did a good thing when I boxed you. When a man's hit himself it sort of drives things home."

"You are right," said Zenas. He was very pale, and his face wore a strange expression.

He looked shocked and exalted. He also had been vanquished, although he bore not a mark on his wiry old body. Thomas Dodd had been subtly victorious. Zenas realized a soreness of his very soul, harder to be borne than all the bruises which he had inflicted on the other's body.

"It isn't Germany's body alone, but her soul we are fighting," he groaned, as if to himself.

"We are going to win," said Marion.

"Win fast enough," said Zenas, "but it's got to be a terrible victory. Germany on the sofa, body and soul!"

Suddenly he turned very pale and James caught him. The old pacifist had exhausted himself. He was helped into his bedroom and Adeline brought him a glass of port wine. He looked up at her after he had swallowed it.

"Sam Buzzy has got to keep his dog at home," said he.

"Lie still now and don't worry," said Adeline, soothingly.

"I am going to collect that demand note," said Zenas. Adeline did not know what he meant.

"That's all right, so you shall. Don't worry," said she.

"How is Thomas going to get home?"

"Marion will drive him in the car."

"I didn't hurt him much?"

"No. Don't you worry."

After the Sylvesters had gone, and Marion had driven off, with Thomas Dodd propped up in the tonneau of the car, James Lord sat by himself in the outer room. He thought it wiser to leave his uncle alone. The bedroom door was ajar and he could hear if he stirred.

James sat with a bewildered face until he heard the

Leicester car return; then he jumped up and opened the door for Marion. Both men tiptoed back into the room.

"I think he's asleep," whispered James.

The two stood looking at each other.

"What possessed him?" whispered Marion.

"Hanged if I know. Say, Marion, it's hard luck. I want to enlist. I don't want to hang around here when it's a war like this war. I'm disgraced for life if I don't enlist."

"I suppose you have to——"

"Support him, yes. But if he would collect a demand note that's due him he would have enough to set me free."

Marion gave a low whistle.

"A demand note?"

"Yes, my uncle Abel's."

"He ought to pay."

"Of course he ought. He would pay, too, but of course he'd get mad. Uncle Abel never paid for anything without raising Cain, and Uncle Zenas is all for peace."

Marion tapped his head significantly.

"I don't know," said James. "Sometimes I wonder myself."

"You needn't wonder," said a voice. "I'm just as right in my head as you are." He was still very pale, old Zenas, standing there in the bedroom door, but he spoke firmly. "I've made up my mind to fight a little for my own rights," said Zenas. "My fight with Thomas turned me clean round. I'm for every man that's able fighting for the country, and fighting for his own rights if he's able. Sam Buzzy has got to keep that dog of his home, and I'm going to collect that note, and— Look here, James Lord, I've got money besides that. You go and enlist, and there will be plenty for you to buy yourself a good kit, everything you want, and you can stay in the army, for all me, as long as you live. Maybe you'll get promoted. I've had money enough all along, only I wouldn't tell because I didn't approve of war. Better hurry and enlist before the war's over."

James looked at him, frightened.

Old Zenas laughed.

"You needn't think I'm crazy," said he. "You enlist, and you fight for all you are worth, if you think anything of me."

"I don't know how to thank you, uncle," said James, in a bewildered fashion.

Zenas looked at the man in khaki, then at his nephew. A strange light was in his eyes. His peaceful acquiescence with the buffets of the century of wrath and terror was gone forever. He was now of his day, the dreadful Day for all the world. He understood. He could not fight the common foe as he had fought Thomas Dodd; he was too old. The din of battle and trench life was not for him, but in him blazed like a torch the war spirit.

"How can I ever thank you, uncle?" James said, again.

"The head of Germania on a charger," said old Zenas Lord.

# XIV. *A SOLITARY*[1]

It was snowing hard, as it had been for twenty-four hours. The evergreen trees hung low with the snow. Nicholas Gunn's little house was almost hidden beneath it. The snow shelved out over the eaves, and clung in damp masses to the walls. Nicholas sat on his doorstep, and the snow fell upon him. His old cap had become a tall white crown; there was a ridge of snow upon his bent shoulders. He sat perfectly still; his eyes were fixed upon the weighted evergreens across the road, but he did not seem to see them. He looked as calmly passive beneath the storm as a Buddhist monk.

There were no birds stirring, and there was no wind. All the sound came from the muffled rustle of the snow on the trees, and that was so slight as to seem scarcely more than a thought of sound. The road stretched to the north and south through the forest of pine and cedar and hemlock. Nicholas Gunn's was the only house in sight.

Stephen Forster came up the road from the southward. He bent his head and struggled along; the snow was above his knees, and at every step he lifted his feet painfully, as from a quicksand. He advanced quite noiselessly until he began to cough. The cough was deep and rattling, and he had to stand still in the snow while it was upon him. Nicholas Gunn never looked up. Stephen bent himself almost double, the cough became a strangle, but Nicholas kept his calm eyes fixed upon the evergreens.

At last Stephen righted himself and kept on. He was

very small; his clothes were quite covered with snow, and patches of it clung to his face. He looked like some little winter-starved, white-furred animal, creeping painfully to cover. When he came opposite the house he half halted, but Nicholas never stirred nor looked his way, and he kept on. It was all that he could do to move, the cough had exhausted him; he carried a heavy basket, too.

He had proceeded only a few paces beyond the house when his knees bent under him; he fairly sank down into the snow. He groaned a little, but Nicholas did not turn his head.

After a little, Stephen raised himself, lifted his basket, and went staggering back. "Mr. Gunn," said he.

Nicholas turned his eyes slowly and looked at him, but he did not speak.

"Can't I go into your house an' set down an' rest a few minutes? I'm 'most beat out."

"No, you can't," replied Nicholas Gunn.

"I dunno' as I can git home."

Nicholas made no rejoinder. He turned his eyes away. Stephen stood looking piteously at him. His sharply cut delicate face gleamed white through the white fall of the snow.

"If you'd jest let me set there a few minutes," he said.

Nicholas sat immovable.

Stephen tried to walk on, but suddenly another coughing fit seized him. He stumbled across the road and propped himself against a pine tree, setting the basket down in the snow. He twisted himself about the snowy tree trunk, and the coughs came in a rattling volley.

Nicholas Gunn looked across at him, and waited until Stephen got his breath. Then he spoke. "Look-a-here!" said he.

"What say?"

"If you want to set in the house a few minutes, you can. There ain't no fire there."

"Thank ye."

It was some time before Stephen Forster gathered strength enough to return across the road to the house. He leaned against the tree, panting, the tears running down his cheeks. Nicholas did not offer to help him. When at last Stephen got across the road, he arose to let him pass through the door; then he sat down again on the doorstep.

Stephen Forster set his basket on the floor and staggered across the room to a chair. He leaned his head back against the wall and panted. The room was bitterly cold; the snow drifted in through the open door where Nicholas sat. There was no furniture except a cooking stove, a cot bed, one chair, and a table; but there were ornaments. Upon the walls hung various little worsted and cardboard decorations. There was a lamp mat on the table, and in one corner was a rude bracket holding a bouquet of wax flowers under a tall glass shade. There was also a shelf full of books beside the window.

Stephen Forster did not notice anything. He sat with his eyes closed. Once or twice he tried feebly to brush the snow off his clothes, that was all. Nicholas never turned his head. He looked like a stone image there in the doorway. In about twenty minutes Stephen arose, took his basket up, and went timidly to the door.

"I'm much obleeged to ye, Mr. Gunn," said he. "I guess I can git along now."

Nicholas got up, and the snow fell from his shoulders in great cakes. He stood aside to let Stephen pass. Stephen, outside the door, paused, and looked up at him.

"I'm much obleeged to ye," he said again. "I guess I can git home now. I had them three coughin' spells after I left the store, and I got 'most beat out."

Nicholas grunted, and sat down again. Stephen looked

at him a minute; then he smiled abashedly and went away, urging his feeble little body through the storm. Nicholas watched him; then he turned his head with a stiff jerk.

"If he wants to go out in such weather, he can. I don't care," he muttered.

It was nearly four o'clock in the afternoon, the snow was gradually ceasing. Presently a yellow light could be seen through the woods in the west. Some birds flew into one of the snowy trees, a wood sled creaked down the road, the driver stared at Nicholas in the doorway, he turned his head and stared again. It was evident that he was not one of the village people. They had witnessed the peculiarities of Nicholas Gunn for the last six years. They still stared, but not as assiduously.

The driver of the wood sled, as soon as he went down the slope in the road and could no longer see Nicholas, began to whistle. The whistle floated back like a wake of merry sound.

Presently Nicholas arose, took off his cap, and beat it against the doorpost to rid it of its dome of snow; then he shook himself like a dog and stamped; then he went into the house, and stood looking irresolutely at the cold stove.

"Should like a fire to heat up my hasty puddin' mighty well, so—I won't have it," said he.

He took a wooden bucket, and went with it out-of-doors, around the house, over a snow-covered path, to a spring. The water trickled into its little basin from under a hood of snow. Nicholas plunged in his bucket, withdrew it filled with water, and carried it back to the house. The path led through the woods; all the trees and bushes were white arcs. Some of the low branches bowed over the path, and Nicholas, passing under them, had to stoop.

Nicholas, back in the house, got a bowl out of a rude

closet; it was nearly full of cold hasty pudding. He stood there and swallowed it in great gulps.

The light was waning fast, although it lasted longer than usual on account of the snow, which, now the clouds were gone, was almost like a sheet of white light.

Nicholas, when he had finished his supper, plunged out again into this pale dusk. He tramped, knee-deep, down the road for a long way. He reached the little village center, left it behind, and went on between white meadow lands and stretches of woods. Once in a while he met a man plodding down to the store, but there were few people abroad, the road would not be cleared until morning.

Finally Nicholas turned about, and went back until he reached the village store. Its windows and glass door were full of yellow light, in which one could see many heads moving. When Nicholas opened the clanging door and went in, all the heads turned toward him. There was hardly a man there as tall as he. He went across the store with a kind of muscular shamble; his head, with its wild light beard, had a lofty lift to it. The lounging men watched him furtively as he bought some Indian meal and matches at the counter. When he had gone out with his purchases there was a burst of laughter. The storekeeper thrust a small sharp face over the counter.

"If a man is such a darned fool as to live on meal and matches, I ain't got nothin' to say, so long as he pays me the money down," said he. He had a hoarse cold, and his voice was a facetious whisper.

There was another shout of laughter; Nicholas could hear it as he went down the street. The stranger who had driven the wood sled past Nicholas's house was among the men. He was snowbound overnight in the village. He was a young fellow, with innocent eyes and a hanging jaw. He nudged the man next him.

"What in creation ails the fellar, anyhow?" said he. "I

seed him a-settin' on his doorstep this afternoon, and the snow a-drivin' right on him."

"He ain't right in his upper story," replied the man. "Somethin' went again' him; his wife run off with another fellar, or somethin', an' he's cracked."

"Why don't they shet him up?"

"He ain't dangerous. Reckon he won't hurt nobody but himself. If he wants to set out in a drivin' snowstorm and tramp till he's tuckered out, it ain't nothin' to nobody else but himself. There ain't no use bringin' that kind of crazy on the town."

" 'Twouldn't cost the town much," chimed in another man. "He's worth property. Shouldn't be surprised if he was worth three thousand dollars. And there he is a-livin' on corn meal and water."

An old man, in a leather-cushioned armchair beside the stove, turned his grizzly quizzical face toward the others and cleared his throat. They all bent forward attentively. He had a reputation for wit.

"Makes me think of old Eph Huntly and the story Squire Morse used to tell about him," said he. He paused impressively, and they waited. Then he went on. "Seems old Eph got terrible hard up one time. One thing after another went again' him. He'd been laid up with the rheumatiz all winter; then his wife she'd been sick, an' they was 'most eat up with medicine an' doctors' bills. Then his hay crop had failed, an' his pertaters had rotted, an' finally, to cap the climax, his best cow died, an' the int'rest money was due on the mortgage an' he didn't have a cent to pay it with. Well, he couldn't raise the money nohow, an' the day come when he s'posed the farm would have to go. Lawyer Holmes he held the mortgage, an' he expected to see him drive into the yard any time. Well, old Eph he jest goes out in the yard, an' he ketches a nice fat crower, an' he kills him an' picks him. Then he takes him in to his wife. She was takin' on terrible 'cause she thought the farm had to go, an' sez he, 'Sukey Ann, I want you to go an' cook this crower jest as good as you know how.' 'Oh, Lor'!' sez she, 'I don't want no crower,' an' she boo-hooed right out. But old Eph he made her go an' stuff that crower, an' cook him, an' bile onions, turnips, an' squash, an' all the fixin's. He said he never felt so bad in his life, an' he never got to sech a desprit pitch, an' he was goin' to have a good dinner, anyhow. Well, it so happened that Lawyer Holmes he driv into the yard jest as old Eph an' his wife were settin' down to dinner, an' he see that nice baked crower an' the fixin's all set out, an' he didn't know what to make on't. It seemed to him Eph couldn't be so dreadful bad off, or he wouldn't have any heart for extra dinners, an' mebbe he had some way of raisin' the money in prospect. Then Lawyer Holmes he was mighty fond of his victuals himself, an' the upshot of it was, he sot down to the table, an' eat a good meal of the crower an' fixin's, an' there wa'n't no mortgage foreclosed that day, an' before long Eph he managed to raise the money some-how. Now if Nicholas Gunn jest had a leetle grain of old Eph's sense, he'd jest git better victuals the wuss he felt, an' let one kinder make up for t'other, instead of livin' on Injun meal an' matches. I ruther guess I wouldn't take to no meal an' matches if my Ann Lizy left me. I'd live jest as high as I could to keep my spirits up."

There was a burst of applause. The old man sat wink-ing and grinning complacently.

"Nicholas Gunn is a darned fool, or else he's cracked," said the storekeeper in his hoarse whisper.

Meanwhile Nicholas Gunn went home. He put the meal away in the closet; he lighted a candle with one of his matches; he read awhile in the Bible; then he went to bed. He did not sleep in the cot bed; that was too luxurious for him. He slept, rolled in a blanket, on the bare floor.

Nicholas Gunn, whether his eccentricities arose from mystical religious fervor or from his own personal sorrows, would have been revered and worshiped as a saintly ascetic among some nations; among New Englanders he met with the coarse ridicule of the loafers in a country store. Idle meditation and mortification of the flesh, except for gain, were among them irreconcilable with sanity. Nicholas would have had more prestige had he fled to the Himalayas and built himself a cell in some wild pass; however, prestige was not what he sought.

The next morning a wind had arisen; it blew stiff and cold from the north. The snow was drifted into long waves, and looked like a frozen sea. A flock of sparrows had collected before Nicholas Gunn's door, and he stood watching them. They were searching for crumbs; this deep snow had shortened their resources woefully; all their larders were buried. There were no crumbs before this door; but they searched assiduously, with their feathers ruffled in the wind. Stephen Forster came up the road with his market basket; it was all he could do to face the wind. His thin coat was buttoned tight across his narrow shoulders; his old tippet blew out. He advanced with a kind of sidewise motion, presenting his body like a wedge to the wind; he could not walk fairly against it.

When he was opposite Nicholas, the sparrows flew up at his feet; he paused and shifted his basket. "Good mornin', Mr. Gunn," said he, in a weak voice.

Nicholas nodded. Stephen's face was mottled with purple; his nose and mouth looked shrunken; his shoes were heavy with snow.

"If you want to go in an' set down a few minutes, you can," said Nicholas.

Stephen moved forward eagerly. "Thank ye, Mr. Gunn. I am kinder beat out, an' I'd like to set a few minutes," he said.

He went in and sat down. The wind rushed in great gusts past the open door. Stephen began to cough. Nicholas hesitated; his face was surly; then he shut the door with a bang.

While Stephen rested himself in the house, Nicholas marched up and down before it like a sentinel. He did not seem to see Stephen when he came out, but he stood before him in his track.

"I'm much obleeged, Mr. Gunn," said he.

Nicholas nodded. Stephen hesitated a minute; then he went on up the road. The snow blew up around him in a dazzling cloud, and almost hid him from sight.

"It's the last time I do it," muttered Nicholas.

But it was not. Every morning, storm or shine, Stephen Forster toiled painfully over the road with his market basket, and every morning Nicholas Gunn invited him into his fireless hermitage to rest. A freezing hospitality, but he offered it, and Stephen accepted it with a fervent gratitude.

It grew apparently more and more necessary. Stephen crept more and more feebly over the road; he had to keep setting his basket down. Nicholas never asked him if he was ill; he never questioned him at all, although he knew nothing about him but his name. Nicholas did not know the names, even, of many of the village people; he had never offered nor invited confidences. Stephen also did not volunteer any information as to his circumstances during his morning calls upon Nicholas; indeed, he was too exhausted; he merely gave his gentle and timid thanks for the hospitality.

There came a night in January when the cold reached the greatest intensity of the season. The snow creaked underfoot; the air was full of sparkles; there were noises like guns in the woods, for the trees were almost freezing.

The moon was full and seemed like a very fire of death, radiating cold instead of heat.

Nicholas Gunn, stern anchorite that he was, could not sleep for the cold. He got up and paced his room. He would not kindle a fire in the stove. He swung his arms and stamped. Suddenly he heard a voice outside. It sounded almost like a child's. "Mr. Gunn!" it cried.

Nicholas stopped and listened. It came again—"Mr. —Gunn!"

"Who's there?" Nicholas sung out, gruffly.

"It's—me."

Then Nicholas knew it was Stephen Forster. He opened the door, and Stephen stood there in the moonlight.

"What are ye out for this time of night?" asked Nicholas.

Stephen chattered so that he could hardly speak. He cowered before Nicholas; the moonlight seemed to strike his little, shivering form like a broadside of icy spears. "I'm 'fraid I'm freezin'," he gasped. "Can't ye take me in?"

"What are ye out for this time of night?" repeated Nicholas, in a rough, loud tone.

"I had to. I'll tell you when I git a leetle warmer. I dunno' but—I'm freezin'."

Stephen's voice, indeed, sounded as if ice were forming over it, muffling it. Nicholas suddenly grasped him by one arm.

"Come in, then, if ye've got to," he growled.

He pulled so suddenly and strongly that Stephen made a run into the house, and his heels flew up weakly. Nicholas whirled him about and seated him on his cot bed.

"Now lay down here," he ordered, "and I'll cover ye up."

Stephen obeyed. Nicholas pulled off his boots, gave his feet a fierce rub, and fixed the coverings over him with rough energy. Then he began pacing the room again.

Presently he went up to the bed. "Warmer?"

"I guess—so." Stephen's shivering seemed to shake the room.

Nicholas hustled a coat off a peg, and put it over Stephen. Then he paced again. Stephen began to cough. Nicholas made an exclamation, and stamped angrily out of the house. There was a little lean-to at the back, and there was some fuel stored in it. Nicholas came back quickly with his arms full of wood. He piled it into the stove, set a match to it, and put on a kettle of water. Then he dragged the cot bed, with Stephen on it, close to the stove, and began to rub him under the bedclothes. His face was knit savagely, but he rubbed with a tender strength.

"Warmer?" said he.

"Yes, I—be," returned Stephen, gratefully.

The fire burned briskly; the sharp air began to soften. Soon the kettle steamed. Nicholas got a measure of meal out of his cupboard, and prepared some porridge in a little stewpan. When it began to boil he bent over the stove and stirred carefully, lest it should lump. When it was thick enough, he dished it, salted it, and carried it to Stephen.

"There, eat it," said he. "It's the best I've got; it'll warm ye some. I ain't got no spirits; never keep any in the house."

"I guess I ain't—very hungry, Mr. Gunn," said Stephen, feebly.

"Eat it."

Stephen raised himself, and drained the bowl with convulsive gulps. Tears stood in his eyes, and he gasped when he lay back again. However, the warm porridge revived him. Presently he looked at Nicholas, who was putting more wood on the fire.

"I s'pose you think it's terrible queer that I come here this way," said he; "but there wa'n't no other way. I dunno' whether you know how I've been livin' or not."

"No, I don't."

"Well, I've been livin' with my half-sister, Mis' Morrison. Mebbe you've heard of her?"

"No, I ain't."

"She keeps boarders. We ain't lived in this town more'n three years; we moved here from Jackson. Mis' Morrison's husband's dead, so she keeps boarders. She's consider'ble older'n me. I ain't never been very stout, but I used to tend in a store till I got worse. I coughed so, it used to plague the customers. Then I had to give it up, and when Mis' Morrison's husband died, and she come here, I come with her; she thought there'd be some chores I could do for my board. An' I've worked jest as hard as I could, an' I ain't complained. I've been down to the store to get meat for the boarders' dinner when I couldn't scarcely get along over the ground. But I cough so bad nights that the boarders they complain, an' Mis' Morrison says I must go to—the poorhouse. I heard her talkin' with the hired girl about it. She's goin' to get the selectmen to the house tomorrow mornin'. An'—I ain't a-goin' to the poorhouse! None of my folks have ever been there, an' I ain't goin'! I'll risk it but what I can get some work to do. I ain't quite so fur gone yet. I waited till the house was still, an' then I cut. I thought if you'd take me in till mornin', I could git down to the depot, an' go to Jackson before the selectmen come. I've got a little money—enough to take me to Jackson—I've been savin' of it up these three years, in case anything happened. It's some I earned tendin' store. I'm willin' to pay you for my night's lodgin'."

Nicholas nodded grimly. He had stood still, listening to the weak, high-pitched voice from the bed.

"It's in my vest pocket, in my pocketbook," said Stephen. "If you'll come here, I'll give it to you, and you can take what you think it's worth. I pinned the pocket up, so's to be sure I didn't lose it."

Stephen began fumbling at his vest. Nicholas lifted a cover from the stove.

"I don't want none of your money," said he. "Keep your money."

"I've got enough to pay you, an' take me to Jackson."

"I tell ye, stop talkin' about your money."

Stephen said no more; he looked terrified. The air grew warmer. Everything was quiet, except for the detonations of the frost in the forest outside, and its sharp cracks in the house walls. Soon Stephen fell asleep, and lay breathing short and hard. Nicholas sat beside him.

It was broad daylight when Stephen aroused himself. He awoke suddenly and completely, and began to get out of bed. "I guess it's time I was goin'," said he. "I'm much obleeged to you, Mr. Gunn."

"You lay still."

Stephen looked at him.

"You lay still," repeated Nicholas.

Stephen sank back irresolutely; his timid, bewildered eyes followed Nicholas, who was smoothing his hair and beard before a little looking-glass near the window. There was a good fire in the cooking stove, and the room was quite warm, although it was evidently a very cold day. The two windows were thickly coated with frost, and the room was full of dim white light. One of the windows faced toward the east, but the sun was still hidden by the trees across the road.

Nicholas smoothed his hair and his wild beard slowly and punctiliously.

Stephen watched him. "Mr. Gunn," he said, at length.

"What say?"

"I'm afraid—I shan't get to the depot before the train goes if I don't start pretty soon."

Nicholas went on smoothing his beard. At length he laid his comb down and turned around. "Look a-here!" said

he; "you might jest as well understand it. You ain't a-goin'
to any depot today, an' you ain't a-goin' to any train, an'
you ain't a-goin' to any depot tomorrow nor any train,
an' you ain't a-goin' the next day, nor the next, nor the
next, nor the next after that."

"What be I a-goin' to do?"

"You are a-goin' to stay jest where you are. I've fought
against your comin' as long as I could, an' now you've
come, an' I've turned the corner, you are a-goin' to stay.
When I've been walkin' in the teeth of my own will on one
road, an' havin' all I could do to breast it, I ain't a-goin'
to do it on another. I've give up, an' I'm a-goin' to stay
give up. You lay still."

Stephen's small anxious face on the pillow looked almost
childish. His helplessness of illness seemed to produce the
same expression as the helplessness of infancy. His hollow, innocent blue eyes were fixed upon Nicholas with
blank inquiry. "Won't Mis' Morrison be after me?" he
asked, finally.

"No, she won't. Don't you worry. I'm a-goin' over to
see her. You lay still." Nicholas shook his coat before
he put it on; he beat his cap against the wall, then ad-
justed it carefully. "Now," said he, "I'm a-goin'. I've
left enough wood in the stove, an' I guess it'll keep warm
till I get back. I shan't be gone any longer than I can
help."

"Mr. Gunn!"

"What say?"

"I ruther guess I'd better be a-goin'."

Nicholas looked sternly at Stephen. "You lay still," he
repeated. "Don't you try to get up whilst I'm gone; you
ain't fit to. Don't you worry. I'm goin' to fix it all right.
I'm goin' to bring you something nice for breakfast. You
lay still."

Stephen stared at him; his thin shoulders hitched uneasily under the coverlid.

"You're goin' to lay still, ain't you?" repeated Nicholas.

"Yes; I will, if you say so," replied Stephen. He sighed
and smiled feebly.

The truth was that this poor cot in the warm room
seemed to him like a couch under the balsam-dropping
cedars of Lebanon, and all at once he felt that divine rest
which comes from leaning upon the will of another.

"Well, I do say so," returned Nicholas. He looked at
the fire again; then he went out. He turned in the doorway and nodded admonishingly at Stephen. "Mind you
don't try to get up," he said again.

Nicholas went out of sight down the road, taking long
strides over the creaking snow. He was gone about a
half hour. When he returned his arms were full of packages. He opened the door and looked anxiously at the bed.
Stephen twisted his face toward him and smiled. Nicholas
piled the packages up on the table and lifted a stove cover.

"I've seen Mis' Morrison, and it's all right," said he.

"What did she say?" asked Stephen, in an awed voice.

"Well, she didn't say much of anything. She was fryin'
griddle cakes for the boarders' breakfasts. She said she
felt real bad about lettin' you go, but she didn't see no
other way, an' she'd be glad to have you visit me jest as
long as you wanted to. She's goin' to pack up your clothes."

"I ain't got many clothes. There's my old coat an'
vest an' my other pants, but they're most worn out. I
ain't got but one real good shirt besides this one I've got
on. That was in the wash, or I'd brought it."

"Clothes enough," said Nicholas.

He crammed the stove with wood and began undoing
the packages. There were coffee, bread, and butter, some
little delicate sugar cookies, some slices of ham, and eggs.
There were also a pail of milk and a new tin coffeepot.

Nicholas worked busily. He made coffee, fried the ham and eggs, and toasted slices of bread. When everything was ready, he carried a bowl of water to Stephen for him to wash his hands and face before breakfast. He even got his comb and smoothed his hair.

Then he set the breakfast out on the table, and brought it up to the bedside. He had placed a chair for himself, and was just sitting down, when he stopped suddenly. "I don't know as it's just fair for me not to tell you a little something about myself before we really begin livin' together," said he. "It won't take but a minute. I don't know but you've heard stories about me that I wa'n't quite right. Well, I am; that is, I s'pose I am. All is, I've had lots of trouble, an' it come mainly through folks I set by; an' I figured out a way to get the better of it. I figured out that if I didn't care anything for anybody, I shouldn't have no trouble from 'em; an' if I didn't care anything for myself, I shouldn't have any from myself. I 'bout made up my mind that all the trouble an' wickedness in this world come from carin' about yourself or somebody else, so I thought I'd quit it. I let folks alone, an' I wouldn't do anything for 'em; an' I let myself alone as near as I could, an' didn't do anything for myself. I kept cold when I wanted to be warm, an' warm when I wanted to be cold. I didn't eat anything I liked, an' I left things around that hurt me to see. My wife she made them wax flowers an' them gimcracks. Then I used to read the Bible, 'cause I used to believe in it an' didn't now, an' it made me feel worse. I did about everything I could to spite myself an' get all the feelin' out of me, so I could be a little easier in my mind."

Nicholas paused a moment. Stephen was looking at him with bewildered intensity.

"Well, I was all wrong," Nicholas went on. "I've give it all up. I've got to go through with the whole of it like other folks, an' I guess I've got grit enough. I've made up my mind that men's tracks cover the whole world, and there ain't standin' room outside of 'em. I've got to go with the rest. Now we'll have breakfast."

Nicholas ate heartily; it was long since he had tasted such food; even Stephen had quite an appetite. Nicholas pressed the food upon him; his face was radiant with kindness and delight. Stephen Forster, innocent, honest, and simple-hearted, did not in the least understand him, but that did not matter. There is a higher congeniality than that of mutual understanding; there is that of need and supply.

After breakfast Nicholas cleared away the dishes and washed them. The sun was so high then that it struck the windows, and the frostwork sparkled like diamonds.

Nicholas opened the door; he was going down to the spring for more water; he saw a flock of sparrows in the bushes across the road, and stopped; then he set his pail down noiselessly and went back for a piece of bread. He broke it and scattered the crumbs before the door, then went off a little way and stood watching. When the sparrows settled down upon the crumbs he laughed softly and went on toward the spring over the shining crust of snow.

# XV. *TWO OLD LOVERS* [1]

LEYDEN was emphatically a village of cottages, and each of them built after one of two patterns: either the front door was on the right side, in the corner of a little piazza extending a third of the length of the house, with the main roof jutting over it, or the piazza stretched across the front, and the door was in the center.

The cottages were painted uniformly white, and had blinds of a bright spring-green color. There was a little flower garden in front of each; the beds were laid out artistically in triangles, hearts, and rounds, and edged with box; boys'-love, sweet williams, and pinks were the fashionable and prevailing flowers.

There was a general air of cheerful though humble prosperity about the place, which it owed, and indeed its very existence also, to the three old weather-beaten boot-and-shoe factories which rose stanchly and importantly in the very midst of the natty little white cottages.

Years before, when one Hiram Strong put up his three factories for the manufacture of the rough shoe which the workingman of America wears, he hardly thought he was also gaining for himself the honor of founding Leyden. He chose the site for his buildings mainly because they would be easily accessible to the railway which stretched to the city, sixty miles distant. At first the workmen came on the cars from the neighboring towns, but after a while they became tired of that, and one after another built for himself a cottage, and established his family and his household belongings near the scene of his daily labors. So gradually Leyden grew. A built his cottage like C, and B built his like D. They painted them white, and hung the green blinds, and laid out their flower beds in front and their vegetable beds at the back. By and by came a church and a store and a post office to pass, and Leyden was a full-fledged town.

That was a long time ago. The shoe factories had long passed out of the hands of Hiram Strong's heirs; he himself was only a memory on the earth. The business was not quite as wide-awake and vigorous as when in its first youth; it droned a little now; there was not quite so much bustle and hurry as formerly. The factories were never lighted up of an evening on account of overwork, and the workmen found plenty of time for pleasant and salutary gossip over their cutting and pegging. But this did not detract in the least from the general cheerfulness and prosperity of Leyden. The inhabitants still had all the work they needed to supply the means necessary for their small comforts, and they were contented. They too had begun to drone a little like the factories. "As slow as Leyden" was the saying among the faster-going towns adjoining theirs. Every morning at seven the old men, young men, and boys, in their calico shirt sleeves, their faces a little pale—perhaps from their indoor life—filed unquestioningly out of the back doors of the white cottages, treading still deeper the well-worn footpaths stretching around the sides of the houses, and entered the factories. They were great, ugly wooden buildings, with wings which they had grown in their youth jutting clumsily from their lumbering shoulders. Their outer walls were black and grimy, streaked and splashed and patched with red paint in every variety of shade, according as the original hue was tempered with smoke or the beatings of the storms of many years.

The men worked peacefully and evenly in the shoe shops

all day; and the women stayed at home and kept the little white cottages tidy, cooked the meals, and washed the clothes, and did the sewing. For recreation the men sat on the piazza in front of Barker's store of an evening, and gossiped or discussed politics; and the women talked over their neighbors' fences, or took their sewing into their neighbors' of an afternoon.

People died in Leyden as elsewhere; and here and there was a little white cottage whose narrow footpath leading round to its back door its master would never tread again.

In one of these lived Widow Martha Brewster and her daughter Maria. Their cottage was one of those which had its piazza across the front. Every summer they trained morning-glories over it, and planted their little garden with the flower seeds popular in Leyden. There was not a cottage in the whole place whose surroundings were neater and gayer than theirs, for all they were only two women, and two old women at that; for Widow Martha Brewster was in the neighborhood of eighty, and her daughter, Maria Brewster, near sixty. The two had lived alone since Jacob Brewster died and stopped going to the factory, some fifteen years ago. He had left them this particular white cottage, and a snug little sum in the savings bank besides, for the whole Brewster family had worked and economized all their long lives. The women had corded boots at home, while the man had worked in the shop and never spent a cent without thinking of it overnight.

Leyden folks all thought that David Emmons would marry Maria Brewster when her father died. "David can rent his house and go to live with Maria and her mother," said they, with an affectionate readiness to arrange matters for them. But he did not. Every Sunday night at eight o'clock punctually the form of David Emmons, arrayed in his best clothes, with his stiff white dickey, and a nosegay in his buttonhole, was seen to advance up the road toward

Maria Brewster's, as he had been seen to advance every Sunday night for the last twenty-five years, but that was all. He manifested not the slightest intention of carrying out people's judicious plans for his welfare and Maria's.

She did not seem to pine with hope deferred; people could not honestly think there was any occasion to pity her for her lover's tardiness. A cheerier woman never lived. She was literally bubbling over with jollity. Round-faced and black-eyed, with a funny little bounce of her whole body when she walked, she was the merry feature of the whole place.

Her mother was now too feeble, but Maria still corded boots for the factories as of old. David Emmons, who was quite sixty, worked in them, as he had from his youth. He was a slender, mild-faced old man, with a fringe of gray-yellow beard around his chin; his head was quite bald. Years ago he had been handsome, they said, but somehow people had always laughed at him a little, although they all liked him. "The slowest of all the slow Leydenites," outsiders called him, and even the "slow Leydenites" poked fun at this exaggeration of themselves. It was an old and well-worn remark that it took David Emmons an hour to go courting, and that he was always obliged to leave his own home at seven in order to reach Maria's at eight, and there was a standing joke that the meeting house passed him one morning on his way to the shop.

David heard the chaffing, of course—there is very little delicacy in matters of this kind among country people—but he took it all in good part. He would laugh at himself with the rest, but there was something touching in his deprecatory way of saying sometimes: "Well, I don't know how 'tis, but it don't seem to be in my natur' to do any other way. I suppose I was born without the faculty of gittin' along quick in this world. You'll have to git behind and push me a leetle, I reckon."

He owned his little cottage, which was one of the kind which had the piazza on the right side. He lived entirely alone. There was a half acre or so of land beside his house, which he used for a vegetable garden. After and before shop hours, in the dewy evenings and mornings, he dug and weeded assiduously between the green ranks of corn and beans. If David Emmons was slow, his vegetables were not. None of the gardens in Leyden surpassed his in luxuriant growth. His corn tasseled out and his potato patch was white with blossoms as soon as anybody's.

He was almost a vegetarian in his diet; the products of his garden spot were his staple articles of food. Early in the morning would the gentle old bachelor set his pot of green things boiling, and dine gratefully at noon, like mild Robert Herrick, on pulse and herbs. His garden supplied also his sweetheart and her mother with all the vegetables they could use. Many times in the course of a week could David have been seen slowly moving toward the Brewster cottage with a basket on his arm well stocked with the materials for an innocent and delicious repast.

But Maria was not to be outdone by her old lover in kindly deeds. Not a Saturday but a goodly share of her weekly baking was deposited, neatly covered with a white crash towel, on David's little kitchen table. The surreptitious air with which the back-door key was taken from its hiding place (which she well knew) under the kitchen blind, the door unlocked and entered, and the good things deposited, was charming, although highly ineffectual. "There goes Maria with David's baking," said the women, peering out of their windows as she bounced, rather more gently and cautiously than usual, down the street. And David himself knew well the ministering angel to whom these benefits were due when he lifted the towel and discovered with tearful eyes the brown loaves and flaky pies—the proofs of his Maria's love and culinary skill.

Among the young and more irreverent portions of the community there was considerable speculation as to the mode of courtship of these old lovers of twenty-five years' standing. Was there ever a kiss, a tender clasp of the hand, those usual expressions of affection between sweethearts?

Some of the more daring spirits had even gone so far as to commit the manifest impropriety of peeping in Maria's parlor windows; but they had only seen David sitting quiet and prim on the little slippery horsehair sofa, and Maria by the table, rocking slowly in her little cane-seated rocker. Did Maria ever leave her rocker and sit on that slippery horsehair sofa by David's side? They never knew; but she never did. There was something laughable, and at the same time rather pathetic, about Maria's and David's courting. All the outward appurtenances of "keeping company" were as rigidly observed as they had been twenty-five years ago, when David Emmons first cast his mild blue eyes shyly and lovingly on red-cheeked, quiet-spoken Maria Brewster. Every Sunday evening, in the winter, there was a fire kindled in the parlor, the parlor lamp was lit at dusk all the year round, and Maria's mother retired early, that the young people might "sit up." The "sitting up" was no very formidable affair now, whatever it might have been in the first stages of the courtship. The need of sleep overbalanced sentiment in those old lovers, and by ten o'clock at the latest Maria's lamp was out and David had wended his solitary way to his own home.

Leyden people had a great curiosity to know if David had ever actually popped the question to Maria, or if his natural slowness was at fault in this as in other things. Their curiosity had been long exercised in vain, but Widow Brewster, as she waxed older, grew loquacious, and one day told a neighbor, who had called in her daughter's absence, that "David had never reely come to the p'int.

She supposed he would some time; for her part, she thought he had better; but then, after all, she knowed Maria didn't care, and maybe 'twas jest as well as 'twas, only sometimes she was afeard she should never live to see the weddin' if they wasn't spry." Then there had been hints concerning a certain pearl-colored silk which Maria, having a good chance to get at a bargain, had purchased some twenty years ago, when she thought, from sundry remarks, that David was coming to the point; and it was further intimated that the silk had been privately made up ten years since, when Maria had again surmised that the point was about being reached. The neighbor went home in a state of great delight, having by skillful maneuvering actually obtained a glimpse of the pearl-colored silk.

It was perfectly true that Maria did not lay David's tardiness in putting the important question very much to heart. She was too cheerful, too busy, and too much interested in her daily duties to fret much about anything. There was never at any time much of the sentimental element in her composition, and her feeling for David was eminently practical in its nature. She, although the woman, had the stronger character of the two, and there was something rather motherlike than loverlike in her affection for him. It was through the protecting care which chiefly characterized her love that the only pain to her came from their long courtship and postponement of marriage. It was true that, years ago, when David had led her to think, from certain hesitating words spoken at parting one Sunday night, that he would certainly ask the momentous question soon, her heart had gone into a happy flutter. She had bought the pearl-colored silk then.

Years after, her heart had fluttered again, but a little less wildly this time. David almost asked her another Sunday night. Then she had made up the pearl-colored silk. She used to go and look at it fondly and admiringly from time to time; once in a while she would try it on and survey herself in the glass, and imagine herself David's bride—a faded bride, but a happy and beloved one.

She looked at the dress occasionally now, but a little sadly, as the conviction that she should never wear it was forcing itself upon her more and more. But the sadness was always more for David's sake than her own. She saw him growing an old man, and the lonely, uncared-for life that he led filled her heart with tender pity and sorrow for him. She did not confine her kind offices to the Saturday baking. Every week his little house was tidied and set to rights, and his mending looked after.

Once, on a Sunday night, when she spied a rip in his coat, that had grown long from the want of womanly fingers constantly at hand, she had a good cry after he had left and she had gone into her room. There was something more pitiful to her, something that touched her heart more deeply, in that rip in her lover's Sunday coat than in all her long years of waiting.

As the years went on, it was sometimes with a sad heart that Maria stood and watched the poor lonely old figure moving slower than ever down the street to his lonely home; but the heart was sad for him always, and never for herself. She used to wonder at him a little sometimes, though always with the most loyal tenderness, that he should choose to lead the solitary, cheerless life that he did, to go back to his dark, voiceless home, when he might be so sheltered and cared for in his old age. She firmly believed that it was only owing to her lover's incorrigible slowness, in this as in everything else. She never doubted for an instant that he loved her. Some women might have tried hastening matters a little themselves, but Maria, with the delicacy which is sometimes more inherent in a steady, practical nature like hers than in a more ardent one, would have lost her self-respect forever if she had done such a thing.

So she lived cheerfully along, corded her boots, though her fingers were getting stiff, humored her mother, who was getting feebler and more childish every year, and did the best she could for her poor, foolish old lover.

When David was seventy, and she sixty-eight, she gave away the pearl-colored silk to a cousin's daughter who was going to be married. The girl was young and pretty and happy, but she was poor, and the silk would make over into a grander wedding dress for her than she could hope to obtain in any other way.

Poor old Maria smoothed the lustrous folds fondly with her withered hands before sending it away, and cried a little, with a patient pity for David and herself. But when a tear splashed directly on to the shining surface of the silk, she stopped crying at once, and her sorrowful expression changed into one of careful scrutiny as she wiped the salt drop away with her handkerchief, and held the dress up to the light to be sure that it was not spotted. A practical nature like Maria's is sometimes a great boon to its possessor. It is doubtful if anything else can dry a tear so quickly.

Somehow Maria always felt a little differently toward David after she had given away her wedding dress. There had always been a little tingle of consciousness in her manner toward him, a little reserve and caution before people. But after the wedding dress had gone, all question of marriage had disappeared so entirely from her mind, that the delicate considerations born of it vanished. She was uncommonly hale and hearty for a woman of her age; there was apparently much more than two years' difference between her and her lover. It was not only the Saturday's bread and pie that she carried now and deposited on David's little kitchen table, but, openly and boldly, not caring who should see her, many a warm dinner. Every day, after her own housework was done, David's house was set to rights. He should have all the comforts he needed in his last years, she determined. That they were his last years was evident. He coughed, and now walked so slowly from feebleness and weakness that it was a matter of doubt to observers whether he could reach Maria Brewster's before Monday evening.

One Sunday night he stayed a little longer than usual—the clock struck ten before he started. Then he rose and said, as he had done every Sunday evening for so many years, "Well, Maria, I guess it's about time for me to be goin'."

She helped him on with his coat and tied on his tippet. Contrary to his usual habit, he stood in the door and hesitated a minute—there seemed to be something he wanted to say.

"Maria."

"Well, David?"

"I'm gittin' to be an old man, you know, an' I've allus been slow-goin'; I couldn't seem to help it. There has been a good many things I haven't got around to." The old cracked voice quavered painfully.

"Yes, I know, David, all about it; you couldn't help it. I wouldn't worry a bit about it if I were you."

"You don't lay up anything ag'in me, Maria?"

"No, David."

"Good night, Maria."

"Good night, David. I will fetch you over some boiled dinner tomorrow."

She held the lamp at the door till the patient, tottering old figure was out of sight. She had to wipe the tears from her spectacles in order to see to read her Bible when she went in.

Next morning she was hurrying up her housework to go over to David's—somehow she felt a little anxious about him this morning—when there came a loud knock at her door. When she opened it a boy stood there, panting for breath; he was David's next neighbor's son.

"Mr. Emmons is sick," he said, "an' wants you. I was goin' for milk, when he rapped on the window. Father an' mother's in thar, an' the doctor. Mother said, tell you to hurry."

The news had spread rapidly; people knew what it meant when they saw Maria hurrying down the street, without her bonnet, her gray hair flying. One woman cried when she saw her. "Poor thing!" she sobbed. "Poor thing!"

A crowd was around David's cottage when Maria reached it. She went straight in through the kitchen to his little bedroom, and up to his side. The doctor was in the room, and several neighbors. When he saw Maria, poor old David held out his hand to her and smiled feebly. Then he looked imploringly at the doctor, then at the others in the room. The doctor understood and said a word to them, and they filed silently out. Then he turned to Maria. "Be quick," he whispered.

She leaned over him. "Dear David," she said, her wrinkled face quivering, her gray hair straying over her cheeks.

He looked up at her with a strange wonder in his glazing eyes. "Maria"—a thin, husky voice, that was more like a wind through dry cornstalks, said—"Maria, I'm—dyin', an'—I allers meant to—have asked you—to—marry me."

# XVI. *GENTIAN*[1]

I⊤ had been raining hard all night; when the morning dawned clear everything looked vivid and unnatural. The wet leaves on the trees and hedges seemed to emit a real green light of their own; the tree trunks were black and dank, and the spots of moss on them stood out distinctly.

A tall old woman was coming quickly up the street. She had on a stiffly starched calico gown, which sprang and rattled as she walked. She kept smoothing it anxiously. "Gittin' every mite of the stiff'nin' out," she muttered to herself.

She stopped at a long cottage house, whose unpainted walls, with white window facings, and wide sweep of shingled roof, looked dark and startling through being sodden with rain.

There was a low stone wall by way of fence, with a gap in it for a gate.

She had just passed through this gap when the house door opened and a woman put out her head.

"Is that you, Hannah?" said she.

"Yes, it's me." She laid a hard emphasis on the last word; then she sighed heavily.

"Hadn't you better hold your dress up comin' through that wet grass, Hannah? You'll git it all bedraggled."

"I know it. I'm a-gittin' every mite of the stiff'nin' out on't. I worked half the forenoon ironin' on't yesterday, too. Well, I thought I'd got to git over here an' fetch a few of these fried cakes. I thought mebbe Alferd would relish 'em fur his breakfast; an' he'd got to have 'em while they was hot; they ain't good fur nothin' cold; an' I didn't hev a soul to send—never do. How is Alferd this mornin', Lucy?"

" 'Bout the same, I guess."

"Ain't had the doctor yit?"

"No." She had a little, patient, pleasant smile on her face, looking up at her questioner.

The women were sisters. Hannah was Hannah Orton, unmarried. Lucy was Mrs. Tollet. Alfred was her sick husband.

Hannah's long, sallow face was deeply wrinkled. Her wide mouth twisted emphatically as she talked.

"Well, I know one thing; ef he was my husband he'd *hev* a doctor."

Mrs. Tollet's voice was old, but there was a childish tone in it, a sweet, uncertain pipe.

"No, you couldn't make him, Hannah; you couldn't, no more'n me. Alferd was allers jest so. He ain't never thought nothin' of doctors, nor doctors' stuff."

"Well, I'd make him take somethin'. In my opinion he needs somethin' bitter." She screwed her mouth as if the bitter morsel were on her own tongue.

"Lor'! he wouldn't take it, you know, Hannah."

"He'd hev to. Gentian would be good fur him."

"He wouldn't tech it."

"I'd make him, ef I put it in his tea unbeknownst to him."

"Oh, I wouldn't dare to!"

"Land! I guess I'd dare to. Ef folks don't know enough to take what's good fur 'em, they'd orter be made to by hook or crook. I don't believe in deceivin' generally, but I don't believe the Lord would hev let folks hed the faculty fur deceivin' in 'em ef it wa'n't to be used fur good sometimes. It's my opinion Alferd won't last long ef he don't hev somethin' pretty soon to strengthen of him up an' give him a start. Well, it ain't no use talkin'. I've got to git home an' put this dress in the washtub ag'in, I s'pose. I never see such a sight—jest look at that! You'd better give Alferd those cakes afore they git cold."

"I shouldn't wonder ef he relished 'em. You was real good to think of it, Hannah."

"Well, I'm a-goin'. Every mite of the stiff'nin's out. Sometimes it seems as ef thar wa'n't no end to the work. I didn't know how to git out this mornin', anyway."

When Mrs. Tollet entered the house she found her husband in a wooden rocking-chair with a calico cushion, by the kitchen window. He was a short, large-framed old man, but he was very thin. There were great hollows in his yellow cheeks.

"What you got thar, Lucy?"

"Some griddle cakes Hannah brought."

"Griddle cakes!"

"They're real nice-lookin' ones. Don't you think you'd relish one or two, Alferd?"

"Ef you an' Hannah want griddle cakes, you kin hev griddle cakes."

"Then you don't want to hev one, with some maple merlasses on it? They've kept hot; she hed 'em kivered up."

"Take 'em away!"

She set them meekly on the pantry shelf; then she came back and stood before her husband, gentle deprecation in her soft old face and in the whole poise of her little slender body.

"What *will* you hev fur breakfast, Alferd?"

"I don' know. Well, you might as well fry a little slice of bacon, an' git a cup of tea."

"Ain't you' most afeard of—bacon, Alferd?"

"No, I ain't. Ef anybody's sick, they kin tell what they want themselves 'bout as well's anybody kin tell 'em. They don't hev any hankerin' arter anythin' unless it's good for 'em. When they need anythin', natur gives 'em a longin' arter it. I wish you'd hurry up an' cook that bacon, Lucy. I'm awful faint at my stomach."

She cooked the bacon and made the tea with no more words. Indeed, it was seldom that she used as many as she had now. Alfred Tollet, ever since she had married him, had been the sole autocrat of all her little Russias; her very thoughts had followed after him, like sheep.

After breakfast she went about putting her house in order for the day. When that was done and she was ready to sit down with her sewing, she found that her husband had fallen asleep in his chair. She stood over him a minute, looking at his pale old face with the sincerest love and reverence. Then she sat down by the window and sewed, but not long. She got her bonnet and shawl stealthily and stole out of the house. She sped quickly down the village street. She was light-footed for an old woman. She slackened her pace when she reached the village store, and crept hesitatingly into the great lumbering, rank-smelling room, with its dark, newly-sprinkled floor. She bought a bar of soap; then she stood irresolute.

"Anything else this mornin', Mis' Tollet?" The proprietor himself, a narrow-shouldered, irritable man, was waiting on her. His tone was impatient. Mrs. Tollet was too absorbed to notice it. She stood hesitating.

"*Is* there anything else you want?"

"Well—I don' know; but—p'rhaps I'd better—hev—ten cents' wuth of gentian." Her very lips were white; she had an expression of frightened, guilty resolution. If she had asked for strychnine, with a view to her own bodily destruction, she would not have had a different look.

The man mistook it, and his conscience smote him. He thought his manner had frightened her, but she had never noticed it.

"Goin' to give your husband some bitters?" he asked, affably, as he handed her the package.

She started and blushed. "No—I— thought some would be good fur—me."

"Well, gentian is a first-rate bitter. Good morning, Mis' Tollet."

"Good morning, Mr. Gill."

She was trembling all over when she reached her house door. There is a subtle, easily raised wind which blows spirits about like leaves, and she had come into it with her little paper of gentian. She had hidden the parcel in her pocket before she entered the kitchen. Her husband was awake. He turned his wondering, half-resentful eyes toward her without moving his head.

"Where hev you been, Lucy?"

"I—jest went down to the store a minit, Alferd, while you was asleep."

"What fur?"

"A bar of soap."

Alfred Tollet had always been a very healthy man until this spring. Some people thought that his illness was alarming now, more from its unwontedness and consequent effect on his mind, than from anything serious in its nature. However that may have been, he had complained of great depression and languor all the spring, and had not attempted to do any work.

It was the beginning of May now.

"Ef Alferd kin only git up May hill," Mrs. Tollet's sister had said to her, "he'll git along all right through the summer. It's a dretful tryin' time."

So up May hill, under the white apple and plum boughs, over the dandelions and the young grass, Alfred Tollet climbed, pushed and led faithfully by his loving old wife. At last he stood triumphantly on the summit of that fair hill, with its sweet, wearisome ascent. When the first of June came, people said, "Alfred Tollet's a good deal better."

He began to plant a little and bestir himself.

"Alferd's out workin' in the garden," Mrs. Tollet told her sister one afternoon. She had strolled over to her house with her knitting after dinner.

"You don't say so! Well, I thought when I see him Sunday that he was lookin' better. He's got through May, an' I guess he'll pull through. I did feel kinder worried 'bout him one spell— Why, Lucy, what's the matter?"

"Nothin'. Why?"

"You looked at me dretful kind of queer an' distressed, I thought."

"I guess you must hev imagined it, Hannah. Thar ain't nothin' the matter." She tried to look unconcernedly at her sister, but her lips were trembling.

"Well, I don't know 'bout it. You look kinder queer now. I guess you walked too fast comin' over here. You allers did race."

"Mebbe I did."

"For the land's sake, jest see that dust you tracked in! I've got to git the dustpan an' brush now, an' sweep it up."

"I'll do it."

"No; set still. I'd rather see to it myself."

As the summer went on Alfred Tollet continued to improve. He was as hearty as ever by September. But his wife seemed to lose as he gained. She grew thin, and her small face had a solemn, anxious look. She went out very little. She did not go to church at all, and she had been a devout churchgoer. Occasionally she went over to her sister's, that was all. Hannah watched her shrewdly. She was a woman who arrived at conclusions slowly; but she never turned aside from the road to them.

"Look-a here, Lucy," she said one day, "I know what's

the matter with you; thar's somethin' on your mind; an' I think you'd better out with it."

The words seemed propelled like bullets by her vehemence. Lucy shrank down and away from them, her pitiful eyes turned up toward her sister.

"Oh, Hannah, you scare me! I don't know what you mean."

"Yes, you do. Do you s'pose I'm blind? You're worrying yourself to death, an' I want to know the reason why. Is it anything 'bout Alferd?"

"Yes. Don't, Hannah."

"Well, I'll go over an' give him a piece of my mind! I'll see—"

"Oh, Hannah, don't! It ain't him. It's me—it's me."

"What on airth hev you done?"

Mrs. Tollet began to sob.

"For the land sake, stop cryin' an' tell me."

"Oh, I—give him—gentian."

"Lucy Ann Tollet, air you crazy? What ef you did give him gentian? I don't see nothin' to take on so about."

"I—deceived him, an' it's been 'most killin' me to think on't ever since."

"What do you mean?"

"I put it in his tea, the way you said."

"An' he never knew it?"

"He kinder complained 'bout its tastin' bitter, an' I told him 'twas his mouth. He asked me ef it didn't taste bitter to me, an' I said, 'No.' I don' know nothin' what's goin' to become of me. Then I had to be so keerful 'bout putting too much on't in his tea, that I was afraid he wouldn't get enough. So I put little sprinklin's on't in the bread an' pies an' everythin' I cooked. An' when he'd say nothin' tasted right nowadays, an' somehow everything was kinder bitterish, I'd tell him it must be his mouth."

"Look here, Lucy, you didn't eat everythin' with gentian in it yourself?"

"Course I did."

"Fur the land sake!"

"I s'pose the stuff must hev done him good; he's picked right up ever since he begun takin' it. But I can't git over my deceivin' of him so. I've 'bout made up my mind to tell him."

"Well, all I've got to say is you're a big fool if you do. I declare, Lucy Ann Tollet, I never saw sech a woman! The idee of your worryin' over such a thing as that, when it's done Alferd good, too! P'rhaps you'd ruther he'd died?"

"Sometimes I think I hed 'most ruther."

"Well!"

In the course of a few days Mrs. Tollet did tell her husband. He received her disclosure in precisely the way she had known that he would. Her nerves received just the shock which they were braced to meet.

They had come home from meeting on a Sunday night. Mrs. Tollet stood before him; she had not even taken off her shawl and little black bonnet.

"Alferd," said she, "I've got somethin' to tell you; it's been on my mind a long time. I meant it all fur the best; but I've been doin' somethin' wrong. I've been deceivin' of you. I give you gentian last spring when you was so poorly. I put little sprinklin's on't into everything you ate. An' I didn't tell the truth when I said 'twas your mouth, an' it didn't taste bitter to me."

The old man half closed his eyes, and looked at her intently; his mouth widened out rigidly. "You put a little gentian into everything I ate unbeknownst to me, did you?" said he. "H'm!"

"Oh, Alferd, don't look at me so! I meant it all fur the best. I was afeard you wouldn't git well without you hed it, Alferd. I was dretful worried about you; you didn't know nothin' about it, but I was. I laid awake nights a-worryin' an' prayin'. I know I did wrong; it wa'n't right to deceive you, but it was all along of my worryin' an' my thinkin' so much of you, Alferd. I was afeard you'd die an' leave me all alone; an'—it 'most killed me to think on't."

Mr. Tollet pulled off his boots, then pattered heavily about the house, locking the doors and making preparations for retiring. He would not speak another word to his wife about the matter, though she kept on with her piteous little protestations.

Next morning, while she was getting breakfast, he went down to the store. The meal, a nice one—she had taken unusual pains with it—was on the table when he returned; but he never glanced at it. His hands were full of bundles, which he opened with painstaking deliberation. His wife watched apprehensively. There was a new teapot, a pound of tea, and some bread and cheese, also a salt mackerel.

Mrs. Tollet's eyes shone round and big; her lips were white. Her husband put a pinch of tea in the new teapot, and filled it with boiling water from the kettle.

"What air you a-doin' on, Alferd?" she asked, feebly.

"I'm jest a-goin' to make sure I hev some tea, an' somethin' to eat without any gentian in it."

"Oh, Alferd, I made these corn cakes on purpose, an' they air real light. They ain't got no gentian on 'em, Alferd."

He sliced his bread and cheese clumsily, and sat down to eat them in stubborn silence.

Mrs. Tollet, motionless at her end of the table, stared at him with an appalled look. She never thought of eating anything herself.

After breakfast, when her husband started out to work, he pointed at the mackerel. "Don't you tech that," said he.

"But, Alferd—"

"I ain't got nothin' more to say. Don't you tech it."

Never a morning had passed before but Lucy Tollet had set her house in order; today she remained there at the kitchen table till noon, and did not put away the breakfast dishes.

Alfred came home, kindled up the fire, cooked and ate his salt mackerel imperturbably; and she did not move or speak till he was about to go away again. Then she said, in a voice which seemed to shrink of itself, "Alferd!"

He did not turn his head.

"Alferd, you must answer me; I'm in airnest. Don't you want me to do nothin' fur you any more? Don't you never want me to cook anything fur you ag'in?"

"No; I'm afeard of gittin' things that's bitter."

"I won't never put any gentian in anything ag'in, Alferd. Won't you let me git supper?"

"No, I won't. I don't want to talk no more about it. In futur I'm a-goin' to cook my vittles myself, an' that's all thar is about it."

"Alfred, if you don't want me to do nothin' fur you, mebbe —you'll think I ain't airnin' my own vittles; mebbe—you'd rather I go over to Hannah's—"

She sobbed aloud when she said that. He looked startled, and eyed her sharply for a minute. The other performer in the little melodrama which this thwarted, arbitrary old man had arranged was adopting a rôle that he had not anticipated, but he was still going to abide by his own.

"Mebbe 'twould be jest as well," said he. Then he went out of the door.

Hannah Orton was in her kitchen sewing when her sister entered.

"Fur the land sake, Lucy, what is the matter?"

"I've left him—I've left Alferd! Oh! oh!"

Lucy Tollet gasped for breath; she sank into a chair and leaned her head against the wall. Hannah got some water.

"Don't, Lucy. There, there! Drink this, poor lamb!"

She did not quite faint. She could speak in a few minutes. "He bought him a new teapot this mornin', Hannah, an' some bread an' cheese and salt mackerel. He's goin' to do his own cookin'; he don't want me to do nothin' more fur him; he's afeard I'll put gentian in it. I've left him! I've come to stay with you!"

"You told him, then?"

"I hed to; I couldn't go on so no longer. He wouldn't let me tech that mackerel, an' it orter hev been soaked. It was salt enough to kill him."

"Serve him right ef it did."

"Hannah Orton, I ain't a-goin' to hev a thing said ag'in Alferd."

"Well, ef you want to stan' up fur Alferd Tollet, you kin. You allers would stan' up fur him ag'in your own folks. Ef you want to keep on carin' fur sech a miserable, set, unfeelin'—"

"Don't you say another word, Hannah—not another one; I won't hear it."

"I ain't a-goin' to say nothin'; thar ain't any need of your bein' so fierce. Now don't cry so, Lucy. We shell git along real nice here together. You'll get used to it arter a little while, an' you'll see you air a good deal better off without him; you've been nothin' but jest a slave ever since you was married. Don't you s'pose I've seen it? I've pitied you so, I didn't know what to do. I've seen the time when I'd like to ha' shook Alferd."

"Don't, Hannah."

"I ain't a-goin' to say nothin' more. You jest stop cryin' an' try an' be calm, or you'll be sick. Hev you hed any dinner?"

"I don't want none."

"You've got to eat somethin', Lucy Ann Tollet. Thar ain't no sense in your givin' up so. I've got a nice little piece of lamb, an' some peas an' string beans left over, an'

I'm a-goin' to get 'em. You've got to eat 'em, an' then you'll feel better. Look-a here, I want to know ef Alferd drove you out of the house 'cause you give him gentian? I aint' got it through my head yet."

"I asked him ef he'd ruther hev me go, an' he said mebbe 'twould be jest as well. I thought I shouldn't hev no right to stay ef I couldn't git his meals for him."

"Right to stay! Lucy Ann Tollet, ef it wa'n't fur the grace of the Lord, I believe you'd be a simpleton. I don't understand no sech goodness; I allers thought it would run into foolishness sometime, an' I believe it has with you. Well, don't worry no more about it; set up an' eat your dinner. Jest smooth out that mat under your feet a little; you've got it all scrolled up."

No bitter herb could have added anything to the bitterness of that first dinner which poor Lucy Tollet ate after she had left her own home. Time and custom lessened, but not much, the bitterness of the subsequent ones. Hannah had sewed for her living all her narrow, single life; Lucy shared her work now. They had to live frugally; still they had enough. Hannah owned the little house in which she lived.

Lucy Tollet lived with her through the fall and winter. Her leaving her husband started a great whirlpool of excitement in this little village. Hannah's custom doubled: people came ostensibly for work, but really for information. They quizzed her about her sister, but Hannah could be taciturn. She did their work and divulged nothing, except occasionally when she was surprised. Then she would let fall a few little hints, which were not at Lucy's expense.

They never saw Mrs. Tollet; she always ran when she heard anyone coming. She never went out to church nor on the street. She grew to have a morbid dread of meeting her husband or seeing him. She would never sit at the

window, lest he might go past. Hannah could not understand this; neither could Lucy herself.

Hannah thought she was suffering less, and was becoming weaned from her affection, because she did so. But in
reality she was suffering more, and her faithful love for her
imperious old husband was strengthening.

All the autumn and winter she stayed and worked quietly;
in the spring she grew restless, though not perceptibly.
She had never bewailed herself much after the first; she
dreaded her sister's attacks on Alfred. Silence as to her
own grief was her best way of defending him.

Toward spring she often let her work fall in her lap, and
thought. Then she would glance timidly at Hannah, as if
she could know what her thoughts were; but Hannah was
no mind reader. Hannah, when she set out for meeting
one evening in May, had no conception whatever of the
plan which was all matured in her sister's mind.

Lucy watched her out of sight; then she got herself ready
quickly. She smoothed her hair, put on her bonnet and
shawl, and started up the road toward her old home.

There was no moon, but it was clear and starry. The
blooming trees stood beside the road like sweet, white,
spring angels; there was a whippoorwill calling somewhere
over across the fields. Lucy Tollet saw neither stars nor
blooming trees; she did not hear the whippoorwill. That
hard, whimsical old man in the little weather-beaten house
ahead towered up like a grand giant between the white
trees and this one living old woman; his voice in her ears
drowned out all the sweet notes of the spring birds.

When she came in sight of the house there was a light in
the kitchen window. She crept up to it softly and looked
in. Alfred was standing there with his hat on. He was
looking straight at the window, and he saw her the minute
her little pale face came up above the sill.

He opened the door quickly and came out. "Lucy, is that you?"

"Oh, Alferd, let me come home! I'll never deceive you ag'in!"

"You jest go straight back to Hannah's this minute."

She caught hold of his coat. "Oh, Alferd, don't—don't drive me away ag'in! It'll kill me this time; it will! it will!"

"You go right back."

She sank right down at his feet then, and clung to them. "Alferd, I won't go; I won't! I won't! You sha'n't drive me away ag'in. Oh, Alferd, don't drive me away from home! I've lived here with you for fifty year a'most. Let me come home an' cook fur you, an' do fur you ag'in. Oh, Alferd, Alferd!"

"See here, Lucy—git up; stop takin' on so. I want to tell you somethin'. You jest go right back to Hannah's, an' don't you worry. You set down an' wait a minute. Thar!"

Lucy looked at him. "What do you mean, Alferd?"

"Never you mind; you jist go right along."

Lucy Tollet sped back along the road to Hannah's, hardly knowing what she was about. It is doubtful if she realized anything but a blind obedience to her husband's will, and a hope of something roused by a new tone in his voice. She sat down on the doorstep and waited, she did not know for what. In a few minutes she heard the creak of heavy boots, and her husband came in sight. He walked straight up to her.

"I've come to ask you to come home, Lucy. I'm a-feelin' kinder poorly this spring, an'—I want you ter stew me up a little gentian. That you give me afore did me a sight of good."

"Oh, Alferd!"

"That's what I'd got laid out to do when I see you at the winder, Lucy, an' I was agoin' to do it."

# XVII. *THE WIND IN THE ROSE-BUSH*[1]

FORD VILLAGE has no railroad station, being on the other side of the river from Porter's Falls, and accessible only by the ford which gives it its name, and a ferry line.

The ferry-boat was waiting when Rebecca Flint got off the train with her bag and lunch basket. When she and her small trunk were safely embarked she sat stiff and straight and calm in the ferry-boat as it shot swiftly and smoothly across stream. There was a horse attached to a light country wagon on board, and he pawed the deck uneasily. His owner stood near, with a wary eye upon him, although he was chewing, with as dully reflective an expression as a cow. Beside Rebecca sat a woman of about her own age, who kept looking at her with furtive curiosity; her husband, short and stout and saturnine, stood near her. Rebecca paid no attention to cither of them. She was tall and spare and pale, the type of a spinster, yet with rudimentary lines and expressions of matronhood. She all unconsciously held her shawl, rolled up in a canvas bag, on her left hip, as if it had been a child. She wore a settled frown of dissent at life, but it was the frown of a mother who regarded life as a froward child, rather than as an overwhelming fate.

The other woman continued staring at her; she was mildly stupid, except for an overdeveloped curiosity which made her at times sharp beyond belief. Her eyes glittered, red spots came on her flaccid cheeks; she kept opening her mouth to speak, making little abortive motions. Finally she could endure it no longer; she nudged Rebecca boldly.

"A pleasant day," said she.

Rebecca looked at her and nodded coldly.

"Yes, very," she assented.

"Have you come far?"

"I have come from Michigan."

"Oh!" said the woman, with awe. "It's a long way," she remarked, presently.

"Yes, it is," replied Rebecca, conclusively.

Still the other woman was not daunted; there was something which she determined to know, possibly roused thereto by a vague sense of incongruity in the other's appearance. "It's a long ways to come and leave a family," she remarked with painful slyness.

"I ain't got any family to leave," returned Rebecca, shortly.

"Then you ain't ——"

"No, I ain't."

"Oh!" said the woman.

Rebecca looked straight ahead at the race of the river.

It was a long ferry. Finally Rebecca herself waxed unexpectedly loquacious. She turned to the older woman and inquired if she knew John Dent's widow who lived in Ford Village. "Her husband died about three years ago," said she, by way of detail.

The woman started violently. She turned pale, then she flushed; she cast a strange glance at her husband, who was regarding both women with a sort of stolid keenness.

"Yes, I guess I do," faltered the woman, finally.

"Well, his first wife was my sister," said Rebecca with the air of one imparting important intelligence.

"Was she?" responded the other woman, feebly. She glanced at her husband with an expression of doubt and terror, and he shook his head forbiddingly.

"I'm going to see her and take my niece Agnes home with me," said Rebecca.

Then the woman gave such a violent start that she noticed it.

"What is the matter?" she asked.

"Nothin', I guess," replied the woman, with eyes on her husband, who was slowly shaking his head, like a Chinese toy.

"Is my niece sick?" asked Rebecca with quick suspicion.

"No, she ain't sick," replied the woman with alacrity, then she caught her breath with a gasp.

"When did you see her?"

"Let me see; I ain't seen her for some little time," replied the woman. Then she caught her breath again.

"She ought to have grown up real pretty, if she takes after my sister. She was a real pretty woman," Rebecca said, wistfully.

"Yes, I guess she did grow up pretty," replied the woman in a trembling voice.

"What kind of a woman is the second wife?"

The woman glanced at her husband's warning face. She continued to gaze at him while she replied in a choking voice to Rebecca:

"I—guess she's a nice woman," she replied. "I—don't know, I—guess so. I—don't see much of her."

"I felt kind of hurt that John married again so quick," said Rebecca; "but I suppose he wanted his house kept, and Agnes wanted care. I wasn't so situated that I could take her when her mother died. I had my own mother to care for, and I was school-teaching. Now mother has gone, and my uncle died six months ago and left me quite a little property, and I've given up my school and I've come for Agnes. I guess she'll be glad to go with me, though I suppose her stepmother is a good woman and has always done for her."

The man's warning shake at his wife was fairly portentous.

"I guess so," said she.

"John always wrote that she was a beautiful woman," said Rebecca.

Then the ferry-boat grated on the shore.

John Dent's widow had sent a horse and wagon to meet her sister-in-law. When the woman and her husband went down the road, on which Rebecca in the wagon with her trunk soon passed them, she said, reproachfully:

"Seems as if I'd ought to have told her, Thomas."

"Let her find it out herself," replied the man. "Don't you go to burnin' your fingers in other folks' puddin', Maria."

"Do you s'pose she'll see anything?" asked the woman with a spasmodic shudder and a terrified roll of her eyes.

"See!" returned her husband with stolid scorn. "Better be sure there's anything to see."

"Oh, Thomas, they say ——"

"Lord, ain't you found out that what they say is mostly lies?"

"But if it should be true, and she's a nervous woman, she might be scared enough to lose her wits," said his wife, staring uneasily after Rebecca's erect figure in the wagon disappearing over the crest of the hilly road.

"Wits that's so easy upset ain't worth much," declared the man. "You keep out of it, Maria."

Rebecca in the meantime rode on in the wagon, beside a flaxen-headed boy, who looked, to her understanding, not very bright. She asked him a question, and he paid no attention. She repeated it, and he responded with a bewildered and incoherent grunt. Then she let him alone, after making sure that he knew how to drive straight.

They had traveled about half a mile, passed the village square, and gone a short distance beyond, when the boy drew up with a sudden Whoa! before a very prosperous-looking house. It had been one of the aboriginal cottages of the vicinity, small and white, with a roof extending on one side over a piazza, and a tiny "L" jutting out in the rear, on the right hand. Now the cottage was transformed by dormer windows, a bay window on the piazzaless side, a carved railing down the front steps, and a modern hardwood door.

"Is this John Dent's house?" asked Rebecca.

The boy was as sparing of speech as a philosopher. His only response was in flinging the reins over the horse's back, stretching out one foot to the shaft, and leaping out of the wagon, then going around to the rear for the trunk. Rebecca got out and went toward the house. Its white paint had a new gloss; its blinds were an immaculate apple green; the lawn was trimmed as smooth as velvet, and it was dotted with scrupulous groups of hydrangeas and cannas.

"I always understood that John Dent was well-to-do," Rebecca reflected, comfortably. "I guess Agnes will have considerable. I've got enough, but it will come in handy for her schooling. She can have advantages."

The boy dragged the trunk up the fine gravel walk, but before he reached the steps leading up to the piazza, for the house stood on a terrace, the front door opened and a fair, frizzled head of a very large and handsome woman appeared. She held up her black silk skirt, disclosing voluminous ruffles of starched embroidery, and waited for Rebecca. She smiled placidly, her pink, double-chinned face widened and dimpled, but her blue eyes were wary and calculating. She extended her hand as Rebecca climbed the steps.

"This is Miss Flint, I suppose," said she.

"Yes, ma'am," replied Rebecca, noticing with bewilderment a curious expression compounded of fear and defiance on the other's face.

"Your letter only arrived this morning," said Mrs. Dent, in a steady voice. Her great face was a uniform pink, and her china-blue eyes were at once aggressive and veiled with secrecy.

"Yes, I hardly thought you'd get my letter," replied Rebecca. "I felt as if I could not wait to hear from you before I came. I supposed you would be so situated that you could have me a little while without putting you out too much, from what John used to write me about his circumstances, and when I had that money so unexpected I felt as if I must come for Agnes. I suppose you will be willing to give her up. You know she's my own blood, and of course she's no relation to you, though you must have got attached to her. I know from her picture what a sweet girl she must be, and John always said she looked like her own mother, and Grace was a beautiful woman, if she was my sister."

Rebecca stopped and stared at the other woman in amazement and alarm. The great handsome blonde creature stood speechless, livid, gasping, with her hand to her heart, her lips parted in a horrible caricature of a smile.

"Are you sick!" cried Rebecca, drawing near. "Don't you want me to get you some water!"

Then Mrs. Dent recovered herself with a great effort. "It is nothing," she said. "I am subject to—spells. I am over it now. Won't you come in, Miss Flint?"

As she spoke, the beautiful deep-rose color suffused her face, her blue eyes met her visitor's with the opaqueness of turquoise—with a revelation of blue, but a concealment of all behind.

Rebecca followed her hostess in, and the boy, who had waited quiescently, climbed the steps with the trunk. But before they entered the door a strange thing happened. On the upper terrace, close to the piazza post, grew a great rose-bush, and on it, late in the season though it was, one small red, perfect rose.

Rebecca looked at it, and the other woman extended her hand with a quick gesture. "Don't you pick that rose!" she brusquely cried.

Rebecca drew herself up with stiff dignity.

"I ain't in the habit of picking other folks' roses without leave," said she.

As Rebecca spoke she started violently and lost sight of her resentment, for something singular happened. Suddenly the rosebush was agitated violently as if by a gust of wind, yet it was a remarkably still day. Not a leaf of the hydrangea standing on the terrace close to the rose trembled.

"What on earth——" began Rebecca; then she stopped with a gasp at the sight of the other woman's face. Although a face, it gave somehow the impression of a desperately clutched hand of secrecy.

"Come in!" said she in a harsh voice, which seemed to come forth from her chest with no intervention of the organs of speech. "Come into the house. I'm getting cold out here."

"What makes that rose-bush blow so when there isn't any wind?" asked Rebecca, trembling with vague horror, yet resolute.

"I don't see as it is blowing," returned the woman, calmly. And as she spoke, indeed, the bush was quiet.

"It was blowing," declared Rebecca.

"It isn't now," said Mrs. Dent. "I can't try to account for everything that blows out-of-doors. I have too much to do."

She spoke scornfully and confidently, with defiant, unflinching eyes, first on the bush, then on Rebecca, and led the way into the house.

"It looked queer," persisted Rebecca, but she followed, and also the boy with the trunk.

Rebecca entered an interior, prosperous, even elegant, according to her simple ideas. There were Brussels carpets, lace curtains, and plenty of brilliant upholstery and polished wood.

"You're real nicely situated," remarked Rebecca after she

had become a little accustomed to her new surroundings and the two women were seated at the tea-table.

Mrs. Dent stared with a hard complacency from behind her silver-plated service. "Yes, I be," said she.

"You got all the things new?" said Rebecca, hesitatingly, with a jealous memory of her dead sister's bridal furnishings.

"Yes," said Mrs. Dent. "I was never one to want dead folks' things, and I had money enough of my own, so I wasn't beholden to John. I had the old duds put up at auction. They didn't bring much."

"I suppose you saved some for Agnes. She'll want some of her poor mother's things when she is grown up," said Rebecca with some indignation.

The defiant stare of Mrs. Dent's blue eyes waxed more intense. "There's a few things up garret," said she.

"She'll be likely to value them," remarked Rebecca. As she spoke she glanced at the window. "Isn't it 'most time for her to be coming home?" she asked.

"'Most time," answered Mrs. Dent, carelessly; "but when she gets over to Addie Slocum's she never knows when to come home."

"Is Addie Slocum her intimate friend?"

"Intimate as any."

"Maybe we can have her come out to see Agnes when she's living with me," said Rebecca, wistfully. "I suppose she'll be likely to be homesick at first."

"Most likely," answered Mrs. Dent.

"Does she call you mother?" Rebecca asked.

"No, she calls me Aunt Emeline," replied the other woman, shortly. "When did you say you were going home?"

"In about a week, I thought, if she can be ready to go so soon," answered Rebecca with a surprised look.

She reflected that she would not remain a day longer than she could help after such an inhospitable look and question.

"Oh, as far as that goes," said Mrs. Dent, "it wouldn't make any difference about her being ready. You could go home whenever you felt that you must, and she could come afterward."

"Alone?"

"Why not? She's a big girl now, and you don't have to change cars."

"My niece will go home when I do, and not travel alone; and if I can't wait here for her, in the house that used to be her mother's and my sister's home, I'll go and board somewhere," returned Rebecca with warmth.

"Oh, you can stay here as long as you want to. You're welcome," said Mrs. Dent.

Then Rebecca started. "There she is!" she declared in a trembling, exultant voice. Nobody knew how she longed to see the girl.

"She isn't as late as I thought she'd be," said Mrs. Dent, and again that curious, subtle change passed over her face, and again it settled into that stony impassiveness.

Rebecca stared at the door, waiting for it to open. "Where is she?" she asked, presently.

"I guess she's stopped to take off her hat in the entry," suggested Mrs. Dent.

Rebecca waited. "Why don't she come? It can't take her all this time to take off her hat."

For answer Mrs. Dent rose with a stiff jerk and threw open the door.

"Agnes!" she called. "Agnes!" Then she turned and eyed Rebecca. "She ain't there."

"I saw her pass the window," said Rebecca in bewilderment.

"You must have been mistaken."

"I know I did," persisted Rebecca.

"You couldn't have."

"I did. I saw first a shadow go over the ceiling, then I

saw her in the glass there"—she pointed to a mirror over
the sideboard opposite—"and then the shadow passed the
window."

"How did she look in the glass?"

"Little and light-haired, with the light hair kind of tossing
over her forehead."

"You couldn't have seen her."

"Was that like Agnes?"

"Like enough; but of course you didn't see her. You've
been thinking so much about her that you thought you did."

"You thought *you* did."

"I thought I saw a shadow pass the window, but I must
have been mistaken. She didn't come in, or we would have
seen her before now. I knew it was too early for her to get
home from Addie Slocum's, anyhow."

When Rebecca went to bed Agnes had not returned.
Rebecca had resolved that she would not retire until the girl
came, but she was very tired, and she reasoned with herself
that she was foolish. Besides, Mrs. Dent suggested that
Agnes might go to the church social with Addie Slocum.
When Rebecca suggested that she be sent for and told that
her aunt had come, Mrs. Dent laughed meaningly.

"I guess you'll find out that a young girl ain't so ready to
leave a sociable, where there's boys, to see her aunt," said
she.

"She's too young," said Rebecca, incredulously and in-
dignantly.

"She's sixteen," replied Mrs. Dent; "and she's always been
great for the boys."

"She's going to school four years after I get her before she
thinks of boys," declared Rebecca.

"We'll see," laughed the other woman.

After Rebecca went to bed, she lay awake a long time
listening for the sound of girlish laughter and a boy's voice
under her window; then she fell asleep.

The next morning she was down early. Mrs. Dent, who kept no servants, was busily preparing breakfast.

"Don't Agnes help you about breakfast?" asked Rebecca.

"No, I let her lay," replied Mrs. Dent, shortly.

"What time did she get home last night?"

"She didn't get home."

"What?"

"She didn't get home. She stayed with Addie. She often does."

"Without sending you word?"

"Oh, she knew I wouldn't worry."

"When will she be home?"

"Oh, I guess she'll be along pretty soon."

Rebecca was uneasy, but she tried to conceal it, for she knew of no good reason for uneasiness. What was there to occasion alarm in the fact of one young girl staying over-night with another? She could not eat much breakfast. Afterward she went out on the little piazza, although her hostess strove furtively to stop her.

"Why don't you go out back of the house? It's real pretty—a view over the river," she said.

"I guess I'll go out here," replied Rebecca. She had a purpose—to watch for the absent girl.

Presently Rebecca came hustling into the house through the sitting room, into the kitchen where Mrs. Dent was cooking.

"That rose-bush!" she gasped.

Mrs. Dent turned and faced her.

"What of it?"

"It's a-blowing."

"What of it?"

"There isn't a mite of wind this morning."

Mrs. Dent turned with an inimitable toss of her fair head. "If you think I can spend my time puzzling over such nonsense as ——" she began, but Rebecca interrupted her with a cry and a rush to the door.

"There she is now!" she cried.

She flung the door wide open, and curiously enough a breeze came in and her own gray hair tossed, and a paper blew off the table to the floor with a loud rustle, but there was nobody in sight.

"There's nobody here," Rebecca said.

She looked blankly at the other woman, who brought her rolling-pin down on a slab of pie crust with a thud.

"I didn't hear anybody," she said, calmly.

"*I saw somebody pass that window!*"

"You were mistaken again."

"I *know* I saw somebody."

"You couldn't have. Please shut that door."

Rebecca shut the door. She sat down beside the window and looked out on the autumnal yard, with its little curve of footpath to the kitchen door.

"What smells so strong of roses in this room?" she said, presently. She sniffed hard.

"I don't smell anything but these nutmegs."

"It is not nutmeg."

"I don't smell anything else."

"Where do you suppose Agnes is?"

"Oh, perhaps she has gone over the ferry to Porter's Falls with Addie. She often does. Addie's got an aunt over there, and Addie's got a cousin, a real pretty boy."

"You suppose she's gone over there?"

"Mebbe. I shouldn't wonder."

"When should she be home?"

"Oh, not before afternoon."

Rebecca waited with all the patience she could muster. She kept reassuring herself, telling herself that it was all natural, that the other woman could not help it, but she

made up her mind that if Agnes did not return that afternoon she should be sent for.

When it was four o'clock she started up with resolution.
She had been furtively watching the onyx clock on the sitting-room mantel; she had timed herself. She had said
that if Agnes was not home by that time she should demand
that she be sent for. She rose and stood before Mrs. Dent,
who looked up coolly from her embroidery.

"I've waited just as long as I'm going to," she said. "I've
come 'way from Michigan to see my own sister's daughter
and take her home with me. I've been here ever since
yesterday—twenty-four hours—and I haven't seen her. Now
I'm going to. I want her sent for."

Mrs. Dent folded her embroidery and rose.

"Well, I don't blame you," she said. "It is high time she
came home. I'll go right over and get her myself."

Rebecca heaved a sigh of relief. She hardly knew what
she had suspected or feared, but she knew that her position
had been one of antagonism if not accusation, and she was
sensible of relief.

"I wish you would," she said, gratefully, and went back
to her chair, while Mrs. Dent got her shawl and her little
white head-tie. "I wouldn't trouble you, but I do feel as if
I couldn't wait any longer to see her," she remarked, apologetically.

"Oh, it ain't any trouble at all," said Mrs. Dent as she
went out. "I don't blame you; you have waited long
enough."

Rebecca sat at the window watching breathlessly until
Mrs. Dent came stepping through the yard alone. She ran
to the door and saw, hardly noticing it this time, that the
rose-bush was again violently agitated, yet with no wind
evident elsewhere.

"Where is she?" she cried.

Mrs. Dent laughed with stiff lips as she came up the steps

over the terrace. "Girls will be girls," said she. "She's gone with Addie to Lincoln. Addie's got an uncle who's conductor on the train, and lives there, and he got 'em passes, and they're goin' to stay to Addie's Aunt Margaret's a few days. Mrs. Slocum said Agnes didn't have time to come over and ask me before the train went, but she took it on herself to say it would be all right, and ——"

"Why hadn't she been over to tell you?" Rebecca was angry, though not suspicious. She even saw no reason for her anger.

"Oh, she was putting up grapes. She was coming over just as soon as she got the black off her hands. She heard I had company, and her hands were a sight. She was holding them over sulphur matches."

"You say she's going to stay a few days?" repeated Rebecca, dazedly.

"Yes; till Thursday, Mrs. Slocum said."

"How far is Lincoln from here?"

"About fifty miles. It'll be a real treat to her. Mrs. Slocum's sister is a real nice woman."

"It is goin' to make it pretty late about my goin' home."

"If you don't feel as if you could wait, I'll get her ready and send her on just as soon as I can," Mrs. Dent said, sweetly.

"I'm going to wait," said Rebecca, grimly.

The two women sat down again, and Mrs. Dent took up her embroidery.

"Is there any sewing I can do for her?" Rebecca asked, finally, in a desperate way. "If I can get her sewing along some ——"

Mrs. Dent arose with alacrity and fetched a mass of white from the closet. "Here," she said, "if you want to sew the lace on this nightgown. I was going to put her to it, but she'll be glad enough to get rid of it. She ought to have this and one more before she goes. I don't like to send her away without some good underclothing."

Rebecca snatched at the little white garment and sewed feverishly.

That night she wakened from a deep sleep a little after midnight and lay a minute trying to collect her faculties and explain to herself what she was listening to. At last she discovered that it was the then popular strains of "The Maiden's Prayer" floating up through the floor from the piano in the sitting room below. She jumped up, threw a shawl over her nightgown, and hurried downstairs trembling. There was nobody in the sitting room; the piano was silent. She ran to Mrs. Dent's bedroom and called hysterically:

"Emeline! Emeline!"

"What is it?" asked Mrs. Dent's voice from the bed. The voice was stern, but had a note of consciousness in it.

"Who—who was that playing 'The Maiden's Prayer' in the sitting room, on the piano?"

"I didn't hear anybody."

"There was some one."

"I didn't hear anything."

"I tell you there was some one. But—*there ain't anybody there.*"

"I didn't hear anything."

"I did—somebody playing 'The Maiden's Prayer' on the piano. Has Agnes got home? I *want to know.*"

"Of course Agnes hasn't got home," answered Mrs. Dent with rising inflection. "Be you gone crazy over that girl? The last boat from Porter's Falls was in before we went to bed. Of course she ain't come."

"I heard ——"

"You were dreaming."

"I wasn't; I was broad awake."

Rebecca went back to her chamber and kept her lamp burning all night.

The next morning her eyes upon Mrs. Dent were wary and blazing with suppressed excitement. She kept opening her mouth as if to speak, then frowning, and setting her lips hard. After breakfast she went upstairs, and came down presently with her coat and bonnet.

"Now, Emeline," she said, "I want to know where the Slocums live."

Mrs. Dent gave a strange, long, half-lidded glance at her. She was finishing her coffee.

"Why?" she asked.

"I'm going over there and find out if they have heard anything from her daughter and Agnes since they went away. I don't like what I heard last night."

"You must have been dreaming."

"It don't make any odds whether I was or not. Does she play 'The Maiden's Prayer' on the piano? I want to know."

"What if she does? She plays it a little, I believe. I don't know. She don't half play it, anyhow; she ain't got an ear."

"That wasn't half played last night. I don't like such things happening. I ain't superstitious, but I don't like it. I'm going. Where do the Slocums live?"

"You go down the road over the bridge past the old grist mill, then you turn to the left; it's the only house for half a mile. You can't miss it. It has a barn with a ship in full sail on the cupola."

"Well, I'm going. I don't feel easy."

About two hours later Rebecca returned. There were red spots on her cheeks. She looked wild. "I've been there," she said, "and there isn't a soul at home. Something *has* happened."

"What has happened?"

"I don't know. Something. I had a warning last night.

There wasn't a soul there. They've been sent for to Lincoln."

"Did you see anybody to ask?" asked Mrs. Dent with thinly concealed anxiety.

"I asked the woman that lives on the turn of the road. She's stone deaf. I suppose you know. She listened while I screamed at her to know where the Slocums were, and then she said, 'Mrs. Smith don't live here.' I didn't see anybody on the road, and that's the only house. What do you suppose it means?"

"I don't suppose it means much of anything," replied Mrs. Dent, coolly. "Mr. Slocum is conductor on the railroad, and he'd be away, anyway, and Mrs. Slocum often goes early when he does, to spend the day with her sister in Porter's Falls. She'd be more likely to go away than Addie."

"And you don't think anything has happened?" Rebecca asked with diminishing distrust before the reasonableness of it.

"Land, no!"

Rebecca went upstairs to lay aside her coat and bonnet. But she came hurrying back with them still on.

"Who's been in my room?" she gasped. Her face was pale as ashes.

Mrs. Dent also paled as she regarded her.

"What do you mean?" she asked, slowly.

"I found when I went upstairs that—little nightgown of—Agnes's on—the bed, laid out. It was—*laid out*. The sleeves were folded across the bosom, and there was that little red rose between them. Emeline, what is it? Emeline, what's the matter? Oh!"

Mrs. Dent was struggling for breath in great, choking gasps. She clung to the back of a chair. Rebecca, trembling herself so she could scarcely keep on her feet, got her some water.

As soon as she recovered herself Mrs. Dent regarded her with eyes full of the strangest mixture of fear and horror and hostility.

"What do you mean talking so?" she said in a hard voice.

"It *is there.*"

"Nonsense. You threw it down and it fell that way."

"It was folded in my bureau drawer."

"It couldn't have been."

"Who picked that red rose?"

"Look on the bush," Mrs. Dent replied shortly.

Rebecca looked at her; her mouth gaped. She hurried out of the room. When she came back her eyes seemed to protrude. (She had in the meantime hastened upstairs, and come down with tottering steps, clinging to the banister.)

"Now I want to know what all this means?" she demanded.

"What what means?"

"The rose is on the bush, and it's gone from the bed in my room! Is this house haunted, or what?"

"I don't know anything about a house being haunted. I don't believe in such things. Be you crazy?" Mrs. Dent spoke with gathering force. The color flashed back to her cheeks.

"No," said Rebecca, shortly, "I ain't crazy yet, but I shall be if this keeps on much longer. I'm going to find out where that girl is before night."

Mrs. Dent eyed her.

"What be you going to do?"

"I'm going to Lincoln."

A faint triumphant smile overspread Mrs. Dent's large face.

"You can't," said she; "there ain't any train."

"No train?"

"No; there ain't any afternoon train from the Falls to Lincoln."

"Then I'm going over to the Slocums' again to-night."

However, Rebecca did not go; such a rain came up as deterred even her resolution, and she had only her best dresses with her. Then in the evening came the letter from the Michigan village which she had left nearly a week ago. It was from her cousin, a single woman, who had come to keep her house while she was away. It was a pleasant unexciting letter enough, all the first of it, and related mostly how she missed Rebecca; how she hoped she was having pleasant weather and kept her health; and how her friend, Mrs. Greenaway, had come to stay with her since she had felt lonesome the first night in the house; how she hoped Rebecca would have no objections to this, although nothing had been said about it, since she had not realized that she might be nervous alone. The cousin was painfully conscientious, hence the letter. Rebecca smiled in spite of her disturbed mind as she read it; then her eye caught the postscript. That was in a different hand, purporting to be written by the friend, Mrs. Hannah Greenaway, informing her that the cousin had fallen down the cellar stairs and broken her hip, and was in a dangerous condition, and begging Rebecca to return at once, as she herself was rheumatic and unable to nurse her properly, and no one else could be obtained.

Rebecca looked at Mrs. Dent, who had come to her room with the letter quite late; it was half-past nine, and she had gone upstairs for the night.

"Where did this come from?" she asked.

"Mr. Amblecrom brought it," she replied.

"Who's he?"

"The postmaster. He often brings the letters that come on the late mail. He knows I ain't anybody to send. He brought yours about your coming. He said he and his wife came over on the ferry-boat with you."

"I remember him," Rebecca replied, shortly. "There's bad news in this letter."

Mrs. Dent's face took on an expression of serious inquiry.

"Yes, my Cousin Harriet has fallen down the cellar stairs —they were always dangerous—and she's broken her hip, and I've got to take the first train home to-morrow."

"You don't say so. I'm dreadfully sorry."

"No, you ain't sorry!" said Rebecca with a look as if she leaped. "You're glad. I don't know why, but you're glad. You've wanted to get rid of me for some reason ever since I came. I don't know why. You're a strange woman. Now you've got your way, and I hope you're satisfied."

"How you talk."

Mrs. Dent spoke in a faintly injured voice, but there was a light in her eyes.

"I talk the way it is. Well, I'm going to-morrow morning, and I want you, just as soon as Agnes Dent comes home, to send her out to me. Don't you wait for anything. You pack what clothes she's got, and don't wait even to mend them, and you buy her ticket. I'll leave the money, and you send her along. She don't have to change cars. You start her off, when she gets home, on the next train!"

"Very well," replied the other woman. She had an expression of covert amusement.

"Mind you do it."

"Very well, Rebecca."

Rebecca started on her journey the next morning. When she arrived, two days later, she found her cousin in perfect health. She found, moreover, that the friend had not written the postscript in the cousin's letter. Rebecca would have returned to Ford Village the next morning, but the fatigue and nervous strain had been too much for her. She was not able to move from her bed. She had a species of low fever induced by anxiety and fatigue. But she could write, and she did, to the Slocums, and she received no answer. She also wrote to Mrs. Dent; she even sent numerous telegrams, with no response. Finally she wrote to the postmaster, and an answer arrived by the first possible mail. The letter was short, curt, and to the purpose. Mr. Amblecrom, the postmaster, was a man of few words, and especially wary as to his expressions in a letter.

"Dear madam," he wrote, "your favour rec'ed. No Slocums in Ford's Village. All dead. Addie ten years ago, her mother two years later, her father five. House vacant. Mrs. John Dent said to have neglected stepdaughter. Girl was sick. Medicine not given. Talk of taking action. Not enough evidence. House said to be haunted. Strange sights and sounds. Your niece, Agnes Dent, died a year ago, about this time."

Yours truly,

"THOMAS AMBLECROM."

# XVIII. *A CONFLICT ENDED*[1]

In Acton there were two churches, a Congregational and a Baptist. They stood on opposite sides of the road, and the Baptist edifice was a little farther down than the other. On Sunday morning both bells were ringing. The Baptist bell was much larger, and followed quickly on the soft peal of the Congregational with a heavy brazen clang which vibrated a good while. The people went flocking through the street to the irregular jangle of the bells. It was a very hot day, and the sun beat down heavily; parasols were bobbing over all the ladies' heads.

More people went into the Baptist church, whose society was much the larger of the two. It had been for the last ten years—ever since the Congregational had settled a new minister. His advent had divided the church, and a good third of the congregation had gone over to the Baptist brethren, with whom they still remained.

It is probable that many of them passed their old sanctuary today with the original stubborn animosity as active as ever in their hearts, and led their families up the Baptist steps with the same strong spiritual pull of indignation.

One old lady, who had made herself prominent on the opposition, trotted by this morning with the identical wiry vehemence which she had manifested ten years ago. She wore a full black silk skirt, which she held up inanely in front, and allowed to trail in the dust in the rear.

Some of the stanch Congregational people glanced at her amusedly. One fleshy, fair-faced girl in blue muslin said to her companion, with a laugh: "See that old lady trailing her best black silk by to the Baptist. Ain't it ridiculous how she keeps on showing out? I heard some one talking about it yesterday."

"Yes."

The girl colored up confusedly. "Oh dear!" she thought to herself. The lady with her had an unpleasant history connected with this old church quarrel. She was a small, bony woman in a shiny purple silk, which was strained very tightly across her sharp shoulder blades. Her bonnet was quite elaborate with flowers and plumes, as was also her companion's. In fact, she was the village milliner, and the girl was her apprentice.

When the two went up the church steps, they passed a man of about fifty, who was sitting thereon well to one side. He had a singular face—a mild forehead, a gently curving mouth, and a terrible chin, with a look of strength in it that might have abashed mountains. He held his straw hat in his hand, and the sun was shining full on his bald head.

The milliner half stopped and gave an anxious glance at him; then passed on. In the vestibule she stopped again. "You go right in, Margy," she said to the girl. "I'll be along in a minute."

"Where be you going, Miss Barney?"

"You go right in. I'll be there in a minute."

Margy entered the audience room then, as if fairly brushed in by the imperious wave of a little knotty hand, and Esther Barney stood waiting until the rush of entering people was over. Then she stepped swiftly back to the side of the man seated on the steps. She spread her large black parasol deliberately, and extended the handle toward him.

"No, no, Esther; I don't want it—I don't want it."

"If you're determined on setting out in this broiling sun, Marcus Woodman, you jest take this parasol of mine an' use it."

"I don't want your parasol, Esther. I—"

"Don't you say it over again. Take it."

"I won't—not if I don't want to."

"You'll get a sunstroke."

"That's my own lookout."

"Marcus Woodman, you take it."

She threw all the force there was in her intense, nervous nature into her tone and look; but she failed in her attempt, because of the utter difference in quality between her own will and that with which she had to deal. They were on such different planes that hers slid by his with its own momentum; there could be no contact even of antagonism between them. He sat there rigid, every line of his face stiffened into an icy obstinacy. She held out the parasol toward him like a weapon.

Finally she let it drop at her side, her whole expression changed.

"Marcus," said she, "how's your mother?"

He started. "Pretty well, thank you, Esther."

"She's out to meeting, then?"

"Yes."

"I've been a-thinking—I ain't drove jest now—that maybe I'd come over an' see her some day this week."

He rose politely then. "Wish you would, Esther. Mother'd be real pleased, I know."

"Well, I'll see—Wednesday, p'rhaps, if I ain't too busy. I must go in now; they're 'most through singing."

"Esther—"

"I don't believe I can stop any longer, Marcus."

"About the parasol—thank you jest the same if I don't take it. Of course you know I can't set out here holding a parasol; folks would laugh. But I'm obliged to you all the same. Hope I didn't say anything to hurt your feelings?"

"Oh no! Why, no, Marcus! Of course I don't want to

make you take it if you don't want it. I don't know but it would look kinder queer, come to think of it. Oh dear! they are through singing."

"Say, Esther, I don't know but I might as well take that parasol, if you'd jest as soon. The sun is pretty hot, an' I might get a headache. I forgot my umbrella, to tell the truth."

"I might have known better than to have gone at him the way I did," thought Esther to herself, when she was seated at last in the cool church beside Margy. "Seems as if I might have got used to Marcus Woodman by this time."

She did not see him when she came out of church; but a little boy in the vestibule handed her the parasol, with the remark, "Mr. Woodman said for me to give this to you."

She and Margy passed down the street toward home. Going by the Baptist church, they noticed a young man standing by the entrance. He stared hard at Margy.

She began to laugh after they had passed him. "Did you see that fellow stare?" said she. "Hope he'll know me next time."

"That's George Elliot; he's that old lady's son you was speaking about this morning."

"Well, that's enough for me."

"He's a real good, steady young man."

Margy sniffed.

"P'rhaps you'll change your mind some day."

She did, and speedily, too. That glimpse of Margy Wilson's pretty, new face—for she was a stranger in the town—had been too much for George Elliot. He obtained an introduction, and soon was a steady visitor at Esther Barney's house. Margy fell in love with him easily. She had never had much attention from the young men, and he was an engaging young fellow, small and bright-eyed, though with a nervous persistency like his mother's in his manner.

"I'm going to have it an understood thing," Margy told Esther, after her lover had become constant in his attentions, "that I'm going with George, and I ain't going with his mother. I can't bear that old woman."

But poor Margy found that it was not so easy to thrust determined old age off the stage, even when young Love was flying so fast on his butterfly wings that he seemed to multiply himself, and there was no room for anything else because the air was so full of Loves. That old mother, with her trailing black skirt and her wiry obstinacy, trotted as unwaveringly through the sweet stir as a ghost through a door.

One Monday morning Margy could not eat any breakfast, and there were tear stains around her blue eyes.

"Why, what's the matter, Margy?" asked Esther, eyeing her across the little kitchen table.

"Nothing's the matter. I ain't hungry any to speak of, that's all. I guess I'll go right to work on Mis' Fuller's bonnet."

"I'd try an' eat something if I was you. Be sure you cut that velvet straight, if you go to work on it."

When the two were sitting together at their work in the little room back of the shop, Margy suddenly threw her scissors down. "There!" said she, "I've done it; I knew I should. I've cut this velvet bias. I knew I should cut everything bias I touched today."

There was a droll pucker on her mouth; then it began to quiver. She hid her face in her hands and sobbed. "Oh, dear, dear, dear!"

"Margy Wilson, what is the matter?"

"George and I—had a talk last night. We've broke the engagement, an' it's killing me. An' now I've cut this velvet bias. Oh, dear, dear, *dear,* dear!"

"For the land's sake, don't mind anything about the velvet! What's come betwixt you an' George?"

"His mother—horrid old thing! He said she'd got to live with us, and I said she shouldn't. Then he said he wouldn't marry any girl that wasn't willing to live with his mother, and I said he wouldn't ever marry me, then. If George Elliot thinks more of his mother than he does of me, he can have her. I don't care. I'll show him I can get along without him."

"Well, I don't know, Margy. I'm real sorry about it. George Elliot's a good, likely young man; but if you didn't want to live with his mother, it was better to say so right in the beginning. And I don't know as I blame you much; she's pretty set in her ways."

"I guess she is. I never could bear her. I guess he'll find out—"

Margy dried her eyes defiantly and took up the velvet again. "I've spoilt this velvet. I don't see why being disappointed in love should affect a girl so's to make her cut bias."

There was a whimsical element in Margy which seemed to roll uppermost along with her grief.

Esther looked a little puzzled. "Never mind the velvet, child; it ain't much, anyway." She began tossing over some ribbons to cover her departure from her usual reticence. "I'm real sorry about it, Margy. Such things are hard to bear, but they can be lived through. I know something about it myself. You knew I'd had some of this kind of trouble, didn't you?"

"About Mr. Woodman, you mean?"

"Yes, about Marcus Woodman. I'll tell you what 'tis, Margy Wilson, you've got one thing to be thankful for, and that is that there ain't anything ridickerlous about this affair of yourn. That makes it the hardest of anything, according to my mind—when you know that everybody's laughing, and you can hardly help laughing yourself, though you feel 'most ready to die."

"Ain't that Mr. Woodman crazy?"

"No, he ain't crazy; he's got too much will for his common sense, that's all, and the will teeters the sense a little too far into the air. I see all through it from the beginning. I could read Marcus Woodman jest like a book."

"I don't see how in the world you ever come to like such a man."

"Well, I s'pose love's the strongest when there ain't any good reason for it. They say it is. I can't say as I ever really admired Marcus Woodman much. I always see right through him; but that didn't hinder my thinking so much of him that I never felt as if I could marry any other man. And I've had chances, though I shouldn't want you to say so."

"You turned him off because he went to sitting on the church steps?"

"Course I did. Do you s'pose I was going to marry a man who made a laughingstock of himself that way?"

"I don't see how he ever come to do it. It's the funniest thing I ever heard of."

"I know it. It seems so silly nobody'd believe it. Well, all there is about it, Marcus Woodman's got so much mulishness in him it makes him almost miraculous. You see, he got up an' spoke in that church meeting when they had such a row about Mr. Morton's being settled here—Marcus was awful set again' him. I never could see any reason why, and I don't think he could. He said Mr. Morton wa'n't doctrinal; that was what they all said; but I don't believe half of 'em knew what doctrinal was. I never could see why Mr. Morton wa'n't as good as most ministers—enough sight better than them that treated him so, anyway. I always felt that they was really setting him in a pulpit high over their heads by using him the way they did, though they didn't know it.

"Well, Marcus spoke in that church meeting, an' he kept getting more and more set every word he said. He always had a way of saying things over and over, as if he was making steps out of 'em, an' raising of himself up on 'em, till there was no moving him at all. And he did that night. Finally, when he was up real high, he said, as for him, if Mr. Morton was settled over that church, he'd never go inside the door himself as long as he lived. Somebody spoke out then—I never quite knew who 'twas, though I suspected—an' says, 'You'll have to set on the steps, then, Brother Woodman.'

"Everybody laughed at that but Marcus. He didn't see nothing to laugh at. He spoke out awful set, kinder gritting his teeth, 'I will set on the steps fifty years before I'll go into this house if that man's settled here.'

"I couldn't believe he'd really do it. We were going to be married that spring, an' it did seem as if he might listen to me; but he wouldn't. The Sunday Mr. Morton begun to preach, he begun to set on them steps, an' he's set there ever since, in all kinds of weather. It's a wonder it ain't killed him; but I guess it's made him tough."

"Why, didn't he feel bad when you wouldn't marry him?"

"Feel bad? Of course he did. He took on terribly. But it didn't make any difference; he wouldn't give in a hair's breadth. I declare it did seem as if I should die. His mother felt awfully, too—she's a real good woman. I don't know what Marcus would have done without her. He wants a sight of tending and waiting on; he's dreadful babyish in some ways, though you wouldn't think it.

"Well, it's all over now as far as I'm concerned. I've got over it a good deal, though sometimes it makes me jest as mad as ever to see him setting there. But I try to be reconciled, and I get along jest as well, mebbe, as if I'd had him—I don't know. I fretted more at first than there was any sense in, and I hope you won't."

"I ain't going to fret at all, Miss Barney. I may cut bias for a while, but I shan't do anything worse."

"How you do talk, child!"

A good deal of it was talk with Margy; she had not as much courage as her words proclaimed. She was capable of a strong temporary resolution, but of no enduring one. She gradually weakened as the days without her lover went on, and one Saturday night she succumbed entirely. There was quite a rush of business, but through it all she caught a conversation between some customers—two pretty young girls.

"Who was that with you last night at the concert?"

"That—oh, that was George Elliot. Didn't you know him?"

"He's got another girl," thought Margy, with a great throb.

The next Sunday night, coming out of meeting with Miss Barney, she left her suddenly. George Elliot was one of a waiting line of young men in the vestibule. She went straight up to him. He looked at her in bewilderment, his dark face turning red.

"Good evening, Miss Wilson," he stammered out, finally.

"Good evening," she whispered, and stood looking up at him piteously. She was white and trembling.

At last he stepped forward suddenly and offered her his arm. In spite of his resentment, he could not put her to open shame before all his mates, who were staring curiously.

When they were out in the dark, cool street, he bent over her. "Why, Margy, what does all this mean?"

"Oh, George, let her live with us, please. I want her to. I know I can get along with her if I try. I'll do everything I can. Please let her live with us."

"Who's *her?*"

"Your mother."

"And I suppose *us* is you and I? I thought that was all over, Margy. Ain't it?"

"Oh, George, I am sorry I treated you so."

"And you are willing to let mother live with us now?"

"I'll do anything. Oh, George!"

"Don't cry, Margy. There—nobody's looking—give us a kiss. It's been a long time, ain't it, dear? So you've made up your mind that you're willing to let mother live with us?"

"Yes."

"Well, I don't believe she ever will, Margy. She's about made up her mind to go and live with my brother Edward, whether or no. So you won't be troubled with her. I dare say she might have been a little of a trial as she grew older."

"You didn't tell me."

"I thought it was your place to give in, dear."

"Yes, it was, George."

"I'm mighty glad you did. I tell you what it is, dear, I don't know how you've felt, but I've been pretty miserable lately."

"Poor George!"

They passed Esther Barney's house, and strolled along half a mile farther. When they returned, and Margy stole softly into the house and upstairs, it was quite late and Esther had gone to bed. Margy saw the light was not out in her room, so she peeped in. She could not wait till morning to tell her.

"Where have you been?" said Esther, looking up at her out of her pillows.

"Oh, I went to walk a little way with George."

"Then you've made up?"

"Yes."

"Is his mother going to live with you?"

"No, I guess not. She's going to live with Edward. But I told him I was willing she should. I've about made up my mind it's a woman's place to give in mostly. I s'pose you think I'm an awful fool."

"No, I don't; no, I don't, Margy. I'm real glad it's all right betwixt you and George. I've seen you weren't very happy lately."

They talked a little longer, then Margy said "Good night," going over to Esther and kissing her. Being so rich in love made her generous with it. She looked down sweetly into the older woman's thin, red-cheeked face. "I wish you were as happy as I," said she. "I wish you and Mr. Woodman could make up, too."

"That's an entirely different matter. I couldn't give in in such a thing as that."

Margy looked at her; she was not subtle, but she had just come out triumphant through innocent love and submission, and used the wisdom she had gained thereby.

"Don't you believe," said she, "if you was to give in the way I did, that he would?"

Esther started up with an astonished air. That had never occurred to her before. "Oh, I don't believe he would. You don't know him; he's awful set. Besides, I don't know but I'm better off the way it is."

In spite of herself, however, she could not help thinking of Margy's suggestion. Would he give in? She was hardly disposed to run the risk. With her peculiar cast of mind, her feeling for the ludicrous so keen that it almost amounted to a special sense, and her sensitiveness to ridicule, it would have been easier for her to have married a man under the shadow of a crime than one who was the deserving target of gibes and jests. Besides, she told herself, it was possible that he had changed his mind, that he no longer cared for her. How could she make the first overtures? She had not Margy's impulsiveness and innocence of youth to excuse her.

Also, she was partly influenced by the reason which she had given Margy; she was not so very sure that it would be best for her to take any such step. She was more fixed in the peace and pride of her old-maidenhood than she had realized, and was more shy of disturbing it. Her comfortable meals, her tidy housekeeping, and her prosperous work had become such sources of satisfaction to her that she was almost wedded to them, and jealous of any interference.

So it is doubtful if there would have been any change in the state of affairs if Marcus Woodman's mother had not died toward spring. Esther was greatly distressed about it.

"I don't see what Marcus is going to do," she told Margy. "He ain't any fitter to take care of himself than a baby, and he won't have any housekeeper, they say."

One evening, after Marcus's mother had been dead about three weeks, Esther went over there. Margy had gone out to walk with George, so nobody knew. When she reached the house—a white cottage on a hill—she saw a light in the kitchen window.

"He's there," said she. She knocked on the door softly. Marcus shuffled over to it—he was in his stocking feet—and opened it.

"Good evening, Marcus," said she, speaking first.

"Good evening."

"I hadn't anything special to do this evening, so I thought I'd look in a minute and see how you was getting along."

"I ain't getting along very well; but I'm glad to see you. Come right in."

When she was seated opposite him by the kitchen fire, she surveyed him and his surroundings pityingly. Everything had an abject air of forlornness; there was neither tidiness nor comfort. After a few words she rose energetically. "See here, Marcus," said she, "you jest fill up that teakettle, and I'm going to slick up here a little for you while I stay."

"Now, Esther, I don't feel as if—"

"Don't you say nothing. Here's the teakettle. I might jest as well be doing that as setting still."

He watched her in a way that made her nervous, as she flew about putting things to rights; but she said to herself that this was easier than sitting still, and gradually leading up to the object for which she had come. She kept wondering if she could ever accomplish it. When the room was in order, finally, she sat down again, with a strained-up look in her face.

"Marcus," said she, "I might as well begin. There was something I wanted to say to you tonight."

He looked at her, and she went on:

"I've been thinking some lately about how matters used to be betwixt you an' me, and it's jest possible—I don't know—but I might have been a little more patient than I was. I don't know as I'd feel the same way now if—"

"Oh, Esther, what do you mean?"

"I ain't going to tell you, Marcus Woodman, if you can't find out. I've said full enough; more'n I ever thought I should."

He was an awkward man, but he rose and threw himself on his knees at her feet with all the grace of complete unconsciousness of action. "Oh, Esther, you don't mean, do you?—you don't mean that you'd be willing to—marry me?"

"No; not if you don't get up. You look ridickerlous."

"Esther, do you mean it?"

"Yes. Now get up."

"You ain't thinking—I can't give up what we had the trouble about, any more now than I could then."

"Ain't I said once that wouldn't make any difference?"

At that he put his head down on her knees and sobbed.

"Do, for mercy's sake, stop! Somebody'll be coming in. 'Tain't as if we was a young couple."

"I ain't going to till I've told you about it, Esther. You ain't never really understood. In the first of it, we was both mad; but we ain't now, and we can talk it over. Oh, Esther, I've had such an awful life! I've looked at you, and— Oh, dear, dear, dear!"

"Marcus, you scare me to death crying so."

"I won't. Esther, look here—it's the gospel truth: I ain't a thing again' Mr. Morton now."

"Then why on earth don't you go into the meeting house and behave yourself?"

"Don't you suppose I would if I could? I can't, Esther —I can't."

"I don't know what you mean by can't."

"Do you s'pose I've took any comfort sitting there on them steps in the winter snows an' the summer suns? Do you s'pose I've took any comfort not marrying you? Don't you s'pose I'd given all I was worth any time the last ten year to have got up an' walked into the church with the rest of the folks?"

"Well, I'll own, Marcus, I don't see why you couldn't if you wanted to."

"I ain't sure as I see, myself, Esther. All I know is I can't make myself give it up. I can't. I ain't made strong enough to."

"As near as I can make out, you've taken to sitting on the church steps the way other men take to smoking and drinking."

"I don't know but you're right, Esther, though I hadn't thought of it in that way before."

"Well, you must try to overcome it."

"I never can, Esther. It ain't right for me to let you think I can."

"Well, we won't talk about it any more tonight. It's time I was going home."

"Esther—did you mean it?"

"Mean what?"

"That you'd marry me anyway?"

"Yes, I did. Now do get up. I do hate to see you looking so silly."

Esther had a new pearl-colored silk gown, and a little mantle like it, and a bonnet trimmed with roses and plumes, and she and Marcus were married in June.

The Sunday on which she came out a bride they were late at church; but late as it was, curious people were lingering by the steps to watch them. What would they do? Would Marcus Woodman enter that church door which his awful will had guarded for him so long?

They walked slowly up the steps between the watching people. When they came to the place where he was accustomed to sit, Marcus stopped short and looked down at his wife with an agonized face.

"Oh, Esther, I've—got—to stop."

"Well, we'll both sit down here, then."

"*You?*"

"Yes; I'm willing."

"No; you go in."

"No, Marcus; I sit with you on our wedding Sunday."

Her sharp, middle-aged face as she looked up at him was fairly heroic. This was all that she could do: her last weapon was used. If this failed, she would accept the chances with which she had married, and before the eyes of all these tittering people she would sit down at his side on these church steps. She was determined, and she would not weaken.

He stood for a moment staring into her face. He trembled so that the bystanders noticed it. He actually leaned over toward his old seat as if wire ropes were pulling him down upon it. Then he stood up straight, like a man, and walked through the church door with his wife.

The people followed. Not one of them even smiled. They had felt the pathos in the comedy.

The sitters in the pews watched Marcus wonderingly as he went up the aisle with Esther. He looked strange to them; he had almost the grand mien of a conqueror.

# XIX. A CONQUEST OF HUMILITY[1]

Two o'clock had been the hour set for the wedding. It was now four, and the bridegroom had not yet appeared. The relatives who had been bidden to the festivities had been waiting impatiently in the two square front rooms of Maria Caldwell's house, but now some had straggled out into the front yard, from which they could look up the road to better advantage.

They were talking excitedly. A shrill feminine babble, with an undertone of masculine bass, floated about the house and yard. It had been swelling in volume from a mere whisper for the last half hour—ever since Hiram Caldwell had set out for the bridegroom's house to ascertain the reason for his tardiness at his own wedding.

Hiram, who was a young fellow, had gotten into his shiny buggy with a red, important face, and driven off at a furious rate. He was own cousin to Delia Caldwell, the prospective bride. All the people assembled were Thayers or Caldwells, or connections thereof. The tardy bridegroom's name was Lawrence Thayer.

It was a beautiful summer afternoon. The air was hot and sweet. Around the Caldwell house it was spicy sweet with pinks; there was a great bed of them at the foot of the green bank which extended under the front windows.

Some of the women and young girls pulled pinks and sniffed them as they stood waiting. Mrs. Erastus Thayer had stuck two or three in the bosom of her cinnamon-brown silk dress. She stood beside the gate; occasionally she craned her neck over it and peered down the road. The sun was hot upon her silken shoulders; the horizontal wrinkles shone, but she did not mind.

"See anything of him?" some one called out.

"No. I'm dreadful afraid somethin' has happened."

"Oh, mother, what do you think's happened?" asked a young girl at her side, hitting her with a sharp elbow. The girl was young, slim, and tall; she stooped a little; her pointed elbows showed redly through her loose white muslin sleeves; her face was pretty.

"Hush, child! I don't know," said her mother.

The girl stood staring at her with helpless, awed eyes.

At last the woman in cinnamon-brown silk turned excitedly about. "He's comin'!" she proclaimed, in a shrill whisper.

The whisper passed from one to another.

"He's coming!" everybody repeated. Heads crowded together at the window; all the company was in motion.

"It ain't Lawrence," said a woman's voice, disappointedly. "It ain't nobody but his father, with Hiram."

"Somethin' *has happened*," repeated Mrs. Thayer. The young girl trembled and caught hold of her mother's dress; her eyes grew big and wild. Hiram Caldwell drove up the road. He met the gaze of the people with a look of solemn embarrassment. But he was not so important as he had been. There was a large, white-headed old man with him, who drew the larger share of attention. He got lumberingly out of the buggy when Hiram drew rein at the gate. Then he proceeded up the gravel walk to the house. The people stood back and stared. No one dared speak to him except Mrs. Erastus Thayer. She darted before him in the path; her brown silk skirts swished.

"Mr. Thayer," cried she, "what is the matter? Do tell us! What has happened?"

"Where's Delia?" said the old man.

"Oh, she's in the bedroom out of the parlor. She ain't been out yet. Mr. Thayer, for mercy's sake, what is the matter? What has happened to him?"

David Thayer waved her aside and kept straight on, his long yellow face immovable, his gaunt old shoulders resolutely braced, through the parlor, and knocked at the bedroom door.

A nervously shaking woman in black silk opened it. She screamed when she saw him. "Oh, Mr. Thayer, it's you! What is the matter? Where is he?" she gasped, clutching his arm.

A young woman in a pearl-colored silk gown stood, straight and silent, behind her. She had a tall, full figure, and there was something grand in her attitude. She stood like a young pine tree, as if she had all necessary elements of support in her own self. Her features were strong and fine. She would have been handsome if her complexion had been better. Her skin was thick and dull.

She did not speak, but stood looking at David Thayer. Her mouth was shut tightly, her eyes steady. She might have been braced to meet a wind.

There were several other women in the little room. Mr. Thayer looked at them uneasily. "I want to see Delia an' her mother, an' nobody else," said he, finally.

The women started and looked at each other; they then left. The old man closed the door after them and turned to Delia.

Her mother had begun to cry. "Oh dear! oh dear!" she wailed. "I knew somethin' dreadful had happened."

"Delia," said he, "I don't know what you're goin' to say. It ain't very pleasant for me to tell you. I wish this minute Lawrence Thayer didn't belong to me. But that don't better matters any. He does, an' somebody's got to tell you."

"Oh, is he dead?" asked Delia's mother, brokenly.

"No, he ain't dead," said the old man; "an' he ain't sick. I don't know of anything that ails him except he's a fool. He won't come—that's the whole of it."

"Won't come!" shrieked the mother. Delia stood stiff and straight.

"No, he won't come. His mother an' I have been talkin' an' reasonin' with him, but it hasn't done any good. I don't know but it'll kill his mother. It's all on account of that Briggs girl; you might as well know it. I wish she'd never come near the house. I've seen what way the wind blew for some time, but I never dreamed it would come to this. I think it's a sudden start on his part. I believe he meant to come, this noon, as much as could be; but Olive came home, an' they were talkin' together in the parlor, an' I see she'd been cryin'. His mother an' I got ready, an' when he didn't come downstairs she went up to see where he was. He had his door locked an' he called out he wasn't goin'; that was all we could get out of him. He wouldn't say another word, but we knew what the trouble was. His mother had noticed how red Olive's eyes were when she went back to the shop. She'd been takin' on, I suppose, an' so he decided, all of a sudden, he'd back out. There ain't any excuse for him, an' I ain't goin' to make up any. He's treated you mean, Delia, an' I'd rather have cut off my right hand than had it happened; that's all I can say about it, an' that don't do any good."

Mrs. Caldwell stepped forward suddenly. "I should think he had treated her mean!" she said—her voice rose loud and shrill. "I never heard anything like it. If I had a son like that, I wouldn't tell of it. That Briggs girl! He ought to be strung up. If you an' his mother had had any sort of spunk you'd made him come. You always babied him to death. He's a rascal. I'd like to get hold of him, that's all. I—"

Delia caught her mother by the arm. "Mother, if you

have any sense, or feeling for me, don't talk so loud; all those folks out there will hear."

The older woman's shrill vituperation flowed through the daughter's remonstrance and beyond it. "I would like to show him he couldn't do such things as this without gettin' some punishment for it. I—"

"Mother!"

Mrs. Caldwell changed her tone suddenly. She began to cry weakly. "Oh, Delia, you poor child, what will you do?" she sobbed.

"It isn't going to do any good to go on so, mother."

"There's all them folks out there. Oh dear! What will they say? I wouldn't care so much if it wa'n't for all them Thayers an' Caldwells. They'll jest crow. Oh dear! you poor child!"

Delia turned to Mr. Thayer. "Somebody ought to tell them," said she, "that—there won't be any—wedding."

"Oh, Delia, how can you take it so calm?" wailed her mother.

"I suppose so," assented the old man; "but I declare I can't tell 'em such a thing about a son of mine. I feel as if I'd been through about all I could."

"The minister would be a good one, wouldn't he?" said Delia.

Mr. Thayer took up with the suggestion eagerly. He opened the door a chink, and asked one of the waiting officious guests to summon the minister. When he came he gave him instructions in an agitated whisper; then retreated. The trio in the bedroom became conscious of a great hush without; then the minister's solemnly inflected voice broke upon it. He was telling them that the wedding was postponed. Then there was a little responsive murmur, and the minister knocked on the door.

"Shall I tell them when it will take place? They are inquiring," he whispered.

Delia heard him. "You can tell them it will never take place," said she, in a clear voice.

The minister stared at her wonderingly. "Oh!" groaned her mother. Then the minister's voice rose again, and directly there were a creaking and rustling, and subdued clatter of voices. The guests were departing.

After a little, Delia approached the door as if she were going out into the parlor.

"Oh, Delia, don't go! Wait till they're all gone!" wailed her mother. "All them Thayers and Caldwells!"

"They are gone, most of them. I've stood in this hot little room long enough," said Delia, and threw open the door. Directly opposite was a mahogany table with the wedding presents on it. Three or four women, among them Mrs. Erastus Thayer and her daughter, were bending over them and whispering.

When the door opened they turned and stared at Delia standing there in her pearl-colored silk, with some drooping white bridal flowers on her breast. They looked stiff and embarrassed. Then Mrs. Thayer recovered herself and came forward.

"Delia," said she, in a soft whisper, "dear girl."

She put her arm around Delia, and attempted to draw her toward herself; but the girl released herself and gave her a slight backward push.

"Please don't make any fuss over me, Mrs. Thayer," said she; "it isn't necessary."

Mrs. Thayer started back and went toward the door. Her face was very red. She tried to smile. Her daughter and the other women followed her.

"I'm real glad she can show some temper about it," she whispered when they were all out in the entry. "It's a good deal better for her."

"Ask her why he didn't come," one of the women whispered, nudging her.

"I'm kind of afraid to. I'll stop and ask Hiram on my way home. Mebbe Mr. Thayer told him."

Delia, in her bridal gear, stood majestically beside one of the parlor windows. She was plainly waiting for her guests to go. They kept peering in at her, while they whispered among themselves. Presently Mrs. Thayer's daughter came across the room tremblingly. She had hesitated on the parlor threshold, but her mother had given her a slight push on her slender shoulders and she had entered suddenly. She kept looking back as she advanced toward Delia.

"Mother wants to know," she faltered, in her thin girlish pipe, "if—you wouldn't rather—she'd—take back that toilet set she brought. She says she don't know but it will make you feel bad to see it."

"Of course you can take it."

"Mrs. Emmons says she'll take her mats, too, if you'd like to have her."

"Of course she can take them."

The young girl shrank over to the table, snatched up the toilet set and mats, and fled to her mother.

When they were all gone, David Thayer approached Delia. He had been sitting on a chair by the bedroom door, holding his head in his hands.

"I'm goin' now," said he. "If there's anything I can do, you let me know."

"There won't be anything," said Delia. "I shall get along all right."

He shook her hand hard in his old trembling one. "You're more of a man than Lawrence is," said he. He was a very old man, and his voice, although it was still deep, quavered.

"There isn't any use in your saying much to him," said Delia. "I don't want you to, on my account."

"Delia, don't you go to standin' up for him. He don't deserve it."

"I ain't standing up for him. I know he's your son, but it doesn't seem to me there's a great deal to stand up for. What he's done is natural enough; he's been carried away by a pretty face; but he has shown out what he is."

"I don't blame you a bit for feelin' so, Delia."

"I don't see any other way to feel; it's the truth."

"Well, good-by, Delia. I hope you won't lay up anything again' his mother an' me. We'll always think a good deal of you."

"I haven't any reason to lay up anything against you that I know of," said Delia. Her manner was stern, although she did not mean it to be. She could not, as it were, relax her muscles enough to be cordial. All the strength in Delia Caldwell's nature was now concentrated. It could accomplish great things, but it might grind little ones to pieces.

"Well, good-by, Delia," said the old man, piteously. He was himself a strong character, but he seemed weak beside her.

After he had gone, Delia went into the bedroom to her mother. Mrs. Caldwell was sitting there crying. She looked up when her daughter entered.

"Oh, Delia," she sobbed, "what are you goin' to do? What are you goin' to do?"

"I am going to take off this dress, for one thing."

"I don't see what you will do. There you've got this dress and your black silk, two new silk dresses, and your new brown woolen one, and your new bonnet and mantle, all these new things, and the weddin' cake."

"I suppose I can wear dresses and bonnets just as well if I ain't married; and as for the wedding cake, we'll have some of it for supper."

"Delia Caldwell!"

"What's the matter, mother?"

Delia slipped off the long shimmering skirt of her pearl-colored silk, shook it out, and laid it carefully over a chair.

"Are you crazy?"

"Not that I know of. Why?"

"You don't act natural."

"I'm acting the way that's natural to me."

"What are you going to do? Oh, you poor child!"

Mrs. Caldwell laid hold of her daughter's hand as she passed near her, and attempted to pull her to her side.

"Don't, please, mother," said Delia.

Her mother relinquished her hold and sobbed afresh. "I won't pity you if you don't want me to," said she, "but it's dreadful. There's—another—thing. You've lost your school. Flora Strong's spoke for it, an' she won't want to give it up."

"I don't want her to. I'll get another one."

Delia put on a calico dress and kindled a fire and made tea as usual. She put some slices of wedding cake on the table; perhaps her will extended to her palate and kept it from tasting like dust and ashes to her. Her mother drank a cup of tea between her lamentations.

After supper Delia packed up her wedding gifts and addressed them to their respective donors. There were a few bits of silver, but the greater number of the presents were pieces of fancywork from female relatives. She folded these mats and tidies relentlessly with her firm brown fingers. There was no tenderness in her touch. She felt not the least sentiment toward inanimate things.

"I think they're actin' awful mean to want to grab these things back so quick," said her mother, her wrath gaining upon her grief a little.

"It goes well with the rest," said Delia.

Among the gifts which she returned was a little embroidered tidy from Flora Strong, the girl who had been engaged to teach her former school.

Flora came over early the next morning. She opened the door and stood there hesitating. She was bashful before the trouble in the house. "Good morning, Mrs. Caldwell; good morning, Delia," she faltered, deprecatingly. She had a thin, pretty face, with very red lips and cheeks. She fumbled a little parcel nervously.

"Good mornin', Flora," said Mrs. Caldwell. Then she turned her back and went into the pantry.

Delia was washing dishes at the sink. She spoke just as she always did. "Good morning," said she. "Sit down, won't you, Flora?"

Then Flora began. "Oh, Delia," she burst out, "what made you send this back? What made you? You didn't think I'd take it?"

"Take what?"

"This tidy. Oh, Delia, I made it for you! It doesn't make any difference whether—" Flora choked with sobs. She dropped into a chair and put her handkerchief over her face. Mrs. Caldwell heard her, and began weeping, as she stood in the pantry. Delia went on with her dishes.

"Oh, Delia, you'll—take it back, won't you?" Flora said, finally.

"Of course I will, if you want me to. It's real pretty."

"When I heard of it," the girl went on—"I don't know as you want me to speak of it, but I've got to—I felt as if —I declare I'd like to see Lawrence Thayer come up with. I'll never speak to him again as long as I live. Delia, you aren't standing up for him, are you? You don't care if I do say he's—a villain?"

"I hope she don't," wailed her mother in the pantry.

"No," said Delia, "I don't care."

Then Flora offered to give up the school. She pleaded

that she should take it, but Delia would not. She could get another, she said.

That afternoon, indeed, she went to see the committee. She had put the house to rights, pinned Flora's tidy on the big rocking-chair in the parlor, and dressed herself carefully in a blue-sprigged muslin, one of her wedding gowns. Passing down the hot village street, she saw women sewing at their cool sitting-room windows. She looked up at them and nodded as usual. She knew of a school whose teacher had left to be married, as she had done. She thought the vacancy had possibly not been filled. Very little of the vacation had passed. Moreover, the school was not a desirable one: the pay was small, and it was three miles from the village. Delia obtained the position.

Early in September she began her duties. She went stanchly back and forth over the rough, dusty road day after day. She had the reputation of being a very fine teacher, although the children were a little in awe of her. They never came to meet her and hang about her on her way to the schoolhouse. Her road lay past the Thayer house, where she would have been living now had all gone well. Occasionally she met Lawrence; she passed him without a look. Quite often she met Olive Briggs, who worked in a milliner's shop and boarded at Lawrence's father's. She always bowed to her pleasantly. She had seen her in the shop, although she had no real acquaintance with her. The girl was pretty, with the prettiness that Delia lacked. Her face was sweet and rosy and laughing. She was fine and small, and moved with a sort of tremulous lightness like a butterfly. Delia, meeting her, seemed to tramp.

Everybody thought Lawrence and Olive Briggs would be married. They went to evening meetings together, and to ride. Lawrence had a fine horse. Delia was at every evening meeting. She watched her old lover enter with the other girl, and never shrank. She also looked at them riding past.

"Did you see them, Delia?" her mother asked in a fluttering voice one afternoon. She and Delia were sitting at the front windows, and Lawrence and Olive had just whirled by the house.

"Yes."

"You kept so still, I didn't know as you did."

People kept close watch over Lawrence and Olive and Delia. Lawrence was subjected to a mild species of ostracism by a certain set of the village girls, Delia's mates— honest, simple young souls; they would not speak to him on the street. They treated Olive with rough, rural stiffness when they traded with her in the one milliner's shop. She was an out-of-town girl, and had always been regarded with something of suspicion. These village women had a strong local conservatism. They eyed strangers long before they admitted them.

As for Delia, the young women friends of her own age treated her with a sort of deferential sympathy. They dared not openly condole with her, but they made her aware of their partisanship. As a general thing no one except a Thayer or a Caldwell alluded to the matter in her presence. The relatives of the two families were open enough in expressing themselves either with recrimination or excuse for Lawrence, or with sympathy or covert blame for Delia. She heard the most of it, directly or indirectly. Like many New England towns, this was almost overshadowed by the ramifications of a few family trees. A considerable portion of the population was made up of these Thayers and Caldwells—two honorable and respectable old names. They were really, for the most part, kindly and respectable people, conscious of no ill intentions, and probably possessed of few. Some of them expostulated against receiving back those vain bridal gifts, but Delia insisted.

Some of them were more willing to give than she to receive their honest and most genuine sympathy, however ungracefully they might proffer it.

Still the fine and exquisite stabs which Delia Caldwell had to take from her own relations and those of her forsworn bridegroom were innumerable. There are those good and innocent-hearted people who seem to be furnished with stings only for those of their own kind; they are stingless toward others. In one way this fact may have proved beneficial to Delia: while engaged in active defense against outside attacks, she had no time to sting herself.

She girded on that pearl-colored silk as if it were chain armor, and went to merrymakings. She made calls in that fine black silk and white-plumed wedding bonnet. It seemed at times as if she were fairly running after her trouble; she did more than look it in the face.

It was in February, when Delia had been teaching her new school nearly two terms, that Olive Briggs left town. People said she had given up her work and gone home to get ready to be married.

Delia's mother heard of it, and told her. "I should think she'd be awful afraid he wouldn't come to the weddin'," she said, bitterly.

"So should I," assented Delia. She echoed everybody's severe remarks about Lawrence.

It might have been a month later when Flora Strong ran in one morning before school. "I've just heard the greatest news!" she panted. "What do you think—she's jilted him!"

"Jilted whom?"

"Olive Briggs—she's jilted Lawrence Thayer. She's going to be married to another fellow in May. I had it from Milly Davis. She writes to her. It's so."

"I can't believe it," Mrs. Caldwell said, quivering.

"Well, it's so. I declare I jumped right up and down when I heard of it. Delia, aren't you glad?"

"I don't know what difference it can make to me."

"I mean aren't you glad he's got his pay?"

"Yes, I am," said Delia, with slow decision.

"She wouldn't be human if she wasn't," said her mother. Mrs. Caldwell was cold and trembling with nervousness. She stood grasping the back of a chair. "But I'm afraid it ain't so. Are you sure it's so, Flora?"

"Mrs. Caldwell, I know it's so."

Delia on her way to school that morning looked at the Thayer house as she passed. "I wonder how *he* feels," she said to herself. She saw Lawrence Thayer, in her stead, in the midst of all that covert ridicule and obloquy, that galling sympathy, that agony of jealousy and betrayed trust. They distorted his face like flames; she saw him writhe through their liquid wavering.

She pressed her lips together and marched along. At that moment, had she met Lawrence, she would have passed him with a fiercer coldness than ever, but if she had seen the girl she would have been ready to fly at her.

The village tongues were even harder on Lawrence than they had been on her. The sight of a person bending toward the earth with the weight of his just deserts upon his shoulders is generally gratifying and amusing even to his friends. Then there was more open rudeness among the young men who were Lawrence's mates. They jeered him everywhere. He went about doggedly. He was strong in silence, but he had a sweet womanish face which showed the marks of words quickly. He was still very young. Delia was two years older than he, and looked ten. Still, Lawrence seemed as old in some respects. He was a quiet, shy young man, who liked to stay at home with his parents and never went about much with the young people. Before Olive came he had seldom spoken to any girl besides Delia. They had been together soberly and steadily ever since their school days.

Some people said now, "Don't you suppose Lawrence Thayer will go with Delia again?" But the answer always was, "She won't look at him."

One Sunday afternoon, about a year after Olive Briggs's marriage, Mrs. Caldwell said to Delia, as they were walking home from church, "I jest want to know if you noticed how Lawrence Thayer stared at you in meetin' this afternoon?"

"No, I didn't," said Delia. She was looking uncommonly well that day. She wore her black silk, and had some dark-red roses in her bonnet.

"Well, he never took his eyes off you. Delia, that feller would give all his old shoes to come back, if you'd have him."

"Don't talk so foolish, mother."

"He would—you depend on it."

"I'd like to see him," said Delia, sternly. There was a red glow on her dull, thick cheeks.

"Well, I say so, too," said her mother.

The next night, when Delia reached the Thayer house on her way from school, Lawrence's mother stood at the gate. She had a little green shawl over her head. She was shivering; the wind blew up cool. Just behind her in the yard there was a little peach tree all in blossom.

She held out her hand mutely when Delia reached her. The girl did not take it. "Good evening," said she, and was passing.

"Can't you stop jest a minute, Delia?"

"Was there anything you wanted?"

"Can't you come into the house jest a minute? I wanted to see you about somethin'."

"I don't believe I can tonight, Mrs. Thayer."

"There ain't anybody there. There was somethin' I wanted to see you about."

The green shawl was bound severely around her small,

old face with its peaked chin. She reached out her long, wrinkled hand over the gate, and clutched Delia's arm softly.

"Well, I'll come in a minute." Delia followed Mrs. Thayer past the blooming peach tree into the house.

The old woman dragged forward the best rocking-chair tremblingly. "Sit down, dear," said she. Then she seated herself close beside her, and, leaning forward, gazed into her face with a sort of deprecating mildness. She even laid hold of one of her hands, but the girl drew it away softly. There was a gentle rustic demonstrativeness about Lawrence's mother which had always rather abashed Delia, who was typically reserved. "I wanted to speak to you about Lawrence," said the old woman. Delia sat stiffly erect, her head turned away. "I can't bear to think you are always goin' to feel so hard toward him, Delia. Did you know it?"

Delia half arose. "There isn't any use in bringing all this up again, Mrs. Thayer; it's all past now."

"Sit down jest a minute, dear. I want to talk to you. I know you've got good reason to blame him; but there's some excuse. He wa'n't nothin' but a boy, an' she was sweet-lookin', an' she took on dreadful. You'd thought she was goin' to die. It's turned out jest the way I knew 'twould. I told Lawrence how 'twould be then. I see right through her. She meant well enough. I s'pose she thought she was in love with Lawrence; but she was flighty. She went home and saw another fellow, an' Lawrence was nowhere. He didn't care so much as folks thought. Delia, I'm goin' to tell you the truth: he thought more of you than he did of her the whole time. You look as if you thought I was crazy, but I ain't: She jest bewitched him a little spell, but you was at the bottom of his heart always —you *was*, Delia." The old woman broke into sobs.

Delia rose. "I'd better go. There isn't any use in bringing this up, Mrs. Thayer."

"Don't go, Delia—don't. I wanted to tell you. He got to talkin' with me a little the other Sabbath night. It's the first time he's said a word, but he felt awful bad, an' I questioned him. Says he, 'Mother, I don't dream of such a thing as her havin' of me, or carin' anything about me again; but I do feel as if I should like to do somethin' if I could, to make up to her a little for the awful wrong I've done her.' That was jest the words he said. Delia, he ain't such a bad boy as you think he is, after all. You hadn't ought to despise him."

"He'll have to do something to show I've got some reason not to, then," said Delia. She looked immovably at the old woman, who was struggling with her sobs. She told her mother of the conversation after she got home.

"You did jest right," said Mrs. Caldwell. "I wouldn't knuckle to 'em if I was in your place." She was getting tea. After they had finished the meal and sat idly at the table for a few minutes, she looked across at her daughter suddenly, with embarrassed sharpness. "Speakin' about Lawrence, you wouldn't feel as if you ever could take him, anyhow, would you?" said she.

"Mother, what are you talking about?"

In a few weeks the anniversary of Delia's defeated wedding came. She spoke of it herself after dinner. She and her mother were making currant jelly.

"Why, it's my wedding day, mother," said she. "I ought to have put on my wedding gown and eaten some wedding cake, instead of making jelly."

"Don't talk so, child," said her mother. Sometimes Delia's hardihood startled her.

Delia was pressing the currants in a muslin bag, and the juice was running through her fingers, when there was a loud knock at the door.

"Why, who's that?" her mother said, fluttering. She ran and peeped through the sitting-room blinds. "It's Mrs. 'Rastus Thayer," she motioned back, "an' Milly."

"I'll go to the door," said Delia. She washed her hands hurriedly and went. She noticed with surprise that the two visitors were dressed in their Sunday best, Mrs. Thayer in her nicely kept cinnamon-brown silk, and Milly in her freshly starched white muslin. They had an air of constrained curiosity about them as they entered and took their seats in the parlor.

Delia sat down with them and tried to talk. Pretty soon her mother, who had prinked a little, entered; but just as she did so there was another knock. Some of the Caldwell cousins had come this time. They also were finely dressed, and entered with that same soberly expectant air. They were hardly seated before others arrived. Delia, going to the door this time, saw the people coming by twos and threes up the street. They flocked in, and she brought chairs. Nothing disturbed her outward composure; but her mother grew pale and tremulous. She no longer tried to speak; she sat staring. At two o'clock the rooms were filled with that same company who had assembled to see Delia wedded two years before.

They sat around the walls in stiff silence; they seemed to be waiting. Delia was not imaginative, nor given to morbid fancies; but sitting there in the midst of that mysterious company, in her cotton gown, with her hands stained with currant juice, she fairly began to believe that it was a dream. Were not these people mere phantoms of the familiar village folk assembling after this truly fantastic manner, and sitting here in this ghostly silence? Was not the whole a phantasmagoria of the last moments of her sweet old happiness and belief in truth? Was not she, herself, disenchanted, with her cotton gown and stained hands, the one real thing in it?

The scent of the pinks came in the window, and she noticed that. "How real it all is!" she thought. "But I shall wake up before long." It was like one of those dreams in which one clings stanchly to the consciousness of the dream and will not sink beneath its terrors.

When Lawrence Thayer entered she seemed to wake violently. She half rose from her seat, then sank down again. Her mother screamed.

Lawrence Thayer stood by the parlor door, where everybody in the two rooms could hear him. His gentle, beardless face was pale as death, but the pallor revealed some strong lines which his youthful bloom had softened. He was slender, and stooped a little naturally; now he was straight as a reed. He had a strange look to these people who had always known him.

"Friends," he began, in a solemn, panting voice, "I—have—asked you to come here on the anniversary of the day on which Delia Caldwell and I were to have been married, to make to her, before you all, the restitution in my power. I don't do it to put myself before you in a better light: God, who knows everything, knows I don't; it's for *her*.. I was a coward, and mean, and it's going to last. Nothing that I can do now is going to alter that. All I want now is to make up to her a little for what she's been through. Two years ago today she stood before you all rejected and slighted. Now look at me in her place."

Then he turned to Delia with a stiff motion. It was like solemn, formal oratory, but his terrible earnestness gave it heat. "Delia Caldwell, I humbly beg your pardon. I love you better than the whole world, and I ask you to be my wife."

"I never will." It was as if Delia's whole nature had been set to these words; they had to be spoken. She had risen, and stood staring at him so intently that the whole concourse of people vanished in blackness. She saw only his white face. All the thoughts in her brain spread wings and flew, swiftly circling. She heard what he said, and she heard her own thoughts with a strange double consciousness. All those days came back—the sweet old confidences, the old looks and ways. That pale speaking face was Lawrence's—Lawrence's; not that strange other's who had left her for that pink-faced girl. This revelation of his inner self, which smote the others with a sense of strangeness, thrilled her with the recognition of love. "A coward and mean." Yes, he had been, but— Yes, there was some excuse for him—there was. Is not every fault wedded to its own excuse, that pity may be born into the world? He was as honest in what he was saying as a man could be. He could have had no hope that she would marry him. He knew her enduring will, her power of indignation. This was no subtle scheme for his own advantage. Even these people would not think that. They would not, indeed, believe him capable of it. The system of terrible but coolly calculated ventures for success was one with which this man would not be likely to grapple. He was honest in this. There sat all the Thayers and Caldwells. How they would talk and laugh at him!

Lawrence turned to go. He had bowed silently when she gave him her quick answer. There was a certain dignity about him. He had in reality pulled himself up to the level of his own noble, avowed sentiments.

Delia stood gazing after him. She looked so relentless that she was almost terrible. One young girl, staring at her, began to cry.

Mrs. Erastus Thayer sat near the door. Delia's eyes glanced from Lawrence to her face. Then she sprang forward.

"You needn't look at him in that way," she cried out. "I am going to marry him. Lawrence, come back!"

## XX.  *THE APPLE TREE*[1]

SAM MADDOX'S house was like a glaring blot on the tidy New England landscape, for the very landscape had been made to bear evidence to the character of the dwellers upon the soil.  There was no wealth in the village, there was even poverty, but everywhere thrift and making the most of little, bringing out of humble possessions the very utmost that was in them for beauty and utility.  When a house was scarcely larger than a child's toy it was white-painted and green-blinded, with windows shining like jewels; when there was only a little patch of yard, it was gay with flowers or velvet-smooth with grass; before it was a white fence or a trim green hedge, outside was a row of carefully tended trees.

But Sam Maddox's house, unpainted since it was built, and that was nearly a hundred years since, sagging as to its roof and its sills, with a scant and ragged allowance of glass in the windows, with the sordid waste of poverty in shameless evidence around it on all sides, stood in a glaring expanse of raw soil, growing only a few clumps of burdocks, and marked in every direction with the sprawling tracks of omnipresent hens.  In the first hot days of May this yard before Sam Maddox's house was a horror, actually provocative of physical discomfort to a sensitive observer. The sun lay on the front of the Maddox house and its yard all day; every detail of squalor, so extreme that it reached the limit of decency, was evident.  Passers-by turned aside; even the sweet spring air was contaminated to their fancy; for it was not in reality; it was only that the insult to one sense seemed to imply an insult to another. In reality the air was honey-sweet; for there was no crying evil of uncleanliness about the place, and in the midst of the yard was a whole bouquet of spring. That was the one redemption of it all. Often one, after looking away, unless he was carping to stiff-neckedness, would glance backward, and the sight of the apple tree would serve as a solace to his very soul, and beauty and the hope of the resurrection would vanquish squalor and the despair of humanity. There was never a more beautiful apple tree; majestic with age, it yet had all the freshness of youth and its perfection. Not one dead branch was there on the tree, not one missing from its fair symmetry. The blooming spread of it was even to the four winds; it described a perfect circle of wonderful bloom. The blossoms of this apple tree were unusually rosy—they were as deep as roses, but with shadows of pearl—and the fragrance of them was exhaustless. The whole tree seemed to pant, and sing, and shout with perfume; it seemed to call even more loudly than the robins that lived in its boughs. The tree was utter perfection, and a triumph over all around it.

On the day in the month of May when the tree was at its best, Sam Maddox sat in the doorway, and his wife Adeline rocked back and forward past the open window. A baby wailed in her lap; she held a cheap novel over its head and read peacefully, undisturbed. Four more children pervaded the yard, their scanty little garments earth stained, their faces and hands and legs and feet earth stained. They had become in a certain sense a part of the soil, as much as the weeds and flowers of the spring. Their bare toes clung to the warm, kindly earth with caressing instinct; they grubbed in it tenderly with little, clinging hands; they fairly burrowed in it, in soft, sunny nests, like the hens. They made small, inarticulate noises, indicative of extreme comfort and satisfaction, like young which are nursed and coddled to their fill. There was very little strife and dissension among the Maddox children in spite of their ill-repute and general poverty and wretchedness. The Maddoxes were pariahs, suspected of all sorts of minor iniquities, but in reality they were a gentle, docile tribe, whose gentleness and docility were the causes of most of their failures of life. Sam Maddox and his brood, lacking that of comfort and necessaries which they saw their neighbors possess, never thought of complaining or grasping for the sweets on the boughs behind their wall of fate. They settled back unquestioningly on the soft side of their poverty, and slept, and smiled, and were not unhappy.

Over across the road Mrs. Sarah Blake cleaned house. She was small and weak-muscled in spite of her life of strenuous toil, which had bent her narrow back and knotted her tiny hands without strengthening them. She staggered out into the hot May sunlight with a great feather bed, tugging it with a grip of desperation on the slack of one end. She dumped it into the midst of the green expanse of her front yard, between a tossing snowball bush and a syringa on one side and a strip of lilies-of-the-valley on the other; then she beat it with half-futile fury, assailing it like a live thing with a cane which her husband had used to walk abroad the year she was married, half a century ago. Sarah Blake was an old woman, although she had never confessed it, even to herself. Her two children were dead long ago, after they were women grown. There was no one except herself and husband, and Edison Blake was much older than she, stronger of body, though with less vigor of mind. All the morning she had been striving in vain to whip up old Edison to the point of enthusiasm in house cleaning. He was lukewarm, not openly rebellious, timid, but covertly dissenting. Whenever her back was turned and she presumably out of hearing, old Edison, who had been considered unregenerate

in his youth, would say something under his breath, and
then glance apprehensively around, and then chuckle with
defiance.

Once his wife heard him. She had left him meekly, to
all appearances, cleaning the parlor windows. The old man
was laboriously wiping off the panes with a cloth dipped in
kerosene, the fumes of which were in his nostrils; he abom-
inated kerosene. He was stout, and his fat, pink face was
beaded with perspiration. He pulled his collar off with a
jerk; then he said something with force. That time his
wife heard him. She had not gone so far as he thought.
She had come in for a clean little broom to sweep the
feather bed, after whipping it with the cane. "What did
I hear you say, Edison Blake?" she demanded. She eyed
him like an accusing conscience. Old Edison gave her one
sidelong glance; then he turned to the window. He cleaned
vigorously; he cocked his head on one side, busily, to see
if a streak remained athwart the sunlight. "You needn't
pretend you don't hear and it wa'n't nothin', Edison Blake,"
said his wife Sarah. "I know you said something you
didn't want me to hear, and now I want to know what it
was."

"What you want to hear for, if it's somethin' you think
wa'n't right?" inquired old Edison, with a feeble growl of
self-assertion.

"I want to know," said she, ignoring the point of his
remark.

"I didn't say much of anything," he hedged.

"What did you say, Edison Blake?"

"I said goll durn it, then, if you want to know," burst
forth old Edison, with the fury of desperation.

"Edison Blake, I don't see what you think is goin' to
become of you."

Old Edison was meek and always in a state of chronic
intimidation by his wife, but all things have a bay. Old

Edison could find his. He did now. He faced his wife Sarah. "It ain't likely, whatever is goin' to become of me, I'm goin' where there's house cleanin', anyhow!" said he.

"You'll go where there's somethin' worse than house cleanin'."

"It'll have to be pooty goll durned bad to be any worse," said old Edison.

He looked steadily at his wife. She yielded, beaten by masculine assertion. She essayed one stony look of reproof, but her pale-blue eyes fell before the old man's, full of shrewd malice and quizzical triumph. She tossed her head and went out with her limp calico skirt lashing her thin ankles in a gust of spring wind. "When you get that winder finished you can come out an' help me shake the braided mat," she called back. She knew that would depress the victor, for she was merciless and miraculously untiring when it came to shaking a mat; she would not release the sufferer at the other end until not an atom of dust clouded the air. This time, however, fate, although an untoward one, interposed. Old Edison stepped in a chair to facilitate the process of cleaning the upper panes of the window, and the chair, dating back to the period of his wife's mother, and having seen better days as to its cane seat, and the old man being heavy, succumbed, and old Edison came with a jolt through to the floor. The thud brought in his wife Sarah, pale and gasping. When she saw her husband standing there in the wreck of the chair she stared a moment, then she spoke. Old Edison was holding to his head in a dazed fashion, not offering to move. "Now you've gone an' done it, Edison Blake!" said she.

"It give way all of a sudden an' let me through, Sarah," said old Edison, feebly.

"Didn't you know better than to stand up in one of them cane-seat chairs, heavy as you be?"

"I didn't know but it would bear me, Sarah!"

"Of course it wouldn't bear you. One of them nice cane-seat chairs that mother had when she was married! I'd ruther have given five dollar than had it happen."

"I'm dretful sorry, Sarah."

"I think you'd better be. Why don't you git out, an' not stand there starin' and hangin' onto your head?"

"My head is kind of dizzy, I guess, Sarah. I can't seem to see jest straight. I come down pooty hefty, I guess."

"You didn't come down on your head, did you? Looks to me as if you'd landed on your feet. That nice chair!"

"Yes, I s'pose I did land on my feet, Sarah, but it ain't them that's hurt, but my head feels pooty bad, I guess."

There was, directly, no doubt that it did. Old Edison turned a ghastly, appealing face toward his wife, who promptly advanced, scolding the while, and strove to extricate him from the broken chair. But that was beyond her strength, and old Edison was unable to help himself, although he was not unconscious. He continued to make feebly deprecatory remarks as he failed to respond to his wife's futile efforts.

Finally Sarah Blake made an impatient exclamation. "Well, I ain't goin' to work this way for nothin' any longer," said she. Then she was gone, not heeding the weak inquiry as to what she was going to do which her husband sent after her.

Straight across the road she raced, with skirts and apron flying to the wind like sails, making pitiless revelations of ascetic anatomy. Straight up to Sam Maddox in his peaceful leisure on the front doorstep she went. "Edison has fell and hurt himself, gone through one of the cane-seat chairs my mother had when she was married," she said, in an accusing tone, "an' he's stuck there in it, and I want you to come right over and git him out. I can't lift him, and he won't help himself one mite."

Sam Maddox raised his shaggy, blond head, and brought his pleasant blue eyes and pleasanter gaping mouth to bear upon her.

"Hey?" he said, inquiringly, with a long, husky drawl.

Sarah Blake repeated the burden of her speech with furious emphasis.

"You want me to come over and help git him out?" said Sam Maddox. Adeline Maddox had come to the door, and the small baby in her arms was uttering wails of feeble querulousness unheeded.

"Yes, I do want somebody to come over an' git him out," said Sarah Blake. "I can't lift him, an' he'll stan' there till doomsday, for all he'll help himself."

"Is he hurt?" inquired Sam Maddox, with some interest.

"Says his head's kind of dizzy; he looks kinder pale. I s'pose he come down pretty hard. He went right through the seat of that chair, an' the cane seat wa'n't broke a mite before."

"I'll come right along," said Sam Maddox, and straightway rose with loose sprawls of ungainly limbs. He seemed a kindly and ineffectual giant when he stood up; he had doubled up an enormous length of limb in his sitting posture.

Sam Maddox followed, with long, languid strides, Sarah Blake, who hopped on before him, like a nervous bird, across the street. After them streamed the Maddox children, a white-headed, earth-stained troop; in the rear of all came Adeline Maddox, her paper novel fluttering, the small baby wailing, her yellow hair flying in strings.

"There ain't no need of the whole family," Sarah Blake called out sharply once, but they came on smilingly.

Poor old Edison Blake was sitting on the ragged edge of the broken chair when they arrived. "I swun!" said Sam Maddox, when he caught sight of him.

He lifted him out bodily and laid him on the lounge, and Sarah got the camphor bottle.

She was not in the least alarmed. "He come down pretty hard, and his head wa'n't never very strong," she said. She bathed his forehead with the camphor with hard strokes; she got it in his eyes, and she pushed back his hair remorselessly. "Keep still. I'm goin' to see to it that you git enough camphor to do some good," said she, firmly, when old Edison pushed her hand away from his smarting eyes.

"You're gitting of it in my eyes, Sarah," he remonstrated, meekly. All his spirit was gone, between the hurt to the chair and himself.

"You keep still," said she, and old Edison screwed his eyes tightly together. His color was fast returning. He was evidently not much the worse, but he groaned when his wife inquired how he felt now.

"Seems to me he'd better keep still awhile," said Sam Maddox, looking at him compassionately. "Seems to me he hadn't better clean winders till he's rested a little whilst."

"We've got somethin' to do beside rest over here," replied Sarah Blake, with unmistakable emphasis. Sam Maddox smiled, and Adeline smiled foolishly and sweetly. They appreciated the sarcasm, and took it amiably.

However, old Edison groaned again, and Sarah left him in peace on the lounge, when the Maddoxes streamed homeward across the street, and she returned to the yard to resume her struggle with the feather bed and the mats.

She was somewhat at a loss when it came to the braided mat which belonged in the sitting room. It was a large mat, and very heavy. She strove to lift it; she could scarcely do that. She strove to shake it; as well try to shake the side of the house. She eyed it as if it were some refractory animal. The negative opposition of inanimate things always filled this small, intense woman with fury. She let the mat slide to the ground; she gave a weary and angry sigh. Then she looked across the street. There sat Sam Maddox on his doorsteps, lazily regarding her. He had certainly seen her helpless effort to shake the braided mat. She stood eyeing him for one minute. Then across the street she marched.

She stood before Sam Maddox, electric, compelling, this small, delicate old woman before this great, lumbering giant of a man.

"Sam Maddox, I'd like to know what you mean?" said she.

He stared at her. "Hey?" he said.

"I'd like to know what you think of yourself?"

"Hey?"

"I'd like to know what you think of yourself? You heard what I said the first time. If you was my son, I'd cure you of sayin' 'hey,' if I killed you. If you hear, why don't you hear? You are too lazy to sense things, even, unless somebody else drives 'em into your head to save you the trouble of takin' 'em in. I'd like to know what you think of yourself?"

"I dunno," said Sam Maddox.

"I guess you don't know. If you did know, you wouldn't keep your settin' long. Ain't you been lookin' over the road at me tryin' to shake that great mat all alone, and you doin' nothin'?"

Sam Maddox hitched. His wife, Adeline, with the baby, came slowly to the front; the earth-stained children gathered round.

"What did you s'pose I was goin' to do?" queried Sarah Blake.

Sam Maddox looked at her with the perplexed stare of a good-natured dog trying with the limitations of his doghood to comprehend a problem of humanity; then he murmured feebly again that he didn't know.

"And me with my husband laid up with falling through one of my mother's nice cane-seat chairs that she had when she was married!" said Sarah Blake, further.

Adeline, who was weakly emotional, wiped her eyes. Sam Maddox, feeling it incumbent upon him to make some response, and finding speech inadequate, grunted.

"Well, ain't you goin' to do nothin' but sit there and stare?" demanded Sarah Blake, with a sort of cold fury.

Sam Maddox rose and shuffled before her, as if essaying a dance.

"For the land's sake! Ain't you got any gumption, no snap at all? Be you goin' to sit there an' see me tryin' to shake that great, heavy mat, an' never offer to raise a finger?"

"Do go over there an' help her shake her mat, Sam," sniffed Adeline.

A look of joyous relief overspread Sam Maddox's perplexed face. He started with perfect assent. "Sartain," he drawled—"sartain."

"I'll make it wuth your while," said Sarah Blake.

Sam stopped and eyed her doubtfully.

"What?" said he.

"I'll see to it you're paid for it."

Sam settled loosely on to the doorsteps again; a look of evanescent firmness overspread his face.

"Ain't you comin'?"

"I ain't workin'," said Sam Maddox.

"Mebbe you think we can't pay enough. I guess we can pay as much as your work is wuth, Sam Maddox. We ain't in the poorhouse yet."

"I ain't workin'."

"He means he don't do no work for money. Don't you, Sam?" inquired Adeline, tearfully. The baby whimpered, and she dandled it with no enthusiasm.

"He won't work for pay?" inquired Sarah Blake, dazedly.

"I don't shake mats for old women for no pay," said Sam Maddox, with who could tell what species of inborn pride or generosity?

"You mean you'd rather come for nothin'?"

Sam nodded obstinately.

"You think we ain't able to pay you?" asked Sarah, jealously.

"Dunno', and don't care."

"You mean you just won't?"

Sam nodded.

"Why don't you come, then, an' not keep me standin' here all day? I want to git that setting room cleaned, if I can, today."

Sam rose again, and slouched across the road in the wake of the little, vociferous, indefatigable woman. He looked, this great, loosely built, ineffectual, blond giant of a man, the very antipode to the woman snapping with her overplus of energy, as she led the way to the scene of labor. He might have been an inhabitant of another planet.

Now, indeed, came a time of trial to Sam Maddox. From where he toiled, in the Blake yard, he could see, like a vision of a lost paradise, his old comfortable doorstep, the doorpost which leaned luxuriously to his back, the warm sunlight which overspread the whole place like a sea of blessing. The clamor of the happy children playing about with an incessant enjoyment of youth and life was as pleasant to him as the hum of bees. Adeline rocked ever back and forth past the window with an inertia of peace, and the great apple tree perfumed and irradiated the whole. Sam Maddox glanced scornfully at the small, reluctant pear tree in the Blake yard.

"What be you a-lookin' at?" inquired Sarah Blake from the other end of the braided mat. "Shake it this way."

"Your pear tree don't amount to much, does it?" said Sam Maddox.

"No, it don't, and they're winter pears on that tree, too. They last till long after Thanksgivin'. I always make sauce of 'em an' have 'em for supper Thanksgivin' night. We don't want much after turkey dinner, an' a little of that pear sauce used to go jest right. I dunno' what ails that tree. He trimmed it up real nice, too."

"Mebbe he trimmed it too much."

"No, he didn't. I ain't goin' to have old, dead branches or spindlin' ones that don't amount to much on a tree in my yard. I believe in keeping trees nice an' neat as well as houses."

"Ain't never tetched my apple tree," observed Sam Maddox, with unusual pride.

Sarah sniffed. "Well, I suppose the Lord looks out for trees, the same as he does for folks, when they ain't got anybody else," said she.

"It's a pretty handsome tree," said Sam Maddox, ignoring the sarcasm.

"I don't care nothin' about the looks of a tree so long as it has good apples. I want apples to last all winter, good, sound ones. I want 'em for my Thanksgivin' pies. I feel thankful for apples like that, but I can't say as I do, if I say just what I think, for them early kinds."

"The apples on that tree would keep if we let 'em, I reckon," said Sam Maddox, "but we don't make pies nor sauce of 'em, and we eat 'em right up. They ain't quite so meller. The children are dreadful fond of them apples."

"I didn't s'pose you did make pies," said Sarah, and she sniffed.

"I never see blooms so pink as them," said the man, gazing with the expression of an artist at the tree.

"I don't care nothin' about blooms; it's apples I'm arter," said Sarah.

That was a red-letter day for old Edison Blake. He fell asleep on the sitting-room lounge, and when he awoke was fully aware that the dizziness in his head was gone. He felt guiltily that he ought to rise and resume his labor, but he could not resist the impulse to remain in his comfortable place a little longer. Sam Maddox passed the open window with a braided mat over his shoulder. Old Edison heard his wife's sharp voice of direction and admonition. "She's got Sam Maddox helpin' her," he reflected. He knew how small an opinion his wife had of Sam Maddox; he knew that he ought to rise, but he lay still. Pretty soon Sam entered the room for a brush. Old Edison lay with eyes wide open, regarding him. Sam paused and stooped over him.

"Better?" he inquired.

Old Edison closed his eyes in affirmation.

"Dizzy feelin' gone?"

"'Bout."

Sam Maddox looked down at the aged, recumbent figure. "Look here," he said. He bent low and whispered, sharply: "Don't you git up. You jest lay low. It's durned hard work, house cleanin'; you're too old. You lay low. I'll stay round and help."

Old Edison looked at him with intensest gratitude; an expression of bliss overspread his face. He smiled the smile of a contented baby.

"Just go to sleep ag'in," said Sam Maddox.

Old Edison closed his eyes.

When Sam Maddox emerged from the house, Sarah Blake inquired how her husband was.

"Looks pretty slim to me," said Sam Maddox.

"Asleep?"

"His eyes was shut; looked as if he was. Seems to me he ought to keep pretty still."

"Guess he can keep still enough," said Sarah. Pretty soon she went in to peep at old Edison. He lay drawing long, even, whistling breaths. When she went out of the room he gazed after her from the corner of one cautious eye.

Sam Maddox worked all that beautiful May day for Sarah Blake. She was the hardest, and, in fact, the only task mistress of life whom he had ever known. Sam had lived somehow without much work. He owned his poor house and lot and apple tree. People who pitied the children of the irresponsible pair assisted them. Once in a while he went gunning and fishing. Somehow they lived and were happy.

When Sam Maddox went home that night, the oldest girl had dug a mess of dandelions, and there was a parcel of cress from the bank of the brook. Somehow there was a loaf of bread, and molasses, and tea. Sam had no idea how they were procured, but there they were. They all ate and were thankful. After supper, in the delicious cool of the day, Sam sat on the doorstep. Adeline put the baby to bed, then she came and sat by her husband's side, her elbows on her knees, her delicate chin in her hands, and her sharp, pretty face upturned toward the ineffable clear pallor of the sky. The children had subsided, and were grouped in a charming little cluster like a bunch of flowers in the yard under the apple tree. And the apple tree was a mystery of whiteness and ravishing fragrance. In the day it had been simply a magnificent apple tree; when the shadows came, it was something more. Sam Maddox gazed at it, and the breath of it came over his senses. He looked across at the Blake house in its tidy yard. There was a light in the sitting room, and a small figure bustled back and forth incessantly past the window. Now and then a larger, taller shape lumbered before the light. There was a sound of a hammer and a sharp voice.

"Old Edison, he's had one day off, anyhow," chuckled Sam Maddox. He stretched his great limbs, which ached with the unaccustomed strain of the day's toil. He continued to gaze reflectively at the Blake house. "Dreadful clean over there," he murmured.

"S'pose so," asserted Adeline, indifferently. There was an angelic expression in her face, upturned toward the sky. Possibly her imagination, from the slight stimulus of a third-rate novel, was making a leap out of her surroundings.

"Says she cleans house once a month from now till Thanksgivin', on account of the dust, an' the winders havin' to be open so much," said Sam Maddox.

"Lord!" said Adeline, indifferently.

"I shouldn't think they'd have any Thanksgivin' when they got to it, workin' so hard and fussin' all the time. I shouldn't."

Then Adeline looked with strong disapproval across at the Blake house. "Doggin' round all day," said she.

"That's so," assented Sam. "It's terrible hard work cleanin' house."

"What's the use? It gits dirty again," said Adeline.

"That's so." Sam looked again at the great apple tree. "Mighty handsome tree," said he.

Adeline looked and smiled. Her face was really beautiful. "Real handsome," said she.

"I don't see no use in waitin' for Thanksgivin', fussin' and cleanin' an' cookin'. I don't see why we ain't got Thanksgivin' any time right along any time of year," said Sam, thoughtfully.

"That's so," said Adeline, nodding happily.

Sam gazed at her. "Seems as if you got better-lookin' than ever," he said. "You ain't tired, be you?"

"No; ain't done nothin' all day. You tired, Sam?"

"Sorter. Hard work cleanin' house."

"You can rest tomorrer."

Sam nodded, still with tender eyes on his wife's face.

The wind blew, and a wonderful breath of fragrance came from the apple tree, and they inhaled it. "Lord! it's a dreadful pretty world, ain't it?" said Sam Maddox, and on his face was a light of unconscious praise.

"Yes, 'tis," said Adeline, and her face looked like her husband's.

The splendid apple tree bloomed and sweetened, and the man and woman, in a certain sense, tasted and drank it until it became a part of themselves, and there was in the midst of the poverty and shiftlessness of the Maddox yard a great inflorescence of beauty for its redemption.

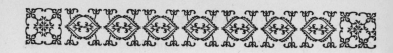

# XXI. NOBLESSE[1]

MARGARET LEE encountered in her late middle age the rather singular strait of being entirely alone in the world. She was unmarried, and as far as relatives were concerned, she had none except those connected with her by ties not of blood, but by marriage.

Margaret had not married when her flesh had been comparative; later, when it had become superlative, she had no opportunities to marry. Life would have been hard enough for Margaret under any circumstances, but it was especially hard, living, as she did, with her father's stepdaughter and that daughter's husband.

Margaret's stepmother had been a child in spite of her two marriages, and a very silly, although pretty child. The daughter, Camille, was like her, although not so pretty, and the man whom Camille had married was what Margaret had been taught to regard as "common." His business pursuits were irregular and partook of mystery. He always smoked cigarettes and chewed gum. He wore loud shirts and a diamond scarfpin which had upon him the appearance of stolen goods. The gem had belonged to Margaret's own mother, but when Camille expressed a desire to present it to Jack Desmond, Margaret had yielded with no outward hesitation, but afterward she wept miserably over its loss when alone in her room. The spirit had gone out of Margaret, the little which she had possessed. She had always been a gentle, sensitive creature, and was almost helpless before the wishes of others.

After all, it had been a long time since Margaret had

been able to force the ring even upon her little finger, but she had derived a small pleasure from the reflection that she owned it in its faded velvet box, hidden under laces in her top bureau drawer. She did not like to see it blazing forth from the tie of this very ordinary young man who had married Camille. Margaret had a gentle, high-bred contempt for Jack Desmond, but at the same time a vague fear of him. Jack had a measure of unscrupulous business shrewdness, which spared nothing and nobody, and that in spite of the fact that he had not succeeded.

Margaret owned the old Lee place, which had been magnificent, but of late years the expenditures had been reduced and it had deteriorated. The conservatories had been closed. There was only one horse in the stable. Jack had bought him. He was a worn-out trotter with legs carefully bandaged. Jack drove him at reckless speed, not considering those slender, braceleted legs. Jack had a racing gig, and when in it, with striped coat, cap on one side, cigarette in mouth, lines held taut, skimming along the roads in clouds of dust, he thought himself the man and true sportsman which he was not. Some of the old Lee silver had paid for that waning trotter.

Camille adored Jack, and cared for no associations, no society, for which he was not suited. Before the trotter was bought she told Margaret that the kind of dinners which she was able to give in Fairhill were awfully slow. "If we could afford to have some men out from the city, some nice fellers that Jack knows, it would be worth while," said she; "but we have grown so hard up we can't do a thing to make it worth their while. Those men haven't got any use for a back-number old place like this. We can't take them round in autos, nor give them a chance at cards, for Jack couldn't pay if he lost, and Jack is awful honorable. We can't have the right kind of folks here for any fun. I don't propose to ask the rector and his wife, and old Mr. Harvey, or people like the Leaches."

"The Leaches are a very good old family," said Margaret, feebly.

"I don't care for good old families when they are so slow," retorted Camille. "The fellers we could have here, if we were rich enough, come from fine families, but they are up-to-date. It's no use hanging on to old silver dishes we never use and that I don't intend to spoil my hands shining. Poor Jack don't have much fun, anyway. If he wants that trotter—he says it's going dirt cheap—I think it's mean he can't have it, instead of your hanging on to a lot of out-of-style old silver; so there."

Two generations ago there had been French blood in Camille's family. She put on her clothes beautifully; she had a dark, rather fine-featured, alert little face, which gave a wrong impression, for she was essentially vulgar. Sometimes poor Margaret Lee wished that Camille had been definitely vicious, if only she might be possessed of more of the characteristics of breeding. Camille so irritated Margaret in those somewhat abstruse traits called sensibilities that she felt as if she were living with a sort of spiritual nutmeg grater. Seldom did Camille speak that she did not jar Margaret, although unconsciously. Camille meant to be kind to the stout woman, whom she pitied so far as she was capable of pitying without understanding. She realized that it must be horrible to be no longer young, and so stout that one was fairly monstrous, but how horrible she could not with her mentality conceive. Jack also meant to be kind. He was not of the brutal—that is, intentionally brutal—type, but he had a shrewd eye to the betterment of himself, and no realization of the torture he inflicted upon those who opposed that betterment.

For a long time matters had been worse than usual financially in the Lee house. The sisters had been left in

charge of the sadly dwindled estate, and had depended upon
the judgment, or lack of judgment, of Jack. He approved
of taking your chances and striking for larger income. The
few good old grandfather securities had been sold, and wild
ones from the very jungle of commerce had been substi-
tuted. Jack, like most of his type, while shrewd, was as
credulous as a child. He lied himself, and expected all men
to tell him the truth. Camille at his bidding mortgaged
the old place, and Margaret dared not oppose. Taxes were
not paid; interest was not paid; credit was exhausted. Then
the house was put up at public auction, and brought little
more than sufficient to pay the creditors. Jack took the
balance and staked it in a few games of chance, and of
course lost. The weary trotter stumbled one day and had
to be shot. Jack became desperate. He frightened Camille.
He was suddenly morose. He bade Camille pack, and
Margaret also, and they obeyed. Camille stowed away her
crumpled finery in the bulging old trunks, and Margaret
folded daintily her few remnants of past treasures. She had
an old silk gown or two, which resisted with their rich
honesty the inroads of time, and a few pieces of old lace,
which Camille understood no better than she understood
their owner.

Then Margaret and the Desmonds went to the city and
lived in a horrible, tawdry little flat in a tawdry locality.
Jack roared with bitter mirth when he saw poor Margaret
forced to enter her tiny room sidewise; Camille laughed
also, although she chided Jack gently. "Mean of you to
make fun of poor Margaret, Jacky dear," she said.

For a few weeks Margaret's life in that flat was horrible; then it became still worse. Margaret nearly filled with
her weary, ridiculous bulk her little room, and she remained
there most of the time, although it was sunny and noisy,
its one window giving on a courtyard strung with clothes-
lines and teeming with boisterous life. Camille and Jack

went trolley riding, and made shift to entertain a little, merry but questionable people, who gave them passes to vaudeville and entertained in their turn until the small hours. Unquestionably these people suggested to Jack Desmond the scheme which spelled tragedy to Margaret.

She always remembered one little dark man with keen eyes who had seen her disappearing through her door of a Sunday night when all these gay, bedraggled birds were at liberty and the fun ran high. "Great Scott!" the man had said, and Margaret had heard him demand of Jack that she be recalled. She obeyed, and the man was introduced, also the other members of the party. Margaret Lee stood in the midst of this throng and heard their repressed titters of mirth at her appearance. Everybody there was in good humor with the exception of Jack, who was still nursing his bad luck, and the little dark man, whom Jack owed. The eyes of Jack and the little dark man made Margaret cold with a terror of something, she knew not what. Before that terror the shame and mortification of her exhibition to that merry company was of no import.

She stood among them, silent, immense, clad in her dark purple silk gown spread over a great hoop skirt. A real lace collar lay softly over her enormous, billowing shoulders; real lace ruffles lay over her great, shapeless hands. Her face, the delicacy of whose features was veiled with flesh, flushed and paled. Not even flesh could subdue the sad brilliancy of her dark-blue eyes, fixed inward upon her own sad state, unregardful of the company. She made an indefinite murmur of response to the salutations given her, and then retreated. She heard the roar of laughter after she had squeezed through the door of her room. Then she heard eager conversation, of which she did not catch the real import, but which terrified her with chance expressions. She was quite sure that she was the subject of that eager discussion. She was quite sure that it boded her no good.

In a few days she knew the worst; and the worst was beyond her utmost imaginings. This was before the days of moving-picture shows; it was the day of humiliating spectacles of deformities, when inventions of amusements for the people had not progressed. It was the day of exhibitions of sad freaks of nature, calculated to provoke tears rather than laughter in the healthy-minded, and poor Margaret Lee was a chosen victim. Camille informed her in a few words of her fate. Camille was sorry for her, although not in the least understanding why she was sorry. She realized dimly that Margaret would be distressed, but she was unable from her narrow point of view to comprehend fully the whole tragedy.

"Jack has gone broke," stated Camille. "He owes Bill Stark a pile, and he can't pay a cent of it; and Jack's sense of honor about a poker debt is about the biggest thing in his character. Jack has got to pay. And Bill has a little circus, going to travel all summer, and he's offered big money for you. Jack can pay Bill what he owes him, and we'll have enough to live on, and have lots of fun going around. You hadn't ought to make a fuss about it."

Margaret, pale as death, stared at the girl, pertly slim, and common and pretty, who stared back laughingly, although still with the glimmer of uncomprehending pity in her black eyes.

"What does—he—want—me—for?" gasped Margaret.

"For a show, because you are so big," replied Camille. "You will make us all rich, Margaret. Ain't it nice?"

Then Camille screamed, the shrill raucous scream of the women of her type, for Margaret had fallen back in a dead faint, her immense bulk inert in her chair. Jack came running in alarm. Margaret had suddenly gained value in his shrewd eyes. He was as pale as she.

Finally Margaret raised her head, opened her miserable eyes, and regained her consciousness of herself and what lay before her. There was no course open but submission. She knew that from the first. All three faced destitution; she was the one financial asset, she and her poor flesh. She had to face it, and with what dignity she could muster.

Margaret had great piety. She kept constantly before her mental vision the fact in which she believed, that the world which she found so hard, and which put her to unspeakable torture, was not all.

A week elapsed before the wretched little show of which she was to be a member went on the road, and night after night she prayed. She besieged her God for strength. She never prayed for respite. Her realization of the situation and her lofty resolution prevented that. The awful, ridiculous combat was before her; there was no evasion; she prayed only for the strength which leads to victory.

However, when the time came, it was all worse than she had imagined. How could a woman gently born and bred conceive of the horrible ignominy of such a life? She was dragged hither and yon, to this and that little town. She traveled through sweltering heat on jolting trains; she slept in tents; she lived—she, Margaret Lee—on terms of equality with the common and the vulgar. Daily her absurd unwieldiness was exhibited to crowds screaming with laughter. Even her faith wavered. It seemed to her that there was nothing forevermore beyond those staring, jeering faces of silly mirth and delight at sight of her, seated in two chairs, clad in a pink spangled dress, her vast shoulders bare and sparkling with a tawdry necklace, her great, bare arms covered with brass bracelets, her hands incased in short, white kid gloves, over the fingers of which she wore a number of rings—stage properties.

Margaret became a horror to herself. At times it seemed to her that she was in the way of fairly losing her own identity. It mattered little that Camille and Jack were very kind to her, that they showed her the nice things which her terrible earnings had enabled them to have. She sat in two chairs—the two chairs proved a most successful advertisement—with her two kid-cushiony hands clenched in her pink spangled lap, and she suffered agony of soul, which made her inner self stern and terrible, behind that great pink mask of face. And nobody realized until one sultry day when the show opened at a village in a pocket of green hills—indeed, its name was Greenhill—and Sydney Lord went to see it.

Margaret, who had schooled herself to look upon her audience as if they were not, suddenly comprehended among them another soul who understood her own. She met the eyes of the man, and a wonderful comfort, as of a cool breeze blowing over the face of clear water, came to her. She knew that the man understood. She knew that she had his fullest sympathy. She saw also a comrade in the toils of comic tragedy, for Sydney Lord was in the same case. He was a mountain of flesh. As a matter of fact, had he not been known in Greenhill and respected as a man of weight of character as well as of body, and of an old family, he would have rivaled Margaret. Beside him sat an elderly woman, sweet-faced, slightly bent as to her slender shoulders, as if with a chronic attitude of submission. She was Sydney's widowed sister, Ellen Waters. She lived with her brother and kept his house, and had no will other than his.

Sydney Lord and his sister remained when the rest of the audience had drifted out, after the privileged handshakes with the queen of the show. Every time a coarse, rustic hand reached familiarly after Margaret's Sydney shrank.

He motioned his sister to remain seated when he approached the stage. Jack Desmond, who had been exploiting Margaret, gazed at him with admiring curiosity. Sydney waved him away with a commanding gesture. "I wish to speak to her a moment. Pray leave the tent," he said, and Jack obeyed. People always obeyed Sydney Lord.

Sydney stood before Margaret, and he saw the clear crystal, which was herself, within all the flesh, clad in tawdry raiment, and she knew that he saw it.

"Good God!" said Sydney, "you are a lady!"

He continued to gaze at her, and his eyes, large and brown, became blurred; at the same time his mouth tightened.

"How came you to be in such a place as this?" demanded Sydney. He spoke almost as if he were angry with her.

Margaret explained briefly.

"It is an outrage," declared Sydney. He said it, however, rather absently. He was reflecting. "Where do you live?" he asked.

"Here."

"You mean—?"

"They make up a bed for me here, after the people have gone."

"And I suppose you had—before this—a comfortable house."

"The house which my grandfather Lee owned, the old Lee mansion house, before we went to the city. It was a very fine old Colonial house," explained Margaret, in her finely modulated voice.

"And you had a good room?"

"The southeast chamber had always been mine. It was very large, and the furniture was old Spanish mahogany."

"And now—" said Sydney.

"Yes," said Margaret. She looked at him, and her serious blue eyes seemed to see past him. "It will not last," she said.

"What do you mean?"

"I try to learn a lesson. I am a child in the school of God. My lesson is one that always ends in peace."

"Good God!" said Sydney.

He motioned to his sister, and Ellen approached in a

frightened fashion. Her brother could do no wrong, but this was the unusual, and alarmed her.

"This lady—" began Sydney.

"Miss Lee," said Margaret. "I was never married. I am Miss Margaret Lee."

"This," said Sydney, "is my sister Ellen, Mrs. Waters. Ellen, I wish you to meet Miss Lee."

Ellen took in her own Margaret's hand, and said feebly that it was a beautiful day and she hoped Miss Lee found Greenhill a pleasant place to—visit.

Sydney moved slowly out of the tent and found Jack Desmond. He was standing near with Camille, who looked her best in a pale-blue summer silk and a black hat trimmed with roses. Jack and Camille never really knew how the great man had managed, but presently Margaret had gone away with him and his sister.

Jack and Camille looked at each other.

"Oh, Jack, ought you to have let her go?" said Camille.

"What made you let her go?" asked Jack.

"I don't know. I couldn't say anything. That man has a tremendous way with him. Goodness!"

"He is all right here in the place, anyhow," said Jack. "They look up to him. He is a big bug here. Comes of a family like Margaret's, though he hasn't much money. Some chaps were braggin' that they had a bigger show than her right here, and I found out."

"Suppose," said Camille, "Margaret does not come back?"

"He could not keep her without bein' arrested," declared Jack, but he looked uneasy. He had, however, looked uneasy for some time. The fact was, Margaret had been very gradually losing weight. Moreover, she was not well. That very night, after the show was over, Bill Stark, the little dark man, had a talk with the Desmonds about it.

"Truth is, before long, if you don't look out, you'll have

to pad her," said Bill; "and giants don't amount to a row of pins after that begins."

Camille looked worried and sulky. "She ain't very well, anyhow," said she. "I ain't going to kill Margaret."

"It's a good thing she's got a chance to have a night's rest in a house," said Bill Stark.

"The fat man has asked her to stay with him and his sister while the show is here," said Jack.

"The sister invited her," said Camille, with a little stiffness. She was common, but she had lived with Lees, and her mother had married a Lee. She knew what was due Margaret, and also due herself.

"The truth is," said Camille, "this is an awful sort of life for a woman like Margaret. She and her folks were never used to anything like it."

"Why didn't you make your beauty husband hustle and take care of her and you, then?" demanded Bill, who admired Camille, and disliked her because she had no eyes for him.

"My husband has been unfortunate. He has done the best he could," responded Camille. "Come, Jack; no use talking about it any longer. Guess Margaret will pick up. Come along. I'm tired out."

That night Margaret Lee slept in a sweet chamber with muslin curtains at the windows, in a massive old mahogany bed, much like hers which had been sacrificed at an auction sale. The bed linen was linen, and smelled of lavender. Margaret was too happy to sleep. She lay in the cool, fragrant sheets and was happy, and convinced of the presence of the God to whom she had prayed. All night Sydney Lord sat downstairs in his book-walled sanctum and studied over the situation. It was a crucial one. The great psychological moment of Sydney Lord's life for knight errantry had arrived. He studied the thing from every point of view. There was no romance about it. These were hard, sordid,

tragic, ludicrous facts with which he had to deal. He knew
to a nicety the agonies which Margaret suffered. He knew,
because of his own capacity for sufferings of like stress.
"And she is a woman and a lady," he said, aloud.

If Sydney had been rich enough, the matter would have
been simple. He could have paid Jack and Camille enough
to quiet them, and Margaret could have lived with him
and his sister and their two old servants. But he was not
rich; he was even poor. The price to be paid for Margaret's
liberty was a bitter one, but it was that or nothing. Sydney
faced it. He looked about the room. To him the walls lined
with the dull gleams of old books were lovely. There was
an oil portrait of his mother over the mantelshelf. The
weather was warm now, and there was no need for a hearth
fire, but how exquisitely homelike and dear that room could
be when the snow drove outside and there was the leap of
flame on the hearth! Sydney was a scholar and a gentleman.
He had led a gentle and sequestered life. Here in his
native village there were none to gibe and sneer. The contrast of the traveling show would be as great for him as it
had been for Margaret, but he was the male of the species,
and she the female. Chivalry, racial, harking back to the
beginning of nobility in the human, to its earliest dawn,
fired Sydney. The pale daylight invaded the study. Sydney,
as truly as any knight of old, had girded himself, and with
no hope, no thought of reward, for the battle in the eternal
service of the strong for the weak, which makes the true
worth of the strong.

There was only one way. Sydney Lord took it. His
sister was spared the knowledge of the truth for a long
while. When she knew, she did not lament; since Sydney
had taken the course, it must be right. As for Margaret,
not knowing the truth, she yielded. She was really on the
verge of illness. Her spirit was of too fine a strain to enable
her body to endure long. When she was told that she was

to remain with Sydney's sister while Sydney went away on business, she made no objection. A wonderful sense of relief, as of wings of healing being spread under her despair, was upon her. Camille came to bid her good-by.

"I hope you have a nice visit in this lovely house," said Camille, and kissed her. Camille was astute, and to be trusted. She did not betray Sydney's confidence. Sydney used a disguise—a dark wig over his partially bald head and a little make-up—and he traveled about with the show and sat on three chairs, and shook hands with the gaping crowd, and was curiously happy. It was discomfort; it was ignominy; it was maddening to support by the exhibition of his physical deformity a perfectly worthless young couple like Jack and Camille Desmond, but it was all superbly ennobling for the man himself.

Always as he sat on his three chairs, immense, grotesque— the more grotesque for his splendid dignity of bearing—there was in his soul of a gallant gentleman the consciousness of that other, whom he was shielding from a similar ordeal. Compassion and generosity, so great that they comprehended love itself and excelled its highest type, irradiated the whole being of the fat man exposed to the gaze of his inferiors. Chivalry, which rendered him almost godlike, strengthened him for his task. Sydney thought always of Margaret as distinct from her physical self, a sort of crystalline, angelic soul, with no encumbrance of earth. He achieved a purely spiritual conception of her. And Margaret, living again her gentle lady life, was likewise ennobled by a gratitude which transformed her. Always a clear and beautiful soul, she gave out new lights of character like a jewel in the sun. And she also thought of Sydney as distinct from his physical self. The consciousness of the two human beings, one of the other, was a consciousness of two wonderful lines of good and beauty, moving forever parallel, separate, and inseparable in an eternal harmony of spirit.

# XXII. *THE OUTSIDE OF THE HOUSE*[1]

BARR CENTER almost always excited the amusement of strangers. "Why Barr Center?" they would inquire, and follow up the query, if they were facetious, with another, "The center of what?"

In reality, Barr Center, the little village where lived the Edgewaters, the Ellertons, the Dinsmores, and a few more very good old New England families, was hardly anything but a center, and almost, regarded geographically, the mere pin prick of a center of four villages. As a matter of fact, the apex of a triangle would have been a more accurate description. The village came first on the old turnpike from the city; Barr-by-the-Sea was on the right, three miles away; Leicester, which had formerly been West Barr, was three miles to the left; South Barr was three miles to the south.

There was a popular saying that Barr Center was three miles from everywhere. All four villages had, of course, been originally one, the Precinct of Barr. Leicester had been the first to revolt and establish a separate township and claim a different name. Leicester was the name of the one wealthy old family of the village, which had bestowed its soldiers' monument, its town hall, and its library, and had improved the cemetery and contributed half of the high school.

Barr-by-the-Sea came next, and that had serious and legitimate reasons for individuality. From being a mere summer colony of tents and rude cottages it had grown to be almost a city, frequented by wealthy city folk, who had beautiful residences along the shore. Barr-by-the-Sea was so large and important that it finally made an isosceles triangle of the original Precinct of Barr. All summer long it hummed with gay life, ending in the autumn with a carnival as a grand crescendo. Barr-by-the-Sea was, however, not the center. It boasted no old family, resident all the year round, as did Barr Center.

South Barr was the least important of all. It was simply the petering out of the Barrs. It was a little farming hamlet which humbly sold butter, fresh eggs, and garden truck to Barr-by-the-Sea for the delectation of the rich folk who dwelt in the hotels and boarding houses and stately residences on the ocean front.

Barr-by-the-Sea was an exclusive summer resort. Its few permanent inhabitants were proud of it, and none were prouder than old Captain Joe Dickson and his wife Martha. The Dicksons lived in a tiny house beyond the fashionable limits. They were on the opposite side of the road from the sea. The house stood in a drift of sandy soil, pierced by coarse beach grass like green swords. Captain Joe, however, had reclaimed a little garden from the easily conquered waste, and his beans, his cucumbers, and his tomatoes were flourishing.

In front of the house Martha had two great tubs of hydrangeas, which she colored a ghastly blue with bluing water from her weekly wash. Captain Joe did not approve of the unnatural blue.

"Why don't ye leave the posies the way the Lord made 'em?" he inquired.

"They have them this way at a lot of the grand places," replied Martha. "The big bugs color them."

"Ruther guess the big bugs ain't any bigger than the Lord A'mighty," returned Captain Joe. "I guess if He had thought them posies would look better blue He would have made 'em blue in the fust place."

Captain Joe, having spoken his mind, puffed his pipe amiably over the tops of the blue flowers. He sat on his bit of a porch, tipping back comfortably in his old chair.

Martha did not prolong the discussion. She was not much of a talker. Captain Joe always claimed that a voyage with him around the world in a sailing vessel had cured her of talking too much in her youth.

"Poor Marthy used to be a regular buzz saw at the talk," he would say, "but rockin' round the world with such a gale that she couldn't hear her own tongue wag, and bein' scared 'most to death, cured her."

Whether the great, primeval noises of the world had, in fact, subdued the woman to silence, rendering her incapable of much sounding of her own little note all through her life, or not, she was a very still woman. She went silently about her household tasks. When they were done there was much mending while her husband smoked.

Over across the road the littered, wave-marked beach sloped broadly to the sea. There were several boats anchored. One was Captain Joe's, the *Martha Dickson*. He had been out in it fishing that very morning, had had a good catch, and sold well to the customers who flocked on the beach when the fishing boats came in. The rich people sent their servants with baskets for the fresh fish.

Joe had sold his catch, with the exception of one fine cod, which Martha was making into a savory chowder. Captain Joe sniffed with pleasure the odor of frying onions which were to make the foundation of the good dish. He gazed at the sea, which now and then lapped into view with a foaming crest over the beach. There was no passing, as a rule. The fine road for driving and motoring stopped several yards before Joe's house was reached. He was mildly surprised, therefore, when a runabout with a red cross on the front, with a young man at the wheel and a pretty young girl by his side, came skidding over the sand and stopped.

"Any fresh fish?" inquired the young man, who was Doctor Tom Ellerton.

Joe shook his head.

"Know where I can get any?"

"Guess mebbe you can get a cod at the third house from me. He was late gettin' in and didn't sell the hull. But you'll capsize if you try to go there in that."

Tom eyed the road billowing with sand. "Sit here while I find out," he told Margy, his sister. She nodded.

After Tom had gone plowing through the sand, Captain Joe rose stiffly. He was not a very old man, but a broken leg had not been set properly, and kept him from his life-work of cruising the high seas.

He limped up to the car. "Pooty hot day," he remarked.

"Very," replied Margy.

"Wish I'd had the fish. Sold all my catch except the cod Marthy's cookin'."

Margy sniffed appreciatively. "A chowder?" she inquired.

Joe nodded. "About the only way to cook a cod. Goin' to have yourn cooked that way?"

"It isn't for us," explained Margy. "My brother is trying to find some really fresh fish for an old lady who is ill. My brother is a doctor. He has just been to see her. She wanted fresh fish, and he said he would try to find some. Their servants are all busy because they are closing the house. They are going to sail for Europe tomorrow."

"What house?" inquired Joe, eagerly.

"The very large house on the ocean side of the road, about half a mile back."

"The one with all them yaller flowers in the front yard, and a garden of 'em on the roof, with vines hangin' over?"

Margy nodded. "That sounds like it," said she. "There are two square towers, one on each side, then the flowers and vines are on the balcony between; and there is a roof garden, too; and there are quantities of beautiful flowers on the grounds. It is a lovely place."

"Know the name of the folks that live there?"

"Willard," replied Margy. She eyed Joe with surprise.

"Lord!" said he. "They goin' away so soon?"

He paid no more attention to Margy, but limped into the house, and the girl heard loud exclamations. Then she saw Tom coming with a fine glistening fish in each hand.

"I have one for us, too," he said as he got into the car. "They are fine fish."

Tom put on power, as he wished not only to deliver the fish to the Willards fresh, but to reach home with his own in good condition, and it was a scorching day. Margy clung to her side of the car as they spun along. After the fish had been left at the grand Willard house, and a beautiful young lady in a pale-blue gown had thanked the young doctor charmingly, and they were on a smooth road, Margy asked Tom why he thought the lame man, of whom he had inquired about the fish, had been so interested in the Willard family.

"Oh, probably he is one of the old residents here. I discovered some time ago that they feel a queer interest in the comings and goings of the summer folks," said Tom. "Their lives are pretty narrow eight months of the year. They have to be interested in something outside themselves. I think lots of them have a feeling that they own a good deal that they only have liberty to look at."

"I can see how a fisherman can feel that he owns the sea," said Margy. "Maybe it is because so many of them are fishermen."

She looked reflective with her deep-set blue eyes. Tom cast a quick glance at her. "Maybe," he said.

Tom was not imaginative. When Margy said things like that he always wondered if she were well. He began to plan a prescription for her as they sped along.

He did not know how intensely Margy had felt that she owned the sea, just from looking at it, when she had sat in the car waiting for him when he was making professional calls, and that her reasoning was quite logical and not unnecessarily imaginative. If she considered that she owned the sea, which is the vast untaxed asset of the world, how much more would the fisherman who got his daily bread from it?

Meantime, the fisherman with whom she had talked was in excited colloquy with his wife in the kitchen and living room of the little house. The room, though comfortable and clean, was poorly equipped, with the exception of various articles that were at direct odds with all else. There was a cooking stove, on which the chowder was steaming. There was a kitchen table, set for a meal with the commonest utensils, save that in the center, ready for the chowder, was a bowl of old Japanese pottery which would have adorned a palace. Martha did not think much of this bowl, which Joe had brought home from one of his voyages. She considered the decorations ugly, and used it to save a lovely one from the ten-cent store, decorated with pink rosebuds. Martha could understand pink rosebuds, but she could not fathom dragons and ugly, grinning faces of Oriental fancy.

There was a lounge with a hideous cover, two old chairs worn into hollows of comfort, two kitchen chairs, an old clock, and a superb teakwood table. Martha did not care for that, either. The contortions of the carved wood gave her a vague uneasiness. She kept it covered with an old fringed spread, and used to set her bread to rise on it. On the mantel, besides the clock and three kerosene lamps, was a beautiful old Satsuma vase, and a pressed glass one, which Martha loved. The glass one was cracked, and she told Joe she did not see why the other vase could not have suffered instead. Joe agreed with her. He did not care much for the treasures which he had brought from foreign ports, except the shells—lovely, pinked-lipped ones that were crowded on the shelf between the other things, and completely filled more shelves which Joe had made expressly to hold them. The shelves were in three tiers, and the shells were mounted on them, catching the light from broken surfaces of rose and pearl and silver. Martha privately considered that the shells involved considerable work. She washed them carefully, and kept them free from dust, but she also admired them.

In front of the outer door was a fine old prayer rug of dull, exquisite tones. Martha kept it there for Joe to wipe his feet on, because it was so faded, but she had a bright red one in the center of the room. Joe never stepped on that until his shoes were entirely clean. He had made quite sure there was not a speck of dust to injure this brilliant rug before he entered to give Martha the intelligence.

"They are goin' away from Our House tomorrow," said he.

Martha, standing over the chowder, turned, spoon in hand. She waved the spoon as if it were a fan. "Before the carnival?" said she.

Martha was a small, wide eyed woman with sleek hair. She was not pretty, but had a certain effect of being exactly in place which gave the impression of prettiness to some people.

"They are goin' to sail for Europe," said Joe.

"I suppose for His health," said Martha. Nobody could excel the air of perfect proprietorship with which she uttered the masculine pronoun. The man indicated might have been her own father, or her brother, or her son.

"I guess so," said Joe. "He has looked pooty bad lately when I've seen him."

"I suppose They are goin'?"

"I s'pose so, because they are closin' the house. That young doctor from the Center stopped out here just now, and wanted to know where he could get fresh fish, and I told him I guessed Mac had some left; and whilst he was gone his sister—she was with him—told me they were closin' the house, and Old Lady Willard wanted fresh fish, and they were out huntin' for it, because all the help was busy."

"That means Old Lady Willard's goin', and Him, and his Wife, and the three girls, Grace and Marie and Maud, and the two little boys."

"Yes."

"And they will take the ladies' maids, and His man. Maybe that pretty young lady that visits there so much will go, too."

"Maybe; and the lady that teaches the little boys will go."

"O Lord, yes! They couldn't get on without her. My! there will be 'most enough to fill the ship."

"About enough to sink my old one I sailed around when you was aboard," said Joe, and laughed.

Martha never laughed. The seriousness of New England was in her very soul. She was happy and good-natured, but she saw nothing whatever to laugh at in all creation. She never had.

"Land, yes!" said she. "You know there wa'n't any room in that little cabin."

"Not more'n enough to hold you and your Bible and sewin' machine," said Captain Joe. He cast a glance at the old sewing machine as he spoke, and laughed again. It was perfectly useless because of that long-ago voyage, and the fact always amused him. Martha considered it no laughing matter. The sewing machine was dear to her, even in its wrecked state. She kept the Bible on it, and a little cup and saucer.

"The chowder's done," said she. "Draw up, Joe."

Joe drew up a chair to the table. "Smells prime," said he. "Guess it's all right."

"Ef your chowders ever wa'n't all right I'd think the sun was goin' to rise in the west next mornin'," said Joe.

Martha ladled the chowder into the beautiful bowl, then into heavy, chipped plates. The two ate with relish.

"Tomorrow's Saturday," said Joe. "That means we can go to Our House come Sunday."

Martha nodded. Her good mouth widened in the semblance of a smile. Her steady eyes gleamed with happy intelligence at her husband.

"It will seem nice," said she. "Land! I'd been thinkin' we might have to wait till 'way into October, the way we did last year, and now it's only the first of August."

"I'm feelin' jest as set up as you be about it," said Joe.

That night all the family from the great house where Tom Ellerton had called went by train to Boston. They were to stay in the city overnight to be ready for the steamer. Not one of the numerous company even noticed Captain Joe Dickson and his wife Martha, who were at the station watching them closely, hearing everything that was said, noting all details—the baggage, the host of servants.

All the servants were to be out of the house next day, the Dicksons heard Her tell another lady who inquired. "Only a caretaker, the same old colored man we always employ," stated Mrs. Richard Willard, tall, elegant, a bit weary of manner. "The servants will finish closing the house tomorrow, then some of them have vacations, and the rest will be in our Boston house. We take only our maids and Mr. Willard's man up tonight. We shall not go to the city house at all ourselves. It will be much more sensible to stay at the hotel."

"Of course," said the lady. Then she said something about an unexpected start, and so early in the season, and Mrs. Willard replied that to her nothing was ever unexpected. That had ceased with her youth, and Mr. Willard was not quite well, and there were seasons all over creation. She said that with a pleasant smile—weary, however.

Martha eyed her keenly when she and Joe, after the train

with all the Willards on board had pulled out, were walking home.

"She said that She didn't look none too strong, and she guessed it was a good thing She was going." Martha said that as if Mrs. Richard Willard, who had never heard of her, was her dearly beloved friend or relative.

Joe nodded solemnly. "She did look sorter peaked," he agreed. "As for Him, he didn't look no worse than usual to me, but I guess it's jest as well for them they're off, let alone us."

The remark seemed enigmatic, but Martha understood. They walked home from the station. They passed the Willard house, standing aloof from the highway like a grand Colonial lady.

"The awnin's are down," said Martha, "and they've begun to board up the winders."

Joe nodded.

"It is unlooked for, as far as we are concerned," said Martha, with a happy widening of her lips.

"Day arter tomorrer—only think of it!" said Captain Joe. "Goin' out fishin' tomorrer?"

"Reckon not; got an considerable today, and I want to git my hair cut tomorrer."

"I'm goin' to trim my bunnit over, and fix my best dress a little, too; and I guess your best suit needs brushin'."

"There's a spot on the coat."

"I'll git it off. Land! I do hope Sunday is pleasant."

"Goin' to be. It's a dry moon," declared Joe.

However, Sunday, although fair, was one of those fervid days of summer which threatened storm.

"It's goin' to shower," declared Martha. She was clad in her best black silk, hot, and tightly fitted, trimmed with cascades of glittering jet. A jet aigrette on her bonnet caught the light. She had fastened a vivid rose on one side of the bonnet to do honor to the occasion. Crowning glory—she wore her white gloves, her one pair, which was the treasure of her wardrobe.

"Better take the umbrell', I guess," said Joe.

"Guess you'd better."

Joe held his head stiffly because of his linen collar. He wore a blue suit much too large for him, but it was spotless. He took the umbrella from behind the door. It was distinctly not worthy of the occasion, although it was entirely serviceable. Still, it was large, and greenish-black, and bulged determinedly from its mooring of rubber at the top.

Martha, as they walked along, looked uncomfortably at the umbrella. "Can't ye roll the umbrell' up tight, the way I see 'em?" she inquired.

Joe stopped, unfastened the rubber strap, and essayed to roll it. It was in vain. "The umbrell' is too thick," he said. "No use, Marthy. It's a good umbrell'. If it showers it will keep it off, but I can't make it look slim."

"Well, don't show it any more than you can help," admonished Martha.

Joe henceforth carried the umbrella between himself and Martha. It continually collided with their legs, but Martha's black-silk skirt flopped over its green voluminousness and it was comparatively unseen.

"I declare; it does seem like showerin'," said Joe.

"You said it was a dry moon."

"Ef thar's anything in nature to be depended on least of anything else it's a dry moon," said Joe, with an air of completely absolving himself from all responsibility in the matter of the moon.

"Of course in such hot weather nobody can tell when a thunder-tempest is goin' to come up," said Martha. She was extremely uncomfortable in her tight black raiment. Drops of perspiration stood on her forehead.

"If we were goin' anywhere else I'd take off my gloves," said she.

"Well, Marthy, long as it's the first time this year, reckon you'd better stand it, if you can," returned Joe. "My collar is about chokin' me, but it's the first time this year we're goin' there, you know, Marthy."

"That's just the way I feel," agreed Martha.

The sun beat upon their heads. "Ef the umbrell' was a little better-lookin' I'd h'ist her," said Joe.

"Now, Joe, you know you can't."

"I know it, Marthy. I can't."

They were now in the midst of a gay, heterogeneous Sunday throng. The church bells were ringing. A set of chimes outpealed the rest. Elegantly arrayed people—the ladies holding brilliant parasols at all angles above their heads crowned with plumes and flowers; the gentlemen in miraculously creased trousers, many of them moving with struts, swinging sticks—met and went their way. The road was filled with a never-ending procession of motor cars, carriages, horses, and riders. Barr-by-the-Sea was displaying her charms like a beauty at a ball.

Many were bound for church; more for pleasure. There were country people dressed in cheap emulation of the wealthy, carrying baskets with luncheon, who had come to Barr-by-the-Sea to spend Sunday and have an outing. They were silent, foolishly observant, and awed by the splendors around them.

Joe Dickson and his wife Martha moved as the best of them. There was no subserviency in them. They had imbibed the wide freedom and lordliness of the sea, and at any time moved among equals; but today their errand made them move as lords. By what childlike sophistry it had come to pass none could tell, but Joe Dickson, poor ex-captain of a sailing vessel, and his wife Martha were, in their own conviction, on their way to reëstablishment in the best mansion on that coast, inhabited by the wealthy of the country.

When they reached the Willard house Joe and Martha ducked under the iron chain across the carriage drive, and proceeded along the glittering smoothness bordered by brilliant flowers, having no realization of the true state of affairs.

"I declare, it does seem good to get back," said Joe.

"It certainly does," said Martha, "and so much earlier than we'd looked forward to."

"I calculated they might stay till late in October, the way they did last year," said Joe, joyously. "Just see that red-geranium bed, Marthy."

"Them ain't geraniums; them is begonias," said Martha, haughtily.

"It always seems to me as if all the flowers was geraniums," said Joe. He laughed.

Martha did not smile. "They ain't," said she.

They passed around to the back of the grand house. The wide veranda was cleared except for two weather-beaten old chairs. The windows, except one on the second floor, were boarded over. The house looked as if asleep, with closed eyes, before that magnificent ocean, a vast brilliance as of gemlike facets reflecting all the glory of the whole earth and the heavens above the earth. The tide was coming in. Now and then a wave broke with a rainbow toss, quite over the sea wall of the beach. The coast in places—and this was one of them—was treacherous.

Captain Joe and his Martha sat down in the rude chairs. Martha sighed a sigh of utter rapture.

"Land! it is certainly nice to be here again," said she.

Joe, however, scowled at the sea wall. "They had ought to have seen to that wall afore they went off," he said.

"Land! It's safe, ain't it?"

"I dunno'. Nobody never knows nothin' when the sea's consarned. Ef they had asked me I'd said: 'Hev a lot of men on the job, and make sure there ain't no shaky places in that 'ere wall; and whilst you're about it, build it up about six foot higher. It wouldn't cut off your view none.' The hull of it is, the sea never quits the job. Everything on earth quits the job, one way or t'other, but that sea is right on, and she's goin' to be right on it; and bein' right on the job, and never quittin', means somethin' doin' and somethin' bein' done, and nobody knows just what."

"I guess it's all right," said Martha. "It ain't likely that they would have gone off and left this house unless it was; and money ain't no object."

"Sometimes folks with money gits the wrong end of the bargain," said Joe. "Money don't mean nothin' to the sea. It's swallowed more'n the hull earth holds, and it's ready to swallow till the day of jedgment. That wall had ought to be looked arter."

There was a sound of the one unboarded window being opened, and it immediately framed an aged colored face, with a fringe of gray beard like wool. The owner of the face could not be seen, and, because of the veranda roof, he could not see, but, his ears being quick to note sounds above the rush of the waters, he heard Joe and Martha talking on the veranda. Presently he came up the veranda steps. He was the caretaker, and his door of entrance and exit was in the basement, under the veranda. He was a tall old colored man with an important mien.

When his head appeared above the veranda floor Joe and Martha rose. "Good day, Sam," they said almost in concert.

Sam bowed with dignity. "I 'lowed it was you," he said, then sat down on a fixed stone bench near the chairs.

"So they've gone," said Joe, as he and Martha resumed their seats.

"Yassir. Mr. Richard is kind of pindlin', and the doctor 'lowed he'd better get away. They went day before yesterday, and all the help last night."

Joe nodded. Martha nodded. They all sat still, watching the waves dash at the sea wall and break over it.

"They had ought to have looked at that wall," said Joe, presently.

The colored man laughed with the optimism of his race. "That wall has held more'n twenty year—eber since the house was built," said he. "Wall all right."

"Dunno'," said Joe.

Martha was not as optimistic as the colored man, but she was entirely happy. "Seems sorter nice to be settin' here ag'in, Sam," said she.

"Yes'm," said Sam.

"We've got a baked fish for dinner, and some fresh beans," said Martha. "We thought you'd come and have dinner with us, the way you always do the first day."

"I 'lowed you'd ask me, thank ye, marm," said Sam, with his wonderful dignity.

"Seems nice to be settin' here ag'in," repeated Martha, like a bird with one note.

"Yes'm." Sam's own face wore a pleased expression. He, too, felt the charm of possession. All three, the man and wife and the colored retainer, realized divine property rights. The outside of that grand house was as much theirs as it was any soul's on the face of the earth. They owned that and the ocean. Only Joe's face was now and then disturbed when a wave, crested in foam, came over the sea wall. He knew the sea well enough to love and fear it, while he owned it.

The three sat there all the morning. Then they all went away to the little Dickson house. The thunder was rumbling in the northwest. They walked rapidly. Joe spread the umbrella, but no rain came. There was a sharp flash of lightning and a prodigious report. All three turned about and looked in the direction of the Willard house.

"Struck somewheres, but it didn't strike thar," said Joe.

When they reached home Martha immediately changed her dress and set about preparing dinner. The two men sat on Joe's upturned boat, on the sloping beach opposite, and smoked and watched the storm. It did not rain for a long time, although the thunder and lightning were terrific. The colored man cringed at the detonations and flashes, but Joe was obdurate. He had sailed stormy seas too much to be anything but a cool critic of summer showers. However, after each unusual flash and report the two stared in the direction of the Willard house.

"Seems as if I had ought to have stayed there," remarked Sam, trembling, after one great crash.

"What could you have done? That didn't strike no house. Struck out at sea. I'm keepin' an ear out for the fire alarm," said Joe.

"Have you got it ready?" inquired Sam, mysteriously.

Joe nodded. He flushed slightly. Sam was under orders to keep secret the fact that the poor old sailorman had the preceding year purchased a fire extinguisher, with a view to personally protecting the House. "You can run faster than I can, and you know how to use it," said Joe.

Then another storm came up swiftly. Martha came to the door. "It's another!" cried she.

Joe rose. "Get it for me, Marthy," said he.

Martha brought the fire extinguisher.

"Guess you and me had better be on the bridge ef another's comin'," said Joe, grimly, to Sam.

The two disappeared down the road in a gray drive of rain. Martha screamed to Joe to take the umbrella, his best suit would get wet, but he did not hear her. Sam went on a run and Joe hobbled after. They stood on the Willard veranda and kept watch. Both men were drenched. The waves broke over the sea wall, and the salt wind drove the rain in the faces of the men.

At last it was over, and they went back to the Dickson

house. The odor of fish and beans greeted them. Martha had continued her dinner preparations. She was not in the least afraid of storms. She, too, only thought of danger to the grand house, but she had great faith in her husband and the fire extinguisher, whose unknown virtues loomed gigantic to her feminine mind.

She made Joe change his best suit, which she hung carefully to dry on the clothesline, and she gave Sam a ragged old suit, and hung up his drenched attire also. "You couldn't do much about taking care of things if you got the rheumatiz," said she.

They ate their dinner in comfort, for the thunderstorm had conquered the heat. Afterward, while Martha cleared away, the men sat on the porch and went to sleep. Martha herself slept on the old lounge. She dreamed that she was on the veranda of the Willard house and she awoke to no disillusion. Next day, and all the following days, for nearly a whole year, she and Joe could be there if they chose. They were in possession; for so long that dispossession seemed unreality.

That was the happiest summer Joe and Martha had ever known in Barr-by-the-Sea. There were long afternoons, when Joe had been out and sold his catch; there were wonderful moonlight nights, when they lived on the outside of the beautiful house and inherited the earth.

The fall was late that year. Long into October, and even during warm days in November, they could assemble on the veranda and enjoy their wealth. There came a storm in October, however, which increased Joe's fears concerning the stanchness of the sea wall. He conferred with Sam. Sam was hard to move from his position that the past proved the future, but finally his grudging assistance was obtained. The two worked hard. They did what they could, but even then Joe would look at the wall and shake his head.

"She ought to be six foot higher," he told Martha.

If Sam could have written, he would have pleaded with him to write the Willards abroad, urging that they order the raising of the wall, but Sam could not write. Joe went to a real-estate agent and talked, but the man laughed at him.

"Don't butt in, Joe," he advised. "Nobody is going to thank you. I think the wall is all right."

"It ain't," declared Joe.

Joe was right. In December there came the storm and the high tide. Joe was up at two o'clock in the morning, awakened by the wild cry of the sea, that wildest of all creation, which now and then runs amuck and leaps barriers and makes men dream of prehistoric conditions.

He hastened along the road, with that terrible menace in his ears, dragging a great length of rope. Martha stayed behind on her knees, praying. Nobody ever knew quite what happened; that is, all the details. They did know that in some miraculous fashion the sea wall of the Willard house had been strengthened by frantic labor of poor men who owned not a stick as valuable as the poorest beam in the house, and that they were urged on by Captain Joe Dickson, with his lame leg and his heart of a lover and a hero. They knew that strange things had been piled against that wall; all the weighty articles from the basement of the Willard house—wood, boats, sandbags, stones, everything which had power to offer an ounce of resistance. They knew that the wall stood and the house was saved, and old Sam was blubbering over old Captain Joe Dickson lying spent almost to death on the veranda where he had been carried.

"Tell Marthy Our House is safe," stammered old Captain Joe. Then he added something which was vaguely made out to be a note of triumph: "The sea didn't git me."

When they took him home to Martha she was very calm. All her life, since she had married Joe, she had had in her heart the resolution which should be in the hearts of the

wives of all poor sailormen and fishermen, who defy the
splendid, eternal danger of the sea to gain their sustenance.

It was Doctor Tom Ellerton, spinning over from Barr
Center, at the risk of his neck and his car, who saved Captain Joe, although the old man was saved only to spend
the rest of his life in bed or wheel chair, and never could
sail the seas again. It was Doctor Tom Ellerton who told the
Willards, and it was they who sent the wheel chair and
gave Joe a pension for saving their house. Mrs. Richard
Willard (Richard had died during their stay abroad) came
out on purpose to see Joe. She was sad, and weary, and
elegant in her deep black.

She told Joe and Martha what was to be done, and they
thanked her and gave her daughter some of their choicest
shells. They were quite dignified and grateful about her
bounty. On the train going home Mrs. Willard told her
daughter that they were evidently superior people. "They
belong to the few who can take with an air of giving and not
offend," said Mrs. Willard.

Neither of them dreamed of the true state of the case:
that subtly and happily the old man and his wife possessed
what they called their own home in a fuller sense than they
ever could. More than the announcement of the comfortable annuity had meant Mrs. Willard's statement that
they would not open the House at all next summer; they
would visit with relatives in the Berkshires, then go abroad.

Joe and Martha looked at each other, and their eyes said:
"We can go to Our House as soon as you can wheel me
over there. We can stay there as much as we like, all one
year."

Mrs. Willard saw the look, and did not understand. How
could she? It was inconceivable that these two people should
own the outside of her home to such an extent that their
tenure became well-nigh immortal.

# XXIII.  *CORONATION*[1]

Jim Bennet had never married. He had passed middle life and possessed considerable property. Susan Adkins kept house for him. She was a widow and a very distant relative. Jim had two nieces, his brother's daughters. One, Alma Beecher, was married; the other, Amanda, was not. The nieces had naïvely grasping views concerning their uncle and his property. They stated freely that they considered him unable to care for it; that a guardian should be appointed and the property be theirs at once. They consulted Lawyer Thomas Hopkinson with regard to it; they discoursed at length upon what they claimed to be an idiosyncrasy of Jim's denoting failing mental powers.

"He keeps a perfect slew of cats, and has a coal fire for them in the woodshed all winter," said Amanda.

"Why in thunder shouldn't he keep a fire in the woodshed if he wants to?" demanded Hopkinson. "I know of no law against it. And there isn't a law in the country regulating the number of cats a man can keep." Thomas Hopkinson, who was an old friend of Jim's, gave his prominent chin an upward jerk as he sat in his office armchair before his clients.

"There is something besides cats," said Alma.

"What?"

"He talks to himself."

"What in creation do you expect the poor man to do? He can't talk to Susan Adkins about a blessed thing except tidies and pincushions. That woman hasn't a thought in her mind outside her soul's salvation and fancy work. Jim has to talk once in a while to keep himself a man. What if he does talk to himself? I talk to myself. Next thing you will want to be appointed guardian over me, Amanda."

Hopkinson was a bachelor, and Amanda flushed angrily.

"He wasn't what I call even gentlemanly," she told Alma, when the two were on their way home.

"I suppose Tom Hopkinson thought you were setting your cap at him," retorted Alma. She relished the dignity of her married state, and enjoyed giving her spinster sister little claws when occasion called. However, Amanda had a temper of her own, and she could claw back.

"*You* needn't talk," said she. "You only took Joe Beecher when you had given up getting anybody better. You wanted Tom Hopkinson yourself. I haven't forgotten that blue silk dress you got and wore to meeting. You needn't talk. You know you got that dress just to make Tom look at you, and he didn't. You needn't talk."

"I wouldn't have married Tom Hopkinson if he had been the only man on the face of the earth," declared Alma with dignity; but she colored hotly.

Amanda sniffed. "Well, as near as I can find out, Uncle Jim can go on talking to himself and keeping cats, and we can't do anything," said she.

When the two women were home, they told Alma's husband, Joe Beecher, about their lack of success. They were quite heated with their walk and excitement. "I call it a shame," said Alma. "Anybody knows that poor Uncle Jim would be better off with a guardian."

"Of course," said Amanda. "What man that had a grain of horse sense would do such a crazy thing as to keep a coal fire in a woodshed?"

"For such a slew of cats, too," said Alma, nodding fiercely.

Alma's husband, Joe Beecher, spoke timidly and undecidedly in the defense. "You know," he said, "that Mrs.

Adkins wouldn't have those cats in the house, and cats mostly like to sit round where it's warm."

His wife regarded him. Her nose wrinkled. "I suppose next thing *you'll* be wanting to have a cat round where it's warm, right under my feet, with all I have to do," said she. Her voice had an actual acidity of sound.

Joe gasped. He was a large man with a constant expression of wondering inquiry. It was the expression of his babyhood; he had never lost it, and it was an expression which revealed truly the state of his mind. Always had Joe Beecher wondered, first of all at finding himself in the world at all, then at the various happenings of existence. He probably wondered more about the fact of his marriage with Alma Bennet than anything else, although he never betrayed his wonder. He was always painfully anxious to please his wife, of whom he stood in awe. Now he hastened to reply: "Why, no, Alma; of course I won't."

"Because," said Alma, "I haven't come to my time of life, through all the trials I've had, to be taking any chances of breaking my bones over any miserable, furry, four-footed animal that wouldn't catch a mouse if one run right under her nose."

"I don't want any cat," repeated Joe, miserably. His fear and awe of the two women increased. When his sister-in-law turned upon him he fairly cringed.

"Cats!" said Amanda. Then she sniffed. The sniff was worse than speech.

Joe repeated in a mumble that he didn't want any cats, and went out, closing the door softly after him, as he had been taught. However, he was entirely sure, in the depths of his subjugated masculine mind, that his wife and her sister had no legal authority whatever to interfere with their uncle's right to keep a hundred coal fires in his woodshed, for a thousand cats. He always had an inner sense of glee when he heard the two women talk over the matter. Once

Amanda had declared that she did not believe that Tom Hopkinson knew much about law, anyway.

"He seems to stand pretty high," Joe ventured with the utmost mildness.

"Yes, he does," admitted Alma, grudgingly.

"It does not follow he knows law," persisted Amanda, "and it *may* follow that he likes cats. There was that great Maltese tommy brushing round all the time we were in his office, but I didn't dare shoo him off for fear it might be against the law." Amanda laughed a very disagreeable little laugh. Joe said nothing, but inwardly he chuckled. It was the cause of man with man. He realized a great, even affectionate, understanding of Jim.

The day after his nieces had visited the lawyer's office, Jim was preparing to call on his friend Edward Hayward, the minister. Before leaving he looked carefully after the fire in the woodshed. The stove was large. Jim piled on the coal, regardless outwardly that the housekeeper, Susan Adkins, had slammed the kitchen door to indicate her contempt. Inwardly Jim felt hurt, but he had felt hurt so long from the same cause that the sensation had become chronic and was borne with a gentle patience. Moreover, there was something which troubled him more and was the reason for his contemplated call on his friend. He evened the coals on the fire with great care, and replenished from the pail in the ice box the cats' saucers. There was a circle of clean white saucers around the stove. Jim owned many cats; counting the kittens, there were probably over twenty. Mrs. Adkins counted them in the sixties. "Those sixty-seven cats," she said.

Jim often gave away cats when he was confident of securing good homes, but supply exceeded the demand. Now and then tragedies took place in that woodshed. Susan Adkins came bravely to the front upon these occasions. Quite convinced was Susan Adkins that she had a good home, and it behooved her to keep it, and she did not in the least object to drowning, now and then, a few very young kittens. She did this with neatness and dispatch while Jim walked to the store on an errand and was supposed to know nothing about it. There was simply not enough room in his woodshed for the accumulation of cats, although his heart could have held all.

That day, as he poured out the milk, cats of all ages and sizes and colors purred in a softly padding multitude around his feet, and he regarded them with love. There were tiger cats, Maltese cats, black-and-white cats, black cats and white cats, tommies and females, and his heart leaped to meet the pleading mews of all. The saucers were surrounded. Little pink tongues lapped. "Pretty pussy! pretty pussy!" cooed Jim, addressing them in general. He put on his overcoat and hat, which he kept on a peg behind the door. Jim had an armchair in the woodshed. He always sat there when he smoked; Susan Adkins demurred at his smoking in the house, which she kept so nice, and Jim did not dream of rebellion. He never questioned the right of a woman to bar tobacco smoke from a house. Before leaving he refilled some of the saucers. He was not sure that all of the cats were there; some might be afield, hunting, and he wished them to find refreshment when they returned. He stroked the splendid striped back of a great tiger tommy which filled his armchair. This cat was his special pet. He fastened the outer shed door with a bit of rope in order that it might not blow entirely open, and yet allow his feline friends to pass, should they choose. Then he went out.

The day was clear, with a sharp breath of frost. The fields gleamed with frost, offering to the eye a fine shimmer as of diamond dust under the brilliant blue sky, overspread in places with a dapple of little white clouds.

"White frost and mackerel sky; going to be falling

weather," Jim said, aloud, as he went out of the yard, crunching the crisp grass under heel.

Susan Adkins at a window saw his lips moving. His talking to himself made her nervous, although it did not render her distrustful of his sanity. It was fortunate that Susan had not told Jim that she disliked his habit. In that case he would have deprived himself of that slight solace; he would not have dreamed of opposing Susan's wishes. Jim had a great pity for the nervous whims, as he regarded them, of women—a pity so intense and tender that it verged on respect and veneration. He passed his nieces' house on the way to the minister's, and both were looking out of windows and saw his lips moving.

"There he goes, talking to himself like a crazy loon," said Amanda.

Alma nodded.

Jim went on, blissfully unconscious. He talked in a quiet monotone; only now and then his voice rose; only now and then there were accompanying gestures. Jim had a straight mile down the broad village street to walk before he reached the church and the parsonage beside it.

Jim and the minister had been friends since boyhood. They were graduates and classmates of the same college. Jim had had unusual educational advantages for a man coming from a simple family. The front door of the parsonage flew open when Jim entered the gate, and the minister stood there smiling. He was a tall, thin man with a wide mouth, which either smiled charmingly or was set with severity. He was as brown and dry as a wayside weed which winter had subdued as to bloom but could not entirely prostrate with all its icy storms and compelling blasts. Jim, advancing eagerly toward the warm welcome in the door, was a small man, and bent at that, but he had a handsome old face, with the rose of youth on the cheeks and the light of youth in the blue eyes, and the quick changes of youth, before emotions, about the mouth.

"Hullo, Jim!" cried Doctor Edward Hayward. Hayward, for a doctor of divinity, was considered somewhat lacking in dignity at times; still, he was Doctor Hayward, and the failing was condoned. Moreover, he was a Hayward, and the Haywards had been, from the memory of the oldest inhabitant, the great people of the village. Doctor Hayward's house was presided over by his widowed cousin, a lady of enough dignity to make up for any lack of it in the minister. There were three servants, besides the old butler who had been Hayward's attendant when he had been a young man in college. Village people were proud of their minister, with his degree and what they considered an imposing household retinue.

Hayward led, and Jim followed, to the least pretentious room in the house—not the study proper, which was lofty, book-lined, and leather-furnished, curtained with broad sweeps of crimson damask, but a little shabby place back of it, accessible by a narrow door. The little room was lined with shelves; they held few books, but a collection of queer and dusty things—strange weapons, minerals, odds and ends—which the minister loved and with which his lady cousin never interfered.

"Louisa," Hayward had told his cousin when she entered upon her post, "do as you like with the whole house, but let my little study alone. Let it look as if it had been stirred up with a garden rake—that little room is my territory, and no disgrace to you, my dear, if the dust rises in clouds at every step."

Jim was as fond of the little room as his friend. He entered, and sighed a great sigh of satisfaction as he sank into the shabby, dusty hollow of a large chair before the hearth fire. Immediately a black cat leaped into his lap, gazed at him with green-jewel eyes, worked her paws, purred, settled into a coil, and slept. Jim lit his pipe and threw the match blissfully on the floor. Doctor Hayward set an electric coffee urn at its work, for the little room was a curious mixture of the comfortable old and the comfortable modern.

"Sam shall serve our luncheon in here," he said, with a staid glee.

Jim nodded happily.

"Louisa will not mind," said Hayward. "She is precise, but she has a fine regard for the rights of the individual, which is most commendable." He seated himself in a companion chair to Jim's, lit his own pipe, and threw the match on the floor. Occasionally, when the minister was out, Sam, without orders so to do, cleared the floor of matches.

Hayward smoked and regarded his friend, who looked troubled despite his comfort. "What is it, Jim?" asked the minister at last.

"I don't know how to do what is right for me to do," replied the little man, and his face, turned toward his friend, had the puzzled earnestness of a child.

Hayward laughed. It was easily seen that his was the keener mind. In natural endowments there had never been equality, although there was great similarity of tastes. Jim, despite his education, often lapsed into the homely vernacular of which he heard so much. An involuntarily imitative man in externals was Jim, but essentially an original. Jim proceeded.

"You know, Edward, I have never been one to complain," he said, with an almost boyish note of apology.

"Never complained half enough; that's the trouble," returned the other.

"Well, I overheard something Mis' Adkins said to Mis' Amos Trimmer the other afternoon. Mis' Trimmer was calling on Mis' Adkins. I couldn't help overhearing unless I went outdoors, and it was snowing and I had a cold. I wasn't listening."

"Had a right to listen if you wanted to," declared Hayward, irascibly.

"Well, I couldn't help it unless I went outdoors. Mis' Adkins she was in the kitchen making light bread for supper, and Mis' Trimmer had sat right down there with her. Mis' Adkins's kitchen is as clean as a parlor, anyway. Mis' Adkins said to Mis' Trimmer, speaking of me—because Mis' Trimmer had just asked where I was and Mis' Adkins had said I was out in the woodshed sitting with the cats and smoking—Mis' Adkins said, 'He's just a doormat, that's what he is.' Then Mis' Trimmer says, 'The way he lets folks ride over him beats me.' Then Mis' Adkins says again: 'He's nothing but a doormat. He lets everybody that wants to just trample on him and grind their dust into him, and he acts real pleased and grateful.' "

Hayward's face flushed. "Did Mrs. Adkins mention that she was one of the people who used you for a doormat?" he demanded.

Jim threw back his head and laughed like a child, with the sweetest sense of unresentful humor. "Lord bless my soul, Edward," replied Jim, "I don't believe she ever thought of that."

"And at that very minute you, with a hard cold, were sitting out in that draughty shed smoking because she wouldn't allow you to smoke in your own house!"

"I don't mind that, Edward," said Jim, and laughed again.

"Could you see to read your paper out there, with only that little shed window? And don't you like to read your paper while you smoke?"

"Oh yes," admitted Jim; "but my! I don't mind little things like that! Mis' Adkins is only a poor widow woman, and keeping my house nice and not having it smell of tobacco is all she's got. They can talk about women's rights —I feel as if they ought to have them fast enough, if they want them, poor things; a woman has a hard row to hoe, and will have, if she gets all the rights in creation. But I guess the rights they'd find it hardest to give up would be the rights to have men look after them just a little more than they look after other men, just because they are women. When I think of Annie Berry—the girl I was going to marry, you know, if she hadn't died—I feel as I couldn't do enough for another woman. Lord! I'm glad to sit out in the woodshed and smoke. Mis' Adkins is pretty good-natured to stand all the cats."

Then the coffee boiled, and Hayward poured out some for Jim and himself. He had a little silver service at hand, and willow-ware cups and saucers. Presently Sam appeared, and Hayward gave orders concerning luncheon.

"Tell Miss Louisa we are to have it served here," said he, "and mind, Sam, the chops are to be thick and cooked the way we like them; and don't forget the East India chutney, Sam."

"It does seem rather a pity that you cannot have chutney at home with your chops, when you are so fond of it," remarked Hayward when Sam had gone.

"Mis' Adkins says it will give me liver trouble, and she isn't strong enough to nurse."

"So you have to eat her ketchup?"

"Well, she doesn't put seasoning in it," admitted Jim. "But Mis' Adkins doesn't like seasoning herself, and I don't mind."

"And I know the chops are never cut thick, the way we like them."

"Mis' Adkins likes her meat well done, and she can't get such thick chops well done. I suppose our chops are rather thin, but I don't mind."

"Beefsteak and chops, both cut thin, and fried up like sole leather. I know!" said Doctor Hayward, and he stamped his foot with unregenerate force.

"I don't mind a bit, Edward."

"You ought to mind, when it is your own house, and you buy the food and pay your housekeeper. It is an outrage!"

"I don't mind, really, Edward."

Doctor Hayward regarded Jim with a curious expression compounded of love, anger, and contempt. "Any more talk of legal proceedings?" he asked, brusquely.

Jim flushed. "Tom ought not to tell of that."

"Yes, he ought; he ought to tell it all over town. He doesn't, but he ought. It is an outrage! Here you have been all these years supporting your nieces, and they are working away like field mice, burrowing under your generosity, trying to get a chance to take action and appropriate your property and have you put under a guardian."

"I don't mind a bit," said Jim; "but—"

The other man looked inquiringly at him, and, seeing a pitiful working of his friend's face, he jumped up and got a little jar from a shelf. "We will drop the whole thing until we have had our chops and chutney," said he. "You are right; it is not worth minding. Here is a new brand of tobacco I want you to try. I don't half like it, myself, but you may."

Jim, with a pleased smile, reached out for the tobacco, and the two men smoked until Sam brought the luncheon. It was well cooked and well served on an antique table. Jim was thoroughly happy. It was not until the luncheon was over and another pipe smoked that the troubled, perplexed expression returned to his face.

"Now," said Hayward, "out with it!"

"It is only the old affair about Alma and Amanda, but now it has taken on a sort of new aspect."

"What do you mean by a new aspect?"

"It seems," said Jim, slowly, "as if they were making it so I couldn't do for them."

Hayward stamped his foot. "That does sound new," he
said, dryly. "I never thought Alma Beecher or Amanda
Bennet ever objected to have you do for them."

"Well," said Jim, "perhaps they don't now, but they want
me to do it in their own way. They don't want to feel as
if I was giving and they taking; they want it to seem the
other way round. You see, if I were to deed over my property to them, and then they allowance me, they would feel
as if they were doing the giving."

"Jim, you wouldn't be such a fool as that?"

"No, I wouldn't," replied Jim, simply. "They wouldn't
know how to take care of it, and Mis' Adkins would be
left to shift for herself. Joe Beecher is real good-hearted,
but he always lost every dollar he touched. No, there
wouldn't be any sense in that. I don't mean to give in, but
I do feel pretty well worked up over it."

"What have they said to you?"

Jim hesitated.

"Out with it, now. One thing you may be sure of: nothing that you can tell me will alter my opinion of your two
nieces for the worse. As for poor Joe Beecher, there is
no opinion, one way or the other. What did they say?"

Jim regarded his friend with a curiously sweet, far-off
expression. "Edward," he said, "sometimes I believe that
the greatest thing a man's friends can do for him is to
drive him into a corner with God; to be so unjust to him
that they make him understand that God is all that mortal
man is meant to have, and that is why he finds out that
most people, especially the ones he does for, don't care
for him."

Hayward looked solemnly and tenderly at the other's
almost rapt face. "You are right, I suppose, old man,"
said he; "but what did they do?"

"They called me in there about a week ago and gave
me an awful talking to."

"About what?"

Jim looked at his friend with dignity. "They were two women talking, and they went into little matters not worth repeating," said he. "All is—they seemed to blame me for everything I had ever done for them, and for everything I had ever done, anyway. They seemed to blame me for being born and living, and, most of all, for doing anything for them."

"It is an outrage!" declared Hayward. "Can't you see it?"

"I can't seem to see anything plain about it," returned Jim, in a bewildered way. "I always supposed a man had to do something bad to be given a talking to; but it isn't so much that, and I don't bear any malice against them. They are only two women, and they are nervous. What worries me is, they do need things, and they can't get on and be comfortable unless I do for them; but if they are going to feel that way about it, it seems to cut me off from doing, and that does worry me, Edward."

The other man stamped. "Jim Bennet," he said, "they have talked, and now I am going to."

"You, Edward?"

"Yes, I am. It is entirely true what those two women, Susan Adkins and Mrs. Trimmer, said about you. You *are* a doormat, and you ought to be ashamed of yourself for it. A man should be a man, and not a doormat. It is the worst thing in the world for people to walk over him and trample him. It does them much more harm than it does him. In the end the trampler is much worse off than the trampled upon. Jim Bennet, your being a doormat may cost other people their souls' salvation. You are selfish in the grain to be a doormat."

Jim turned pale. His childlike face looked suddenly old with his mental effort to grasp the other's meaning. In fact, he was a child—one of the little ones of the world—

although he had lived the span of a man's life. Now one of the hardest problems of the elders of the world was presented to him. "You mean——" he said, faintly.

"I mean, Jim, that for the sake of other people, if not for your own sake, you ought to stop being a doormat and be a man in this world of men."

"What do you want me to do?"

"I want you to go straight to those nieces of yours and tell them the truth. You know what your wrongs are as well as I do. You know what those two women are as well as I do. They keep the letter of the Ten Commandments—that is right. They attend my church—that is right. They scour the outside of the platter until it is bright enough to blind those people who don't understand them; but inwardly, they are petty, ravening wolves of greed and ingratitude. Go and tell them; they don't know themselves. Show them what they are. It is your Christian duty."

"You don't mean for me to stop doing for them?"

"I certainly do mean just that—for a while, anyway."

"They can't possibly get along, Edward; they will suffer."

"They have a little money, haven't they?"

"Only a little in savings bank. The interest pays their taxes."

"And you gave them that?"

Jim colored.

"Very well, their taxes are paid for this year; let them use that money. They will not suffer, except in their feelings, and that is where they ought to suffer. Man, you would spoil all the work of the Lord by your selfish tenderness toward sinners!"

"They aren't sinners."

"Yes, they are—spiritual sinners, the worst kind in the world. Now——"

"You don't mean for me to go now?"

"Yes, I do—now. If you don't go now you never will. Then, afterward, I want you to go home and sit in your best parlor and smoke, and have all your cats in there, too."

Jim gasped. "But, Edward! Mis' Adkins—"

"I don't care about Mrs. Adkins. She isn't as bad as the rest, but she needs her little lesson, too."

"Edward, the way that poor woman works to keep the house nice—and she don't like the smell of tobacco smoke."

"Never mind whether she likes it or not. You smoke."

"And she don't like cats."

"Never mind. Now you go."

Jim stood up. There was a curious change in his rosy, childlike face. There was a species of quickening. He looked at once older and more alert. His friend's words had charged him as with electricity. When he went down the street he looked taller.

Amanda Bennet and Alma Beecher, sitting sewing at their street windows, made this mistake.

"That isn't Uncle Jim," said Amanda. "That man is a head taller, but he looks a little like him."

"It can't be Uncle Jim," agreed Alma. Then both started. "It is Uncle Jim, and he is coming here," said Amanda.

Jim entered. Nobody except himself, his nieces, and Joe Beecher ever knew exactly what happened, what was the aspect of the doormat erected to human life, of the worm turned to menace. It must have savored of horror, as do all meek and down-trodden things when they gain, driven to bay, the strength to do battle. It must have savored of the godlike, when the man who had borne with patience, dignity, and sorrow for them the stings of lesser things because they were lesser things, at last arose and revealed himself superior, with a great height of the spirit, with the power to crush.

When Jim stopped talking and went home, two pale,

shocked faces of women gazed after him from the windows. Joe Beecher was sobbing like a child. Finally his wife turned her frightened face upon him, glad to have still some one to intimidate.

"For goodness' sake, Joe Beecher, stop crying like a baby!" said she, but she spoke in a queer whisper, for her lips were stiff.

Joe stood up and made for the door.

"Where are you going?" asked his wife.

"Going to get a job somewhere," replied Joe, and went. Soon the women saw him driving a neighbor's cart up the street.

"He's going to cart gravel for John Leach's new sidewalk!" gasped Alma.

"Why don't you stop him?" cried her sister. "You can't have your husband driving a tip cart for John Leach. Stop him, Alma!"

"I can't stop him," moaned Alma. "I don't feel as if I could stop anything."

Her sister gazed at her, and the same expression was on both faces, making them more than sisters of the flesh. Both saw before them a stern boundary wall against which they might press in vain for the rest of their lives, and both saw the same sins of their hearts.

Meantime Jim Bennet was seated in his best parlor and Susan Adkins was whispering to Mrs. Trimmer out in the kitchen.

"I don't know whether he's gone stark, staring mad or not," whispered Susan, "but he's in the parlor smoking his worst old pipe, and that big tiger tommy is sitting in his lap, and he's let in all the other cats, and they're nosing round, and I don't dare drive 'em out. I took up the broom; then I put it away again. I never knew Mr. Bennet to act so. I can't think what's got into him."

"Did he say anything?"

"No, he didn't say much of anything, but he said it in a way that made my flesh fairly creep. Says he, 'As long as this is my house and my furniture and my cats, Mis' Adkins, I think I'll sit down in the parlor, where I can see to read my paper and smoke at the same time.' Then he holds the kitchen door open, and he calls, 'Kitty, kitty, kitty!' and that great tiger tommy comes in with his tail up, rubbing round his legs, and all the other cats followed after. I shut the door before these last ones got into the parlor."

Susan Adkins regarded malevolently the three tortoise-shell cats of three generations and various stages of growth, one Maltese settled in a purring round of comfort with four kittens, and one perfectly black cat, which sat glaring at her with beryl-colored eyes.

"That black cat looks evil," said Mrs. Trimmer.

"Yes, he does. I don't know why I didn't drown him when he was a kitten."

"Why didn't you drown all those Malty kittens?"

"The old cat hid them away until they were too big. Then he wouldn't let me. What do you suppose has come to him? Just smell that awful pipe!"

"Men do take queer streaks every now and then," said Mrs. Trimmer. "My husband used to, and he was as good as they make 'em, poor man. He would eat sugar on his beefsteak, for one thing. The first time I saw him do it I was scared. I thought he was plumb crazy, but afterward I found out it was just because he was a man, and his ma hadn't wanted him to eat sugar when he was a boy. Mr. Bennet will get over it."

"He don't act as if he would."

"Oh yes, he will. Jim Bennet never stuck to anything but being Jim Bennet for very long in his life, and this ain't being Jim Bennet."

"He is a very good man," said Susan with a somewhat apologetic tone.

"He's too good."

"He's too good to cats."

"Seems to me he's too good to 'most everybody. Think what he has done for Amanda and Alma, and how they act!"

"Yes, they are ungrateful and real mean to him; and I feel sometimes as if I would like to tell them just what I think of them," said Susan Adkins. "Poor man, there he is, studying all the time what he can do for people, and he don't get very much himself."

Mrs. Trimmer arose to take leave. She had a long, sallow face, capable of a sarcastic smile. "Then," said she, "if I were you I wouldn't begrudge him a chair in the parlor and a chance to read and smoke and hold a pussy cat."

"Who said I was begrudging it? I can air out the parlor when he's got over the notion."

"Well, he will, so you needn't worry," said Mrs. Trimmer. As she went down the street she could see Jim's profile beside the parlor window, and she smiled her sarcastic smile, which was not altogether unpleasant. "He's stopped smoking, and he ain't reading," she told herself. "It won't be very long before he's Jim Bennet again."

But it was longer than she anticipated, for Jim's will was propped by Edward Hayward's. Edward kept Jim to his standpoint for weeks, until a few days before Christmas. Then came self-assertion, that self-assertion of negation which was all that Jim possessed in such a crisis. He called upon Doctor Hayward; the two were together in the little study for nearly an hour, and talk ran high, then Jim prevailed.

"It's no use, Edward," he said; "a man can't be made over when he's cut and dried in one fashion, the way I am. Maybe I'm doing wrong, but to me it looks like doing right, and there's something in the Bible about every man having his own right and wrong. If what you say is true, and I am hindering the Lord Almighty in His work, then it is for Him to stop me. He can do it. But meantime I've got to go on doing the way I always have. Joe has been trying to drive that tip cart, and the horse ran away with him twice. Then he let the cart fall on his foot and mash one of his toes, and he can hardly get round, and Amanda and Alma don't dare touch that money in the bank for fear of not having enough to pay the taxes next year in case I don't help them. They only had a little money on hand when I gave them that talking to, and Christmas is 'most here, and they haven't got things they really need. Amanda's coat that she wore to meeting last Sunday didn't look very warm to me, and poor Alma had her furs chewed up by the Leach dog, and she's going without any. They need lots of things. And poor Mis' Adkins is 'most sick with tobacco smoke. I can see it, though she doesn't say anything, and the nice parlor curtains are full of it, and cat hairs are all over things. I can't hold out any longer, Edward. Maybe I am a doormat; and if I am, and it is wicked, may the Lord forgive me, for I've got to keep right on being a doormat."

Hayward sighed and lighted his pipe. However, he had given up and connived with Jim.

On Christmas eve the two men were in hiding behind a clump of cedars in the front yard of Jim's nieces' house. They watched the expressman deliver a great load of boxes and packages. Jim drew a breath of joyous relief.

"They are taking them in," he whispered—"they are taking them in, Edward!"

Hayward looked down at the dim face of the man beside him, and something akin to fear entered his heart. He saw the face of a lifelong friend, but he saw something in it which he had never recognized before. He saw the face of one of the children of heaven, giving only for the sake of the need of others, and glorifying the gifts with the love and pity of an angel.

"I was afraid they wouldn't take them!" whispered Jim, and his watching face was beautiful, although it was only the face of a little, old man of a little village, with no great gift of intellect. There was a full moon riding high; the ground was covered with a glistening snow level, over which wavered wonderful shadows, as of wings. One great star prevailed despite the silver might of the moon. To Hayward Jim's face seemed to prevail, as that star, among all the faces of humanity.

Jim crept noiselessly toward a window, Hayward at his heels. The two could see the lighted interior plainly.

"See poor Alma trying on her furs," whispered Jim, in a rapture. "See Amanda with her coat. They have found the money. See Joe heft the turkey." Suddenly he caught Hayward's arm, and the two crept away. Out on the road, Jim fairly sobbed with pure delight. "Oh, Edward," he said, "I am so thankful they took the things! I was so afraid they wouldn't, and they needed them! Oh, Edward, I am so thankful!" Edward pressed his friend's arm.

When they reached Jim's house a great tiger cat leaped to Jim's shoulder with the silence and swiftness of a shadow. "He's always watching for me," said Jim, proudly. "Pussy! Pussy!" The cat began to purr loudly, and rubbed his splendid head against the man's cheek.

"I suppose," said Hayward, with something of awe in his tone, "that you won't smoke in the parlor tonight?"

"Edward, I really can't. Poor woman, she's got it all aired and beautifully cleaned, and she's so happy over it. There's a good fire in the shed, and I will sit there with the pussy cats until I go to bed. Oh, Edward, I am so thankful that they took the things!"

"Good night, Jim."

"Good night. You don't blame me, Edward?"

"Who am I to blame you, Jim? Good night."

Hayward watched the little man pass along the path to the shed door. Jim's back was slightly bent, but to his friend it seemed bent beneath a holy burden of love and pity for all humanity, and the inheritance of the meek seemed to crown that drooping old head. The doormat, again spread freely for the trampling feet of all who got comfort thereby, became a blessed thing. The humble creature, despised and held in contempt like One greater than he, giving for the sake of the needs of others, went along the narrow footpath through the snow. The minister took off his hat and stood watching until the door was opened and closed and the little window gleamed with golden light.

## XXIV. *THE GOLD*[1]

THE Colonies had but recently declared war with the old country, and Abraham Duke being an able-bodied man, although no longer young, was going to fight for the cause. He was fastening on his old sword, which his father before him had wielded well, and his wife Catherine was standing watching him, with an angry cant to her head. "Wherefore cannot you tell me where the gold is, Abraham Duke?" said she.

Abraham Duke regarded his wife with stern melancholy, and his glance of fixedness in his own purpose was more impregnable than any fort.

"I can tell you not, Catherine," replied he, "because no man can tell any woman anything which he wants not the whole world to know, and there are plenty of evil-disposed folk abroad in these troublous times, and 'tis for your own sake, since, in case robbers come, you can tell them without perjury that you know not where the gold is."

"For *my* sake!" returned Catherine, with a high sniff. "You tell me not for fear I shall spend the gold, and you always loved gold better than your wife. You fear lest I should buy a new gown to my back, or a new cap ribbon. Never fear, Abraham Duke, for I have gone poorly clad so long that, faith, a new cap ribbon even would frighten me."

"I have given you all that I could, Catherine," returned Abraham, gravely.

"But now that you have all this wealth, five thousand pounds, you hide it away, and tell me not where it is—me, your wife, who has kept your house for scarce anything save a poor measure of daily bread, all these years. You wrong me, Abraham Duke."

But Abraham Duke only kept his mouth shut more tightly. He was perhaps ten years older than his wife, but he was handsome, with a stern, almost a sad, majesty of carriage. It was only some few weeks before that the money, a legacy from his father in England, five thousand pounds in gold, had come on the English ship *The Queen Mary*. It was the day afterward that he had sent his wife away by stagecoach fifty miles inland on a visit to her sister, Mistress Abigail Endicott. He had charged her while on her visit to say nothing about the five thousand pounds, but well he knew that she had talked of nothing but the gold, and had bragged much, and now, when she had returned and her husband was about to join the army, the gold was hidden, and she was to know nothing of it and have nothing of it all to spend until her husband's return. He regarded her at the last with the sort of restrained tenderness of his kind. She was still a most charming woman to look upon, fair-skinned and fair-haired, and, in spite of her complaints, attired daintily, although she had spun and woven the blue petticoat which she wore, and worked herself the lace kerchief which veiled her bosom, and the cap which crowned her fair head. "When I come home, you shall have what you will to spend," said he, "but not now. Now is a time when a good wife needs nothing except the wherewithal to live, with her goodman away and war in the land."

"Abraham, tell me where you have hid the gold?"

"I will not tell you, Catherine," said Abraham Duke, and now he was all equipped to start. "If, perchance, I should never come back, you may go to Parson Rawson, who holds a sealed letter for you, but in no case will he give it to you unless I fall and he has ample proof of it. He has promised me upon his honor, and no man living ever knew Parson Ebenezer Rawson to forswear his word."

"And in the meantime, while you fight I am to stay alone at home and starve."

"There is no need for a woman of industry to starve in a good home, with a bound boy to cut wood and dig the garden for her, and cows and sheep and chickens," said Abraham.

"But should the enemy come and take them all, as they may do, since we are on the seashore!" cried Catherine.

"In that case you will go to your sister, Mistress Endicott, in Rexham," replied Abraham. He was advancing toward his wife for a decorous last embrace, should she be disposed to yield it in her rancor, when little Harry Evarts, the son of Abraham's friend and neighbor, the goldsmith, came rushing in, and he was all bloody, and his pretty face was deadly white, and his fair curls, like a girl's, seemed to stand up and wave like plumes over his head, he was in such a fright. Then Catherine Duke forgot the gold, for she had no child of her own, and she loved the boy. "Harry! Harry!" she shrieked, running to him and holding him to her breast. "What is it, child? Speak! Are you hurt?"

"Father! father!" gasped the boy, and then he hung almost lifeless on Catherine's arm.

"What ails your father? Speak!" cried Catherine.

"Father is killed," replied the boy, faintly.

"Killed! What, your father killed! Abraham, do you hear? Joseph Evarts is killed. Hear what this child says! Run, quick, Abraham!"

But when Catherine turned to look at her husband there was no one there, and she for the moment thought nothing of it, inferring that at the child's first word he had hastened to see what had happened to his friend.

But Abraham Duke did not return, and it was known

on good authority that he had never set foot in Joseph Evarts's house to ascertain what had happened to him, but had made his way straight out of the village to the army, the company of which he was a member being assembled in Suffield, about ten miles away.

Catherine, although she had had the difference with her husband concerning the hiding of the gold, felt hurt that he should have slipped away in such wise without a word of farewell while she was in such anxiety over the bereft child, but she had no suspicions then, or afterward, and nobody spoke of suspicions to her. But suspicions there were, although they slumbered in the general excitement of the war and the ever-recurring rumors of a ship of the enemy in sight and about to land in the harbor of the little village of South Suffield. It was said that Abraham Duke was the last one seen entering and leaving the house of Joseph Evarts the evening before his dead body was found by his little son, who was returning from a visit to his grandmother; his mother was dead. Little Harry Evarts had, indeed, found the door of his home blocked by something, and pushed with all his childish strength, and found, when the door yielded a gap, that it was the body of his father, dead of a sword-thrust in the side, which blocked the door. Evarts had been a goldsmith by trade in the old country; since he had been in the new, finding little opportunity for the exercise of his craft, he had supported himself and his little son by working his farm. It was held that Abraham Duke had gone the night before to bid him farewell. Mistress Prudence Dexter, who lived next door, had distinctly seen him enter and leave, and she had seen no one else that evening, and it was bright moonlight and she had been sitting beside her window with no light, to save candles. Still, in spite of the sinister report, Abraham Duke's standing—he was tithingman in the meeting house, and esteemed by all—and the utter absence of any known motive served to keep the suspicion well within bounds, and would have done so even had not everybody's mind been distracted by the war and the rumors of strange sails on the horizon.

Meantime Catherine Duke lived on alone, save for the bound boy, who was none too bright as to his wits, although strong and a good worker, and night and day she searched for the gold, which she was confident her husband had hidden somewhere about the house, if he had not buried it in the field. Her husband had not been gone twenty-four hours before all the usual hiding places of treasure were overhauled, such as old teapots, the drawers of dressers, secret drawers, and the clock. She searched the clock particularly, since she heard that her husband had been seen coming from Joseph Evarts's with some of the works of the clock that night before he went away. Prudence Dexter had averred that she had distinctly seen the dangling pendulum of a clock from under Abraham's cloak as he went down the street.

Catherine, knowing that the dead man, Joseph Evarts, had been a cunning workman in many ways, thought that he might have rigged for his friend a secret closet in the clock, and she searched it well, but found nothing. She thought that it might have been possible for her husband to carry the main body of the clock under his cloak, for the purpose of the secret closet, but, although she sounded every inch and poked the inmost recesses of the clock well over, no gold did she discover. She therefore let it be, ticking with the solemn majesty of its kind; it was an eight-day clock, taller than a man, standing like Time itself in the corner of the living room, and casting a shadow like the shadow of a man across the floor every morning when the sun shone into the room. But she searched, after she had searched the clock, every inch of the house. She even had the hearthstones taken up, she and the dull-witted bound boy, working by candlelight, with the curtains drawn, that the neighbors might suspect nothing, and she replaced them in a masterly fashion; for Catherine Duke was in reality a masterly woman. And then she had out many of the chimney bricks, as many as she dared, and she even had up some of the flooring, but she found nothing.

Then she and the bound boy dug up the cellar bottom, and then the bound boy plowed every inch of land which had hitherto remained uncultivated. She could do that openly, and people began to say that Catherine would make more of the farm than her husband had done. But the land that was too stony for the plow she was more secret about, she and the boy digging it up by moonlight and replacing the sods.

Once she ventured forth with a lantern in her impatience, but the light, seen flitting along the field near the shore, occasioned a rumor in the village that a ship of the British had landed and a drum beat to arms. Then all the old men and boys left in the place sallied forth, and Catherine and the bound boy, whose name, which belied his character, was Solomon—last name he had none at all that anybody knew, for he was a foundling—had hard work to reach the house undiscovered, although she blew out the lantern and scudded for her life with her petticoats lifted, while the boy sped with her, the more afraid that he knew not what he feared.

However, all Catherine's searching came to nothing, although she worked hard—and hard work it was, with what she had to do on the farm. No woman in South Suffield was considered a better housewife than she, and she had to live up to her reputation. She and the boy sheared and washed sheep, and she spun and wove the wool. She tended the flax and made of that lengths of linen cloth; she made her soap and her candles, and kept her house as neat as wax, and all the while the search for the hidden gold was in her mind. Many a time in the dead of night would she, lying awake and pondering over it, and striving to place her own mind in the attitude of her husband's when he had hidden the treasure, think of another place where she had not looked, and be up, with her candle lit, and over the house, in her bedgown, to find nothing at all.

Catherine grew old with the loneliness and the ever-increasing wrath with her husband, who had so mistreated her after her years of self-denial and toil for his sake. The sense of injury is like a fermenting canker in the mind when once it is allowed to work with no protest. Catherine's pretty, round face grew long and sour, her smooth forehead knitted. Her blue eyes got an expression of sharp peering which never left them. She even looked at her friends as if she suspected that the hiding place of the gold might be in their minds. And yet all the time she had in reality no desire for the gold itself, for she had enough and to spare. Had she found the gold she would directly have hid it again and spent not one shilling until her husband's return, but the sense of injury ever spurred her on with a goading which almost produced madness. She asked herself over and over why she should not know —why her husband, for whom she had saved and toiled, could not have trusted her? Of a Sabbath day, when she went to meeting, she regarded the parson, Ebenezer Rawson, with a covert hatred, since he held the sealed letter, and had been trusted to a greater extent than she. Sometimes, although in spite of her wrath and sense of ill treatment, which warped her mind, she still loved her husband and prayed for his safety, the imagination would come to her how, in the case of his falling before the enemy, she should go to the parson and demand the sealed letter, and know at last what she had a right to know—the hiding place of the gold.

After her husband had been away some six months and she had had one letter from him, with not a word about the gold, she dressed herself in her best—in her red cloak, which she had had as a bride and kept carefully, and a hat with a plume which would have become her had she not gotten the expression on her fair face of the seeker after dross, which disfigures more than aught in the world— and she made her way to the parson's house. He was a widower, and always had a kindly word for a pretty woman, although esteemed, as her husband had said, a man who kept his own counsel. Past the parson's house-keeper, an ancient aunt of his, declaring that she had need of spiritual consolation, and leaving her staring, sus-picious because of the red cloak and the plume, she marched into the study, lined with books which damned all man-kind by reason of the love of God, according to the tenets of the day, and she found the parson at his desk, with his forehead knitted over the tenthly of his next Sabbath day's sermon. And then calling to her aid old blandishments of hers, she beset the parson for the letter, although the conditions of its delivery were not fulfilled, and she gave good and sufficient reasons why she should know the se-cret, since lately the rumors of the enemy on the coast had increased, and she argued that she should know the hiding place of the treasure, that she might bury it safely away from the greed of the redcoats.

But Parson Ebenezer Rawson, who was a handsome man in a powdered wig, and had something of the diplomat in him, only laughed, and spoke to her with a pleasant chid-ing, the while he noted that she was no longer, in spite of her red cloak and her feather, as goodly to see as she had been, and had an apposite verse of Scripture concerning the frailty of the flesh and the evanescence of beauty enter his mind.

"Mistress Duke," said Parson Rawson, "it truly seemeth to me that, since you yourself cannot find the gold, no safer hiding place can be discovered from the enemy."

Catherine blushed high with anger. "But I am in want of goods for household use," said she. In response to that, Parson Rawson surveyed her rounded form and the sumptuous folds of her red cloak, and said that he could not betray his trust, since his word, once given, was like a lock and seal upon his soul, and that did she want for the necessaries of life he would advance the money needful to her upon a loan.

At last Catherine Duke went away, still unsatisfied, and she walked—for thoroughly feminine she was—with a graceful movement, being conscious of the carriage of her head and the folds of her red cloak, until she was out of view of the parson's windows, and then she broke into an angry switch, and she even wept like a crossed child, as she went along where there were no houses.

Before she came to her own house, some quarter of a mile distant, she had to pass the house where Joseph Evarts had lived and wherein he had come to his death by foul means. Catherine Duke was not a nervous woman, nor timid, but as stanch and stout-hearted as woman needed to be in those times. Still, for all that, and although she had not heard of the suspicions which were directed against her husband, she never passed this house without an involuntary quickening of her steps, especially when it was nightfall, as now, and she was alone. The house had remained deserted since poor Joseph Evarts's dead body had been carried forth from it, for the little boy had been taken to live with his grandmother in an adjoining town. Now, in this gray, weather-stained house seemed to abide the spirit of mystery and murder, and to glare forth from the desolate blanks of its windows upon all passers-by. Thus Catherine Duke, stout-hearted as she was, quickened her steps that evening, and scudded by in her red cloak, with her best plume waving in the breeze; but as she passed she gave a terrified roll of her blue eyes at the house, and she could have sworn that she saw a gleam of light in one of the rooms of the second story. She looked instinctively at the opposite side of the road for a light which could produce a reflection, but there was no house there, and no bonfire. She looked again, and it seemed certain to her that there was a candlelight in the east room on the second floor.

Then she fairly ran, for a vague horror was upon her, and it seemed to her that she heard footsteps behind her, although, when she reached her own door and turned around, with the latch in her hand and Solomon gazing at her from the lighted living room, there was not a person in sight on the road, which made a sharp turn a short distance from the Duke house. That turn swerved the road from the sea, and gave room on both sides for houses. The Evarts house was on the sea side of the road. All that could be seen from the front door of the Duke house was the desolate, moaning waste of waters, which had largely acquired a terrible significance as a possible highway for the enemy, and the road, with no dwelling as far as the turn. Catherine called Solomon to the door. "Look," said she, sharply, "and see if you can spy out anybody on the road."

Solomon came and stood beside her, projecting his simple, gaping face, with its prominent light-blue eyes, into the gathering gloom, and whimpered—for he had some vague idea that he was being blamed, and he held his mistress in awe—that he saw no one. "Go as far as the turn in the road," said Catherine, imperiously, "and see if you see anybody; and, if you do, come back quickly and let us lock the door."

Solomon started, although he was afraid—for he was more afraid of his mistress' anger than of any unknown quantity—but she called him back. "If you see no one on the road," said she, "keep on until you reach the Evarts house, and look and see if you spy a light in the east chamber." Solomon sped away, although his legs trembled under him, for the fear in his mistress' heart infected his own.

Catherine went into the house and hung on the porridge kettle, and very soon Solomon came back, saying that he had seen no one, and there was no light in the east chamber of the Evarts house, but there was a boat moored behind the house, on the seashore.

"You cannot have seen rightly," said Catherine, for now her confidence had returned. "You saw the old wreck that has lain behind the house for the last three years."

"Nay, mistress, 'twas a boat," persisted the boy; but when Catherine insisted that he had seen wrongly, he yielded and agreed with her, and said it was the wreck, for he had no mind of his own when the pressure of another was brought to bear upon it.

But the poor lad was right, and it had been well for poor Catherine Duke had she heeded him and taken the candle gleam in the chamber of the deserted house and the boat on the sand behind it as a warning, instead of recovering her bravery of outlook and going about her evening tasks as usual. After supper she set Solomon to paring apples to dry, and she herself spun at her flax wheel. They found her hard by it the next day, and she was murdered even as Joseph Evarts had been; but she had not come to her death so easily, for she had been tortured first, and there were the marks of fire on her feet and hands.

As for the bound boy, he had leaped out of the window as the men beat down the door, and he had sped away on his long legs, with what little wit he had ever owned wellnigh gone forever. When he was found and brought back, he shook like one with palsy, and he went through his life so, and he could speak only in disjointed stammers. As for answering questions to any purpose, there was no hope of it from him, although the people gathered some confirmation of what they at first suspected, that Catherine had been first tortured to make her reveal the hiding place of her gold, and then, when she did not reveal it, as she could not, poor soul, she was finished.

Then the whole house had been ransacked for the gold, but the robbers and murderers found it no more than Catherine had done, although people were not sure of it. Indeed, it was said by many that the men, who were supposed to have come ashore in the boat which had been moored behind the Evarts house, and which had been seen by a man passing as well as by Solomon, had found the gold and taken it away. Catherine had talked much, to her own hurt, about the treasure, and there were stragglers from the army, as well as the enemy, to fear. Some said they were British soldiers who had come ashore in the boat, and some said they were men from the Colonial army, a company of which had been recently stationed for a short time at Suffield, but no one ever knew certainly.

When Abraham Duke came home, with only one arm, having lost the other by a British shot, he found a deserted home and a devastated farm, for there had been a raid by the enemy after Catherine's death. They had left the house standing, with its contents, but the livestock had been taken.

Abraham lived on alone, and worked his poor fields painfully, being so crippled with only one sound arm and hand, and he barely kept soul and body together, for, if the gold had not been stolen, he made no use of it. Sometimes the neighbors, albeit grudgingly and doubtfully, being still uncertain as to whether he was hoarding his treasure or not, came and helped the poor man with his scanty harvesting.

However, they seemed to meet with but little gratitude, for Abraham Duke, always taciturn and cold of bearing, had become more so. He spoke to no man unless he was first spoken to, and then he made scant reply. And although he still attended all the services on the Sabbath day in the meeting house, he had given up his office of tithing-man, and would not have it; and people said he had doctrinal doubts, because of his afflictions, which were not to his credit, even if he was innocent of the crime which those who were more ready to think evil laid at his door.

As time went on, people looked more and more askance at him, for his face grew more and more bitter and forbidding, even terrifying. The children became afraid of him, and gradually the old suspicion became more assured. He was held (although no one had any proof, and, there being no motive for the crime, there was no talk of bringing him to justice) as a man accursed, and when he was helped it was more and more grudgingly and with serious doubts as to the blessings to be received for the deed.

Joseph Evarts's son had grown up, and he was living in his father's old house with his grandmother, who still lived, although very old, and never did Abraham Duke pass the house that he was not conscious of the young man's eyes upon him. Abraham had become aware of the suspicion, and it looked more keenly from Harry Evarts's eyes than any other's. Abraham rarely looked the young man in the face, for it had become to him the face of an avenging fate. He went past the house with his head bent, but always he knew there was an eye upon him—if not the young man's, his grandmother's, for she too suspected, and voiced her suspicions openly. Her old face, set in the narrow window frame, was as malignant as a witch's upon Abraham Duke passing by, and he felt it, although he did not look up.

Affairs grew worse and worse with him. Rheumatism

beset him one winter, and he was crippled with that, as well as his maimed arm and his age, for he was now an old man. He sat all day by his fireless hearth; for it was often fireless, since he could not cut wood nor hire it cut, and often he went a day without food, for he was more and more abhorred for the shadow of suspicion of an evil deed which had fallen upon him. Old Parson Rawson had died years before. He had given up the sealed letter to Abraham when he returned from the army, and Abraham had taken it without a word, and nobody knew what had become of it.

Abraham Duke lived on, hanging to life with a feeble clutch, like an old leaf to an autumn bough, and he was near eighty, and suffering all that one could suffer and live. He was slowly freezing and starving to death, and the occasional aid from his kind only served to prolong his misery. At last, when he was eighty, there came a fierce winter, and one morning Harry Evarts, who had lately married, and whose heart, embittered with suspicion and the desire for vengeance, was somewhat softened by the thankfulness for love, thought of the old man, and, walking down the turn of the road, and seeing no smoke from the chimney, he returned home for his hand sled, and drew a good store of firewood, with a basket of provisions, to the Duke house.

It was a bright, freezing morning, a day glittering as if strung with diamonds, and the wind from the north was like a flail of death. Harry Evarts shuddered as he dragged his sled up to the door of the Duke house, and he hesitated a second for dread of what he might find when he entered. Then he heard a sweet voice from behind calling, and the girl he had married came running to join him, her fair face all glowing with the cold.

When she came alongside, Harry pounded on the door, and a horrible, dull echo, as of the vacancy of death itself, came in their ears. The young wife, Elizabeth, caught hold of her husband's arm, and she was almost weeping. "Oh, Harry! oh, Harry!" she whispered. "The poor old man must be dead."

Harry shut his mouth hard and pounded again, and again came the echo like a voice of desolate mockery from the outside of life. Then Harry shut his mouth harder, and opened the door, which was unlocked, as if the old man had left it on the latch for death, and he entered, Elizabeth shrinking behind him.

And on the hearth sat old Abraham Duke, frozen and starved, but his face had an expression of such exceeding peace and humility that even the girl was not frightened, but she began to weep bitterly. "Poor old man! oh, poor old man!" she sobbed. "And he does not look, dead, as he did alive."

The room was full of brilliant sunlight, but bitter cold, and on the hearth were only ashes, but the andirons and the tops of the fire set caught the sunlight and glowed warmly. So also did the ornaments on the desk and the highboy and the clock, and the pendulum of the clock, which still ticked, seemed to swing in an arc of gold. Harry was deadly white, standing looking at the old man on the hearth. Elizabeth continued to sob; then, being led by her sweet, womanly instincts, she went nearer to the old man, and placed one of her little hands with a caressing gesture like a blessing on his sunken forehead. Then she started. "Harry," she said—"Harry, there is a letter in his hand."

Harry did not stir. He was thinking of his father, and how he had come home to find him lying dead across the door.

"Harry," said the girl again, "there is a letter." Then she reached down and softly took the letter from the dead man's hand, which seemed to yield it up willingly. "Harry, the letter is for you!" cried Elizabeth, in an awed whisper.

Then she handed the letter to her husband. "Open it," said she.

"I can't," said the young man, hoarsely, for he was fighting a fight with himself.

"I will open it!" cried the girl, who was full of quick impulses, and she broke the seal. There were only a few words in the letter, which was, in fact, more a memorandum than a letter, and she read them aloud: "The andirons, the fire set, the handles on the highboy, the handles on the desk, the trimmings of the clock, the pendulum, the trimmings on the best bed, the handles on the dresser, the key of the desk—Gold."

"My father did the work; he made the things of gold instead of brass, and he *knew!*" exclaimed Harry.

The girl was ghastly white. She continued to look with a wild gaze of awful understanding at the old man sitting stark and dead on his fireless hearth, where he had sat so long with the great god Mammon, whom he had not dared command to his own needs lest he destroy him. She reflected how he had sat there and starved with his wealth glittering in his eyes, and she also reflected, considering the look on his dead face, that perhaps his earthly retribution had won him heavenly peace. But she shuddered convulsively, and the gold light reflected from the tops of the andirons seemed to wink at her like eyes of infernal understanding and mockery. She looked at the letter again, and called out its contents again in a voice shrill with hysteria: "The andirons, the fire set, the handles on the highboy, the handles on the desk, the trimmings of the clock, the pendulum, the trimmings on the best bed, the handles on the dresser, the key of the desk—Gold."

"My!"

"Don't you think I've done pretty well?"

"Sarah Bannister, you know as well as I do, it is wonderful!"

The two women stood in the best parlor, a long room, furnished with aggressive plush and mahogany, and onyx tables, and a marble Clytie drooping her head impudently in her out-of-place state in a New England parlor. The room was chilly in spite of the radiators, glaring with gilt in the most conspicuous wall spaces. Every piece of furniture—old-fashioned square tables, chairs, and piano—was covered with dainty things, large and small, of all colors and fabrics.

"To think you made everything here with your own hands!" commented Miss Lottie Dodd. She was a distant relative of Mrs. Bannister's, who lived with her a month at a time.

"Yes, and the worst of it is, it isn't quite a week to Christmas, and I haven't got the things done yet."

"Land! I should think you had enough here for the whole town."

"I'm giving to about the whole town this year. Then, you know all our cousins out West, and the raft of relations we never see except at our funerals, that live in Watchboro, and Center Watchboro, and South and North and East."

"I didn't know you remembered them Christmas."

[1] *Copyright, 1919, by Harper & Brothers.*

"I don't every year, but this time I was so forehanded I thought I'd put them in with the rest."

"You don't mean to say you are remembering all the Rice family?"

"Yes, I am."

"Not all those children?"

"Oh, I've got the children's presents all ready; it's the older folks' I haven't got done. I have planned a lot of drawnwork."

"You do that so beautifully," said Lottie. She was a tiny woman snugged in a lavender wool shawl. The tip of her sharp nose was red. Her blue eyes were tearful, from cold and enthusiasm. Lottie was prey to enthusiasms, even petty ones.

"I've got a lot more to do. I sha'n't try any different patterns from these here; the same with the knitted lace. That will make it easier."

Sarah Bannister clipped the last word short with a sneeze.

"Sarah, you are catching cold in this room."

"Don't know but I am. It never will heat when the wind's northwest. It's bitter outdoors today, too. The snow hasn't melted one mite. Look at those windows all frosted up."

"Well, Sarah, we better be going back to the sitting room, where it's warm."

"Guess we'd better. I was going to look a little longer. I don't seem to see some things I know I've got. I do feel some as if I were catching cold. Hope to goodness I don't— just before Christmas, too. I'll get Henry to bring in some wood for the sitting-room hearth fire."

"I sort of wonder sometimes why you and Henry don't keep a man to fetch and carry," said Lottie Dodd, as the two entered the sitting room, meeting a gust of warm air, scented with geranium and heliotrope from the window plants. "Henry is quite some older than you, and it's beginning to show."

"Oh, Henry's perfectly able to do what little chores we have. Men want some exercise."

They sat down. Sarah Bannister began to crochet, a neatly rolled-up ball of finished lace bobbing as her fingers moved. Lottie worked laboriously on a blue centerpiece.

"It certainly is lucky you are so well off, Sarah."

"Yes, I realize it is. Henry never saved much, but I have enough for both, thanks to poor father. I never spend a cent but I think of him. He used to talk so much to me about not being extravagant."

"Oh, Sarah, as if anybody could accuse you of that!"

Sarah started, but she continued talking. "Poor father used to say—I remember as if it were yesterday—'Sarah, it's easy enough to get money, for those who have the right kind of heads, and work, but it takes more than heads to keep it. That's a gift.' "

Lottie Dodd, impecunious, who had never benefited much from Sarah's riches, except in the somewhat negative way of food and cast off clothing, looked reflectively at the large, flat, rather handsome face.

Sarah stared sharply at Lottie, who did not speak. Silence and immobility make a fool inscrutable.

Sarah suspected. "Now, you wouldn't believe, Lottie Dodd, how little some of these things in there"—she shrugged her shoulders toward the parlor—"cost."

"You don't mean it." Lottie's voice was as blatantly innocent as a lamb's.

"Yes, I bought a lot at the five-and-ten-cent stores, and I had nice pieces of silk and satin and lace, and I mixed them in, and you'd never know. I thought of poor father every minute I was in these five-and-ten-cent stores."

"They would have just suited your dear pa."

Again the look of suspicion was in Sarah's eyes, to disappear before the other woman's innocent expression. Then the doorbell rang with a loud clang.

"Sakes alive! Whoever can that be, such a cold afternoon?" said Mrs. Bannister.

"Maybe it's a peddler."

"Well, if it is, he vamooses. I never will allow a peddler in my house." Sarah Bannister sneezed three times.

"Let me go to the door," said Lottie Dodd. "You have caught cold, sure as fate. Let me go, dear."

In Lottie's voice was the faint, very faint inflection in which she betrayed her consciousness that she was a year and a half younger than Sarah. To Lottie that meant, when she so desired, the feebleness of age for Sarah, juvenile agility for herself.

Sarah recognized that inflection. "I rather guess I'm as able to go to the door as you," she retorted. She thrust her face almost into the other's in a way she had when irritated.

"It was only on account of your cold, dear," protested Lottie, shrinking back.

"I haven't got any cold. If you're trying to wish one on me, you can just stop. Sneezing don't prove you've got a cold. Hm!"

"Why, Sarah!"

Sarah stepped majestically doorward as the bell rang again. She walked on her heels as she had a trick of doing when feeling unusually self-sufficient. Lottie peeked around the curtain over the pots of geraniums, but she could see nothing. She could hear voices, and the wind came in the cracks of the sitting-room door. The front door closed with a bang, and Lottie darted back to her chair. She expected to see Mrs. Bannister enter irate after turning away a peddler, but after Sarah entered a young girl, hardly more than a child.

"Go right to that hearth fire and sit down and get warm

through," ordered Mrs. Bannister. She spoke in a stern voice, but her speech ended in a beautiful cadence. When the child was seated before the fire, which Sarah stirred to a higher blaze and piled with more wood, she gazed at the young face reflecting the red glow, and smiled in a way that made Lottie gaze wonderingly at her, and suddenly remember that years ago, so many years that she had forgotten, Sarah Bannister had lost a daughter about the age of this girl. Meantime Sarah Bannister was removing the girl's extraordinarily shabby hat, and pulling off gently her shabbier coat. The girl resisted the last a little, and her small timid voice murmured something about her dress.

"Never mind your dress," said Sarah. "You will get warmer with these off."

As she spoke she laid the coat and hat on a chair, rather gingerly. Such rags as the coat disclosed, such rags of a red silk lining, and such a sinfully draggled feather decked the old hat. Sarah turned to look at the girl. Lottie was looking. Lottie had her mouth slightly open. Sarah gasped. The girl sitting there, meekly, almost limply, was a darling of a girl (judging from her little face). It was very pale now, but with the velvety pallor of a white flower. Her hair lay in soft rings of gold shading into brown about her small head. She wore her hair short, and it made her seem more a child. Her dress was torn about the sleeves and gaped where hooks were missing, unless pinned with obvious pins. Her little hands were stiff and red, and one continued to clasp cautiously the handle of an unspeakably shabby old bag. Suddenly she looked up, first at one, then at the other of the faces regarding her. She looked with perfect composure, so perfect that it directly made her seem older. Her great blue eyes had a womanly wise cognizance of the two women.

"How old are you?" demanded Sarah Bannister, suddenly.

"Thirteen last May," replied the girl. Her voice was charming, with a curious appeal in it. She seemed to be begging pardon for the fact that she was thirteen last May.

Sarah Bannister, her face working as if she were about to weep, went to a little china closet, and presently came back with a glass of homemade wine, and a square of sponge cake on a pink plate.

"Here, drink this and eat this cake," said she. "It will do you good."

She set a small table beside the girl and placed the wine glass and the cake on it.

"Thank you, ma'am," said the girl. She began to eat and drink rather eagerly. She was evidently famished, but very gentle about it. She still retained her hold of the bag.

Lottie spoke for the first time. "What have you got in that bag?" said she, rather sharply. The girl flashed her blue eyes at her in a frightened but defiant way.

"Things to sell," she whispered.

Lottie looked at Sarah. So she was a peddler, after all. Sarah did not return Lottie's glance. She spoke to the girl.

"When you have finished your cake and wine, and get real warm, I will look at the things you have to sell," said she, softly.

"Thank you, ma'am."

Lottie began to be aggressive. "What is your name?" she asked, peremptorily.

"Don't speak so sharp, Lottie," said Sarah. "You will scare her half to death. She's nothing but a child. She was half frozen. She was standing there on the doorstep, shaking from head to foot, poor little thing, half dressed, too, on such a day as this." Sarah glanced at the heap of wool and red silk rags on the chair, and remembered a nice thick wool coat in the closet of a certain chamber.

Lottie asked again, but more gently, "What is your name, little girl?"

"Joan Brooks."

"Oh, I know her," said Lottie, with an accent of slight scorn. "Her father's that broken-down minister. He fills the pulpit sometimes when Mr. Whitman has bronchitis."

"He preaches very well, too," said Sarah, kindly.

"Father is not broken-down. He stands up as well as you do," said Joan, unexpectedly. Then she began to rise. "Where is my coat?" said she.

"You sit right down, child," said Sarah. "She didn't mean a thing. Of course your father isn't broken-down. We always speak that way of a minister who don't preach regularly."

"Father used to preach regularly," said the girl, eagerly, "but after we moved here the church he came to preach in burned down."

"That was the little Hyde's Corner church," interpolated Lottie. Sarah nodded.

"He preached regularly there," stated Joan, "until the fire."

"What does your father do now?" asked Lottie.

"He preaches for other ministers a great deal, and betweenwhiles he goes about taking orders for a beautiful book on the Holy Land."

Lottie looked at the geraniums, and her lips moved inaudibly: "Peddler."

"We don't have as much money as we did before the fire," stated the little girl, "and we don't have much of anything to give away. That is why—" She stopped.

Sarah caught up the bag, which Joan had placed on the floor beside her.

"Well, let us see what you have to sell," said she.

Sarah opened the bag and Lottie stood looking over her shoulder.

"My!" said Lottie, "what lovely drawnwork, and it's just

the same pattern as that bureau scarf you made for your cousin Lizzie, too!"

"And I wanted one like it for her married sister, Jennie. How much is this, Joan?"

Joan mentioned a price. Lottie paled, and her mouth dropped when Sarah Bannister, so careful of money, said she would take it. She also bought for a large sum a beautiful tablecloth with embroidered corners for the minister's wife.

"That's just like the one you made yourself for Mrs. Lester Sears," said Lottie. She thought Sarah Bannister must be losing her wits. "There's that same cornucopia in one corner, and cluster of daisies in another," she mentioned, feebly.

"I know it," said Sarah, defiantly. "Why shouldn't it be the same? It's a common pattern. I made that tablecloth for Mrs. Sears because she was so good when I was sick with the grippe, sending in things 'most every day. I wanted to make something for the minister's wife just as nice, because she and Annie Sears are so thick, and because we all know the minister isn't very popular, and I feel sort of sorry for her, but I didn't have the time or strength to make it. This is a real godsend."

"You'll have to tell her you didn't make it," remarked Lottie, maliciously.

"I am not in the habit of either telling or implying a lie," replied Mrs. Bannister. Then she turned suddenly to Joan. "My dear, who made these pretty things?"

Joan crimsoned, then paled, but she lifted clear eyes of truth to Mrs. Bannister: "A lady."

"What lady?"

"A lady."

"But what is the lady's name?"

"I would rather not tell her name."

Sarah looked at Lottie and spoke with lip motion: "Her mother."

Even skeptical Lottie nodded. What so likely as that the broken-down minister's wife might do this exquisite work, and send her little daughter out to sell it?

Sarah was examining the tablecloth. "I am sure it is a little different from mine," she reflected. "The bunch of daisies is larger."

Lottie nodded. "Looks so to me."

Sarah laid down the tablecloth and took up some knitted lace. "This is almost exactly the pattern of mine, and I did want to knit some for Daisy Hapgood. I am so glad to get this."

The more Sarah Bannister bought, the more the little girl's face beamed. Her cheeks flushed; her blue eyes gleamed. Sarah kept gazing at her with loving admiration. As she bought everything in the bag, Joan seemed fairly quivering with delight. She held her pretty upper lip caught between her teeth, lest she break into sheer laughter.

"I will take this handkerchief with the embroidered G," said Sarah. "It is just what I wanted to tuck in a letter to Ella Giddings."

"I thought I saw one in the parlor just like that," said Lottie.

"So you did, similar. Mine has a queer little quirk at the top of the G, and that is for Emma Gleason. I wanted to make another for Ella. Lottie, do you mind going upstairs and bringing down my little black silk shopping bag? My purse is in it. I don't want to go through that cold hall. I have got the grippe; I almost know it," said Sarah, when the bag was empty.

While Lottie was gone, Mrs. Bannister and the girl added up items rapidly on the back of an old envelope. Sarah was economical with paper. Sarah added with zeal, and her hand was over the sum total, and she had time to shake her head

with finger on lips when the door opened. The girl nodded.
She was only a child, but she understood. The other lady
was not to know what the things cost.

Lottie cast a sharp glance at the gleam of white paper in
Sarah's cautious hand. "Whatever made you hang that bag
up in the closet, when you always keep it in the top bureau
drawer?" said she. "I had an awful hunt. Thought I never
would find it."

"I remember hanging it there when I hung up my coat
when I came home yesterday," replied Sarah, calmly.

Sarah loosened the strings of the bag. Lottie watched
like a cat. Sarah took out her nice black leather pocketbook.
Lottie craned her neck. Sarah bent over the pocketbook,
hiding her proceedings, counted out money, folded it in a
nice little roll, and gave it to Joan.

"There," said she, kindly. "That is right. Now you
had better run and give it to your mother."

"I shall not take this money to mother," said she. "She
will not expect it. It is my money. Father and mother
wish me to be independent. I have this money for Christmas presents and I shall have to see to them myself."

Joan rapidly slipped into her ragged coat. Sarah thought
of the warm one upstairs, but did not somehow feel like
mentioning it.

"You mean to say you don't tell your mother about this?"
said Lottie.

"Mother does not wish me to tell her everything," said
Joan. "Father does not, either. They say I should lose
my individuality."

"No danger, seems to me," said Lottie. When the girl
had gone and was disappearing down the road, a red rag
from the silken lining of her coat blowing back stiffly in the
icy wind like an anarchist flag, the women stood at the window, watching her.

"She is a darling little girl," remarked Sarah, with an absent air.

Lottie looked at her. Directly there came before her mental vision the freckled face, the long nose, the retreating chin, the weak eyes and stiff, sandy hair of Sarah's departed daughter, long in her little green grave.

"She thinks this beautiful girl looks like her," Lottie reflected.

Directly Sarah spoke in a breaking voice, and tears rolled down her cheeks. "She is the living image of my Ida."

Lottie lied for the sake of her own heart. "Yes, so she is," said she.

"Then you saw the likeness?"

"How could I help it?"

"Want me to take these things into the parlor and put them with the others?" offered Lottie. "You mustn't go in there with such a cold as you've got."

"I'll put them in the secretary, here," said Sarah. "There's one drawer without a thing in it. I want to look them over again, and everything will have to be done up and addressed out here, anyway. Remind me to send to the store for some more Christmas ribbon tomorrow morning."

Sarah folded the dainty things she had bought and laid them carefully away in the secretary drawer, then she seated herself in her rocking-chair and took her pocketbook out of her black silk bag. She looked up and saw Lottie's sharp eyes turn away. She laughed and the laugh had a tang in it.

"Well, Lottie," said she, "if you want so much to know what I paid for the things, I am perfectly willing to tell you, although I cannot imagine why you want to know. I am not in the least curious, myself."

Lottie flushed suddenly. She tried to smile. "I ain't curious," she replied. "I never was. What makes you talk so, Sarah? It sounds sort of hateful."

Sarah paid no attention. "The things cost just twenty-three dollars and seventy-nine cents," said she, coolly.

"My goodness!"

"Yes, just twenty-three dollars and seventy-nine cents." Very swiftly Lottie sped her own little shaft.

"Why, Sarah Bannister, I never knew you spent as much on Christmas presents in your whole life. You have never had the name of being as free as all that."

"I didn't deserve it," said Sarah. "All those things made up in the parlor there didn't cost fifteen dollars. I told you they didn't cost so much, and they didn't."

"And you laid out all that money on these things?"

"I didn't have to do the work on these, and the work means a good deal when you are tired out and coming down with the grippe. And, besides"—Sarah hesitated; then she finished with defiant accent—"when I saw that darling little girl, the exact image of my dear lost Ida, I felt almost ready to mortgage the place to buy her out."

"Well, all I can say is, I am beat," remarked Lottie. "If anybody had told me that you would spend twenty-three dollars and seventy-nine cents buying Christmas presents from a peddler, I should say if you did you had gone plumb mad."

"She wasn't a peddler, Lottie. That girl is the daughter of a minister of the Gospel."

"Minister of the Gospel! He ain't preaching. He's peddling books."

Sarah began to speak, but the door bell cut her short.

"Who in the world is coming now?" she murmured, and smoothed her hair and straightened her apron strings.

"Another nice peddler, maybe," said Lottie. "Don't put your pocketbook away, Sarah."

Sarah looked at her reproachfully, and coughed. "Will you go to the door?"

Lottie went, her head erect. Directly the door was opened

Sarah heard a loud, very sweet, very rapid voice, and knew the caller was Mrs. Lee Wilson. Mrs. Wilson danced in ahead of Lottie, who followed her sulkily. She did not like Mrs. Wilson, who was so much prettier than she ought to have been, considering her years, and so much gayer and livelier, that it seemed to give grounds for distrust. Mrs. Wilson slipped back her handsome fur neck piece, disclosing a deep V of handsome white neck, which Lottie glanced at, then openly sniffed. Then she spoke in a voice which seemed drawn out like thin wire. The voice had hissing sibilations.

"Don't you feel cold, Mrs. Wilson?" said Lottie.

Mrs. Wilson laughed. She understood. "Oh no," said she, sweetly. "I never catch cold with my neck exposed. Don't you think I am lucky to have a neck good enough to keep up with the styles? A woman does look so old-fashioned now, with a high collar."

Lottie flushed. "I care more about decency than I do about style," she snapped. Her animosity was no longer disguised.

Mrs. Wilson laughed again. "Well, it is nice to have a neck long and thin like yours in case the styles changed, and they are bound to, and I look like a freak with a high collar," she said, good-naturedly. "But, Sarah Bannister, and you, too, Lottie, I didn't come here to discuss low necks and high collars. I came here about that Brett family. You remember the talk when the father ran away and left those six children, after the mother died of quick consumption?"

"I thought an aunt came, or something," said Sarah.

"So she did, and stayed quite awhile, and then there was a report that she had gone away and taken the children. You know at first we thought the town would have to do something about it."

"Didn't the aunt take them away?" asked Lottie.

"Why, no, it seems she didn't. The minister's wife saw

the oldest girl—she's a pretty little thing, you know—dragging a small one on a sled yesterday. She said both the children looked well dressed and well nourished, but the eldest girl wouldn't tell her who was looking after them."

"Guess the aunt came back," said Lottie, rather indifferently. Lottie was always indifferent when it came to large families of the poor. It had always vaguely seemed to her like something immoral.

Sarah looked interested. "Why, it seems as if the aunt must have come back," said she, "if they looked as well as you say. How old is the eldest girl?"

"Oh, they are all young. She can't be more than eight, a very pretty child with red-gold hair. They are all shy; won't talk. What I came about—" Mrs. Wilson hesitated a moment. She colored a little and laughed confusedly. "Well," she said, finally, "I suppose we have all been rather lax about those children. I had a letter from Mrs. S. Walsingham today, and how she had heard of the case I don't know, but she had, and—she reminded me very politely, but she reminded me all the same, that she was making an annual donation to the Ladies' Aid Society for just such cases. She said she presumed her letter was useless, for doubtless we had already looked into the case. She knew we hadn't. Somebody in this town has told her."

Lottie nodded her head in a sidewise direction. Mrs. Wilson laughed. "I dare say you are right," she agreed. "Emmeline Jay and her mother are always on the watch ever since they stopped going to church because they thought the minister before this one preached at them all. Well, anyway, Clara Walsingham wants to know, and, of course, she has a right."

"Just like Clara to write that sort of a letter," said Lottie. "Why can't folks come right out? I hate beating around the bush."

Mrs. Wilson giggled. "As for me, there never was a bush

handy to beat around. I had to come right out and say my say. Well, the fact is not a woman of the society knows a thing about these Brett children, and who is going to begin? I would, but my little boy is sick and I suspect measles. I can't carry measles into a poor and deserving family. The minister's wife says she would right away, but her sister with her four children has come to spend Christmas with her, and she has her own three and no help. She says after Christmas she can do anything."

"I'd go tomorrow," said Sarah, reflectively, "but I think I have taken cold, and—it seems selfish, but I must get my presents off. I got rid of working on more, for I bought a lot, but I have a quantity to do up."

The two women looked at Lottie. She sat with her chin high, gazing out of the window.

"Christmas is right here, next week Thursday," remarked Mrs. Wilson, helplessly.

"If my cold is better I will go and see these children tomorrow, presents or no presents," said Sarah firmly.

Lottie looked over her shoulder at her. " 'Twon't be any better. You've got fever now. Look at your cheeks."

As Sarah could not very well look at her own cheeks, and there was no mirror in the room, she gazed at Mrs. Wilson for confirmation.

She nodded. "Your cheeks do look pretty red," said she.

"I'll wait and see how I feel in the morning," she said as Mrs. Wilson rose to go.

In the morning Sarah was no worse and no better. The weather was severe. The wind was very high. Sarah decided to have Lottie bring the presents out from the icy parlor and see if she could not get them ready for mailing during the day.

"By doing that," said she, "I can have tomorrow to go and see those Brett children. Of course, something can be hung on the Sunday-school tree for them, anyway, and it can be seen to that they come, but I don't feel right to wait till after Christmas to do more than that. They may be suffering."

"Guess they're all right," said Lottie. "When there's such a tribe as they, somebody bobs up and looks after them."

Lottie deposited with care her first load of dainty things from the parlor. Sarah, muffled in a white wool shawl, sat out of the draught from the open door. Lottie went back and forth. She laid things on the table, the sofa, on chairs.

"Well, this is all," she said, finally.

"All?"

"Yes, I've brought out everything. You haven't things put away in other places?"

"No, only those I bought from the little girl yesterday. They are in the secretary drawer."

"Sarah Bannister, where is that beautiful embroidered tablecloth that we said was so much like the one you bought?" said Lottie, suddenly. "I don't remember bringing it out. No, don't you go to handling all these cold things. I'll look myself."

Lottie examined everything. Sarah watched. She was rather pale. Finally Lottie came forward and stood before Sarah with a determined air. "That tablecloth ain't here," said she.

"It must be."

"It ain't. When I look I look. It ain't."

Sarah stared at her.

"Some other things ain't here, too," said Lottie.

"What?"

"A lot of doilies, a lot of other things."

Sarah gasped. "Where do you think?"

"Sure you ain't put them away in other places?"

Sarah shook her head.

"Which drawer in the secretary did you put those things you bought from that girl?"

"Lottie!"

"Which drawer?"

"I don't see what you think that has to do with it."

"Which drawer?"

"Next to the top one," Sarah whispered, feebly.

Lottie crossed the room, her skirts swishing. She returned after two trips and laid the soft piles of dainty handiwork in two chairs before Sarah.

"These ain't cold," said she. "Now let's look over these things. Here's the tablecloth you bought."

"I don't see what you mean."

"Look at it; look real careful."

Sarah took the square of glistening linen, with its graceful embroidery, and examined it. She lingered long over one corner. Her lips tightened. She folded it carefully. "Lay it over on that other chair," said she.

Lottie obeyed. She looked a little frightened.

Sarah went on, examining one article after another. Lottie laid one after another on other chairs.

"There are still four more things missing," said Sarah.

"What?"

"That large centerpiece, really the best thing I had. I meant that for Clara Walsingham. She always sends me such beautiful presents. Then I don't see that blue sweater I knit for the Langham girl—Sally, you know—and I don't see the white Shetland shawl I crocheted for Grandma Langham. That was large and I couldn't fail to see it. And—I don't see the pink bedroom slippers I made for Cousin Emma's daughter Ruth."

Sarah's voice broke. She passed her handkerchief across her eyes.

"Don't you cry and get all worked up. It will make your fever higher."

"I haven't told you," moaned Sarah, weakly.

"What ain't you told me?"

"I haven't told you that the tablecloth I put in the secretary drawer, that I bought from that dear girl, who looks so much like my own daughter who passed away, is the tablecloth I made."

"You sure?"

"Yes, I found the place in the horn-of-plenty where I made a mistake and had to rip out something and work a leaf to hide it."

"Sarah Bannister!"

"I made all the other things I bought, too," said Sarah. "I had ways of telling."

"Are you sure?"

"I wish I wasn't."

"What are you going to do?"

"I don't know anything I can do."

Lottie, who had not received anything except a high-school education, but was usually rather punctilious about her English, forgot all caution. She sprang into a morass of bad grammar.

"She had ought to be took up!" she said, with decision.

"Lottie, that darling little girl!"

"Darling little limb of Satan!"

"She looked so—"

"If you say another word about her looking like your Ida I shall begin to wonder what your Ida really was. Likening your own flesh and blood to a thief and a liar!"

"Come to think of it, she didn't lie. She wouldn't tell the name of the lady who made the things."

"Oh, well, if she only stole, she ain't quite so bad. I shouldn't wonder," returned Lottie, sarcastically, "if there wan' goin' to be no question of brimstun' for jest plain stealin'."

"Why, Lottie, how you do talk! What has got into you?" Sarah said, weakly. Then she began to weep again.

The doorbell clanged. Lottie ran to the window and peeked.

"It's a man," she whispered. "Wipe your eyes, Sarah. It's the minister. I know him by his pants. He's the only man that don't go to the city to work that wears creased pants in the morning in this town. Wipe your eyes, Sarah. You don't want him to see you've been cryin'."

"I don't care," wept Sarah. "I'm going to tell him the whole story and ask for his advice. What's a minister for? He can offer up the question to the Lord in prayer."

"If he don't offer it up to his wife, it's all right," Lottie said in a loud whisper, on her way to the door. When she returned, the minister, Silas Whitman, followed her. He had removed his topcoat and appeared clad in clerical black, shabby, but tidy and beautifully kept. Silas Whitman's salary forced careful keeping and nearly prohibited expenditure. He was a very small man, fair, with high, light eyebrows, and light hair growing stiffly from his forehead. As a result, he had a gentle, surprised expression. He took a chair near Sarah Bannister, and she went on at once with her story. Silas listened, and his expression of surprise deepened to one of positive pain.

The minister was not exactly a success in this particular parish. He realized it forlornly, but saw no way out. He was a man whose genuine worth and attainments were dimmed by his personality. He was like a rather splendid piece of trained mechanism doomed to one track, which did not allow him to even use many of his abilities. He was overeducated for the little New England village; he was overinformed; mentally he towered among them like a giant among Lilliputians. There was not among them a man or a woman to whom he could betray his everyday thoughts of the great present of the world. Not one could have understood. During the war he had done his best to discharge his duty to his God and his country among a people whom the war, in spite of their Red Cross work and their contributions to the Expeditionary Forces, never reached. It came the nearest to reaching them when the profiteers hid the sugar and the scarcity began in the stores, when Mrs. A couldn't make currant "jell" and Mrs. B couldn't make peach preserve, and Mrs. C and all the rest of the alphabet could not bring sweet cake to the Ladies' Aid parties, when the men missed the sugar from their coffee; then it seemed to the minister as if through the fruit and pickle season his good New England people peered out and up, almost enough to smell powder and hear the roar of the cannon. At that time the minister preached two war sermons to full congregations, and had hopes. However, after the fruit season, the people settled back in their ruts of the centuries.

Silas, sitting there listening to Sarah's strange story, considered how she was shocked out of her tracks now, but how soon she would regain her step. It seemed a pity. Just now she was dramatic and interesting, and at the crucial moment of the tale, when Sarah had missed the four treasures, the doorbell rang, and Lottie, peering out of the window, announced, "It's her."

"I am so glad you are here," Sarah said to the minister; then, in the next breath, she plucked at his sleeve as the door opened, and begged in a whisper: "Better let me speak to her first. She's only a child."

The minister nodded, and Lottie re-entered, leading Joan, or, rather, pulling her, for the little girl seemed to resist.

"Come here, dear," said Sarah. "Don't be afraid. Nobody is going to hurt you."

The little girl, carrying her bag, which did not seem so full as yesterday, allowed Sarah to put her arm around her.

"Now, dear little girl," said Sarah, and her voice trembled, "I must talk to you, and—"

The child interrupted. "What is the matter?" she inquired, with the sweetest air of pity.

"The matter?" murmured Sarah.

"Yes, ma'am, the matter with you. You have been crying and look worried."

"So I am," said Sarah, stepping into the open emotional door. "I am worrying about you."

The child regarded her with great, blue, troubled eyes. "I am very well, thank you," said Joan. "Please don't cry any more about me. I haven't any stomachache, or toothache, and I said my prayers this morning, and there's nothing ails me, truly."

Sarah gasped. "Do you feel that you have done just right?"

"Yes, ma'am."

"Are you a little girl who loves God?"

"Yes, ma'am."

The minister's face twitched. He coughed quickly and drew out his handkerchief and blew his nose. Lottie eyed him sharply. Sarah looked bewildered. The minister looked from her face to the perfectly open, ready-to-answer one of the child, and he coughed again.

"What have you got in your bag today?" Sarah inquired, rather hopelessly.

"The other things to sell."

"What other things? Open the bag!"

The girl obeyed at once. She drew forth, one by one, the missing articles of Sarah's collection. She eyed them admiringly. "Pretty," she commented.

Sarah stared.

"Why don't you speak right up to her?" said Lottie.

The little girl stared at her and smiled sweetly. "If you please, ma'am," she said to Sarah Bannister, "I am very busy this morning."

The minister swallowed a chuckle. Lottie looked at him.

"Joan," said Sarah.

"Yes, ma'am," said the child, looking up brightly.

"I have found out that you had sto—taken all those things you sold to me yesterday from me. You sold me my own things."

The little girl gazed. "I am real glad you found out so soon," said she.

"My goodness!" said Lottie.

Sarah gasped. "Why?"

"Because I was afraid you wouldn't."

Sarah stared at her, quite pale.

"I would have told you this morning if you hadn't found out," said the little girl, calmly. She took up the center-piece which she had brought and looked fondly at it. "This is real handsome and I think you must have worked real hard embroidering it," said she. She added, "This is five dollars."

"You aren't going right on selling me my own things?" gasped Sarah.

"I must sell them to you. I couldn't afford to give them to you, and I mustn't sell them to anybody else."

The minister spoke for the first time. "Why not?" he asked.

She looked wonderingly at him. "It wouldn't be right. Are you the minister?"

Silas replied that he was.

"Then I am surprised you didn't know it wouldn't be right, and had to ask me," remarked Joan.

"Why wouldn't it be just as right to sell to anybody else?" asked Sarah.

Joan looked as though she doubted her hearing correctly. "Why, they are your own things," she said simply.

Lottie came forward with a jerk of decision. "Now you look right at me, little girl," said Lottie. "Do you mean to tell me you don't know it was wrong for you to come here and sell Mrs. Bannister all this stuff?"

"It is hers," said Joan. She looked puzzled.

"Then, if it was hers, why didn't you let it alone?"

"I wanted to sell it. I wanted the money."

"What for?"

"All those poor little Brett children."

"The Brett children?"

"Yes, ma'am. Their mother died and their father thought he'd like to go and live with another lady, so he got married and the other lady didn't want six children so in a bunch, and so he didn't worry any more about them, and they were all starving to death and freezing, and there are two just little babies. And so I have them to take care of, and I can't earn money, for I am not old enough, and this is the only way, I decided, and I have just begun, and it works perfectly lovely."

"Goodness!" said Lottie.

Now the Rev. Silas Whitman realized that he must enter the field or be thought a quitter by two of his parishioners.

"Come here, little girl," he said, pleasantly.

Joan went smilingly and stood at his knee.

"Now, my child, listen to me," he said. "Didn't you know it was wrong for you to do such a thing? Don't you know you ought not to take anything whatever that belongs to other people and sell it to them?"

"They are all hers."

"Then why ask her to pay for them?"

"I wanted the money for the poor little Brett children and there wasn't any other way."

"But why should she have to pay for her own things?"

"Because she hadn't given any money to the Brett children, and I didn't begin to ask what they are worth."

"Don't you know it is wrong?"

"No, sir."

"Do you realize what you have done?"

"Yes, sir."

"Tell me what."

Joan looked up in his face and smiled a smile of innocent intelligence. "I opened one of the long windows in her best room," said she, "and I took those things I sold her yesterday and these I brought today, and I hid them in the Brett house. Then yesterday afternoon I packed them very nicely in the bag. I couldn't get all the things in, so I had these left over, and I came and sold them."

"Do you think she is going to pay you any more, you little—" began Lottie, but Sarah hushed her.

"I am not going to pay her, but I am going to give her some more money to buy things for the Brett children," said she.

"And you don't think you have done wrong?" persisted the minister.

Joan looked at him wearily. "They are her own things and she has them back, and she has paid me the money, and you heard her say she was going to give me some more, and it is for the Brett children. I haven't done wrong. The lady didn't give the money in the first place to the Brett children, so, of course, I had to see to it. And now she has her presents all back and everything. I think I must go now or I shall have no time to buy some meat and cook the children's dinner."

Sarah opened her black silk bag and handed a bill to the little girl. "Kiss me, dear," she whispered.

Joan threw both arms around her neck and kissed her, over and over.

"Will you come and see me?" whispered Sarah, fondly.

"Yes, ma'am; I'd love to."

They all stood at a window watching the child go down the path. Suddenly Silas Whitman began to speak. He seemed unconscious of the two women. He watched the little girl, the red silk rag from her coat lining streaming, march proudly away with a curious air, as if she led a platoon, not as if she marched alone.